HOUSE OF BOREAL
THE HAIDREN LEGACY

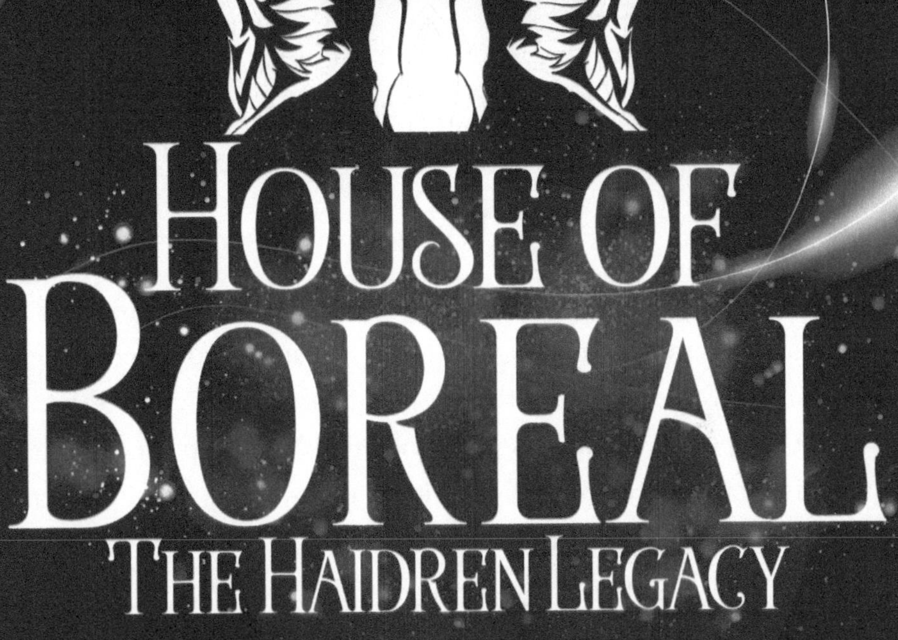

HOUSE OF BOREAL

THE HAIDREN LEGACY

3

K.L. KOLARICH

ISBN: 978-1-7354606-8-0 (e-book)
ISBN: 979-8-218-32013-3 (Paperback)
ISBN: 978-1-7354606-9-7 (Hardcover)

Cover Art & Design: Fiona Jayde Media
Interior Book Design: Brent Spears

Printed by Rogue Kite Publishing, in the United States of America.

First printing edition 2023.

www.TheHaidrenLegacy.com

For my parents,
who taught me to chase the truth and never its counterfeit.

"What light befalls, there sprouts growth, and what grows will surely transform; a transformation irrevocable and unafraid of its shadow."

- Psalm of the Brightling, Sword Age

N
W
E
S
ORALLACH MOUNTAINS
Ciann
GULF OF SAOIRSE
ILIAS OCEAN
Lempeii
IKAIKA COVE
HOUSE OF PILAR
Gakoshū
Vien
KHÀN RIVER
Jol'Nune
RAZÔUEL
ORYN
Halona
MWORRA
Yowekao
HOUSE OF DARAKAI
Calluc
ANDWELE MOUNTAINS
Faraji

DRYSTAN SEA
TEVÁAR
Sovllim
HOUSE OF BOREAL
Odetha
Aksel's Keep
Roûwen
BALMUN CHANNEL
NUORIC RIDGE
Isle of Viridis
LAKE VASIL
THE WASTES
Port Tadeas
Port Niall
VALLEY OF FAHIME
THOARNE BAY
Arune
YACHEL RIVER
Province of Hildur
Province of Wendylle
Outer Proper
Province of Galina
Port Khmer
YAKILA RIVER
Inner Proper
Province of Uriel
HOUSE OF BASTIION
THIA
Province of Agoston
EINDRULLA PLAINS
MIRAJII FOREST
YAKOV RIVER
Rian
WETLANDS OF HAGARH

SCAN ME

- Allöh'jomn'yeh -

Equip your journey out of the known and into the Other by enlisting
the regional glossary, hosted both online and after the epilogue.

For a more immersive reading experience, explore
the world of Orynthia outside the pages at
www.TheHaidrenLegacy.com
for instant access to a treasury of THL resources.

- Tredae'Aurynth -

Prologue

A knowing chill seeped through his cloak, hard and callous at his back, entombing the figure in a past that should have stayed forgotten.

The tattered fabric slithered across the marbled floor where he soundlessly rounded an identical column inside the darkened Arune estate. He hesitated and listened intently. Its servants long in their slumber, the gaudy corridor was empty of the raucous it had once corralled. In its vacancy, silence was the figure's only companion, escorting him through the maze of sleepy halls, barren except for the recollected echo of clinking glassware, haughty society, and their ineffectual chatter.

A phantom to their spectral dance, the figure skated the wall toward an ornate set of doors. Moonlight sparkled off the mosaic scroll of the trim work. His eyelids chafing, he blinked at it miserably; the brilliant threshold was one he'd hoped to never cross again.

Clicking the latch ajar, the figure succumbed to his torment; the dreaded moment had arrived to confront the life he'd deserted on the other side.

Neglected books loomed above his shadowed hood. Starlight streamed through the row of towering windows, bathing his feet like it had on the first occasion it'd hosted his company. The figure assessed the room. Mire swam through his insides as he instantly lamented his course. The Hastings library stood unchanged by the quarter of a century he'd buried behind him. But as he stood amid its stale musk, it was as if no number of years had passed at all. The tall but quaint space was enclosed by intimate tiers of dust-laden quartz shelves, their contents undisturbed by age or interest. That was the same too, inviting the figure to smirk. Gregor loathed books—except for the accolade of their accumulation during an era when such artifacts were rarely written or discovered.

He was always the fool, the figure recounted, eyeing the gilded baubles and bookends. Between them, stacked for Gregor's leisure, were leather-bound gems, diminished to relics within a mausoleum of counterfeit treasure.

Lifting the worn heel of his boot, the figure trudged through time, advancing down an aisle of volumes as he inhaled the melancholy of their antiqued perfume. The scabs at his nostrils split apart and he savored the scent longingly. But pain quickly replaced his euphoria in exhale. Such fleeting, unmerited pleasure was not why he'd come, not why he had run from Port Khmer and away from his mistress's charge.

The figure's half-hearted grin plummeted as he lowered his gaze.

Beneath his threadbare clothes, trepidation raced his marred flesh in a brisk tingle when he stalled at the end of the costly shelving. Preparing himself, he looked up with excruciating slowness until his gaze settled on the place where he'd first seen her.

Raggedly, his breath hitched.

He fixated on the emptiness behind an unused desk, and it was as if she were still there, boldly perusing the subject matter of an adjacent shelf. The figure tore his vision from her absence. His sinuses swelled and moistened, burning from a rush of unreserved feeling when he instead turned in the other direction and plodded along the wall of vellum codices. With a harsh sniff, he bored his sights onto their weathered spines, searching the ledge where the cursed item belonged. That was his singular purpose, he reiterated to himself. Though most of the titles were frayed and flaking at the edges, the figure retraced his steps with shameful accuracy, his transgressions reenacting his habitual journey to the spot he sought.

The secret space they'd shared so senselessly in those early days.

His gloved forefinger ached as the figure skimmed along the unmarked books, their bindings too old to bear their naming. Cocking his head, he peered across the glittered moonlight, spying where the dust coating was thinner than that of its neighbors. The figure reached for the familiar codex—his preliminary connection to her—grateful for the layer of battered leather separating his doomed flesh from its touch. He started to scoot it out from its snug seating.

A tremor shot through his hand, and the figure lingered in his partial success, unready to reopen its pages.

To reenter the clandestine world of his and his beloved's creation.

An intelligent, provocative, irresistible world etched within a few inches of allowance.

How he'd poured himself into those margins, well before Korbin had ever adopted his father's battle-ravaged reign. Then throughout the initial fight for peace… when far from the frontline, Gregor's coastal estate in Arune had been deemed to be the court's safest haven. They blurred together, the countless seasons the figure had been forced to sojourn among the nobility in this vapid crypt. But how he'd come to yearn for it. To plant his feet upon this very marble, just to repeatedly tuck these well-loved pages back into place, ravenous for her every response.

In unmatched agony, the figure tested a glance beyond the edge of his hood and locked it again on the lonely desk. This time, he dared not look away.

For just a moment—one indulgent, monstrous moment—he let the stain of his crimes bleed away, staring where she'd once stood. His eyes grew aflame, unable to shed the tear he felt departing his soul. Within seconds, the figure was enraptured by Alora's immortalized picture. As if she were a ghost in his haunt, he watched her like he had that life-shattering evening of Korbin's regal soiree—an event neither had wished to attend, thus had found themselves disappearing into the same disregarded library, sheltered from every ounce of courtier folly.

Human softness cracked open inside him as the decades faded, blending into the plaster. The vaulted walls swallowed the figure until he was only a man, smiling at the most mesmerizing woman all knowledge and wisdom could affirm.

A man who'd once had a name.

"Yancy nonsense," the foreign maiden grumbled, shoving the squat compendium onto the bookshelf with zeal. Candlelight gleamed off the swing of her strange platinum hair, bound in a loose plait, as she grabbed another title and cursed aloud.

Her exasperated huff echoed under the dome and over the quartz case he loitered behind, bringing an uptick to his already-intrigued grin. It wasn't shyness hiding him there, rather the tier of chronological anthologies he perused to quell his rising boredom. Better a moldy memoir from the Staff Age than that of a thoroughly inebriated haidren to Bastiion.

To the point, a subsequent snort sounded from said haidren's desk.

Brow quirking, he again peeked over the barricade of literature and found the Boreali al'haidren rifling through the ambassador's varied volumes, which decorated his uncluttered workspace. Frustrated, she was visibly unimpressed. Her features were fair as the moon, and he studied them in amused silence. Despite her station, she was a subject like any other, he surmised. Then again, they both were. He too was locked away from his contemplative nest. Although, tonight the crown's cage was finally proving more beguiling than that of his birds.

"Ock!" A book plopped onto the desk. "Rubbish, the lot of it!"

The young al'haidren stepped forward, then hesitated and pivoted on her heel. A crease wrinkled her forehead. Carefully, her slight hands straightened the stack back into rights, tidying it before she moved onto the next collection.

He refocused his thoughts on the anthology in hand and discreetly turned a page. It hosted diaries of a burgeoning Ethnicam. More like delusions, he thought with a chuckle, given the drunken diplomacy of the adjacent rooms.

He heard her sharp intake. "Who's there? I demand you make yourself known."

Even this deep in the provincial circle, he was unaccustomed to the authority in her tone. She was much haughtier than they'd described. Though people, specifically Unitarians, rarely invested attention on those with whom they found little commonality. With a bemused slanting of his head, he snapped the crumbling pages shut and crept around the shelving.

"I regret to disrupt your quest, Lady Boreal," he remarked, suppressing the spring in his lips.

Her own pastel mouth fell ajar as quickly as it resealed, smoothing her countenance to resemble the same fine statuette at her rear. The delicate beading of her gown refracted patterns across the sculpture's white surface when she sidled in place, knitting her fingers together over her slender middle.

He lifted his gaze from it. "We've not yet had the occasion to meet. I am—"

"I know who you are," the al'haidren blurted, then bit her lip, her eyes widening. Something sparkled in her right iris, alarmingly brighter than the other, when it caught the starry shine through the tallest windows. "But I... I did not hear your approach?"

Curiously, it was stated like a question, as if she ought to have sensed his footing over the loudening revelry coursing through the doors.

Unsure what to make of it, he mused aloud, "In escape, I admit I came on a quest of my own."

"You do not approve of Korbin's party?" she asked, her watch meeting his more directly. It was certainly eerie to hold; in that much, the rumor-mongers were correct.

"Well, we are at war. Seems an odd excuse for a waltz." He treaded closer, as not to shout across the library, and cocked an ear toward the muffled holler. "That is... if they're even employing the musicians anymore."

"Gregor's father doesn't seem to have ever employed his desk," she stated with an unexpectedly dry wit. Gracefully, the al'haidren skirted her alabaster fingers atop a plush, wingback chair. Her hand fluttered upward at her comment. "Meh fyreon—forgive my untoward candor."

Nearly giving himself away, he tightened his smile, taking her in. She reminded him of a pristine ice sculpture melting in agitation, only to apologize to the sun for its mess.

"Since we are here, might I help you discover something more worth your effort?" he suggested, gesturing toward the surrounding shelves.

She dragged a finger along the panel nearest her person and idly asked, "Do you read often?"

Succumbing to his grin, he did not respond but lowered his head to shield her from it. Charmed by her attempted poise, he watched her through the sheet of cropped, black hair that swung forward. She didn't need to try so hard, and yet she did so brilliantly. At his wordlessness, the al'haidren's feigned nonchalance abruptly dissolved and she glanced up—mortified, given the lovely bloom across her steep cheeks.

"Stupid question. Of course you do…" Her voice trailed off, indicating not the anthology in his grasp but the layers of gray silk enveloping his slightly older frame.

Tucking it behind him with both hands, he positioned himself to walk alongside her down the row of books, genuinely intrigued. She was an endearing perplexity—a segregant from court but a product of it nonetheless. "Do you maintain a favorite subject?"

"Herbology, mostly," she said studiously, recovering from any remnant embarrassment to fall in step with his unhurried stride. "Medicinal journals… and hints of animalia, when it serves."

Remembering propriety, he upheld the gap between their elbows. Whereas through the corner of his vision, he tried not to linger on her hip and the allure of its mathematical sway beneath her skirts, a task that he repeatedly failed during their brief voyage to the opposing wall.

"I share your interest, on the last subject specifically," he remarked, stopping before the assemblage of codices he'd discovered the week prior. "These should be more to your liking."

He reached up to make a recommendation, and the al'haidren did the same, causing them to bump their knuckles over the same inconspicuous spine. There was nothing noteworthy about it. The codex was bound and plated in alder, its navy dye dinging to brown along the decayed border, thus they'd both chosen it for no reason at all. And for no reason, at least none uttered aloud, they let their hands mingle there longer than they ought.

Warmth streamed into his skin for the few breaths her fingers remained against his. With a nervous laugh, the al'haidren retreated.

"Bolaeva," she said, pointing clumsily at his selection. "Erm—please do, I mean."

He tilted the codex out of socket, smirking that she'd tendered him a translation. "Trust that I am well acquainted with your tongue, Lady Boreal."

Overlooking how close she stood, he turned and spotted her stunned expression where that exact tongue was coyly caught between her teeth. Lashes more translucent than her tresses, accented by her dusky-lilac dress, shuttered over her Northern eyes at the unintended, double meaning of his statement. He squinted at them in the sparse light. It wasn't an illusion, he realized, admiring the extraordinary shading of their heterochromia. One dazzled like opal, pairing the other as blue as the Ilias Ocean.

Under his audacious examination, the al'haidren bit her lip and twisted her face aside, backlit by the cloudless night. Too fixated on her profile as he cataloged every quirk, every twitch of expression, he finally remembered the codex weighting his palm.

"Here," he said, more fascinated by her being than any book. "Take it first, then deliver me your thoughts."

She reached for it but then, withdrawing, brushed her neckline self-consciously and toyed with the trim. Staring into the darkened hills outside, she whispered, "We shouldn't develop a confidence beyond necessity… no matter the loneliness outside this room."

Sadness seemed to weight her otherwise-alert countenance. Because of the war, King Aquila's summons had sequestered her with the others under his son's countryside protection, to preserve Prince Korbin's future Quadren. The al'haidren had been at the Hastings estate no more than three days. And three nights was all it had taken to learn the lonely quality of its corridors.

This he knew firsthand, having been confined to them even longer.

As he considered her, hope sprung from an untapped depth and occupied what used to be his empty, isolated refuge. She was an anomaly to the aristocracy, but so was he. Together they made an impossible equation. Yet before he could attempt to solve it, he gently pushed the codex into the al'haidren's care with surprising desperation.

"War has stolen much, leaving behind few minds worthy of consultation," he softly remarked. She returned her attention to him, and he cherished every glimmer in her stare. "Do we not deserve that comfort at least?"

The al'haidren's peculiar irises darted to the air beside his face, as if she expected to find something floating there. A furrow nestled above the bridge of her delicate nose. With two concentrated blinks, she shifted her footing and replied, "Wem. Maybe we do."

Relief blew past his lips. "I'm so glad to hear it, Lady Boreal."

The sweetness of pine and bramble teased his nose when warily she took the codex, sparking another fleeting brush of fingertips as she murmured, "My name is Alora."

While it was already known, he still anchored onto every poetic syllable. He split a wider grin and replied in kind, "They call me—"

A click and a clang tore the figure from his reverie.

Throttled back into the present, he seized the grimy codex against his hollow chest and reeled into the blackest shadow. He batted his scabbed lids. His tear ducts were afire, giving no pardon to his sorrow where he shrank behind a towering shelf. It was reckless, disgraceful even, to have dwelled—a fool's errand, were it not for the text pressed over his dead heart.

Beneath the hood, the figure strained to focus on the clatter echoing off the library's eastern wall. Voices, whispering urgently, accompanied the screech of sliding furniture. He inched around a column, keeping out of sight.

Protruding from the molding angled a small, concealed door—one he'd not noticed, despite the hundreds of times he'd walked past its well-hidden hinges.

And out from its opening crawled a queen on her hands and knees.

Crouched outside the squat passage, Gregor scooted a chair farther out of the way and quickly extended Lourissa his hand. "Hurry, before we wake the groundskeepers. They will be up soon."

"And we thought the days of this tunnel were behind us…" she replied, accepting his help to stand. A candle resting on the ground illuminated the mud caked halfway up her imperial skirts, which matched the soiled commoner's boots that shuffled under her hem. "But you're right. Even the servants cannot know my whereabouts now."

The years had been kind to Korbin's widow, opposed to the merciless pop of Gregor's knees when he clenched the molding and joined her upright. He shook out the stiffness of his leg when someone resembling a child popped out of the hole after Lourissa.

"Don't worry, Queenie," piped a petite Darakaian, scuttling to rise. "I'll tell your king cub of our sneakies from Bastiion proper. Tell him of our kwihila getting into fancy man's fancy lair."

Gregor frowned at the youngling. The figure could not tell what the person was—boy or girl, child or adult—except that the trio had been traveling together at the behest of Lourissa's son. A wise decision, to remove her from a kingless court.

"Shores of Aurynth, these old bones!" A large-toothed Boreali woman finished their party, emerging through the wall. From her plain dress and apron, stained but neatly tied, the figure assumed she was a maid of sorts… though not nearly fine enough to have been in the service of their queen.

"To the doors there," Gregor directed hushedly.

Slinking back, the figure kept to the darkest pools across the floor.

The odd ensemble migrated toward the exit. Nearly there, Lourissa let the two surpass her steps and reached for Gregor, delaying him.

Her chestnut waves, threaded with silver, framed the palpable panic contorting her face as she started to cry. "Korbin didn't prepare him for any of this, Gregor. I cannot lose my son too."

The figure glowered at Gregor's hand when it encompassed hers on his arm, a show of genuine friendship he'd not once experienced from the man. "Our boys will be safe in the North. All of them."

"Thank you." Lourissa nodded. Even her sniffling was dignified. Her capacity to feel and forge ahead had held truer than it had in years past. "You've kept my family's secrets for a long time."

"Just as you've kept Cyra's and mine. Come now," he said, giving her a gentle nudge toward the hall. "Korbin would want you to rest."

The codex burned against the figure's gloved palm as he watched them depart the library.

Twisting away, he plunged through the hidden passage and into the deep. The cold stone widened, and he tore past its crags. His legs thrummed as he ran into the lightless hollow, uncaring as to where it led. He needed to get out, to get farther from this resurrecting life.

It was all too close. Too real.

After crashing through a trap door, he rolled into an open field under the stars. The figure scrambled for the codex among the grasses and thumbed through its antique pages with fervor, tearing them in haste. Margins scribbled with sweet nothings blurred by as he tracked their numbering, getting closer and closer to his damnation.

Overhead, a familiar screech pierced his ears just as he stopped, and his stomach lurched forth. Black-brown bile soaked the ripped binding where he examined it in fear.

There was a page missing.

The page that had started it all.

Only three people knew of its existence: two by possession and a treacherous third, someone Alora had never learned had been told.

The figure outheld his forearm, awaiting Amaranth's sharp talons. The hawk landed with a painful sting where she grappled onto his sores. He brought his disfigured nose to her beak, dreading his next breath.

"Search for your sister in the skies. She will lead to where we must go."

CHAPTER ONE
LUSCIA

Luscia smeared the dollop of yolk yarrow onto the stubborn gash that split the warrior's forehead in two. It carved an ugly valley down his umber, sweat-soaked skin. Nearly a week aboard the stolen brig and the enclosed air had fermented into a dank, overcrowded fetor, doing little to encourage his healing—nor that of the many others dozing in their hammocks, cramming the tight space beside his every moan and whimper.

The man shivered as she unstuck his braids from where they'd dried into her previous application. At least he was allowing her to help at all; not every member of his pryde did, not once they'd awakened to their pains after the raid in Port Khmer only to find the frightening and fabled haidren to Boreal nursing their wounds in the darkness.

Glistening against her knees, Luscia's apothecary had been thrown open for enlistment. The spice of the maroon-hued Viridi chest countered the reek of his pus-coated stitches—not that it varied much from the general odor of the entire deck. They were over capacity as it was, and with so many warriors unable to handle a mop, their unwashed gore seeped into the wood planking, marinating the unplanned voyage in foul reminiscence.

Inside the Viridi chest, the Northern jars jangled with the side-to-side groan of the ship, adding a rhythmic *chink* to the jostle of salt-rusted lanterns strung overhead. Luscia assessed her vial of ennus thorn. It was too depleted to spare, not when the last barbs were needed for a vital elixir she'd soon need to recreate. She instead selected something ordinary to dull his ache, though its effectiveness would leave him wanting.

Lumin-laced specimens sparkled from the jumble of glassware, enlightening her quick work on the souvenir down the man's forehead. His pain was made worse, she sensed, by the treason of his own House, having been Darakai, under the deceitful command of Nyack Kasim, who had marred the warrior. The House of Darakai had cut him down and turned him into a runaway in his escape across the unforgiving waters of Lake Vasil. He no longer resembled who he was born to be. He'd become an outlaw, just like Luscia.

Just like their king.

She caught the near-empty jar of horned thissleweed when it rolled down the floorboards of the orlop deck with the ship's exaggerated heel. The waves had worsened. A nervous flutter passed through her belly as she uncorked the jar and crumbled the common wilted weed onto the warrior's stitches. They were not far, Luscia knew, now that the winds chilled the surface above and the churn had deepened below. The harrowing, spectacular shift of nature had thwarted sailors for centuries, including their own renegade host, Rafe Nabhu. Quirking her Boreali ears, she heard the gaudy captain barking in preparation to his crew over the rumbling snores that surrounded her.

"By your estimation, Lady Boreal, is the warrior more likely to walk ashore or expire in the coming hours?" Hachiro Naborū-Zuo hunched lower, querying over Luscia's shoulder.

His bedside manner was as insensitive as his notetaking. He coarsely scratched onto the ledger he used to track the recovery of the injured, something she'd not asked him to do. And yet there he had appeared at her side, enrobed in the amber silks of a shoto acolyte—still bearing the grisly exploits of Khmer—quill in tow, as if planning to attend an elite lecture. From the second morning aboard and in the days that followed, Sayuri's inquisitive brother had shown no interest in terminating his uninvited observation, against Luscia's ritual request. Consequently, Hachiro hovered annoyingly close as she resettled the thissleweed among its fellow herbs and shut the apothecary with a terse *snap*.

"I'm afraid you pose an unproductive inquiry, one only the warrior may answer," she answered dryly, lifting the Viridi chest. By Aniell'si-laem—His grace alone—it had survived their race from the docks, along with a few horses and meager supplies. But after tending two injured prydes, the rarities housed within her apothecary's inventory were dangerously depleted. "Besides, Lord Pilar, the expiration of others is not the sort of thing we should be concerned with right now."

"On the contrary, that is precisely what is of concern, given the emptiness of this mysterious crate you won't permit me to analyze," Hachiro said into his ledger, adding to his notes. "You ought to ration. We've lost six and three-quarter subjects."

"Patients, not subjects, Hachiro." Luscia dropped the formality and batted a tawny tangle out of her gaze. She picked up a bowl of bloodied water to stack it atop the locked chest. "And… Your math doesn't make any sense. We've lost a warrior every day since Khmer."

The shoto'shi-turned-interim-haidren blinked at her bundle of materials and back at her blankly, offering no aid except in reply. "A correct assessment." Hachiro tapped the parchment with his quill, then pointed it toward the injured warrior. "And by the law of averages, this man is three-quarters on his way out."

When will you be on the way out? Luscia ground her teeth. She was ashamed to admit that by the third afternoon saddled with his company, she'd started to miss his sister—a fact even more regrettable than whatever came out of his mouth.

With a sigh, Luscia ducked beneath a swinging lantern and side-stepped the shoto'shi's expectant stare, trying to offer him a modicum of patience. She again prayed that Sayuri had made it to Ira's country estate with Tallulah and the queen, and that the little Darakaian scout hadn't murdered the rightful haidren in transit.

It'd be a plausible mistake… Sayuri's snobbery was hardly any better, merely enough for Luscia to wish the rightful haidren would return to the Quadren from whatever ruse had confined her to her apartments in Bastiion.

Then again, maybe Luscia was losing her edge. It'd been a long week.

I just need to see dry land is all. And an inch of personal space, she thought, chiding herself as she looked back at where Hachiro harmlessly stood beneath a low-hanging rafter. Brushing the underside of the timber beaming, his stiff, inky hair seemed to permanently stick up on one side, courtesy of another night in a roughhewn hammock.

With her inflection tired but gentle, Luscia told the shoto'shi, "People are not numbers. I'm learning more and more that when mortals' averages are stacked against them, they are prone to surprise us."

Hachiro angled his head. The tuft of hair defied gravity as he mulled her statement over in the same unrushed, academic manner she imagined he'd exhibit within the philosophic halls of Gakoshū.

A characteristic tic quivered his cheek, causing one eye to squint. He hugged the ledger and replied, "You submit that people are variables, rather than rules."

"Wem—yes. That is what I'm saying," Luscia confirmed.

"Then what of the rules of inheritance? Because this debacle with Lord Darakai—"

"The king asked you join him on deck for the crossing, did he not? Surely you don't want to miss that," Luscia said briskly, disinclined to discuss the Southern haidren called Zaethan Shà, or the scandal of his parentage.

"Oh, the crossing! A phenomenon indeed." Hachiro fished his odd monocular device from the dirtied pocket of his robes. After sliding it over one ear, he clicked through the lenses and snapped the blue disk into place. It magnified one of his golden-brown eyes as he blinked like a bug from the marshes. "We've not a moment to waste!" He scurried toward the ladder, stooped at its base, and retrieved a filthy rag off the floor with the end of his quill. Delicately, he added it to the pile in Luscia's arms. "I recommend you don't dawdle, Lady Boreal."

Not for the first time, she clamped her jaw and steeled a breath. Luscia's feelings for Sayuri grew fonder and fonder as her sibling climbed the ladder, gratefully out of sight.

Luscia carted the bundled heap toward a snug workroom, tucked behind the hatchway to the upper decks, where she hoped to tidy before the event took place. Luscia had never witnessed it herself. Having been raised within the strict boundary of the Boreali peninsula, she was looking forward to not only seeing the ship carve through the natural marvel but also the looks on everyone's faces as they did. The break in the lake had caused plenty of skittish rumor among the crew—just as it'd done for ages, warding off outsiders from the Isle of Viridis and the mythic highlands beyond. In that sense, nature was doing its job, ceding to the High One's will for the protection of Luscia's people.

She chuckled as she stepped over a cot and rounded a pillar encased in mildew. Legend could incite as much terror as it could hope. What everyone feared was nothing more than the mixing of two worlds not meant to collide. Slipping into the workroom, she glanced up, and her chuckling trailed off.

It was already occupied.

With his trim hip leaned against the splintered counter stood Hachiro's rejected topic of discussion.

When she sighted him, Luscia's chest involuntarily caved behind the bowl she carried atop her apothecary, but forcing her posture upright, she shook off every impulse to retreat. She was a woman, not some feeble girl, and, right now, a woman who needed access to the counter he'd commandeered. Impatiently, she readjusted her bundle in hand and waited in loaded silence for him to finish.

The quiet was worse, considering the room was small, granting little place for her eyes to linger anywhere but onto the very haidren she'd been trying to avoid.

Zaethan Shà made no effort to rush—immune, as if uninspired to flee. Her nearness was doing nothing to him. Mere feet from her, he did not acknowledge Luscia while he carefully rewrapped the bindings around his slit palms, a tribute to the defeat of his rival, Wekesa, on the docks in Port Khmer. Zaethan had disposed of a murderer that night, after having discovered it had been his challenger, not Salma Nabhu, who'd poisoned King Korbin.

Worse, the king's demise had been at the behest of Darakai's chief warlord, the man who had pretended to be Zaethan's father and who had killed Zaethan's mother upon his birth. He'd used the twisted event for his own duplicitous devices: the plot of regicide, the machinations of war, and the absolute ruination of his should-be son.

All these revelations had cut a forever reminder across Zaethan's hands. With a heavy exhale, Luscia considered she ought to relieve him of the scars. That was… if he'd even allow her attempts.

It wasn't a massive ship, and she wasn't dumb. He'd been avoiding her too.

Misinterpreting the sound, Zaethan shoved his old dressings into a pile of dirtied tools, gruffly clearing off the limited counterspace. "There, uni? I'll be done and out of your way in a moment."

Anticipating the bite in his tone, she calmly deposited her things beside him. One of them had to remain civil. And as his haidrenship was currently under speculation, Luscia supposed it fell to her to set Quadrennal standard. They were still peers after all, be it peers who could no longer look each other in the eye.

She spied the jerk of his movements while she cleared the items off her apothecary. Snatching a clean wrapping from the counter, he pivoted away from her and began to bandage his other hand. His sheepskin breeches creased with his shifting, hugging the muscle of his thighs in her periphery. She was surprised he still wore them, given their origin, so she assumed his traditional gunjas must had been ruined beyond repair during the assault. Untucked, a flimsy linen shirt floated out from under Declan's borrowed jacket, swaying with the revolutions of Zaethan's arm. Unlike the breeches, the quilted, navy jacket was too short for his considerable height, though his biceps filled the sleeves as well as the brawny najjan to whom it belonged.

The fit is irrelevant, Luscia admonished herself, anchoring her attention back to the bone lock and its matching skeletal key, which she produced from beneath her belted, olive tunic—another article of clothing donated by a member of her guard. It too fit just fine, not that it mattered. The Quadren was on the run for their life, and the portrayal of her shape from within an oversized linsilk shirt should have been the last issue consuming Luscia's thoughts. Yet at that precise moment, it was nearly all that did.

Perturbed, she lifted the chain over her gathered tumble of hair. Luscia stifled the urge to fidget with the sterling collar of Creyvan's tunic once the key was free from her neck.

Pegging his wrist against his abdomen, Zaethan twisted forward again and severed the leftover binding with his teeth. He grunted when the fabric tore. The spare landed beside her apothecary. With it came a sickly-sweet waft, overpowering his woodsy aroma of smoked cedar, a memorable scent she'd been trying to ignore.

"It's infected," Luscia muttered, sliding her key into the lock.

He knotted the binding clumsily, having pegged the ends between the counter and his hipbone. "It's nearly healed," he snapped.

"Is that so?" Luscia turned toward him and folded her arms. "Prove it."

"I don't need to prove anything to you."

Without meeting his gaze, she bore into the measured rise and fall of his chest, sloppily on display beneath the untoggled jacket, as he'd not bothered to lace his shirt. "Niit, not if you lose that hand to gangrene."

Incrementally, Zaethan lowered. His breath ruffled the rebellion of her blondest fly-aways when he stated flatly, "I'm good with both hands. You should know."

Luscia flattened her lips, choosing to believe he was referencing their trainings and nothing more. "Your sword arm still belongs to the king, does it not? He will want me to look at it."

"Well, I've been doing just fine without you." Zaethan's breathing picked up, defying his impassive reply.

Her eyes squeezed shut with the sting. *More* was exactly what he'd been referencing. Reopening them, she sternly gestured toward the stool in the corner. "Of that I am certain. You are a capable man, one who would never allow a personal matter to disarm his countless faculties. Bolaeva, Lord Darakai. Please sit."

It angered him, the logic in her request. She could tell by the reluctance of his bootheels, as after a few tense moments, they dragged him backward and onto the stool.

Luscia parked before him. She remained standing, reluctant to kneel like the last occasion she'd tended his injuries. Repeating those events was no longer an option.

One transgression deserved grace. But a second, its stain.

The haidren to Boreal could not bear both desire's stain and the seal of the woman she was to embody. Luscia would not endanger her calling again. In outstretching her hand for his, it struck her that it was the first time they'd been alone since she'd explored the breadth of him… since she'd come back to her senses before it had been too late.

She willed away her blush when Zaethan begrudgingly complied and hoisted his wound into the space between them. Despising the subtle shake of her thumbs, Luscia loosened the bandage and unraveled his handiwork, avoiding the feel of his calloused skin as much as able, beautiful though it was. The lantern above them illuminated the reason for so much debate, transforming Zaethan's cross-caste lineage into a spice field of copper undertones. The identity of his real sire, whether unknown or undisclosed, had left him fatherless and without the pure ancestry needed to claim his House, despite Dmitri's protest otherwise. All the Quadren knew for certain was that the seated haidren was not the product of two Darakaians, as he had been led to believe, but instead that of an eliminated predecessor and a nameless Unitarian. Thus, the issue of his haidrenship remained. Luscia tried not to admire his disowned flesh, radiating the warm hints of turmeric, cinnamon, and star anise. She hardly knew why it made any difference anymore.

Nyack Kasim had seduced the chieftains into sedition. And where the War Council no longer wanted his fake heir, the House of Darakai needed him just the same.

So did Dmitri.

Zaethan said nothing when she spun toward her apothecary and unlatched it. She dug out the last remnants of kaléo flower along with an unsoiled cloth. Returning to him, she cleaned the cut of debris, causing him to hiss. Luscia focused on the ship's noise, not on their history or the way she felt him watching her in their present. She had left that behind, entombed it deep within herself, when she'd accepted Marek's kurtfierï, tied about her wrist.

Zaethan didn't ask what the token meant. Nor had she told him.

And in that, it was serving its purpose.

The beading of her father's cuff jostled while she ground the swollen stamen between her fingertips. Zaethan clenched and unclenched his opposite hand upon his thigh. Snowy pollen peppered his infection, and she prayed that the dusting, enriched by lumin, would be enough to cure it. With the binding in hand, Luscia rewrapped his palm with methodical detachment.

She was almost finished when she heard his lips part.

"Are you sure you can do this with me?"

Luscia froze mid-knot. A sickening wave of shame and regret overtook her cheeks as Zaethan all but repeated his words from the inn, after she'd ripped herself from the heat of his arms. *You mean you can't do this with me.* The echo lashed her ears. A Darakaian, cross-caste or otherwise, would never understand the impossible position he'd put her in that night.

Their friendship, were she to classify its complexity as such, had never been particularly cordial. But this strained animosity over the last week had become more unbearable than how they'd first begun. He hadn't known her at the start.

He barely knew her now.

And yet the allegation behind his every phrase hurt worse than any derogatory slur.

Finally, Luscia elevated her chin and met his sage-green eyes. They tensed. Something akin to hatred sharpened their vibrancy in wreath of verdant daggers, each arbor out for blood.

She cinched the knot pointedly and said, "I'm sure."

His hand kept still, but with catlike control, he eased his upper body lithely away from the wall. Perched on the stool, Zaethan inched his face to just below hers. His sable, ropelike locs were gathered high, though a few fell over his brow, pierced by a set of golden rings.

Luscia didn't move as his decorated brow arched rebelliously.

"Prove it."

While her throat thickened, her focus descended toward his shapely lips, which under her attention, ticked at their corners. Over the creak and moan of the ship's activity, she heard his pulse quicken. Or maybe the rushing beat belonged to hers…

Submit emotion to reason, her aunt cautioned in her mind.

Leveling her shoulders, Luscia released the binding and looked him square in the face. "I believe 'tadöm' is the word you are looking for, Lord Darakai. It is how we thank each other in the North," she acerbically said. "You will soon find yourself safely there, indebted to use it."

Stepping back, she swiftly locked the apothecary and resituated its bone key between her breasts, inside the tunic.

"Your mask is cracking, Maji'maia," he told Luscia to her back.

She swiveled on her heel. "Excuse me?"

Arrogance plucked his features as Zaethan tapped his bottom lip in mock consideration. "Uni, that mask you wear. I wonder which of us will be more shocked at who you really are beneath it… once it breaks."

Her nose buckled indignantly, to his apparent delight. Luscia stormed toward the slim door. She recognized he was hurting… was swimming through a river of heartache. But he was holding two conversations at once, one of which she had not agreed to have.

And if he insisted on speaking in translation, then so could she.

"Your wound will lessen over time, Lord Darakai, if tended properly. The scar will heal to nothingness until eventually, it will be as if none of this"—she sliced the air between them—"ever existed."

Luscia stomped into the sea of cots and hammocks and rushed between them as if she could run away from the swell raging inside her. She seized a rung of the ladder and scrambled for the hatch, the portal to where she belonged. Her place was not below, where things were forged in secret. That had been rendered inconsequential, and she had to let the inconsequential go.

She had to let *him* go.

They were clashing currents, like those battering the hull—the mixing of two worlds that was never meant to be.

The ties of Marek's kurtfierï smacked the final rung, and Luscia paused there. For Boreal, for her people, for Aniell… She would give up what she must. *Who* she must. Reshaping her expression, she climbed higher into the daylight.

The haidren inside did not look back.

Chapter Two
Zaethan

Once, twice, three times his head thumped against the mildewy slats where he sat in defeat. Zaethan couldn't even name what game they were playing anymore. Her definitions were always changing, just like her rules. He didn't know what Luscia Darragh Tiergan was playing at, except that after the hatchway smacked shut behind her, he had once again lost.

Balanced on the stool, Zaethan's stare seared the low ceiling of the workroom while his fingers toyed with the frayed threads of his bandages. He released a bitter laugh at the absurdity of his position, teetering on a half-busted stool like some pathetic, abandoned pup.

This entire time he'd thought it had been him rejecting her…

When all along, it had really been the other way around.

"Depths, that's a sour joke," Zaethan muttered to his lonesome. Kumo would love it—were Zaethan to eventually share the punchline with his beta.

Maybe the highlander haidren was justified to reject him. He was no one, after all. Technically not even her equal. His newfound illegitimacy had secured that too, stripping not only his right to inherit his late mother's haidrenship but the right to be in the same room as the successors of her peers—a parting gift from his father-pretender. The very man—ano, the very traitor—whose forces had hounded them across the realm and onto a stolen merchant ship. In the process, he'd reduced Zaethan to nothing, a cross-caste without name or lawful title. Whatever he had, he'd been allowed to keep either out of pity or the sheer stubbornness of those who still cared for him.

Pity, more like.

With a frustrated grunt, Zaethan plied himself off the stool. Unlawfully titled or not, there were two prydes left under his command. More, if Yousif Shà, his uncle and Dmitri's appointed commander supreme, was successful in his covert mission to rally further support among the militia. But those forces were thinly spread across Orynthia's outermost reaches. It could take months to learn the news, if they survived long enough to hear it.

Those with Zaethan on the ship deserved an alpha zà worthy of their sacrifice, having turned with him from their mutinous chief warlord and, consequently, the House of their homeland. He knew more than anyone that to break from Nyack Kasim, to move against him in any way, was to break from Darakai. Zaethan bore enough scars to boast it, meaning the only "Darakai" his prydes had left to claim stood aboard this blasted brig.

A brig that was currently heeling more exaggeratedly than the showmanship of its captain.

Gripping the edge of the counter, Zaethan pulled himself through the threshold with a murderous scowl, dodging the bins and empty growlers that barreled into his path. He knew exactly who this show was for, and for the last time, he meant to put it to a stop.

Zaethan climbed, bypassing the vacant galley, as every able-bodied man was already above deck. He wasn't even to the main before a ration of last night's gruel dribbled down the ladder rungs. Evading the mess with a curse, Zaethan opted to haul himself through the final hatch by his elbows, snagging the planks and using his bootheels to lurch himself upright into an open-air gangway. Its base was coated in a chunky slurry of barley, pig's feet, and a sort of gelatinous noodle Zaethan did not wish to identify, all generously provided by his gigantic beta slumped against the adjacent bulwark.

"I'm going to kill him, Ahoté." Kumo wiped his mouth, revealing a green tinge. "I'm going to ring his flamboyant neck—"

Without warning, the ship's severe tilt switched, shooting the beta like a cannon across the gangway. He slammed into the opposing bulwark with a thud and spewed more of his insides. Zaethan had been told by the first mate—an odorous fellow more beard than teeth—that tacking was necessary for them to sail upwind, but he doubted the drama of it all was just as crucial as the actual zigzag maneuver through the chilling waters.

Toeing by a half-digested chunk, Zaethan patted Kumo on the shoulder promisingly. "Don't worry, cousin. I'll do it for you."

He wedged past and stepped out into the sun. Combing through the chaotic scuttle, Zaethan pinned his sights higher, toward the quarter-deck. He stormed the length of the brig beneath its canopy of rippling sails and cut aftward through the commotion until he halted at the base of an ornate stair. Above it, Salma's ridiculous nephew directed his crew from behind a giant spinning wheel, touting an equally ridiculous tricorn hat.

Resembling a squadron of eyes, a billow of peacock feathers batted the wind behind Rafe Nabhu's tawdry grin as he shouted something to his svelte guest atop the commanding deck. His hearty chortle gratingly carried for miles. Zahra did not seem amused nor impressed. That much pleased Zaethan, though it did little to dampen his escalating ire for the man. Nabhu been at it for days, laying it on Zahra at every turn—physical turns—as the rest of the vessel suffered his theatrics and her even-more-frequent dismissals.

A one-handed sailor, with rigging coiled around his stump of an arm, scampered past Zaethan when the ship tacked onto its other side with overstated flourish. Spare barrels rolled after him only to shatter against the railing. As he speared another look at the brass-buttoned captain, all Zaethan could think of was the distemper of his Andwele stallion, crudely boarded in the hold below.

"Zahra!" he barked with more gusto than the brewing winds. "Get your skinny legs down here now and leave the pirates to their pirating!"

"Privateering, Lord Haidren!" Nabhu called, pinching his fingers as if he'd heard a bit of out-of-key music. "How many times must I remind you, it's *privateering?*"

Returning Zaethan a biting grimace, his third bypassed the wafting hem of the captain's lavishly plum frock coat. As it lifted, the floral brocade of the coat's lining disputed Nabhu's insistence that his business ventures were at all legitimate. Even full-blooded Darakaian, no breakaway afforded a nobleman's clothier on a seaman's wages, not unless said breakaway came into questionable sums by questionable benefactors. And by the look of Nabhu, a strange mix of opulence and drudgery—a contrast more befitting Rian than the Vasil—this break-away seemed quite comfortable with his benefactors indeed.

Zaethan eyed Zahra as she descended the steps, and he shot back at the captain, "How many times must I remind you that as a criminal, your definitions are worth shtàka, Nabhu?"

Affronted, Rafe Nabhu spun his hips with the wheel, to better face Zaethan from above, and a chorus of protest rang out across the deck. He splayed his widespread fingers over his heart. "My Lord Haidren— if I still ought to call you that, yeah?" His rod-thin, ebony mustache twitched when he winked mischievously. "I'm a breakaway. I'm a priva-teer! But never a criminal." Nabhu swatted his frock with bravado and anchored a fist onto his bizarre, Andwele-stitched buckskin waistcoat. "Ano, it is my patrons who are the criminals, the rebels of House and court. Why… individuals such as yourselves!"

When Zahra hit the bottom step, Zaethan tore his ire from the man to address his third.

But before he got a word out, she thwacked him. "Eh! You call these legs skinny?"

"Uni, they're withering away, standing around with that would-be yancy." Zaethan grinned and poked the meat of her sturdy thighs, concealed inside her breezy gunja pants. Then, backhanding her leg, he ordered, "Go, rhaolé ono. Hurry, before you turn into his seafaring wench."

Owàa's late-afternoon shine settled on her chicory-shaded scalp when she leaned in. As it was freshly shaved, her Southern tattooed runes were on bright display. "More like he'd be *my* wench, yeah?" Zahra flashed her teeth and, strutting past him, went to see to the horses.

"Keep it smooth," he called, a final warning to Nabhu. "There is royalty aboard."

From the quarterdeck, Salma's nephew poked his head over the helm as Zaethan crossed starboard. Twin braids escaped the docked curls Nabhu had stuffed beneath his hideous hat. The beads jangled against his dark neck when he hailed with cheer, "And what royal rapscallions you are!"

Zaethan scrubbed his face as he ducked eagerly under a line, away from the stern. Near the crowded mainmast, he sidled past the stout, ginger shadowman, offering him a mutual grunt. Zaethan was wearing the man's clothing, short as it was. The least he could rumble was an excusable hello in the highlander's trek to rejoin his own haidren and her guard, huddling portside. Not far behind trailed her wolx. Tarrying after the shadowman, it pressed its hulking weight against Zaethan's leg, leaving the stamp of its dampened fur.

The smell with it.

He sneered, wicking the secondhand sea spray from his breeches. Ahead, Zaethan spotted Dmitri, nestled under the shadow of the foremast with Hachiro. Their king was chatting with the shoto'shi animatedly where he stood, swaddled in blankets, as he pointed toward the horizon. The farther north they traveled, the faster autumn was befalling their party. His friend was already missing his gratuitous, out-of-season fires. Zaethan was certain it would be Dmitri's first request once they landed on the strange shores that awaited them.

Coming up to the pair, he instantly regretted it.

"So it is when the two bodies coincide that the clashing occurs?" Dmitri asked Hachiro.

The last thing Zaethan needed was another lecture from their resident librarian in ladieswear. Cruelly, his lectures were the only thing left in abundance on the ship.

"Precisely, Your Majesty. The freshwater current drives northward and, at a specific point, contests the salinity surging southward from the

Baemun Channel, forming a salt barrier across the lake." The shoto'shi motioned out over the waves as Zaethan settled in on Dmitri's opposite side. "Being more a freshwater sea with a brackish rim, the Vasil provides a remarkable habitat for its incompatible species."

"Zaeth, marvelous timing. Hachiro was just explaining what we are about to witness." Dmitri returned his attention to the vast blue. "But the barrier runs the entirety of Boreal's southeastern border. Would it not be more natural for it to form higher up, in the mouth of the channel?"

"Therein lies the phenomena, My King." Hachiro clicked an orange lens over his eye, as if Dmitri's face would change in its view. His faint brows sputtered with his furious blinking. "In fact, an inverse phenomenon exists to the west, where fresh founts and runoffs pour into the Gulf of Saoirse, creating a mirrored effect that has spun a sort of legend among sailors… hence its naming."

"The Ghostly Gate. That does make sense now," Dmitri replied, disregarding the tangible shift among the crew at their backs. They'd hushed, save the nervous chitter that lifted the sails like the incoming gusts, stronger and cooler than those just minutes prior. "And being too different in composition, the waters can never mix then?"

Over the taffrail, the shoto'shi flipped open his journal. "In time, the denser, more fortified water comes under the less substantial and, in lifting it up, assimilates the foreign into itself." His scrawny forefinger drew circles over a diagram for Dmitri's viewing, but Zaethan was fixed on the opposite piece of parchment and an odd set of data recorded there. "Eventually the two become united—"

"Is that…" Zaethan's voice rose among the deck's uncharacteristic quiet. "Hachi, is that a *death chart*?"

Recognizing the names of his kinsmen, he gradually dragged the journal closer, down the rail, as Hachiro said, "For the purpose of my and Lady Boreal's treatment, it's imperative we record such morbid details, Lord Darakai."

"Mm." Zaethan nodded, then abruptly ripped out the page. After crumpling it into a neat ball, he balanced it over the binding and scooted the journal back to its owner. "Don't do that, Hachi."

Microtremors erupted through the unusual stubble of the shoto'shi's lean cheeks as he scrutinized the ball, then Zaethan. Hachiro emitted an insulted squeak. But at Zaethan's unyielding glare, he backed away with caution. It was an overcrowded deck, and within moments, he'd find another audience for his tactless lessons.

That was if the sailors didn't throw him overboard during his opening statement. That they hadn't had been a favor to Zaethan on more than one occasion.

"He means well," Dmitri peacefully said, interjecting over the folds of his thick knit blanket. He tightened it around his increasingly slender frame. How it seemed to have dwindled so much in the span of a week was starting to concern Zaethan, even more than the darkening hollows beneath his moss-and-oak-hued eyes.

"His kakk is almost as unbearable as Ira's…" Zaethan spun and assessed the deck, not finding the Eastern haidren near the open casks of ale by which he usually lounged. "Depths, where is that yancy now, getting initiated as a cabin boy?"

"While Ira does enjoy sporting their—what he calls—'swabby getup,' the job involves far too much manual labor, I'm afraid." A wry grin cracked Dmitri's regal facade as he inclined his head toward where a pair of cabin boys were grappling with the rigging. "Nevertheless, it appears Ira has moved up in rank. Maybe you should follow his lead, Zaeth."

His grin widened, flashing the whites of Dmitri's pearly teeth, when Zaethan stalked his friend's forefinger toward the quarterdeck. The captain had relinquished the helm to his officer. Yet in the helmsman's shadow, Ira's swinging arms cut through the sea breeze with each jerky rotation of the man's steering. A red kerchief was tied at Ira's bronze neckline, as if he'd earned enough sweat to soak it. Beside him, Nabhu coached his mock motions to become as broad and grand as his own.

Zaethan moaned and pivoted back toward the taffrail. "That's a disaster waiting to happen."

"On the contrary, I think they were made for each other." Dmitri chuckled. Casting it over the darkening waters, his countenance quickly sobered. "At least one of us is relishing this turn of events."

Zaethan's smile faltered. His boyhood friend was eroding away, leaving behind the sculpted sadness of a betrayed king. He wasn't eating, not that Zaethan could blame him when their only choice of sustenance was mopping the deck after Kumo's seasick farewell. But that was not the reason behind Dmitri's failing appetite. He'd nearly lost his kingdom. The court was now in question, barring whatever loyalty was still maintained among the self-serving vipers occupying the Peerage of Nobility. Zaethan knew Dmitri feared for his mother's life above the loss of his crown. And until Dhalili met them in Boreal—if she made it to the highlander border at all—Zaethan suspected little food would be touching his plate.

There was another shout at the helm, and suddenly the ship tacked to the other side. Zaethan seized the black-and-gold finial atop the railing and rushed to catch his tired king. Inside his arms, Dmitri stopped their fall with his ornamental walking cane.

As to not be overheard, Zaethan whispered over his friend's wool-swathed shoulders and into his ear, "You should not be up here when it's like this."

"It's a lovely day, Zaeth. Clear skies abound."

"Eh, if one can stand unaided beneath them."

"I just wanted to see it for myself."

Zaethan relaxed his hold into a brotherly stance but did not trust their footing enough to let go entirely. "Rafe Nabhu is going to sink us before the Ghostly Gate has the chance," he growled. "Boreal better be close behind. Owàa knows I can't go another day without boxing him."

"Oh, we're not sailing to Boreal, Zaeth." Dmitri's gaze swung aside in earnest. "We can't, not yet."

"What do you mean, we can't—"

A violent gust threatened the foremast, rippling the sails, as if the earth were shoving the brig and its passengers back to Port Khmer. Zaethan tensed his grasp on the decorative finial. Uneasy, he twisted, finding the entire deck crew holding their collective breath. Even their ever-boisterous captain, Rafe Nabhu. Without word, the Darakaian breakaway lowered his spyglass and measuredly reached for his helmsman.

Telling spindles traced Zaethan's spine before the foreboding stillness broke.

"There death awaits!"

"Pray to the Fates!"

Timorous and terror-stricken, mortal men shouted their warnings all around as the winds whistled for their advance. Its bite whipped between the masts, driving many of the crew both port and starboard to lean over the lacquered taffrail and behold the roiling deep.

Something slapped against Zaethan's back, causing him to jump, then realize it was simply Takoda Muthwali's heavy-handed greeting.

The warrior's braided rows bobbed into view. "Alpha Zà." He hastily bumped his fist to his chest in respect.

Flanking him was Kai Wakhan—alpha of the Mirajii Pryde—who seemed equally eager to witness the crossing. He hardly looked his station, with his busted leg still trapped in a splint. They must have dragged him off his cot and up from the bellows. Inclining on a crude crutch, Kai resembled Dmitri, half-supported by Jabari Ulumb under his free arm.

"Fates curse the hillman who drinks of the two-faced sea, Alpha Zà," Jabari chattered in his broken Yowekaon accent. The long-limbed warrior then inhaled an abrupt gulp of cool air. Under his mop of curls, his strained hickory cheeks puffed like a squirrel's with his held breath.

Kai popped the crutch between his teeth and superstitiously wafted his fingers up and off his forehead, as to invite the spirits to pass over him. Reclaiming the crutch, the lesser alpha said to them lowly, "What kakka-shtàka witchery did this to the Vasil?"

His voice carried fear as well as wonderment. An unnatural depiction reflected in Kai's deep-brown eyes. Zaethan finally turned toward the waves.

Dividing the lake, so infinite it should never be called such, stretched an inexplicable rift as far as he could see.

Zaethan gasped, unable to stopper his disbelief. Below his grip on the railing, freshwater slopped the hull. Its bright, silty crests were a stark cerulean contrast to the darker, fast-approaching azure line across the lake. Ahead, the choppy saltwater forged a clear boundary, separating Boreal from the rest of Orynthia and splitting his world—and his past—from the future of hers. Zaethan didn't look back at Luscia across the deck but instead across her Ghostly Gate, and it stretched for miles. The sky cast a mirror overhead, its blues darkening into a thunderous shelf of uninviting cloud cover.

The ship groaned as they pierced the Gate and charged through the spectral sight. Like his neighbors, Zaethan nearly toppled over to catch a better glimpse into the mysterious ravine as it passed beneath their feet. Without thought, he imitated Kai's gesture and waved off the spirits. As did his Darakaian pryde along the railing.

Swimming under the surface, like a constellation trapped inside the boundary of unmixable brine, were swirling pinpricks of bioluminescent light.

It was the kind he'd seen—and cursed—glittering within the jars of Luscia Darragh Tiergan's apothecary.

"Alpha Zà…" someone said to Zaethan as he closed his mouth. "What the Depths is *that*?"

Sending his eyes toward the front of the ship, he stopped. His breathing, his response… everything. In an instant, every inch of his hard-trained body became acutely aware of how small he really was—a no-name cross-caste unmeant for these lands.

For in all the facets of his convoluted life, Zaethan had never faced anything so dreadfully colossal as this.

"If you believe in the Fates, beg them for hérumaa now," he told his men with a tremor. "May they grant us mercy for coming to this forsaken place."

Not far beyond the brig's enduring sway awaited a mountain of mist that ran the length of the Ghostly Gate. Emerging from the sea, waterspouts whipped off the surface, clawing toward the heavens in a furious dance. Light flashed within the haze—the shadows so steep, not even the sun dared to cross them. And as to what perils lurked beyond, Zaethan was truly afraid to find out.

Chapter Three
Zaethan

Drumfire filled the air, struck with mallets of thunder. Another hostile wave battered the bow, drenching the brig and its motley team in a frigid brine. Deadly winds lashed their rain-slickened cheeks as they fought the temper of an unmatched tempest.

Among a scurry of bodies, both sailor and warrior alike, Zaethan heaved the rigging to brace the sail against the next berating gust. The violent upsurge nearly toppled him. He yelled a warning to the toothless man at his rear, but the storm swallowed his voice as it left him. Soaked to the soles, Zaethan skidded down the weather deck as the ship rolled at a dangerous angle. He caught the lacquered base of the mainmast underfoot, then held fast with one heel against the wood and his other planted on the planking at a dangerous slope.

The sailor behind him was less lucky. Screaming, he was sent flailing across the deck and only caught the laddered shroud right before he flew into the cold and merciless deep.

Zaethan swore through the downpour with enough description to make the regulars at The Veiled Lady blush, the hollow haven of a night-caller's arms a faraway shelter compared to the fury of Boreal's sea and sky. Chaotically, the crew handed off their lines fore to aft, tying them about their waists in a desperate dance. Expletives more colorful than his own spilled from Zaethan's battered companions as they hastily secured themselves to anything they could find. And corrupting the chorus of terrified shouts came the jubilant laughter of a maritime maniac.

Rafe Nabhu was going to get them killed.

The unhinged pirate captained them into the storm with sheer delight as he dangerously dodged between the waterspouts. Screens of water splashed from both above and below, but through the torrent, Zaethan's anger was fixed on the single spray of peacock feathers behind the helm. Whipping after Nabhu's tricorn hat, the soppy plumage waved like a flag of deranged victory. In a burst of mirth and gusto, he cranked the wheel with booming glee, sending Zaethan and the crew sliding starboard as he repeatedly tacked the ship left to right into the murky unknown.

Following the lead of the nearest sailors, Zaethan threw his body windward, steadying the changing position of the sail to keep it from ripping, as others did upon the foremast.

"Shtàka, Alpha Zà! We were better off in Khmer!" Takoda hollered across the decking over the wailing wind. Peppering the crew, members of his and Kai's prydes whooped their agreement.

"Oh rhaolé," Zahra barked from where she was wedged between two beefy sailors manning the jib sheet. "Go on! Go take a swim and cry about it to your mhàddas!"

Zaethan frowned, nearly tripping over a canvas that had been half-battened over the hatches. There hadn't been time to complete the task, lest it be the last thing the man assigned to it ever did in his life. Water was pooling around Zaethan's ankles even as it gushed back into the Vasil through the scuppers. Kumo had gotten Dmitri—along with the others—to his cabin just before the waters had turned over and poured from the sky. Zaethan doubted Kumo was looking over their king now, given the volatility of his sea-sickened gut.

"This'll be our last," the sailor behind him vowed. Fear grated his voice. "There's a river of bones beneath us, lads. Nary a man reaches the Ghost Coast when he's meant to sink at its gate."

"Àla'maia save us!" a cross-caste deckhand cried to Zaethan's left, just as a wave crashed over the taffrail.

The boy's Andwele prayer was drowned with his grip on the line. The knotting around his waist slackened, and seeing him almost swept away, Zaethan shot out his hand and caught him by the back of his slippery belt. Relief burst past his lips.

But with the next wave, the leather slid through his fingers and the deckhand was lost.

Zaethan batted his lashes as a tornado of water ripped across the surface, narrowly missing the ship. A very real distress rattled his limbs, and he searched the colossal hills of the rolling tide. Each wild crest added to a calvary of white-capped horses, trampling the boy under them to his death. Were he to search the trample any longer, Zaethan knew it would take him next.

"Best make yer peace with it now, Haidren."

Zaethan revolved toward the gruff sailor sharing his line. His square of missing front teeth beckoned like a tunnel to their doom. The sailor's skin pleated at the narrowing of his bloodshot eyes before they sprung wide and daunting.

"Something—someone—does not want us here!" A fistful of seaweed hung over the man's brow, shrouding his eerie warning. Iridescent lines shimmered across the tangled vegetation under a crack of lightning. Yet when the thunder clapped and the brightness dissipated, returning them to the mist and shade, the seaweed's unnatural twinkle remained.

Rain pelted Zaethan's face. He leaned closer and squinted. Bewildered, Zaethan lifted his fingertips to retrieve the sparkling weed off the sailor's dubious expression, but a rush of water toppled over them and stole it off the sailor—stealing the legs beneath them both too.

Thrown onto his backside, Zaethan trundled onto his elbow and attempted to rise. Disoriented, he sloshed through the pooling as the clouds raged overhead. Another break of lightning illuminated the deck and, in a brilliant flash, glinted off a series of witchiron blades speared in row against the forecastle. Pointed and curved toward the Depths, each free-standing crescent wraith was planted between the shadowmen. With their eyes shuttered, they stoically sat side by side, tied together on a bench instead of on their feet like the rest—their haidren locked squarely between them.

The earth clamored, yet they were seated in silence. And within their silence, their pale lips never ceased moving.

Zaethan slapped the water with a growl. He gripped forearms with the sailor and helped him upright, incensed that the shadowmen couldn't be bothered to assist in the deadly battle to get to their own shores. He'd sacrificed enough men in the past week. At this point, everybody was critical, and their numbers were even more stretched with the highlanders contented to let Zaethan's do the fighting for them.

The deckhand was buried somewhere below, in a soilless grave. Zaethan's spirit chafed when bravely he freed himself from the safety line and wrestled his way toward the steps of the quarterdeck.

Seizing every baluster, Zaethan tugged himself up the stairs. Nearing the top, he bellowed to the captain, "Doru! End this, Nabhu. It's not worth the king's life! Turn us back! We will find another way!"

"I expected more faith from you, Lord Haidren," Rafe Nabhu called from the helm. A huge grin upheld his sharp mustache, contesting the utter terror of his crew. "Do you not see it?"

"See what!" Zaethan climbed the final steps.

A wet palm hovered before his eyes. Helping him to stand, Nabhu rotated Zaethan by his shoulders, pointing far past the bow and into the clashing horizon. "The hand of God."

Raising his sleeve, Zaethan sheltered his gaze from the hammering droplets and scrutinized the waves. A spindle of lightning split the heavens. It was then he noticed that not everything out there was warring underneath them. Jutting from the roiling surface were five obsidian megaliths, where the colossal rock, irregular and jagged, stood out from the seawater. Disturbingly, one stone was segregated from four of descending height—a natural hand clawing up and out of the Depths—and at the center, the emerging fingers encompassed a gap barely large enough for a ship.

Zaethan wheeled toward Nabhu. "Ano zà, we are *not* sailing through that death trap!"

Nabhu gave Zaethan's shoulder a patronizing squeeze and patted him across the chest. "Watch me!"

The pirate chuckled confidently before pulling away. Giving a sharp whistle, Nabhu reclaimed the wheel from his helmsman with a lurch underfoot and guided the brig straight toward the menacing monument. In a chain response, sailors heaved the rigging with the revised course.

Zaethan clamped onto the taffrail and looked upon his own warriors. Unlike their rigor, the highlanders were rested in place, utterly unbothered, their blades anchored beside them. The only hint of the storm's interruption was the rigidity of their postures, as the haidren to Boreal and her shadowmen braced themselves upon the bench in unspoken meditation. Shaking his head, Zaethan pushed off the railing, but Nabhu's first mate threw him a line, nodding for him to promptly knot himself to it.

Everything seemed to blacken. Savage swells broke against the stones, worsening as the ship neared the natural opening. Under Nabhu's command, screams rang out from his crew, who were struggling to control the sails. Zaethan's footing slipped at a perilous angle when the breakaway captain cranked the wheel and aimed them toward the narrow passage. Suddenly, the vessel was sent heeling.

Zaethan cleaved to the railing. Sheer terror ripped through his chest as staring down, he was practically perpendicular to the waters. The dark waves clapped below, clamoring for him to fall just a bit farther…

Nabhu released a diabolical roar, and Zaethan was flung aside, away from the sea. He scrambled onto his bootheels when he realized the ship had been righted once more. And letting his head fall back in relief, he saw that an enormous megalith arched overhead.

Above it, the clouds lessened their hold, clearing to reveal the makings of a hard-earned sunset. As they passed the monument's backside, the megalith's glistening surface mirrored the abrupt calm, reflecting an undulating picture daubed in coral, teal, and marigold. The sailing smoothed under the high-reaching rock thumb. Ornamented in dangles of weed and sea vine, rain dripped onto Zaethan's already-drenched locs. He turned in place atop the quarterdeck. Zaethan's jaw slackened at the scene behind them, where the wall of lightning and mist flickered its farewell.

His stunned surveyance dropped to the row of shadowmen before the forecastle. Together and all at once, their Northern lips stilled. At the center, Luscia's lashes shuddered apart, and her steady gaze met Zaethan's. He couldn't miss the brightness that danced within her right iris. Down her either side, her guard followed suit, their eyes opening like a string of blue-green candles. Across the decking, she gifted him a stern nod, as if she'd had something to do with their miraculous survival.

From the unmissable hitching of her chest, Zaethan considered with a shiver that maybe she had.

He broke from her lingering watch. Zaethan freed himself from his leash and ordered his third, who was spitting up saltwater on the main. "Zahra! See to the king immediately. Jabari, rhaolé ono—to the animals."

"Uni zà, Alpha Zà!"

"This time if Hellion kick the hillman, the hillman kicking him back!" Jabari promised, trudging after Zahra down the hatch.

Zaethan rang out his hair, genuinely concerned for the stallion as well as the warrior. The horses had not fared well on this journey, and if they outlived the storm, Hellion would be sure the first human he saw paid for it.

A brass-buttoned, sopping mess, Nabhu strutted toward Zaethan, pounding the planks. The feathers of his hat hung flaccidly, though his smile could not have been more virile. Zaethan would have punched it off him had they not been inexplicably standing on both feet.

"There lies the Isle, Captain!" his navigator declared and tossed a rusty telescope to Nabhu.

He didn't need it, for even Zaethan could make out the tall island in the looming distance, coupled by an equally lofty but smaller islet, safeguarding its southern coast.

"The Isle of Viridis…" Nabhu's mustache twitched smugly as he told Zaethan, "This story is going to pour me a shot of bwoloa in every port for years to come."

"If I don't ring your neck first. You endangered our sovereign for *drink?*"

The pirate threw an arm around Zaethan, which he attempted to shirk.

He failed.

"Eh, yeye qondai, Lord Haidren,. A taste of home is worth endangering everything," Nabhu said.

"Ano zà. Not when it wears a crown."

"Headwear aside"—he pulled Zaethan in—"hewe hai Darakai, yeah?"

Zaethan clamped his jaw, and he spied the breakaway from the corner of his eye. "You abandoned Darakai. You're its defector."

"And you its bastard, *my Haidren*," Nabhu stated. "But let me tell you a secret… Darakai beats outside her borders. See, she beats for us now!"

The pirate snapped to the rhythm of his pryde warriors, huffing and hauling the lines in unison among the blended crew. Zaethan shoved out of the captain's soggy embrace, entombing the hurt of a home lost to him forever.

It certainly wasn't here, on this ship with Rafe Nabhu.

Zaethan suspiciously asked, "How did you know how to get to the Isle?"

Giddily, Nabhu's teeth shone wide. "I didn't," he answered, spreading out his hickory-hued fingers. "But sometimes the divine reaches for us, and when it does, I know better than to blink."

Zaethan folded his arms and muttered, "Will the divine alert the shadowman shrine that we come in peace? I bet two rounds of bwoloa they already have arrows aimed at our throats."

"They'll know," Nabhu stated. Stepping back, he flapped out his coattails dramatically.

Zaethan arched a brow. "I highly doubt that." He knew the highlanders better than most of his brethren—knew how little they warmed to outsiders docking in their business.

"Hmph." The pirate pondered. Pitting his fists upon his hips, Nabhu cocked his chin up toward the crow's nest. "Your y'siti haidren told me they would know. And I'm guessing that's how."

"Don't call her that," Zaethan snapped, tracing Nabhu's line of sight.

Noxolo—the shadowman who'd endured the Mirajii Forest with he and Ira—had climbed into the barrel atop the foremast. In a gallant sweep, he raised his crescent wraiths, crisscrossing them high above the bloated sails until they caught the sinking sunlight. A brilliant beam ricocheted off the witchiron. Having scaled the shrouds, Declan and the flaxen shadowman did the same, the rope ladder in one grip and a wraith in the other. Together, they refracted a diadem of golden light about the brig.

A timed thumping pulled Zaethan's awareness lower. Beside his haidren, the fire-headed captaen was pounding his kuerre against the wood. As was she.

Somehow, the sound carried for miles. And in one mesmerizing, abiding voice, the Boreali started to sing.

The Quadren gathered in Viridis's shadow upon the unwelcoming dock. By the lone boat slit and spiked portcullis waiting to be dropped over the winding steps that led into the belly of the steep cliffside, the Isle obviously did not intend to receive visitors on this side of the Vasil, but rather to defend against their number. Being one of them, Zaethan butted his frame in front of Dmitri's. His friend wouldn't perceive the hostility of the tense exchange between the najjani sentinel and his runaway haidren.

Zaethan had learned her tells. The way she rolled her bottom lip during their soundless communication. How her nostrils flared as she measured her breaths to keep calm. The micro-quirks of her head whenever she heard something she did not like... The foreign shadowmen had tells too—a tapping finger, a tendon jump, or the way the one seemingly in charge stepped forward to almost imperceptibly tower over her. Each sign leaked forth shortly after the highlanders had knelt and kissed the backs of Luscia Darragh Tiergan's hands. From the moment she'd made it clear that the entire group were to walk onto Viridis alongside her, their conversation had gone silent.

The warmth in her kinsmen's delivery with it.

Zaethan presumed it'd turned to ice after the sentinels had spotted the kuerre hanging from his belt.

Luscia's guard formed a broken semicircle at her back, Captaen Bailefore closest to the argument. Her massive wolx paced around their strained hush. His snow-white ears jerked with the debating tones. The shadowman cut off her next comment, motioning sharply to the lead sentinel in some sort of directive, causing Zaethan to wonder how much authority Bailefore held in this place. As the two spoke over her, Luscia bent her chin a fraction.

She did not like that one bit, he thought, stifling a smirk.

"Hachiro, do you happen to know the theme of this discourse? I'm afraid I don't see the issue," Dmitri quietly inquired to the shoto'shi.

There was a quaver in his voice. The temperature was dropping with the sun. Zaethan would have offered the quilted jacket off his back had it not formed a puddle beneath him on the dock.

Pages rustled behind them. "My records indicate that no outsider has ventured onto the Isle since the late Staff Age," Hachiro answered from his kakka-shtàka journal. "As the Ethnicam has not known such peace in the ages since the Mworran Wars, I suspect the Order of the Najjan is not eager to test it."

Beside him, Kai leaned impatiently on his crutch. "The y'siti have always held the strictest border."

Zaethan shot him a murderous look. The lesser alpha shrank back, visibly regretting his use of the derogatory term.

"The Ethnicam Accords were set up to preserve the Houses' power over their purebred subjects," Dmitri quietly explained to Kai. "Otherwise, two or more Houses would be forced to share governance over the same cross-caste subject."

"Uni, but unlike the other Houses, they don't even allow traders to come ashore," said Kai. "Money equals more power, yeah? What's a bigger driver than power?"

Their king considered his response. "To the Boreali? Historically, faith."

"Fear," Zaethan said as he lowered his gaze.

Ahead of them, Luscia gestured at Dmitri, then again toward the head sentinel. The stranger was spectral looking, resembling the nightmare of Darakaian cubs, with tiny, faintly glowing stones embedded in his skin. They descended in a thin stripe from each eye as if he were permanently weeping. He was built like a tree, and his blond beard had been twisted down to his embellished belt. As they spoke, the head sentinel shrugged off her point—whatever it was.

Her messy mane was pasted to the sharpness of her features. Clearly angered, she rose onto her toes, gaining an inch.

Zaethan didn't envy the man, Owàa help his resolve. However, knowing she could injure any of them, he couldn't understand why she allowed her inferiors to stand in her way.

"Well, I'm not looking to invade. Not in that sense, at least," Ira interjected. The yancy straightened his stupid kerchief and cricked his neck. "I'll be happy with a warm bed at this point. And some ale. And perhaps the comfort of a very special friend." Twisting, he scrubbed the air in front of Zahra, who was leaning against a post of the gangplank. "No offense to your many scary selling points, dear."

Zahra sucked her front teeth, making it clear she couldn't wait to sell Ira to the first trader she found.

"Her offer wasn't on the table," Zaethan barked.

His third winked menacingly. "I'd break his table."

Ira stroked the fine hairs of his arm. "My exact fear, as I wouldn't fare well with the splintering—"

Zaethan jerked the yancy front-facing, away from his third and the dozens of weary faces collecting behind her set shoulders. Everyone wanted off the boat as much as Zaethan. From the top, Kumo—a mountain amid boulders—rammed his way down the gangplank toward Zahra, his complexion still harboring its sickly tinge. The beta needed something in his stomach before it emptied itself again.

They all did.

The wet material was squelched against his spine as Dmitri, surely aware of the same, grew restless behind Zaethan. With a gentle nudge, he pushed him out of the way, and with his ornate cane, their king clacked forward to where the Boreali were huddled.

His friend steepled the walking stick under both hands, waiting patiently.

"It is a bit brisk here, isn't it? Lady Boreal, might you bring me into the fold before the hypothermia sets in?" Dmitri requested diplomatically. He masked his sarcasm only slightly, and it was heard loud and clear where their words were not.

"Of course, Your Majesty," she replied promptly and aloud, stepping back so he could come forth. Luscia laced her fingers together, becoming taller next to him. "As I was saying, Taemplar Carrick, being an officer of the Order, you are in no position to turn away the king of Orynthia, nor his officials, no matter the soil on which he steps."

The half dozen Boreali flanking the shadowman grumbled among themselves as his mouth resumed its noiseless rebuttal.

"Wem, they can, and they will," Luscia replied.

"Viridis is in part its own. You know we do not speak for our master, Ana'Sere." Taemplar Carrick stiffened stubbornly. He then extended Dmitri a belated bow. "My King, you and your Quadren may seek refuge on the Isle, but this is sacred ground, and the lowborn must remain on their ship."

"Lowborn!" a member of Kai's pryde shouted. "These walking corpses question *our* birth?"

Discontent arose from those in earshot as Dmitri raked his face. Nodding, he said to the obstinate shadowman, "I recognize that is a great compromise for you. However, as these brave men and women are here at your mercy, I trust you will do them the decency of supplying food and blankets to this dock."

Taemplar Carrick bowed his head in agreement.

"There are three mounts boarded in the hull. They might be injured." Zaethan rubbed his palms anxiously. "Shamàli, if you could see they're tended on dry land…"

After a long pause, one loaded with harsh study, the Boreali officer repeated the gesture. He mouthed something in witchtongue, and two shadowmen left him for the foreign vessel. Without watching them plow through the crew up the gangplank, Taemplar Carrick led the way under the sliding grate.

Zaethan pushed Ira and Hachiro after their king. The metal grille blasted to the ground the minute they entered the tunnel, and with a meager grimace toward both Kumo and Zahra through the lattice, he'd no choice but to leave them behind, trapped on the brig.

Yet for some reason, it was he who he felt was imprisoned, not his pryde. Should anything go awry, those he cared for most could leave.

Ahead, Dmitri's unkempt waves shuffled in and out of sight between a hedge of unidentified shoulders as he embarked deeper into a fortress not their own. Zaethan did not blink. Unlike Nabhu, he did not trust the divine—just the rush of his feet, keeping pace with his friend's decisive lead.

A downcast king, shepherded by a company of criminals. The only king Zaethan would follow anywhere… even into the clutches of the House of Boreal.

CHAPTER FOUR
LUSCIA

A parade of eager footfalls echoed off the moss-roofed stonework. Beneath their soon-to-be sanctuary, the air boasted the citadel's ancient fortitude, enveloping king and Quadren in the scents of calcified rock, cold waters, and ripened algae. Erected during the Spire Age, the tunnel had been built by Luscia's forebearers. The stones they'd laid had witnessed much, and since the writing of the Accords, not one had been altered. Everything was exactly the same, and she'd stridden it before. Yet as Luscia stalked Taemplar Carrick's lead underground, she felt herself unfamiliar.

Because it was not the Isle that had changed.

It was her.

She knew she would be unrecognizable to the Order now; Luscia had returned to her brethren only to defy their law. A closed border was one of the most fundamental creeds within the House of Boreal. Safe-guarding the coastline from the heights of Viridis, these warriors were the enforcers of the ordinance and therefore maintained the sternest interpretation of the principle that upheld it. No foreigner had come ashore in centuries, whether too scared or too smart to try. It was a serious statement, what she'd done in bringing the Quadren there, in that way. One that would not be dismissed or cleansed from her legacy.

Luscia hadn't left the Isle as a mere al'haidren. She'd left it as one of their own. She had left as *najjan*.

But that was not how she'd returned.

Luscia caged her expression, reining in the disharmony of relief, resentment, and shame. It wrestled within her more mightily than she'd anticipated. After all, she'd had a whole week to prepare her case while trapped aboard the stolen brig. Though nothing, no clarity of morning or insight of night, could have readied her heart to receive the accusa-tion of infidelity that had leaked from the eyes of every najjan who'd greeted her on the dock.

Defiantly, perhaps with more strength of spirit than she possessed, Luscia elevated her chin with the arrowing of her spine. The realm was bigger than this island. Orynthia was faltering. People were dying, and more than once, she had nearly died alongside them.

May the High One judge me where He must and grant me grace where He mustn't, Luscia repeated to herself, for it was only Aniell who should be entrusted to do either.

Not Taemplar Carrick, however esteemed the officer might be.

Aksel hugged her hip, trotting along the narrow walkway with enthusiasm. She couldn't blame the lycran. He'd not made the best passenger, as the crew eventually had had to stow him in the first mate's cabin to keep the beast from destroying their dwindling supplies amid his daily, stir-crazed frenzies. His hulking weight nearly pushed her into

Marek, who was shielding her stride from the channel that flowed to their left and the glimmering ïlarith eels lurking just below the surface.

She used to sneak down there to observe them, to admire their soft, pulsing light in such a dank and dark setting—especially at the vulnerable age of fifteen, when her world had lost its own brilliant hope. She felt a kinship with the eels swimming in circles, down there in the bowels of something great. Like Luscia's own story, that of the ïlarith was not as lovely as it appeared. No matter how celebrated, nothing ever was.

Unexpectedly, Marek's hand touched hers, granting the slightest of assurances where it swung. While the brush was subtle, her men would see it, were they to look. The kurtfierï bound to her wrist reminded Luscia that there was nothing to conceal, correcting her instinct to withdraw. Behind Dmitri, who was voicing his many curiosities to the taemplar, Luscia glanced up at the captaen of her guard and forced an anxious smile.

Marek's head dipped, although his focus was fastened ahead. His pinky finger crooked around Luscia's. "Let them spin their conclusions. We will set them to rights. Your breach is our breach too," he whispered lowly, quieter than the current lapping in from the Vasil through the metal grate. "Se'lah Aurynth, your men and I are with you in this, Luscia."

Her chest tightened, and her voice dropped even lower than his. "Niit, not all of you."

Gradually, Marek's stubble skated his shoulder. He looked toward the rear, where Creyvan was murmuring with a pair of local najjan. Unlike Nox and Declan, who closely shadowed her and their captaen, Creyvan had broken off into a private discussion. Even Luscia could not discern his wording over the clatter and commentary of the others, but she sensed it was less than supportive.

"Our brödre's attitude will recover once he is reunited with Böwen," Marek replied with a faint sigh.

It'd better recover, she thought. Creyvan had been harboring the same foul distemper since leaving Bastiion that summer for the coronation tour. Its foiling had not helped matters. Instead, the duplicitous turn of events had only soured his view of the other Houses more. Luscia lifted up a prayer that his twin had arrived in Roüwen with her lady's maid as planned. They needed Böwen and soon, before the damage to Creyvan's nature—once jubilant and kind—was irreparable.

"Get up, Hachi," Zaethan snarled behind her. His recent adoption of Ira's nickname for the shoto'shi had become more regular, as did the impatience in his use. "I'm hungry and don't intend to teach you how to fish for my next meal."

Pivoting, she watched as Hachiro dangled his quill over the ledge and into the water, baiting an ïlarith. Fading in and out, the eel's blush glow intensified as it drifted directly beneath him.

Dropping out of Marek's grasp, Luscia promptly pushed past her guard. "Lord Pilar, do not touch what you don't understand!"

Perched inside his capacious robes, the shoto'shi clicked a purple lens over his monocular device and said in an insulted puff, "A benighted presumption on your part, Lady Boreal. I've translated many ancient documents mentioning ïlarith, credibly more than yourself—"

Luscia lurched him away from the water before a row of fangs burst from below and snapped after his hand. "The eels bite," she told him while he gulped in her arms. "Now, to Lord Darakai's point, do get up."

Crowding the shadows, Creyvan sneered between his two new confidants, evidently amused by the shoto'shi and the near loss of his limb.

She slid out from under Hachiro and marched to her wayward

guard. Lacing her fingers, Luscia let the admonishment escape her lips with little kindness. "We are to protect them from what we know and what they do not. Wem, Creyvan?"

His gaze flitted to either warrior, as if they could answer for him. His smirk slipped, though a slight, rebellious screw of his mouth remained. "Wem. Meh fyreon, Ana'Sere."

She turned before she could behold his golden head bowing in respect. Ahead, Marek's countenance darkened, a captaen brewing a punishment. *Waedfrel,* she considered. Creyvan was Marek's problem to fix now.

The group came toward a steep, winding staircase. Moisture trickled down the stones where Luscia started her ascent with the other haidrens. By the third step, Zaethan came shoulder-to-shoulder with her, the sea-soaked fabric of his borrowed jacket seeping against the sleeve of her own.

"If your shadowmen don't send their promised provisions, Hachi won't be the only eel bait needing rescue. The crew is starving. Depths, more clemency was granted to the livestock than the people who got us here—not that you did anything to help us live through it," he stated harshly.

"This was the best I could negotiate," Luscia said, her reply saltier than Boreal's southeastern coast. "Be grateful I didn't leave you behind."

The Southern haidren scoffed. "I thought you were supposed to be in charge here."

"Were you in Darakai?"

Zaethan sniffed. "Things in that House were—"

"Different? Complicated? Wem. So too here," she snapped, and clutching the underside of her brother's rigged gauntlets, she momentarily considered sending a dart through his boot for the unceremonious interrogation. She'd left enough scars on his feet. What was one more?

Skipping steps at a time, Luscia climbed higher, escaping his company.

Rejoining Dmitri toward the front of their makeshift party, they entered a vaulted antechamber. A set of heavy doors soared high above them. The rare maroon wood, streaked with black petrification, was carved in rings of Boreali psalms, foretelling the history that lay beyond it. Viridi history. Luscia's history.

It was the Order's oldest credo, that which was sang over every najjan upon their final evaluation on the Isle, gated the entry—the same credo that had been sung over her.

Weh yeyisha'shadü tredae lim Lux.

We live in the shadow to walk by the Light.

Taemplar Carrick reached for the handle.

Luscia swung around to both Ira and Hachiro. "Hands to yourself and touch nothing," she said, eyeing the shoto'shi, who, undeterred by the weak torchlight, was already transcribing the psalms into his journal.

"My hands are reserved for your service, gosling." Ira winked rakishly, as if he weren't a disheveled heap.

Heatedly, Luscia speared the Unitarian haidren with a glare, acutely aware of the disturbed looks from their najjani escort. Her lips buckled, and before she could do it herself, Zaethan snatched the yancy by the base of his neck.

Glowering at Ira, he confirmed for her and her men, saying, "Uni. No touching."

She granted a stiff nod toward the taemplar. After asking their king to step back, a pair of his najjan seized the archaic doors. At the resonating groan, Luscia breathed deep and steeled herself for their parting... for the approaching disappointment of her feared and formidable brethren.

The strip of warmth between the doors spread wider. Luscia felt

Marek's hand shielding her spine, and she closed her eyes, letting him guide her forth.

With a gasp, Dmitri exclaimed in front of her timorous steps, "By the Fates!"

"Your Fates hold no authority here, My King," responded Taemplar Carrick. "Boreal is Aniell's alone."

At the mention of the divine, Luscia knocked her head back in petition to the High One for courage.

The Northern grandeur reflected the rest of the citadel. Boreali craftsmanship was nothing like that in Bastiion or Darakai. An old devotedness swelled in Luscia's nose, causing her to sniffle, as she beheld the symbols of what she'd taken for granted during the three years she'd called the Isle of Viridis home.

Vaulted and interlaid in stonework, the soaring ceiling was upheld by a labyrinth of outstretched branches and mossy vine. Rafters of living Viridi wood beckoned those beneath to glance toward Aurynth, for soon the starlight would pierce the canopy through the abundant apertures that dotted the rooftop. When it streamed in, it would depict the constellations in their design.

"Is that the Necluda arrangement?" Hachiro asked, recognizing the celestial patterns above. He jotted something in his journal. "I'd not realized the Boreali attribute their destiny to the night sky."

"We don't worship ourselves in the stars, Lord Haidren," Taemplar Carrick responded in her stead, his Northern patois thick with derision. His tone was unsurprising, given the notorious talï prayer stones planted in his skin, denoting his Orallach origin. "We worship the One who made them. Within each constellation reads a promise. And there we remember Aniell."

Hachiro's curiosity quickly concentrated elsewhere.

Setting the scenery aglow in a pearl-and-periwinkle haze was a succession of lumilores, just like the one weighting Luscia's pocket. Yet unlike her own, these precious stones had been chiseled into the images of heroes who'd come before. Statues were mounted along each wall above flickering sconces. The heat from each flame danced in the hall's draft, awakening each lumilore with the breath of the najjan.

Marek's lips hovered over her unkempt tresses when he leaned closer. "Look at them, Luscia."

Warriors of all ages were littering the hall, having poured in from the adjoining corridors and training spaces. A battalion of sharp eyes locked onto Luscia and her captaen behind the king of Orynthia. They might not recognize Dmitri Thoarne, with his being so new to the throne, but Luscia Darragh Tiergan—their seated haidren and the daughter of Boreal's Clann Darragh— was unmistakable in their midst. In passing, Luscia inclined toward more than a few, remembering them personally. The intricate threadwork of their linsilk garb contested the sweat clinging to most of their brows. This isle demanded much, a taxation the Quadren had interrupted by their unorthodox visit.

On either side, unsheathed, luxiron weaponry fenced her ragtag group where they progressed down the forested hallway. Like falling rain, some of the najjan bent a knee—not to their king nor the taemplar beside him.

They were kneeling for Luscia.

"Ana'Sere," they murmured in congress, their foreheads pressed to the hilts of their blades. Their voices layered over each other, the intonation of those who'd once saved her from despair by giving her a sword and the name of najjan.

In shock, she peered up at Marek, who was already peering back. His usually stark features were split by a boyish grin. It crinkled the sparse freckling around his cerulean eyes, transforming his entire face as it brightened with pride.

A mass fled Luscia's hip when Aksel tore for the school of children, who'd trickled in through the hedge of adult legs. Her lycran licked at their cherubic cheeks as they flocked to his enormous, fluffy tail. The miniature of his or her senior, each child was suited in linsilk sparring gear, a small-scale kuerre belted at each waist.

"There are children on the Isle?" Dmitri questioned Taemplar Carrick, dodging their giggling horde.

"Püpils, Your Majesty." Modifying her position, Luscia eased between him and the officer. "The citadel is not simply a fortress. It's also a proving ground. Most enlist during the formative years, sent by Boreali parents in the hopes that their son might join the Order as one of the chosen aelect."

"Is that what you all are?" Dmitri asked the surrounding najjan. "The chosen aelect?"

Luscia snapped for Aksel to rejoin her. As he trotted away from the children, she spied a young girl, her ginger hair secured in a tight plait. She was the lone female among their fledgling number. Offering her a knowing wink, Luscia extended an open hand, inviting the girl to walk with her haidren.

The child broke into a beaming smile, exposing her missing front tooth, and at the jealous whine of her male peers, she skipped to take Luscia's fingers before asking for her instructor's permission.

Luscia swung their conjoined hands as they strolled and explained to Dmitri, "Wem, in a fundamental sense, all najjan are the aelect. While at the command of our Clann Darragh, the Order of the Najjan is governed by a master, many of whom you see commemorated in this very hall." Pointing at the row of lumilore figurines, she saw the quizzical interest tugging the bridge of Dmitri's fine nose as he tried to work out the source of their radiance. "Taemplars are the highest-ranking officials within the Order of Hosts, based here on the Isle. Those like

Taemplar Carrick can be identified by the najjani brooch they wear. Where the taemplar sports three branches on his cloak pin, that of an armaeger bears two."

With his head turned, Taemplar Carrick lifted the braid of his blond beard to show Dmitri the luxiron, penannular brooch adorning his chest. An open circlet, its lustrous pin was fashioned to resemble a trio of Viridi branches, the edges smoothed and sealed to prevent the corrosion of whatever it clasped. To his left, another najjan walked backward to better display his brooch for their king's examination. A rank lower, the middle-aged armaeger tapped the twin boughs reverently. His was the exact pin Marek had been sporting when she'd first been introduced to him on the Isle.

One of the youngest to ever receive it, Marek had properly earned his former title. She'd made sure of it. Given they were only four years apart in age, the master had briefly assigned Marek as her initial instructor.

The arrangement had not lasted long.

"Below the armaegers reside the bulk of the najjan, our chosen aelect," Luscia said for Dmitri. "A single branch, no less worthy. Aniell knows it is a feat to receive one."

In consideration, her king motioned over his heart. "Captaen Bailefore and your najjan… They do not wear the same insignia?"

A dignity not her own bloomed from Luscia's middle as she explained, "Marek is a Set Apart Steward—one of few, handpicked by my father and the master for the assignment to a dedicated unit, such as my personal guard."

"The others and I are considered the Ranger Aelect," Marek said over her shoulder. "We prefer not to draw attention to ourselves, Your Majesty, so it is counterintuitive to wear the brooch. You'll soon see our pin resembles the antler of a reingafier. Within our own borders, we are freer to bear it."

Dmitri draped his arms behind himself thoughtfully. "I appreciate your clarification, Captaen. Lady Boreal. So little is known about the operation of your military force."

Despite his relaxed facade, Luscia detected the shiver he failed to suppress. Autumn had not fully fallen, and he was already fighting its chill. The knot reformed in her stomach as they navigated out of the populated hall and down a corridor toward the senior dormitories.

Forcing her optimism, Luscia squeezed the young girl's hand enthusiastically and added "Marek was named captaen over my guard after he was already an appointed armaeger within the Order. His is a double honor, rare even among the elite."

"Truly?" Their king shook out his dusky waves, thoroughly impressed. "You can't be older than I, Captaen Bailefore. That's remarkable indeed."

Her focus flitted again to the kurtfierï wrapped around her wrist. She couldn't deny that her father had approved of Marek's courtship for good cause. His Bailefore lineage alone was desirable in a suitor. The venerated family dated back to the days of Tiergan the First. That Marek lived up to the expectation of such a surname only added to his well-sought-after qualifications—qualifications that Boreal's haidren should seek in whoever was to sire her an heir.

Successors didn't produce themselves on their own, especially those of pure Tiergan descent, no matter the Higher Gifts she might possess. And given Dmitri's lackluster pallor, Luscia would soon need a Boreali partner to help her produce an heir to safeguard her king's. That was if they could eventually deliver him to his wedding.

Or Luscia to hers.

The lacing of her father's cuff seemed to constrict, and Luscia had the sudden itch to loosen it.

"Where are your women?" Zaethan shouted from the back.

Those at the front halted at the haidren's tactless query. Luscia's face went hot. He'd been successful at keeping Ira and Hachiro silent for so many minutes, Luscia had almost forgotten the remainder of the Quadren was even there.

"Boreali women are too bright for Southern eyes. You best avert them, lest you'll be blinded," the taemplar warned, an audible growl rumbling his middle-aged timbre.

Zaethan scoffed. Flippantly, he signaled back toward the legendary hall. "Here, among your 'chosen.' Where are they all?"

Taemplar Carrick resumed his clipped pace. "The women are at home," he replied to Zaethan with a pithy shrug, as if their whereabouts should have been obvious.

"Your haidren isn't at home. Was she not chosen?" Zaethan asked the group.

The question left a void only her voice should fill.

Two bodies away, she heard Declan awkwardly clear his throat.

Luscia bristled. Running her palm against the young girl's head, she handed her off to another najjan before anything irredeemable was said. She waited for him to get the child out of Boreali earshot before she spoke. In this matter, her men would not do it for her.

"Women have bolstered the aelect for centuries, however brave and uncommon their desire to do so," Luscia said politically as their procession stalled before a row of unoccupied dorms. The doors were ajar, and clean, downy beds awaited their guests. "Most women choose a different path. Now, the king and I need to speak with the master. Immediately. If you will feed and clothe the haidrens, we will take our leave. You"—she pointed at one of the armaegers—"collect a cloak for His Majesty."

With another shudder, Dmitri rebutted, "That's not necessary—"

"Bolaeva, brödre, the best you can find," she instructed the warrior, who, after a brief bow, set off in the opposite direction. The finest would be the warmest, and Dmitri would need it before the evening winds overtook the citadel.

Declan, carting her apothecary chest, disappeared into one of the dorms. Unable to collapse in it, exhausted as she was, Luscia motioned for Noxolo and Creyvan to get some rest while their captaen remained. Marek would have to serve as escort.

As well as witness.

"A bed! Come al-along, Hachi." Ira yawned and waved at the sleepy shoto'shi. "But don't get any ideas. You're not the special friend I had in mind."

Cleaning the smudges from his monocular device, Hachiro sluggishly trailed after him into the room. "My shoto prime says ideas should never be suppressed."

"Your shoto prime never lost a quarter of his inheritance in Port Niall…"

The chatter of the eccentric pair disappeared behind a heavy door, to the appreciation of everyone on the other side. However, in the threshold of the neighboring dorm, Zaethan lingered against the maroon frame, his arms crossed. His bright, green eyes narrowed at her in wordless challenge.

He didn't want to be separated from Dmitri. But this was her domain, not his.

"Taemplar Carrick," she said, stifling a vengeful sneer. "Assign sentinels to bookend this corridor. You know, *for the haidrens' safety.*"

Zaethan smacked his lips at the reference to her first night in Bastiion, when he'd done the same under that very poor pretense.

"Wem, Ana'Sere," the taemplar agreed.

Satisfied, Luscia signaled for Marek to spearhead the way to the master's sanctum. Dmitri did not lag in imitating his long strides, picking up his cane to follow.

She marched by Zaethan to join the swift departure. Yet without warning, he caught her by the elbow, holding her back.

Commanding and sure, his hold on her was not rough. "What you said earlier… about the women. I'm glad you didn't choose a different path, Maji'maia."

His comment rankled her. Luscia cocked her head. "My path is my concern. How is it yours?"

His ringed brow arched as Zaethan's bright irises roved the landscape of her face in a seconds-long crusade. "A different path would diminish my personal experience of Boreali women. And I'd like to keep it intact."

Luscia snaked out of his warm grasp. And gradually, he let her go. Free, her feet stayed planted, locked there by his unreserved meaning. She took him in, leaning there so carelessly, so comfortably, while his intent was anything but.

"The master does not wait for Darakai, Ana'Sere," Marek called from the corridor's bend.

The captaen's summons carried a caution. His simple phrasing weighted the air, charging it with the pressure of a promised storm, one they both knew had less to do with the man in reference than the one with whom she was currently speaking.

A defiant blush scaled her throat, masked by her jacket collar, like her scar. Bidding him no farewell, Luscia deserted Zaethan where he stood, thinking not of the haidren nor the captaen, but of the redheaded girl she'd sent away—the undiminished spirit she had willingly returned to a ministration of men.

The taemplar was right. The women *were* at home. They were exactly where they belonged. Because Luscia was on the Isle of Viridis, right in their midst.

CHAPTER FIVE
LUSCIA

"He and I are not as you assume," Luscia advised Marek, in a tone too clipped and quiet for their king to overhear. Her steps were fluid in her upturned boots. Stroking the warm solrahs pierced through her septum, she suppressed her embarrassment during their brisk walk toward the master's secluded sanctum. Luscia didn't need to aggravate the issue by provoking Dmitri's opinions about her delay.

Those implied by her najjani captaen had slandered her enough.

"Your conscience belongs to the High One, Luscia," Marek replied under his breath as his smooth strides perfectly paired hers in the most irksome manner. "It does not yet matter what I assume."

But it will, she added silently. Wedged between him and her sovereign, Luscia's grimace fractured her delicate poise as they passed under an entangled archway of Viridi boughs. Pillar to pillar, the leafy wood knit the ancient stronghold together so firmly, it was as if the earth itself would have to perish for it to crumble. She envied the permanence of the inlaid stones they passed. How sure and supported each was, never doubting the purpose of their creation or the shape into which they had been formed.

As they were haidrens of two opposing Houses, there were endless situations when Luscia would be coerced into spontaneous discourse with the likes of Zaethan Shà. She wasn't going anywhere, nor was he—not unless Dmitri authorized Zaethan's full-blooded cousin and beta, Kumo, to inherit his rightful Darakaian seat. Thus, their discourse was unavoidable, a job requirement she couldn't shirk simply because she begrudged its recurrent necessity. And whatever errant undercurrents might bubble to the surface during such discourses, none were subject to Marek's unsolicited input.

Yet.

As he'd so tactfully pointed out.

Covertly, Luscia's reproof swept off her tongue in an icy gust. "Niit. Do not patronize me, Marek. Not *here*. Not on our own sacred soil." She tut-tutted for Aksel. The huge animal scampered behind, happily squeezing his haunches into the meager gap, driving Luscia and the captaen another foot apart.

Pressed aside, Marek blustered out a sigh. The shoulder of his linsilk coat raked against the mossy stonework. "It's getting late, and Aurynth knows the offense was unintended. My intention was never to criticize…"

Irritable, she glanced up when he trailed off. Marek's thin lips sheepishly rolled under. He tucked a crimson tangle behind his ear and, high above her head, offered Dmitri an uncomfortable nod.

"Have you been doing that this entire time, you two?" their king suspiciously asked before succumbing to a yawn. Refurling his brow, Dmitri's hazel eyes narrowed, darkened by the lavender depressions he tried to rub away, despite his fatigue. "I'm aware you Boreali have superior hearing, but I hadn't comprehended that it made all of that"—he wagged his finger between them—"so imperceptible. I cannot begin to convey how unnerving that is to witness."

"Meh fyreon, Your Majesty." Luscia tipped her head down, mortified he was only then noticing their capacity to converse below his detection. She'd done it hundreds of times in his presence. "Bolaeva, please forgive our disregard for your sovereignty. We will refrain from speaking so softly in the future. I even pledge my men to it."

"No need to put yourself on trial, Lady Boreal. I only meant that it was rude," he said. They stalled before an imposing gated archway of luxiron metalwork. "As am I, turning up uninvited at your master's door."

The iron, fashioned into branches like those on a najjani brooch, was so interwoven, one could barely see through the barrier except for the pinpricks of illumination flickering behind it. There needn't be a lock, for no najjan entered the master's domain without urgent cause or invitation. Luscia had attended it only once, when she'd arrived on the Isle with her father for her unconventional deposit into the care of the Order of the Najjan.

She found it poignant, the parallels of her unfortunate return.

Without comment or delay, Marek clicked the gate ajar, permitting the trio inside. They'd taken not two steps before Dmitri's cane clattered to the whirls of inlaid stone. Luscia caught his arm and steadied his footing. Her king's chest heaved erratically.

She knew it had nothing to do with the weakness of his lungs.

Luscia stared into his wide eyes instead of what they beheld. The reflection of a thousand moons waltzed across his earthly irises. From them, a look of pure wonderment spilt down his face as he regained his royal composure.

Teeming the shadow, intrusive whispers played at her ears, toying with her tolerance. Luscia shook her head fervidly and refused them, while holding Dmitri. The murky pictures in her periphery quivered as the Sight menaced her vision.

But she refused that too—just as she'd done since Rian, unready for what it might bring.

Dmitri clutched her arm when Luscia joined him in gazing upon the light-bearing tree fixed at the center of the master's sanctum. The undressed roots were uncorrupted by their centuries. Inside the walled atrium, at furled angles, the tree sprawled out from innumerable crags that interrupted the swirling design upon which they stood. Most of its roots were large enough to serve as benches or even hollowed into tunnels. Boreali proverbs stretched beneath the toe of her mud-caked boot. The script was etched in a massive corkscrew, guiding visitors around the base of an ageless, gnarled trunk.

Its breadth was that of ten broad-shouldered warriors.

Unlike the maroon striations of the Isle's native Viridi trees, streams of lumin glittered within the bark of the master's living monument. Its countless boughs crowded the open canopy, nearly blotting out the brilliance of Aurynth's Watchman where it hung in the heavens. Instead, the tree spread out its own starry tapestry. Luminescent leaves, bespeckled by their natural radiance, adorned the branches, boasting the same vibrancy as the day the tree had been uprooted from the Dönumn's holy bank. Replanted there at the beginning of the Spire Age by Tiergan's eldest grandchild—he who'd established Viridis—the tree stood a symbol of the najjani credo. Throughout the generations, every master had knelt in the pool of that ethereal glow. Holding their decisions to account, the tree showered najjani leadership in an ever-lasting reminder of the shores they were oath-sworn to shield.

And of another oath made deeper inland—a reminder of the Dönumn Lux itself.

Above them, a million leaves fluttered against the highland breeze in an orchestral ensemble. Luscia's head tipped back, and she welcomed the unending praise for their Maker. The tree's applause rustled an intense devotion inside her bones. The sound beckoned Luscia. Like calling to like, it was inviting her back to the land of mystery and myth.

Her vision shuddered once more, teasing the veil between this dimension and the *Other*. Luscia blinked, stubbornly regaining control. An unwelcome tickle dusted her nape. Then another. Then the whispers loudened in a rush.

"Luscia…"

"Luscia…"

She swatted them away with her free hand, earning a disconcerted frown from Marek, who'd swooped to their king's aid at his opposite elbow.

"Relent, Luscia…"

No pain accompanied the lumin's call. Yet a harrowing flash of Port Khmer did.

Fear had rippled through Luscia then, when the voices had commanded her to tear a man from a rooftop and plunge him to this death. That same fear quaked through her again, in the middle of the master-secluded refuge. The lumin had spoken to her in Port Khmer, just like it had in Rian and the Mirajii Forest. It'd protected life. It had stolen it too. It had guided her and shielded her, but through the most chilling and unnatural manifestations—manifestations that Alora taught as never having been recorded. A haidren's Higher Gifts were said to be unique, distinctive to each direct descendant of Tiergan, though always bound by a concurrent set of limitations.

Meaning it was not her Higher Gifts that were unnatural… It was Luscia.

She'd lost the case of her aunt's tonics in the Quadren's escape. Since taking the last dose, her lifelong episodes and their torment had presumably vanished. Whereas in the absence of pain, the *Other* was only oppressing Luscia more, a disturbing fact she could not currently explore on Viridis.

Nearly drawn into the Sight, Luscia squeezed her lashes shut, causing her eyes to water, and gritted her teeth as she barricaded herself against the veil splitting inside her mental scape.

Niit, niit, niit, she mutely demanded.

Outraged, the whispers rose overtop each other. And then, with a distinct and familiar *pop*, they deserted Luscia until all she heard were the ragged exhales of her stupefied king.

A bead of sweat rolled down her neck. Luscia composed her panicked expression, ignoring the way Marek searched its every crevice in concern.

"You let me prattle on about the weeds in my garden when this… Luscia, in all my life, I had no idea…" Dmitri's jaw slackened. Twisting, her king retreated from her and quirked his chin, as if he'd never fully seen her before. Dmitri never had, not wholly. His contemplation locked onto her right eye, the eye of Tiergan. He flicked his troubled gaze toward the tree and back, piecing their opalescent hues together.

Luscia withheld her breath.

Apprehension began to formulate beneath his furrowed brows.

Visibly shaken, Dmitri steadied his hold on the handle of his byrn-nzite cane. Surely the empty vial tucked in his pocket had swum to the forefront of his mind, along with the contents he so frequently consumed. He had learned the truth of its making that late, melancholy night huddled inside her byumbé in Faraji—the five drops of her blood she'd added to his elixir. Luscia could almost see the cogs of his thoughts clicking into place, as the king of Orynthia suddenly realized that something within the Northern tree was beating through his Unitarian veins. That the same something within her and Alora was what had kept his heart from failing.

Luscia nodded at him soberly. "Wem. Prepare yourself, My King," she said carefully. "This is only the threshold."

Boreal was still to come.

"Master Rohan." Marek cleared his throat and dipped his upper body in a haste bow. He did not rise before Luscia could turn on her heel.

A man surfaced from the most shaded corner of the atrium. His masterful steps, artfully wrapped in their linsilk bindings, were barely audible, even to Luscia's ears. Their meeting had disturbed him after all, she saw by his meditative attire. An intricate, sleeved robe hung off Master Rohan's stalwart shoulders. The beige material floated airily as he glided toward them, its sacred symbols encouraging her to bend. But Luscia stopped herself, remembering she needn't bow. Not anymore.

Fleeing her side, Aksel padded up to his old acquaintance. Her najjani mentor raked the strip of russet fur along the lycran's spine in a friendly hello. It'd always surprised her that the master had agreed to house an overgrown wolx pup with the Clann Darragh's fifteen-year-old daughter. Perhaps Aksel was the real reason he'd even allowed her to stay.

"Allöh'jomn'yeh, Captaen Bailefore. Yours is an unforeseen home-coming." Master Rohan removed his linsilk hood, and in a descent too graceful for his years, he lowered onto his knee. "My Haidren,

Ana'Sere." He swept up the underside of Luscia's palm and pressed the back of it against his furrowed forehead, dipping so humbly that the graying ginger curls tied at either side of his head mopped her soiled feet. The uncut gems threaded through his beard jangled against her boot. Each precious stone had been blessed in ceremony by her own aunt, no doubt. Parting Luscia's hand from his age-specked skin, the master of Viridis inclined just as deeply toward Dmitri. "Meh fyreon, Your Majesty, for my postponement in receiving you. I was praying in the high place," he explained, referencing the citadel's topmost, north-facing tower. "Taemplar Carrick conveyed you came by merchant ship. I would be remiss not to ask how it managed the crossing."

He rose as Dmitri responded with a tired chuckle. "By the will of a madman known as Rafe Nabhu."

"By petition," Luscia stated more accurately, catching Marek's eye. It was the High One's passage to grant. She and her guard had given Nabhu's crew more in prayer than they could have strapped to his lines.

"Then lothadim'Aniell that He answered your plea, Ana'Sere. Nevertheless, I've yet to learn why it is you came to Viridis at all—and sailed with a company of brigands, rather than a regiment of soldiers." Patiently, Master Rohan crossed his wrists, tucking them into the excess of either sleeve. The delicate outer garment was deceiving. Like any good najjan, between the sheepskin breeches and loosely woven tunic, he'd hidden at least half a dozen blades along his middle-aged physique. "Was the coronation tour not to winter in Pilar, then travel to Boreal through the Valley of Fahime? You know that even our own merchants cross the border by land."

"And a far more preferrable route that would have been, had Darakai's chief warlord not hunted us all the way into the Yachel River," Luscia replied, unable to hide the hostility in her tone. Master Rohan's sharp gaze strained while she continued. "That is why we are here. Why we resemble the very dogs he tried to capture." She lifted the hem of her filthy clothes. "And why we have fought for our lives, simply to get the Quadren here to fall under the mercy of Boreal. War has been declared on the throne of Thoarne, Master Rohan. Ours is the only House able to shelter the king amid this concerted coup to overthrow his reign."

Partnering Dmitri's recollection of events, Luscia told the master of their excruciating journey to Port Khmer. How with the support of Pilar's chancellor, Nyack Kasim had orchestrated an unsanctioned treaty with Orynthia's cannibalistic enemy, Mworra, in an attempt to strongarm Dmitri into breaking his betrothal and declaring war on their ally Razôuel. That the War Council had been rallied after their chief warlord had publicly pinned King Korbin's assassination on a smuggler's falsified collusion with the Zôueli queen—when it was really Nyack Kasim, her accuser, who had arranged the late king's poisoning all along.

"My entire regiment had been turned, riddled with soldiers loyal to Nyack Kasim or whatever bribe he'd promised for their treason. My Quadren tried to lose our trackers in the wetlands as we fled for Khmer," Dmitri said, the nightmare still engraved in the healing scrapes and scratches peppering his chin. "Surviving a final strike there in port, we made it to the ship moored to your dock. The Quadren and I were the lucky ones. So many loyal pryde warriors who'd come to my defense were not. I will carry their courage to my grave…"

Mournfully, their young king kneaded his temples, as if he could rub away the anguish of their dying cries.

Luscia understood. They echoed within her too.

She cupped Dmitri's elbow once more and gently guided him forward when Master Rohan started to pace within the rings of stone around the base of the enormous tree. His generous sleeving drooped back as the leader of the najjan reached into the branches and absently let his fingertips sweep the sparkling leaves in consideration.

"Was the ship's captain prevented from sailing into Thoarne Bay in escape, Your Majesty?" The bioluminescence shadowed the master's wiry brows, making them appear bushier where they scrunched together. "Surely your army in Bastiion could better defend the crown from insurgents than a few dozen infirmed warriors and a vessel of pilfered goods."

The walking cane clacked with Dmitri's burdened steps. "In theory, yes," he said. "However, as no one in Bastiion has learned that whilst in Faraji I announced Yousif Shà as my new commander supreme, the Orynthian army still believes it reports to the authority of Nyack Kasim. You're right, Master Rohan, in that my remnant force is too outnumbered. His lies know no bounds and therefore could sink my ship before we ever made it into harbor."

Together they circled the tree again as he processed the information. The elder najjan steepled his calloused fingers.

"It worsens, Master," Luscia said, preparing him for their greatest danger yet.

"Ykah lö? Ana'Sere, what could possibly be worse than leaving the entire Orynthian military under the command of a traitor?" Beneath his coppery whiskers, Master Rohan's masked reproof coasted past his arrowed fingers. Himself the equivalent of a general, he did not agree, Luscia discerned, with their decision to bypass the crown city. "Isn't that the purpose of the Peerage of Nobility, to strengthen the king's claim to sovereignty whenever it is threatened?"

Behind her and Dmitri's strides, leather creaked when Marek adjusted his sword belt uneasily.

"Wem, when the Peerage has not itself been infected by a virus darker than conventional ploys for power."

Master Rohan stopped altogether. "Tell me."

"There is one they call the Obscurer, an unidentified leader who has been gaining disciples from all classes, and rapidly, from varied corners of the realm. And with his resource and influence, he is weaving unspeakable destruction." Swallowing, she suppressed the picture of Omun, the savaged warrior who'd bled into her lap in the arena. Or the archway of bodies strung up in Hagarh, all filleted by the same monsters she'd killed near the wetland border. But that detail Luscia would reserve for her father and the elders, as she could only hope they would know what to do about it. "So now you see, Master, even if we could reenter Bastiion unharmed, there would be no way to decipher who within the Peerage is operating for the throne and who for the cult. It has already been confirmed that Nyack Kasim has been indoctrinated; he too bears this 'Obscurer's' strange symbol. Were we to uncover how many disciples reside inside the proper, or even the palace alone, without an army, we would likely be prevented from having them charged and find ourselves arrested all over again."

"Shores of Aurynth…" Master Rohan combed the exposed tail of his long, tightly bound beard. "You mean that at this moment, all of Bastiion might be governed by a court of converts?"

"Wem," Luscia, Marek, and even Dmitri professed in unison.

The master of Viridis covered his mouth in shock. Eventually, he lowered his hands and caught Luscia's in his. "You are our guide. Consult your Eiide Corün, Ana'Sere. Bestowed upon you, it is yours now." His eyes stretched fervently, as if he imagined the Wreath of Wisdom was adorning Luscia's tresses instead of her aunt's. "Relay whatever you need, and I will do my best to provide it."

"Asylum—for king and Quadren, along with our rescuers—in Boreal," Luscia declared without hesitation. "And your permission for Captain Rafe Nabhu to sail us there."

Aksel encircled their quartet, pressing his sea-dampened coat against Master Rohan's legs as he mulled over her bold, possibly revolutionary, request. A wet impression soaked the thin robe. The master scratched the lycran's ear nonetheless and tendered Luscia a promising nod. "Asylum I cannot grant… but the passage to plea for it, I can."

Luscia squeezed his hand in fervent thanks, her grip tired and weary. "Tadöm, Master. That is all I require."

"Lodging on the Isle," Dmitri suddenly said. Using his cane, he took a meager step in front of Luscia. "For the pryde and crew."

The master politely inclined toward the king. "Niit."

"They are heroes who are presently sleeping like peasants, Master Rohan," Dmitri rebutted disbelievingly.

"Perhaps." He decisively slid his wrists back inside his either sleeve. "But we both know full well that the Isle of Viridis was written into the gray of the Accords, neither within nor wholly without the realm's jurisdiction. This citadel has not been breached by the Ethnicam in over a hundred years. Trust me, My King, it will bode better for your subjects when they entreat the elders if we reserve some semblance of najjani tradition tonight."

Dmitri's lean jaw clamped before he said, "Then tadöm to you for the hospitality you have shown to my *few*. Let us hope they relay in word what cannot be done for the rest in deed. Captaen Bailefore." He swiveled toward Marek. "I think I am ready to retire alone now. Please lead the way."

Stoically, Master Rohan watched the king make his sleepy but curt departure.

Luscia twisted toward her old teacher diplomatically. "It has been a trying journey. The king—"

"We are permitted our emotions, Ana'Sere, especially when we disagree," Master Rohan interrupted, looking past the gate toward the hazy cast of the corridor's lumilore sconces. He emitted an uncharacteristic sigh. "I'm told the haidren to Darakai carries our sacred luxiron. I pray this is a fiction."

Luscia forced her eyeline upright, refusing to buckle under the same questioning she'd endured on the dock. "As I explained to Taemplar Carrick, the kuerre was a gift—a lifesaving one at that."

"While it is not mine to try you, Ana'Sere, I cannot protect you from those in Roüwen who will," he warned.

The looming scrutiny of her late judgments had not been lost on Luscia in the least. The elders would not agree with her reasoning behind the infraction. Each would surely view it as a transgression against her own kind.

But it wasn't, she'd come to understand. That kuerre had spared Zaethan's life more than once. And in teaching him how to use it, it'd spared her too—in deeper ways the elders could never comprehend.

"I am prepared to answer for what is right." Luscia planted the soles of her feet steadily. "And will not cower when I'm interpreted as wrong."

Master Rohan offered a meek smile. "Wem. In that regard, I'm proud you've not changed." He reached into his pocket and pulled out something folded inside a piece of embroidered, sterling linsilk. "You'd left the Order so soon after your evaluation, you've likely forgotten what was always awaiting your return."

At his urging, Luscia took the small bundle from him and unfolded the featherlight material. She blamed her exhaustion when her eyes started to well.

Inside her palm rested a luxiron brooch.

Her brooch.

"Like our Isle in the Accords, just because you exist outside of us does not mean you have not been grafted into us either."

A tear escaped, though she hated its fall, and it tinkled against the metal with a chime only she and the master could hear. It sprinkled the single branch of the chosen aelect. Though set apart from any other, Luscia's was decorated with a leaf, expertly mosaiced in crushed lumilore.

As she released a happy laugh, her breath awoke the spiraled pattern of glowing pebbles. From underneath, Master Rohan elevated her hand until it was backlit by the sanctum's timeless tree.

Her leaf blended into the backdrop of its shimmering tapestry.

"You are our guide now, Ana'Sere," he said again and closed his rough fingers over hers around the najjani brooch. "But se'lah Aurynth, may you never discount everything else you have strived to become too."

The unfiltered sunrise streamed through the tall clear windows of the püpil conservatory. Luscia balanced atop the child's klödjen within a yellow beam of cloudless morn. She was not much larger than a child, thus the flattened circumference that ringed the training device was scarcely undersized. It fit her small feet just as snugly as it had when she was fifteen.

Though, Luscia was much better at not falling flat on her face these three and a half years later.

She teetered, not from a lack of balance but intentionally, rolling out her nerves with the bend of her knees. They were soon to set sail. It'd only been one night since her reunion with the citadel and the memories it sheltered. Luscia absently thumbed the polished brooch that pinned her rabbit-collar cloak over the corseted olive jacket and women's sparring breeches she'd borrowed from another najjan—rare it was to find one of her sex and stature.

Sounding from the entrance, someone's knuckles knocked the lichen-sheathed bark of the timber framing. Luscia glanced over her shoulder. With one arm crossed, Marek leaned against the Viridi tree, which fanned into a lofty web of sparse limbs high above his position in the otherwise-empty doorway.

He grinned and tilted his forehead at the brooch. "Well deserved."

Luscia rotated her neck back toward the series of windows and the gorgeous view of the rippling Vasil. "Grant me a few more minutes. I'm unwilling to leave yet."

"I never thought I'd hear you say such words about this place, especially to me."

She heard his laugh as his footfalls rounded the klödjen. Coming into her periphery, Marek folded both of his arms. Legs widened, he planted himself at the edge of the chalk circle, adopting the very stubborn stance he used to.

How her younger self had always endeavored to break it.

She'd been so angry back then. Rebellion was a way to fight back—against anyone—after what had happened. On too many occasions, Luscia had tried to dismantle the armor of assuredness Marek had always carried. The same he did still. But it'd never come off, despite her unending outbursts or complaint to Master Rohan. All well deserved, for his arrogance and approach. Marek challenged her like any other püpil in those early days, before she'd demanded another tutor. He'd cracked the feidierdanns until her feet had bled. He had once forced her to dive through the ice until those same feet had frozen numb.

Marek had treated Luscia the same as his other students—or so she'd thought.

Only in hindsight could she grasp how many times in class he had made her go first just to curtail her strain. Or in endurance training, he had prolonged the struggle of those whose turns came afterward.

He'd tried to make things easier for her. Even in her adolescence. Her whining for his replacement had only bought her the stricter instruction of another. With it, harsher expectation.

Separated from her, Marek had not overseen her trial on the klödjen. A different armaeger had assumed that particular responsibility, along with the remainder of her education on the Isle.

And she'd broken her own father's record because of it.

"I'm feeling nostalgic," Luscia admitted, rocking so that the globe rolled directly opposite him.

Neither were as they had once been. Yielding, she inhaled his familiar hints of pine. As her eyes took him in, she absorbed his picture in the new dawn.

Never afraid of her estimation, Marek skewed his angular face, and the corners of his slim mouth curved more the longer she stared. He'd dressed in a similar fashion. His own penannular brooch, its pin that of a curved antler, shone off his chest where it glinted in the sunlight. Its variance in design was subtle. The luxiron tusks, like those of a reingafier, crisscrossed the base of the gleaming circlet, distinguishing Marek as the captaen of his dedicated field unit. It was evident, his pride in finally be allowed to wear it again—not as an armaeger but one of the Ranger Aelect, for he'd braided his hair up so tightly that not one scarlet lock obscured its uncommon insignia. His cheeks had never looked so fiercely cut, suggesting he was the stunning statue of a man, rather than the genuine article.

Luscia's stance softened unwittingly.

He *was* genuine.

"Why did you do it," she quietly inquired, gesturing toward her feet on the klödjen. "Why was it you who stepped forward, who'd volunteered to attend to me during that trial?"

She could still remember it… him bending to his knees to clean the pool of urine when she'd no longer been able to withhold it. By the fourteenth hour of immobile torment, most had succumbed. Nearly each and every püpil. But Luscia had given in to her bladder much earlier than her fellow recruits. Without that initial mortification, Luscia would not have uncovered the most important rule to the klödjen trial: it was easier to sustain one's position when honest about one's nature.

The others had not realized the same, fighting their every spasm and ache—not wanting to be humiliated—until one by one, they fell from their klödjens.

But as Luscia had outlasted them all, repeatedly pissing herself onto the stone floor, it'd been Marek who had stooped while their kinsmen had snickered.

He'd tended to her throughout the entirety of the trial, sponging her drinks of water whenever her lips grew parched, never succumbing to the lure of his own slumber. He had stayed there, day into night, seeing day's reprise, before she finally faltered during her twenty-sixth hour.

Marek had provided her all that… even when she'd disrespected him.

"I volunteered because I knew you needed someone faithful," he replied, leaving his typical post to perch just below her chin. His aquatic-colored eyes flashed as he stifled his broadening smile. "A man who would stand by and not rest until you accomplished what it was you needed to."

"Even though it meant getting your hands dirty?" Luscia arched a brow, feeling spirited.

But Marek did not take her playful bait. Rather, he reached up and slipped a stray fall of blonde back into her collection of metal-ringed twists. His fingers descended her ear in a delicate graze. Pausing, he adjusted the trim of her collar, pulling it neatly as if readying her to brave the homey chill outside. Segregated by the fur, his touch passed over her scar and it ran the length of her arm.

"Enjjen anar. To none other, my Luscia," Marek replied, reciting his courtship words. "No matter the mess, I will always be there to help you clean it up."

Luscia deflated beneath the heavy shroud of the luxurious, unstained cloak. While noble in intent, his response was unsatisfying. For whatever reason, she suddenly felt as if they were once more speaking in a puddle of her filth. "Is that what we are sailing into now, another one of my messes?"

His smile renewed, and he brought her hand to his mouth and gave it a tender kiss. "Why don't we find out together?" Marek asked, retreating so she could descend the klödjen. "My Haidren, are you ready to depart?"

Luscia peered through the glass and into the daylight, then anchored onto the strip of sacred land in the distance. "Wem. That I am."

Chapter Six

The apartment was sterile. Stale though freshly cleaned. Empty but primmed with opulent detail. The walls were swathed in costly silk curtains, softening the rigidity of even costlier oil canvases. More museum than manor, the architectural appendages reminded the figure of a cadaver dressed for its funeral—fashioned into an imitation of life, while impotent to exhibit it.

He flexed his nostrils. Hit by a cloying tang of myrrh, ginger, and pyeiitoon pepper, the figure choked back the incongruous aroma of Western burial spices, which he then spied had been set to smoke inside a tall, silver incense burner nestled in the corner.

The Pilarese apartment even smelled like a funeral. Outside, a flutter of wings against the glass was followed by a disgruntled squawk. Amaranth smelled it too.

The figure carefully revolved inside the cage of straight lines. Not one possession had been staged out of place or at a dissenting angle. The owner would undoubtedly notice any piece moved an inch outside its proper standing. After wrapping his battered cloak about his waist, the figure knotted the hem so as not to disturb anything. The itchy material shrouded the cursed codex he carried strapped against his chest. It was a grim paradox, how something so small and benign had proven so heavy. As each moment passed, the pages of the codex, ruined by his and Alora's first relentless exchanges, burned an unfillable cavity into his withered heart. Words, verses, and promises that should have never been inked soaked past his sternum. Their poison was pitiless and taxed the figure's every step across the expensive, Vienese hand-tied rug.

He deserved this torment.

He was its author.

Artifacts shadowed the domed common room in a mirage of dark and ambiguous shapes. Though deprived of candlelight, the figure did not bother with any of the sconces at his disposal. He did not need their aid. Nor did he want it. The figure belonged to the darkness, and for his mistress's sake—for the sake of everyone she loved—it was his responsibility to ensure that his darkness never entered the light again.

To his left ran a shelf of rare vessels, varied in origin, era, and typology. On evident display, the sequence posed a covetable collection, no doubt intended to both intimidate and allure whichever political power was made to sit and negotiate directly opposite its showcase. A gilded Zôueli vase, crimped along the neck, outshined its elder sibling from the Scourge Age—a squat decanter plated in Pilarese lettering. The sale of either could feed a family for a decade, not that those who bought such things ever counted the cost of their next meal. Farther down was an even more precious, chipped clay urn. Remarkably, it must have been preserved from a tribe in the Spear Age, when humanity, reborn from earth's wreckage, had rediscovered its dependency on dominion and war. Instead of passing it, the figure lingered and crooked his head within the threadbare hood. Beside the urn rested a modern amphora. It was no older than the Shield Age, but its antiquity was far less noteworthy than the two coiled luxiron branches serving as its handles.

Witchiron—as the realm so jealously branded the superior, strictly regulated metal of the North—was there, inside one of the most prestigious palace residences.

Wary, the figure backstepped from the shelf, surprised not only to discover a stolen Boreali amphora among the number of collectibles but that its wealthy collector had valued the piece so equitably alongside his more sought-after relics.

Because someone with a commoner's understanding of luxiron would not. The only people who chased the bootleg metal were those in the military. But the amphora was no weapon… not to the ignorant.

Ignorance equated apathy. Once a wonder was understood—once it was priced—it was pursued. The inkling of a hundred spider legs skittered up the figure's spine.

Adopting a lightness of foot, gifted not by his natural birth but that which had come after, he crept out of the domed space and into a hallway of paintings toward an adjoining study. Apart from size and allotted bedrooms, apartment layouts were roughly identical throughout the Western wing of suites, though the figure had seldom spent time in them. There'd been little incentive when his true interests had lived and laughed outside an uninspiring, well-dressed box.

Alora used to despise her box, her inherited walls of routine orthodoxy and stagnation, doldrum and impersonal description. Yet it was his transgressions, not hers, that had ultimately driven her back into the barren box and locked her inside. And with it, her spark, that twinkle of innocent rebellion he'd encountered in a duke's library, had been snuffed out forever.

Bitterly, the figure clicked a set of doors ajar and entered an even dimmer room than the previous. His lids scraped his irritated eyes as they adjusted to the scantly windowed study. By happenstance or design, the space was surrounded by floor-to-ceiling bookshelves, piled under heaps of scrolls and orderly texts that obstructed the glass panes.

The musk of parchment and knowledge permeated the study, incensing the apartment's real fortune. The collection had to be the largest outside Gakoshū, the City of Learning. Unable to stop himself, as a puppet on a string, the figure slowly removed his glove. He hardly noticed the strip of skin that tore off with it. Enthralled, he lifted his blistered mitt and barely stroked the brittle cusp of a single scroll.

Genuine treasure never tarnished. For when read, its value was immortalized.

As was its wickedness.

Outside the glove, the odor of his prolonged decay overpowered the archival notes, reminding the figure of his true purpose in being there. Through the peppered moonlight, he slunk toward the lone desk at the center of the study. Aside from an inkwell and quill, the surface was bare, belying the infinite hours it was indeed put to use. An ornate rod overhung the corner of the desk, empty of its feathered hunter. A pair of thin, leather jesses dangled off the raptor's perch.

Constraints the hawk no longer required and hadn't for twenty years.

Angered by the sight, the figure gnawed a scab clean off his lip and, savoring the fresh metallic stream, indelicately gripped the handle of a desk drawer. He wrenched it toward himself, but it wouldn't budge. He tried the second. Then the third. It too was locked so securely, the wood was nearly cemented shut.

The figure slammed his gloveless palm against the desk. Pus and blood were smeared where he lifted it away, having burst a boil atop the grain. Frustrated, he wadded his cloak and diligently wiped it clean. His objective was to evade leaving a trail. Staining the desk was no less counterproductive than busting it into a pile of shards.

Rounding it, the figure ran his scarred fingertips along the underside, in search of a key. Nothing. Moving about the study, the figure scrutinized the plaster exposed between the shelving and marbled trim, seeking out discrepancies in the texture. Minutes went by. No trace of trick paneling. He pulled up the rug, but there lay nothing but a dead beetle. His anxiety arose, for unfamiliar with the servants' schedule, he could be interrupted any second. The figure paced.

Then he stalled before the only painting in the room.

He tipped the artwork off the wall, scanned the backside of the frame, and growled. It was smooth. When he let it go, the thick, gold scrollwork thudded against the plaster.

Thoroughly puzzled, the figure retreated and leaned against the front of the desk. The painting it faced was beautiful and expertly executed. Prominent even, unlike its subject. In a splay of vivid color, it did not depict the magnificent pillars of Gakoshū nor the exalted stands within the halls of the Shoto Collective. In fact, the canvas was not at all what one would expect Chancellor Tetsu Naborū, sil'haidren to Pilar, to daily behold.

Instead of glory and accomplishment, the painting portrayed a rural harbor outside Lempeii. The figure released a shallow, controlled breath when it dawned on him.

The painting was a personal commission.

His mind raced, rethinking his approach to uncovering something so ordinary, so unpretentious, as a desk key. Looking back at the picture of the rustic shoreline, a boyhood rhyme, one taught by his crotchety tutors, sent ripples through his memory. He heard his own youthful voice, a modest, pure sound he'd thought forgotten with his name, reciting the childlike proverb:

Listen as the teacher speaks.

Patience before havoc wreaks.

What asked within exists without.

An open mind should know to doubt.

Exists without…

It was almost too simple, but taking a chance, the figure aborted the study and plunged into the common room outside. Hood falling backward, he cradled his temples as he tried to recall the tricky phrasing of the second stanza.

The right masquerades its left.

Where false wisdom commits theft.

He spun aside to face the row of ancient vessels gracing the leftward wall.

Imitation a clever art.

When answers locked outside the heart.

His lips almost curled. The figure shifted focus from one artifact to another as he reexamined their detail once again, looking for an impostor. The market for forgery never died, not since its height during the Scourge Age, having served many masters amid the Mworran Wars.

Without delay, he cautiously picked up the Pilarese decanter and scrutinized the lettering. Using the nail of his forefinger, one of the few not yet shed, the figure scratched at the gilded inlay. Imported from the gold-rich lands of Razôuel, the plating should have been softer, were it authentically refined. Whereas imitation leaf, embraced by charlatan brokers, incorporated a percentage of silver alloy.

Only the best forgeries imitated substance as well as style. And this antique lettering did not flake.

Seeing no alternative, the figure was about to smash it when the final stanza of the rudimentary rhyme returned to him.

Humility guides this quest.

Knowledge waits at its behest.

What the student seeks can be found.

Not in the clouds but near the ground.

He set the decanter down and his eyes fell upon the plain, rectangular box resting on the table below. Covered in stout bronze pyramids, the piece was nothing special, just like the painting. A corner was cracked, and clues of Pilarese craftsmanship clung to its age-worn angles. It was more than an artifact. The box was an heirloom.

Hurriedly, the figure removed the lid.

Empty.

Vexation simmered his senses. Riddles had never been his forte. And he'd even less patience for them now. Holding the lid, he repeated each line.

Not in the clouds but near the ground…

The figure stooped and searched the bottom of the tabletop. When he found it free of compartments or hidden lips, his eyes resentfully rolled toward the ceiling.

His mouth parted. Burrowed into the underside of the lid was a mortise key.

After snatching it from its holding place, the figure got up, reeled around the bend, and flew into the study. He unlocked each drawer and rummaged through the contents as quickly as possible. Spare quills. A monocular magnifier. Wax sealant. A sickening stench wafted from the last drawer, where the figure pushed aside a marrow pipe and the accompanying jars of milky syrup. Beneath the street drug was a stack of old vellum, stained by the sticky opiate. His stomach sharply twisted. With shuddering fingers, he picked up the papers.

Flipped upside down, he sensed the thing's nearness before he turned the stack over, exposing the topmost scrap. The codex saddled against his sinking chest seemed to scream after its lost member. On the vellum, ramblings in alternating handwriting were hatched across the columns of tiny, printed characters. But it was the faded symbol he'd left inside the margin that bored into his soul—an infinite figure eight, turned on its side and divided by an introduced lifeline.

The vellum quivered within his grasp. He should have burned the original back then—when it had only been a theory—like she'd begged him to. But he'd been a fool, a selfish, deluded, murderous fool, who'd believed it was his hypothesis to test.

Pages rustled as he shuffled through the thin stack, finding each to be a worse revelation than the last. The figure held onto the desk, and he shakily spread the contents out before him in a web of his undoing. Fragments of his earliest research, toiled in desperate notes and senseless diagrams, blared up at him in accusation. In horror, he stumbled back, away from it all, in disbelief. He'd only mentioned the codex once. Not everything else. Not to anyone.

Which meant that following his downfall, it'd been discovered.

All of it.

He'd unmade himself into a monster, and his replicas had begun populating the realm. The crueler, more animalistic creatures had birthed from one wayward objective, an objective that had been further perverted and exploited, to a malevolent scale he could have never imagined.

That objective was going to destroy the world.

The figure scraped at his balding scalp and screamed. The scream held no sound, for it was too terrible, too visceral to pronounce. He collapsed onto his knees as it departed him. And not for the first time in his darkened exile did he so profoundly wish he were dead.

An unexpected *bang* crashed into the painting of the harbor from the suite on the neighboring side. The figure's head snapped up. After scrambling the vellum papers into a pile, he seized the mortise key and resecured the desk drawers, ensuring everything had been left in its rightful order.

About to exit the study, he hesitated. Out of momentary curiosity, the figure pressed his head against the plaster and listened intently. A muffled, predatorial gargle met the inflamed tissue of his ear. Disturbed, he pulled off when another item collided into something else, accompanied by a woman's piercing shriek.

The rush of attendants could be heard advancing through the corridor.

Ahead of their arrival, the figure swept into the hall. He returned the key to its hiding spot in the common room, paid one last lingering glance to the humble Pilarese heirloom, and noiselessly slithered through the terrace doors and onto the balcony.

Amaranth greeted his hurry with a wide flap of her lavender wings. Anticipating his movements, she launched into the cooling night air as the figure clutched a baluster of the byrnnzite cupola and vaulted onto the strip of palace rooftile. He scaled the ledges, hauling himself toward a lower tower overlooking the southern gate.

The figure hooked his leg over a stone railing and rolled onto the veranda of the royal aviary.

Cracking the gate, his intuitive hawk flew in to join the colony of predatory birds. Most of the nobility's sporting falcons were hooded and housed in tight, bordering mews. Unlike their taming, Amaranth favored the open, and she landed on an empty bow perch. She ruffled in an agitated shake, a grumpy warning that she would rather feast with friends than travel afar. Her summer molt had not yet concluded, confirmed by the few distal feathers missing from her wings and tail. She was in no mood to fly, but there wasn't time to get her acquainted with the idea. Time was of the essence.

In need of a new anklet, the figure promptly searched a crate of falconry fittings. Amaranth had pecked the last to shreds, another testament of her seasonal, scruffy temperament.

Finding one, he clasped it onto her ankle, receiving a perturbed snap of her hooked beak. He fished a graphite stick from his cloak folds and, trembling, spread a rumpled piece of parchment atop the workbench.

In blunt penmanship, he jotted down the overdue news of Darakai's treason and their leveraging Mworran tribesmen. Of Nyack Kasim and his rumored disowning of Cyra's son. Of the creature in Port Khmer and the Quadren's impending arrival from across Lake Vasil.

Of Luscia's courage, and his last observed state of her slow-dying king.

Spasms fired through the figure's stomach, preventing him from writing what he must, that which mattered more than anything listed before it. They'd shared their secrets for so long, he and his Alora. Throughout age and evolution, together they were the keepers of their own certainty. But each secret was a lock and every lie its key. Once too many were swallowed, eventually a keeper's insides were going to rupture. Something he would not be able to endure, for it was *she*, not him, who'd been left to deceive everyone of the figure's death.

That he'd been barely more than a stranger.

That he'd not committed an atrocity worse than death, for her.

When he'd departed the land of the living, he had deserted his love to face the fallout alone. And deserted still, everything was about to unravel at Alora's cherished, lonely feet.

The graphite hovered in place, as if not writing the words could erase his stain. Ultimately, the figure inscribed the most hair-raising warning onto the parchment.

Tetsu learned our truth.

CHAPTER SEVEN
ZAETHAN

"I'm beginning to think blue is your color, Zaeth. Fits in so nicely with the scenery."

Shoulder-to-shoulder at the edge of the Order's harbor, Zaethan speared Dmitri a wry look, thoroughly unamused. Draped in a downy silver-and-cream cloak, his friend motioned toward the sparkling waters and smirked behind the mantle of tawny fur that spared his kingly neck from the brisk, morning breeze.

Zaethan tightened his folded arms against the cold descending the steep peaks of the Isle. He plucked the velvety fabric over his bicep flippantly. "I fit in like you in a whorehouse. Depths, they've bundled us a whole season ahead of themselves," he muttered, begrudgingly grateful for the warmth of the padded gambeson coat that hugged him at the waist. Buckled asymmetrically across his chest and stitched in sterling thread, it was noticeably bulkier than anything their Boreali escorts had adopted for the sail across the sapphire divide.

Imitating everything that surrounded the remote Isle of Viridis, the daylit horizon was dressed in a thick fog. Whatever life lay beyond, it was alien and accustomed to frost.

All these shadowman—these *najjan*—certainly were.

The fair-skinned warriors fenced him and Dmitri atop the planking, as they distributed supplies and rations between the small fleet of bizarrely shaped longships moored to the north-facing docks. Before him, Zaethan's pryde warriors also hustled, though far more suspiciously, among the najjani throng. It was the largest number of Northern faces he'd ever seen at once, along with the largest display of witchiron ever brandished in the open. As they strode by, the high-landers took equal note of the kuerre that openly swung at Zaethan's hip, adjacent to his Darakaian kopar against the other. Anger was plainly written in their collective scowls.

Zaethan leveled his stance under the disgusted stare of the nearest shadowman. He was a clean-shaven member of the lesser aelect, given the style of his brooch, and was carting a bin of donated vegetables across the dock. The knot of wheat-colored hair wobbled atop his crown when sucking his teeth at Zaethan, the shadowman shook his head in passing.

Fellow probably would have spit on him too, were their king not downwind.

Alighted by the morning, their activity brought to mind the swarm of albino locusts that infamously fell upon Faraji when he was a boy. The najjan were themselves a swarm, just as pale and destructive as that one had been, albeit more lethal. Sheathed crescent wraiths crisscrossed each of their backs in a bladed wingspread he did not dare approach. The hair stood along Zaethan's nape, and not from the chill.

His Darakaian warriors were painted in equal unease. As the master's promise had been fulfilled, they too were outfitted for weather less forgiving than this. With stolen glances partnered by haste sidesteps, the members of his prydes warily migrated around the najjan—the same deadly men whose clothing they wore—and onto the boats as directed.

Not far from Zaethan's stiffened position, Nabhu's brig swayed on its lines in the deceptively calm waves. He'd been permitted to sail around the north side of the Isle to deposit the Darakaian forces onto the meager strip of land that supported the harbor, and a designated wall of najjan had awaited those coming ashore between the piling, ensuring that no one crossed the clear boundary of their *blessed* Isle.

"This is kakk. Their treatment of us doesn't exactly scream fealty to the throne, Dmitri," Zaethan said, his nostril furling while he watched a shadowman break from the stoic row and heed a brusque warning to an offloading warrior, who had clearly gotten turned around. "Boreal calls Darakai mongrels. Barbarians. But even the House that betrayed you threw a feast for your guests."

"Better a crumb with the true, than a feast with the false, Zaeth." Dmitri's tone dropped, but his meek chin popped over the wispy fur mantle resolutely. "Kings should not be quick to judge. Facts get distorted by emotion, and I think an even temper is our only hope to disclose them."

Zaethan snorted. He'd been spouting things like that lately, his friend, ever since Port Khmer, as if the ambiguous maxims were sayings he had read and intentionally recited to coach himself. Dmitri was obviously rattled. Perhaps made unconfident in his own ability to rule.

He had been thrown into the regency after his father's murder with nothing but mountains of ledgers and the journals of dead kings and queens to help him make his decisions. It'd been wearing on him, deepening the dusk beneath his eyes and crisping his jawline from the most recent pounds he'd shed. Already a thin man, Dmitri couldn't afford to lose them—not in Boreal, if indicated by their ample attire.

The Quadren was there to advise. But Zaethan was aware his friend inherited an even heavier anchor of responsibility, one buried deep down to which the haidrens had never been privy. And unless Dmitri fully let them in—let *him* in—Zaethan would not be able to help his king haul that anchor home.

"We've proven ourselves, my prydes and I," Zaethan responded lowly. Sidling an inch closer, he tilted his head downwind. Scanning the foreign docks, he found Zahra and Kumo offering aid to the najjan bringing the horses aboard one of the boats. In a flash, his third showed her hands in surrender at something the Northerner had said and slapped Kumo to yield in kind. "If this plan fails… if the Darakaian fighters are shunned at the coast… you will be losing your most loyal protection in your most vulnerable state."

"I know my priorities. And I won't compromise them." Dmitri nodded toward Zaethan's beta, who had stomped off, away from Hellion's newest keeper. "You have my word, brother."

Zaethan sniffed gruffly, the impossibilities of the situation playing out before him. "Still, meme qondai, I know that you may be forced to. You need refuge. You need rest. And you need the House of Boreal to back your return to Bastiion when we've gathered enough intel to attempt it. So, *if they shun us*…" he said through his teeth, "I take the prydes to Rian. Rally more with Yousif and wait for you to send Dhalili to me with instructions. Uni? Agreed?"

His friend's hazel irises speared him from the corner of his eyes, an abrupt liveliness in their hue. Dmitri was not a fan of the idea.

Nor was Zaethan.

Heaving a loaded sigh, Dmitri released his arm from the weighty cloak and reached around to clasp Zaethan's shoulder tightly. "Agreed. A king must always have a contingency plan, however unfavorable. Nonetheless, as in all my contingencies, you leaving my side is to be avoided at all costs. Is that clear?"

"Uni zà, if it is a cost we can pay." Zaethan inclined his head grimly.

"Good. Now don't bring it up again until I'm unconscious. Let the prospect disturb my dreams instead," Dmitri said. His pallid lips recovered their youthful grin and he let go, retreating his fingers beneath the material. "Ah, I see Captain Nabhu has acquired the stores he requested. A rather finicky list, if I recall. Although, in exchange, he assured the najjani master that he'd be off and coasting the Vasil by noon."

Nearing them, the breakaway in question advanced from a perpendicular dock. Wedged between the crate of gear under one arm and his pardoned aunt on the other, Rafe Nabhu strolled in spritely conversation with the haidren to Boreal, as if on some gallant promenade. Beneath the brim of his idiotically plumed hat stretched a rakish leer. Denied by Zahra, he'd found a new victim for his bombastic charms, it seemed. Zaethan considered what a charity it'd be if he were to smack the expression off his wafer-thin mustache, then in his animated gait, Nabhu's spray of peacock quills smacked Salma for the fourth time. Battling seasickness for most of the journey, the former madam hadn't come up for air in days.

It was a shame the reprieve would be so short lived, regardless of how many feathers she'd been made to swallow.

Confused, Zaethan turned toward Dmitri as the mismatched trio approached. "They aren't coming with us? I thought you'd negotiated the crew's passage with our own."

"That I did," he replied, shrugging. "But Nabhu didn't want it. You know the superstitions. Apparently after sleeping under the stars last night, the crew is too spooked to go any further."

Zaethan scratched his stubble and concealed his smirk. Having believed them himself, he was well acquainted with the stories of the highlanders—tales of bloodletting, occult moon rituals, and eating the hearts of the young. They were endless, and for once, he was grateful such frightening chatter existed. Because Zaethan couldn't wait to be rid of the man. Frivolous and foolhardy, Rafe Nabhu was a wild card. In Zaethan's experience, those rarely played in his favor.

No matter what happened on the Ghost Coast, the voyage there had just gotten a little bit lighter.

"Be nice," Dmitri chided, smiling wide when Nabhu towed his aunt onto the main platform.

Stopping beside them, Luscia angled her body away from Zaethan and told their bundled king, "The najjan are prepared to depart when you are, Your Majesty."

Commencing good-byes, Salma broke from her nephew and strutted toward Zaethan with the same command she'd been known to exhibit inside her decadent brothel. Her tiers of belted quilting bounced about her full figure as she caught his fingertips. "Tell me you'll miss me, Jaha. How will my freedom look without you, eh?"

"A lot more lucrative, I'd guess," Zaethan replied with a wink.

The notorious madam—and revealed confidant of the mother he'd never met—laughed warmly at her disreputable penchant for profit. "Cyra's industry shines through you. And by Owàa, I hope it never fades. Ano zà." Salma placed a slow kiss on Zaethan's either cheek. In pulling away, her dark curls tickled his skin when she whispered,

"Don't believe their lie, Jaha. Being cross-caste is our bounty, not our curse."

Her palm, its lineage and shading as mixed as his, lingered, cupping Zaethan's countenance. A flicker of pride flashed through her mossy eyes. He sensed it wasn't him but her long-lost friend she held there. With a final stroke of her thumb, Salma presented him a pleased chuckle and resaddled herself around her nephew's elbow.

"Tadöm, Captain Nabhu, for your service to the crown. It will not be forgotten by the Quadren anytime soon," Luscia expressed to the renegade sailor with a diplomatic air.

Dmitri nudged Zaethan's side expectantly.

He clicked his tongue at Nabhu's ridiculous getup. "I mean, how could anyone forget all that?"

Rafe Nabhu tipped his tricorn hat for Zaethan. "Shàla'maiamo, Lord Haidren." Then toward Luscia. "Maji'maia."

Zaethan's mouth screwed at the use of his pryde's nickname for her, despising how it lolled off the man's tongue.

"Should this Quadren thing not work out, there's always a life of piracy."

"You told us you were a privateer," accused Luscia.

The breakaway crooked a dark finger underneath her sharp chin. "That's just a figure of speech, darling. You can't believe everything you hear."

She smacked him off. "I heard it from you!"

"And what a lovely time we've shared, but I'd better run. Aunt Salma?" Nabhu directed her toward the brig's gangway.

His walking stick hit the wood, and Dmitri hurriedly took off after them. "Captain Nabhu, a word about that job…" He glanced back when Zaethan made to follow, adding a clear "alone" as he crossed the planks and called for Ira as substitute.

Engrossed in an improvised game involving the toss of some pebbles and the blowing of a leaf overtop them, the yancy haidren reluctantly tore from his gambling against Jabari and Takoda. Sprinting to Dmitri's side, if one could call that scamper a sprint, Ira joined their king in private discourse with Nabhu—the exact opposite picture of "alone."

Forehead down, the yancy nervously clung to the snuff canister draped about his neck as he walked with Dmitri and his rushed wording.

What could Ira possibly offer a covert assignment that Zaethan could not?

"Don't take it personally," said a husky voice behind him. "He won't tell me where he's sending Nabhu's crew either."

"Sending—" Zaethan clamped his lips shut, irked that Dmitri would be keeping secrets, much less after the discussion they'd just finished. He pivoted on his heel and pointed over Luscia's head, changing the subject. "A dozen vessels in your najjani fleet, that's it? We expected to be impressed by your Isle of Viridis."

Her icy, unevenly colored eyes narrowed. "Have you not learned? One najjan is worth twenty of you. You see twelve ships." Luscia cocked her hip. "I see two hundred and forty."

Zaethan arched a brow. "That's arrogant."

Hers arched back. "That's math."

Freeing a growl of exasperation, he clutched the hilt of his gifted kuerre and stomped down the docks toward a grouping of his own kind, where one man was worth the same as the next.

Zaethan had always hated math.

Specifically, hers.

Ahead, Sayuri's brother was huddled beside the tottering hull of one of the unusual, single-masted longships. Surging from the current, the stern platforms rose higher than the narrow, oar-ridden deck. The sides were sheeted with undulating scroll and whittled figures.

Conversely, the prow soared and curved inward, reminding Zaethan of a toboggan—an unusual toy Dmitri had received during a record snowfall one winter, from the now-sil'haidren to Boreal. The pristine meadow of white had melted by the following morn. Nevertheless, slathered in sludge, he and his friend had still recruited that toboggan to slide through the garden's subsequent mush. In truth, that was the only snow Zaethan had ever touched, outside the dustings drawn in pictures.

Mirroring the prow, every ship was outfitted with a hooked ram, similar to the toe of each najjan's upturned boot. He'd always assumed the design was to better catch the stirrups of a saddle, but he wondered if the purpose was somehow twofold.

By the spreading of Hachiro's thumb and forefinger, he appeared to be measuring the angle along the sweeping, ornamental mural carved across the length of the boat. Zaethan could hear his calculated ramblings as the shoto'shi transferred data into his kakka-shtàka journal. Not in the mood for more of his charts, or their prophetic death tolls, Zaethan swooped down in passing and wrenched Hachiro up by the collar of his ocher robes.

"Playtime's over," he said. Zaethan located the ship holding Kumo and thrust the scrambling shoto'shi in that direction. "Onto the boat, Hachi. Rhaolé, pick up your feet."

Snapping the colorful lenses one by one over his monocular device, Hachiro sputtered, "But—but the arithmetic. It wasn't finished!"

"We're leaving. Arithmetic solved."

"You don't understand, Lord Darakai." Peering back, he showed off an eye magnified twice its natural size. It blinked fitfully. "The Boreali vödalera is a physicist's dream! Translating as 'water sleigh,' the hull is fashioned to both withstand the fiercest tempest as well as navigate the shallowest inlet—"

Zaethan caught the shoto'shi when he stumbled within the opulent volume of his robes. "Is it soundless?"

"Well, given the communal and often boisterous heave of the rowers—"

"Shh. If you're quiet enough, we can put it to the test." He prodded Hachiro over the gunwale and into the bench queues. "Can't deny your research a good test, can you, yeah?"

"Oh, one should never do that."

After plunking Hachiro down directly behind the mast, Zaethan hopped over the rower stations toward the stage of the prow. On his heel, a swarm of colorless, armored bodies piled onto the longship as well. Zaethan's leg stiffened as he hoisted it over the frontmost bench. He'd never had so many shadowmen positioned at his back.

Zaethan snuck a glance over his hunched shoulder. In joining him aboard, he'd only heard the jostling *chink* of their witchiron.

He'd not heard their feet.

Gripping the elaborate gunwale, Kumo communicated much the same by the roving whites of his rounded eyes. "I don't like it, ano," his beta grumbled when Zaethan anchored a bootheel upon the half deck where Kumo stood. "They don't act like men, Ahoté. They act like this mist, yeah? And now, they have us wrapped in their witchery."

Kumo jabbed his thumb toward the foggy expanse, where the waters were swathed in unnatural clouds, as if the hem of the sky had hung too low, modestly concealing the North.

Zaethan broke from the ominous view and glanced past Kumo's arm, at his prydes scattered down the harbor of loaded "water sleighs." On the next longship, Dmitri crowded the same half deck with Luscia and her Captaen Bailefore. Zaethan watched as his oldest friend tugged his flapping cloak taut and worded some confirmation to her, the inscrutable haidren to Boreal.

Against her wild, tawny mane, her frame of bone-white hairs was a reckless diadem thrashing in the breeze. She was an empress of the untamed, leading from a helm of everything to the contrary. Secrecy clouded her stark features, just like the land from which she hailed and to which she was returning.

Her face disappeared when she twisted away toward one of her kinsmen.

Zaethan's eyes tore from the neighboring ship. He examined his beta—his cousin—hiding his fear and reservation. "For the king, we go where he must. Even into Boreal."

"Ano zà, Ahoté." Kumo deliberately brought his fist to his chest. "We go where *you* must."

His beta kept it over his heart, even as the najjan discharged their horns.

The hauntingly harmonic signal quaked Zaethan's bones, and the longship lurched underfoot, commissioning them into the echoing unknown.

Birdsong heralded them through the cool vapor, foretelling that life indeed stretched beyond the shroud of the notorious Ghost Coast.

As it cleared, Zaethan's legs threatened to give way where he took it in from the head of the surging vödalera. His vision was overwhelmed by the sheer green of it all. Zaethan, physically stunned, blinked to be sure. He shuttered his lashes again, absorbing the verdant tints and tones, a foreign brilliance that quite possibly did not exist outside of the microseconds between his every astonished blink.

On faltering footing, Zaethan rocked with the waves as they neared the place of perpetual myth. The birthplace of dark fable and superstition. The backdrop to his childhood nightmares and his awakening worries.

The very land he'd suggested they bring his king.

Orynthians did not tread into the North. They dared not knock at the mist's doorway, for were it to open, it might never close.

Boreal lay bare before him now, taunting Zaethan and his unwelcome knocking—the gall of a disowned, Darakaian cross-caste. As a warrior, an alpha, a *son*, he had devoted his life to fighting what he hadn't met before this day, and here it stood, mocking his inability to move.

Because even at the pinnacle of his hatred… He could have never pictured this.

Swells beat the soaring mountain of striated stone that rose from the Vasil. Armored with natural, daunting juts no less argent than the purest alloys, the silvered rockface upheld an imposing grandeur so separate from the red-flushed Andwele Mountains or the comprehensible sprawl of the Eindrulla Plains. Zaethan's disparity—and that of his homeland—hung in the air, blunt and unabashedly. It crisped every particle under the immense sky, too big and too blue to absorb, which crowned a forested land of dramatic, sweeping slopes. Snow-dusted alps climbed like reaching giants toward a deity he did not know. Their monolithic caps stood unseen, disguised in an ever-changing mystery he could not name.

This was alien canvas, fascinating yet ferally serene, where every paradox was drenched in a languid shadow, skimming the heights beneath a fleece of stark-white mist.

"Did she describe this to you, Ahoté?" Kumo breathed heavily beside him, his huge hand dropping from where it masked his beard.

Zaethan closed his mouth. Salt cased his lips. In reply, the same whispered wonderment slid from him. "Ano zà, cousin. Not once."

He wasn't sure if his beta even heard his answer over the choral ho and heave of the najjani oarsmen at their backs, who were vigorously rowing toward a narrow beach tucked between opposing cliffs. The shining strip of land was guarded by two colossal warriors, cut from the mountain and fashioned for eternity within the steep, ascending boulders. In their unrelenting hands, their intersecting wraiths impaled the bluffs, casting gigantic hexes over the sand. The sunlight pierced each stone warrior's subservient kneeling pose. Zaethan's head fell backward as the fleet of vödalera neared land. Bearing the image of their najjani brethren, the twin statues were bowing to no one except the vast open—to an apparent nothingness outstretched above them all.

He swerved his neck reluctantly away from the striking sight and toward Luscia, the one to whom it belonged.

Luscia Darragh Tiergan hovered over the waves. Her arm was outspread like the wing of a descending dove, where with one foot planted on the gunwale, she dangerously hung off the prow of her longship. Set and undeterred, the haidren's gaze was unwavering. And glistening her reddening cheeks, her tears were streaming in offering to the wind.

It was the first time he'd ever seen her cry. Zaethan hadn't been sure she could.

And he was powerless to discern why he thought it so lovely.

The waters shallowed, and the foamy tide washed the hull. Zaethan heard Dmitri's yelp when still a fair distance from the coast, Luscia plunged into the frigid, rippling froth to swim the remainder of the way toward her homeland. Her hulking wolx jumped in shortly after.

Splashing trailed her procession, for without urging or delay, her men too abandoned ship, and all five eagerly dived into the breaking waves of the Vasil.

Her dark-blonde head broke the surface and dripped a glossy veil as she emerged in a waded march toward the shore. The fleet soon gained on her and her guard's trudged advance. Zaethan's vödalera passed them, grinding to a halt atop the smoothly graded beach. As most were desperate to finally touch dry land, the Darakaians did not need any order to disembark the boats. Along with his prydes, Zaethan backed from the prow and found Hachiro, swaddling his journal in his sleeves as he waited to be assisted. With a meager eyeroll, Zaethan offered the interim haidren a hand and helped him over the gunwale into the few inches of standing water.

Ice, or what felt like it, encased Zaethan's ankles when he jumped in after Hachiro. Shells crunched under his feet, and the cold soaked through his boots, causing him to promptly lumber up the sugary, pearlescent sand. He rubbed his biceps and crossed in front of the long-ship, hoping to locate Dmitri among the witchiron-wielding number. But as soon as Zaethan came to the other side, he halted, for the busy crowd of Boreali shadowmen had abruptly parted.

Out of the Vasil, their haidren's feet touched the sand.

Their sudden silence coaxed him to try to listen too. Luscia's lips did not cease. Whether prayer or incantation, repeated Boreali phrases flew from her mouth in hushed sprints while she strode straight past the najjan's reverent watch. Uneasy murmurings arose from Zaethan's prydes where they littered the outskirts, and unturning, he knew well why.

Tears streaming, the haidren to Boreal's eyes were bright and gleaming, giving her left iris the sheen of the cobalt waters sloshing behind them, and her other, the optical prism of her sword. Yet in addition to the beauty of the kuerre stitched in its scabbard at her hip, her right iris emitted a light of its own.

Just as it'd done inside the War Council's bunker… in Marketown, the night of Lord Ambrose's demise. Or that awful, unforgettable day in their abandoned training room.

Even the evening of their king's eighteenth birthday… when Zaethan had evicted its youthful sparkle under a firework-flooded sky.

No longer a strange child but an even-stranger woman, Luscia led her men farther up the beach toward the tallest timberline he'd ever seen. She fell onto her knees. Bending her drenched body, she drilled her wet arms deep into the sand until they were swallowed to her shoulders. Slowly, ardently, Luscia bowed her forehead to the ground, expressing her recitations in some private rite.

Within minutes, her muffled sobs filled the coast.

Compelled by her weeping, her five najjan sank to their own knees, their faces meeting the seat of hers. Nervously, Zaethan sidestepped when every shadowman on the beach unsheathed their crescent wraiths and, with a shrill chime, knelt wherever they stood, planting their blades into the soil as if to imitate the very statues overseeing their arrival.

Like weeds in a manicured meadow, Ira, Hachiro, Zaethan, and his prydes gawked as the stanza of a once-sung ballad lifted off the prostrate Boreali and rumbled up the cliff face.

Rul'lothadim Aniell,

Rul'lothadim, on high.

Under no compulsion, Zaethan found himself lowering. He touched the earth and rolled the soft, translucent grain against his thumb. Out of amazement, or apprehension, he dug his fingertips lower into the fine sand.

Zaethan's mouth fell ajar.

A gentle vibration, barely detectable, enveloped his skin to the rhythm of their song. Timidly, he withdrew his hand, though not before the briefest jolt tingled its departure. His face wrenched in question. In ludicrous doubt.

It could not be.

Boreal was singing too.

For in concert with nature's instruments, Zaethan sensed that rather than clamoring for the outsiders to run, the land was summoning them to dwell.

CHAPTER EIGHT
Luscia

They'd packed up their camp on the beach, and though they were hours into the Quadren's morning ascent through the highlands, Luscia continued to press her prayer against every tree she crossed up the craggy mountain pass.

The elevations rose steeply. Her touch grazed the next holdre-heiim—a native giantling among the woodland, just like the one planted in the master's sanctum. Covering them in both blessing and confession, she treasured the rough reception of its plated bark. "Meh fyreon, Aniell," Luscia whispered contritely, pouring out her many failings and the innumerable missteps she'd made since parting from His lands. Happening upon the next tree, she graced it with a declaration of gratitude. "Tadöm, Aniell. Rul'lothadim, on high."

Stares accumulated from her foreign guests, noticeably shot between the hoofbeats of the few horses they'd retained. Walking alone, she ignored them. Her lycran had abandoned her to the roving wilds and its infinite feasting. Aksel had suffered enough, having been cooped up on a rogue ship like a black-market beast in a criminal's caravan. He deserved to run free. And she was pleased the lycran had, jealous of him as she was.

Luscia roamed without a horse, having opted to hike among the nature. She weaved off the main path, in and out of sight, as she repeated the ritual near the front of the party. Her eyes felt chapped, not from the beautifully brisk air but the tears that'd only ceased once darkness had fallen and she'd finally drifted off to sleep. It had been uncontainable, her outpouring upon their return. Luscia would never forget that feeling, how her heart had catapulted out her chest ahead of the vödalera, as if it were a lamb being called by its shepherd.

Nor would she forget what had followed. After she'd dived into the physical world, she'd broken through the *Other* instead. The moment would never quit her... Luscia had entered those ice-cold waters, and within the sheer seconds caught beneath the tide, her vision had erupted into the Sight.

She'd been such a fool to neglect it.

In an underwater masterpiece, lumin had plaited the waves toward Boreal's shore. Sparkled among the fish like waggling jewels. Shimmered within the veins of the dancing seagrass and over the slickened rock beds blanketed in algae. When Luscia had surfaced, when her eyes had crested the waterline, she'd not been ready for the pure, unadulterated spectacle of it all.

The threads were consuming, more concentrated than Luscia had ever understood. Because she'd not tempted to *see* during her Ascension ceremony—her final moments in Boreal—as her aunt had instructed, Luscia had departed blind to what the Higher Gifts promised her when leaving its soil. Here, the lumin skated the cliffsides… upheld its majestic peaks and precipices with unfiltered grandeur. Glittered the mammoth najjan in robes of light where they forever defended the centuries-tread mountain pass. Frolicking in the open, the hallowed light energy saturated the canopies of the loftiest holdreheiim as a hovering pasture, through the very treetops that had sheltered her forefathers since the dusk of the Spear Age.

Or maybe even longer ago, long before their illumination was ever resurrected in Tiergan's flesh.

As haidren, Luscia was expected to speak for the threads… to commune and then interpret them for her people. Yet she'd fled the lumin time and time again. In some ways, for good reason. The whispers from the *Other* had returned and berated her while she'd been in the process of assembling her tent—a dangerous anomaly she was not supposed to hear. However, in other ways, Luscia's reasons were not nearly good *enough*. She had eventually shuttered her Sight on the beach, but she recognized it had been wrong, so wrong, to stifle her Sight completely. Luscia still needed answers about the uncontainable forces that plagued her Gifts. After Port Khmer, she needed those answers more desperately than ever. But they would not be learned through her absolute withdrawal from the *Other*.

In that, Luscia had failed her people anew. Thus, in the lumin's midst, as she traipsed through their Maker's courtyard, she pleaded her penitence and gave thanks for whatever mercies it received.

Luscia's palm scraped the massive breadth of another holdreheiim, citing her heartfelt prayers.

"Depths, is she still talking to those kakka-shtàka shrubs?" Zaethan's beta asked from behind her, someone down the line.

There came a perturbed huff. "She speaks on their behalf," Marek curtly replied.

Luscia anticipated a terse remark, too quiet for Kumo's hearing, then recalled she'd not been the only one to promise to abstain from covert speech within their king's presence, who rode not far ahead of the captaen in their najjani convoy. Straddling Harmonia, Dmitri was carried by the gray Andwele mare. The horse was the pictured inverse of the stallion beside her. On the far side of the trail rode not her king's oldest friend but Kai, the injured alpha collected from the Mirajii. Guiding the horse from the ground instead walked the man who'd bred both stately steeds in Halona, the very foothills that considered him an outlaw.

Luscia shifted among the tree trunks and tinkered with the beaded kurtfierï about her wrist, decidedly averting Zaethan Shà's intermittent looks through the stallion's reins.

Such looks were unfruitful, however fleeting.

She ducked out from under a limb laden with long pinnate leaves, resembling not quite needles or petals but rather something in between. Fondness crooked her lips sweetly. The ancient foliage had always reminded her of eagle feathers when she was a girl. Consequently, Luscia had once convinced Phalen to construct her pretend wings of fallen branches. Even then her brother had demonstrated his penchant for overachieving, for in the end, the leafy wingspan had stretched taller than them both put together.

Orynthia's king harbored a kindred awe, where angling upward at the tangle of mighty boughs, Dmitri's nape had converged with his plush cloak collar. High above them, rivaling the impressive stories of his royal palace, grommets of infinite blue dotted the breezy pavilion of whistling leaves. The undersides crafted a decorated quilt of emerald-and-jade luster. Splintering the heights, divergent sunrays descended upon the party, casting them in a tunnel of golden beams.

"It's a marvel!" Dmitri proclaimed as he peered overhead, having inherited the childlike wonder his late father had once exhibited in a ballroom, when he'd gushed over Luscia's hybrid wolx and his profusely bushy tail. "And they grow even bigger, you say? Until today, I'd never believed a tree could tower over a hilltop."

Upon the saddle of Luscia's dappled mare, parchment was made to shuffle at his inquiry. Hachiro read from his codex. "*Holdreheiim, the rumored behemoth of the North, said to survive interior cut and design—*"

"The tall one talked to the trees too," Zaethan said, disinterested in the librarian's dissertation. "Did it all the time when we were in the Mirajii Forest."

"Yes, the lanky lunatic! He tried to kill me with his adverse berries too!" Ira piped up from the shared saddle, unlacing his arms where they were hooked around the generous pleats at Hachiro's waist. "It's a miracle I'm even here to tell the tale!"

"We've heard plenty about your tail…" grumbled Zaethan.

Luscia mouthed her next prayer as her gaze curiously fell onto Noxolo—the tallest among them—who strode between Creyvan and Declan, behind the Quadren's mounts. In their frenzied flee from Darakai, she'd not asked too many questions about her guard, nor the week they'd spent apart.

His najjani brooch, showcasing the pin of the Ranger Aelect, curved like a reingafier's antler and shone off Noxolo's reinforced linsilk jacket under the patches of mottled midday sun. Covering its proud glint, his long arms folded over the insignia when he admitted, "Wem, I spoke to the trees. They supplied the berries I had to live off. Was a better alternative than a whining yancy and his Darakaian bloodhound. A piece of my sister's driest jerky offers more desirable conversation than these two."

"Well, by the Watchman!" Declan walloped Noxolo across the gut in jest, for his thick arm didn't meet the taller najjan's chest. "What *doesn't* a man desire off the stalwart Dierdre Egon? A hefty handshake? A burly blush?" Splitting a playful grin—the kind he'd not worn since their initial trek to Bastiion that spring—Declan cupped an ear over his bush of frizzed ginger braiding. "I think I hear your sister's well-built wares, calling all the way from Ödetha's market!"

A preemptive chuckle escaped Luscia, comforted to see their banter had restored upon their own soil. She'd missed it dearly. Declan took a generous gulp where he walked. His belly puffed out over his belt as if he were a famed minstrel about to share a stage-favored ballad and let loose a new deafening verse about poor Diedre Egon.

Noxolo's lengthy nose hooked miserably. "Oh, for the last time, enough of this dumb ditty!"

His disapproval did not stop Declan in the least. Nor did Luscia want it to.

Her plump red cheeks glow like no other.
Sent from Aurynth, said so my mother.
'Tis a larger lass gives greater rush.
But a shorter man who makes her flush.

Noxolo made as if to dislodge something rotten from his mouth while laughter erupted down the traveling party. Some of the najjan recited it along the way. The ditty earned a few reluctant sniggers from even the sternest and most scraped among the two prydes. Maintaining a conscious distance, the Darakaians nearly doubled the number of those remaining najjan who were acting as Quadrennal escort toward the ruling city fortress of Roüwen, home to both Boreal's high clan and Elder Enclave.

A nervous pulse shot through Luscia's stomach, but she repressed it, stepping over a moss-encased log, and emerged from the brush to rejoin her men in their gaiety on the trail.

"I admit," Dmitri said, shifting atop his saddle, "it is a catchy addition to the tune."

Hachiro had twisted atop his horse as well, angling his journal and quill around Ira's slender torso. "As to the optimal female measurements referenced in the third stanza, what was that exact height?"

"Ock!" Declan flew his freckled hand well above his stout build. "The bigger the better, Lord Haidren!"

More laughter flooded the steep pass. It was the most unified the blended forces had acted since battling for their lives and that of their communal king. Their amusement boomed over each other in a pleasant melding so loud, Luscia didn't even hear her lycran when he scampered out the neighboring thicket, his muzzle stained in conquest, and straight to her side.

Nor did Luscia hear the approach of those who accompanied him.

"Surely that would cause complication without a ratioed schematic between partners—"

The shoto'shi mumbled the rest of the sentence to himself, unable to suppress it midway, when between a set of enormous tree trunks, the greenery parted for a fearsome man on horseback. Partially plaited, his long silver hair hung past the shoulders of his trim and tidy linsilk jacket, barely concealing a najjani brooch identical to Marek's.

The collective laughter died off, the Darakaians leading the silence.

His face was pleasant but stern, fissured with the unspoken confidence a man earned instead of boasted. Luscia had never deciphered the mature lines that fortified his unsmiling countenance any differently. Still, when he opened his mouth, his greeting voiced a smile just the same.

"Allöh'jomn'yeh, Ana'Sere. Your Majesty. May peace convene with you all," Emiere Tallaesen said, translating for the outsiders, and lowered his head first toward Luscia, then toward Dmitri. The captaen of Alora's personal guard cut an imposing figure of the Order, from the faded, slit of a scar that disfigured the corner of his lips—an unfortunate encounter with luxiron during his youth—to the set of throwing knives he kept holstered down the stamped leather shoulder straps of his wraith sheaths. Behind the older najjan, horse snouts prodded the bushes as more men just like him appeared in arrival. "My Haidren, we've come to usher you home to Roüwen."

In surprise, Luscia came beside the Andwele mare, nearer her king.

Dmitri sputtered as he ran a hand through his hair. "While I'm pleased to see you again, Captaen Tallaesen, how could you have possibly known about our coming?"

She was wondering the same; the Quadren's exact whereabouts were supposed to be secret. Had the breakaway captain Rafe Nabhu betrayed them, he wouldn't have known where the vödalera fleet would land. Even Master Rohan couldn't have gotten word to Roüwen so quickly.

Because Luscia was traveling with his messengers.

"Ana'Mere—our sil'haidren," Emiere replied, clarifying for the others, "foretold it." His green gaze, as vivid as the canopy above, landed on Luscia. "Told us she sensed a disturbance in the threads."

Like her aunt had often commanded her to do, Luscia teased her Sight into the *Other* where the lumin wafted through the wood, completely *undisturbed*. Blinking, she returned in front of the veil. "The disruption was oddly specific."

At the charged tilt of her head, Emiere adjusted in his saddle. Subtly, maybe even subconsciously, his eyes flitted overhead toward a string of birds flying from one side of the trail to the other.

Her aunt had a bird of her own, one that often bore missives from the unknown—one Luscia swore she had spied in Faraji.

A solidifying distrust plucked the stiffness down Luscia's spine. But she mastered her expression. Many watched it closely. They could not be permitted to witness the bloom of her budding anger.

Alora hadn't sensed the threads. She'd had her niece followed.

The Sight overwhelmed her the second they crossed into Roüwen, and this time, Luscia let it have its way. In celebratory ribbons of light, the lumin decorated her homeland, mimicking those of linsilk and wool being flown by the Boreali citizens that crowded the road. Though her companions could not behold it, the resplendent vision was unfolding before them. It was there.

And it was glorious.

Lumin illuminated the twilight settling over the city. Between her and her najjan, stationed on either side, threads paraded alongside Luscia as if they were members of the royal procession, twirling and floating in joyful patterns throughout the street. Except, the threads were not the only bearers of the *Other*. Merely its guardians. Here in the highlands, the lumin was born from that which flowed beneath the surface, and thus the light energy was seeded throughout. Forming ethereal torches as far as her eye could see, the lumin spread up and outward, dressing the monolithic holdreheiim.

Like an otherworldly vining, the threads branched into the trees, where together they upheld a rising borough of nested homes, swing bridges, and shimmering stone colonnades.

I'm really here, Luscia thought, nearly overturned. *I'm in Roüwen.*

The people cheered. It came as an anthem pulsing within the *Other*, the sound blurring inside her ears. Under the aura of twinkling threads, a lake of faces had converged for her and the king's unplanned yet no-less-jubilant welcoming. Between the fence of amassing bodies, the road seemed to narrow the closer the Quadren neared the town square. It was as if the entire nation was pressing in from every angle.

A perturbed yip rivaled the volume. Luscia lifted her hand accordingly for Aksel to squeeze his broad frame in against hers. When she pet him, marks of lumin glittered throughout his downy coat. Though the lycran's tall ears twitched erratically, his hackles did not rise.

Aksel too was where he belonged.

Fringe tickled her forehead when they passed under rows of swaying white tassels, strung from various dwellings within the heights. Each silk cord represented a Boreali family, and each knot a prayer. The festive tassels would only multiply with the days approaching Ana'Innöx. Some were braided, though most others were threaded with chimes. Billowing through Luscia's unbrushed mane, the wind swept Roüwen with reassuring bell tones as if to acknowledge her kinsmen's every appeal.

At the wind's fleeting touch, flecks of lumin were awakening along the strands.

Mesmerized, Luscia's vision brimmed with moisture as it had on the beach. Her legs progressed forward as the cheering faded and whispers overtook their place.

"*Relent, Luscia,*" the threads called in haunting harmonies. "*Relent and reach…*"

Although she was surrounded by hundreds, perhaps thousands, she couldn't stop the way her fingertips obeyed and reached into the crop of prayers. Heat zapped her skin when it met the fringe, and both alarmed and intrigued, Luscia jerked her hand back against her chest.

"It's Böwen!"

Creyvan's yell burst through her daze. "Brödre!"

She snapped out of the *Other,* all its secrets dissolving behind the veil. *Tadöm,* she thought, thanking the High One for letting her escape it without issue. Her fingertips thrummed, still warm as if she could feel the forces she no longer saw.

Marek sidestepped into Luscia when out of nowhere, Creyvan shoved between them from behind. In an ecstatic rush, the najjan hopped over a wine cask that'd rolled into the street. His upturned boots smacked the metallic, mineral-rich gravel as Creyvan beat the rest of her guard toward a sandy-bearded man, who was grinning ear to ear among the throng.

Forgetting the threads, Luscia abandoned all her Quadrennal decorum, for her own footfalls were scurrying out of line and straight toward Böwen too.

Böwen's turquoise eyes shined when his mirror image reached him. His twin clutched his skull in both palms and shoved their broad foreheads together. Soon, Luscia caught up to their reunion. Childlike laughter cradled the deadly duo. Creyvan's hands raked the other Tearlach brother, as if he meant to ensure he wasn't imagining that Böwen was truly there.

"Allöh, Ana'Sere!" Böwen yelled, his neck wrangled within his brother's embrace, one of his arms still pinned back in the crowd. Their months of separation were logged in the new inches of flaxen hair that dusted his tunic collar. "We thought you wouldn't come until spring!"

Luscia opened her mouth to respond, but a mousy voice stole her interest. Or, rather, that it was no longer mousy at all.

"We're so happy you're here, Lady Luscia!"

"Mila!" Luscia exclaimed when her palace attendant appeared beside Böwen. "Shores of Aurynth, you both made it!" She engulfed the girl in her arms, relieved to see her alive and well. Better than well, given the healthy pink to her fair, cross-caste cheeks, which were fuller than when they'd last seen each other in Bastiion. Luscia stepped back and took hold of her normally underweight arms. She grinned at the muscle she was gripping inside Mila's woolen dress sleeves. "Waedfrel, Mila. You look well. You look strong."

Appearing older herself, Mila stood sturdily and lovelier than ever. Boreali bangles jingled when she tucked a raven lock bashfully behind her ear. It was surprising that Mila wasn't yet used to the attention. Possibly the only cross-caste on the entire peninsula—aside from the haidren to Darakai—the rare contrast in her features made her a dramatic rose among a field of fair-headed wheat. Luscia wasn't the only person to notice either.

Creyvan pivoted toward the source of his unfettered infatuation— the girl he'd criticized Luscia for sending away to safety, and whose absence had unbearably soured his disposition. Though he couldn't seem to formulate an audible hello, Creyvan's parched stare drank Mila in, like she was the only thing to saturate it.

Mila, however, didn't appear to notice. Not that she ever had before. "Tadöm, milady. I'm becoming strong… day by day, thanks to you." Her deep-cobalt eyes lowered demurely toward her hand, which was enfolded in another's. "And to my Böwen."

Luscia felt her brows climb, with as much happiness as she was baffled.

"Been training her, like you tasked, Ana'Sere. She's a marvelous student." Böwen proudly showed off the fresh callouses on Mila's palm. With a smitten smirk, he kissed the roughness and let go.

Creyvan gaped at his brother's abruptly emptied grasp as if it still held her there. Böwen reached around him for a second embrace.

Only one of them was smiling.

With the turn of events undoubtedly awkward, Luscia was grateful when Marek leaned in to give a quick, affectionate slap across Böwen's forearm, which still encased his crestfallen twin. Voicing their quick plans to meet again later, the captaen gently cupped Luscia's lower back and said, "Come, Luscia. Not much further, the Clann Darragh awaits us."

Marek herded her and her lycran back into the rippling procession. The Quadren, steered by their najjani escort, had pressed on toward the continuously tended basin of fire, fixed at the heart of Roüwen. A statue—almost as giant as the najjan cut into the cliffsides—soared out of the pastel flames. Sculpted droplets beaded off his bared torso where the Boreali forefather reached toward Aurynth. Over the sacred pyre and around the fountain it alighted, braided filament was strung high, spindling up into the trees. The swaying spokes hoisted a hundred lumilore votives, where strung starlight illuminated the city center's daily bustle and trade.

Hurrying forward, Luscia rose onto her toes as she navigated between the horses. Her hand found Marek's amid the loudening festivity. She smelled the flaming basin before it fully came into view. Its herbaceous aroma was more fragrant than the purest extracts in Orynthia. A perfume of berry, sap, and pine soothed Luscia's nostrils, calming her return. Not far in the distance, the lavish heap of lumin-rich incense burned within the ever-burning pyre, spitting brilliant sprays of lavender and teal in its eternal dance.

Hollers sounded among those at the front to make way, dispatching horses and footmen to the roadsides.

Dashing forth from below the blaze ran her father.

A heavy, exquisite cloak battered the air as Boreal's Clann Darragh, their appointed *mighty oak*, deserted his post of authority for his daughter. Without a word, Luscia dropped Marek's hand and raced past those who still littered her path. Her father's strong arms stretched farther than the Eindrulla Plains—farther even than the unabashed, toothy smile that split open his burly beard to release a joyous, earth-shaking roar.

In a crash, Luscia was lifted off the ground and into his unrelenting hold. So much shorter than her only living parent, she couldn't even scrape the pebbles with her toes when the renowned Orien Darragh swung her in circles.

Pressed against his stalwart frame, she felt his hearty laugh boom through her bones.

"Meh lu'Lycran… My darling, little wolx." Her father cradled her crown in a desperate, crushing manner, which relayed his fears that he might never again would. "Tadöm, Aniell. Tadöm for bringing my daughter to me safe and whole."

Luscia's legs swung side to side. Shoving his face into her hair, he kept expressing his thanks to the skies.

"Allöh, Fappa," she said with a chortle and patted his meaty back. "Fappa, put me down. The Quadren… The king."

"Wem, if I must." Her father set her on the road but imprisoned her hands just to plant a kiss upon them each. As the last time they'd spoken, his eyes were misty beneath his full, graying brows. "I don't know why you are here so soon, and we will hear of it soon enough. But whatever the circumstance, lu'Lycran, you have filled me with such gladness this day."

"I am filled with it too." Luscia squeezed her father's grasp, then looked toward the emptiness beside him. "Fappa, where is Phalen?"

"Being a better diplomat than I," he replied with a wink, caring for court politics even less than his daughter. He ticked his brow at the faint outline of her brother, Phalen, buried among a group of newcomers.

Someone had to represent the family.

At least it's not me for once, Luscia supposed.

Aksel circled them both, and her father stooped to pet the snowy fur of the grown pup he'd saved and given to her. The movement stifled the next question burning Luscia's tongue.

Upon the fountain steps awaited her aunt.

Slowly, Luscia moseyed around her father as he gladly greeted Marek. The men's polite exchange faded behind her as she stepped farther into the light of the crackling pyre toward her predecessor.

Alora's fingers remained laced together, her posture neither rigid nor entirely relaxed. Her scrutiny descended on Luscia. Effortless and plain, it lacked any elaboration, like the immaculate hem of her modest linsilk gown.

"Allöh'jomn'yeh, Ana'Mere." Luscia stared through her lashes as she dropped in a hesitant half curtsy. Although, she rose almost as soon as she sank.

As Luscia had become haidren, it should have been the other way around.

Yet Alora stayed where she stood, on higher ground. "Niece," she said, instead of a more proper greeting. Her mismatched irises brightened. Strained inside the *Other*, they swooped about Luscia.

Her suspicion was evident.

As was it mutual.

Luscia neglected the instinct to humble her own posture. She was not the only one holding back information anymore.

The glimmer waned from Alora's Tiergan eye as she deserted the Sight, apparently unsatisfied by whatever she'd seen. "We are late," she announced, picking up her skirts. She gestured toward the variegated stone stair that enwrapped the most ancient holdreheiim in Roüwen. "You have been summoned to the Grand Tabernacle."

"But we've only just arrived—"

"With a barbarian brigade at your back. Your activities—your every choice outside our border has consequence within, niece. *Especially* within." Alora's chin lifted as Luscia's fell. "Se'lah Aurynth, Luscia. Until those shores, I don't know what else to do with you," her aunt softly admonished. Exhibiting a restrained tenderness, Alora fleetingly reached down to tidy Luscia's collar where it covered the ugly scar on her neck. "Pray the Enclave is more compassionate than I. Before their congress, my sympathy will be of no aid."

Luscia's resentment toward her aunt dissolved, succumbing to the pit of nerves that brewed in her belly. She'd thought she would have had at least the night to prepare. But as they paced in pregnant silence toward the base of those sanctified steps, Luscia begged the High One that *veriidim*, the pure, untainted truth, would be made evident.

For whether the Elder Enclave chose to believe their haidren or not, the truth was going to be bled out on their altar just the same.

CHAPTER NINE
ZAETHAN

Entering Roüwen was like untangling an infinite knot—and just as aggravating too. Zaethan slapped another dumb tassel out of his face, only to walk nose-first into a second. Then a third. And, as if the imagined Fates had ordained it, an endless jungle of cordage thereafter.

"Depths!" Kai cursed from atop Hellion, hunching over in the saddle to dodge a cluster of miniature bells. "What kind of moron drapes this shtàka in the middle of the road?"

"Don't try to understand the Boreali. It'll just leave you nursing a headache, a bruise, and a bottle of bwoloa, more confused than before," Zaethan replied to the recovering alpha. He tightened his grip on Hellion's lead, avoiding a brush against Kai's busted leg where it hung out of the stirrup, still trapped in its splint. As he meandered his horse through the foreign street, it struck Zaethan he was probably wiser to have remained on foot, unlike his peers. Upheld in the saddle, the bordering Boreali would assume the darker rider to be the haidren to Darakai.

And by Owàa, they did not look happy about it.

Although thousands in the city had joyfully flocked along the bizarre highway, their joy was in no way meant for Zaethan or his comrades—maybe not even their king. Instead, the heralding cries trailed *her*—their prodigal haidren—as she paraded by them. Hands as colorless as Luscia's strained to touch her in passing. Some even grazed her profoundly native clothing. The Boreali articles, like these people, had never met a different country or culture.

Had they seen you in Darakai, Maji'maia, he spitefully mused to himself.

Luscia didn't even seem to notice how the people yelled after her when she hurried ahead with her shadowmen toward someone else within the crowd.

An accompaniment of Northern fiddlers and flutists enthused her homecoming celebration. Over the music and shouting, Dmitri hollered, "I think it's all rather charming—if a bit obtrusive." He ducked around an especially low-hanging tassel that skimmed Harmonia's haunches. By his besotted grin and emergent dimple, their king had overlooked the subtle shift among the nearest highlanders that crammed the roadside, as well as the chilling pale stares that pierced the rest of his Quadren. So too the harsher scowls the Boreali reserved for the contingent of Darakaian militia, which was warily hugging the rear. "I'm sure there's some explanation for the bizarre display, but there is a rustic loveliness to the whole construction, is there not?"

Zaethan scratched his jaw. The stubble was beginning to itch mightily. He eyed the unbelievable heights from which the strange, woven cords were strung. "If by 'rustic,' you mean weird and arcane…"

"These might be a custom correlated with the upcoming 'Ana'Innöx,'" Hachiro suggested from his shared saddle. A spasm rippled his cheek as he squinted through the declining sunlight at the crinkled pages of his blasted codex. "Translates to *Great Harvest*. It appears as a holiday concurrent with the autumn equinox, Sire, but there is no further note expounding on its meaning within my limited references."

"Thank the F-Fates for th-that! Going numb on this horse is th-thorment enough." After spitting out a wad of Hachiro's stiff, black hair, Ira adjusted his expression, which hovered just above the shoto'shi's unkempt crown. His tongue spluttered over his slim lips in disgust. "Whenever I next want to forage among someone's brush, Hachi, I can promise it won't be yours. Oh, what now?" The yancy bucked under Zaethan's perturbed glare and jabbed his ringless fingers toward the saddle mate in front of him. In recent wager, Ira had forfeited most of his courtly ornaments to Takoda. "In spite of my foraging prowess, Hachi wouldn't even enjoy it!"

"I would not enjoy it," the shoto'shi stated, distractedly turning a page.

"Muzzle yourselves," Zaethan growled. Cautiously, he tried to decipher the outline of a strange, looming monument through the sheet of dangling cords—along with the persons congregated at its base. "These people aren't like us." His guarded watch traveled skyward, into Roüwen's interconnected web of nested homes. "They can hear *everything*. Not another word until we know what we're walking into."

He'd heard and repeated the far-fetched stories of the Boreali—had believed most of them too. They were terrifying. They were fanciful.

They spoke of a nation nestled among the birds and clouds. Yet in all of the fear-driven fantasy, Zaethan would have never dreamed the enormity of what soared above him now. It was inconceivable.

Disproving those fabled roosts—as if the Boreali were mystical pigeons, who lived inside crude hovels of twig and straw—spires of inlaid stone steps ascended in colossal coils up the Northern tree trunks. Zaethan estimated each was the breadth of fifty men, had he enough warriors to measure hand-in-hand around the bases. Instead of simple rope and ladder, complex turbines ran parallel between the stair flights, where the intersecting wheels were anchored along the bark, rotating in overflowing pailfuls. Zaethan soon concluded that the intricate system powered the local forges and mills on the ground. The water must have been distributed down the inhabited heights from reservoirs somehow, throughout the gargantuan canopy.

Though his anxiety multiplied with each step deeper into the Boreali domain, so did his awe.

In place of buildings, Roüwen boasted a rookery of structures that had been cored out from within its trees. Lustrous verandas, supported by witchiron balusters, were shrouded under twisting vines, encircling what looked like shops and residences alike in a branch-bearing stateliness. The network seemed to soar for miles. Overlapping swing bridges linked the verandas together across their perilous voids. At the idea of traversing one, Zaethan's palms slickened on Hellion's reins. He swallowed hard and returned his focus forward, back to the hard, tangible gravel underfoot. He'd always considered himself suited for heights.

Evidently that was not the case.

From his vantage in the street, the most impressive of these extended structures towered over the city center, fixed around the greatest of trees. Through the dwindling tassels, Zaethan could make out a veranda like no other. Its gem-encrusted columns stretched multiple stories, upholding a dazzling awning. Lit by outdoor lamps, tiers of decorated fabric descended like waterfalls, garbing the bark in a jewel-toned tapestry. The colors were swept at steep angles to conceal whatever lay inside.

Directly before the edifice, whatever it may be, ascended a glistening monument—a man, sculpted from limestone or saltrock shot out of a fountain. An eerie, otherworldly flame consumed the statue's lower body as it appeared to claw out from an erected silver basin. He'd never seen fire that color, or a lack of it, before. It was wrong. Zaethan shivered under his coat.

Backlit by its glow stood the sil'haidren to Boreal.

The older woman's study was as generous as her steeled lips. Beaded and buttoned to her neckline, she stood an iron lady, reflecting the city lights in her iridescent gray gown like his gifted backsword. A cool sensation scraped at Zaethan's nape when he guided the fragmented Quadren past her and around the fountain, then slowed to a halt. He rested the horses between the flaming statue and what resembled a tavern excavated unto the foundation of the adjacent tree.

Zaethan cagily descended and hitched his reins over a post. Leaving Kai to slide off the saddle on his own, he aimed for their king. "Easy does it," he said, stabilizing Dmitri as he pushed off the heavy cloak and swung his leg overtop Harmonia. They'd been riding for so long; everyone's limbs were bound to have melted to marmalade.

"Oh, allowed to speak again, are we?" his friend sniped, dropping onto the street, his walking stick in tow. For a fraction, Zaethan rethought his earlier directive, but he soon spotted the boyish grin softening Dmitri's sharp profile. "Did we lose Luscia to the masses, or was she—"

An elated, masculine roar spun them both on their heels to witness a boulder of a man running in full sprint toward the haidren in question.

A cavity reopened in Zaethan's middle. Raw and unhealed, it stung brutally.

The brazen love that radiated from the highlander's roughened face was coarse salt on the wound. When the two collided, the finely stitched, gauzy robe he wore overtop his traditional tunic engulfed Luscia in a misty cloud. His thick arms scooped her up and off the ground. He held her so securely that one would have had to pry them apart with a wrecking bar.

Zaethan stared at the pair. His shoulders vacantly sagged, as she was twirled in loving circles in the middle of the city street.

The man was her father.

And his shameless display was more foreign to Zaethan than any creed or coloring ever could be.

Eyes stinging, Zaethan ultimately looked away and beyond his shoulder, where upon it, Dmitri's hand descended without comment. He was given a tender squeeze. Instinct wanted to shirk his friend and storm out of sight. However, he couldn't. Zaethan's cruel fraud-of-a-father had murdered Dmitri's genuine one. Both fatherless, there they stood—on cold, unfamiliar ground—together and undivided.

Nodding at no one, Zaethan clasped Dmitri's wind-bitten fingers over his shoulder. Such friendship should never be shirked.

Dozens of shadowmen spilt around them, escorting the prydes off the main road and toward the place where the Quadren was dismounting. Well, most of them. Hachiro had elected to remain in saddle, so as not to interrupt his scrupulous notetaking where he had his journal steadied against the horn. A self-proclaimed student of spirits, Ira unsurprisingly spotted the library of abandoned pints that had been left littering the tables inside the neighboring tavern. When Ira's eager feet took off in that direction, Zaethan broke from Dmitri and swiftly snatched his slender arm. He planted Ira in place. Haidren or not, a drunk yancy was even more offensive than a sober one.

Given the disgusted expressions that decorated the gathering shadowmen, who were herding the Darakaian warriors in from off the main highway, the House of Boreal was already sufficiently offended without any lewd, long-winded toasts from Ira Hastings.

The king of Orynthia had stuck the tip of his tongue out. "Does the air taste odd to you, Zaeth? Clean but… prickly?"

"Clean but prickly," said Ira. "Same, I suspect, as their women."

A couple large najjan turned on their heel with retaliation in their eyes.

"The air tastes cold!" Zaethan said even louder and reeled Ira closer. "Shut up now."

He kept leash of the haidren as he tallied Zahra, Kumo, and the rest among the cluster, ensuring his own were accounted for. Both hurriedly pushed forward toward him. But his beta and third were quickly blocked by a squadron of shadowmen just as a youthful, fair-haired boy entered the Quadren's makeshift circle.

Pale as the next Boreali and of average stature, his coal-sullied attire said little to the adolescent's station or why he was there at all. Though in his bold approach to their king, his eyes divulged his identity well before his name.

The young man bent a knee. "Allöh'jomn'yeh, King Dmitri. May peace convene with you all, my Lords Haidren," he said with a respectful incline toward Zaethan, Ira, and Hachiro—who, disinterested, was still scrawling atop his horse. The befalling dusk caught like lightning across the stranger's right iris. Identical to his sister's, it held the same opalescent sheen as the kuerre warming Zaethan's sheath. The young man rose off his knee with a genuine smile. "My name is Phalen Darragh

Tiergan, son of the Clann Darragh. From my family to yours, you are most welcome to Roüwen."

Freckling peppered his nose, though his overall features were several shades lighter than Luscia's. Zaethan hadn't realized how much the Southern sun had altered her coloring. He'd heard her sibling's name only once, from one of her stories—a heartbreaking one at that. Twisting his neck, Zaethan searched until he found Luscia climbing a massive stair across the square with her aunt, well away from him and the Quadren.

Rotating toward her brother, Zaethan crossed his arms. Phalen's grin had lessened, proving the shadow on his cheek was not a dimple but a speck of soot. His champagne-shaded brows were pinched, the hairs so translucent they revealed the crimps in his skin. The boy was fixed on the najjani sword Zaethan carried. Curiosity sparkled where Phalen's kinsmen had showed concern or disdain.

Nevertheless, how Zaethan came to own the witchiron remained unasked.

"Allöh and tadöm," Dmitri replied, in the boy's language. "Luscia has long sung your praises, Phalen. It's a privilege to finally make the acquaintance of such a talented innovator."

Weary of diplomacy and small talk, Zaethan waved at the only Boreali present—the armed shadowmen penning their Quadren like sheep. "Where are your leaders?" he flippantly demanded. "The king of Orynthia is at their door. The least they can do is greet him obligingly."

"Well…" Uneasily, the youngest Tiergan rubbed behind his ear, where his head was shorn on its sides. "Our leaders are very eager to welcome him, along with his Quadren. Just, uh… up there." Phalen threaded his fingers together and pointed them toward the gem-columned edifice in the treetops. "Bolaeva, if you'll let me show you the way."

Zaethan didn't know what that place was, but he knew he didn't want to wander into it alone. He cast an arm across Dmitri defensively and motioned with the other for his beta and third to be allowed through the human barricade. "Let them pass. My men go where I do."

"Niit." A burly shadowman spun around toward Zaethan. "In that you are mistaken, Lord Haidren. They do not."

"Zaeth, we will do as they request and sort out the insult later," Dmitri commanded quietly. Then, boosting his voice, he said, "Phalen, bolaeva, please lead us forth."

Reluctant to leave his warriors, Zaethan held Kumo's anxious eyes, and after swiping a palm down his chest, Zaethan patted the air near his belting, signaling his order to quell the angst of his and Kai's prydes. He needed everyone to lie low. Without such an order, an uprising might easily erupt in their alpha zà's absence.

He, Ira, and Hachiro trailed Dmitri's sweeping cloak through the city center and toward the monumental winding stairs. Having migrated off the highway, people were crowding the base. Their chatter was thick and animated. Zaethan shrugged by a gaggle of ruddy-cheeked barmaids as he climbed after his king.

"I must ask, Phalen, why doesn't Boreal outsource these holdreheiim? So grand and abundant, it would make for rich trade," Dmitri marveled aloud from farther ahead.

Traveling up and down the tree, citizens moved out of his way without being told. "It cannot be lumbered. The timber shatters upon falling. Besides, the fibers crumble once you cut them off from the root, so to use it, the wood must remain living," he answered with a simple shrug. "Holdreheiim are only as strong as they are upright."

With a pang, the drudgery reminded him of Làtoh Ché, in Faraji. While he was accustomed to taking endless steps, Zaethan felt himself smaller and smaller. As they went higher, he glimpsed between the suspended votives at just how huge the statue rising out of the basin really was. His vantage shifted with the curving stair. Firelight flickered off the Northern stone as if it were crushed crystal, almost like the first few layers were transparent—a detail he did not consider picturesque, but disturbing. Though the imposing figure carried no weapon and its blank eyes were directed toward the darkening sky, Zaethan felt them watching his careful ascent.

"Who is that?" Hachiro inquired of their guide.

It might have been the first occasion Zaethan was glad for his over-active mind.

"Tiergan the First." Putting his upturned boot on the topmost step, Luscia's brother had brought them as high as the gem-laid veranda. It was smaller than it had seemed from the ground. He said with a gentle bow, "Unascended, I can only take you as far as these doors."

Dmitri quirked his chin at the boy. "Phalen, are we in some sort of trouble?"

"Aniell'silaem… by His grace, I really hope not."

CHAPTER TEN
ZAETHAN

Not once had Zaethan ever wondered what the inside of a tree looked like. Nor was he eager to revisit nature's bowels ever again, given the eerie ambience of his first encounter.

With his palm enfolding his other wrist, Zaethan feigned composure. He'd been brought into the heart of the occult. Everything within this place was peculiar. His body could sense it, even if they'd plucked out his eyes. The hairs stood at attention down his forearms, under the Boreali jacket. And though his elbow had subconsciously nestled against Dmitri beside him, Zaethan most consciously kept it there.

Reticence spellbound them all, enthralling each haidren in varied manners. Zaethan heard Ira, withdrawn toward the back, rocking on his bootheels, along with the swinging clink of the chained snuff canister he was surely clasping. On Dmitri's opposite, Hachiro was nearly silent, except for the incessant click of his monocular device. The shoto'shi shuffled through the colored lenses, and slack-jawed, he blinked up into the massive growth rings of the living wood high overhead—more precisely, the lustrous lettering between its darkened bands. The carved dome formed a bowl of reflective Boreali script—a system of strange glyphs, each curled like the tail of a najjani whip. The writing wound around the enormous chamber and cast a shimmering sphere over the clustered spot where Zaethan and the Quadren had been ushered. He couldn't say what the Northern words meant, but isolated from the one haidren who could, he didn't appreciate how naked he felt being surrounded by their lamplit inscription.

The walls seemed thick, as there were no windows. With it being so dim inside, he could only make out the initial rows of local audience that thronged the back wall. The limited light source came from a succession of eyelet lanterns, dangled over an elevated, rounded chancel. The seats were grouped in star-pointed sets of five, save a more elaborate, empty chair upon a platform off to the side. Four clusters made twenty-one seats in total, yet most of the groupings were only semi-occupied. The few leaders present waited in pinpricked shadow.

At least he had one thing in common with the Boreali; everyone appeared just as delighted to be there as Zaethan.

It was the central feature that had captivated Dmitri, for with his hand poised over his mouth, the king hadn't looked away from it since they'd entered into the so-called Grand Tabernacle.

Twin spindles of water trickled in from above—their origin, Zaethan couldn't tell—and rained onto a sort of shrine, its peculiar design simultaneously majestic and crude. The continuous waters brimmed two golden bowls, set apart and placed upon a slate of unhewn stone. They were of average size, as if laid for an arcane dinner. Gentle ripples overflowed the metal down a mound of nature. Rootage and exotic flora unlike anything Zaethan had ever seen spread over the vibrant moss. For wherever the waters touched, the matted leafing had sprung up, and the flower petals had teased apart.

At their nourishment, the nature was set aglow.

Zaethan would have cursed the sight, had he not already spied similar herbs radiating inside Luscia's many secreted jars. Whatever the element was, she'd used it to heal him on more than one occasion.

The bioluminescence brightening the flanks of the mound reminded Zaethan of a warrior's pauldrons, were the uncut stone a set of shoulders, and the bowls atop it, three heads of the same ancient being. Because a third bowl, fashioned from the same translucent rock as the statue of Tiergan the First, resided between those of gold.

That bowl was bone dry.

And Luscia was standing before it.

The doors to the Grand Tabernacle reopened, groaning for her personal guard. As they infiltrated the chamber, Zaethan noticed the faintest crook of her neck. At it, and the order she likely uttered, her shadowmen soundlessly fenced the Quadren, sheltering them from the onlooking Boreali who lined the back wall. Declan, her favorite henchman, came behind Zaethan's right shoulder. Noxolo, the platinum pillar, behind his left. It was only then Zaethan gathered that they too were weaponless. He could not spot a single blade inside the tabernacle, not even one of their own.

Equally unarmed, Captaen Bailefore entered in after with Luscia's father—the man heralded to be their reclusive leader, not only of Roüwen but the entire House. As his son's in the square, his garb said little of his elevated status, barring the delicate robe that outside seemed common, but inside hung more like ceremonial uniform. Her father inclined his ear toward Captaen Bailefore, allowing him to finish a statement. The fragile linen was a sail off his broad frame as he walked alone toward the helm of the half-empty seats. Stripped of the exuberance he demonstrated in the streets, the Clann Darragh slowed as he crossed his daughter.

He did not acknowledge her in the dimness.

Boreal's sil'haidren exited the shadows and rounded the room. Zaethan's suspicion tracked her as she neared and reservedly motioned for Dmitri. "Bolaeva, Your Majesty, please come forth beside the haidren to Boreal."

Hesitant, his friend gripped his walking stick, having employed it for the majority of the tree-stair. They were all worn out, their king most exhausted of all. However, Dmitri complied and followed her hand toward the space next to Luscia.

The dynamic had shifted. As did her men at his back. Nervously, Zaethan glanced again toward the stone bowl and swallowed.

The sil'haidren deserted them. Aside, she stationed herself behind the vacant chair. Forged from witchiron, the seat mirrored the reduced light in curling bands, for it'd been fashioned to imitate twigs growing up from the wooden stage. She did not sit. Instead, the sil'haidren gripped the iron chairback, giving Zaethan the impression the seat was no longer meant for her but her niece. The older woman's face retreated, along with her thoughts, back under the shrouded gloom.

Zaethan tilted his head backward and asked Declan as quietly he could, "Why is this room so unlit?"

The ginger replied in a harsh whisper. "The truth shines brightest in the dark."

Surprised he even answered and uneased by his response, Zaethan listened as the chamber hushed to hear the barest footfalls when Luscia's father strode up to the opposite edge of the bowls.

"Boreal's Elder Enclave greets in peace our king and his Quadren." His voice was solemn and robust; it fell weightily into the crevices, commanding their hollows. "We are eager to hear your testimony, of that which has brought you to Boreal out of tradition's turn. But first, we must put to test she who bears it." His deep-blue eyes, the skin about them pleated by maturity and discomfort, avoided his daughter as he rotated toward the star-pointed groupings and those seated beneath each enchained lantern. "The Enclave is inadequately numbered. In the absence of our joint eldership, this quorum bears witness behind me, Orien Darragh—her high clann, her governing overseer... her *mighty oak*.

"From the Drystan Sea, peaceably hail the elders of Clan Ödetha," he pronounced, bending toward the sole man who represented the region, alone amid its four vacant seats.

The elder's alabaster fingers were laced calmly over his belting, dissimilar to the hostility that seeped from the palest trio their Clann Darragh pointed out next.

"From the Orallach Mountains, peaceably hail the elders of Clan Ciann."

The trio stood out from the other leaders. Their unfriendly expressions were painted in luminous designs, the same as Zaethan remembered Luscia wearing up her neck at the solstice ball. Lucent stones embedded their cheeks in descent from their unblinking eyes.

They were still. So unnaturally still.

The Clann Darragh introduced another underpopulated pod, boasting only two elders in attendance. It was the only group to include a woman.

"Gathered from the upland and inlands, peaceably hail the elders of the lesser clans. And gathered from our own ground, peaceably hail the elders of High Clan Roüwen."

Zaethan presumed the fifth, unoccupied, seat was intended for Orien Darragh himself. All present, the other four elders of Roüwen appeared to meditate over their steepled fingers, as if anticipating something significant.

Luscia raised her arm over the stone bowl fixed between the pattering rainfalls. Her back was pitted toward Zaethan. He couldn't see her boldness, but he heard it clearly in her unshaken voice. "Meh'dajjeni Dönumn, weh'dajjeni Lux," she said above the muddied murmurs among her packed audience. "I freely offer my testimony to the Enclave, for their strength is mine. There is no need to demand it from my body. May veriidim, may the *untainted truth*, be liberally spilt."

Her father finally looked at her. An unfiltered distress gripped his eyes. Under his coarse beard, Orien Darragh's lips had flattened in an unbreakable line, much like hers often did whenever she was forced to yield in a disagreement. But her father unclasped the hand behind his back and produced a long, slender knife.

The bowls were an altar.

What in the dark Depths? Zaethan took a half step forward.

Declan's sudden grip on his bicep halted him from going any farther.

Held over her offered palm, the corrosive blade sparkled as luminously as Zaethan's confiscated kuerre. Her flesh would not heal smooth from this rite but be forever scarred, like the witchiron mark down her neck.

A whine came from the rear. "Why he'd have to sneak a knife into the party?" Ira squeaked past his snuff canister. "Things were just calming down…"

Zaethan shot a scowl over his shoulder at the yancy, but her startling assurance was a gentle balm to Ira's restless rocking. "It is all right, Lord Bastiion," she said without looking and elevated her palm higher.

Her father took her hand, and closing his eyes, he secured it over the altar. Opening them, he stated, "Luscia Darragh Tiergan, Ana'Sere and haidren to Boreal, you stand accused of having committed unfaithful acts against your House: the defilement of our borders with unsanctioned outsiders. Of acts against the Dönumn and Aniell: the adulteration of our sacred iron with those outside the covenant."

Her messy braids fell forward as she bent in acknowledgment of her charges.

Orien Darragh's hold on the knife wavered in the air. "Pricta'siim, may the High One prove your defense."

Zaethan held his breath as her father hastily kissed her palm.

Then he slid the knife across her skin.

The smell of the caustic cut, burning and bubbling, bloomed throughout the chamber. But without a hint of her promised pain, Luscia made a fist and drained her blood into the stone bowl. Against its constant stream, she spoke.

She told of their tour.

Of Darakai's sedition and Pilar's funding. Unsanctioned naval contracts and Mworran conspiracies. Rigged challenges for the militia. Kasim discarding Cyra's bastard, Zaethan Shà. Poisoned plots. Innocents indicted. The regicide of King Korbin Julius Thoarne.

She told them everything—everything except those nights she'd spent blade to blade in Zaethan's arms.

Regardless, he knew he would serve as a symbol of both Darakai's failing and the leader—the liar, the murderer—who'd broken the Ethnicam Accords and persuaded his House to act against the throne. Elder eyes of sapphire, emerald, and steel swerved toward Zaethan throughout her account, sometimes angered, oftentimes confused.

But Zaethan was no longer concerned with them. He was concerned with Luscia's blood, pooling enough to be seeping through the crevices in the bowl. His head tipped sideways with its falling droplets. Zaethan's mouth fell ajar. Whatever vine, leaf, or petal her blood touched would spring to life and blossom more brilliantly than anything else in the room.

As the organic light intensified more brightly and widespread down the mound, the Boreali observers muttered between themselves more loudly than before, suggesting they'd not expected that phenomenon to occur—or at least, not so spectacularly.

A frenzy clacked at Zaethan's left, where Hachiro shuffled through his monocular lenses in haste and disbelief. "No, surely not. What is the experiment unfolding before us? I'd like to replicate it myself," he whispered to Noxolo, the shadowman closest to his analysis. The shoto'shi rummaged for his journal and flipped it open. "Describe how the contraption is erected…"

"Niit, it is not a contraption. Or an experiment," Noxolo said, quietly bending lower to fold Hachiro's journal shut before pointing his lanky forefinger toward the gleaming structure. "*That* is the Prajja'Ve-riidim, the Altar of Truth—the untainted truth, where Aurynth flows into the bowls of gold." Another finger joined to demonstrate the twin waters escaping from above. "For the High One gives the truth of heaven and of earth. In the divide, the accused gives the truth of man. If her testimony is false, the veridaedill—the teller's bane planted below—will shrivel and wilt. To be proven true, the lumin in her blood must bleed in harmony with her words, rousing the veridaedill to life."

Zaethan twisted, discovering a proud, toothy grin widening Noxolo's stork-like appearance.

"Our Ana'Sere was just proven. Indisputably so."

"What the Depths is lumin?" Zaethan bluntly asked.

"Hm." Noxolo rolled his lips under, as if stumped, then replied with a shrug. "It is the proof."

Returning to his full height, Zaethan heard his flaxen companion whack Noxolo's arm disapprovingly. He also heard Noxolo whack him back even harder. Whatever their dispute, it was ended before it'd begun.

"Will we have to go next?" Ira asked Noxolo timidly, plucking at the bronze skin of his wrist. It'd gone a bit pallid. "You know, I don't really think I'm in season right now. My 'lumin' is not ripe at all."

"Swallow your blasphemy," the golden-haired shadowman warned through his teeth. "Your yancy refuse will never pollute our altar—"

"Creyvan, outside. Crestï," Captaen Bailefore gruffly ordered the fellow, cutting him off before they drew more notice away from Luscia's final account.

She finished her testament on the string of cross-caste corpses they'd exposed in the summer and their slaying of Felix Ambrose, leading her into their discovery of the cult that'd turned him into the monster he'd become. "Somehow the Obscurer has birthed these… creatures. Creatures that are created from something vile—unnatural, wrong, utterly devoid of human light." She was tapping her chest, over her heart. "Immediate measures must be taken to thwart the Obscurer's increasing destruction. Therefore, to evade his detection, we request full asylum for king and Quadren, as well as for the loyal Darakaian warriors who fought to get us out of Port Khmer and be here today. Here in the safety of Boreali protection, we plan to strategize together with the Elder Enclave, the Order of the Najjan, and eventually, with Razôuel."

Luscia indicated Dmitri's opportunity to interject. "Wem, yes, that's right," he said in a respectful bow to the stone-faced elders. "My marriage contract with Bahira'Rasha is still intact, and I intend to leverage Zôueli aid. Once our trusted scout rendezvouses with us, correspondence can covertly be sent to the queen. If members of the Peerage have shifted their allegiance to the Obscurer, like those spearheading insurrection within the Orynthian legions, then retaking Bastiion will require najjani forces indeed. But I don't intend for those forces to march alone."

The Clann Darragh paced behind the altar, combing his beard. His countenance was severe. Revealed by the blood-lit greenery, his disturbed frown only deepened with each new piece of intel. He turned to appeal his kinsmen in their seats. "Weh'dajjeni Lux." He said the Boreali phrase with finality.

While Zaethan recognized it, he'd yet to hear it translated.

"What say the Enclave?"

The middle-aged elder from Clan Ödetha unlaced his fingers, having not moved during Luscia's testimony. "Ana'Sere, why did you not deposit the prydes in Port Tadeas, or another village outside our border? Ethnicam tradition permits only king and Quadren on Boreali soil, and that is with permission. If your purpose is to uphold the Accords, why break them?"

"The Proper and Mirajii Prydes fought valiantly not only for *us*, Elder Yarlven, but *against* their own chief warlord. They are considered fugitives. And now need great care and recovery from those who ought to give it."

Staring out from the middle of the Ciann representatives was the most senior of the Enclave, given the long white tail of his plaited beard and how the patterns framed the caverns of his time-sunken cheeks. Cold and sharp, his gaze was fastened on Luscia. It speared Zaethan, then moved back to its original target.

"Your motives are already justified by Aniell. I merely wish to understand them further, Ana'Sere," Elder Yarlven calmly expressed.

"Each House has always sacrificed for the throne of Thorne. Darakai included. What makes these events so different?"

Zaethan was done with this unnecessary debate. "It's different because if they were caught wherever you'd prefer we dumped them, my warriors would be coerced and tortured into betraying the king's position! If you hate having guests so much, then help us keep our being here a secret!"

The crotchety elder from Clan Ciann hobbled to stand. The strength of his shout was a shock to many. "The cross-caste pretender will keep silent during these proceedings!"

"Yet he is right," Luscia stated with a half turn toward Zaethan. "The haidren to Darakai is right, Elder Morratagh. Our priority is the king, and he alone. Withholding asylum from the prydes will put him in added danger, more than you realize. If I could be allowed to describe the horrors we faced along the way—"

"This is a quarter quorum, Ana'Sere." Elder Morratagh, whose reproof sounded as old and gritty as dirt, waggled a patronizing finger at Luscia. "We are not here to debate statecraft, simply your culpability in the unlawfulness that brought it all about."

Zaethan saw she was angered by the elder's treatment. She ought to be. He didn't understand why she was suppressing it in the slow rise and fall of her shoulders until she clenched her fist tighter, increasing the stream of blood over the bowl.

She didn't yell back in defense. The vine intensified its shine, proclaiming it for her.

Some elders rearranged uneasily in their seats. The lone woman, situated among those representing the lesser clans, cleared her throat. "Perhaps the prydes can remain in Roüwen under the strict stipulation of the city limit. The king and his Quadren ought to be hosted by the

Clann Darragh, per tradition of His Majesty's coronation tour." She bowed her graying head toward Luscia's father. "And the Darakaian warriors perhaps hosted by Roüwen's most gracious households."

Silk and linen rustled as the citizens squished at the opposite end of the chamber squirmed under her suggestion.

Not one *gracious household* volunteered.

"No bastard shall stay under the same roof as the haidren to Boreal."

Every person in the tabernacle swiveled toward Luscia's aunt, for she'd not uttered a word until that moment.

"Given the issue of his illegitimacy, I recommend he be housed elsewhere, with the rest."

Heat slapped Zaethan's cheeks.

Dmitri struck his byrnnzite cane upon the wood floor. "That is a preposterous assertion. Zaethan *is* the haidren to the House of Darakai!"

"Which Darakai?" The elderly man from Clan Ciann hitched his white brow. "There seem to be two."

"The one we left unburied in Port Khmer!" Zaethan barked, his chest heaving.

Luscia's henchman stepped up and positioned his bulky frame partly in front of Zaethan. "The Athdara household will host the haidren to Darakai," Declan declared, to the astonishment of many. "My family will be honored to shelter him and his pryde leadership."

The Clann Darragh emitted a gusty exhale. He paced back toward the altar at the middle of the Grand Tabernacle and tapped the spot on his chest where the najjan pinned their brooch. "Tadöm, Declan Athdara, for your example. It is decided; refuge must be arranged for the king and his party. Wem, his *entire* party. Boreal cannot reject them in this dark hour. So says the High One," he proclaimed through the chamber. With a strip of linen he'd tucked in his belt, Luscia's father tenderly wrapped the fabric around her wound, putting her bleeding to a stop. "This quorum is closed. Tredae'Aurynth, meh Ana'Brödre."

Dmitri resumed a quiet discussion with Luscia and the Clann Darragh, as her guard steered Zaethan and the others out through the enormous, intricately carved doors. He massaged his brow, uneager to return to the veranda or its overlook of the terrifying drop to where he'd hitched the horses, too many stories below. It was well after sundown, and the moon would be of little help navigating the labyrinth of bridges and stairways outside.

"Oh my," Hachiro said to somebody.

Zaethan ran into the shoto'shi's back, as he'd frozen just beyond the threshold. He regained his balance. His vision cut past Hachiro into an alien terrain, as his limbs went liquid. Dumbfounded, he set the blinking Westerner back onto both feet.

"Oh my," Zaethan said too.

The highlands were incandescent.

Covered by night, Boreal did not miss the sun; its forest was lit from within.

Luminous streaks twinkled throughout the bark grooves, brightest at the tree bases where the gargantuan roots were buried under beds of lambent lichen. Colors were unveiled in a pastel kaleidoscope, the flowers disrobed in freckled luster, gleaming no more beautifully than the bouquets of fungi illuminating every bird and accustomed passerby. All around him, exiting the Grand Tabernacle, the Boreali went about their evening routines as if it were nothing. As if they weren't traversing beneath a windswept ovation of shimmering, light-stricken leaves. Down in the square, their footsteps supported an unheard heartbeat pulsing throughout the stonework and up the numerous staircases that stretched for the stars.

The truth shone brightest in the dark.

A stray leaf blew across Zaethan's cuff, and he caught it. He twirled the thing by its stem, ogling the glittering veins.

If this was the truth… then what was the lie?

CHAPTER ELEVEN
LUSCIA

Though her anxiety had not quelled—nor would it, given the state of the realm—her entire body relaxed against her younger brother's arm in deep, contented breaths. Luscia hadn't sighted Phalen until she'd been released from the Grand Tabernacle, where he had been impatiently waiting outside. She clasped onto him as they climbed toward the lofty veranda of their childhood home, Phalen dousing her in rushed updates of Roüwen's local gossip the entire way. She hardly heard it. A part of her was still unconvinced he was even real, that his large frame held the same whimsical boy she'd said good-bye to in the spring.

Possibly her most favorite person in the world, he had grown so tall, and she'd missed it. Missed every day that'd sharpened his plump cheeks into the adolescent blades that had trimmed the youth from his unfinished masculinity. Unlike Luscia, their mother's gentle face was preserved in Phalen. Whereas their father stretched in Phalen's wide shoulders, the confidence of his broadened gait, and most unbelievably, the dramatic drop in the pitch of his enthusiastic monologue.

His silly grin was unchanged though, still as crooked and off-kilter as ever.

Tadöm Aniell for that, she thought, fondly gazing up at his unaffected smile and its matching sooty smear.

Phalen would soon be sixteen—in just a handful of weeks, she realized, suddenly remembering the calendar, though not entirely certain of the day itself. There remained only the crumbs of childishness about her brother. And leaning against him, Luscia hugged the muscle of his enlarged bicep tightly, thoroughly unready to let him or his childhood go.

"Then the Connells got into a bidding war with the Macnüds, but the Athdaras refused to sell the goat to either family. None of them speak to this day," Phalen finished saying when they'd climbed to the top of the terrace landing. Dappled under the nightly luminescence, a mischievous twinkle shone in his eyes, both blue and Tiergan.

Luscia was unsurprised by the story's ending; Declan's parents were an austere pair. If they wouldn't sell a goat to an unworthy owner, she doubted they'd appreciate their son having volunteered their uptight abode to a team of Darakaian squatters.

"But that was all forgotten once your mixed maid turned up to the Caellaighs with her Unitarian mother and cross-caste sister. Fappa had to force the Caellaighs to take them in. Set your guard Böwen off like Zôueli boom powder—exploded, right there on their porch! I could hear his shouting all the way from my forge!" Phalen sounded all too giddy about the ordeal. Though to his defense, isolation within Boreali borders often came at the price of provincial boredom.

Luscia brushed the smudge of coal off his buff leather vest and asked, "Have you heard much of their travels? I sent them away during a dangerous time in Bastiion and worried their journey's hardships might have been riskier than the political consequence—"

"No politics in the house." Their father stepped up from the immense stairway. Dodging a spindle of tinkling chimes, he came to where Luscia and Phalen loitered before a set of emerald doors seated in the flickering bark.

Each were complexly carved with a raised mural, same as those decorating the najjani vödalera ships. However, this one was forebodingly unique. The image of a splintered oak tree sprawled upward and outward over the threshold, bearing tribute to their father's Darragh heritage.

Aksel's abundant tail lapped her thigh. The lycran's eagerness was evidence he'd not forgotten his earliest home with Luscia, as a pup. The home was haunted by so much memory, and Aksel had swiftly become her solace inside.

Once she'd been able to fall asleep within its walls again.

Twisting on her heel, Luscia discovered their king had stalled some steps lower, where he was huddled over a leafy sprout with Hachiro. There was nothing spectacular about the craggy vegetation except that, at the hour, it glowed. In essence, Dmitri had merely been captivated by another weed, just as the dozen he'd stopped to inspect along the spiraled trek toward the Clann Darragh's manor—once he and Hachiro had accepted the lambent quality of the stone itself. Given his worsening fatigue, Luscia had expected Dmitri to struggle with the perpetual incline. Her home was one of the highest in all of Roüwen. But her king had wanted to examine every analogous detail along the way.

It'd been a tedious stroll.

And none appeared more ready to end it than the haidren to Bastiion, who yawned against the vined banister behind them.

"I don't care if I have to degrade myself to warm Hachi all night," Ira tiredly drawled, rubbing the side of his unshaven face. "Just promise me there's a soft bed and a stiff drink on the other side of that scary door."

The shoto'shi clicked a blue lens over his magnified bug-looking eye and gathered his dirt-encrusted robes to stand. "Your dignity lacks the performance to sell it, Lord Bastiion. Besides, I find it disturbing how you talk in your sleep. In graphic detail, I might add. I've begun sketching diagrams but can never seem to finish before you change topic."

Hachiro proceeded to showcase such diagrams—undressed bodies posed in the strangest positionings—as Dmitri, completely mortified, fumbled the journal shut. "My goodness, Lord Pilar!"

"Well for starters, you had it upside down," Ira corrected him.

Blinking, the shoto'shi cracked the parchment apart and flipped his head aside at the drawings. "Vexingly inconclusive," Hachiro muttered and nestled the closed pages against his tightly buttoned torso.

Releasing a grumble, Luscia descended a step, keen to get Dmitri out of the befalling chill. His cheeks, though blushed from embarrassment, had held a feverish pink for some time. "I assure you there is plenty of room for everyone. Your Majesty, bolaeva, it is growing bitter outside," she said, offering him a hand up.

"Ah, right you are, Lady Boreal."

"Waedfrel. After you, My King." Her father beamed as he pushed in the doors. "It will be good to see the place full again."

Luscia followed the clack of Dmitri's cane into a den of much-needed warmth. In the foyer, she dragged in a deep inhale, the kind that tested her lungs, and nearly puffed out the comforting notes of resin and nixberry with her long-withheld relief. Aksel trotted into the towering space as if he owned it, fleeing beneath her fingertips. But Luscia dusted them over her heart as her head tipped back.

She'd forgotten how lovely it really was.

Like all dwellings in Roüwen, the manor occupied the hollows of a living holdreheiim. However, while the tree's exterior was preserved and unfettered, apart from the manmade additions that jutted the heights, the interior was a homage to traditional Boreali craftsmanship. Smooth nooks and platforms were sculpted in seamless, languid transitions from the outer walls, whereas the spiraled rafters and winding beams were constructed of stouter woods such as maple, oak, and pine. Gnarled pillars of the holdreheiim had been left intact, supporting the inner structure like bones instead of branches.

A corkscrewed staircase was planted at the center of the den. The halved-log steps toured guests upward between the manor's varied levels. Made of twisting boughs, the handrail seemed to be rippling, doused in iridescence, and opposite the staircase, a fireplace mosaiced in lumilore pebbles heated the main floor.

Before the contained flames rested her father's armchair, draped in her mother's spotless cream shawl.

Luscia shuffled her feet toward it while Dmitri and the others explored the residence. She hesitantly reached for the linsilk swath. Her mother's totem survived as a respected entity in their midst. Thumbing the silver-and-rose beadwork along the trim, the pattern emulating the natural elegance of highland ferns, Luscia let it slide out of her grasp. Eoine Darragh Tiergan was no longer with them. Nor would she return to this plane, no matter how profoundly her father ached for Eoine to spin into his lap once again, gaily laughing as if her mind were whole—not tormented.

A heavy kiss pushed through the mess of hair atop her crown. "Meh fyreon, lu'Lycran," her father murmured as his enormous fist gently enclosed around her palm, the one he'd wrapped it in bloodstained linen. "My duty has scarred you twice over. Once by my negligence, and today by my care."

Luscia turned and peered up at him. Orien Darragh, whom she used to consider the strongest man alive and, in many ways, still did, fought back the moisture gathering along his woodsy lashes. His stress was apparent. Coarse and tawny, his hair had exponentially grayed during their months apart.

"Fappa." She reached up and tugged the braids hung down either side of his mouth like she had as a young girl, cherishing his reluctant chortle. "I've been learning a lot as haidren. Faultlessness scarcely leaves us unscathed. In fact, it's usually the opposite."

His beard tickled her forearm when he nodded and straightened the luxiron solrahs through her septum. "You share your mother's perception of adversity," he said, his tone as proud as it was melancholy.

"Just as I share your sundown hanker for mulled wine. Does Arlette have any simmering?"

Catching her wrist, he turned over his own cuff, tied there by Marek. Beads of stained glass beside those of stippled ceramic were knitted along the overlapping rawhide bands. His unkempt brow arched hopefully. "Do I spy a cause for celebration?"

Luscia stared at Marek's accepted kurtfierï. She'd seen them speaking—no doubt about such courtship developments—upon their arrival. "Niit, not yet. But perhaps in time there will be."

Her father's countenance folded in hearty wrinkles. "Arlette!" he shouted, for their live-in housekeeper. When the elderly woman didn't respond, Boreali hearing aside, he stormed in the direction of the kitchen. "Bolaeva, Arlette, your best wassail for my daughter! And by the Watchman, I forbid you tossing those awful nettles into it…"

"Luscia?" Phalen called to her, already halfway up the staircase with their drowsy new tenants.

She motioned for her brother to continue climbing. "Wem, let's get everyone to bed, shall we?"

"Does that mean you're coming with?" Ira swung around eagerly.

"To my own quarters, Lord Bastiion."

"Is that Arlette available then?" he asked as alternative, hiking toward the second level.

Phalen, baffled by the yancy's lewd demeanor, coughed back a snicker. "Maybe if you remove her wooden teeth first."

Luscia batted Ira aside while he seemed to consider it. Old Arlette didn't deserve any indecent advances, although Ira absolutely deserved the fork she'd aptly stick in his side. "Ahead, you will take that eastward room—alone. Lord Pilar, there is another bedroom opposite Phalen's you can seize," Luscia directed Hachiro, who wordlessly slumped toward the promise of rest. She kissed Phalen on his much-too-leaned cheek in a hurried good-night and with some gentle guidance, Luscia steered Dmitri on up to the third story.

Aksel happily padded up the steps in front of her. To his beasty chagrin, they couldn't exactly have shared a hammock on Nabhu's brig. Overgrown and overspoiled, the lycran was a furry two-hundred-pound brat leading them to plush victory. Luscia could see it in the lazy lolling of his tongue; he was going to steal the blankets tonight too.

The next circular landing was much grander, as it hosted the primary bedrooms. Three in total: her father's master suite and two twin abutting. Windows showered the upper steps with Roüwen's natural luster. It was said that Boreal knew no absolute darkness, for even its night wielded inherent light. In reality, Boreal hosted the dark's most genuine form, no different than the unlit lowlands.

That kind of darkness the sun could never shine away; that kind warred over the humanity of men.

Her chest constricted as her attention scanned the trio of doorways and anchored onto the third. An iron padlock was installed on its front. Only Luscia knew where its corresponding key was stored—the meager consolation her father had reserved, for her alone, in the aftermath. She gripped the handrail firmly, her nails picking at the fissures in the woodgrain.

It'd been nearly four years since she'd stepped inside that room.

A millennium would have to pass before she ever did again.

"Which is yours, Lady Boreal?" Dmitri abruptly asked, jolting Luscia from her darkened reverie. "I'm perplexed that your brother doesn't reside on the same floor as you and the Clann Darragh."

"He used to," she replied, her voice faraway and as hollow as the holdreheiim. "You will take my room to the left, Sire. I hope you find it to your comfort."

Luscia made to leave, to escape the unexpected choking sensation she swallowed down, but Dmitri contested, "I can't put you out, Luscia… After everything you've organized on our behalf, you've at least earned your own long-awaited bed."

She glanced up the staircase at the final floor. "Aksel and I will take the aerial loft. Don't fret for our comfort. It's the best view in Roüwen." Luscia winked and, bidding him a good rest, assured him, "I need to brew your next batch of elixirs." She threw her hand up to his protest. "Niit, you know it's overdue. At my knock, I'll deposit the vials in your quarters after dawn."

"More reason to stay in here yourself, where your supplies are already kept. Why can I not take the room adjacent yours?"

She swallowed again, her gaze traveling past the tip of his cane to the locked door. With a steely resolve, Luscia wrenched her collar over her throat.

"Because that room shouldn't exist. Good night, Your Majesty."

Luscia's legs dragged behind her like anvils, either from undeniable weariness or a very deniable reluctance to conclude the evening with a visit to her aunt.

She'd have to face it alone. Alora had never cared for Aksel, particularly not in her home, which was the principal reason why Luscia had ultimately moved back and taken Phalen's room after those initial weeks she'd slept under her aunt's cover.

Sporadically, lanterns had been looped among the suspension cabling between Roüwen's unfelled structures. The lamplight was intended for the twilight hours, given how at night the moon rivaled the glimmer of the canopy itself. Scattered among the swishing boughs, toads croaked their forlorn reception to Luscia as she strolled across the connected swing bridge to Alora's private lodgings. Isolated from the main manor, her aunt had long lived in what had originally served as additional guest housing. The arrangement suited Alora's preference. She remained close to the family yet detached in her thicket of drying herbs and undisturbed ongoings.

Luscia preferred it that way too.

Alora's squat veranda was cluttered with overflowing pots, possibly the singular aspect of chaos within her otherwise orderly environment. The lush and well-nurtured plants unfurled over their ceramic rims in twinkling shoots. Northern ivy crept up the furrowed bark of the slimmer holdreheiim that housed her accommodations. Rhali blooms dangled like slender bells over the threshold, whereas kaléo flowers flourished in copious red-violet bursts around the vaulted windows. A candle had been lit and set to wait on the other side of the panes. Its portentous flicker illuminated the window's delicate tracery.

That flame would endure till morning, had Luscia not opted to come. She almost hadn't.

But Alora had as much to answer for as Luscia—Boreal's newly maimed haidren—even if there was no Enclave to wield the teller's knife or witness the questioning.

Luscia braced her nerves. With a slow intake, she flexed her unhealed palm and made to knock, but her aunt's voice creaked through the wood.

"It's beneath you to loiter, niece."

Biting the meat of her cheek, Luscia obligingly popped the latch and crept inside. A meadow of aromatic bunches—seven-pointed drösarra, fennel, lacey gilead, and common rue—swung from the rafters, causing her to duck as she moved toward Alora's quaint seating area, set before a modest, crackling fire.

Atop its roughly wooden mantel gleamed a decorative miniature; a jade bowl rested between two others leafed in gold. An opulent, household replica of the Prajja'Veriidim, the Altar of Truth, there on display in the house of someone who so rarely divulged it.

Luscia repressed her snort of irony.

Steam wafted from a cast-iron kettle where it steeped upon the modest table. The setup was snugly propped between two plushily upholstered chairs, though three were in attendance. For warming her perch in the corner, a lavender hawk was idly preening herself. Luscia's eyes narrowed at the correspondence-carting anklet that jingled over Amaranth's hooked talons. Someone had surely followed the Quadren all the way to Port Khmer, reporting uncountable insights directly to Alora. And someone had used that exact bird to do it.

Luscia did not wait for an invitation to claim the empty seat, an action she wouldn't have taken before the summer.

Under her unbound, whitening tresses, Alora's thin brow arched, having taken note of the small rebellion. Nevertheless, her aunt poured Luscia a hot cup of Viridi tea and scooted it forward. She did not speak as Luscia took a lengthy sip.

The minutes ticked by.

Luscia broke their unnerving silence. "It was an insult to Dmitri to force a member of his Quadren into the charity of my guard."

"It was an insult to Boreal to have shared so much with that member," Alora replied. She unlaced her fingers to serve herself more tea.

Luscia bit her lip. The hostility behind her aunt's meaning was palpable, though it was unclear if she implied Luscia's handing over a luxiron kuerre to Zaethan Shà or something more forbidden. Her eyes darted toward Amaranth. The letters carried by that hawk could have contained anything. And there were things far more damning than sharing a sword.

Her aunt's nose uplifted as she continued. "The young man's illegitimacy is becoming public, Luscia. A finite stain on King Dmitri's legacy. As sil'haidren, I cannot allow it to stain you as well by your sharing a roof with that cross-caste. Whoring out your weaponry was scandal enough."

Luscia tried her best to keep still and not squirm. There was no sense in defending an act already absolved before the elders—tadöm Aniell. Regardless, her jaw steeled at her aunt's crass phrasing. "The past months have required unprecedented compromise," Luscia said, then plucked the threading along the bloody scrap tied about her cut. "You should also learn I've accepted Marek as a suitor."

"A telling leap in conversation."

Luscia glanced up sharply. While no clear accusation was verbalized, it was most certainly spoken. Alora's right iris sparkled overtop her teacup. There was something exacting inside her opaline scrutiny, fueled by an undisclosed stress. In the firelight, Luscia spotted how creped and saggy the skin of her aunt's neck had become, as if whatever she was hiding behind her eyes was feeding off her seemingly ageless vigor.

Though their knees were a few feet apart, the woman Luscia thought she knew felt miles away.

"I simply thought you'd be glad to know—"

"Wem, I am glad for it," said Alora. "The Bailefores possess a strong heritage, and through you, Marek would therefore possess even stronger heirs. Something our line needs in the coming era… sooner rather than later if your summary of the realm bears true. You shouldn't delay the marriage."

You should not have had me followed.

Alora must have detected that the conversation continued in Luscia's head. "Leverage wisdom, Luscia. A date should be set."

Rich, coming from a woman who never got married, Luscia wished to say.

But didn't.

The fire popped. Luscia flicked off a wayward ember. "Capriciousness is the enemy of reason," Luscia stated, quoting her aunt, and pulled more threads off her crude bandaging. They'd formed a pile on her thigh. "Such covenants should never be rushed, not when there is so much hanging in the balance—as my summary in the tabernacle did attest."

Alora's eyes tapered at their corners. However, with a terse sigh, she pushed a jar toward Luscia, a stubby spoon already wedged under the lid. From its punchy scent, the healing poultice was freshly made.

"Strip off that filthy rag and apply this." Aggravation replaced any concern in her aunt's instruction. Rejoining her hands over her neatly robed middle, Alora asked, "Due to your premature arrival, how many vials of tonic remain in the case I'd assembled for His Majesty's tour? Have you been compelled to increase your dosages during all this recent strain?"

Luscia mastered her breathing so as not to give herself, or her tonic-free revelations, away. She'd not experienced an episode in weeks, not since Faraji. At least not in the painful sense. Incidents that had been strange and scary? Very. Astonishing and alarming? Absolutely. But outright painful? Nothing, apart from the pain of knowing there was a falsehood, a purpose unrevealed, dividing Luscia from the maternal figure who'd prescribed her to drink said tonic her entire life.

"The case of tonics got left in Faraji, during our escape," Luscia steadily replied. "To the king's blessing, my apothecary was recovered. His elixirs were unaffected by the loss."

Luscia sensed the sudden shift before it flashed across Alora's gaze. Their shared lineage glowed in the dimness, alert and exhaustive, as her aunt scoured the air about Luscia's tense posture. She felt the particles vibrating against her skin. The intimate sensation lifted the hairs on her arms, as if the threads were pushing through from the *Other*. But she did not respond to their invitation. Luscia dared not enter the Sight in front of her mentor.

She couldn't trust what they'd both see behind the veil. Or that Alora's seeing it was safe to begin with.

"You've gone unmedicated this entire time?" her aunt asked, an icy grate to her every consonant. Her chin dipped, and her line of questioning adopted a curiously careful inflection, the tone one might use when approaching a rabid wolf. "You must have suffered greatly then… Have you not, niece?"

Hearing voices. Manipulating matter. Butchering men with the metaphorical snap of her finger. And unable to confide in anyone about it?

Suffering sounded about right.

"It has been excruciating," Luscia replied. "But I've returned here, to your administration, so there is nothing to fear anymore, is there?"

She could hear her own heartbeat over the prolonged disquiet.

Alora surely heard it too.

The flame flickered over her aunt's sharp features, her ivory skin made into cheesecloth that stretched over barbed fencing. "Niit, there is not. I ought to brew your immediate replacements."

Gripping the chair edge, Alora stiffly got up. Squeezing past Amaranth's perch, she whispered an absent-minded "heh'ta, dearest" to soothe the hawk when it restlessly tousled her molting wings.

Sliding to the nearby counter, Alora reached for various herbs like a puppet, as if marionetted by habit instead of actual urgency.

Luscia's aunt was Boreal's most gifted healer, and yet she'd never relayed the ingredients of the mysterious tonic to her protégée. Luscia had always yearned to learn it. To try to classify the elements and technique required, Luscia used to watch Alora's hands.

Now, she watched everything else.

Alora hunched, her back toward the fire as she ground a clipping beneath her pestle. There was an evasive curve to her aunt's slim shoulders that Luscia had never noted before. She tore a bulb off the potted yolk yarrow with an anxious *snap* and squished it in her fist, draining the milky residue into the mortar.

Leaning forward, Luscia tested her aunt's composure. "We spent time with the mudmen during our escape... Do you know why they have a luxiron spear in their possession?"

There came a loaded pause. Whether a sign of Alora's foreknowledge or genuine shock, Luscia wasn't sure.

Alora then lit a match, tossed it into the mush, and ground the ingredients more forcefully. "There has always been black-market trade of our artifacts, Luscia. As haidren, you should have better educated yourself on Orynthia's corrupt commerce."

Luscia let the criticism roll off. Creeping toward the edge of her seat, she said, "Their leader… the high matriarch… She has Tiergan eyes."

The pestle clattered against the lip of the limestone bowl. "That's impossible."

"And yet she met me inside the Sight."

Sidelong, Alora spun; her hip pressed against the counter. "How could you possibly endure it," she posed, "if you did not have your treatments on hand?"

Luscia's breathing sped, but she held her aunt's stare. "Sacrifices were made for the survival of all. How could our lineage bear markers so far south? The Gulgons' high matriarch described the lumin as a 'Sacred Wind.' Their people follow its path. If I'm to be educated on commerce, should I not be equally educated on history?"

"Then the lore bears sincerity," Alora said, more to herself than Luscia, and turned back to her work.

"Which part exactly? Because they called me their cousin."

She'd picked the topic for its unpleasant inference. How willing would Alora be to answer an issue of antiquity? That of the present was sure to be more tight-lipped.

Although, Luscia was itching to learn exactly *that*—how a migratory and primitive people had received Boreali weaponry and Tiergan eyes. They even had identical engineering that hoisted Gulgon villages up out of the swamp.

At the counter, Alora's grinding resumed. "There is an alternative legend to which you've always heard," Alora reluctantly began, whipping a towel over her shoulder. "Lore teaches that after the death of Tiergan, his child was killed. Another lore later emerged that the Wrathling had *not* been executed, but banished. That Tiergan's murderous child left our shores, never to return. Perhaps the Wrathling landed in Hagarh. Woe to the mudmen if it had."

Luscia stroked her mouth in thought. She recalled the legend, the original at least, wherein Tiergan the First had been slain by the hand of one of his four recorded children—better known as the Wrathling. She pushed her disbelief aside and considered the implications to the present.

"If that is the case, then the Gulgons *are* our cousins. Meaning they have been excluded from their inheritance in Boreal." Mind spinning, Luscia sputtered, "Why, they've been cut off from the Dönumn—from the source itself!"

"If the mudmen were sired by the Wrathling, they hail from a murderous line and should stay cut off. Furthermore, we know cross-castes cannot inherit the Higher Gifts, thus they've no purpose in Boreal."

"But in Hagarh, I witnessed the matriarch—"

"I said they *cannot!*" Alora slammed her hand against the counter.

Luscia flinched, unsure what she'd said to invoke so much anger.

Her aunt repeated the words a few more times to herself. With frightening calm, Alora re-sorted herself. She brought the hand to her mouth and blew a type of power over her concoction. "Yet again, your priorities are misaligned, niece," she said curtly. "The bigger concern is your upcoming obligation to your people, now that you are here for your first Ana'Innöx as haidren. You will have to relay to the king that you'll soon depart Roüwen without the Quadren."

Already half off the chair, Luscia bolstered onto her heels. "I'm not going anywhere without the king. His regime is too fractured for us to be splintering apart now. Surely an exception can be made, given the circumstances."

Alora balled the towel and faced her. "Outsiders are forbidden from the keep. Boreal's haidren cannot be heard purporting such shocking suggestions. You serve your House and Aniell before all others."

"I serve Aniell by not deserting His appointed king."

"Do not let your affections dissuade you from your duty, Luscia. Affection is a poison if it blinds you," Alora said through a tightened mouth. "The sacred affair is not for them."

"Niit." Luscia widened her legs. The cut over her palm stung through the soothing paste. "I won't leave him."

Sucking in her bottom lip, Alora turned to indignantly pour the finished tonic into a set of clean vials. The glass clinked under her shaking; her emotion was unmistakable, for she was a woman who never shook.

Her aunt shuffled the vials into a velvet sack, strode forward, and proffered them on a string to Luscia. "Boreal deserves a haidren who can deny herself the delusions that plague every other person sitting at that pentagonal table," Alora snapped. Her Tiergan eye blazed as she spoke from both sides of the veil. "Fail to deny yourself, then you have already failed all of Boreal. You *are* going to fulfill your duty at Ana'Innöx. We will discuss it again when your mind returns to you. As you said, niece, it has not been right for some time."

The sack of tonics fell into Luscia's hand with a loaded *chink*.

They might as well have been bricks.

Aksel's snout was cold and wet where he prodded it deeper against Luscia's linsilk robe. He was happy to be home, content in his fleecy sprawl across her lap. She gazed out an open window in the aerial loft. Her legs had gone numb a while ago, but she didn't care.

Luscia's chin settled onto the tendons of her hand, which too had lost feeling. Her heavy exhales sprouted goose bumps along her skin. She tinkered with a vial propped on the ledge, just as she had for the last hour. Her forefinger teetered the uncorked lip of the vial back and forth, with her two choices. Weighing them, she watched the thick, plum sewage skate the glass.

She had so much to prove. To her House, to her family, to her king…

For that, Luscia could drink it—deny herself as ordered and protect this one delusion. Alora was right. Everyone on the Quadren maintained a delusion of some kind… Perhaps this was hers. Throughout girlhood, she'd always trusted her aunt implicitly. Done whatever she'd dictated. To be *right*. To be virtuous and true. So, Luscia could regress into the safety of her long-medicated naivete and become the girl Alora had raised. Luscia could "relent" as the voices had whispered to do, so that maybe she'd never have to hear them again. She could choose pain over fear. Control over chaos. Ignorance over doubt.

She could prove to be the haidren everyone seemed to be searching for.

Or…

Luscia tilted the vial on its other side.

She could smother the delusion.

A different wind swept through the windows with the rush of a thousand wings. Warm and comforting, it bathed her cheeks, tingling her flesh. Though she was not *seeing* the lumin, she felt it there. The threads always were. As the tingling departed, her decision was made.

Luscia tipped the vial and drained Alora's tonic over the ledge.

A girl proved who she was to other people. A woman proved it to herself.

Chapter Twelve

Rain slithered down the stark, black beams unique to the quaint village of Littleling Eaves. Of all Agoston's settlements, it was the least suspecting—simple, picturesque people from a uniformly picturesque countryside. Inside their idyllic homes, the villagers slumbered, snugly unaware that a resurrected nightmare lurked beyond their windows.

The lonely oil lamp outside the inn fizzled to smoke, for under a moonless sky, the proprietor had been long lulled to sleep. Intently, the figure studied the door as he scratched the side of his blistered face. A sheet of crusty flesh came away on his glove. Out from under the overhang, he extended his hand into the downpour, rinsing his humanity off the leather. He hadn't even felt it come loose.

The figure gathered his weather-beaten cloak over his sore knees and resettled against the slick, pristine plaster. It was the prize of Littleling Eaves, kept immaculately white for the rare, bypassing pleasure of their duke. Or, to the recollection of few, the even rarer visit of a king.

Nested in the cross braces, Amaranth ruffed her feathers, objecting to the wetness of the season. Autumn settled lazily in the plains. With it brought a sogginess despised by the figure and the Pilarese hawk alike. By his whistle, Amaranth retreated her wings back into the shadows. He'd missed her. Greatly. Though the bird's return was poorly timed, and it'd been a risk to let her accompany his hunt that night.

She wasn't the only one who had.

Stately and statuesque, her sister was perched on the neighboring roof. He kept hidden from the opposing hawk. Naturally, her loyalties had shifted during their decades apart. The same could be said of her master, who delayed somewhere inside the inn. From her anklet dangled an inconsiderate strap. The figure's incisors pierced his bottom lip when the hawk shook out her foot. Whipping the roof slats, the falconry jess would likely snag the next rough edge she encountered. Iron soaked the figure's mouth; he should have saved them both. Should have freed her from the second cage, questions about his survival be damned—

His fixation jolted toward a movement farther down the street. Hastened footsteps were all but smothered by the unrelenting pitter-patter of rain, but as the hooded individual scurried up to the inn's doorstep, they fumbled for a keyring and sneaked inside.

The figure boosted off his heels and skated through the puddles, himself a shade bleaker than the darkness. Anticipation enlivened his bones. Saliva lathered his teeth once he'd sighted his prey. It was why he'd trailed Tetsu all this way into the quiet countryside of Agoston—his carriage having been stowed off the main highway and out of the village sight.

In her last letter, Alora had suspected Tetsu's conspiration with an underground cabal. Its leader was known only by an indecipherable alias: the Obscurer.

If Pilar's sil'haidren and ruling chancellor of the Shoto Collective *was* such a disciple, then the grotesque creatures might be the emerging instruments of a secret society—a society comprised of masked members within Orynthia's elitist underbelly.

If so, the operation was feeding on the figure's exhumed transgressions. The new currency, possibly in the hands of this Obscurer, was no longer locked in a tomb where the figure thought he'd laid his past self to rest.

He should have buried his feelings for her there too.

At the notion of his mistress, he lingered on the stoop. Rain pelted his back as he focused on the unlatched handle. The figure swallowed his slavering and, with it, the eagerness to chase whomever Tetsu was to meet.

He did not wish to return inside; the figure did often enough in his dreams.

Surrendering, he creaked the door on its hinges. His head hung low. The empty foyer had not changed over the years, nor had the duke of Agoston, a notably traditional aristocrat with a well-known predilection for tulips. Though out of season, the bulbed petals were everywhere, carpet to ceiling. Tulips decorated the wood paneling in an oppressive floral motif that pointed toward the rented rooms above. The figure gradually traveled it up the stairwell, fearing when the scrollwork would end.

Of the dozen rooms available, only a scattering of doors were closed along either side of the hall. Few stayed in Littleling Eaves, least of all the nobility, making it an ideal destination for those hellbent on avoiding them.

He walked on, trying to forget what it had been like to walk behind the comfort of her unhurried gait down the same hallway. Avoiding the swollen, yellow vase atop the upcoming table—from which he'd once discreetly stolen a freshly cut stem—the figure foolishly averted his eyes to the opposite threshold.

The doorway was ajar; a slivered portal he could not shut. Inching closer, he became fixed on the half-timbered windowpanes along the exterior wall.

Water beaded the glass.

The figure's feet denied him, trapped between his decades of torment. It had been raining that night too.

He closed the door behind him with a rush and a click, then planted his drenched head against the wooden barrier. Alora had spun round; her fingertips halted in the unthreading of her bodice. His hair dripped over his crested brow and the wistful smile it surely partnered. Unlike her, amid the disorganized frenzy, he hadn't bothered to change.

Alora whipped a frayed blanket off the provincial bed and covered herself, her cheeks ripening as embarrassment colored her skin in the loveliest stain. "What are you doing in here!" she worriedly hissed.

"I thought you'd be impressed I managed it. Would you prefer that I leave?" While he asked it in jest, his nerves sputtered at the terrifying possibility he'd overestimated her affections. Simply holding them was danger enough.

Sheepishly, Alora bit her lip and admitted, "Niit." She gestured toward the hall. "Korbin and the others?"

"Typical newlyweds. Korbin passed out with Gregor over their cheese platter, to Lourissa's dismay... A shock she didn't leave it swimming in the

street," he replied, his hands knit behind him as he took a watchful step deeper into her room.

He circled the foot of the bed, granting her ample space. It was the first time they'd ever been alone in such personal quarters—the atmosphere so very different than that of an archive or aviary. The overall smell was much improved at that.

"I'm grateful for a storm of this magnitude. It afforded me a bed so early in his tour," she said, sitting slowly onto its edge, graceful and birdlike. The mattress barely depressed under her weight. Since her Seating, she had become his swan in a lake of civility. And within her brilliant, incandescent eyes, he so often took flight.

"Might I sit with you?" He nodded toward the bed, as it was the only place he could.

Wide-eyed, Alora ogled his attire, forming a puddle at his feet. "You're soaking wet!"

"Yes, well," he said, grimacing at his heavy robing, "I can take it off if you like."

The room went quiet. He glanced up and found her blush had traveled into her parted lips. His own wording replayed in his ears as his gaze traced the subtle pout of her mouth.

He'd never had time for such things before… but he'd be a fool not to want them now.

Alora threw her face aside, hiding the spirited tint along her delicate features. "It's fine," she said and smoothed the coverlet beside her thigh. She produced a brittle book from under her pillow. It was their codex. "Did you come for this?"

He was relieved to see it safe from the deluge outside. Gently, he sat a few inches away. "You rescued it."

"I couldn't bear to lose us," replied Alora as she stroked the well-cher-ished binding. "Not when I've discovered myself in these pages."

"Then I propose a deserved trade." He revealed the single tulip he'd been carrying at his back. "For I believe tonight, Lady Boreal, you have rescued us both."

Accepting the flower, Alora brought it to her nose and smiled softly. She scooted the codex toward him across the bed.

He flipped it open and caressed the old, fragile vellum, its margins cluttered by her newest musings and witty correspondence. Comments concerning music. Poems exploring both doubt and devotion. A few jumbled verses recounting the crossing of a recent comet. He emitted a chuckle, having spotted an errant doodle of Gregor struggling to mount his horse.

Folding it shut, he fondly laid it to the side. He could hardly wait to revive its riddles.

"How I adore your mind," he replied. Narrowing the space between them, he gently sifted her unburdened curtain of pearly blonde hair off her temple, allowing the smooth strands to pass through his fingers as if it were the costliest silk.

Unexpectedly, her face turned inward against his palm as it lowered.

His heart lurched. His body stilled. As he cradled her smooth cheek, his breaths started to match hers, increasing in rate and sum. "I mean it. To the depths of me, I love your mind, Alora."

Alora blinked at him, her eyes shining with either fear or consequence, or both, as her voice scarcely rose above a murmur. "I think I love… you."

The floorboards creaked when, against his own restraint, he leaned in until his lips hovered atop hers. With the slightest uptick, she pressed against them.

Nature unfolded him. The years of their expressive intellect, profound debate, and the passion it all had restored set him afire. He slid his grasp behind her head and held her close, closer than any philosophy or praxis. Cupping her face, he bathed in her tangibility. She was the constant. The pages, the politics… Everything else, diminishing variables.

He broke from their long-awaited kiss to daringly ask, "I can steal away before the dawn. Shall I stay?"

Her nuzzled nod was confirmation enough for his body to overcome his better judgment. He began to peel off his soggy, outer robe. Free of a shirt and in nothing but his breeches, he laid her back onto the sheets.

"Wait…" She repeated his name and gently guided him onto his ribs so that he lay beside her.

"If you'd rather I go—"

"Heh'ta, stay the night through," she requested, rubbing her hand atop his shoulder. Gooseflesh followed its trail. "But nothing more can happen."

Nestling against the pillow, he said, "Is nothing happening now?" But the quirk in his grin faltered when her eyes started to shimmer. "What is wrong?"

"Do you remember the revelation I told you about… about my blood?"

"About the 'lumin,' you mean—"

"Shh." She hurriedly covered his mouth, trapping a reiteration from crossing his lips. "You promised you wouldn't tell a soul."

He scooped up her fingertips into his. "Of course not."

"If Eoine does not soon wed, then…" she said, her voice hitching, "then I will have to marry first."

The gears in his mind whirled to action, unable to accept that she could be taken from him before he even tried to keep her. "Marry me," he boldly begged. "We will find a way. Petition the Peerage."

But her face crumpled, and she started to cry. "Only two of the same can produce an heir of Tiergan, and the line must continue for Korbin and Lourissa's children." A tear slid from her luminescent right eye. "I cannot afford to bear someone's child who is unable to succeed me, however… however much I might wish to."

"Alora," he soothed, holding her fast.

"In Boreal, it would destroy us both."

He understood that she was different, unlike any other person he'd ever meet, and she would need a partner of equal fiber, of equivalent exception, to form a future. Yet the thought of another man, some highlander of acceptable descent lying in his place, rent a valley through his soul.

"What is it that you once wrote, 'is not the answer to everything seeded in our soil'? What if… What if I could formulate a way for us to be together, even in hiding? Somehow introduce the lumin into my system progressively, or perform some sort of transfusion—"

"Don't even speak it!" Tears rolled from under her lashes more fiercely than the storm raging outside.

"Forgive me." He pulled her closer so she could cry into the crook of his neck, his arms stretched securely around the sorrow he shared. "Forgive me, Alora," he said again as he kissed her head. "Just know that I would do anything for us to stay like this."

"My dearest." Squeezing his torso, Alora's hold rivaled his. "I would keep you forever if I could."

The figure panted against the doorframe. Shame came like a filthy shower. He deserved the pain, to suffer this heartrending anguish. He deserved everything, even her pledge to keep him there to endure it for as long as she could.

He stumbled backward, away from the reminder. There came a scrape from the end of the hall.

The room was closed off, though unable to trap the muffled argument inside. Soundlessly, the figure vaulted for the beaming overhead. With his scabbed ankles hooked around it, he swung his body overtop and shimmied to where the sound was leaking through a grate in the plaster.

Pressing his nose, whatever skin and cartilage stood intact, against the metal grill, he peered inside.

A man scrambled across the floor and grabbed a turned-over table for support. By his dress, he was of noble station. With his velvet hood thrown back, his balding scalp shone Unitarian bronze in the candlelight. Wedges of bread littered the rustic floorboards—a knife glinting a few inches from his reach.

"It will do you no good, Gaius," warned Tetsu as his sinewy form, wading in tiers of white, circled the cowering lord. Hands clasped, Tetsu tapped his hooked, silver nailpiece over his other hand like a raven clicking its talon. His jaundiced neck tilted to its side. "It is simple. Vote correctly. Convince your peers from Agoston to vote correctly. It would be so regretful for your next shipment of playthings to turn up at the wrong duke's estate. We mustn't let anyone see how young they all are, hm? Your family would be ruined. Your wife and daughters reduced to swine."

The apparent Duke Ambrose, so much older than the figure recalled, flashed his scowl at Tetsu. "The life of a pig is better than this! You've taken my son, my future!"

Tetsu squatted inside his billowing robes. They fanned around him as he wrenched the duke's liver-spotted forearm and stripped the sateen coat sleeve up to his elbow. The figure gripped the beam. Its edges snapped in his grip.

Branded into the duke's flesh was his symbol: an endless life loop with one dividing line through its intersection.

"Like you, Gaius, your son made an oath to the Obscurer. Felix owed him a debt." Tetsu's yellowed teeth showed as he pierced the sharpened tip of his nailpiece into the symbol. "Would you like to pay yours?"

The duke of Agoston whimpered as he profusely shook his head. Tetsu removed his metal claw. His yancy victim clutched his forearm where blood trickled from the puncture.

"Good. Then he is pleased with you, Gaius." Rising, Tetsu pet the man's head with a sickly fondness, the way one might pet a dog. "You serve an important role in the induction of the Obscurer's incarnate kingdom. Bolster the Peerage's confidence in the Shoto Collective, and you will be elevated in his sight."

Incarnate kingdom, the figure silently repeated.

A kingdom incarnate of what?

"And—and I'll be rewarded?" the duke sputtered on his knees, grappling for Tetsu's hand.

Tetsu pricked the underside of the man's wrinkled chin and sloped it upward. His dark, angular eyes flashed within their brothy whites. "With all the playthings you so desire."

A grin stretched the duke's face with vile gleam. He sat in a greedy daze as Tetsu's chancellor robes whooshed by without farewell. As he departed the room, the revolting stench of pipe marrow rose into the rafters, thickening the air about the figure's position. He tried not to gag.

Halfway down the hall, Tetsu twirled. However, his suspicious study did not climb higher than the cedar wainscoting. The figure's panic awoke. Along Tetsu's face a tendon twitched in confusion. A tic shuddered his slim brows. More twitches fired as frustration invoked an uncontrolled series of blinks.

The figure stared at Tetsu, finally recognizing him.

At last, the sil'haidren resembled his authentic self.

Tetsu's blackened tongue flailed from his mouth, stained by whatever substance he'd recently consumed to subdue the facial tics. He shook out his cheeks and spun forward, absconding down the stairwell and into the night, the inn and its inhabitants none the wiser.

The figure dropped to the rug and took after him, but instead of taking the door, he careened himself out a window and flipped onto the rugged rooftop. In the slickened street, Tetsu embarked toward his carriage. He pulled out a leather pad and flapped it across his shoulder. Within seconds, Amaranth's sister descended onto it.

Dread caught in the figure's ravaged throat. He could not kill him, not yet. He couldn't stop whatever was in motion, not when the superior villain was still unknown, and Tetsu the conduit to his heinous society.

The figure clucked for Amaranth. The hawk latched onto his arm, her talons crafting new scars among his tissues. He was damned, and because of him, so was Orynthia.

Inside this very inn, the figure had promised Alora he would never tell.

But he had told. Once, to accomplish his own ends. Spoken as mere theory in a single discussion about a false mutation in birds, he'd introduced the concept of lumin. A light-bearing anomaly that affected variants in the blood.

It had been Tetsu who'd hypothesized the genetic bridging. To what extent, he hadn't then known. But Tetsu knew it now.

And so did the Obscurer.

Chapter Thirteen
Zaethan

When Zaethan cracked an eyelid to his first morning in a Boreali home, he found himself face-to-face with a meddlesome squirrel nibbling the edge of his mattress.

Well, he *thought* it was a squirrel. That was what its black body most resembled, despite the crest of auburn fur ridging its backside, reminding Zaethan of the summer Dhalili had sported a dainty mohawk. He flattened against his pillow. Zaethan watched the rodent and its three shaggy tails flit back and forth as it hungrily plucked dried herbs through a hole in his highland bedding. The wide-eyed critter squeaked as it chomped contently. At least someone appreciated the tufts poking through the fabric and into Zaethan's back all night long. He certainly hadn't.

He flicked the squirrel off when it started to dig around his locs, unbound and splayed over the edge. With a squeal, it scurried up the windowsill whittled into the tree within which he'd slept. On his ribs, Zaethan replayed the events that'd landed him inside it, still unable to fathom how it'd all come to pass. He'd awoken in the highlands, on a bed of fragrant herbs belonging to a member of the haidren to Boreal's personal guard. His old self would have laughed—or screamed—at the notion. Yet there he was, breathing in the oaky resin of a home that while hollowed out was not dead, but very much alive. The spiraled woodgrain stretched overhead like an ancient cocoon. He wondered if the Boreali often felt like larva. So small and finite compared to their quarters. Zaethan said as much aloud, only to realize he was alone.

Kumo's bed lay empty, apart from the deep depression of a warrior too big for its timber frame.

Crisp air blew in from the open window, which Kumo had left ajar. Neither had ever slept in a place so stripped of humidity, or in his beta's words, so *naked*. Succumbing to the dawn, Zaethan lifted off the mattress and cracked his spine. At a brisk breeze, he looked down.

The air wasn't the only thing naked.

He hardly recalled undressing, having been so exhausted. Zaethan scrambled about, peeking under the bedframe to locate his clothes, grimy as they were from their endless journeying. Popping up, he saw a clean stack folded atop the chair near the door. Beneath it rested a pair of upturned boots.

Zaethan ground his teeth. But as his gooseflesh spread southward, he snatched the lambskin breeches and simple gray gambeson off the chair before he or his Southern roots shivered in retreat. After buckling the straps across his chest, he shoved his numb toes into the boots, thoroughly surprised by how comfortably they fit.

He tempted the heavy door open and was greeted by the unexpected sound of clinking crockery and tersely shushed giggles.

Steam fled from the Athdaras' kitchen at the end of the knobby hall. Stomach rumbling, Zaethan followed his nose to the egg-shaped threshold. A giant, bubbling pot occupied the iron stove—as did a short stack of bowls, for most were already enlisted to feed his pryde leaders, who were seated at the spacious main table. The Athdaras didn't breakfast with them and instead clustered themselves among the chairs collected at the farthest counter. The lady of the house, an unpleasantly stern woman wrapped in a woolen shawl, watched her Darakaian guests eat, like a vulture atop her stool. Meanwhile, her children suppressed their playful chuckling between her and her husband's unhappy scowls.

Zaethan winked at the pair of ginger-headed boys, ducking behind their cups and bowls. They were the only ones to have noticed his entry. Both looked young for their parents, who together appeared to have been chiseled from an ice-capped tundra.

Cross-armed, Lord Athdara resembled his son by his bristly cider-colored beard and thickset shoulders, which he'd hunched over his untouched meal. Zaethan wondered if he was a shadowman as well or the master of some other trade. He wound in place, not finding Declan in the room with his family. Perhaps he'd not yet awoken. Given the revulsion plastered onto his parents' faces… perhaps he thought it best not to.

Zaethan's stomach again growled. Apparently too consumed by the advantages of the throwing knife over the traditional Yowekaon blow dart, Kai and Zahra didn't ease their animated debate while their alpha zà wandered toward the stove.

"Ahoté! You're finally up. We thought the chill had seeped into your dreams!" Kumo hailed over his spoonful of slop and slid down the bench to make room. There was already plenty, as the family in residence preferred their corner.

"Not quite. Owàamo, cousin." Zaethan yawned and, turning, offered the same to his rigid hosts.

Unmoved, Lord Athdara grunted in response. His wife, though, bounced off her stool the moment Zaethan reached for the ladle.

"Niit, niit!" She waved her hands, speckled with age and rust, shooing him away from the pot. He dropped the ladle and awkwardly obliged. Her icy-blue eyes locked onto Zaethan as she grabbed an empty bowl and meticulously spooned a few helpings into it.

She handed it to him, and he took it, then inclined gratefully toward her. The lady of the house spun and immediately went to wash the ladle, as well as her own hands, and dried them on her apron. Then, she placed the newly cleaned utensil in the pot as if he'd never touched it.

"That makes more sense…" Zaethan grumbled to himself and sat across from Kai. The lesser alpha's splinted calf was propped on the bench between him and Zahra. Zaethan angled his spoon at it. "Eh, fancy a stroll on that leg? Or would you rather we leave you to the warmth of our caretakers?"

"Depths, ano." Kai shook his short locs. A look of dread overcame his already-enlarged eyes. "I think the cubs are plotting my disembowelment over their porridge. Little cutthroats."

Zaethan leaned past the alpha, observing the boys and their mischievous slop-stained grins as they took turns spearing each other in their middles. Catching his attention, the youngest, probably five years, jabbed his spoon across the way at Zaethan like a sword.

The cub erupted in laughter.

"Uni, they're hardened criminals." Zahra rolled her honey-hued eyes. She chucked a hunk of seedy bread at Zaethan's head. "Here. Tastes better with that."

He peered down at the mush, understanding it was a creamed oat of some sort. What he didn't understand was why it was green. Or spotted with brown.

Witnessing her move, one of the Athdara boys threw his own bread at his brother. Their father slammed the arm of his chair, silencing their mirth.

It was the first sense of familiarity Zaethan had had that morning. The man who'd raised him would have never allowed such childishness over breakfast—not that Nyack Kasim had often deigned to share the meal with him. Empathetically, Zaethan winked at the youngest cub, then set his mind on the pryde.

"We need to find the others today, yeah? They have us scattered. I think Takoda and Jabari were taken a few houses… uh, trees… down the way. Did anyone see where Sadik and Yhona went?" Zaethan asked the table.

"Ano," Kumo replied through his chews, "but someone said the rest of the prydes are staying with less important families. Sounded like we got the best digs."

"Hmph." He snorted. "Begrudgingly gotten, that is."

Zaethan admitted the Athdara dwelling had a certain gnarled charm, with its wool-woven rugs and knotted, twisting pillars. It was a just shame that the occupants weren't as toasty as their crackling hearth.

He bent lower over his bowl—a silly instinct, as he suspected their Boreali ears heard everything anyway. "Once Dhalili arrives, I'll want to send some of you in an envoy with her to Razôuel, yeye qondai? The king's message is too important to leave a single scout unprotected.

Until Boreal decides where it stands with the Quadren, I hate to admit it, but the Zôueli may be Orynthia's best defense from itself."

"Uni, wewe qondai. We know she can't do it alone," Zahra agreed.

Kai nodded. "Eh, though she'll kick and scream to do it that way."

"Well, she does bite." Kumo rolled back his shirtsleeve—also unsoiled and lent from their hosts—to reveal an old scar in the shape of a set of small teeth, courtesy of Dhalili's stubbornness.

"Let's just lay low, uni? Play by our keepers' rules. Stay within Roüwen's boundary," Zaethan ordered them. "Tell the prydes to be patient, to rest and wait. No trouble. Boreal can't see us as a threat if their elders are to offer us aid."

Kumo sat back. A weak smile relaxed his mountainous bearing. "Not so restless anymore, are you, Ahoté? Is the bobcat at home in the highlands?" he teased.

Zaethan shoved off his underlying suggestion. "We can't afford to be restless, cousin. We have to be smart."

The front door opened and closed, and he heard a clambering from the foyer. All four of them sat up as a series of heavy footfalls came down the hallway toward the kitchen.

Declan filled the rounded threshold. He mouthed something to his parents in witchtongue, below Darakaian earshot. They did not seem pleased.

Nor had they all morning.

Shorter though amply broader than Zaethan, Declan strode forward, his elbows grazing either beam, and deposited a pelt-wrapped package onto the table with a metallic thud.

"She demanded it be returned to you," the shadowman said gruffly, pointing at the item.

Excitement fluttered through Zaethan's chest as he flipped the hide aside to uncover his confiscated kuerre. Kai whistled at the sight, probably having never been so close to the rare weaponry before. The elder Athdaras stood from their posts, arguing under breath to each other and their son, when Zaethan reached out and stroked the blade. The radiant, opalescent iron thrummed under his touch, more alive than he'd remembered.

Something inside the metal had awoken in Boreal.

"She still wanted me to have it?" Zaethan asked, then looked up at Declan. "Even after what they did to her in the Grand Tabernacle?"

Having stood over the kuerre, he hit a blockage beneath the table with the toe of his boot. More giggles ensued from whichever cub had crawled beneath.

In Boreali, Declan quieted his parents' rebuttal and replied, "My Ana'Sere said '*the haidren to Darakai earned this mystery, and it will not be taken from him.*'" Kneading the base of his meaty neck, the shadowman held Zaethan with his steely eyes and smirked. "I'm beholden to agree with her. Take what is rightfully yours… Just do her a favor and don't flaunt it around the city—least of all in front of Captaen Bailefore." Declan then kneeled and reached under the table to grab his brother by the belt. He hoisted the child like a rucksack as he jerked his chin toward the curved backsword, implying Zaethan were to carry it at his own risk. "She'll defend your possession. Little else."

Zaethan retrieved the kuerre. Ignoring the skeptical hook in Zahra's brow, he grabbed the hilt unrelentingly in his grasp. In a matter of weeks, he'd lost nearly everything he'd ever gained. Had titles and heritage stripped from his soul. And yet on merit alone, his once-enemy had presented that forbidden sword to him twice.

It was an enigma, and so was she.

But they were in Boreal, a land where enigmas were purged from their haidren's own palm. Zaethan held her blade close, its value steeper than any weight in gold.

Part of him suspected it might be the last thing Luscia Darragh Tiergan ever gave him.

"What would one game of motumbha hurt, eh? We're packed into this place like Kumo's gullet after he spies a rack of smoked ox," Takoda complained as he fiddled with a circlet of bells. The warrior could never help himself, having idly reached for one to jangle—a strange bit of jewelry that'd been cropping up across trading benches in the days that had passed.

The trinket vendor smacked his fingers, wiping hers off the minute they disappeared behind her booth.

"Ow! That was harder than last time!" Takoda threw the woman a dirty look. "Listen, Alpha Zà, we can only walk this same kakka-shtàka market so many times."

"It's an agora, not a market," said Hachiro pointedly as he purchased one of the belled bracelets. "Tadöm, madam." He dropped a few crupas into the middle-aged vendor's ashen hand. How he still had coin to spend, Zaethan didn't know—or care, so long as it kept the shoto'shi occupied.

Jabari leaned over the shoto'shi's newest purchase and tapped one of the bells, while their grouping walked on. "Too many chimes in the market maze," he said, swooping his fingers over his bouncing curls to superstitiously wick away any spells. "Buy a bell, belong to a witch, Haidren of West."

"I belong to the Shoto Collective." Hachiro huffed in annoyance.

"Obviously, your understanding of the skin trade is rudimentary at best. I have a spare piece of literature on the legalities somewhere…"

Jabari scrunched his dark nose. "Better a book than a bell, but a ball better than a book. Motumbha match explain this for the squinty haidren, Alpha Zà."

"Ano zà. Again," Zaethan said, pinching his temples. "The outskirts of Roüwen aren't spacious enough to play without crossing into unapproved territory."

"Nevertheless," Hachiro stated, interjecting more conversationally than normal. "Exercise has proven an effective treatment for the Darakaian temperament. Aggressive impulse is the pitfall of your House, so perhaps a game—"

"No one is playing motumbha," Zaethan said through his clenched jaw. "Not unless you're going to be the thing they beat around the field."

The shoto'shi smacked his thin lips. "You can see, Lord Darakai, how your untreated aggression only leads to…" He sputtered when Zaethan sidestepped in front of him threateningly. Hachiro blinked four times. "To… more traffic violations."

Zaethan sniffed and rebound his locs, striding onward. As a favor to Dmitri, he'd agreed to adopt Hachiro in his daily walk, the same his pryde took every day through Roüwen's congested assembly. Zaethan had long since regretted the charity.

He speared a glance through the bordering macramé tapestries, seeking the king who'd saddled him with such a nuisance. Thousands of people packed the path unwinding on the other side, Dmitri wading somewhere among their number with Luscia and her father, no doubt. Woven in similar patterns to the drapes in the Athdara household, the tapestries formed falling hedges along the pebbly footpaths that connected the traffic between the city's innumerable, hollowed-out trees. Empty of their bases, the expansive, lichen-peppered trunks had been cored into giant, mythic archways to better welcome the busy shoppers. Boreali of all ages and class migrated through the arcades. The enormous rootage excavated, it was as if giant holdreheiim hands had been erected on all fingertips, propped high off the forest floor.

Inside those shaded cavities, the more established business bustled.

Zaethan and his fellows ambled behind the masses into another unearthed gallery. To his left, a cobbler hammered boot soles across from a tailor's shop. On his right, a carpenter sawed away at a post, jesting with his neighbor, the silk broker, who fanned out swaths of elegant fabric like billowing sails before vats of sparkling beads. While too restrained to be considered extravagant, every garment—every single good was of exquisite caliber. Their craftsmanship dictated even the most conventional items as finery.

Everything told the same story in Boreal, though no one would share what it was.

Here, the echoes of barter, labor, and clinking commerce boomed within the tree base like they were contained by a wooden kettledrum.

The "agora," as Hachiro termed it, functioned as just that: a sprawling, interconnected hub of artisan culture and trade. He'd learned the highlander highway cut through the peninsula, serving as a rock bed for the Boreali populace. In Roüwen, everything—every home and shrine—was roosted above it. Zaethan knew, having strolled the agora for a week. By the Enclave's statute, there was nowhere else the Darakaians could go.

The shadowman trailing their every step made sure of it.

Zaethan was uncomfortably conscious of the man's nearness, his hover an armed pestilence, never less than ten paces behind. They seemed to rotate wardens among the Quadren and prydes. However, that shadowman had been assigned to observe Zaethan most regularly. Perhaps ten or fifteen years older, he was tall like Noxolo Egon, though ruddier than the crotchety Lady Athdara. He reminded Zaethan of an overgrown carrot. That was how he told them apart. It was his least favorite produce, randomly sprouting up at the most irritating times— and heavily fortified produce at that. The one who followed him last evening resembled an old, white gourd. The one the morning prior, a disgruntled yellow squash.

Zaethan quirked his head, dodging a massive ornamental rug strung high, not having pieced it together until that moment: each were ingredients in Uriel pie.

In Zaethan's periphery, the shadowman's crescent wraiths glinted where they crossed over his back. The unmistakable blades pointed at a poignant reminder of the disparity in weaponry between North and South. The ordinary kopar stuffed in its sheath swayed against Zaethan's thigh in humorless challenge. It stood no contest.

A gaggle of young women flurried around Hachiro toward the tailor's shop, separating the Darakaians from their watcher for a few flashes. But out of a pocket of shade, the big warrior reemerged in the flanks, closer than before. Zaethan flexed his fist, where off his other hip, the hilt of the kuerre swung in disguise. Having wrapped the blade in reinforced strips of something called linsilk, the uncut gemstone set into the pommel was his only najjani craftsmanship on display.

Zaethan didn't intend to wield the kuerre. Nor did he intend to have it stolen from his room either.

The shadowman paced with them through the cloistered gallery across a row of overflowing crates. Cupping the pommel, Zaethan dared a direct look into the man's cold, callous eyes. His blotchy cheeks pinched, and he sneered at the hilt under Zaethan's palm.

The covering wasn't fooling anyone.

"I must say, Lord Darakai, that your boorish intimidation tactics grow tiresome." Hachiro yammered on in a manner that suggested he'd never stopped talking. "Threats have no place in modern diplomacy."

Zaethan tore his focus from the watchful shadowman. He stepped over the hem of Hachiro's vivid orange robe.

Must be nice, having your things laundered.

Zaethan led them out of the tree base and onto another sunny, tassel-framed pathway. "Well, get used to them, *Lord Pilar*. That's all diplomacy really is."

His shoulder hitched a fraction. Pale faces flooded the lane. Typically, a Boreali passerby would grant the Darakaians space, but recently their number seemed to increase, causing some to rub elbows on the street. The highlanders didn't appear concerned for their safety as much as their cleanliness. Sounds of disgust partnered most accidental touches, many disconcerted Boreali scrubbing the invisible muck off their sleeves as they went on their way.

Herded to the edge of the path, Zaethan clasped his hands together, out of the way, as they strode by a line of elderly lacemakers. The silken threads in their care were more fragile than their wrinkly expressions, which sharpened when Zaethan wandered by the creaky rocking chairs. Behind their snow-white heads, another swarm of young, linsilk-clad clanswomen fawned over a yard of lace stretched between them. Its sheen was as shimmery and intricate as stained glass. A doe-eyed, dark-blonde woman caught his gaze. Hers were gentler features, innocent even. She was more traditionally beautiful than her haidren, though far less fearsome. Her lashes fluttered over the lace. Zaethan dragged his face away before he heard the pack's girlish tittering.

He couldn't blame them, trapped on this chilly peninsula with ashen men. After all, he had been labeled a *pretty thing* by the madam of a brothel.

"Eh, I see Kumo and Zahra," said Takoda, pointing through the crowd.

Zaethan jogged after him, between the people.

"They're up ahead, in that smithy they like so much!"

Zaethan grinned, pleased to reunite with his pryde leads. But at the lack of uninvited analysis, he swung around, searching for the haidren to Pilar.

Back by the lacemakers, Hachiro Naborū-Zuo was inspecting the nimble activities of an elderly woman, who did not seem to appreciate the way he was scribbling down her every fidget. Across from the unkempt shoto'shi, the same group of clanswomen exchanged smitten whispers among themselves. Zaethan's mouth fell when one winked at the Westerner—not that he detected it.

Apparently Zaethan was *not* so pretty.

Takoda jogged back toward him, averting a brush with a Boreali man carting a wheelbarrow. "It's getting kind of creepy, uni?"

"The way Boreali women keep ogling the librarian?" Zaethan tossed his hand toward the spectacle, absolutely dumbfounded.

"Ano. How the Boreali keep multiplying. There's got to be another few hundred here since yesterday!"

"Apparently, they're on some sort of pilgrimage. Roüwen must be a waypoint. Hachi!" Zaethan barked to the other haidren.

Hachiro whipped around; his inky cowlick defied gravity where it stood out on one side. One eye, magnified three times the size of the other, blinked in surprise behind his green lens. Dipping side to side in his strange, Pilarese double bow, he bid farewell to the lacemakers and scurried down the path.

Leaving behind the many disappointed coos of his female admirers, of course.

"Rhaolé. Move it. You can talk to your fan club later." Zaethan bunched his robing over the shoto'shi's scrawny spine and propelled him through the crowd.

"It's not my fault I have a perfectly symmetrical face, Lord Darakai. I'm told women like that sort of thing. You haven't suffered this infuriating misfortune, as one of your ears sits higher than the other."

With a snarl, Zaethan steered them toward the specialized smithy.

It'd become one of the warriors' preferred pastimes—watching how the witchiron was hammered and forged into its coveted shapes. Luxsmiths, they'd learned they were called, were set apart from local blacksmiths, their work far more prized than any horseshoe. These craftsmen were guardians and sculptors, toiling over the rarest of metals inside the bases of trees. Yet instead of vendor booths, the cavernous arcade was packed wall-to-wall with specialized forges. Battered anvils, corroded chisels, and hard-worked mallets burdened the benches.

They could hear the insatiable sizzle of a sword being quenched when they approached a familiar hearth manned by the youngest luxsmith in the vicinity. Zaethan bumped his beta in the bicep as he came beside him and Zahra. Huddled off to the side, they observed while an adolescent withdrew a white-hot spear of witchiron—or "luxiron," as the Boreali preferred—from the forge. The opal fuller had melted into a river of diamonds. It refracted the roaring blaze over the spectators in a shower of stars.

Releasing a whistle, Zahra clapped for the young man, even though she'd seen him do it many times over. He pivoted and wiped his coal-smattered chin with the back of his sweaty forearm. His mismatched irises beamed in triumph.

"Nearly there." Phalen Tiergan panted, then with a fanatical, toothy grin, he thrust the blade back into the flames. "Not ready until we can paint Aurynth across the ceiling!"

Jabari moved toward the bench, his lanky fingers flitting over a cooled set of daggers that flashed a light of their own. "Uni, sparkle like Àla'maia's court—"

Iron whined. The lurking shadowman had released his crescent wraiths and aimed them at Jabari. Activity in the smithy halted. Mallets and tongs clanked to the ground as some of the luxsmiths traded for something sharper, brandishing their own blades.

"Doru, doru." Zaethan threw out his hands. "Nothing was touched. Jabari, just step away from the daggers, yeah? Nice and slow."

Crescent wraiths were inched closer. The apple of Jabari's throat became a fishhook, dipping up and down through his skin as he swallowed sharply and slid his heel over the woodchipped floor.

The son of Boreal's Clann Darragh opened his mouth to speak, but he didn't get the chance. Outside, a shriek pointed every blade toward the street.

CHAPTER FOURTEEN
LUSCIA

"So they all make this expedition every year? Entire villages just pick up and leave?" Dmitri asked and took another bite of his apple, gawking at the throng of new pilgrims squeezing onto the busy market lane.

Arm in arm, Luscia guided her king along the lengthy line to the alehouse where it wrapped around the square. "Wem, the able-bodied families who can make the journey. It's a fair distance to Aksel's Keep, though one we Boreali know well. All westbound pilgrims stop in Roüwen to replenish their road supply. And to purchase ornaments, of course, to celebrate Ana'Innöx once they get there."

"Remarkable." A distinctive dimple puckered Dmitri's cheek as he offered a passerby a sincere smile. He pitched his byrnnzite cane toward the increased number of decorated tassels descending from the skyward homes. The braided prayers had multiplied as many traveling relatives arrived. "The translation eludes me. This annual 'Ana'Innöx' is what exactly?"

"The Great Harvest," Orien Darragh answered for Luscia. Her father strolled with them, a stately bear among festive woodland. "The autumn equinox is a holy time for our people, Your Majesty."

Astutely, he glanced at Luscia over their king's mussed waves. Her father rarely made that face, the order behind it clear and precise. His crystal-blue eyes smothered her commentary.

In infrequent agreement, Luscia knew he held solidarity with her aunt in the matter—that the beauty of Ana'Innöx should remain a mystery for the Boreali alone, just as it had for the centuries preceding this one. According to Luscia's betters, such greater truths were not for the Quadren, or their displaced king.

But she wasn't so sure anymore.

Luscia took in her kinsmen greeting their old friends with a kiss. Countless reunions crowded the streets. Hers were a people blessed by their seclusion, free and wholly ignorant of the dark forces that were stealing the same from those outside their iron border. Luscia had seen the depravities of Marketown—where the poor and maligned were reduced to footstools. She'd witnessed the abuse of the proud and the deception of those powerful enough to grind warriors into fodder for a war not yet begun. Luscia had seen unparalleled evil ravage the wilds and innocent souls consumed by its hunger.

The other haidrens had seen the same.

Dmitri's Quadren had been bitten by a mortal venom. Should they not also experience its cure?

Thoarne himself was the only Orynthian regent to behold what lay within Aksel's Keep, for Aksel Bailefore nor his mighty keep had yet been established. It was there, on the banks of that hallowed fount, where history had forever been altered. There, where Thoarne's royal line had been saved.

And there, the line of Tiergan reborn.

With a tickle to her temples, her vision flickered where she stood. A momentary flash of the *Other* draped the city square in luminescent threads, flitting and frolicking over the Boreali travelers. The lumin twinkled under the patches of sunlight. Above the fountain, it clustered more contently around the multicolored flames, where fluttering like butterfly wings, the threads flew at Tiergan's stone feet.

Whispers swished her ears with the movement of the fire.

"Relent and reach, Luscia…"

She swiped away the noise as if it were a buzzing bee and made to turn toward Dmitri. But her heart sputtered, bridling a rush of anxiety, when a thread more brilliant than the others rose over the far side of the gold basin.

The harbinger thread seemed to stare at Luscia through the ghostly flames. Her feet turned to ice.

It hadn't visited her since Port Khmer.

Drowning out the cheery melody of the day, the supernatural voices harmonized more loudly.

"Relent and reach for what will not rust…"

Luscia loosened her grip on her king's arm and forced herself to breathe normally so as not to raise his alarm—or that of her najjan, shadowing them through the crowd. With immense pressure behind her eyelids, she willed the veil to close. A screen reluctantly slid across her mind. Yet as her Sight was locked away, she felt the lumin pressing in from the other side.

Lightheaded, Luscia was grateful for the masses. Her hearing rebalanced, and she returned to herself. Fiddles were played. Carts skidded by. Bushels and hampers grazed Luscia's elbow in the haste of many Boreali on their holiday errands, as if nothing had happened. The pilgrims paid Luscia little interest. She took no offense; she could barely distinguish the three feet in front of her.

"My daughter—my haidren—is a crucial participant this year. It is her inaugural harvest," her father went on to say, his wording vague though weighted with pride.

Luscia made sure he caught the jerk of her chin and, she hoped, not the bead of sweat that escaped her plaited hairline. She hadn't found the occasion to tell Dmitri she must leave him behind in Roüwen. In her gut, the idea of embarking alone still seemed wrong, no matter how she tried to convince herself otherwise.

"Oh, I see. Likewise, I harbor holy devotion for my own garden in Bastiion. Positively sacred, my Hildurean roses—as fickle as they are divine." Tugging his fur cloak higher against the afternoon air, Dmitri's umber brows squished together in curiosity. "What is it you harvest in Boreal this time of year, Clann Darragh?"

Orien Darragh ran his thick fingers through the tangles of his beard—stalling, no doubt—while he scanned the square over the heads of many. His eyes widened. "Ah! I see the eldership from Clan Ciann have arrived. We must make the proper introductions, Your Majesty. Come, come." He waved. The ermine tails of his cape dusted the gravel as he wove through the assembly toward the opposite side of the fountain.

Dmitri hopped out of the way for some bleating goats and a frazzled herdsman and eagerly followed.

Out of habit, as well as dread, Luscia flattened her collar over her scar when she spotted which elders had clustered at the base of the Grand Tabernacle.

All three stood out like portraits of the past. Talï descended from their stern eyes. Ever-painted, iridescent designs swirled about the archaic prayer stones. Their garb was far less adorned than the majority of the worship-minded, who, having dressed in their finest, filed by the elders up the monumental stair. Instead of linsilk, the men from Clan Ciann sported rough woolen tunics over kidskin pants, an elder's hem so long it met the ground. Though, it was the geometric patterns that'd been easiest to spot from a distance. Homespun and loom-stitched, the layered style was so traditional, it had not evolved in centuries.

Neither had those who wore it.

From behind, Luscia caught Noxolo's groan when the crowd, realizing who they were, quickly parted for her. Her sentiment was the same, not that Dmitri heard it; Nox had made no such promises regarding *his* volume. Marek, however, was equally bound by his plastered smile as Luscia was to hers. And she skillfully sharpened it for one najjani guard huddled among the visiting elders.

Her guard.

With one leg comfortably braced against the lowest steps, Creyvan was not in the alehouse, where he should have been babysitting the haidren to Bastiion's binge with Böwen. Rather, there he was outside, conversing with the leaders of the Orallach. They were angled together, their gestures mirrored in their shortness. By their intense nodding, Luscia had no doubt that they swung toward the same side of whatever issue they were heatedly discussing. It was a dangerous affiliation for Creyvan to make, given the zealotry of the only surviving clan across the strait.

The rest had not been granted the same privilege.

"Ciann always sends their elders to travel with the Enclave into the keep," Luscia explained in Dmitri's ear as they neared, and the grouping suspiciously broke apart.

Creyvan swiveled in surprise, nearly tripping on his heel. Her razor-sharp grin pinned her rogue najjan. Misplaced favor directed misplaced footing—a tenet any of the aelect ought to observe and one Luscia would score into his fresh-shaven face later if she must.

Averting the threat in Marek's glare, a force she felt shading her back, Creyvan patted his chest, clearing his throat as he visibly backpedaled from the elders and stomped straight for the alehouse.

Luscia's father stretched over and cupped the clammy hands of the elder whose tunic hem hung limply over his upturned boots, exhibiting more enthusiasm than she'd ever seen him show for the man. "Allöh'jomn'yeh, Elder Hinrük! Elders Dagmar and Kalf." Orien bowed his stature respectfully toward the other two, though as the highest clansman, he needn't lower for anyone but the king. "Rul'lothadim Aniell, how blessed we are that King Dmitri and his Quadren have come to Roüwen during such a celebratory season. It is not often a regent meets with those from the Orallach seaside."

"Allöh, gentlemen," Dmitri said, greeting them kindly in Boreali. He planted his cane in front of himself. "Tadöm, thank you for sharing your city with me and my party. We are most grateful to be here."

The elders' gazes were as cold and watery as the Drystan Sea. Dodging their stares between themselves, they looked as if they had no intention of sharing anything with a Unitarian, no matter his crown. Elder Hinrük grunted and offered Dmitri a rigid bow. Muteness followed.

Her father smacked his lips, offended. "I trust you remember my daughter, your haidren?"

Elder Hinrük's regard slumped below Luscia's elevated chin. She held it there for what felt like an eternity, just as she'd done three and a half years ago under the Enclave's examination. Luscia thanked the High One she'd chosen a surcoat that day; its formality provided a stiff shield that clasped over her disfigured neck. Back then, Elder Hinrük had argued that just like her scar, the trace of Tavish filth would not fade from her once-pristine flesh. That because she'd been assaulted by Prince Darcain, Luscia was sullied. Tarnished. And therefore, that her haidrenship should forfeit to her brother, who, in the eye of Hinrük, was clean.

As he was the speaker of his clan, most from Ciann had agreed. As fundamentalists, they would. But so had other elders within the Enclave.

Some who still did.

That was the permanent injustice of rape—not the innocence robbed but the shame sowed in its place. All it had taken were a few malicious words to water her seeded self-revulsion.

His had been a short-lived campaign against Luscia, put to a stop by her aunt. Clan Ciann was influential, powerful even. Though in their piety, they had one thing to lose, the medal of morality—a self-given medal that Alora could strip them of at any time. Powerful people were often afraid of the anointed. No matter their bearing and no matter their wealth or accomplishment, the one to whom influence was bestowed always garnered more esteem than one who imposed their influence on others. As Alora had been the acting descent of Tiergan, as well as a virtuous woman who'd remained untouched, Elder Hinrük's case had quickly been crushed. Yet here it resurfaced, on the steps to the Grand Tabernacle. Alive and well in his pitiless eyes.

"Wem, weh haidren, the purported friend of Darakai. We look forward to meeting with you properly, Ana'Sere," Elder Hinrük said, granting her a scant bend of his head. His thin, wheaten hair was greased back like yarn to be counted, having come up short. "Ciann is eager to hear your justification for the sacrilege on our soil."

His attention flitted beyond her, to where Luscia was sure dark bodies peppered the public. Because the prydes were sequestered to the main portion of the city, their presence was obvious among the pilgrimage.

Marek stepped up at her right. His taut leather jacket sleeves rasped when the captaen rolled his shoulders back protectively.

The elder gave a derisive snort.

"Change ordained is not always a threat," she stated daringly.

"Niit, not to her who ordains it."

Her father hissed a warning. "Hinrük—"

"Then let me fetch an unchanging figure for you. I believe that is Ana'Mere just over there." Disentangling her arm from Dmitri's, Luscia hotly excused herself.

Her palms prickled. Static kissed their surface as Luscia stormed through the lively crowd to where she swore she'd seen the pendulum of Alora's long platinum braid swinging in pursuit of a candlemaker's stand. Luscia sped toward the only woman who could put a man from Ciann in his place.

"Luscia…"

"Relent, Luscia…"

With an exasperated growl, Luscia swatted the air. Her Sight wavered once more, a picture of the *Other* and its languid threads flashing in and out, before she closed in enough to reach for Alora's shoulder.

Except, it was not her aunt's face that turned around. Luscia let go. "Oh! Meh fyreon—"

"Mamu!"

Noxolo darted around her like a swallow coming to roost and took the woman, presumably his mother, in his arms. Luscia stared in wonder at how akin she appeared to Luscia's aunt. Their eyes weren't the same, of course, but the pitched cheekbones, the delicate nose… Even the daintiness of her ecstatic smile had fashioned her into a true doppelgänger.

She could make easy crupas off that, Luscia thought. On the road to Aksel's Keep, pilgrims wouldn't know the difference between a fake blessing and a real one—were she to exploit their faith.

"Mamu, meet our haidren!" Noxolo exclaimed, spinning her proudly toward Luscia.

Basketed by his lanky arms, his mother gave a clumsy curtsy. "Ana'Sere, we did not expect to see our son this year." Her cheeks puckered under her happy tears. "Aniell bless you, meh haidren, for bringing him home for Ana'Innöx. Bolaeva, here, take a token of our gratitude." Lady Egon handed Luscia a pack of their infamous jerky—or what Luscia assumed was jerky.

"No token necessary, Lady Egon."

"It will bring us honor for others to sight it in your hands," she insisted. At Luscia's quizzical look, Lady Egon's shoulders hunched as she leaned closer. "It's worse this year, meh Haidren. Few will trade with us. The elders from Clan Ciann say we are too close to Tevaár's coast. That pilgrims from Ödetha are unclean."

Then I must be filthy, Luscia thought. "Wem, they have a fondness for describing other people that way." She shot a scowl toward Lord Hinrük where he still conversed with Dmitri and her father. "I will make certain they are spoken to about this issue."

Lady Egon shook her head, suddenly frazzled. "Oh, ock. Don't trouble yourself over us. We didn't mean to report a formal complaint!"

Not many did against Ciann. Once the complainant's reputation was damaged, they never reported much of anything ever again.

"That's our haidren's job, Mamu. Wait, Dierdre is here too?" Noxolo broke from his mother when a tall, attractive redhead wandered away from a band of fiddle players.

"Nox!" His sister dumped her swollen knapsack on the street. Knowing the Egon family, it was probably full of meat, most unappetizing in origin.

She jumped for him in a skyward hug. Together, the siblings loomed over their mother. Poor Deirdre Egon, about whom Luscia had heard more than a couple of stories. She did not at all resemble the young woman her najjan had depicted. Deirdre's light-copper plaits framed a rosy, cherubic face—a face boasting only one chin, not the several she was so often ascribed.

Deirdre was soon resettled on the ground by her thrilled brother. By Luscia's estimation, she must have been as tall as Marek and clearly a hunter's daughter. Deirdre's leggy frame was flattered under her simple traveling tunic by a utility belt festooned with skinning knives cinching her long torso.

Luscia twisted for her captaen. Given the way Marek's mouth hung agape, she expected he thought the same. She wasn't particularly jealous of how he was looking at Dierdre, like how after a devastating winter, one marvels at a flowering field on a spring morn. Luscia had been looked at like that once before—kneeling on the dirt-caked floorboards of a shabby inn.

It signified little.

Marvel didn't always come from the right person.

Luscia reached for Marek's hand in an uncharacteristic breach of public affection. "Waedfrel, we're pleased to meet you both," she said to Noxolo's family.

"Wem." Marek gulped loudly. "Waedfrel indeed, ladies Egon."

Spreading her hem, Dierdre curtseyed low, replying to Luscia, "Rumor of your beauty does you no justice, Ana'Sere." Her observation traveled to the kurtfierï tied around her wrist. "But I see some rumors are true enough. We are so happy for you." Politely, Deirdre peered up at Marek. "Erm—for you both."

The wind picked up as the captaen wrapped his other hand around Luscia's, cradling it whole. Murmurs licked her ears.

"Reach for what will not rust, Luscia…"

Sweetly, Lady Egon touched her heart. "Courtship is such a memorable season for a young couple—"

At an earsplitting *crack* and a hiss of leaves, Luscia threw her head back and saw an enormous branch plummeting straight for Deirdre. Her eyes widened. So had Deirdre's.

In a blink, the *Other* shrouded Luscia's periphery with muted haze. Suddenly, behind the veil, threads of lumin skittered from her body toward the falling limb.

Whispers rushed into roars. A bracelet of glory snaked around her free wrist, statically charged and ablaze. The harbinger thread screamed.

"Relent and reach!"

Cowering under her own arms, Noxolo's sister screamed too.

"Move!" Luscia yelled, throwing her hand out in fright for Deirdre.

Light blasted from her palm in a gust. The threads bowed like a buckler, thrusting Deirdre into the candlemaker's stand. Wax pillars toppled her collapse moments before the branch impacted the earth and shattered right where she'd been standing.

Luscia's Sight dissolved as startled shouts poured from every angle. Lady Egon ran to her daughter, with Noxolo right behind. The candlemaker hollered at all three over his ruined merchandise.

But Luscia panted in shock at her seemingly ordinary palm. Her other, sweat-slickened hand was squeezed. Hard.

She regarded the gobsmacked captaen at her side. Marek's fingers raked his crimson hair as he stared at the empty space before him, then at the holdreheiim branch, splintered to a mulch heap across the path.

Finally, at Luscia.

"Is that… Shores of Aurynth, Luscia," Marek said through a heavy breath. "Is that what you always *see*?"

A loosened lock tumbled past Marek's brow in the breeze. Behind it, a relic tide surfed his glowing irises.

He had glimpsed into the *Other*. In a miraculous daze, Marek lifted their conjoined hands.

He had glimpsed it through her.

Hush settled over the moorland. Its wispy blades of grass were untrampled and deserted of men, except two of her own, who'd rooted themselves as silent fixtures in the setting. Even the crickets had stifled their twilight melody. Every creature was at attention. Watching. Waiting.

It'd taken hours of coaxing to get her there, well out of sight. Marek had been relentless since miraculously glimpsing the *Other* through her touch. He wanted to see it again.

And he wanted to see what Luscia could do inside it.

Aksel's snout rested on his outstretched legs, reminding her of the night he'd witnessed her initiate the Sight outside Bastiion. That clearing felt ages away. So did the girl who'd conjured it. Her lycran blew out, more impatient than the bugs.

Luscia's bootheel skidded backward over the dampened heather, tempting the ring of stones Declan had laid. She sensed his shadow lurking outside it. His sturdy presence hid within the shawl of mist that had enveloped the whole mauve-dusted plateau, sheltering their activity from those who would condemn it.

I just might condemn it too, she confessed.

"Just breathe," Marek said from the center of the containment that circled their feet. She shifted hers anxiously. The traditional sparring sphere was intended to pin her focus to the danger within, though she knew it would come from without.

She exhaled slowly. The tip of her nose went fuzzy, tempting the fabric of the *Other*. The threads were excited for some reason. Luscia closed her lids, then reopened them with her mind's eye. A lumin field waded between her and Marek, uncoiling over the rocks and into the mist. Together, the threads pulsated in rhythmic shudders, like the atmosphere were drumming its fingers expectantly. For what, she was scared to learn.

Nerves chewed at her middle, but she nodded at her captaen nonetheless.

"All right, brödre." He signaled Declan, while his attention remained locked onto Luscia. "Do your worst."

The muscle along Luscia's neck stiffened. Her body was primed for anything to attack.

Initially, nothing did.

Then a dark wad shot out from the fog and burst across Marek's face. He spit dirt, rolling it distastefully off his tongue.

Aksel yipped at the captaen from his bed outside the ring. Apologizing, Luscia winced. "I knew this was a stupid idea. Niit, we shouldn't be doing this anyway—"

"I can't unsee it, Luscia," Marek said, his jaw so firmly set, it carved a new horizon. "I cannot."

"They're probably wondering where we are."

With a tenacious sigh, he scraped the dirt off his lips. "Let them wonder. Something special happened to you—has *been* happening to you. We try again." He raised his voice for the unseen najjan. "Preferable with something inedible this time!"

A low chuckle rumbled the southward gloom. In misty beams, the lumin vibrated with Declan's sound of delight.

Inside the ring, they both stilled. An owl hooted at the burgeoning sunrise.

From the east, a stick whizzed into the circle and struck Marek over his kneecap. Luscia's arms hung limply where she stood like an idiot as he grimaced in pain. Admittedly, the throw had had some power behind it.

"Marek, meh fyreon. It's just not going to work. I don't know how it happened before. Or if it should ever happen again!"

He shook out his leg and marched toward her. His steps were almost silent, despite their strong sense of purpose. "Luscia." Marek lowered his face, sweeping up the apprehension in her eyes with her hands. "My Ana'Sere, I don't know either. Here's what I do know: Aniell made these hands for something we don't understand. Declan and I serve *you*. We aren't going anywhere. Stop fighting whatever the High One is trying to do. I can believe in you… but so must you."

Marek lightly kissed her fingers before walking back to his station at the center.

With her Sight tethered in the *Other*, Luscia watched the tangles of lumin drift aside for him to pass. The harbinger thread had not joined them on the moor. In its absence, Luscia wasn't sure if she was disappointed or relieved.

"Relent and reach," she said, repeating its mantra in a trepid whisper. "Reach for what will not rust." Aniell knew she'd battled whatever this was her entire life. She had medicated it and buried it down so deeply, the Sight had to scrape its way painfully out of her skull.

Yet she wasn't drowning herself any longer. The tonic had been dumped. There was no hiding anymore. There was only Luscia and the threads.

Relaxing her form, she nodded once more at Marek.

Luscia flexed her fingers inside the glittering web. She sought any microshift among the threads. Her palms grew warm, like the solrahs in her septum. Then, like a single string tugging from a hem, a stitch rippled through the web seconds before another stick broke from the mist and sailed for Marek's head.

She threw out her hands, willing the threads to unite and shove him aside. A jolt, hot and cold at once, ran down her arms and fled her palms in a prickling, euphoric rush. As a current rolling the Vasil, the lumin swooshed from either side of her body, and the threads arrowed for Marek.

Their light-bound rupture collided with a smash.

But the captaen did not fall; Marek, rumpled and wind-blasted, did not move an inch. Instead, he stood speechless, gaping at his feet. Her aim must have faltered. Because there at his boot toe lay the stick, fractured to pieces.

Declan raced up the moor. The stocky najjan dropped onto his heavy knees and cradled his freckly cheeks. Out of nowhere, he shrieked with laughter—a delirious punch to the stillness.

"Ykah lö? What in Aurynth's eye?" Declan picked up the twig, or a piece of it, and shucked it at Luscia.

Clumsily, she caught it.

"Ana'Sere… The others have to see this."

Luscia gasped, more from fear than fatigue, scared what the bit of wood foretold of her future—and for Boreal. Haidrens didn't manipulate. Descendants of Tiergan didn't exert.

Not since the firstborns; not since his Brightling.

Nor the Wrathling thereafter.

Luscia clenched her fingers around the fractured twig. Phantom pins and needles prickled her skin from its wash with the lumin. She was unable to comprehend it—to even pose the absurdity of its significance. Tiergan had fathered a child of bright.

As he had a child of wrath.

So which did that make her?

CHAPTER FIFTEEN
ZAETHAN

Zaethan slipped out of his room, careful to coast the door noiselessly into its frame behind him. He toed his way down the crooked hallway toward the kitchen, a charming place when Lady Athdara was not around.

Skirting the table, he brushed the macramé curtain aside and climbed through the window, then scoured the misty grounds in search of a certain ginger shadowman below. Zaethan had spent the daybreak with an eye pressed under his door, watching for foot traffic, after enduring the fifth breakfast without Declan. Five bowls of barley slop had been uncomfortably swallowed as Zaethan had tried to navigate Declan's miserable family dynamics without the buffer of their absent host. Lady Athdara had started making him and the others wrap their cutlery for disposal once they'd finished—afraid of some sort of Darakaian transfer, no doubt.

Zaethan's poor spoons, mummified for simply having touched his lips—lips that boasted a merit of their own, not that Lady Athdara would ever find out.

She should be so lucky. He scowled, dropping his eyes to the edge of the square. *Uptight shrew probably hasn't cracked a smile in years... or anything else.*

Shuddering at the image, Zaethan tapped the glass proudly when he spotted Declan weaving through the agora's northern district. That was not too great a challenge, given it was vacant at the hour. He turned from the panes, but his hip clumsily thumped the glass.

From the hall came a boyish giggle.

Zaethan looked up and saw a set of dainty fingers hugging the trim work. A little freckled nose peeked around the corner.

Depths.

Hurriedly, he disentangled the hilt of his kuerre from where it was knotted in the spindly curtains—to the welcome of more giggling. Another head, identically russet and disheveled, popped out above the younger brother's.

Shtàka, now a second sounding alarm.

Their children were sprouting like weeds. Married to such a straight-laced woman, Lord Athdara must have really known how to woo.

Zaethan hustled past the stove and toward the snug foyer. The two infantries in the trenches crawled after him as if it were a game he'd not agreed to play. Hands on his hips, he turned with a grumble toward where the apple-cheeked boys were chuckling on the floor, wooden swords in hand. The youngest cub had lost another tooth, the gap front and center. Cupping their chins, they knocked their bared feet together mischievously. Their parents were going to hear about Zaethan's outing the moment he left.

Spilling through the windows, the rising dawn dappled their floorboard front line. He considered the boys and lifted his brow.

No matter the House, most cubs were the same…

They weren't loyal in the least.

Zaethan knelt, pointing toward either hilt strapped at his sides. He then pointed at their toy weaponry and bowed his head the way he might for a pair of generals. Zaethan mimed his fingers waltzing out the door. Bringing one to his mouth, he signaled for covert quiet—a universal gesture, no matter the language. The cubs mirrored him, holding up their tiny forefingers, playing along.

Getting up, he reached for the handle with one hand, his other hauling his boots. Zaethan winced when the joints creaked, and he teased the door to freedom. Glancing back at his unreliable comrades, Zaethan propped the door with his heel. He bumped a fist to his chest in Darakaian salute. The funniest feeling washed over him as the boys clenched their fists and did the same.

Lady Athdara was going to loathe it.

Nearly as much as Zaethan loathed her.

Having sprinted through the agora to catch up, Zaethan was hesitant to cross the established boundary. Between the slits in the tasseled tapestries, he lingered at the edge of town, watching Declan disappear over a steep rise and into the highland forest.

Zaethan had told his prydes not to pass outside Roüwen's permit, yet there he—their supposed illegitimate leader—caught himself in deliberation. Quadrennal diplomacy dictated each foreign haidren should observe all House-imposed statutes. Then again, Boreal's haidren had broken many in Faraji.

Tapping a fingertip on his lambskin breeches, Zaethan peered over his shoulder at the empty street, then took an unlawful step off the path.

Someone had to balance the political scales. Blame the Fates if it had to be him.

Once he confirmed no one saw, he trudged higher through the moss beds. Dew wicked off the leather weave of his borrowed boots. Zaethan hooked its peculiar, upturned toe over a gargantuan root. Sunlight filtered in copper and canary-yellow beams from the shady, holdreheiim canopy. The leaves were already changing, some in shades so vibrant, Zaethan had only ever sighted them at a royal ball. Towering above, the mighty trees flaunted their court of colors—velvets and satins brandishing more opulence than any yancy frock could hope to possess.

Zaethan crested the ridge and tucked himself behind a holdreheiim. Farther into the woodland, Declan had also paused, presumably to do his business in a bush. He didn't move except to tilt his head. Impatiently, Zaethan shifted his weight, accidentally snapping a twig.

He swore under breath, then returned his gaze to the brawny shadowman, who'd surely heard.

Declan didn't turn to see who'd made the noise, but merely patted the nearest tree—as his haidren had done after landing in Boreal—and continued on his way.

He knows he's being followed, Zaethan decided. He picked up his pace, the twigs be damned.

For nearly an hour, he tracked Declan uphill to where the trees eventually ceded and gave way to a heather-clad moorland. The nearest plateau stood a shrine beneath the bright, cloudless sky. Around it, boulders jutted at varied angles and pitches, most aimed inward. Zaethan maintained his distance as he climbed after the shadowman toward the top, then stalled a few yards behind him when at the rim, he'd stopped and folded his thick arms.

In the middle of a manmade circle paced his haidren. Leafy greens littered the ground. So did a couple of beat-up cabbages. Balling her fists, she kicked the dirt and loosed a frustrated howl. Heather pelted Noxolo's feet where he and the flaxen twins were assembled outside a circle of stones.

"Shtàka!" She stomped by them. "This is maddening!"

In Declan's shadow, Zaethan tracked her angry figure. She'd peeled off layers despite the cold. Saturated in sweat, the sleek, well-fitting tunic hugged the curves of her figure.

"I don't think you're throwing your authority behind it every time." Captaen Bailefore strode forward from the opposite end inside the ring. With him, he carried a loaded sack and a long-suffering frown.

Begrudging to admit it, Zaethan knew that feeling well.

"How many times do I have to tell you? I'm not in charge! The threads do what they want!"

"Maybe we should work on your negotiation skills, Ana'Sere," Declan called, a one-sided humor lilting his voice.

Luscia's tail of messy plaits lashed her ribs when she spun toward her dutiful henchman. Her strange eyes speared Declan before they slid behind him toward Zaethan. Resembling an angry, albino mouse, her features scrunched with rancor.

He loved making that happen. Zaethan offered her a cheeky grin. "Owàamo, Maji'maia."

Luscia's mouth parted, but it was her captaen who spoke first.

"What are you doing outside the city? How dare you breach the border just to continue to harass our haidren!" Captaen Bailefore stepped in front of her and gestured like one commanding a wolfhound. "Turn around and return to your kind."

Perfectly timed, her enormous wolx scampered up the moor and rounded Zaethan. The beast's profuse tail slapped his leg in a proper greeting. Zaethan wondered, if Captaen Bailefore's face turned any redder, might blood shoot from his nose?

He didn't see any shame in tempting it, and therefore petted the wolx's ear as if they were old friends. "A shame the Boreali are not better known for their hospitality. I was considering returning next year…"

"Does your obsession know no bounds?" the captaen shouted.

"Obsession?" Zaethan scoffed. He jutted his thumb toward Declan. "He invited me."

"That I did not, niit."

Arching his neck, Declan winked at him. In response, Zaethan crossed his arms, plenty confused.

"Then how did he get here?" Luscia questioned her shadowman.

Declan shrugged. "Snuck right past me. I'm afraid you taught him too well, Ana'Sere."

"Careful." She threw him a slanted look.

Captaen Bailefore stormed at Zaethan. "Leave before I make you start walking, Lord Haidren." He leveled his sharp, pale nose—still bare of its imagined blood-rush—with Zaethan's. Dropping his timbre, the captaen said, "You know that I can, and you know that I will, for her. Go back to the city now."

Hot breath, more measured than was normal, wafted over Zaethan's face. Slowly, he reached up and gave it an unhurried scratch.

"It's fine. He can stay." Luscia groaned, her sentiment loaded with defeat. As the captaen reluctantly backed off, she locked her arms overhead and plodded back into the circle. "Aniell knows it won't make a difference either way. I haven't done anything worth snitching."

Distractedly, she waved for the long-limbed shadowman to cross over in place of Declan, who'd assumed a position alongside the stones. "Nox, bolaeva… just keep Lord Darakai quiet."

Honoring her request, Zaethan wordlessly strode off to the side. The wolx padded along with him. He sat and leaned against one of the boulders, unsure what he was about to witness. Whatever it was, it didn't sound like they wanted anyone else to witness it either. Apparently the war-tainted animal held no such qualms when it plopped down, arranging itself against him. Downy fur blanketed Zaethan's shoulder. Noxolo trotted over and settled on his other side, though Zaethan was a bit more preoccupied with the size of the wolx's serrated teeth and their unfavorable proximity to his head.

Within the ring, the captaen fixed his footing, likely so as to not put his back toward their unwanted guest. He reached into the burlap sack and produced a fresh head of cabbage, then took a breath. At Luscia's nod, the captaen threw it into the air.

Her hands shot out.

The cabbage thudded to the ground.

"Was something supposed to occur?" Zaethan murmured to Noxolo.

"Wem," he confirmed. "But even so, her attempt must be kept confidential."

Rolling his eyes, Zaethan stretched his legs out over the heather, crossing them. "They always are, aren't they?"

Noxolo's interest was clearly piqued, but Zaethan paid no mind and regarded Luscia. She was rubbing her temples, her streaks of bone-white hair sticking there from renewed perspiration. When she looked over, he felt the weight of his eyes on her hands as Luscia pressed them down her tunic front, straightening it. She did the same with her squat collar.

She shook out her palms and motioned for another cabbage. The captaen obliged, pitching it high. At the last second, Luscia glanced back at Zaethan. His breath hitched. He didn't blink. Determination flared in her eyes as it had in their private trainings. She swung her face forward and, lifting her chin, threw out her hands.

Static sparkled over their surfaces.

With a clunk, the cabbage hit the ground in one piece, albeit missing a fair amount of leafing. Zaethan scooted forward, more than intrigued.

Luscia bobbed on her heels excitedly. Her grin swung toward Zaethan, slipping when it did. A stubborn grimace overtook it. "Another," she told the captaen.

Obliging, he released a third. Then a fourth. Each time, the unnatural static across her palms grew brighter. On the sixth launch, light flashed with her motion—like a glare over a sunlit pool—and with a crack, the cabbage fell, split in two.

Her shadowmen cheered. Together, the twins rushed to ogle the busted vegetable. Zaethan palmed his unshaven jaw. He found no explanation for what had happened. It wasn't witchcraft; there were no charms, no cauldrons about. It was just Luscia.

Luscia and a light.

He captured Declan's silver eyes as the shadowman proudly clapped for his haidren. *This* was why he'd allowed him to follow. Her temperament had switched—had hardened with Zaethan there. And apparently, so had the outcome.

Zaethan fell back against the boulder.

"I know," Noxolo said to him in as much awe, "Ana'Sere is a gifted woman… but this… This is incredible. A thing of lore."

He had no response to give. He simply propped his elbows on his knees, more alert than ever.

Zaethan had to see it again.

As the twins returned to the outskirt, Luscia crouched defensively. "Throw it at me," she ordered the captaen.

"Luscia, that may be a little premature."

"Throw it at me!" she yelled.

Sighing, the captaen tossed the dirtied cabbage toward her, the force behind it a whisper on the breeze. She stretched her hands for it, but it casually sailed past her arm. Had it hit her, she wouldn't have even stumbled.

She was allowed to bruise.

Like him, she was made tougher for it.

Zaethan snorted to himself. He would have chucked that cabbage with all his might.

"Ykah lö?" Noxolo rolled his head aside. "What, have you some commentary to share?"

He flicked his wrist dismissively. "He's much too soft on her. It's like they've never met." Zaethan pointed to the kakka-shtàka cuff around her wrist—its implication undefined yet more than understood. "Why would she shackle herself to someone who poses no challenge?"

"It's not a shackle. It's a kurtfierï," the shadowman said matter-of-factly.

"Which is what exactly?"

"A token of courtship, between the captaen and Ana'Sere," Noxolo explained.

At the glib confirmation, Zaethan mastered his expression into a mask of disinterest. It was as he'd expected.

"She's accepted him as her suitor. The cuff belonged to her father, the Clann Darragh."

His attention migrated to Captaen Bailefore, who was low-lobbing cabbage after cabbage toward Luscia. Zaethan had never been envious of the man. There was no sense starting now.

"Couldn't cough up his own gift? Your captaen is a real winner."

"Well, he gave correctly," said Noxolo in Bailefore's defense. "The suitor must make his case to the patron of her family before he can present his kurtfierï. The token is proof he has been ratified by those she respects most. That his pursuit is worthy of her."

Zaethan stroked the wolx's snout and let out a grim laugh. "That's antiquated. She can choose for herself."

"Of course she can." Noxolo's long, granite face contorted as if the statement were absurd. "And she did choose. It took her six months to agree."

"Then what's the point? Why the charade?"

"Isn't it obvious?" he asked, turning his lanky body toward Zaethan. "A man can't fall from a posture of humility. He's already bent a knee. It's easy to feign humility in front of a woman when she's watching for it. It's a lot harder to really exemplify it by submitting to the rejection of those who can't give you what you want, only prevent it altogether. Ana'Sere deserves nothing less. And in the captaen, that is what she's found. You should be happy for them. To the Boreali, it is considered a valiant match."

Before them, the next cabbage cracked in half. Hung on Noxolo's explanation of the highlander custom, Zaethan hadn't even been watching.

Luscia ran toward Captaen Bailefore and leaped at him for an ecstatic hug. The redheaded shadowman clutched the base of her nape, laughing into her ear.

Zaethan wasn't so needed after all.

He lowered his eyes from their embrace, an embrace he'd spent countless evenings in the Andweles making easier for her to endure. Before Faraji, Luscia had hardly touched anyone.

My contribution to the Ethnicam, he thought bitterly. "Have they set a date?"

Surprisingly, Noxolo snorted.

Zaethan perked up, to his chagrin, and immediately compelled himself to slouch.

"Setting a date is a semantic at this point. But Aniell'silaem, by Aurynth's grace, I expect it will be announced soon."

A cabbage sailed through the air and struck Noxolo in the ribs. Bringing their conversation to a close, the shadowman scrambled to his feet, outraged.

"Hey, Nox!" Across the moor, Declan prepared to hurl another. A twinge of disgust screwed his already-crooked nose. "What the Depths happened to your sister?"

A growler was slammed to the table, yellow yarrow-mead sloshing everywhere.

Hachiro made a note in his journal as he dabbed the liquid off the lacquer. On the page stretched a new graph—this one charting their companions' rapid consumption and their rate of intoxication. A disinterested glance confirmed it. The Boreali were winning. On the bench across Zaethan, Declan's jaunty gaze was bright and clear as ever.

Beside him, Kumo and his half-emptied growler swayed in place, having tried to keep up.

One of the twins—Böwen, the only present and more genial of the two—blew out in disappointment. "He's too plastered to do an avalanche now! You were just supposed to slip him enough courage, Declan."

"Uni, I c-can do it!" the muscular beta replied with a hiccup, not knowing what it was.

Neither did Zaethan. Though from the giddy expression that spread over Böwen when the shadowman grabbed two fresh pints from the growing collection at the middle, it probably wasn't favorable to Kumo.

"On the count of three, you're going to chug with Böwen," Declan explained. Under his wiry beard, his mouth curled. "One, two—"

Kumo beat him to three. Eye glazing, he proudly wiped off his foamy mustache.

Right before Böwen headbutted him.

"Oh, I get it now…" Beside Zaethan, Takoda scratched the rows of dark skin visible between his braids. "Because you're so snowy, it's like an avalanche coming down. That's crafty, yeah?"

Böwen held his growler, unamused.

"That's not why it's called that?" Takoda asked.

At the end of the table, Jabari planted his skinny elbows down and nodded at the beta sympathetically. "Meme qondai. Blizzard craft the mountain, but mountain craft the hillman. Step too loose, his feeties always freeze."

Kumo gripped the tabletop as his forehead tilted farther toward the lofty ceiling, too incapacitated to disagree.

"Statistically, your beta will be falling over within the next round. Might want to fetch him a cushion of some sort," Hachiro suggested over his rewetted quill as he added another hatch mark to the graph with sterile exactitude.

"One should always keep a cushion on hand, Hachi." Partly rising, Ira wiggled his emptied glass for the barmaid to come and refill his red wine. He was the only patron in the alehouse drinking it.

She wedged her figure through the tables, a thickset, curly-haired woman with as little patience for the yancy as she had for his ever-twiddling fingers.

"I appreciate that the women here carry their own cushion. Very pleasant layer about their bottoms. Advantageous, for whenever and *however* they're inspired to fall."

With her hand perched upon her rounded hip, the barmaid turned the pitcher and doused his arm. She then stormed off.

Affronted, Ira dabbed the wine across his sage-colored sleeve and called after her, "Lucky for you, madam, I look even better in burgundy!"

Most ignored the yancy's foolhardy drivel. Behind Ira, the alehouse was teeming. Alongside their traveling kinsmen, shadowmen swarmed the long, timber bar top that curved with the rustically scored, interior walls. Each inbound face was paler than the next. Gathering in droves, these pilgrims were another kind of avalanche, packed beneath the twined rafters. Consequently, Zaethan's table had formed a sundry company—a glimpse of the Ethnicam in one unusual sitting. Part Darakaian and Boreali, spiced with dash of Unitarian snobbery and Pilarese pester, it was probably the most altogether Orynthian group the barkeep had ever served.

Deserting them that evening to meet with the Clann Darragh, Dmitri had deposited his non-Boreali haidrens with Luscia's guard, under the mistaken knowledge that they would be left in safe—sober—hands.

By their current condition, he'd been very wrong.

Naturally, Zaethan's pryde had wanted to tag along. It wasn't every day one guzzled questionably strong mead inside the hollow of an enormous tree.

From Kumo's other side, Zahra reached around the beta and swiped the drink Declan had placed before him. "Doru, big man. Let me take that off you," his third said, bringing it toward her mouth just to toss it over her shoulder, just as she'd been doing for hours with her own.

Zaethan smirked. Smart, his third. He would be sorry to lose her once his scout arrived.

"I have a query for you, Lord Bastiion," said Hachiro, switching through his monocular lenses over the frothy surface of his untouched growler. "The math has kept me up at night in mulling the whole notion over."

"I'll solve it for you. Yes, three is the superior equation." Ira clinked his glass against the shoto'shi's stationary pint.

With his chin tucked, Hachiro glanced up. "Noble inbreeding was outlawed centuries ago. So how do you avoid incestuous entanglements if you have so many unidentified half siblings riddling Unitarian society? The countryside is a small community, the court even smaller. Mathematically speaking, the venture behind your father's genetic pervasion presents you a ghastly set of odds."

Zaethan choked on his drink. Takoda slapped his back. He looked to Ira in panic, the room suddenly shrinking in his periphery.

It was no secret that the yancy had inherited his rakish ways from Lord Hastings. Zaethan had heard too many stories over too many resented waltzes. A charlatan in his own youth, Ira's father had fostered quite a reputation among the now-middle-aged duchesses, breaking a number of hearts during King Korbin's early reign. Impregnating others. Zaethan knew this. He'd just never considered the facts in relation to each other.

Or in relation to him.

Salma had told Zaethan that Cyra wouldn't name the man before her cross-caste son was born, and she'd been killed. But she'd named enough.

He was Unitarian.

And he'd been in Bastiion… a man his mother might have interacted with regularly.

Gregor Hastings could easily be Zaethan's father.

He felt sick. Zaethan balled his fist against his teeth and turned away as bile rose. *Ano…* Believing himself Darakaian, he had never pled to anyone for anything before, but he did then. Zaethan pled with all his might. *Depths, ano zà.*

As he turned back, Zaethan stared at Ira—anew and absolutely horrified.

The yancy shook out his hair and grabbed a loaf from the basket between them. He cut it in two with an easy chuckle. "Well, does halfsies ever really count?"

"Wem!"

"Uni zà!"

Hachiro clicked off his monocular device. "That would by definition be the issue, yes."

At the table's resounding affirmative, Ira gingerly scooted the bread halves back together, rejoining the loaf whole. He dusted off his fingers. His amber eyes rounded at a different loaf resting in the basket. "Thank the Fates that the North serves up other varieties altogether." Ira reached to take one. "Ooh, rye!"

Rapidly, Declan jerked the basket away. "The rye is not for you."

Desperate to put a stopper to the Hastings spread, Zaethan swapped the yancy's wine for a tepid mug of water that no one wanted. "Here. There's an unquenchable passion born from restraint, yeah? It will do you good in Boreal."

Not yet recovered, Kumo teetered forward. "Speaking from experience, Ahoté?"

"Just making a point." Zaethan grated his clenched mouth. "You should know, Big Kumo. Dhalili says your *big kwihila* hasn't been quenched in some time."

"Uni, and it'll be some more time still," warned Zahra, shoving Kumo when he suggestively knocked her elbow—something his sobriety wouldn't have the courage to attempt.

Ira's protest died under Declan's menacing glower. "Our abstinence it is then." He proffered his cheers and sourly smacked his tongue on the water. "As delicious as we are lonely."

Suddenly, Böwen stood and waved at someone.

His mirror self emerged from the crowd. Though the other twin approached bereft, his face darkened by a swath of unbound, chin-length hair, as if he'd been tearing his hands through it. Behind him strode Captaen Bailefore. His expression exuded the complete opposite.

"Congratulations, Böwen. Truly waedfrel." The captaen shook Böwen's hand and dragged a stool to the free end of the table.

The twin shared no such wishes, whatever they were for, and instead marched straight past his brother for the bar.

"Brödre, heh'ta. Creyvan—" Böwen fired up from the bench to chase after him. "Creyvan, just let me explain!"

Awkwardness descended the table. At the head, Captaen Bailefore grabbed a growler and knocked back a swig. His oceanic eyes were dual tempests aimed at Zaethan over the rim. "Sometimes the girl's intended for another."

Like a lord seated at the head of his own table, the captaen took an easy second sip.

A scene, so different than this, flashed in front of Zaethan. Ivory palms sliding up his thighs. Being scooped off the floorboards. Her nails skating his abdomen, clawing for more. Her breath panting against his neck.

Except the scene wasn't his anymore. It belonged to the captaen.

And so did she.

Her suitor wasn't a cross-caste; he couldn't be the bastard son of some drunken yancy. Zaethan slunk his eyes toward the haidren to Bastiion across the table, who was an infamous product of disaster and debauchery—just like himself.

Captaen Bailefore knew exactly who and what he was in this world.

Zaethan Shà couldn't claim either.

CHAPTER SIXTEEN
Luscia

His weight was overpowering. Luscia struggled against his slimy hold on her still-ordinary, unfortified wrist, her sobbing muffled beneath his other greasy palm. Salt and savagery blighted her mouth as she wailed against his immovable Tavish flesh. She hadn't wanted this when she'd smiled at him.

She'd wanted to be good—what the elders had asked for.

Luscia gagged, thrashing inside the prison of his muscled legs. Her bare feet raked the belting pulled down to his ankles, breaking a toenail. Filthy tangles hung into her eyes, his hair soiled by perversion and too much ale. A liquor-lathered tongue slid up her cheek with the hot slaver of a deranged animal, and a part of her disintegrated under his trail of reeking saliva. Her fingers were caged, but she fought with all her might to stretch them toward *her nightstand. Just a little farther toward Ferocity or Benevolence—her mother's daggers—lying across the surface.*

Trapping her wail behind his harsh grip, she bit the revolting skin that smothered her teeth. He let go of her wrist and punched her in the hip. Luscia wheezed behind his cupped hand. He punched her again, and bone cracked. Misery devoured her side. There came a scramble and a clatter, and he suddenly had Ferocity sizzling her throat in a sickening caress. The stench of her own char suffocated her nostrils. She was going to be ruined; she was going to die. Inside, she was already dead—

"*Luscia…*"

Her eyes shot open, bathed in the turmoil of her dreams. They had plagued her nightly since she'd come home. On her bedroll, Luscia curled inward and wrapped her arms around Aksel, weeping against his soft, snow-white fur, same as when she was fifteen. Because it wasn't a dream, not really; it was a memory.

A memory burned into the mangled tissue down her throat.

Stirring from his phantom adventures, the lycran gave a drowsy whine, and his hindlegs ceased their tremors under Luscia's tightened embrace. She burrowed her nose against his neck, and the vibration of his content, foxy purrs—a soothing trait preserved within his split, war-tainted genes. Reliving their sad routine, Aksel sleepily nibbled her on the shoulder, grooming Luscia clean of her unseen wreckage. Everything was still there, it seemed. The years had not yet washed it away.

"*Luscia…*"

A whisper lured her face from the safety of Aksel's coat. Hesitantly, she blinked into her Sight, the veil within her mind slipping aside more easily in such a despondent state.

"*Luscia, arise…*"

The *Other* blossomed throughout the aerial loft. Lumin twinkled overhead. Glittering along the joints and rafters, its threads languidly twisted in the air underneath the canopy of gem-knit netting. Luscia's mother had strung it there for her and Phalen during their early childhood. The loft was their special place, where anything could happen. Seated under a magical awning, she would cradle them in magical stories. Eoine had always told the fantastical as if it were truth. Behind her wayward wisps of pearly hair, her Tiergan eyes would light in a way her sister's, Alora's, never could. But less fantastical, the truth was far uglier than they'd ever imagined. In all ways, Luscia was proof.

Sometimes, her mother had talked about the threads.

In the end, she'd shrieked about them too.

Luscia veered from the memory-ridden ceiling and the lumin galivanting there, just to see more floating in through a tall window, left ajar.

She didn't remember having opened it.

I must get out of this house.

To Aksel's dispute, she rolled onto her knees and got up. She cinched her robe, stuffed her feet into her boots, waded through a sloppy array of pillows, and snuck down the staircase. At the base, she wavered, staring at her former bedroom.

Padlocked, the door might as well have been a portal to the Depths.

"Luscia…"

"Niit. I don't want to hear you anymore!" She hissed at the lumin taunting her ears. Swishing her hand, she scurried lower through the house. So as not to wake her father or guests, Luscia soundlessly lifted onto her toes, personifying the shadows. She flew out the front door as fast as she could.

Not that the lumin had listened… for there, its threads were waiting in the breeze, ready to embark into the wilderness too.

Staircases and swing bridges blurred as Luscia descended into the woodland brush. She compressed her lashes, binding the veil and extinguishing her Sight, as she ran through Roüwen's lichen-lit darkness. Her feet knew the way. They had even when they'd been half their size, carrying Luscia to the safety of her favorite forested hideaway.

Not far outside the city, she finally slackened her strides, coming near it.

Time had not aged her girlhood refuge. Many a midnight, Luscia used to sneak away and run off, pretending to be one of the whimsical sprites or heroic beasts from her mother's tales. A sword and a doll in hand, she used to play within the same hovel, draped under those same glowing mosses. A pitched, star-brushed tent had preserved the active imagination of a child… before the woman who'd inspired it had perished.

The lacey, ghostly overgrowth was spread across a piled palisade of fractured giants. There was good reason that holdreheiim were never logged. The massive trees were devastated on impact—a reminder to all Boreali that they were made equal in weakness. No matter how great, the mightiest among them broke just the same.

Crouching on all fours, just as she had at nine or ten, Luscia ducked under the natural netting and crawled into her hideaway.

Only to halt midway inside.

"Allöh, lu'Lycran," her brother stated, cozily curled up in the corner atop a twig-framed cot, padded with nettles. Phalen's sooty fingertips were crooked around a sketchpad and a shard of kohl. "I was wondering when you'd show."

"This was always *my* spot," Luscia replied. "What are you doing here?"

He scratched the round tip of his nose, leaving there either a trace of kohl or soot as he continued to draw. "Aurynth knows, you forfeited all your property in leaving. And the sibling handbook is very clear about squatter's rights."

"We never wrote a handbook."

"Something I'm correcting in retrospect." Phalen smirked. The dim, leafy glow made his ivory skin look like crushed lumilore yet pristine, for nothing had ever marred it. Her brother scooted aside an inch, making room for her on the cot. It was a comical effort, considering how severely he had to slouch just to fit. "I sketch in here sometimes when I'm lacking inspiration. This is where I got the idea for your radials." Proudly, he held up his hand to show her the rootage he'd boredly entwined below his knuckles. "Been coming since that summer Alora made you stop."

His faint brows knit together apologetically at the mention. Their aunt had never appreciated Luscia's less useful talents, such as impersonating a wolx in the dead of night when she'd ought to have been in bed.

After their mother's passing, Alora had convinced their father that permitting such errant behavior would only sprout more issue for his daughter in adulthood. In truth, young Luscia had only wanted to escape the confusion of her grief, to a place where she'd once felt anything was possible—to where the remnants of Eoine's happy fantasies might have sprung up, resurrected and alive, among the bright highland wilderness she'd notoriously adored. Wherever Alora saw medicine, her sister had seen magic all around.

But Alora had corrected that too.

Eoine was gone. And consequently, so was her every fiction.

"Wem, well, Aunt Alora was just jealous we wouldn't admit her into our pack." Luscia grabbed his socked ankle and rattled it. "She was never that good at howling."

Phalen grinned overtop his parchment. Without warning, he rounded his characteristically broad lips and let loose a wolfish howl.

Giving in to his playfulness, Luscia joined him. Their song to the Watchman dwindled into chuckles. His sketchpad shook with his too-wide shoulders, and sneakily, she tried to steal a glimpse at his work.

"It's not done yet!" Phalen cried, snapping it backward only to smack her hands with it. "Shores of Aurynth, all this holy haidrenship has really gone to your head. You'll see it when it's ready for wielding, along with the rest of your peasants."

Dissatisfied, Luscia shot him a dry look and slunk back against the hovel's half-rotted wood. "You're a cruel brödre. You could really provide me some distraction."

"How I missed you too."

"I mean it, Phalen… It's only been a fortnight here. I've not been sleeping that well."

He didn't reply right away, and she stared into her lap at a loss. His toe slipped beneath her thigh in solidarity.

"I hate walking past it too."

Luscia turned her neck aside. Phalen's eyes widened like a heavenly puppy's, stretching so sincerely, he nearly resembled the boy who'd stood in her doorway wailing that night—her twelve-year-old brother who'd screamed for their father to come save her.

She laced her arm under his propped legs and shook her head. "He'll never move from that house, even after everything. It was the last place he saw her." With sadness, Luscia said to her brother, "And I can't take that from him. Or you."

"Or *you*," Phalen said, his sketchpad tucked under his chin. It was as square as their father's.

Her voice cracked as she whispered to him, "I'm really glad you're here with me."

"Same." Phalen leaned over and kissed her on the cheek. He sat back, curiously tapping his pad and its secret designs. "If I let you keep the finished weapon, will you come somewhere with me? I want to show you something."

It was an easy choice. "Deal."

Luscia scooted off the cot's edge and out of the hideaway, into the open woodland.

Her brother popped out after. Getting onto his feet, he waved for her to follow him eastward with a snort. "Sucker. I was going to give it to you anyways."

Luscia traced the footprint in the dirt, scrutinizing its human shape under the cast of Phalen's lumilore.

"When did you find this?"

The added illumination shifted with his nervous stance. "Only a couple nights ago. But it's been bothering me ever since."

"It is strange, I grant you that," Luscia replied. "Though some pilgrims do choose to bypass Roüwen altogether on their journey to the keep. You know that."

"Wem, but do they do it barefoot? And look at this…" Phalen beckoned her to rise, flashing the lumilore over the trodden footpath some yards farther up, where the prints ceased altogether. "It's like the person just disappeared. Or leaped into the trees. Alora says the Higher Gifts will manifest differently between us. Now, I've not yet ascended, but you tell me, almighty Ana'Sere, can *you* make that jump?"

Following his fingertip, Luscia judged the distance between the last visible track and the lowest hanging branch, still quite a way up. She trudged to the base of the common tree—a determined maple among the holdreheiim—to better judge it against her own height, putting a hand to her forehead. Luscia stepped back to answer Phalen.

She screamed when something cold scurried across her skin. Phalen rushed over and pointed his lumilore higher. Forebodingly, her stomach crammed up before the light even hit the bark.

Inches from her face, the tree was covered in horned beetles. Black and red, scaly, south-dwelling beetles.

Phalen raised his stone higher. "Huh. Those don't belong in Boreal."

"Get back." Luscia drove Phalen in a forcible retreat away from the sight.

The instinct to protect her brother armored her limbs. The picture of her ripped tent unearthed in her memory, when defaced in the Unitarian lowlands, the same type of beetle had withered out of its menacing void on the spring road to Bastiion.

Though she could not explain it, Luscia perceived a malevolence crawling up that tree. Consuming it. Enshrouding the light-bearing nature with a blight of skittering legs and clicking wings.

It had stalked her into Boreal. It had been stalking her ever since she'd left.

✦

She was frightened. She was fatigued. Out of habit, Luscia averted her burdened gaze from the padlocked room when she soundlessly passed it on the third level. She towed herself up the final flight toward the aerial loft and the lycran-compressed bedroll awaiting her. Behind that door might have stood a fine bed, but she'd rather slumber on the floor for the rest of eternity than ever occupy it again.

Back pains and all.

Her upturned boot caught at the top of the staircase, and she nearly tripped over a quilted bundle. Out of the folds twisted a cap of carob hair, followed by a listless yawn—both belonging to her king.

"I deeply apologize, Lady Boreal. Meh fyreon," Dmitri groggily apologized in Boreali. Balled under his blanket, he forcefully coughed into his fist. There was a sticky rattle to it, far more congested than what Luscia had recently heard. "It's not my intention to intrude; however, I've just been having trouble sleeping alone, and well… I suspect…" He yawned again. His inhale was noticeably wheezier than his exhale. "I suspect that from… the inkblots staining his night shirt… Hachiro is drafting a dissertation on my sleep patterns."

Luscia let out a weakened laugh, if just to conceal her newfound anxiety. He sounded awful. Bending, she encouraged Dmitri to lie still so she could carefully drag him overtop the blankets and farther into the spherical loft. The crystal-laced canopy sparkled upon his Unitarian forehead, as if he were a portion of sun-bleached sandstone dotted with mica. He was far too pale.

Wrenching the chain of her skeleton key out from under her mink robing, Luscia gathered some pillows from where her mother had always stored her bounty of cushions. Gently, she scooted a plump, lambskin pillow under his dampened head. Luscia's hand came away slick with his sweat.

Through insipid lips, Dmitri mumbled, "It is as you said in Boreal… so very cold…."

Luscia snapped for Aksel to get up off the mat and immediately huddle beside her cocooned king. The lycran obliged. Circling his feet, Aksel plopped onto the floor, stretching his overlarge paws across Dmitri's shivering toes. Meanwhile, Luscia hastened toward the short table where she'd set her Viridi chest.

She creaked open the restocked apothecary and nicked a barb of ennus thorn. A nutty scent she'd come to loathe flaked off the stalk when she flattened it. These smells only foretold of his eventual passing, and Luscia could hardly bear it. She ground the ennus into a sandy powder—like bonemeal—and dripped in the nixberry. Wrinkling her nose, Luscia stonewalled her emotion as she struck a long-stemmed match and lit a candle. The room didn't need it, given Roüwen's inherent glints. But he did. He needed everything she had to give.

In a counterclockwise swish, she gradually cocktailed in the eüpharsis precisely according to her aunt's strange and complex protocol. The extract simmered into a gelatinous slime within the glass, turning it darker. She set his elixir on the table.

Hoisting it over the beaker, Luscia went to prick her forefinger with the bloodstained tip of the skeletal key. Instead, she wavered.

Five drops of blood. No more. No less.

Though the effects were waning and his endurance from such doses had declined, Alora's elixir had always bolstered Dmitri's fight against his spreading consumption. Yet her aunt had also directed Luscia to abide by another instruction. She'd ordered her to drink oppressive tonics—tonics Luscia had been pouring out her window.

Upon his first taking, Dmitri had sworn that Luscia's batches were stronger than Alora's. Maybe somehow, her blood was too.

Tiergan blood would always rise to save that of Thoarne. The life-force in her veins would be no different. Defiantly, she plucked her flesh and squeezed.

Three. Four. Five…

Six.

When she swished it, his elixir took on its normal, plummy hue, seemingly no different than if she had stopped when she was supposed to.

Luscia dribbled the promising liquid into a clean set of vials and clicked her case shut. She carried one to where she knelt beside Dmitri. Cautiously, Luscia guided it into his mouth. Her heart hammered her chest as she waited.

Her king stirred, the thin surface of his eyelids fluttering. A healthy flush blossomed over Dmitri's cheeks, and Luscia released a ragged breath. It hadn't killed him. He was all right.

Meticulously, she hovered over his nostrils, straining her Tiergan ears, but his wheeze was hardly there. Luscia doubted even a normal Boreali would be able to perceive the congestion subsiding in his lungs. A puff escaped Dmitri when he blew her dangling hair off his lips.

Her king's eyes cracked open. "Why do you smell like nettles?"

Luscia grinned, thoroughly relieved, and pushed off her knees. "I went for a walk. The highlands are full of them," she retorted as she gathered her own bedding. Across the spiraled woodgrain, Luscia positioned herself near his head, her feet pointing in the opposite direction so that in resting there, she could look him in the eyes while maintaining decorum. It was a habit she'd always treasured in Dmitri. No matter his circumstance or position, he always observed decorum, especially with her.

She pulled a blanket over herself and nested onto her bedroll, facing him upside down.

"You're much better company than Hachiro," Dmitri tiredly whispered. His single dimple cratered his cheek in melancholy. "And no matter the loneliness, I know better than to tempt a knock at Ira's door."

Luscia snickered. A pillowed valley separated their noses. Overtop it, she counted the reflection of each gemstone inside his softened eyes. Stripped of his regality and crown, he seemed so mortal, so frail. "We've both known isolation for a long time. We are alike in that way."

"Except only one of us by choice, Lady Boreal," said Dmitri tenderly. "And that is where we differ."

"How so?"

"Tonight, you walked alone. Whereas I walked to you."

Though his expression was open and kind, it pierced her spirit like a barb. Luscia shifted away and blinked at the twinkling ceiling. Dmitri was possibly the only other person who understood what it was like to know exactly who they were from the moment they were born, and the weight behind an isolated identity. But he was right; that was where they differed. Where he coped through dependence, she coped through detachment. Ironically, they both still carried the burden regardless.

"Have you ever felt, deep in your bones, that you were meant to do something great?" Luscia quietly asked. "I feel that responsibility every day, and each night, go to bed feeling a failure for it."

"Hm." She heard him sigh. Luscia looked back at Dmitri as he said, "I had so many dreams for Orynthia. Great plans I'd intended to set in motion. Yet at the start of my rule, each is being thwarted before I've even begun. The responsibility I carry with me into my slumber is suffocating. But does that mean I stop carrying it? Surely not. How dare I give in to my adversaries when there are so many more people involved, working together just outside my purview to over-throw them?" He stared at her earnestly. "Perhaps you are not a failure, Luscia. Perhaps you are just unable to see how you are a success."

"What if I'm never able to see it?" she said on an exhale, terrified to propose it. "And I feel this… this crippling insufficiency my whole life?"

Dmitri slipped a hand from his quilted cocoon. Gradually, unassumingly, he reached across the gap and swept a strand of hair out of her eyes. "Don't you know, every seedling sprouts from darkness." He removed his elegant fingers without a touch to her skin and tucked them under his chin. "Planting *is* an act of greatness. The rain comes in its season. The sun, on its course. Sometimes… Sometimes we don't get to see what we grow, Luscia." His irises glistened, taking on the shade of soil more than the verdant splendor he so often cultivated in his gardens. "Sometimes our time is cut short in the field. So we must plant greatness wherever there is room, because one day, it may *feed thousands*."

Tears spilled onto the back of his hand as her king smiled weakly at her. Having blotted her own, Luscia took her thumb and wiped the murky pools under his eyes.

"I so fear that day," she said, choking up helplessly. "I fear what the world will look like without you in it."

He captured her hand and glided it with his, back under his soaked chin. "Fear is a paralyzer; it will render you lame, unable to take the path you were long intended to tread. Just promise me you won't walk it alone."

Against the bedroll, Luscia nodded. Her grip tightened around her king's where they innocently lay there in her childhood theater.

"Promise me… Promise me the other thing too, Luscia," Dmitri uttered drowsily, his eyelids succumbing to his exhaustion. "I have to hear you say it aloud."

With a hoarse gulp, she leaned over and pressed a mournful kiss against his balmy forehead. Then Luscia whispered into his ear what it was he needed to fall asleep. "I promise to make sure you wake back up."

CHAPTER SEVENTEEN
LUSCIA

She clamped the arm of the celebrated chair, her nails digging angrily into the minor pocks that scored the metallic wood. Their forebears had shaped it into being, forged the luxiron to imitate the resplendent texture of the living bark that sheltered them, a relic worthy of Boreal's then and future haidrens.

Under the twinkling lamplight, Luscia composed herself, trying to make those forebears proud—to embody the predicted poise and grace they'd once envisioned a daughter of Tiergan might usher into their Grand Tabernacle.

When, in actuality, that very daughter was about to lose it.

"Submit emotion to reason," Alora advised, her tone so curt and discreet that only one sharing her revered blood could hear it. She casually bent down to drape a fur stole over Luscia's shoulders in feigned concern. Her hands stilled there, pressing down in caution. "Yeh'dajjeni Dönumn, niece. Our haidren's strength comes from His gift alone. As such, the elders will not listen to your festering outburst."

Funny how I must listen to theirs. Luscia grunted at the hypocrisy when her aunt reluctantly resumed her standing as sil'haidren, behind the prominent seat of sculpted boughs. One would have assumed that a place so hallowed would be quieter. Acting as both Boreal's judicial and theological governors, the Enclave met in the Grand Tabernacle to weigh major cases, settle clan disputes, and administer the moral tenets as interpreted by their acting haidren, the only individual among them able to discern the lumin and its communicative threads. When dispersed, each elder was expected to uphold the haidren's interpretation just the same.

Unfortunately, most elders did not live in Roüwen. And as the journey to their respective clans was long, there lay an exceeding amount of room for overall opinions to re-form along the way. In imposing their amended ethos onto their clans, many elders returned to the Enclave throughout the year even more solidified in their original stance on any number of topics—usually, a litany of them.

Hence the yelling.

Elder Sheridwen was bellowing again, so much that Luscia was forced to mutely track the trajectory of his spittle to where it was landing pointedly on the Prajja'Veriidim.

"These barbarous lowlanders should surrender to immediate confinement or accept extradition from the House of Boreal! Wem,

I say! How can the Darakaians be trusted when they cannot observe a simple boundary line?" He continued his heated rant, pacing before the altar of unhewn stone and sleeping foliage.

Indeed, Luscia could empathize with his position, however insultingly posed. It was becoming increasingly difficult to defend a group who refused to abide by the single rule given upon their offered asylum: stay within the city limits, and not a step outside.

Her focus scrawled vexingly toward the haidren to Darakai, where he and the rest of the Quadren sat in line with their king on the opposite side of the altar. On the end, Ira Hastings twirled his elongated snuff canister against his lips, likely huffing the residue off its gilded exterior. Draped around his neck, its chain jangled with the incessant tapping of his bootheel. The yancy didn't like conflict. Luscia had quickly realized it during their months together, and having been made to bleed out in front of him had only intensified his aversion in the Grand Tabernacle.

Conversely, Hachiro wasn't helping his nerves, for next to him, the shoto'shi was sure to jot every bit of conflict down. With each errant glance over Hachiro's ink-filled parchment, Ira's tapping grew faster and more distracting—for Hachiro would occasionally jab the point of his quill against Ira's bouncing thigh. As the Enclave's yelling ensued, the cycle only repeated itself.

To their rear, the public's space was completely vacant, as it was a closed session. Even her own guard stood outside.

The hoisted lanterns spotlighted the Quadren as if under interrogation before the gathered elders. Sacred stanzas spiraled the tabernacle walls inside the ancient holdreheiim, preaching both mercy and justice. They did little to suppress the Enclave's vitriol. Instead, the iridescent script cast a cool lamination over Dmitri's tensed knuckles as he deliberately knit his fingers atop the byrnnzite cane, propped across his lap. He was a blatant disparity to the Southern haidren directly at his right.

Zaethan's features were puckered, pulled even tauter by his locs when he'd rebound them tightly for the second time. His chest heaved under the buckled straps of his claret linsilk jacket. The crosswise quilting puffed like his cheeks whenever he jeered at an elder—usually stating something insensitive, as if he were not sitting right there. She wasn't sure why Zaethan looked so angry, having already taken full responsibility for the reckless infraction. It was Luscia who deserved to feel anger. She who deserved to roll her eyes, cross her arms, and brood contemptuously. For it was *she*, along with Dmitri and her father, who had employed the last fortnight meticulously preparing to speak to the fully assembled Enclave.

And this misconduct was most definitely *not* the issue they'd planned to raise.

"Again… It was an innocent pastime, yeah? A game of motumbha in the woods," Zaethan barked. Though his foot was carelessly hitched over his knee, he'd planted himself against his chairback, his entire posture fixed and rigid.

"A *game* says the interloper!" argued Elder Sheridwen, garnering echoed heckles from his counterparts, also representing Clan Roüwen. "And was it you, their haidren, who in rebellion to Boreali headship, granted your prydes this added liberty on our soil?"

Zaethan's next exhale was a promised gale. His mouth strained, almost as if his tongue was in defiance with his lips, as he said, "Yes, uni. As I've previously confirmed for that one. And the elder before him."

Dismissively, he pointed at Elder Tabish and Elder Ejnarök at the center of the elevated chancel, where the two elderly men were bent in shared commentary atop their clan's star-shaped perch.

Luscia thought Zaethan should be grateful. At least detention for the pryde was on the table. Elder Ejnarök had advocated a worse and far more permanent punishment. In Elder Sheridwen's scenario, the warriors kept all their toes.

Near them, a hunched leader—lacking an arm lost to the Shield Wars—stood from among his quintet of lesser clans.

"Then explain to us the reason you'd defy the House that has afforded you refuge," said the elder as he indignantly resettled into his seat, waving with his only hand for Zaethan to answer.

Luscia eyed her father, who respectfully nodded at the man, playing the unbiased high clansman the Enclave had appointed him to be. In turning, he caught her gaze. A repressed sigh deflated his baluster-like shoulders.

Things were not going well.

Her father's lips parted, but it was Zaethan who spoke. "Warriors are bred for activity. Strip them of their kwihila—their victory—of that fundamental function, and they unravel."

Murmurs coalesced among the lofty seats and the devout Boreali who occupied them. Some elders were comforted by the statement; others, seemingly enraged.

Clutching his cane, Dmitri rose without the help of it—another consolation of Luscia's added drop of blood. Because of her meddling with Alora's stringent formulation, their king's stance was firm and steady, his cheeks bronzed by the sun-pleased complexion of his Unitarian pedigree. Luscia smiled bittersweetly, despite the fruitless arguments circulating the background.

He looked vigilant. He looked alive.

"As king, I entreat the Clann Darragh to overlook this initial test, considering the much greater trials at hand. These Darakaians are not your enemies," Dmitri told the Enclave, whose chatter simmered under his regal address into silent yet renewed mumblings. His sharp profile tipped crossly at the clear sight of them communicating beneath his common register. Yet they were not in his domain but that of Boreal, and there, the elders could talk however they pleased. "These Darakaians are your allies as much as they are mine. Further subjugation would be counterintuitive to my Quadren's purpose in speaking with you today. Does your own haidren not agree?"

Lined in fox fur, his robe swished the floor as he turned toward Luscia—the wood at his feet chronicled in endless rings by the centuries it had suffered. Patiently folding both hands atop the handle of his cane, Dmitri awaited her endorsement.

So did the Enclave.

Their unwavering eyes were heavy, the multiplied expectation pressing down on Luscia. She nervously toyed the beaded fringe of her aunt's stole. The elders wanted her to disagree—to affirm and reinforce an issue of Boreali doctrine—so they could justify expelling the prydes. Their motive was wrong. Understandably, her people viewed the Darakaian trespass as a direct blaspheme to their terrain, a disruption to its order and purpose. On its face, the doctrine was clear: Boreali ground was sacred, and the Darakaians were not.

Biting the meat of her cheek, Luscia replayed the events of the night prior, when her brother had shown her the strange foot trail and the adjacent tree covered in foreign beetles. She'd been so certain of what she had seen and sensed there that during her entire walk home, she had been determined to immediately bring it to the Enclave's attention the next morning. Though, that had been before she'd learned the prydes had broken the perimeter. Perhaps those erratic tracks had been partly wiped out amid their wild sport. Darakaians were known to play barefooted at times, although never in such brisk climates. Perhaps they'd embarked farther than the elders even realized, all the way toward her childhood retreat.

Logic dictated it was plausible, too plausible for her mind to fabricate it into something worse. Perhaps she'd grown so accustomed to evil chasing her heel that Luscia was starting to see it everywhere she turned.

Perhaps it'd been easier to see an evil in the woods than the evil in the mirror, etched down her throat... or entombed behind a padlocked door.

Luscia straightened her embroidered collar and flicked her gaze toward the Quadren. In Dmitri's shadow, Zaethan had bent forward, his elbows atop his knees. His brow rippled like Viridi tea whenever it was blown upon. He offered her an incredulous look at her pausing.

She didn't understand it either. It was just an innocent game, like he'd said.

Alora's near-inaudible admonishment blistered her ears. "Luscia, you are to provide an answer—"

"A clemency should be granted to the Darakaians, as Aniell first grants His clemency to us," Luscia said suddenly, sitting up taller. She heard the linsilk rustle when her aunt adjusted herself disapprovingly behind her chair. "We convene today to discuss the reign of King Dmitri Korbin Thoarne. The threats to his throne are far more nefarious than any of these lesser transgressions. For that cause, let us release all unworthy distraction into the cleansing tide that laps Aurynth's shores." Clemency would not easily pacify the elders, least of all Elder Hinrük and his incensed supporters from Clan Ciann. She swiveled her neck to confront the grumbling Enclave and locked onto her father once more. "Might we commence with your blessing—yeh'daeünna— Clann Darragh?"

Hiding the proud glint in his eye, her father pushed off his knees and stood. The ornaments twisted throughout his graying beard clinked as his commanding frame stepped down onto the open floor. "Wem, meh'daeünna'yeh, Ana'Sere. My blessing you have," he replied, his voice as warm and severe as the fires of Phalen's forge. Her father tread before the Enclave's segregated chancel, well out of the shadow of its star-shaped perches, steps above those being questioned. There the Clann Darragh faced down his peers.

"Esteemed brödre… When our brave king sailed for our coast, he fled with him the last remnants of the age. Under the Watchman's everlasting lamp, he survived high treason. Betrayal by Darakai's chief warlord."

Many elders spat to the side at the mention of Nyack Kasim—the notorious warmonger from the South.

"Imprisonment upon the order of his War Council. A far-reaching insurrection that hunted him through the wetlands and off the rotting edge of Port Khmer. Nyack Kasim prepares for war against our ally, Razôuel. And with the aid of the Mworrans!"

Almost in unison, the elders swept their fingers off their lips, as if the cannibals were too wicked to speak of.

Her father went on. "The crown city might already be lost to King Dmitri's enemies, for they remain unmasked across Orynthia. Thus, he cannot return alone. We cannot let him, whom we are sworn by Aniell to protect, march on Bastiion insecurely, not when even darker fiends circle about the throne like carrion birds in his absence. The Obscurer arises and is inducting followers into his treacherous cabal. His influence has corrupted those from every class. The marshal of His Majesty's own regiment was converted into this heinous scheme."

There were sharp intakes among the Enclave when her father spun round and gestured toward Dmitri, who was standing resolutely with his cane.

"Even the chief warlord of Darakai himself! According to inbound reports, such as those given firsthand by my daughter—our consecrated haidren…" His voice wavered upon his reference to Luscia's attack in Rian. He had shown more than a little difficulty absorbing the graver dangers she'd encountered outside his protection. "This Obscurer is not satisfied with his mortal agents. By some means, he has resurrected creatures of old. Conceivably war-tainted, his predators are being dispatched to ravage the countryside and are populating in number. As great as the Obscurer's reach, his dark capacities prove even greater."

Luscia felt Alora grab her chairback as if to steady herself. She peeped over her shoulder and up at her aunt.

The eyes of Boreal's sil'haidren were closed. Although her face had frozen whiter than snow, Alora's chin was trembling.

Luscia shifted her attention back over the Enclave, to those brimming with apprehension, upset, and fear. However, unlike the rest, a palpable skepticism seeped from the perch fixed farthest from her own.

It belonged to Clan Ciann.

Her father cast his thick arms overhead, miming the unrolling of Aurynth's tapestry and its endless chronicle. "The fabric of Orynthia is unraveling, brödre. Peace won by those within this very tabernacle is being foiled and frayed by those in the Ethnicam who wish to destroy it. Here, at the end of the Stag Age, our king has placed his trust in Boreal and her najjani forces. Once more it has fallen to *us*—we children of shadow and light—to intercede on Thoarne's behalf. I ask the Enclave now; what say you?"

The dust of her father's speech had barely settled before a younger man stood among the lesser clans. He wore a frown less furrowed than his heavily wrinkled peers. He could not have been more than ten years Luscia's senior, his youth poorly veiled by his eagerness to speak before those more seasoned. "In honesty, Clann Darragh, these claims seem far-fetched to the extreme," he said with a nervous laugh. His ice-colored eyes darted toward elders Morratagh and Hinrük from Ciann. While Luscia knew the lesser clans were the most remote, and therefore uninformed, she had not realized they were also Boreal's most easily manipulated. "We upland and inlanders submit the need for… caution… when rushing our najjani elite into a hypothetically hostile city."

Through the dimness, Elder Hinrük sneered, presenting a portrait as ugly as it was fleeting, when the man sat and the murmurs around him recommenced with freshened fervor.

Better to stay silent if another will voice the controversy instead.

Luscia narrowed her gaze. *What are you playing at now, Hinrük?*

Her vision flickered unexpectedly, and the Sight consumed her view. The inside of the Grand Tabernacle crackled. Erratic threads appeared, overtaking the room as they quivered and coiled above the Enclave. Though, the flash lasted no longer than a moment, for Luscia immediately wrenched the veil to the *Other* closed, snuffing out the lumin's incandescent light. Panicked, she held her breath. Alora was too close. And given Luscia's current, unorthodox experimentation with the threads, she could not risk drawing their attention when her aunt was surely passing in and out of the *Other* herself—as she'd so adamantly coached Luscia to do.

Her fingertips prickled where she cupped them over her chair arm, clenching the luxiron. Anxiety tightened Luscia's throat in the hopes Alora could not sense the abnormal sensation. How Luscia was starting to feel the threads, active and alive and all around. Stranger, she was starting to feel the lumin within herself. It was occurring more and more with each additional morning she spent with her men in hiding, up on the deserted moor. Were Luscia found out, there was no telling what penance Alora might recommend to the Enclave.

Rolling her right hand over, she stared at the nasty scar cut across her palm—and the second, placed on her body by the luxiron of a loved one. If she'd been cut for her uprightness, just as she'd been cut for another's wrong, how much more would they make her bleed for what could not be defined?

"Niit. The uplanders most certainly do *not* agree with the inlanders, meh Clann Darragh," announced Elder Olwyn from the lesser clans. Though graveled from shrewdness and age, her brusque voice sliced through, being the only feminine pitch within the Enclave. "Nor did we interpret the reported danger to the realm as *hypothetical.*"

"This foe and field may look different, but I give you my word that these dangers are as real as those faced on the battlefield with my father, King Korbin," Dmitri stated, solemn but bold.

From Clan Roüwen, Elder Tabish blew his overgrown whiskers out of the way to declare, "The word of our haidren should alone convince!"

Luscia boosted her chin at the unexpected defense by the decrepit elder. While a sheer sapling to its maturity, he seemed more ancient than the holdreheiim in which they congregated. His feeble hand shook long after he'd dropped it exasperatedly back into the crook of his gaunt lap. Tadöm Aniell that being an heir of Tiergan, she was witness enough for one of her own clansmen, aside from her father.

The biases of Roüwen's other three still appeared fenced.

"Upon their last return, our fur traders did relay what we thought to be outrageous talk about a Unitarian cult," Elder Yarlven said. He stroked the plump, pumpkin-hued braid at his chin while his brethren from Ödetha nodded in agreement. "Picked up the rumor in a few port towns. By the Watchman, could this be the Obscurer's secret faction?"

A few uplanders, along with the smug men from Ciann, wagged their hands in mockery at Elder Yarlven. The stronghold of north-eastern coast, Ödetha commissioned more merchants than the other the Boreali clans put together. And while almost as secluded in nature, its members often received the fastest—and oftentimes only—news from Orynthia, making their farthest clan the most associated with the realm. As such, Ödetha was commonly discredited by zealots like Elder Hinrük. What any sane person would characterize as an asset, Hinrük and his sycophants dubbed a compromise of virtue.

"And did your traders speak of monsters in the night?" he finally asked. The talï prayer stones sparkled down each side of his nose as he goaded Elder Yarlven.

But old Elder Ejnarök came to his aid. "Wem… I do recall Tearlach's son, a guard to our haidren, Ana'Sere, mentioning his encountering a strange beast on the road to Roüwen with that mutt of a girl. Unseemly business, that whole situation with the Caellaigh family—"

"She is no mutt!" Luscia pounded her fist before she'd fully comprehended his bigoted words. "Wait, ykah lö? You mean Böwen and Mila fought off one of these terrible creatures themselves?"

"I suppose, but that was not the cause of the vulgar scene outside the Caellaigh door." He leaned aside toward Elder Sheridwen. "I always did envy the veranda though. A shame it's so undignified now…"

Alora's hand fell upon Luscia's shoulder, this time more forcibly. "Remember your role, niece. It is not for us to interfere until called upon."

"Brödre, bolaeva," her father implored the Enclave.

With a stubborn huff, Luscia leaned back and watched him beseech those who did not deserve to hold the same authority.

"We have established the viability of creature and cult. His Majesty's reign must be safeguarded by the blades of Viridis before a rebel war breaks out against Razôuel."

Elder Yarlven again stood. "Then we must put forth the issue to the najjani master at once."

"Amid a House-wide pilgrimage?" Elder Hinrük snickered. His lackeys, elders Dagmar and Kalf, jumped to join him in rising atop their designated perch. "Devoted as I am, Thaddeus Rohan travels to the keep every year. A few elders can broach it with the master during Ana'Innöx and see if he shares their concern."

Elder Morratagh's knees popped when he matched their mulish stances. "The outlaw king can reign from Roüwen under Boreali guardianship until the najjan are convinced of the path forward, as did his ancestor Thoarne during the epoch of Ana'Alïstria. Perhaps this shall be to the glory of King Dmitri—"

"The Great Reclamation is the glory of the past, Morratagh!" their Clann Darragh boomed. Impatience leaked from her father's countenance, his head shaking with Luscia's. "King Dmitri is our future, and his throne is in Bastiion! I too believed in our total seclusion, but look what it has caused. I sent my daughter into a decay I did not understand. You fear this temporary mixing with the Ethnicam? A further step onto unsacred soil? Imagine a civil war!"

"While I appreciate your conviction, in that your fealty is not to me alone, I must plead for swifter action." Dmitri took a few steps forward, closer to the Prajja'Veriidim and its falls of trickling water. "Time is not our intercessor, gentleman."

Luscia's heart dropped because she knew he meant it in more ways than one.

"My King, the sparrow is swift, but the owl is smart," said Elder Tabish, concurring with Clan Ciann. "Boreal must seek wisdom and counsel before partaking in a brash retaliation—"

"Owàa enchained! Do you hear yourselves?" Zaethan tore out of his seat, nearly tipping it over in his march to Dmitri's side.

Roüwen's eldest waggled his crooked finger down at the Southern haidren. "The Darakaian crossbreed will muzzle his sacrilege, lest we pull his teeth!"

"Elder Ejnarök!" exclaimed Dmitri and Luscia's father in unison.

Emblazoned, Zaethan only strode farther around the altar and toward the base of the chancel. "People are dying out there. They died just to get him—*your king*—here, to you. Loyal Darakaians like Machàkwe, my mother's lowly bondservant, who positioned himself for execution just so that we could escape the Andweles! And what, now you want to twiddle your thumbs? Ride out your holiday, yeah? You, the honorable, fearsome… superior Boreali?" Sarcastically, he plucked the fabric of his Northern jacket, a cool contrast to his heated complexion. He then shoved his forefinger up at the Enclave. "You're a House of hypocrites. Frauds."

Alora's hand tightened, still clutching Luscia's shoulder. The room exploded for the umpteenth time, and Zaethan waved them off, strolling to the other side of the room to cool off. He pitched his hands on his trim hips, his thighs taut and primed for a different kind of combat inside his restrictive, lambskin breeches.

Luscia's cheeks flushed when his wide-set stare stabbed her from under the shadow of his ringed brow. He had stated the exact things she wanted to say but couldn't. Shouldn't. Would never.

"Meh fyreon," Dmitri said, apologizing in Boreali with a disheartened exhale. "Forgive my haidren to Darakai and his explosive yet acerbic passion for my behalf."

"We will pray for the lives lost, Your Majesty. And for those left in the jeopardies of evil," Elder Hinrük stated, his half bow silky and dripping in artifice.

"Oh good, that's what we need. More words." Zaethan laughed darkly from the shadows. "*We will pray…*"

Dmitri outstretched an arm to subdue him. "Zaeth, please—"

"His faith is weak, Sire," said Elder Hinrük. Smugness curled his thin upper lip like a sugary, yolk yarrow tuile—had it spoiled under the sun.

"Only as weak as your spine." Zaethan turned, starting to walk back toward Clan Ciann's perch.

Shirking her aunt's repressive hold, Luscia took to her own feet before he did something rash. The pads of her fingers burned. She scrunched her fists, and louder than she ought, Luscia suddenly declared, "We will act in faith and prudence alike! The owl is shrewd because it knows when to wait and when to strike, Elder Morratagh. The Quadren can wait for Ana'Innöx, for it is only another fortnight away, but we must approach Master Rohan united."

Pasting a smile on her increasingly haggard face, Alora stepped up beside Luscia, her unruly successor. By the rigidity of her aunt's posture, Luscia doubted the act was to spare her reputation as much as it did Alora's.

Amid the masculine grumbles, Elder Olwyn rose. "Ana'Sere," she said, clasping one well-trained hand serenely atop the other. "Is uniting with outsiders a compromise of faith or a fulfillment?"

Luscia could hear her aunt's jaw locking. Tiergan ears heard every-thing—disappointment above all.

On the spot, for the Enclave had quieted, awaiting the assured controversy of her answer, Luscia swallowed roughly and looked at Dmitri. His wavy hair fell over his desperation, worsening with her delay. But to her chagrin, her wanton gaze migrated behind him. To the brute who'd birthed the reason for her every delay. She did know what it was to stumble in her conviction. What it meant to question, even as her belief deepened and her conviction steeled.

He was a steep valley… a foothold of the scariest nature.

He made her doubt her every step.

Luscia swallowed roughly, for as haidren, she didn't have the luxury to doubt. "I think there is considerable nuance in answering that question, Elder Olwyn."

Her focus veered when dubiously, Dmitri stepped back on his heel. "Is there indeed, Lady Boreal?"

"Ock! We do not seek to hear *your* thoughts, Ana'Sere, but that of the threads!" Elder Hinrük yelled. "You are just their pretty mouthpiece—"

"And their interpreter," Alora finished brusquely.

Hinrük's watery, gray eyes bulged at her uncharacteristic outburst. He blubbered a retort, though whatever vile words he'd boiled together were doused as the doors to the Grand Tabernacle came crashing in.

The room spun toward the burst of commotion, a riot rushing straight toward the Quadren. An unusually tall, redhaired man led the charge with a bloodstained, linsilk scarf in tow.

Sharing the reflex, Zaethan ran and pushed Dmitri behind the Clann Darragh as Luscia leaped off the platform.

"Where is he!" the pilgrim screamed, his timbre as jarring as the tears down his lean face. "Where is the demon who let this happen to her?"

With a cry, he charged Zaethan but was thwarted by the locked arms of an equally tall najjan, holding back the violence.

"Nox!" Luscia barked. "What is happening?"

His eyes were stippled in red. Noxolo opened his mouth. The most agonizing sound escaped as he twisted his grasp and scrunched the gore-splattered scarf. "It's meh mamu, Ana'Sere. My mother is gone."

CHAPTER EIGHTEEN
ZAETHAN

The Boreali were a hailstorm, battering in from the balcony outside the Grand Tabernacle. Through the massive, thrown-open doors, their enraged torches gleamed off the gem-clad columns with a blinding fury. The men shook their fists. The women sobbed. Together they had fought to apprehend Zaethan—a near success had Luscia's guard not rushed in to intercede, defending the Quadren against their own civilians.

For a society so professedly self-disciplined, they formed a mob as well as any other.

Worried for Dmitri's sake, Zaethan would have relished the irony were it under different circumstances. He didn't disclose his observation, not to his friend or his neighbors. None of the adjacent elders would see the humor. They were too busy recoiling from their people.

Or from Zaethan, whenever their elbows accidentally touched.

Having been shoved behind the menacing glint of Declan's crescent wraiths, still sheathed over his wide back, Zaethan squared his body before his king. Intermittently, he twisted past his shoulder to relay the happenings to Dmitri, for his vantage had been blocked from the slim ravine that separated the Quadren from the throng. It was an odd display. Protesters on the one side, armed warriors at the other, yet in the middle, their Clann Darragh stood in an absurd embrace, trying to soothe the crazed man who'd initially attempted to throttle Zaethan. He didn't argue… didn't fight.

The attacker had his head buried in his leader's chest. And there, he openly wept.

His leader wept with him.

An extraordinary type of authority had suspended the hysteria and kept it at bay, one that Zaethan had never seen enacted in either Darakai or Bastiion. None of the witnesses made to interrupt, despite their clamor. The Clann Darragh had a forearm folded over his clansman's nape so that his much-broader frame could absorb each emotional wave and blubber. His gray-streaked hair drew a curtain over their private dialogue as he leaned down to speak unceasingly into the attacker's ear. But no matter what was stated between them, it was no use. He appeared to be inconsolable.

Given their identical builds, the man was presumably Noxolo's father. Yet rather than any of a shadowman's specialized getup, he wore a beaver-skin coat and a belt fashioned entirely of knives. A comparable belt hung off the hips of the pretty young woman crying a few feet away, with Luscia.

Luscia showed no such feeling, having turned into a marble cast of herself. Her stark features were unhidden by her normally chaotic hair. She'd tamed it into a neat plait for the Enclave that day—a style unpalatably reminiscent of her aunt's—and it slicked her iciest wisps back from her uniformly colorless face. It had been drained of life, emphasizing her dense brows like runes on a tombstone.

But for whose grave, he was unsure.

Her aunt broke from the huddle around Noxolo to relay something to the Clann Darragh. After a pregnant pause, Luscia's father gestured for both Captaen Bailefore and the crestfallen shadowman. They nodded in some accord, and he released the attacker, calling something in Boreali toward those blocking the entry to the tabernacle.

Captaen Bailefore strode over and addressed Declan. "Grab Creyvan. We're going to start the search for Nox's mother. The family found her scarf and some scuffed tracks. I've tasked Böwen to escort Ana'Sere home with the king's Quadren." He glanced around until he spotted Ira and Hachiro cowering together at the base of the chancel. The captaen grimaced. Then, fleetingly, he spared another quick look at his haidren. "I don't think she should bear reliving this tonight."

I don't think she should bear your making decisions for her, Zaethan almost said. But he stayed quiet, gleaning information instead and seeing it wasn't exactly a good night for a stroll outside. A woman was missing, and the Darakaians were being accused… or so he'd gathered.

He was going to kill Jabari for orchestrating that kakka-shtàka motumbha match. That was if Roüwen's local butcher didn't do it first.

"Shtàka," Declan swore, inviting Zaethan's surprise at the shadowman's use of the Unitarian curse. "All right, wem. I'll rally everyone toward the wood. I assume we will begin along the eastern outskirt?"

In lieu of responding, the captaen pivoted on his heel just seconds before the angry crowd rippled under the Grand Tabernacle's enormous threshold. Citizens parted across the balcony, allowing a team of sterner shadowmen to pass through. Their wraiths were drawn in a menacing wreath around whoever was being herded in their custody. A fury of Boreali taunts and jeers assaulted the unit—and were met by equally contemptible threats in Andwele.

Zaethan's heart raced. Ducking beneath arms, he fled containment behind Declan and an older shadowman and rushed forward. He skidded to a halt when he saw that within the weaponed sphere, Zahra was bound at the wrists. Next to her, his beta's corded throat was locked between a pair of witchiron arcs.

Kumo swallowed, the panicked bob reflecting in the blades' opaline sheen. "Sorcerers snatched us right off the street, Alpha Zà!"

He stepped closer, but with a predatory hiss, one of the shadowmen raised his kuerre, forcing him into retreat. Zaethan's lip buckled at the fair-skinned man. Without breaking eye contact, he demanded to his beta, suddenly frightened for the welfare of his prydes. "Where are the others?"

"Locked inside their dwellings. We only left to, uh, well to warn you there was a mob coming."

"Depths, were you harmed? Did they mark you?"

"Ano." Kumo attempted to shake his head but couldn't. "But yeye qondai, you know how Zahra is. She didn't submit so easily."

"'Tis a weak man's scratch, yeah?" Zahra hollered from behind, then charitably spat a wad of insult onto the nearest shadowman's blade. She smirked as her dribble slid off and onto his Northern boot.

In sidestepping, Zaethan saw that scarlet dripped from a bubbling slice across her bicep, soaking her ruined jacket sleeve. That was no scratch at all. His belly roiled with a hot surge at the sight of her injury.

Zaethan's hand sailed for the hilt of his sword. A roar of exasperation tore from his lips when he remembered that unlike the shadowmen's who'd just entered, *his* weapons were not permitted inside.

"What is the meaning of this?" Dmitri's voice defied the noise when their king broke from his security. "Clann Darragh, tell your men to release these Darakaian heroes at once!"

Luscia's father approached without her, as she remained fixed, almost in a trance beside the crying girl.

"Meh fyreon, Your Majesty. And to the Lord Haidren," he wearily said to Zaethan. "It seems they were apprehended for their own safety. I regret the hysteria has placed a target on their backs." Scrubbing his face, the Clann Darragh motioned for the shadowmen to lower their witchiron. As they did, one tried to remove Zahra's binding, but with a snarl, she jerked away for Kumo to free her instead. "I suggest the three of you remain here, indoors, until our search party departs the town square."

Foisting his cane, Dmitri sputtered. "Clann Darragh, the haidren to Darakai is not your prisoner—"

"We didn't do this!" Zaethan snapped, defending himself.

Boreal's leader closed his stormy eyes. The pleats around them quivered. Reopening those blue gales, a deep-seated sorrow laid anchor in the corners of his mouth as he gently replied, "Wem, Aurynth knows this was not your doing… which makes it all the more heartbreaking. Bolaeva, please excuse us."

He made his leave, ushering Nox and his grief-stricken father with him, toward the doors. In his wake, the Enclave timorously followed the masses outside. Muttering in hastened winds to each other in passing, several elders tossed their sneers at Zaethan.

He sneered right back.

When the room was all but cleared, its liturgy emptied and hollow, only Luscia and her captaen remained with the Quadren. He carefully wrapped an arm about her waist. At his imploring, Luscia's feet shuffled across the stone despondently, like her heart had been stolen and only her animated bones remained.

"This is a disaster," Dmitri grumbled into his hands. "We'll need to mull with the Quadren how to prevent this setback with the Enclave…"

He kept talking, yet Zaethan was swept up in Luscia's leaving… in her sadness and how swiftly it had rendered her lame—the only setback that mattered in that moment.

Zaethan ran onto the balcony and called down to the Clann Darragh, stories lower among the assembling crowd. "Let us join you!" His bellow resonated off their gigantic trees and glowing fungi. "If you mean what you say, Clann Darragh, then let us aid your search. Under armed guard." Zaethan showed his hands in surrender.

Descending the stair in her captaen's care, Luscia unexpectedly twisted round, her countenance empty except for the spark of defiance that inched her away from his hold. She worded something to Captaen Bailefore, pointing below. Luscia's spine visibly arrowed, and her steps resumed ahead of his.

Turning, he scanned Zaethan where he leaned over the prominent balustrade. Bailefore sucked his teeth, assessing Zaethan, as he angled his head. Seconds later, his mouth folded scornfully.

Like the Darakaians atop the balcony, the captaen and his kinsmen in the square awaited their Clann Darragh's answer. Zaethan barely heard when it was given, but they did.

And so much louder than he.

His boots squished the mosses as he trampled the night alongside Declan in a slow, diligent trudge. The heavy gloom could not be called dark, not in a land that stoked its own embers. Somber lights had awoken within the fluted bark of each goliath; it scaled the trees, lustrous toadstools, and glistening bonnets. Whisked by the breeze, unlike those dead underfoot, the clapping leaves were fighting their change into their autumn shades of darkened rust.

Though the nature was eerie at the hour, it was intensified by an army of stone-wielders breathing life into their palm-sized pebbles. He'd seen Luscia do it once, in the tunnels of Faraji. Everywhere, pools of light spattered the earth, shining in all directions and occasionally causing a nocturnal vine to shrink and slither out of sight.

To Declan's grim amusement, it spooked Zaethan every time.

Together, Boreali men and women sifted through the undergrowth, some calling out the woman's name and others keeping soundless as the wind. But none were so silent as Luscia and her family.

A way off from where Zaethan trekked beside Kumo and Zahra, the Clann Darragh migrated through the wood like a monument among men. His children strode hand-in-hand on his either side, the woman's bloodied scarf carried limply in Luscia's grasp. Their attention was not shared with those around them but fixed forward on a path of their own.

The reaction didn't fit—at least not in Zaethan's understanding of the facts. For as the story went, Lady Egon had vanished while foraging among a wild, well-frequented berry patch. Without sufficient tracks, for the forest floor was mostly concealed this season, there was little evidence that she hadn't just walked off. Nothing except for the blood staining the sole article she'd left behind.

As he climbed over a fallen log, Zaethan noticed that when the hulking wolx padded toward the somber trio, Luscia raised her head off her father's arm and let the beast scent the scarf.

He wasn't the only one scenting it. In Zaethan's periphery, Declan's freckled nostrils flared with his own exploratory inhales.

Warily, Zaethan widened the gap between them.

The wolx afforded his mistress a raspy howl and ran on ahead, his bushy, amber-streaked tail disappearing beneath the fern-choked brush. Alone, Luscia lowered her cheek once more against her father.

"Were they close, she and Noxolo's mother?" Zaethan couldn't help but ask her most faithful shadowman. Having kept a handful of her secrets—some including Zaethan—Declan was sure to know.

He stayed quiet. Declan's focus steadied on the cast of his lumilore and the fat, gnarled roots it exposed. Then, in an order to the flanking shadowman, he said, "Creyvan. Take them westward."

Creyvan did not seem in agreeance. His already-foul disposition worsened by the spasm through his arched, blond brow. "Niit, Declan, you cannot!"

"Your arse lost its right to argue weeks ago. Now get." Declan waited until Creyvan stubbornly steered Kumo and Zahra out of earshot—at least, to any lowland standard. "This is not the first search party through Roüwen's wood. Nor the first under such conditions," he said with a burdened sigh. "When I was a boy, there was a local prophetess, who hailed from the highest family. She was beautiful, a woman who was always robed in unfettered kindness, the kind usually only seen in our young. In her early life, she was praised, revered even, for her prophecies because they always came true. Aurynth-sent, we believed them to be. Her father had the gifts of a renown seer, you see. As such, she married well. Had children. Her two were the purest joys of Roüwen. To this day, I cannot remember a happier time in Boreal.

"But happiness is like a stream. It is always shifting, ever changing. And so was she, the prophetess. One winter, she started shrieking in the square, arguing in the snow with things no one could hear or perceive—not on our side of the veil, at any rate. A month later, she came into my father's forge and seized a knife off his anvil. Waved it violently, only to harm herself more badly than anyone else." As they walked together, Declan woefully shook his head and slit his palm across his navel. His hand stalled over his wide belt. "I will never forget the color of that—pooling the ice in front of my fappa's workbench. It hadn't melted until the next spring.

"As her mind deteriorated, the prophetess started to abscond into the wilds for hours at a time, always returning scraped and bruised with the light of dawn. Ten years ago, she never returned.

"People say she went to dance with the threads." Declan twirled his fingers listlessly, as if Zaethan understood the provincial idiom, the *threads* they so often cited in Boreal. "Some say that she was running from something. Others, that she was running toward it. We don't know, niit—only that her body was never found. And that when the search for it was performed, a bloody scrap of dress was the only evidence they ever uncovered."

Zaethan chewed on Declan's tale. Admittedly, its particulars were ominous, though not exactly unusual in wild terrains. It wasn't unusual in Faraji for a hunter to boast about scavenging the mountain only to be found gutted by his prey weeks later. However, not all predators left their dead out in the open but dragged it to their dens in the crags. Maybe the woman's death, and the mystery surrounding it, had simply incurred more mania due to her notoriety than that of any animal strike.

He followed Declan through a tunnel of bowed, mossy limbs. Out the other side, he waited for a small group of Boreali to pass them. "Somehow, I sense I'm missing your point."

The shorter shadowman halted. "That prophetess was my haidren's mother."

Zaethan felt the muscles in his face falling. While he knew she'd too suffered a loss, he hadn't dreamed of all the pain that had paved the way for it. Suddenly, a more rendering truth punched him in the gut.

Luscia's mother had been taken from her just like his.

And now she was making herself retrace those steps all over again, for the sake of Nox.

Overcome, he stared at Declan. A knowing frown was nested within the shadowman's burly beard. He patted Zaethan's back, where it was bent under the weight of Luscia's pain-ridden past.

They took no more than three steps before the wolx's piercing howl splintered the night. Declan instantly yanked him backward. "Heh'ta," he said, halting them. Declan pivoted southward, where a few shadowmen had run toward the wolx and retrieved something from the undergrowth.

They held up a strip of fabric.

"More bloodshed," Declan said with an unnerving uplift of his nose.

Yards away, one of the shadowman brought the strip to his tongue. Zaethan's stomach rolled when the man tasted it. He gave word to his partner. Gasps were heard throughout the vicinity.

"What is it?" Zaethan asked.

"The blood... It isn't just Boreali."

Worn and splintered, the Quadrecipher stretched between its quiet stewards where it lay unfolded across the bed. Zaethan lounged against the headboard beside Dmitri. He chewed his thumbnail as he considered the pentagonal board and the faded crest of his Darakaian panther.

Absently, Zaethan rotated the reed paneling back and forth—being probably the first of cross-caste descent to disgrace it.

He didn't know what role he was filling anymore, as a so-called haidren nor as a man. The only thing he could rightly claim was the friendship that'd placed him there, not the dull ink of his House. Zaethan held a title without meaning, a militia without allegiance… a succession without sire. He had everything in part and yet nothing to give. He had nothing of consequence to aid Dmitri in this ongoing match of political checklerule, a duplicitous game Zaethan was lousy at playing even when it was just wooden pieces on a plate. And so there he sat, a man as useful as the pillows piled on the end of his king's bed.

Fleetingly, his watch flicked up toward Luscia, where she was enfolded stoically on the footboards. Hitched above, a gem-laced net cascaded down around the group in an ethereal canopy, reminding him most maddeningly of the Boreali bride she would soon become. Zaethan rubbed his eyes, holding his breath for a mere second of respite. Disregarding the few possessions Dmitri had strewn about his lodgings—a leather journal here, a potted catastrophe there—the entire room smelled of juniper and rain.

It wasn't lost on him that the bed was really hers. Not for a second.

"Drink up, grumpy cup." Ira rammed a decorative tea glass, taken from a shelf, into Zaethan's hand, having filled it with a green herbaceous wine instead of its intended contents. "Your face is depressing me. Beauty is a gift, Zaeth. Don't squander it for the rest of us."

Zaethan quickly knocked the glass back, revolted by the flavor as much as the flattery, for it might have come from his sibling. "Depths, that tastes of pond scum."

"Tannins of lichen," Luscia said softly, pulling everyone's interest. It was her first utterance since Dmitri had opened their midnight session.

In a mirrored position at the foot of the bed, Hachiro immediately jotted the note down.

"Pond scum, Sire?" Ira offered a second to Dmitri, having poured for them before himself, a petty and rare sign of personal progress.

Dmitri shook his chin from atop his forearms, which basketed his slender knees. He'd rolled up his embroidered silk shirtsleeves—a clear sign of his frustration, having shirked his favor of blankets in a room so temperate. That he'd allowed his never-dying fire to fizzle into embers posed as much a surprise as his inexplicably sun-soaked cheeks.

Another awkward silence ensued. Zaethan took a sip of the earthy wine, regretting it instantly. "You said little to the Enclave tonight."

"It was a risky exchange with the elders, and we've already enough on the line," Dmitri replied. His dark waves tumbled forward and concealed his evident displeasure. "In the economy of speech, the tongue can either rob or invest. A king should speak frugally so he knows what he spends."

Zaethan rolled his eyes at his friend. Dmitri was doing that thing again, as if he were coaching himself through his own reign. "Then thank the Fates that I'm no king."

"Aren't we all a little kingly… in our *own* way?" Ira smacked his lips after a healthy gulp.

"Ira."

Dmitri's reprimand had an odd bite.

At it, the Unitarian haidren clutched his snuff canister uncertainly. "Never mind that seditious thought. We're all rather dull."

"Lord Darakai spoke enough for the whole Quadren," Luscia retorted into her lap.

She was hurting, he knew, her husky voice not so far away as her criticism. Ano, *that* came closer than his nose. Dubiously, Zaethan searched her, then the room, the scum-drunken yancy being the only one to meet his eye.

"Oh, I thought you were a very passionate orator. I especially enjoyed the bit when you tipped over your chair. Such rugged drama." Ira wriggled his fingers. "It was like watching an opera but wherein I was made to sit fully clothed through the entirety of the third act."

Zaethan felt sick and not for the wine. He set it grimly aside on the nightstand.

Hachiro steepled his quill over a strand of calculations on the parchment. "To Lord Darakai's assertion, I concur that no resolution was achieved except to wait until after an event we are not authorized to attend. Given the Enclave's strong partisan record, the odds do not favor us in their impending dialogue with the najjani master."

"You make math sad," said Ira, frowning at the shoto'shi over the silvered rim of his glass.

"How could you possibly estimate that, Lord Bastiion? Had integers any emotion, you'd still the inability to properly calculate them."

Hachiro resumed his inked scratchings, oblivious to his own insult. Zaethan would have cracked a much-welcomed smirk, were it not for the dejection of his friend and sovereign stewing at his side.

"Lord Pilar is correct. The elders are unlikely to side with us now," muttered Dmitri. "Not after the motumbha match you allowed and what the Boreali found of that poor woman in the woods. That just reinstated their every suspicion—"

"I did not allow it," Zaethan snipped.

Luscia's expression was blank, except for the brilliance of her incompatible irises. The right sparkled when she asked, "You were just covering for the pryde?"

"They wanted to play a stupid game," he replied, tired by the futility of the topic. "After their sacrifice in Port Khmer, you would have covered for them too."

She swallowed, sitting straighter. "Wem, that I would have."

"How are the shadow—the najjan—even able to consider refusing their king?" Zaethan's half-bound locs rustled as he shook his head in sheer astonishment. No one else seemed to be raising the most absurd question in the room. "You're the king," he petitioned Dmitri. "You basically own them."

Baring his dimple, Dmitri barked a bitter laugh. "Darakai taught us to never think like that again. I don't own the Order of the Najjan, not quite. Treaty language can be a lot trickier than you think."

"There is an interesting clause written into the original agreement between Boreal and Bastiion, which was later grandfathered into that of the Ethnicam Accords." Hachiro produced a small, battered booklet from the folds of his ocher robes. After licking his thumb, he paged through the pocket codex. "It preserves the najjan's ability to refuse marching orders, and their troops, should Orynthia's cause conflict with their first fealty."

"First fealty?" Zaethan questioned. "Their fealty is to the throne!"

"In some measure. Boreal's history with the crown demonstrates as much," explained Dmitri. "Still, Boreal's *primary* fealty is to their High One… If the Enclave or Master Rohan determines my cause somehow betrays the House's core tenants, they are lawfully permitted to refuse military support. Aid in all other forms to Orynthia is guaranteed, but the Order of the Najjan may lay down their arms wherever they see fit."

Zaethan's forehead crumpled. "Well, that's a kakka-shtàka deal!"

"Hence why the king called it 'tricky,' Lord Darakai," Hachiro said again, shrinking under Zaethan's glare.

"This is why I have to attend Ana'Innöx," Luscia stated soberly.

"I must sway Master Rohan into committing his najjan before he is convinced otherwise."

"Then persuade your father to let us accompany you there, Lady Boreal." Dmitri leaned forward, pleading to her across the Quadrecipher. "This is my realm. My responsibility. My seed to plant, Luscia. Do not take that from me now."

It passed between them, another of their private codes—a message to which Zaethan did not carry the cipher. Her head slanted to the side as her face contorted. Loyalty to her House competed with the throne. That, Zaethan could undoubtedly decipher, for he had felt the same strain in Darakai.

"How did your predecessors handle a separation during their coronation tours?" Ira asked her. "Surely this is not the only holiday in the Boreali calendar."

"It is the only requiring my travel outside Roüwen, which would have been avoided altogether, had our tour not gone awry. Per tradition, the regiment would have stayed in a long-term camp along the southern border. Only king and Quadren were to sojourn here, to the high clan. That's how it happened during King Korbin's tour."

"Though few are left to recount it," Hachiro noted amid his superfluous blinking. "Being that only the sil'haidrens to Bastiion and Boreal outlived their Quadrennal counterparts. My uncle, Tetsu Naborū, had not assumed his seat, for his brother, Akito, was not yet deceased and therefore still occupied it. Nor had Nyack Kasim attended King Korbin during that time, as he had not yet murdered his wife."

Luscia awoke from her stupor. "Lord Pilar!" She admonished him fiercely. "There is a way to state things, and that was not it!"

Hachiro blinked at her. "Matters of historical importance should always be recounted as accurately and unbiasedly as possible."

"It's fine." Zaethan waved it off. "I agree with the librarian."

"Thank you, that is generous, Zaeth. This Quadren doesn't have the luxury of any more needless backbiting. Unification is our only hope now." Dmitri cradled his head in his hands, then looked up at her, the only person who could secure that unity. "Can you not see it, Lady Boreal? I am not operating in contention with any higher fealty… I am here, prostrate before you, begging for its help."

Her thick brows knotted together. As if anguish were threaded between them, Luscia said nothing.

Dmitri sighed, and his shoulders rounded in defeat. "I cannot force you. This session is closed. Please, everyone, leave me to my thoughts."

As they slowly got up and slid off the bed, Zaethan lingered, but his friend signaled for him to leave too. He trailed the other haidrens to the circular landing. Luscia started up the steps to a higher portion of the fine, holdreheiim manor. Sleepily, Hachiro and Ira took to the opposite stair, their muffled bickering fading lower into the story below.

Instead of following their descent, Zaethan whirled angrily and climbed right after her.

Gripping the slick, twisted handrails, Luscia charged him where she had spun. "Heh'ta. Stay where you are."

He did not. Zaethan slunk his feet higher. Aggravation coiled his muscles. She could fix this for them, for Dmitri, but for whatever reason—but after everything they'd endured together—she wouldn't.

Luscia clutched that blasted band around her wrist, posturing it between them like a shield when Zaethan came to stoop a log lower. He sucked in through his teeth at the cuff. Still of dominant height, he leveled his mouth with hers.

He felt the pulse of her sprinting breaths beating his lips when she said, "Return to Declan—"

"Keeping this gap will only make things worse, Maji'maia." He hated how sentimental it sounded, implying himself as much as the Quadren. "Why are you refusing him?"

"I can't give him whatever he wants. I'm not like you."

"Oh, is that it?" Zaethan balked. It stung, being referred to like a pet. "I get that tonight was hard, but you can't just recoil—"

"Don't conflate your needs with his, Zaeth," Luscia spat. Barbs shot from her gaze in clear warning.

They landed true.

He held a hand up like he wanted to shake her. "You know what? Since coming here, it's like you've been trying to mask everything we've built. Masking yourself for who, the Enclave?"

Luscia boosted her chin. "I am their prayer—"

"You are their puppet. Eh, look at you…" He flicked that horrendously tight braid draped over her shoulder.

She jerked away, tempting from him a dark chuckle starved of delight.

"You're gladly cinched and bound by their strings, yeah? When from where I'm standing, you hold all the power. A kind of power they can't even imagine."

"There is no power outside the trust of my people."

"Then you will never have enough," Zaethan whispered, having experienced how easily one could lose it. They were bonded by loss, her and him. Maybe that was the crux of it all—why she was so afraid of the elders' judgment, of their disapproval. It'd befallen her mother. And in memory, it had never left. He backed off, to her audible exhale, talking in his descent. "It goes both ways, Maji'maia. We have to trust you too. So, start giving us a reason to before we stop."

Zaethan's heel hit the landing as at her neck, she fondled the trim of her stiffly pleated gown. Navel to throat, the bodice and sleeves were buttoned so unforgivingly that the picture of her once tumbled over laughing in a pair of borrowed gunjas was a suffocated dream.

"Uni, rhaolé. Hurry and tighten that collar before anyone sees you behind it."

The statement dripped poison from his tongue, and he meant its every sting. Life hurt. *His* life hurt. But this, here and now, mattered more. She was playing the coward, a role too taut for her skin—a role they had spent countless hours on that bluff in Faraji in order to shake. But this time, the cowardice would cost Dmitri everything, and her nothing.

He'd knowingly struck a nerve. Luscia's grieved eyes shot toward something at Zaethan's rear. Wordlessly, she fled to her haven upstairs, leaving him alone.

Like a coward.

Fuming, he rounded onto the other stair and paused, noticing an intimidating padlock on an adjacent door. It was witchiron-clad, another impenetrable lock—one of her many, by his estimation. Zaethan lumbered down the steps, wondering what it contained… if it was being hidden from the world or merely herself.

CHAPTER NINETEEN

Lawlessness devoured the streets. Cries of pain and pleasure coaxed the figure's scalded ears, inviting his baser self to join the Unitarians in their rampant debauchery.

Citizens ran wild through the alleyways, spilling drunkenly onto the main thoroughfares, their laughter both hysterical and hazardous. Men teetered out the windowsills of the overrun night dens, unable to pay their debts to the gambling houses next door. Bottles were broken and punches were thrown as customers traded their coin for the comfort of false company.

The scene stampeding the mounds of glass below them was no

better. Merchants shouted after their midnight shoplifters, having their stalls stripped of their crates and commodities. Another street over, a silk-clad yancy squealed like a piglet as he ran down Butcher Row clutching his hand—rather, the stump where his hand used to be, before he'd pilfered a basket of fish he could've easily afforded.

Throughout his schooling, the figure's tutors had often debated the goodness of mankind. Though, wrapping his scratchy cloak about his blistered flesh, he doubted those renown philosophers would ever electively tread Marketown at midnight, where they'd see the answer on full display. Wickedness was inherent. Goodness was taught. Why support so many laws if it wasn't the case? For when their enforcement was lifted, the hell of humanity always broke loose.

Commerce in the crown city was quickly unraveling into a sport of survival. Had the oil lamps burned out and the nightlife reduced to its array of garbage fires, the figure might have believed he was stooped under a dingy awning in Rian. Such anarchy governed the merchant state in the plains. But he knew these ancient cobbles underfoot—and the prosperous vermin who skittered across their every intersections— far too well.

Here lay the heart of Bastiion.

A heart without its king.

People perished wherever lacked vision and those pledged to protect it. History had proven so time and time again. Because civilizations didn't die overnight, but gradually. Eagerly. Gluttonously, ever unsatisfied.

The figure found Bastiion no different. Before him, the streets were choking on society's own filth. Just like the House's richer provinces, Marketown too had forfeited its much-needed bridle to the North; the city's insatiable appetite had become free to cannibalize itself with decadence and delight. The Proper Pryde had absconded to Boreal with

Alora's niece, and there was no one left to police the classes from their mutual destruction—no one except the opportunistic few, those who profited most by stoking the chaos.

And stoke it, they did.

He dodged a swath of tattered fabric and weaved between butcher blocks to evade a trio of cackling warriors. For days, the Darakaians had been arriving in droves, posing as diplomatic envoys, tradesmen, or even civilians. Their small army permeated the populace in disjointed packs, bloating Marketown from the slums as far as the Drifting Bazaar. A woman shrieked when one of them grabbed her by her hips in passing. As the figure kept walking, her shrieks only loudened.

A violent city called for violent patrol, the kind Nyack Kasim would willingly offer to a desperate Peerage, in spades.

The figure pinched a raw scrap off a bloodstained counter and sank his fangs into the cold meat, slinking forward within the shadows, making his way toward the Morrow District. He assumed the Pilarese chancellor would be returning to those yellowed, vapor-filled tents, like he had every evening preceding it.

Tetsu Naborū's addiction seemed to have worsened during the last fortnight, while he'd traveled alone through the provinces on a bizarre tour. The figure did not know what to make of his covert visits to various nobles—having blackmailed some and bribed others. The upcoming vote about which they spoke was mystery. Backroom politics was an artform, and Tetsu had fashioned himself into a virtuoso long before he'd replaced his brother on Korbin's Quadren. Yet after his recent dealings in Galina, he'd circled back into Bastiion's sickened underbelly, where those mortal pleasure tents awaited his patronage.

Hugging the buildings, the figure eyed a gang of Unitarian sentries across the cobbles. They'd cornered an elderly skinner who'd refused to hand over his earnings. By the gloss of the royal signet on their armor, each was still on duty.

He growled when the sentries picked up the old man and stripped down his breeches, copper coins clinking beneath his genitals, at their feet. They laughed at his nakedness and tossed him aside, then, grabbing a torch, one went to light his stand on fire.

The figure bared his teeth and sprung from the grimy wall. And just as his heels left the ground, a runaway cart—ablaze and led by a screeching donkey—tore through the street. Merchants and their poorest customers alike were chasing the thing down. At their advance, the figure lurched around the corner.

His back thudded against the stones inside the alcove. Alora panted against his arms, still caged around her. He snaked them tighter about her bodice, feeling no desire to let go. The two were well hidden from her fellow haidrens in the corridor.

"The Quadren is going to find out." She let her head slink back onto his shoulder. "How the king doesn't see that there's been something between us since before his coronation—"

"Is a testament to Korbin's roving eye." He swept a few of Alora's frazzled hairs back into sorts with her sleek, ashen plait. His thumb lingered on her temple before it swept below her chin, and he tilted her face around toward his.

Alora did not hesitate. Melting into his embrace, she kissed him until he was sure they were both lightheaded. For years, that was all they'd had to share—kisses refuting the laws of space and time. On most days, that was enough.

His lips chased after hers once they'd broken apart. He cherished the melody of her chuckles as she stifled them against his chest. Alora so rarely showed mirth in public. Its every exhibit had become a private and precious showcase just for him, outplaying the grandest orchestras in the palace.

She was his favorite instrument, his favorite musician, and his favorite song, all composed into one brilliant person.

He knew then—as he'd known plenty times before—that he'd do anything for her.

Alora's unearthly eyes, an opal beside an ocean, flickered at him while her pale, elegant fingers traced his jaw, meeting the rough resistance there. He'd been running late that morning, hurrying to scribble his counter notes within the margin of their battered codex, and had forgotten to shave—or had at least used the occasion as an excuse not to. She touched him more whenever he didn't.

Alora glanced toward the hall with a playful smirk. "I love you, dearest, but we cannot stay in here all day. Aniell knows Tallulah will be expecting me soon. She gossips more than a fishwife from Clan Ciann."

"Maybe that's why no one will marry her," he leaned in and said, then nibbled her ear playfully. "I always thought it was those unfortunate teeth."

She smacked him lightly. "You are wicked. I mean it; I have to go."

"Meet me in the library tonight."

"Don't I always?" Smoothing the folds of her glittering dress, Alora glided out the alcove, but with a twitch of her head, she stopped to listen intently. She jolted back inside, her cheeks aflame.

Troubled, he drew her behind him and positioned himself at the threshold's edge. Voices cradled the corridor where a few haidrens lingered outside the Quadrennal chamber. His hearing was nothing compared to Alora's, and so he strained to listen. Soon, his face grew hot too.

"Get that bitch in line, Gregor," said Nyack Kasim, the newly elected replacement from Darakai. Not even a full year since his wife's passing and the warlord posed less a mystery than he did a menace. "The war is over. There's no more excuse. We want a piece of the witchiron trade. Get her to lift the Boreali embargo once and for all."

"Convince her and you'll be handsomely rewarded, Lord Haidren."

The smooth invitation came as a curious surprise.

He inched his foot over the threshold to spy Pilar's rising star, its most famous shoto prime, Tetsu Naborū, openly conspiring with the other two. But free of his ever-present acolytes, who tended to snake like a golden academic tail wherever he went, the shoto prime was alone.

Tetsu wasn't expected to have left Gakoshū… nevertheless arrived at court.

"Boreal would never give up their military advantage," snipped Gregor Hastings. "Least of all to you. Besides, you're delusional if you think I'm the one who holds sway over the sorceress."

The young warlord sucked his teeth. "You've known the y'siti the longest. Find her weakness and exploit it. Otherwise, I won't just exploit yours." He puffed his chest at Gregor. "I'll nail it to a tree and leave it for dead."

Alora gripped his arm from behind.

He twisted, his heart sinking with her deflating stance.

Her thin brows were puckered in fear. "If Korbin discovers us, I'll be ruined. Everything I have, everything I've become, will be stripped from me until I'm left standing bare before my whole House. If he tells the clann or the elders…"

Collecting her hands, he kissed her knuckles one by one. "Korbin would never betray you like that, Alora. You attend Lourissa. You even delivered his son."

Grief clouded her irises over another. "I wish I could have delivered her too."

"You cannot cure someone of themself. Cyra made her choices, just as she chose for us to leave the child with that horrible man." Swallowing his misgivings, along with the constant regret he carried for honoring the late haidren's dying wish, he pivoted back toward the corridor.

He nervously watched as Tetsu slipped his hands into either belled sleeve and migrated the haidrens down the row of tall windows. Memories of Cyra dissolved when a budding smirk sliced the shoto prime's imperial veneer.

"You'll eventually learn, gentlemen," Tetsu crooned. "My plans are never shortsighted."

A stray bottle thudded against his boot. The figure took an acidic gulp of reality, returning to himself and the chaos echoing throughout Marketown.

Mingling with the darkness, he stifled the latent impulse to breathe as he merged into the river of smoke. It reeked like trash and sweet perfume. The air trapped within the Marrow District clung to his threadbare clothing, trying to seduce him into believing the sickly smolder could take away his pain. But the figure was not like the bloodshot yancies who deliriously lumbered in and out of those discolored tents. They could forget their sins and escape it all, after a mere inhale or two.

Forgetting was the gambit of men. Not of monsters.

Halfway down the soot-caked alleyway, the figure ducked low, finally sighting Tetsu Naborū enter the mouth at the opposite end. He stole a glance at the moon's position in the bleak sky.

The chancellor was late.

Tetsu swept through the smoke. Whatever he pulled alongside him was hidden by its height. Through the haze, his taut complexion was sallower than usual, the jaundice nearly encompassing what used to be the whites of his still-sharp eyes.

Creeping around the swaths of canvas and hide, the figure kept pace with Tetsu's advance toward a squalid tent nested between two decrepit buildings. When he stopped to look through the gap at the chancellor, his stomach nearly tripped over his feet.

Across the way, it was a child with Tetsu.

The boy—Unitarian, by his dainty tanned features—limply held onto the chancellor's hand. His empty expression did not falter as words were exchanged and the tent flap opened for them to enter. Mechanically, his little legs propelled him inward, as if practiced at doing so.

A growl hungrily awoke the lifeless chambers inside the figure. Children performed one function in places like the Marrow District, functions born from the vilest imaginations of those who could afford their funding.

His bootheel had already left the ground when Tetsu followed in after the boy. The figure jumped for a taut clothesline, and slinging himself overtop, he launched off toward the pocked masonry. He caught the fissures, scaling the side like a nightmarish beast toward the tent. Between the crooked walls, the figure landed on the other side in a predatory crouch.

Candles silhouetted the occupants with a nauseating glow, as if bile had been smeared along the interior of the canvas. Tetsu gave instruction to the dealer, and the bubbling of marrow ensued. Soon thick smoke was coiling out a hole at the top of the tent. Over the simmer, the figure then heard another person enter off the street.

The newcomer thumped onto a mattress.

"Leave us," Tetsu briskly ordered the marrow dealer, to which there came no argument. Two adult shadows remained, with that of the boy unmoving between them. Through the canvas, the other man reached toward him, but with incredible speed, his wrist was ensnared.

The chancellor held it in place. "We have a deal then, Darius?"

"You want to do it here? Now?" Darius asked. His lilt had the impatient whine of someone used to getting their way.

"The ritual cannot wait. Give yourself over to the Obscurer, and you will receive your eternal reward," Tetsu said persuasively, bringing the man's arm slowly down around the boy's waist. "Imagine it, Darius of Hildur. Imagine how many more darlings you could collect with the gift of immortality."

Earl Darius—a member of the Peerage of Nobility—smacked his lips eagerly. The earl's shadow scooted closer beside the child.

The trio of outlines sharpened as the figure's pupils dilated. His fangs achingly broke the surface of his gums, and the figure's sticky breath fanned the canvas.

"The Obscurer will never deny you whatever you desire. Nay, whatever you *deserve*," the chancellor promised. "He asks only that you serve him in return. Can you do that, Darius?"

"Yes," the earl raggedly vowed and hurriedly stripped back his shirtsleeve to bare his forearm. His other hand began to caress the boy. "Yes, do it now."

Tetsu unloaded something from within his robes and uncorked it. The fire backlit his hooked nailpiece when he raised it high. Liquid dripped off the tip. "Oh, Darius, immortality costs a lot more than that…" In a blink, the chancellor yanked him by the hair. Against the earl's screams, Tetsu carved his metal talon down the earl's neck. "We must become before we can begin. State your vow while your tongue still attends you, Darius."

"I—I pledge myself to the Obscurer!" he cried.

Finishing the ritual, the chancellor chanted over his nailpiece in a language the figure could not distinguish; its form was so ancient, the syllables overcrowded the human mouth. The figure winced from the syllables, unable to help how his limbs automatically shuddered in retreat. He caught his balance when the intonation stopped.

Sworn into the cult of the Obscurer, the earl pasted his hand against his spasming neck, gasping as Tetsu capped his mysterious jar and rose off the mattress.

"You are to assemble the Peerage once we proceed with the Obscurer's bidding," Tetsu commanded. His shadow bent to retrieve a reed-thin pipe from the central marrow stand. He took a low drag and set it back down. "Enjoy yourself, Darius. And don't leave a mess."

With a swish, the tent flaps were opened and closed. The figure sprung, primed to chase after the chancellor. But the clink of an unbuckling belt raked his fervor back toward the tent.

Children performed one function in the Marrow District.

His humanity surged and abated in a savage tide. The figure seized the canvas with a roar. He ripped the tent wall in half. In a maddened rush, he stormed the earl, his sateen jacket already stripped over an unbuttoned, brocade vest. The figure constricted his legs around his reedy torso, ready to snap the earl's ribs.

Darius's screams were a thrill to the figure's ears as he pierced his fangs into the tendons of his shoulder and spit a fleshy chunk onto the ground. Flailing, the earl slammed them both into an old bureau, dirtied dishes clattering in shards. The figure squeezed Darius's throat, relishing the crunching of his cartilage. Then he saw the wound gushing just below his jaw.

Wickedness poured from a bloody figure eight, divided by a single gash.

Darius hadn't been inducted as another follower. He was to become a creature like the rest.

The figure foamed at the mouth in fury, the taste of terror and shame bathing his tongue, when he heard someone swallow hard. With a snarl, he glimpsed up from his prey.

The boy stared at him blankly, his eyes wide but barren. Like the figure, they'd already seen too much.

"Run." Hot spittle dripped into the earl's wound when the figure warned in a guttural voice, "Run away from me."

Blinking, the child snapped out of his daze, knocking over the pot of bubbling syrup as he fled into the street.

Darius begged through his wet gasps. But the figure ignored his pleas. They were both abominations now, demons bred by their own unmaking.

He plunged his fangs ruthlessly into the cursed sinew and drank it in as he wound his gloved fingers lower, below the earl's belt. The figure clawed after the engorged tissue while Darius screeched. There came no cry from Amaranth. No call from the heavens to make him break off before the massacre began. After tearing the lump from Darius's body, the figure took the flaccid muscle and smothered the earl's screeching until it stopped.

Goodness was learned. Without a guide, it could be unlearned too.

CHAPTER TWENTY
ZAETHAN

Zaethan lumbered to the top of the moor, bracing against the midmorning crisp. His thumb ached. He brought it to his mouth to nurse the gash but remembered the shadowman who'd licked it last.

Made queasy all over again, he spat the clotted blood into a bed of heather.

While the bubbling cut wasn't deep, it was disproportionately painful, having been made by witchiron—an added penalty the armaeger who'd wielded the dagger had seemed to enjoy. Though not as much as Zaethan, when after tasting his blood, said armaeger had declared him not guilty before the packed square of Boreali onlookers. To their consternation, Zaethan's sample did not match the droplets of evidence, be they animal or human, found in the wood. Neither had the sample of any Darakaian who'd been made to stand in the incriminating line.

With a grimace, Zaethan bound his wound in the scarf Lady Athdara had miraculously afforded him. He'd found it dangling from his door handle like a farewell gift, half expecting it to have been hexed or cursed, though no less cursed than the crone's entire House and their primal process of elimination.

After all, it was Lady Athdara who'd been the most disappointed by the verdict, proving that in Boreal, it was more suitable to board a murderer than let a dirty cross-caste serve himself porridge.

Getting maimed served a suitable reason for his being late that morning, Zaethan supposed. Not that anyone had really missed his attendance. Stuffing his hands into the pockets of his quilted tunic, he approached the posse of shadowmen where, dappled in cloud cover, they encircled their haidren's sparring sphere.

She did not sound happy inside it.

Unless, of course, hers were shouts of glee. It was hard to tell the difference these days.

He stopped alongside Noxolo. The willowy shadowman had his long arms crossed, his countenance crestfallen and subdued. In Zaethan's periphery, he could only spy Noxolo's beaky nose, extending past his screen of loose platinum hair.

They stood there, neither acknowledging the other.

Zaethan broke the silence. "Eh, I'm… *sorry*… about your mhàdda." He shifted awkwardly, still uneasy using the apologetic phrase. His heritage might not be entirely Darakaian, but his roots were through and through.

"Tadöm," said Noxolo. He did not look over, or downward for that matter, at Zaethan. Rather, he focused ahead on Luscia and her failed attempt to thwart the cabbage her captaen had thrown at her. "My family will continue the search around Roüwen until we depart for Ana'Innöx. Then, we'll carry the investigation westward."

Zaethan regarded the man who'd fought with him in the Mirajii Forest. Gone were the stripes of his killing. His spine was bowed and unburdened by the glorious weapons he'd earned. He was a reaper reduced to a shell.

Sorrow was the great equalizer; it maintained no allegiance or exception. Zaethan had never felt so comparable to the shadowman than standing elbow-to-elbow, together unarmed and at a loss.

He quietly offered to Noxolo, "My beta and I can join your search this afternoon, if you'll have us."

"Wem, waedfrel. The more eyes the better, however ordinary yours may be," Noxolo replied. In a flash, he struck out his hand and caught a wayward cabbage before it struck Zaethan in the face. Noxolo tossed the undestroyed vegetable back at his captaen.

Gingerly, Zaethan distanced himself from their privileged ring of stone and wandered toward his preferred boulder along the outskirt. With a friendly yip, her massive wolx appeared and sprinted around the bend. His thickening, wintry coat ruffled as he trotted alongside Zaethan's heel. At least someone was happy to see him.

Bracing against the boulder, Zaethan slid his backside down its rockface and sagged against a cushioned patch of heather. It was damp. The melted frost sadly soaked his behind. Legs outspread, Zaethan glowered at the upturned boots and the highlander leatherwork that cupped his cold toes.

His feet looked ridiculous.

And so did he.

Zaethan didn't know why he kept coming there, to the moor, only that Luscia kept permitting it. He'd been doing that a lot lately, aimlessly turning up in places for no reason. These mornings were a silly allowance on her part, for thus far, he served her no purpose except to proffer an occasional snide remark or two. With a sigh, Zaethan ripped up the grass and spindled it between his fingertips. He didn't serve much purpose anywhere anymore.

Above, Owàa soared in the sky, the sun basking Zaethan's knuckles and their mixed coloring in bright mockery. He flexed his fist. How could he have never seen it before? The vibrancy of his sage-green eyes, the cinnamon patina encasing his bones... Had he wanted to be the son of the fearsome Nyack Kasim so badly that he'd been blinded to the obvious?

Had everyone else?

Meme ano'qondai, he confessed to himself in his mother's tongue. Not for the first time, he wished Cyra had lived to hear it. Maybe then he'd understand why she'd kept her child's story a secret. Why she'd buried it with her, never to be told.

"Glad to see you were exonerated."

Zaethan jolted in place, not having heard Declan's unnerving approach. The shadowman's studded tunic *chinked* against the rock when he folded his burly arms and leaned against it. His antlered cloak pin gleamed nobly off his barreled chest. Being a stout fellow not much taller than his haidren, Declan watched her training proceed at vantage not much higher than Zaethan did while sitting.

"Your mother doesn't share the sentiment," said Zaethan dryly. He lifted his bandaged thumb. "In an impassioned speech, she'd urged them to cut the whole thing off, just to be sure. Less of my appendages to touch her kakka-shtàka spoons."

Heartily, Declan laughed.

Zaethan did not.

Another rogue, unimpeded cabbage sailed through the wide open and smashed against the boulder. It rained a harvest. Zaethan swiped the colorful leaves off his forehead, adding to the stray shoots of indigo, fuchsia, and orange that quilted the ground.

Creyvan—the distempered shadowman—snickered across the moor. He was a twit, easily the least helpful of her private guard. For whatever reason, the golden-haired warrior presented the biggest issue with Zaethan's being there, even more than his captaen did. Creyvan was always primed with comment, as untranslatable as it was underhanded.

The sound of Creyvan's satisfaction, whatever his words entailed, died off when his bearded twin muttered a stiff rebuke.

Zaethan thought a stiff punch to the gut would've yielded better results.

Inside the stone ring, Luscia was bent over. She smacked her thighs in frustration. "Meh fyreon, meh fyreon." The haidren blurted her terse apologies to both Declan and Zaethan as she wiped her brow and turned away.

Her back was as drenched as Zaethan's, and not from the frost.

Sweat pasted her silvery sparring garb like a second skin to her strong figure, embellishing the material's natural shine as much as the shape beneath it. Linsilk, he'd heard it termed in town—a lustrous textile that glistened like meadows dressed in dew. Though militaristic in its cut and design, the tunic had an appliqué trim that sparkled with her brusque movements. It flared off her waist, markedly girded by a masculine set of wide leather bands.

Like her gear, everything caught the light in Boreal... down to the insignificant threading of Zaethan's borrowed coat. In a land incapable of true darkness, he suddenly wondered if that was the point… if their every composition was less a refinement than it was a recital.

Luscia shattered that idea when she gave an infuriated, ear-blistering screech.

Hitching his knees, he studied her tiresome pacing over the horizon of his interlocked fists. She'd made little progress during the near two weeks they'd been stealing away to the moorland. The strange forces Luscia had brandished that initial day were unlike any heinous fable he'd heard about the elusive Boreali and their rumored occult, tales of human sacrifice, moon rites, and blood spells. But unabashedly before his eyes, she'd committed none of those things.

She was brilliant and breathtaking. Yet whatever Luscia was trying to wield, whatever power she clearly possessed, it had fallen asleep—most likely lulled listless by her Captaen Bailefore, who nursed his haidren's self-pity in the same way Ira nursed his gambling habit, incessantly and without moderation.

In a huff, Luscia squatted in place. She squeezed her skull between her hands.

Captaen Bailefore marched through the torn heather and stooped before her. A fresh cabbage was wedged under his arm. He stroked their symbol of engagement, strapped about her wrist. "There is no pressure here, Ana'Sere. We will go at your pace."

Zaethan couldn't help but snort.

"Something amiss?" Declan inquired. "Bolaeva, do share."

"He's still pulling his punches. It's obvious she's triggered by danger, to herself or someone else. That reflex will just fade the more he puts off increasing the stakes."

"Aye, he pulls them," the shadowman agreed, his accent crispening day by day with the weather. "But se'lah Aurynth… Until those endless shores, it is against our najjani oath to harm her."

Zaethan rolled his eyes. "He's harming her right now. She's not made of glass. Too much longer and she'll believe she's just that."

"The captaen serves her faithfully" was all Declan said in response.

"Yeah, can't wait for the wedding." Zaethan muttered. "Should cause quite the stir, given how Bailefore's fashioned her into his child bride."

"Ock! They're not betrothed."

Formulating his snide reply, Zaethan suddenly looked up at Declan. "They're not?"

"Niit, Lord Haidren." A grin teamed in the corners of the shadow-man's steely gaze as he repeated himself slowly. "They are *not* betrothed."

Zaethan clambered onto his heels. He stretched across the boulder, keeping his tenor as hushed as possible. "Then what the Depths does that ugly thing mean?" he asked, tapping his own naked wrist yet implying the eyesore around hers.

Declan's response was low in kind. "It means nothing is casual." He pointedly arched a rusty brow, the kinky hairs blending into his furrowed freckles. "Not any longer."

Zaethan glanced aside, mainly to avoid the shadowman's probing stare. He'd been posted outside the room at the Scaly Stowaway that extraordinary—and excruciating—night in Port Khmer. As Declan could overhear things yards away, it was no mystery to him what had happened between the haidrens inside.

Especially when their bench had dented the wall.

Zaethan's focus drifted with Luscia as she stomped toward the opposite side of the training circle.

"Define casual," he said.

"Ana'Sere will only entertain formal suitors moving forward. She's accepted the captaen's kurtfierï," Declan replied. "It's not his fault no others have come forward to add theirs."

Tearing his attention from her crouched stance, Zaethan speared Declan with his stare. "She can wear more than one?"

"Oh, aye." Declan confirmed with a nod. "Meh mamu wore seven, used to be a looker herself."

Zaethan doubted that, for Lady Athdara resembled a troll.

"She finally decided on meh fappa once she could no longer walk under the weight of her eighth kurtfierï."

Zaethan's forehead rumpled, confused by her selfish timing. Not to mention the pomp and circumstance of it all. It wasn't exactly the best season for a mass wooing. "Why now? Why would she start accepting suitors amid so much discord? The Quadren faces enough worries as it is."

"Hm… why indeed." Declan pawed the wiry braids dangling off his chin. His tone suggested he need not suppose an answer, for he already knew one. Flattening his broad back against the boulder, the shadowman tilted his head of knotted curls toward Zaethan. "It calls to mind of when I was a wee lad, and my Great-Aunt Matilde came to live with us."

Clenching his jaw, Zaethan sensed the launch of some pointless parable. The Boreali weren't capable of candor.

"Rickety old thing, Auntie Matilde." Declan continued. "Would always wake up black and blue, her legs covered in bruises. It took us months to realize that she had a serious sleepwalking problem. Fappa was beside himself. Didn't know how to protect her from her own missteps. So, one day, at a loss, he simply told my Aunt Matilde what was going on. And do you know what she did?"

"Obviously not," Zaethan said tersely.

Catching the rising sun, Declan aimed his sky-stroked stare at

Zaethan. "She took a rope and bound herself to the footpost so that she wouldn't wander into the wrong bed."

With an intrigue-filled tilt of his jaw, Zaethan narrowed his eyes at the shadowman before he shifted them sharply toward the sparring ring and the woman commanding it. Declan was sly; he would never betray his haidren's purposes.

But Auntie Matilde just did.

Beads dangled from the leather bands secured around Luscia's thrashing wrist as she argued with her Captaen Bailefore, whom Zaethan had thought she was set to wed. Suddenly, he saw her actions in a new dawn. She was a follower of rules. Rules were Luscia's security and therefore her protection, especially in Boreal. Whatever the court-ship custom entailed, it prohibited her from going too far with another man. Prohibited her from wandering toward someone like Zaethan.

Which meant she wanted to.

So badly that she'd anchored herself to a dead weight named Bailefore.

With his tongue, Zaethan probed the inside of his cheek, watching them interact. The captaen was placating her excuses again. Even in argument, Luscia's body language seldom squared his. Together, their shadows painted dissatisfaction over the piles of unaffected cabbages. She saw them coming every time, yet Bailefore could not rouse that bright mystery within her.

Zaethan's lips twisted in a smirk. Rousing her was what he did best.

"He's afraid to hurt you!" Zaethan shouted. Saddling his back against the boulder, he smugly crossed his arms. "Eh, or are you afraid too, Maji'maia?"

He didn't hide his delight when her eyes flared from across the moor. Haughtily, Luscia pitched her hands upon her sturdy hips.

Captaen Bailefore turned and brandished his weapon at Zaethan.

The attempted intimidation was weak, for he was also brandishing a cabbage. "You are a guest here, Lord Haidren. Not an equal!"

"Marek," Luscia said, reaching over to subdue him. However, doubt had seeded in the corners of her expression. It rolled her lips inward. Pinched the crease above her nose.

Her doubt bloomed when she peeked up at Zaethan.

"It could work, Ana'Sere," Declan unexpectedly said from his right. "One proven method for another."

Guardedly, Zaethan slanted aside, suspicion in his voice. "Why are you backing me?"

"Niit, I'm not backing you." Declan shrugged. "I'm backing *her*."

"Fine. Wem. We'll try it," Luscia said, backing away from her captaen.

Bailefore chased after her steps, his lips flying without sound.

"I said, *we will try*, Marek!" She silenced his witchtongue objection, motioning for him to exit the ring and hand the cabbage to Zaethan.

Zaethan kicked off the boulder, flexing his shoulders as he strode toward the circle's rock-studded rim. Captaen Bailefore met him there in passing. Distain flattened his mouth when he shoved the cabbage not into Zaethan's opened hands but straight to his chest. It knocked him back an inch, taking the wind with him. Bailefore's eyes turned to ice as he stalked past Zaethan in a crimson blur and joined his shadowmen along the outskirt.

Zaethan didn't care. Nor was he sad to see him go. At the edge, he asked her bluntly, "Your men, they will not interfere, ano?"

Luscia stretched her neck. In the breeze, her braid of alder and ash waved, the banner of her own army. She tightened her closed-off stance and scanned her men, granting them the order. "Niit. They will not interfere."

"Good."

Zaethan dropped the stupid vegetable. Instantly, he stooped and stole a rock from the boundary line, then stormed toward Luscia.

"What are you—"

He hurled the rock—to her visible astonishment, at rapid speed. Having hunted with the slingshot in his youth, Zaethan was a fairly good shot—even as a cub.

She sidestepped.

But not in time.

Cupping her bicep, Luscia clutched the fresh tear in her thick tunic. Blood dribbled between her fingers. "Ow!" she angrily cried.

Her men hurried to the rim, crowding it. Zaethan lifted his brow at her. With a growl, Luscia jerked her head at them, signaling their retreat.

"You could've given me some warning, *Lord Darakai*," she seethed. "Shtàka!"

"Warning." He grunted. "You never used to need that. But eh, maybe you're too soft now, Maji'maia. Maybe the puppet needs her cabbage stew," Zaethan said, baiting her as he nicked a few more stones off the ground. Big ones too.

Shadows veiled her face when she tucked her chin. The pearly wake of her right iris sputtered as she said threateningly, "I am not a puppet."

"Right now, you're my puppet."

"I am no one's puppet!" Luscia shouted.

At her back, her snarly braid rose in a way that defied the wind. The hairs of his arms puckered beneath his coat, commanded by another force charging in the air around them.

Zaethan chucked his second rock with ease. Luscia spun with liquid grace and crouched in the heather—an ethereal beast among the thorns—as it cruised overhead.

He skidded his boot forward. Incrementally, she snaked backward on her heels. Had his horsehair lead been knotted about her waist,

Zaethan would have heaved the rope mercilessly. It made him mad, her regression.

Damn the highlands. Damn them to the Depths.

Instead, he started to circle Luscia. Here and there, Zaethan clicked for her like he would after a pony.

Her eyes hunted him beneath her brows. "Don't you dare."

He clicked his tongue again.

Slowly, Luscia lifted from the silky undergrowth. Zaethan charged her, then cut left, and rolling onto his hip, he hurled another rock. It pummeled her straight in the ribs, possibly causing a fracture.

She'd heal. Certainly faster than he had after she'd fractured his.

Luscia howled from her belly, rough and incensed. He didn't stop but snatched an even larger rock from his feet and lobbed it at her. Undeterred, she bull-rushed him and, throwing up her hand, sent an angry shockwave through the open.

A disk of iridescent light flashed against the thrown rock like a shield manifested out of nothingness. The thing burst into bits.

Zaethan staggered in awe. He ran his fingers between his locs.

Yet she hadn't noticed why. With a scream, Luscia sprinted under the pebbled rain at Zaethan.

Bracing for impact, he swept one heel, ducked, and caught her by the middle, swinging them both aside. Using her feet, Luscia pushed off his thighs. She wrapped a leg around him as if he were a post, and managed to shimmy onto his back.

Her forearm ruthlessly hooked around his windpipe as she roared into his ear, "I am no puppet!"

Wheezing, Zaethan enlisted an old move, thrashing them both down to the earth so the impact would break her hold—and were she a normal human, also her spine. Scaping onto his feet, he wrenched her upright, reversing their positions. He snaked an arm across her wide belting, the other up toward her neck. Zaethan cupped her chin, savoring the way his hip bones dug against the top of her buttocks. Forgetting their audience, he couldn't help the way his forefinger crept across her bottom lip.

He chuckled contently as she bucked inside his arms. "If you're no puppet, then why am I the one holding your strings?"

Her movements liquefied. Unable to see her face, as her crown was wedged against his throat, he felt Luscia's mouth part. His heart pounded as his finger slid a fraction inside and touched her tongue.

Suddenly, Zaethan shrieked in pain.

Luscia swiveled. Scarlet basted her mouth, and with unnatural velocity, she slid her trick-blade under his chin. He'd forgotten she was still wearing the blasted rings, just like he'd forgotten she was a biter.

"Why am I the one holding yours?" Luscia countered.

"Feels good, uni?"

The palest platinum along her hairline lifted and swayed. Her nostrils flared. "Hear me when I say, Zaethan Shà… that I am *no one's* puppet."

"Yet you dance so well on the Enclave's stage—"

There came a *whish*, a ghostly gust of energy that emitted off her and rattled his bones as it passed through his body in an exhilarating burst. Beyond Luscia, the stones of the boundary line had risen a foot off the earth in a hovering circle.

He scarcely heard her men's gasps in the background.

"I said I am no one's puppet," Luscia warned through her clenched teeth.

Zaethan pushed against her witchiron blade, ignoring the sizzle of his flesh. "Ano zà, Maji'maia," he said in seriousness. He tipped his forehead toward the rocks suspended around them. "You are absolutely not."

Her eyes enlarged, and the stones instantly clattered to the ground. Shock, fear, and excitement at her own handiwork skated across her gawk all at once. With an abrupt click, Luscia retracted the blade and dropped her arm, though she stayed just as close, studying Zaethan in confusion rather than her own triumph. "I spoke to my father," she said at random. "He has finally acquiesced to allow you all to come with us to the keep for Ana'Innöx. The Quadren will stay together, per its wishes."

"If you want my prydes to trust you, *this* is what they need to see." Zaethan whistled at the busted rubble.

Luscia ignored his suggestion. "We have created a way to take you there. But you're not going to like it."

"Going to make me your prisoner?"

She twined her arms behind her back, putting feet between her and Zaethan. "Something like that."

"Well," Zaethan replied with a devilish smirk. "It wouldn't be the first time we tied ourselves together…"

Appreciatively, he watched her depart, then turned to gather his things—a bit of thrill in his step that had not been there that morning.

The last thing he remembered were the knuckles of Captaen Bailefore's fist.

CHAPTER TWENTY ONE
LUSCIA

"This is insulting."

"Only by your own estimation, Lord Darakai, which we've established holds much less bearing in Boreal than you think it ought," Luscia replied, already tired of, and therefore apathetic to, his characteristic grumbles. "I warned you would not like the Clann Darragh's terms. You can take it off again when we make camp. Yeh'maelim for that, by the way. That particular reprieve took a heap of convincing on my part."

She spied him in her periphery, not wanting to indulge the matter, though he could not see her do it from where he was bound to the saddle atop his Andwele stallion. Hitched to her mare, Luscia led them along the hoof-beaten trail. Zaethan's full lips buckled into a sullen pout beneath the ribbon of linsilk covering the upper half of his face.

As she'd sufficiently argued, there was nothing insulting about wearing a blindfold in another House's territory.

The nightcap pulled overtop his blindfold, however…

That might have been overkill.

Chiefly because it belonged to her housekeeper, Arlette—a hardy woman who found equitable insult in his wearing it.

Luscia conquered her features and stifled a laugh at the long-tailed stocking. Its wool was stitched in highland designs of jade and cream. Zaethan's locs had stuffed the hat into a plump sack over his shoulder, the gilded tassels wisping over his chest. To her father's point, the Enclave would not concede for one measure of discretion, but two. The road to Aksel's Keep was nearly as secret as the keep itself. If one secret must be revealed, even in part, the elders could be comforted that those to whom it was revealed would be unable to find it again.

She didn't know why Zaethan still bothered complaining. He'd sported the cap just the same the day prior, as the one before that. One would have expected a warrior of his brutal breed to be more distressed by the linsilk strapped about his wrists, tethering him to the horn of his saddle. Luscia thought it perplexing that it was his eyes, not his hands, that he most prized.

At the pop of his jaw, she knocked her head to the side. He was stretching out his face again. The indigo stain escaped the blindfold, blotting the swollen skin of Zaethan's accentuated cheekbone. She'd refrained from offering one of her salves, or even the simplest of treatments, from her apothecary out of respect for Marek, the man who'd put it there. The bruise was not hers to remove.

Riding closely beside him, Luscia glanced at her captaen on her left. His sight tore from his marking on the haidren beyond her.

Half-bound and ornamented in sterling cuffs, Marek's hair blew with the falling leaves in autumnal gusts. Under the beams of golden sun, his dark-red strands lit like rubies. Luscia had to admit it served an attractive clash against his angular, ivory features.

Somehow being here… being home… Marek had grown more handsome than ever.

And Luscia didn't know what to do with that.

With a slight incline of his head, Marek said in an almost-inaudible resonance, "He deserved it, Luscia."

She nodded in reply. "Wem, he did."

"I was in my rights."

"Wem, you were."

It was the reason Luscia hadn't let it cause issue between them. And why since quitting Roüwen, she'd opted to position herself as a levelheaded barrier between her recognized suitor and their diplomatic companion. Mutual respect could only exist if it upheld the boundaries of both parties, especially in matters of the heart. As she wore only Marek's kurtfierï, no other man within the House of Boreal was permitted to speak to her so provocatively as Zaethan had. Luscia was no longer free in that sense, a decision she'd made with that exact objective in mind. That he was an outsider, albeit one with title, only added injury to the offense.

Zaethan's legitimacy still being in question was Marek's saving grace. While he'd operated within the rights of courtship, he'd certainly tested those of the Ethnicam in striking the haidren to Darakai. Tadöm Aniell that Zaethan had concealed the origin of his injury from Dmitri, having sputtered some nonsense about his sleepwalking into the wrong bed instead, preventing further discord among the haidrenship. That prevention had taken little coaxing from Luscia.

She suspected Zaethan wished to disclose their indelicate history to their king just as much as she did.

Alternatively, had their king not insisted Zaethan retain his seat on the Quadren, there would've been nothing to protect him. The bruising could have been far worse. There was severe imbalance between the strength of a highlander and the jaw of a lowlander. As a captaen of the najjani Ranger Aelect, Marek had really been holding back.

Her cheeks bloomed from the memory of Zaethan's salacious words. Luscia was still ashamed. Yet her blush had less to do with the content of his words than his words being made public. What had been said before her najjan could not be unheard.

Even by Luscia's ears.

A brazenness had rebirthed in Zaethan over the course of recent days. Sparked from where, Luscia was not certain. But on the moor, she'd felt that spark ignite something within her too… felt its command wrench aside the veil and burn within the *Other*. It'd harnessed the threads without her comprehension. It split stone and raised it off the earth like schoolyard charms strung on chords of glittering lumin. Such power was beyond those of the Higher Gifts.

Or so she'd thought. Luscia didn't know what to do with any of that either.

"Tadöm," Marek said, reaching over the beat of their horses' hooves for her hand. She let him take it, and his aquamarine eyes locked on hers as he scooped up Luscia's palm and kissed it reverentially. He held onto her fingers, sweetly letting them sway in tandem over the leafy road for those behind them to see.

After a few minutes passed, Luscia gently withdrew and readjusted her hold on the reins.

Windchimes rang from the rustic canopy in shimmering steles, each bearing an engraving that told a tale of old. In that way, their songs were sang by an undying orchestra. A company of cardinals trumpeted their accompaniment to the jabbered fluting of squirrels. Sweeping boughs creaked as their leaves clamored their rustling percussion. In unity, the highlands sang for their Maker, heralding the advent of His people as they embarked toward the keep.

Dmitri broke in with a human refrain. "Lady Boreal, how long did you say it takes to pilgrim to this stronghold of yours?" Their king lifted his slender thighs a fraction and stood in Harmonia's stirrups. A linsilk blindfold and corresponding nightcap identical to the other haidrens, as well as the pryde warriors toward the rear of their party, partially obscured his pained expression. "I presume this constant incline is something every Boreali man must get used to."

Marek chuckled with a knowing grin. "Trick is in the breeches, Your Majesty."

Luscia felt her cheeks heating more brightly.

The captaen stabilized the lead between his chestnut horse and the famous argent Andwele mare. In his fidgeting, Dmitri's hat drooped forward, the mink trim comically framing the button of his olive nose.

"Unfortunately, the weeklong climb to Aksel's Keep is defined by its elevation, not its distance," Luscia said to her king.

"Ah, Aksel, like your beastly wolx. Did his namesake once reign from these mounts?" Dmitri fondly asked, but a hoarse cough escaped him on the last word.

Luscia focused on him intently. The temperature was rapidly dropping with their climb. Perhaps she needed to tweak his elixir upon their arrival. Add more blood even.

"Aksel is a forefather," Marek stated but promptly mouthed for Luscia's distracted affirmative to continue.

She supposed they weren't breaking Dmitri's rule concerning their volume if he couldn't sight the betrayal of their lips. At Luscia's instruction, Marek went on.

"During the heart of the Spire Age, while Bastiion crafted her gates and palace jewel, Aksel championed the najjan through the second largest battle in Boreali history. After which, he oversaw the construction of the keep so that such battles would not be repeated. That is why in honor of his wish for peace, it bears his name today. We remember Aksel's cause during Ana'Innöx, just as we pay tribute to the cause of Tiergan the First."

"Well, I am eager to set eyes on it. The scale must be remarkable to harbor so many of your kinsmen. I can hear that the road is even more crowded than yesterday." Dmitri was correct. Narrow as it was, the trail was packed with chattering pilgrims and jangling supply carts as the Enclave's party had caught up with those families who'd gotten a late start on their journey. "But I'm still unclear what it is you actually harvest during these festivities. No one seemed to pack anything beyond our rations. Is it a crop local to these altitudes?"

"Of a sort..." Luscia said, stopping Marek from divulging much more.

"They're back!" Böwen yelled from where he toted the weirdly quiet haidren to Pilar.

Luscia twisted in her saddle. Evidently, the best way to shush Hachiro Naborū-Zuo was to take away his quill. Riding near them, Declan towed the haidren to Bastiion. Given that he was slumped over atop his bay mount, his snores fanning the fluffy lining of his slouched nightcap, all one had to do to shush Ira was swaddle him like a newborn.

Along the road's bank, scouts emerged from their search among the bordering wilds, their horses' legs raking through the lagoon of citrine-and-amber leaves. At the helm rode Noxolo and his despondent father, Eitri Egon. Already a man made to look even thinner by his height, Lord Egon had diminished during the last weeks over losing his wife, exposing him rusty and gaunt. Like Noxolo, he was fast fading with the hope that they would eventually find her. Following his son's lead, they steered the search party toward the elders, clustered near the front of the Enclave precession.

Aside from Creyvan, whom Luscia had suggested accompany them, for she couldn't trust his mouth in front of the Quadren anymore, the search party was largely comprised of talï-decorated, wool-coated men from Clan Ciann. It was an organized show of patriotism, no doubt, to better spin the prior perception of their prejudicial treatment against those precisely like the Egons from Clan Ödetha. Ciann may have been run by zealots, but they were smart about their zealotry. One couldn't impose a fanaticism if one couldn't be well received. And right now, all needed to be received by Master Rohan in order to persuade him to either grant or withhold najjani support in Dmitri's plight.

Luscia included.

Crossing his short, stubby arms over his saddle horn, Elder Hinrük listened complacently as Noxolo debriefed her father and aunt. There was little care for Lady Egon in his empty, gray eyes—nothing except a self-serving satisfaction that it was he who searched for the woman, not Luscia or those in her political camp.

While Noxolo understood that Luscia's first priority was to king and Quadren, the people looking on would not, an angle Elder Hinrük was nursing like a sectarian saint.

Like leavened bread, Hinrük's countenance puffed with contrived concern as he chimed in with something as unhelpful as it was long-winded. Even Emiere, the long-esteemed captaen of Alora's guard, wasn't buying his yeasty facade. His horse stomped under the gruff najjan as Emiere stared down the elder with the same acrimony he would a chipmunk chewing on his shoe.

From their grouping, Noxolo looked over and miserably shook his head to the question unspoken by her entire najjani guard. His face was as pale as his hair.

"I'm worried for him," Luscia said in a distant voice.

Marek sighed and leaned across to stroke her arm in comfort. "He will endure this, Ana'Sere. He can and he must… Se'lah Aurynth."

No one should have to endure this, she thought. Luscia was all too familiar with the agony of losing a parent. But to have them ripped away without any closure, without any explanation, was what was unendurable. The questions never found the grave. They haunted its surface forever. The similarities between the vanishing of Lady Egon and Eoine Darragh Tiergan were too distinct to ignore. Yet were Luscia to give them any more credence, she might entomb herself in the very madness that'd stolen her mother long before she'd left.

"The delusion is helping him, I think," Declan added gruffly.

Luscia shifted toward him. "Delusion?"

"Oh, you haven't heard?" Böwen scratched his short beard and leaned forward, over his horse's neck. "Nox thinks his mamu was taken by an eldertross." As if in flight, Böwen swooped his flattened palm down and plucked the air. "*Pop*. Just like that."

Her face scrunched at the gruesome idea. "But that's not any better than the possible realities."

"Except in that it can't possibly be true," Declan said.

Luscia's shoulders fell.

"What is an eldertross?" Hachiro instantly perked up behind Böwen, his spine erect as he tipped his cap-covered ear their way.

"A terrible, legendary creature hailing from the bleakest alps of the Orallach Mountains," Luscia replied. As he'd kept himself so quiet, she decided she ought to throw the shoto'shi a morsel of knowledge. "The Boreali who could master the eldertross flew them into combat.

Bearing the hooked beak of a raptor, the savage talons of a vulture, and a monolithic body like an eagle, it was said that the wingspan of an eldertross could shadow an entire company of soldiers on the battlefield."

"And that when night fell, none saw it coming," Böwen excitedly said, "for its blackened beak and inky feathers were molten into its snow-white breadth. But you'd be dead before you ever glimpsed it!"

Sensing a conclusion to the elders' conference with Noxolo and Lord Egon, Luscia urged her mare onward. "As the stories go, the eldertross had giant horns like an alpine ibex, arching backward for their rider's control. The stories also bode that they would dismember enemies on command."

"Oh, dear." Hachiro squirmed against his silky restraints. "I admit I'm not very fond of that."

He leaped when Böwen exclaimed, "And they breathed fire too!"

"Well, the mythology remains a bit muddled. Eldertross died off by the late Spire Age." Luscia aimed her gaze on the men cloistered ahead. "But let us never forget the ruthless nature of their riders."

"Who was that?" the haidren to Pilar asked.

Luscia's jaw set firmly. "Clann Ciann."

The night air brimmed with the cool and contented laughter heard only on the road to Ana'Innöx.

Their camp was boxed by pilgrims. Most kept their distance, either out of respect for the Quadren or wariness for its foreign members. Hunched upon a log in front of a homey fire, Luscia polished her najjani brooch with meticulous care. She lovingly swept the leather shammy over the single leaf on her cloak pin, while in her mind, she paced in and out of the master's sanctum. He'd bestowed Luscia the brooch with its unique design for a reason. Where some balked at her appointment to the Order, Master Rohan ordained it fully. She was haidren, yet she was also najjan.

Unless, of course, Master Rohan had only been humoring her.

In positions of power, one could never be sure.

"Are you done with that?" Kumo's thick thumb jutted down to her half-emptied bowl, his large frame squatting in the dirt.

She hardly remembered the beta sitting on the log in the first place.

"Better steal it before Aksel does," said Luscia. Heating her toes, the lycran was mauling a bone from an earlier conquest. Between his snarling and serrated teeth, the thing was stripped.

Leery of the lycran, Kumo swiped the lukewarm bowl of grouse stew.

"He's pretty good, your haidren," said Böwen to the beta, above her head. Sharing his kit with her, he was cleaning his blades beside Luscia. The najjan pointed his dagger through the dancing flames at those sparring on the opposite side.

Between the array of hide tents, Zaethan and his third were squaring off Declan. Her favorite najjani guard split a grin. The weapons glinted beautifully in the firelight as he brandished his crescent wraiths against the pair menacingly.

Like Declan, Zaethan carried a blade in either hand: a gifted kuerre in his right, a Darakaian kopar in his left. He faked a charge, then twirled aside more gracefully than Luscia would've expected, granting his partner a clear opening to strike.

"Wem, brödre," she softly admitted. "He is waedfrel."

Zahra rushed in and, hooking his wraith aside with her sickle sword, made to bludgeon Declan with her spiked shield. Luscia smirked. Unlike her alpha, Zahra was unaccustomed to the aerial style in which he used the force to bounce off the earth and wing around the warrior in a seamless semicircle. Declan landed behind her. Before she could turn, he clocked her in the back of her skull with his central hilt.

Zahra dropped her shield and cradled her head.

The pair of redheaded boys huddling in front of the tents jumped joyfully for their older brother's success. Moments later, their tent flap slapped shut. Declan's parents did not share their children's enthusiasm.

"Oof." Kumo winced. He called to their third, "Tucked your kwihila in too tightly for the night, uni?"

Across the way, Zahra offered the beta what Luscia presumed was an obscene gesture when crooking her middle and forefingers, she faux-spewed them from her nose.

Zaethan kicked the Darakaian shield out of the combat zone. He flexed his shoulders and cocked his head for her to back off, leaving him to defeat Declan alone.

Foot over foot, the burly najjan stalked him in a ring. Zaethan lashed his kuerre and sliced through the top of Declan's boot. However, Declan hopped on the blade, lurching Zaethan downward, and body-slammed him into the pile of leaves.

The najjan rolled off. With a groan, Zaethan popped his spine and regained his footing. He then boosted his mismatched weaponry once more.

Böwen set his dagger on the log and folded his arms in interest. "Got a bit of a chip on his shoulder, hasn't he?"

"Chip? Ano," Kumo stated between sloppy chews of the partially eaten grouse. "That's a kakka-shtàka boulder right there. Ahoté… He always needs to prove himself, yeah? Especially when he thinks no one is watching, even when he was a cub."

Luxiron clashed as Declan swooped under Zaethan's arm and playfully elbowed him in the kidney. Doubling over, Zaethan puffed, but after sucking in a renewing breath, he whipped his kopar, pulling the najjan down by the ankle.

Trundling through the leaves, Declan flipped onto his heels and rammed Zaethan into a tree. He stepped back and allowed the haidren to pant against the bark.

He chuckled when not two minutes later, Zaethan got right back up.

"All right, someone has to make this a fair fight," Böwen said, grabbing his sword from where it leaned in its scabbard against the moss-laden log. He bounded around the fireside and invited Zahra to reenter the combat with him.

"Never thought I'd see my pryde sparring with shadowmen." Still holding his spoon, Kumo rolled a short twist of coarse hair between his fingertips. "Or sharing stew with Boreal's Maji'maia…"

Maji'maia.

Luscia stilled, hearing the Andwele nickname anew. It was Kumo who'd given it to her, after all, and his haidren who'd adopted it. Zaethan had called her that too many times to count. But he hadn't used it every time.

He hadn't used it in that gorge in the Mirajii Forest.

Not when they'd thought they might have been separated for good.

"Kumo," she said, tilting her chin a careful inch. "If I ask you something, will you tell it to me plain?"

"Eh… That depends, Maji'maia." The beta took another scoop of his food. "But I'll give it a Darakaian try."

Luscia focused on the wood burning brightly among the base of the kindling. She lowered her hand to stroke her lycran between his large ears, pulling courage from Aksel's warmth. She abruptly asked, "What does *Domàa'maia* mean?"

Kumo choked. "Where—" He cleared his throat and pounded his chest brusquely. "Where did you hear that?"

"Your haidren called me that once."

"Eh, that… That was just a slip of the tongue, so… kàchà kocho."

Glancing over, she found Kumo awkwardly stirring his stew. There was nothing left but broth.

Luscia shifted her body and mustered her most imperious stare. "What does it mean, Kumo?"

His gigantic frame seemed to fold on itself with one heavy sigh. Kumo looked down into the bowl for many moments. "It is Owàa's name for Àla'maia," he reluctantly said. "His *lover moon.*"

Luscia's lips parted, then shut. Eventually, all she seemed to be able to say was a callous "I see."

Her eyes took to the flames again, her mind spinning with them. She recalled Takoda's tale of their sun and moon. How the illusory Fates had imprisoned Owàa in their service, clipping his wings and enchaining him to the Depths so that he'd rise just high enough to see his lover every morning.

Maybe it had been a slip of Zaethan's tongue.

Her heartbeat ravaged her ears because… because maybe it hadn't been.

Luscia gasped as something akin to happiness soaked in sorrow washed over her. It doused her throat. She sought her stiff jacket collar and loosened it under her rabbit capelet, to breathe better. In a treachery of their own, her eyes wavered above the sparks and embers.

There Zaethan marched between his contenders. Having been knocked in the mouth, he turned and dabbed the blood with the back of his fist. He found her staring.

And letting his weapons hang at his sides, he slowly bit his lip and stood there smiling.

"Maji'maia…" she heard Kumo say.

Luscia tore herself away from his leader. The beta's round features were contorted, the whites of his eyes cinched with worry.

Kumo shook his head and whispered, "He has a heart like Owàa. Don't make him clip his wings for it."

Just then Zaethan hollered, when caught off-guard, Declan's luxiron cut through his tunic sleeve. He took another hit to his side and was beaten down. Bleeding from his bicep, he got back up.

Drinking him in, her heart sank, anchored to the fabled pit in Owàa's story. Luscia clutched the banded kurtfierï at her wrist, needing its restraint more than ever. There was joy to be found in submission, she understood, for self-control was not a selfish gift. Discipline was not the enemy of freedom.

It was the protector.

Dalliances were so dangerous because they sacrificed everyone's future for the individual present. And it was that principle to which Luscia clung, for by the High One, discipline must protect her and him from destroying what was most precious about themselves.

Kumo was correct about his cousin. Zaethan Shà would wield his freedom just to get up again and again for what he wanted. He'd push against every statute in every society until he could fly no more.

Luscia stood from the log and doused the fire without warning. She snapped for Aksel to follow her into the solace of her tent. There and only there could Luscia curse the person who dreamed—if only for a second—of ever taking Zaethan's wings away.

Chapter Twenty Two
Zaethan

His bones ached atop Hellion, unable to see why it was they'd stopped so abruptly. It offered Zaethan some reprieve at least. Dmitri was right about the angle of the ascent. He awkwardly adjusted his numb nether in the saddle—along with the tender bits in front—as he heard a creak of leather nearby. Suddenly, the lengthy woolen cap was stripped away. Cold air blasted his forehead.

And then, like falling water, the smoothest silk slid down his nose when someone ripped the blindfold off his face.

The first thing Zaethan saw were the twined tails of Declan's bushy beard. "Got to wait for the herd," he said, bunching the materials into a satchel bloated with supplies.

Disoriented, Zaethan cricked his neck and let his eyes adjust to the brightness. Though mist waded between the curled roots of the holdreheiim, trees that somehow grew even grander in the uplands, the sky was clear and stark blue from where it could be seen through the canopy's festooned lattice. Macramé tassels spindled from above, exactly like those the Boreali had left hanging in Roüwen. Trinkets and talismans chimed off their intricate knotting. Overhead, light refracted all throughout the wood in bewildering timber prisms.

His sight had been stolen from him for a near week. Although the road was crowded, the pale pilgrims pressing in from either side of the craggy highway, traipsing beneath their dangling prayer charms, felt more of an intrusion than it had when the Quadren had first navigated the streets of Boreal's high clan. Here in the wilderness, it was as if he'd discovered something private, where it was strung in the open.

"We've not yet made camp. Why am I seeing all this?" asked Zaethan.

"You should thank Aniell she is *letting* you see. Like I said," Declan replied, tugging on the lead rope to rotate Hellion toward the head of the party, "we have to wait for the herd to pass."

In turning, Zaethan realized the Enclave's traveling party was stalled near the crest of an upcoming ridgeline. Carts and wagons congested the highway. Pilgrim traffic had bottlenecked at the top, where beyond those amassed on foot, a procession of majestic beasts larger than deer or even caribou, migrated across the road—each boasting a pair of thin, sharp tusks and a single mooselike antler between its fur-laden ears.

Or what Zaethan could only categorize as an antler, for it more resembled a battering ram.

"That's one big cow." From Zaethan's side came the groggy voice of Ira Hastings. The Unitarian haidren shook out his rumpled, dark mahogany-brown hair. "I was gifted a cow by another earl once," he idly said to no one in particular. "I think we ate it with some Wendyllean jellies too. Lovely spread, much like his sister."

Grimacing, Zaethan barked, "Ira!"

People had swiveled around, their pious disapproval etched in the wintry folds of their faces. The Boreali had a soddy sense of humor. And whenever he was childminding the yancy, Zaethan's was just as short lived.

"Niit!" exclaimed Böwen, whose steed was drawing the yancy's reins. Apparently, he'd pulled the unwanted straw that morning. The shadowmen had been taking turns. "We don't eat reingafier!"

"Well, the lycran might," Declan muttered dryly.

"The lycran is a fiend." Böwen tapped his antlered cloak pin keenly. "The reingafier is a steward, like we Set Apart Stewards of the najjani Ranger Aelect. It is the noblest animal to descend the Orallach."

"Hmph," his twin grumbled in his slump behind them. "Is it noble to sneak out of a lady's tent in the wee hours of the morn now, brödre?"

Declan cut his horse around toward his fellow shadowman. "Ock! Enough with the girl, Creyvan!"

Zaethan's attention drifted from their squabbling as it sank into tones too low for his interest or strain. From what he gathered—when not mentioned in witchtongue—said girl had once been maid to their haidren, but one would have supposed her to be the queen of Razôuel.

They'd been fighting about her all week.

He swung about, seeking Kumo and Zahra. He worried for Kai and how the alpha's still-healing leg had fared on the uphill journey. Together, his militia leaders were lost among the warrior stampede toward the rear, where the prydes were filed between strings of wraith-toting shadowmen.

Midway, Zaethan found her instead.

Herded on horseback, Luscia and her family stood out from their most prominent kinsmen, even among the elders' brigade. While her aunt was also adorned in more finery than usual, Luscia was dazzling, head to boot. Beading encrusted her steep collar down to her taut jacket sleeves, which swelled elbow to wrist in a frothy, gem-toned labyrinth. A long gossamer cape, riddled in the same radiant patterns, swooned off her erect shoulders and draped the hindquarters of her dappled mare.

Her stoicism was plain, stripped free of her wild locks. Like her, they'd been tamed into a precise waterfall of intricate braiding down her back. Luscia no longer resembled a warrior who could be baited into skating through the mud by the sheer insults of someone so ordinary as Zaethan.

Ano, he thought. *She is regal.*

She was a princess without a principality.

Though, she wore its crown rested in her tresses—however humble the entwined, witchiron circlet was. It graced her head, much like her aunt's and her brother's. However, Zaethan noticed the same could not be said of her father, who in his rugged wolf-pelt cloak was clearly in the lead. It was as if only one side of Luscia's heritage was being honored, yet Zaethan could tell neither why nor in what respect.

Her chin was stiffly raised. Zaethan knew he did not exist to her in this moment. Luscia's posture stated she knew exactly who she was and why she was there. For that very reason, he found it that much harder to look away.

"In all my days…" Dmitri's utterance reluctantly snapped Zaethan toward his king, who was being attended to by her cohort of influential riders. Unlike Zaethan, his bronze hands had been unbound, and a prominent, fox-fur robe knitted with gemstones surprisingly graced his frame. It was the first time the Boreali had presented him like a king since crossing the border. "Zaeth, have you—" His friend let out a chafed but cheery cough. "Have you ever dreamt of such a place?"

Zaethan followed the angle of his fascination. His gaze widened with Dmitri's.

The herd had cleared. In the distance unfolded a meadow, dressed in emerald and white. At the end of the sprawling field was an enormous, stories-high visage of a bearded man sealing off every conceivable access to the mountain. Moss and rootage foamed from the giant's mouth, an engrossing omen poured out into the wild. From his eyelets, the glossy, silvered rock cried glittering tears—the most reflective water Zaethan could imagine—that fed into a moat of segregation along the base of the summit. It rippled an otherworldly line, keeping the ordinary from encountering whatever lay beyond.

That's it. That is Aksel's Keep, he realized, his mouth slackening.

Zaethan swiveled toward Declan, his current keeper. "How will we get through? There is no entrance."

"The ways of the High One are unseen," the shadowman replied as he leaned closer. "To go further, so yours must be also."

Suddenly, the woolen cap shuttered his eyes, and the world returned to black.

The ground wobbled beneath him as Zaethan was ushered to step down. He sensed they were on the water by the buoyancy underfoot and the rushing sound that echoed from every angle. The air smelled off too. A mineral-rich perfume had filled Zaethan's nose, a not unpleasant yet overpowering odor one sniffed upon retrieving a bucket from the bottom of a coppered well.

His caretaker guided him to sit on an equally wobbly bench and released the grip on his elbow. And once more, the ridiculous stocking cap was yanked off.

Confused, Zaethan found himself stuffed with other people on a kind of ferry, but not on any river to which he was accustomed. For in gazing up, he saw a pasture of rocky pendants spearing toward his head.

The river was underground.

Above, the stalactites were striated in resplendent veins of unmined ore. Zaethan could not name it, but it was assuredly valuable. The Boreali didn't trade the resources they most prized. It would fetch a heap in Marketown; craftsmen shopped with their eyes as much as anyone else, and Orynthia's most greedy would certainly salivate for a fleck of the frosty ore hidden there. Bone white, it shimmered against a webbing of bizarre beads that dangled among the deadly spikes, as if the subterranean shaft had been draped with a roof of blue-green crystals. Warm mist curled up Zaethan's back from the water and coalesced under the lambent, teal aura that lit the entire cave system softly aglow.

"Lune-worms? Ah… as I suspected," said Hachiro, confirming the source of bioluminescence with the individual pressed against Zaethan's opposite side. Shoots of the shoto'shi's black hair scraped Zaethan's chin, when like a spiney tumbleweed, he stuffed himself back into place atop the ferry bench to resume his notetaking.

Zaethan popped his knuckles. Someone had given Hachiro his kakka-shtàka quill.

Turning in the snug space, he made to say as much to his neighbor but lurched backward after sighting him.

To say that the shadowman was leering at Zaethan would have been miraculous, given that he had no eyes. Or rather, he did, but they were trapped behind screens of smooth skin melded over, brow to cheek.

Glowing slit stones were implanted in his flesh, descending from the pupils he no longer employed. Disturbingly, the shadowman twisted his short blond beard at an angle, as if to examine Zaethan through the unnatural barrier of flesh.

Somehow, he was certain the man could.

Zaethan gulped.

Unable to shirk the shadowman's fixation, he glanced about the ferry, seeing that Ira too had been wedged farther down the bench. Standing shoulder against shoulder on the tight ferry were a sampling of elders, as well as Luscia's guardsmen, except for her captaen. She must have boarded another vessel with Dmitri—perhaps the ferry ahead. The underground river was littered with incoming travelers being escorted from a set of inscribed stairwells. Zaethan could not discern how the passageway connected to the surface, only that the pilgrims kept brimming the mouth of it.

Thick ropes were strung above him. What he guessed was a pulley system appeared to link the ferries in line together. Those clustered at the middle reached up and walked their hands one over the other in tandem, heaving the vessel into motion. Their lips moved too, though Zaethan couldn't hear it coming from their mouths, but rather from the cave walls. Their spellbinding song, told in a tongue he did not share, reverberated throughout the chamber, ushering their multitudes down a river of skyless starlight.

Releasing the drenched rope, Declan elbowed his fellow Boreali and wiggled forward. Böwen thereafter. They both were a welcomed display as Zaethan's eyes adjusted to the spectral darkness. A contrast to their conventional appearance, the other shadowmen posted around the ferry bore more resemblance to the spooky figure next door.

Zaethan released a shallow breath when his creepy neighbor shifted to face Declan and Böwen instead.

"Allöh'jomn'yeh, Armaeger Lancil," Declan said formally to the sightless warrior.

Stoically, the armaeger nodded at them both, though only Declan had spoken.

At that, Zaethan tried to put another inch between him and the unusual shadowman, stepping onto Hachiro's roomy robes. He cleared his throat uneasily.

Declan leaked a sly grin. "Ock, it's all right. Tenders of the keep make a *special* pledge to watch and listen before all other acts—including my sorry invitation for small talk."

"Pretty hard pledge to fulfill, factoring in that whole… situation." Zaethan gestured toward the shadowman's fused skin.

"Yes, explain how the procedure is performed." Hachiro popped around him, primed to write. The feather of his quill tickled Zaethan's mouth. "And the tissue, from where is it retrieved?"

Zaethan growled. "Owàa's chains, Hachi!"

Noiselessly, and with eerie speed, the disfigured shadowman rotated and broke his wordlessness. "Do not blaspheme the River Lux, lowlander." The lethal arcs of his crescent wraiths were directed at Zaethan from above the shoulders of his pewter-and-snow-laced tunic. Moisture spat and crackled against the corrosive edge of each lustrous blade, hovered over the steam of the unusually warm waters.

"As I keep repeating, Lord Darakai." The shoto'shi not-so-inconspicuously breathed into his ear. "The House of Boreal is a true theocracy. Best play along with their unfounded superstitions, lest we be tossed overboard with the rest of their good sense."

As Hachiro's feather climbed farther into his nose, Zaethan ripped the quill out of his grasp, and instead of at its owner, he chucked the annoying thing into the river.

Rapidly, the shadowman speared out his arm and caught it midair—right before a mammoth eel shot out of the twinkling waters. Snapping its jaws after the quill, the eel narrowly missed his alabaster fingers.

Without comment, the blind shadowman returned the quill to the stunned haidren to Pilar.

Declan chuckled at Zaethan's face. "It is not with sight that we see in the darkness." He then tapped the corner of Hachiro's journal. "Oh, and it's taken from the left arse cheek, by the way."

If one didn't need their eyes to see—to move with such alacrity—one wasn't human. Not entirely. The "tender" of the keep couldn't be. Zaethan tempted another peek toward the shadowman.

He was already staring back.

"Ever intriguing," Hachiro replied, scribbling enthusiastically. "The male posterior is a plentiful source, no doubt—"

"Where is my king?" Zaethan briskly asked Declan.

"Beside Ana'Sere at the helm of the next ferry," he replied, confirming Zaethan's suspicions. "Naturally, our haidren and her family should sail into the keep alongside the captaen's eldest brother."

"His brother?"

"Wem, the captaen is a Bailefore."

Böwen crossed his arms as his golden brow arched higher. Under the lune-worms, his curious expression took on a sickly, bluish hue. "Aurynth's Watchman… Have you not yet put it together, Lord Haidren? Captaen Bailefore is descendent of Aksel. His family have been the warden to this keep every generation since his death."

"The captaen's brother just assumed his position as the shepherd," Declan said. Reverence soaked his enunciation, smoothing out his words.

"Shepherd of what?"

Declan and the other guard looked at each other with weighted pause. Eventually, Declan responded. "The shepherd of everything you are about to witness on this mount."

The mist cloyed Zaethan's neckline, a deceptively warm yet tightening noose, cinching with every surmounting unknown that awaited him at the end of the river.

The fate of the realm, of Dmitri and his Quadren, was in the hands of those who never gave straight answers. He felt it then—twining about his throat—just how steeply priced the gamble they'd made that night in the Scaly Stowaway really was, when choosing to flee to Boreal. It wagered on a people he did not know, from a land he might never understand. And were they to ever part their mists fully for an outsider… Zaethan very much feared what he'd find.

"Aksel's Keep is possessed by these Bailefores then?" Hachiro queried overtop his binding.

"Possession is of no consequence here," Böwen said. He released a forefinger from his fisted chin to gesture upstream toward the next shrouded ferry. "My point was that inferior only to the line of Tiergan and Ana'Sere herself, the Bailefore name is the most renowned throughout Boreal. Aniell knows he would never tell anyone, but even being the second son, our captaen was made famous the day he was born."

Zaethan walked behind the captaen and his brother, assessing the new "shepherd" who had sent everyone abuzz. It put Zaethan on edge—the silent slip to his gait as he led their king's party through a vast courtyard within the keep… how his serene voice babbled like a brook when he leaned down in deference to speak to his haidren, who strolled between him and her Captaen Bailefore. Their likeness was unmistakable, though the elder brother was broader in the ribs and boxier in the jaw. The tactical arsenal strapped about the shepherd's trained build promised violence when his peaceful mannerisms portrayed anything but.

It was confusing. And Zaethan hated being confused.

He decelerated and instead fell in step with his fellow Darakaians toward the back, most of whom were preoccupied with the peculiarities of their overcrowded cage.

Pilgrims bustled throughout the metropolis of ringed holdreheiim, the people eagerly convalescing around an immense stone dais exalted at the center. Where Roüwen was a forested fortress, Aksel's Keep contained a grove within itself, completely fortified by the same striated stone left unmined in the caverns. These glittering walls were a collage of engraved histories. Some of the muralled battlements were timeless, erected by nature's hands; others served as the bridges of men.

Music rallied from nowhere and everywhere at once. Lutes, fiddles, chimes, and deep-bellowing drums carried around the travelers as they returned to their skyward villa. Built in a massive circle, rings of timbered dwellings encompassed the courtyard, interconnecting the holdreheiim into one harmonious, hollow column. The vine-shrouded railings faced inward, whispering a skin-crawling caution up Zaethan's spine.

Whatever event was to unfold at the top of that dais beckoned spectators.

Contrary to his beta, and even his third—to her usual denial—Zaethan was not swept away by the enchanting ambience, the ribbons and tassels fluttering off every carved balustrade, or the leafy autumnal draperies woven with gem-cut totems and charms.

Even a gold-plated cell was still a cell, one the Darakaians had just gotten themselves locked into.

"Six stories. Ano—seven," Zaethan murmured to Kumo and

Zahra, correcting his count of the massively ringed verandas. Over his hunched shoulder, he took inventory of the distinct lack of gateways along the exterior wall, at least any that he could trace through the trees. "I don't see another exit besides the gate to the river grotto. Yeye? Either of you?"

Zaethan whacked Kumo, retrieving his attention.

"Oh, ano zà. Meme ano'qondai, cousin, but I think we, uh… I think we might be trapped."

"They dragged us from our jail yard just to bring us to this overpopulated prison. Shtàka." Zahra's gold irises tapered after a family hustling by, both mother and father carefully shielding their horde of cubs from a brush with the dirty Darakaians. The older woman hobbling her girth after them spat toward Zahra's feet and grumbled something in passing. "These moody mystics don't even want us here, yeah? So then why *are* we?"

"Alpha Zà." Jabari thrust his head of coils between Zaethan and Zahra. "Fancy doors for fancy feet ahead. Taking cubs a looksie but keeping others out. See? Hillman track elderman tricks before the elderman track him first."

"No clan elder is trying to track you down, Jabari, you paranoid Yowekaon," Zaethan griped, sidestepping just enough to covertly sight a pair of ornate doors cast in witchiron and set into a protruding stone socket amid the lower stories of the enormous villa.

To Jabari's account, the doors were heavily guarded. A dozen sightless shadowmen bookended the entrance to whichever few were allowed access. One by one, elders were excusing themselves from their haidren's company to reunite with their wives and children. At their Clann Darragh's nod, they escorted their families toward the doors and discreetly, worshipfully even, removed their shoes despite the cold and slipped inside.

As their group came closer, Zaethan stilled, looking between the barrage of busy legs. A humble row of boots rested before the shadowmen. Ironically, it was the most powerful who had taken them off.

"I tried to convince her to let you stay with us," someone randomly said.

Zaethan whirled on his heel.

Luscia's brother stood off to the side, his fingers happily knit before him. He wore a slanted smile. It suggested he felt nearly as awkward as the Darakaians who'd stepped away to grant them room.

He scratched his clean-shaven scalp just below the stout knot gathered at his crown. His witchiron circlet cradled it. He pressed his palm against his bead-covered jacket. "I'm Phalen… Phalen Tiergan?"

Zaethan shifted his weight. "Uni—yes, I know. We've already met."

"Well, I'm usually covered in soot. Never hurts to double-check." His unusual eyes sparkled unevenly under his faint brows. "I merely wanted to let you know that I asked her to reconsider. Not all of us are such traditionalists. It's unfortunate, the issue of your…"

"Birth?" Zaethan bit out. He felt the boy's aunt watching him from where she shadowed Luscia, made taller by the vigilant hawk perched on her shoulder. Zaethan didn't ask to which "her" Phalen had referred.

He wasn't sure he wished to know.

"Those doors," Zaethan said instead. "Where do they lead?"

Phalen sighed, causing his faintly freckled smile to hook even more crookedly. "Niit. That, I'm afraid, *no one* agreed to. Come," he said and jerked his head in the opposite direction toward a corkscrewed, timber stair. "Let me walk you and your friends to the Athdaras' lodgings. From what I heard, you could use an extra endorsement with the lady of the house."

Zaethan snorted but obliged, trailing Luscia's brother through the gathering masses. He was different than his sister, more a straightforward kind of person who seemed to carry out matters for the simple joy of doing them and nothing more. No agenda. No smoke and charade.

Quite different from her indeed.

As they marched up the packed stairs, it was not lost on Zaethan the way the young man habitually looked back at him, inquiring about his prydes and their comfort in Boreal. Or the minor twerk to Phalen's neck every time they bypassed a hateful discussion about Darakai along the way.

Neither was it missed that he'd stopped in his tracks, if but for a moment, when a pilgrim had spewed something under breath about the bastard haidren cross-caste once known as Zaethan Kasim.

✦

Phalen's peculiar bode of support proved as ineffective with Lady Athdara as Zaethan's attempts to keep Declan's little brothers from crawling all over him at the dinner table.

While the accommodations were snug, they were crammed with company. Helpings of cousins—up to his third removed, according to Declan—were gathered like cooked carrots down the impossibly long benches. Zaethan and his leads stood out like charred beets among their festive feast. He teased a smirk at Kumo when one of the boys scuttled between his boots.

His beta's big cheeks rounded, stifling a chortle.

They'd never seen so many redheads in their life.

With a hoot, Zahra tossed Zaethan another griddle cake. He reached around the smaller, squirrely cub who had stood on the bench to better tinker with the twin rings pierced through his brow. As he stretched across a platter of braised venison, there came a tug from the base of his nape.

Zaethan swiveled around. "Boo!" he exclaimed to the cub on the floor behind him.

The boy released one of his dreaded locs and giggled against the wall. Zaethan then chomped the air after the brother's runaway fingers as they scurried together into their dungeon beneath the table.

Those above it were far less amused.

Women flanked Lady Egon—presumably her sisters, for they all looked the same to Zaethan. They glowered over their tight-lipped chews and, with shaking heads, rushed acidic whispers into each other's ears. Adding nothing beyond a humph and haw, Lord Egon listened vigilantly, for his mustache didn't leave the rim of his growler.

"What happened to this?" Zahra asked at random, raising the loc the boy had dropped. It was shorter than the rest, nibbled chunks of hair missing.

Zaethan grabbed it from her. "That stupid rat!"

"*That stupid rat!*" the Athdara boys sang.

"Scüries." Declan harrumphed down the bench. "Mangy shrub-busters. Those three-tailed pests litter our house in Roüwen."

One of the ladies shrieked and clawed at her heart when the littlest cub shimmied up Zaethan's leg.

The boy weaseled into their guest's lap unexpectedly and started clanking the spoons in swordplay. But that was not why Lady Athdara shot to her feet, pounded the table, and screeched for her son to get off their guest. It's also not what made him burst into tears when he slid down.

Zaethan's lip curled as he followed suit. Wadding his napkin, he freed himself and marched toward the door, though not without slamming the soiled fabric pointedly beside her plate. "To wash it clean once I've left the room," he said and stormed onto the terrace.

Outside, the evening had fallen with a shock, the cold causing

Zaethan to stuff his hands under his arms as he stomped down the walkway of the third story. He hugged the bark of the holdreheiim, dodging people as best he could. It did not stop them from saying what they did. To the Boreali, he was just "Darakaian swine," like the rest.

He spotted the end of Kai's crutch where he was huddled against the railing with Takoda. Sidling up to them, Zaethan thrust his elbows overtop the rail. He was angry. He was overrun. And he was much too tired to stew about either.

"Eh, owàamo, Alpha Zà," the alpha of the Mirajii Pryde said. Kai cocked his chin. "Your night as rough as ours?"

Zaethan blew out a breath. "I swear that woman has already dug my grave somewhere in the woods."

"You're too pagan for this ground!" Takoda laughed bitterly as he drummed his fingers on the wood. Each had been awarded with Ira's lost jewels. His deep eyes followed a man who passed before he asked, "Alpha Zà, do you know what they are doing down there?"

Over the railing, Zaethan saw that pilgrims were congregated in the courtyard on their hands and knees. However, they weren't praying… They were planting. Their arms were buried in the dirt, stuffing a trench around the base of the stone dais. Tied to their ankles, bells jangled as cubs ran ahead of their parents to offer a spare vegetable or a stalk of grain.

He understood why his men were uneasy. "Those are everyone's rations. We won't have enough for the journey home."

"Unless some of us are never to return…" Takoda eased off from the railing. Below it, a few clanswomen were scattering dried red flowers around the raised platform.

Their offering looked like sprays of blood.

"I'm pretty sure that's an altar," said Kai, a tremble in his tenor. His overlarge eyes swerved toward Zaethan. "Alpha Zà, tell me you know what the Boreali are planning to sacrifice here."

His mouth went dry. "Ano… meme ano'qondai…"

Takoda's hand found Zaethan's forearm. It constricted in panic as the warrior stated, "What is more precious than a king?"

Chapter Twenty Three
Luscia

Prayers strummed her stirring lips as Luscia entered the Sanctuary of Scribes. Her frail notes harmonized with the unceasing song of the dozens who rested cross-legged before their squat pedestals, the age-old hymn anointing the barest voids of the lengthy echo chamber.

An ensemble of tinkering goosequills, trickling water, and turning pages brought the carefully oiled walls to life, reverberating off their wine-hued wood. Luscia was essentially striding through an ancient drum. Inside, the acoustics were well-preserved. Nothing had been altered since the Spire Age. Still cradled by the timber of the first Viridi tree ever brought to the keep, the sanctuary by design stood more akin to a modest manger than any temple.

After all, the words studied and transcribed there were for the nour-ishment of a people. Not their pride.

The stone walkway was stamped in psalms and carved a dividing line under the arched, wood-slat ceiling. Scribes flanked it in rows of ten. They numbered twenty in all, in balance to the Enclave they served. Folded in linsilk robes, they intently focused on their translucent vellums and epochal texts. Steam rose off the warm, shimmering waters that trickled through the roof and into the golden basins fixed between each stone pedestal. There, the truths of Aurynth tested the truth of man as it was being written—yet another parallel to the Prajja'Veriidim inside the Grand Tabernacle.

At the end of the chamber rested the overseeing sage, as gray as the tablet he translated. Together Boreal's wisest sang in concert with their concentration. The music departed their hunched bodies, beau-tiful as it was profound. Mortal melodies made full and melancholy by each singer's confusion, by their understanding… by their wrestle and their wonder.

The scribal sect sang for Aniell. And undergirding their echo, as in their lumin-laced bones, He was singing right back.

Luscia thought it surreal that long ago, Aksel Bailefore had chanted the same while treading the pulsating stonework underfoot. Her toes wiggled inside her upturned boots as she walked, each tingling from their closeness that morning to the Dönumn's precarious bank. She'd chosen to exhaust half the day there, having hoped its waters would calm the anxiety thrumming inside her middle. But the feeling hadn't fled Luscia in its holy presence. The feeling had only increased and continued to compound as she meekly approached her king, knowing full well why he had commanded her to a meeting.

Not asked….

Not requested…

Commanded.

At the opposite end of the sanctuary, a faded floor-to-ceiling mural of an arrow-pierced man emerging from a pool ornamented the barrier between Dmitri and the site of its inspiration. Though he did not know it, that single barrier was far more literal than he could ever imagine. It was as close to the consecrated fount as the Enclave would allow Luscia to take him.

For the fount lay just on the other side.

She had not fought the elders' ruling. Truth was precious… dangerous and, in that, vulnerable to the abuses of a king or his Quadren. Alongside her kinsmen, Luscia served an ultimate sovereign, one who had little use for a crown yet claimed every throne in His kingdom.

The historic picture outlined Dmitri's gaunt shoulders, the violent angles evident even through the bulk of his fur mantle. With his hands cupped behind his back, Orynthia's outlaw king stared up at the central story etched onto every Boreali heart—its original madder, lichen, and lazurite dyes the only source of dedicated color in the room.

Delicately, Luscia came beside him.

Moments passed before Dmitri's head shifted to the side and he asked, "Is your faith a painting or a song, Lady Boreal?"

She stammered. "I'm not sure I follow, Your Majesty."

His elegant fingers moved toward the mural consuming his stare. "Well, a painting is concrete… tangible, comprehensible, for it is set and finished," he said. "Whereas a song, while arguably more evocative, is far less realized."

Thrown by his query, Luscia eased her weight onto her other heel. Dmitri was not notably religious. At least, not outside his precautionary visits to the Temple of the Fates in Bastiion. Her own faith was so different from his; that was if he really ascribed to it. To Luscia, belief was scored in the spirit, and to describe that so mundanely seemed borderline profane.

She answered him honestly while peering up at the image of Tiergan the First. "Faith is hard to categorize."

"Especially when I have placed it so preciously in other people," said Dmitri tersely, without looking to her. "I've found my belief in them can be quite isolating, Lady Boreal."

"Belief may be an independent feat, but faith is always communal."

He made a weak, uncharitable noise. "You mean, in the same way you've refrained from communing with Master Rohan?"

Luscia's stomach dropped when her king turned and confronted her. Lavender stained the taut skin that pinched his rich, hazel eyes. Dmitri's dark lashes were stuck together in sparse clumps, as if they'd dried that way after a wash of tears.

"My word in coming here was sincere, Your Majesty," she replied, imploring him. "It is our tradition at Ana'Innöx that the najjani master meets with the eldership of each clan before the presiding haidren. I'm obligated to wait my turn is all, while my other duties are being fulfilled—"

"What duty is more important than protecting Orynthia from usurpers!" He coughed in frustration. Her focus latched onto the yellow sputum he dismissively wiped off his mouth. "Nyack Kasim is set to march on Razôuel, Luscia. Razôuel, our *sole* ally. When Zaeth's scout at last returns, what word am I to send to them, hm? That I beg the queen for aid without the ability to grant it in return because my haidren to Boreal can't be bothered to cut in line?"

"Wem, I understand, but my argument for the najjan will be heard more effectively in due course. If you can wait for me to speak with Master Rohan—"

"It takes a lot longer to speak than it does to strike." Her king grabbed Luscia by the biceps, shocking her with his unconventional touch. "We don't know if and where Darakai has mobilized their Mworran legions, but we do know that the chief warlord will not hesitate to strike once he has them in place. Orynthia cannot afford *your* hesitation. I command you. No, I outright beg you, Luscia… entreat the master to dedicate his najjan tonight."

She wanted to vomit. Met with his unadulterated desperation, she knew full well she couldn't soothe it the way he wished. Her vows would not allow it. Not yet.

Luscia swallowed roughly, having never denied her king anything before. Her jaw shook when she said as respectfully as possible, "Tonight is the fete."

His grip dropped from her rigid arms. "You are refusing the direct order of your regent… for *merrymaking?*" Dmitri backstepped a portion, coughing more as he shook his hardening frown left to right. It had drained of its newfound warmth; his disappointment radiated from the haggard face of a beggar rather than the fullness of a king. "Boreal was supposed to be Orynthia's salvation," he whispered. In despair, his voice became so small that Luscia was probably the only person in the entire sanctuary who could hear it. "I thought I could trust you. But you're serving your own agenda just like everybody else."

She plunged her hand into her heavy pocket and trapped the pouch of freshly mixed vials between his palms. Luscia held them together with all her might. "We are going to save our people—Boreal, the Quadren, all of us. I promise you salvation *is* coming."

"Even my body is growing weary of your broken promises," he said, pulling his fingers tiredly out of her hands. The glass jingled as Dmitri waved the pouch with her failing assurances. "Soon, there won't be anyone to inherit what you say you're going to save. My time is running out. Fast."

She couldn't stop her lips from asking it. "And if it does?"

Dmitri's jaw set harder than Orallach ice. He snatched his walking cane from where it was propped against the wall. "Every king has a contingency plan, Luscia. And I *can* promise, I will never forgive you if I'm made to leverage mine."

Red peppered his paled cheeks. Boiling with mistrust, the king of Orynthia spun on his heel.

His leaving assaulted her heart like an unquenched storm. Abandoned there before the very picture of her own salvation, it thundered and raged inside her being—a timeless dichotomy that every Boreali haidren had endured before she'd inherited the mysterious seat. She could not temper its demand nor the depression it waged. Luscia could only withstand its surmounting gale, meditate on the conviction beneath her feet, and pray she would not falter.

Luxiron urns were tipped and poured over her bared arms. The cleansing, mystical water splashed to the warming stone pedestal, comforting Luscia's soles. Her toes nakedly poked past the exquisitely beaded sheets of her gossamer gown. Like mirror-spun cobwebs, the pearly linsilk glittered at her no matter the angle. She fidgeted under her handmaidens' tender toweling—having been washed in their sight. Every squirm shivered the strips of tiny bells that were tied waist to ankle beneath Luscia's filmy layers.

She swore the perpetual tinkling was louder than any gong.

Luscia offered Mila a nervous smile, relieved she'd been allowed to include a familiar face in the sacramental preparation for the evening's much-awaited fete.

Imitating a ripple from the place she stood, candle flames danced in symmetrical circles behind Mila as she threaded a cloth between Luscia's fingers. Three fair-haired girls moved around the pair, picking up their brushes and dabbing them into gold-plated bowls of iridescent paint. Together, they decorated Luscia in elaborate, shimmering designs. The youthful handmaidens moved smoothly and steadily. After all, chosen from the best families, they'd been painting such things their entire lives. Composed of crushed lumilores and Boreali herbs, perfumed by chalky ennus and glowing eüpharsis pods, each swirl that coated Luscia's skin symbolized the lumin itself, active and alive within her very-anxious being.

"I am proud to share this Great Harvest with you," said Luscia quietly. She locked onto Mila's eager, deep-sea eyes. As Northern cross-castes were generally barred from the border, it was her first Ana'Innöx—and her first true encounter with their homeland and the people who sprouted from its shores. As Luscia was participating as haidren, in other ways it served as her first Ana'Innöx too. "Tadöm for letting me steal you from Böwen tonight. I know you've surpassed my menial tending. I just, well… I suppose I just needed a friend here."

"Once a palace attendant, always your attendant, Lady Luscia." Her rosy lips cast a sweet grin. She gently slipped Luscia's radials on toward her knuckles with care. "I may not know where my place is, but I know it's near you."

Luscia sighed as another girl palm-rolled her wild tresses into long twists, thick enough to stitch and thread with gemstones toward the ends. "Mila, you cannot know how often I agonized after sending you away from Bastiion. The threats that must have barraged your journey. And to brave them in such a condition…"

She would never forget finding Mila like that—crumpled in shame, her dress in tatters, and at Lord Felix Ambrose's feet. Just the thought of him made Luscia sick. Made her want to kill him all over again.

Though he'd later mutated into something far more monstrous than the predator inside that courtesan alcove, turning him to dust had been too good for the late earl of Agoston.

"Niit, milady," Mila replied. Her newfound accent chimed confidently off her tongue. "It was you who'd saved me from much worse. All of us, really. Even my little sister, for you'd given us Böwen. I don't think my mother would have ever recovered, had he not rescued Kellen from that heinous creature during our trek through the Valley of Fahime—"

Luscia waved off the girl who was embellishing her toes and bent down atop the pedestal. "There was another devoid creature that far north in the valley?"

"Wem." Mila nodded. "It stalked us all the way toward the border. Böwen tried to tell the Enclave about it when we arrived, but they only cared to argue about my ancestry."

Concern grappled Luscia's gut, turning it upside down. But before she could ask more, the rounded door creaked open, and her aunt emerged from the deeper hollows of the ancient stronghold. Her approach was inaudible, except for the bell-laden anklets jangling with her footsteps.

There would be nothing silent about Aksel's Keep that night.

"Allöh'jomn'yeh, Ana'Mere." The serving girls greeted her in reverent unison. They broke away from the pedestal as their sil'haidren padded authoritatively into the sanctified space.

For a woman so fine and who'd seemed to have grown so frail, Alora had an unassertive presence that commanded the air's every particle. Luscia felt her approaching occupation sweep her painted forearms—felt it stirring behind the veil, swishing through the threads. But she was too afraid to open her Sight to the *Other*.

Her aunt was already there.

And were they to meet on that mysterious light-charged plane,

Luscia suspected that her secrets, her potentially heretical secrets, might be revealed. Her handle on the lumin and her unsanctioned exercise was neither safe nor comprehendible. Even if it were, Luscia's burgeoning power could get her banished—possibly even killed, were someone like Elder Hinrük the high clansman and not her father.

Yet Luscia wasn't the only one hiding in plain sight anymore. For whatever purpose, Alora had been lying too. About Luscia's lifelong episodes. About the tonics that were supposed to prevent them. She collected critical news from suspicious sources and withheld intel from their king.

Had at times withheld from Luscia.

With her stare fixed ahead, Luscia wrestled the rippling in her mind, tugging the veil tightly closed, as she fought the urge to see her aunt in her truest form.

As Alora planted herself behind Mila's shoulder, her right iris spun and shone with the same luster as the markings laminating the crinkled skin of her neck. The designs spread all the way toward her pinched temples. Her study was caustic as it scaled Luscia's person.

Mila needn't be told to move, for she readily sidestepped and melted into the candlelight maze.

Luscia wished she could steal away too.

Within seconds, her aunt murmured for one of the girls to redo a smeared trace of artwork over the unsheltered scar along her successor's neck. Gave further instruction to comb out a selection of hairs, yet twist others more securely. Releasing a loaded exhale, Alora requested a cloth, and at the rim of the pedestal, she stretched onto her own bare toes.

"When we are clean, we shine as we ought," she mused aloud and polished the luxiron solrahs pierced through Luscia's septum. Though muted in pattern, Alora's frothy linsilk skirt swished when she retreated to her original footing, a healthy yard from the niece she had raised.

"Tadöm, aunt," Luscia said and straightened to her full height.

Alora's eyes broadened almost imperceptibly. She hiked her nose a fraction in response. Her own solrahs gleamed with the micro-movement, just like the floor-length veil of gemstones that cloaked her steely-white hair. In another glimpse, she might have easily resembled a widow.

Motioning for the handmaidens, she advised them, "Lift the Eiide Corün over the haidren's head. Wem, do it carefully."

Heralded the haidren's Wreath of Wisdom, the Eiide Corün was nestled onto Luscia's head, over the luxiron circlet. Slowly, the crystalline strands descended either side of her face in shimmering curtains so long, their tips fringed the corseted stays that crisscrossed her navel. She'd not worn the legendary headdress since her Seating, at Dmitri's coronation. It was heavy, though not nearly as heavy as the imperviable repute of the woman from whom she'd inherited its load.

"To the right—there. Now she's perfectly suited for an event of such glory," said Alora.

Luscia softened under her aunt's rare praise, only to completely deflate a moment later.

"Tonight is the only opportunity our brethren receive to see a hint of what lies beyond the veil. Even if our haidren refuses to pass beyond it herself."

Shtàka, she knows I'm avoiding her within the Other, Luscia thought as she rooted herself in place. Fidgeting would only spur her aunt's investigation.

The fete was of pivotal importance. Though no one truly saw the threads like the heirs of Tiergan the First, once a year at Ana'Innöx, the Boreali caught glints. And in them, they caught hope. Luscia could envision it as if she were still an ordinary little girl, instead of an anointed woman, how the night would annually light up over Alora, dependably and responsive. How it'd shudder amid Boreal's cloud of colors. Those faint sparks were the only evidence of Aniell's lumin her people had ever had since the Brightling—Tiergan's most faithful heir, the one who'd established the ritual centuries ago—had walked among them.

"In the spirit of good health, I'm leery to test the Sight, Ana'Mere. Not when we are on the precipice of the very glory you speak."

Alora's thin lips pursed skeptically while her radiant gaze sailed about Luscia's uneasy form, reading the tone of the threads as she'd so often described doing. It wasn't the first time Luscia felt contempt for that unique attribute of her aunt's Higher Gifting, not sharing it herself.

"Depart from us," Alora stated, dismissing the handmaidens yet still hooked onto Luscia. "Find your families before the fete. Tredae'Aurynth, ladies."

They flitted out the back door. Mila was last to leave. Luscia forced a grin, regrettably sending her off to freedom.

When the hinges squealed shut, Alora stuffed her fingertips behind the sash at her middle. She exposed a vial. Luscia's heart thudded when she came forward and held it out for her to take. "I should have considered the stress of the fete," said Alora. "Here, I carried a spare dose in case of any incidents. We cannot let you falter on the dais, nor can you avoid the *Other* out of fear. Not tonight."

Luscia's hands remained at her side. "I took a dose just yesterday," she made herself say, despising the taste of falsehood.

Every drop made them more alike.

"A special blend to boost the effects, not endanger them," her aunt replied, hoisting the vial higher.

Gradually, Luscia grabbed it, so as not to betray the fact that her last dose had really been in Darakai. She hadn't consumed the tonic in two months—a not-so-curious correlation to the timing of her last episode.

Her aunt waited for her to bring it to her mouth.

Luscia's fingers clenched rigidly around the glass. "Niit," she whispered.

She stepped closer to the pedestal. Alora's faint brows plunged into a ravine of disappointment. "Weh'dajjeni Dönumn, weh'dajjeni Lux, Luscia! You are a vessel identical to these urns, *not* the water within them. Or have you forgotten what is at stake?"

"All of Orynthia is left to fall apart while I bear that burden every day, for Boreal. For Aniell!" Luscia burst aloud. "Of course I know what is at stake!"

"And yet you brought the king so close to its shoreline," Alora accused.

Her cheeks reddened, toasted by a confusing flare of shame and determination. "He didn't see it," Luscia told her aunt. "He hasn't learned what's on the other side of the wall."

"And he shall not," Alora abrasively declared. "You've imperiled us enough by bringing them here—by circumventing my voice of reason with your father. The Enclave is in absolute upset. Pray tonight allays their storm, niece."

Defensively, Luscia caged her arms. "The High One knows I couldn't fracture the Quadren any further."

An unusually bitter smirk contorted Alora's faintly feathered lips, then after a moment, she asked, "Do you remember the parable of the farmer and his apple?"

"You know I do." She nearly scoffed. Every child was taught that folk story early in their principle—one repeated by all three of Luscia's parental figures, including her aunt.

"Allow me to complete your adornment and dress you with its

wisdom before you lead our precious people this evening, in my place." Alora paced about the pedestal, deliberate yet unrushed, despite the thousands celebrating clamorously throughout the courtyard.

Luscia set her teeth.

"There was once a man in a hungering village. At the center of the square, the elders brought grain from their stores to feed the people. Lines formed to the end of the farthest holdreheiim, and among them stood the tallest tree for miles. Within its canopy, the man saw hanging a golden apple. Its flesh cast a mouthwatering gloss as the line continued to grow, but instead of adding to its number, the man toiled through the afternoon, climbing up the tree's heights. As the sun set, he eventually claimed his prize.

"He bit into the fruit, and it was delicious—better than he imagined. The man finished his meal, belly full, and returned to the square. But upon arriving, his stomach turned over, betraying him in pain, for the grain was all gone. The sweetness on his tongue quickly soured." Alora stopped just below Luscia's stony chin. "Because in chasing what he himself craved, he had doomed his entire family to starve."

Luscia blinked back hot emotion and pledged. "I would never let my family starve, Ana'Mere."

"Words that only the dawn can corroborate," her predecessor replied, seeding worry in Luscia like the Boreali who had sacrificially seeded the soil outside.

She heard their hope, their expectation, thundering through the walls and into her heart.

And it scared her.

It scared her more than any man or the blade he brandished. Gulping, Luscia's fist coasted over Ferocity, her mother's dagger, strapped to her thigh beneath her gauzy skirts.

Alora guided the vial in Luscia's hand upward. "You have started to crave many things, Luscia." A tear glistened her blonde lashes, disturbing her grave composure. "And when we crave what we should not, everyone you love starves for it. So, drink your portion, lu'Lycran, and feed them what you know to be right."

Rattled by her aunt's intensity, Luscia gingerly set the vial against her lips and tilted it back. She hated how the astringent fluid rushed over her tongue like an unsolicited houseguest.

With a nod of relief, Alora helped Luscia down to the floor and escorted her to the primary threshold toward the balcony. But her aunt did not follow any farther. Instead, Alora gestured to be left in private.

"Se'lah Aurynth," she whispered to herself.

Luscia finished the proverb when her aunt did not. "Rul'Aniell."

The masses roared when Luscia pushed the doors apart. Glancing back, she saw Alora pressing a hand to her stomach as if she too had become sick. The bewildering posture of her predecessor made Luscia queasier than ever. Facing forward, she sucked in a breath and made for the entwined stairs. At the top she turned back, fleetingly alone.

Sticking a finger down her throat, she spit her aunt's tonic onto the timber of their ancestors and into her own shadow.

Saddled upon mammoth reingafier, Marek and his elder brother flanked the dais where Boreali from across the highlands festively pressed in. Luscia begged Aniell that the optic would serve her with the elders of Clan Ciann. It'd been his idea, one she was unsure would work.

Segregated from the rest of the Enclave, they'd sheltered themselves under the far terrace, no doubt foretelling her assured missteps. Just as his valiant descendants beside her, Aksel Bailefore had too hailed from the bitters of the Orallach range. It helped that Aksel had flown the last eldertross into battle at this very site. Thus, the image of the Bailefores' support should be strong, strong enough to thwart even Elder Hinrük's most poisonous reservations about Luscia and the disgrace he loved to remind others that still lingered under her camouflaged scar.

Between the sparkling curtains of the Eiide Corün, Luscia stole a look up at the seventh, topmost story. Her father loomed behind the railing. Unbridled, his enormous smile beamed across the courtyard. Though she faced him, the giant of her youth, she felt his pride at her back, holding her upright. Boreal's Clann Darragh waited where he stood between skirting drummers and hornists, their mallets and ram's bone primed for her signal.

As if they did not exist, Luscia lowered onto her knees. Her adornments tinkered against the stone where she spread out her palms. At her touch, the rock pulsed, alighting the psalms escribed upon it. Forehead bowed, Luscia mouthed her prayer to Aniell… her petition to not fail.

The veil in her mind parted not aggressively but hospitably. Warmth trickled down her prostrate arms as her tears streamed down her nose.

"Relent, Luscia…"

The lumin hummed in her ears, whereas everyone else had grown quiet and somber. Before their watching stares, Luscia arose to her feet and scanned the pool of floodlit faces. Threads wavered over the courtyard in a spiraled, dazzling cyclone her people could not see.

But they would.

Soon they would glimpse the truth. On earth, as was in Aurynth.

"Relent and reach for what will not rust…"

Shudderingly, Luscia breathed out and lifted her heel, then stomped it on the ground. Bell tones ricocheted down her leg. The tiny, unimportant sound challenging the keep's still temper.

The bright energy quivered, the lumin made excited and alight. *This is it*, she thought. This was the purpose of her haidrenship. She stomped again and the winds picked up, not unnaturally, for creation's participation was more natural than anything the world had ever known.

On her tongue, Luscia tasted the scum of her aunt's tonic.

Dmitri had asked her what it was they harvested at Ana'Innöx. There was but one thing Boreal could truly give their Maker: praise.

And praise could not be founded on a lie.

Chapter Twenty Four
Zaethan

Another bushel was deposited near the end of their table. The Boreali made no secret of its contents. Purposely untied, the drawstrings hung limply where the fabric had been rolled back. As to what it contained, Zaethan's best guess was pounds of spice, for the powder inside was a shock of bright orange against the otherwise rustic setting. It spread a savory musk in his vicinity. Straining his neck, Zaethan lifted an inch out of his highbacked chair to spy the contrasting load of brilliant teal that bookended their table.

A Boreali dressed in white was posted behind each burlap sack. They ringed the terrace in perfect sequence about the keep's rising tiers.

At a glance, it looked as if the arms of the highland forest were wrapped around its people, its monstrous limbs dotted with eager sprites.

The Boreali were waiting for something.

Or someone.

Below, the clans had converged in a chaotic mingle of merrymaking and song, despite the threat of snow. Bits of it sprinkled down under the bountiful glow of an unabashed amber moon. Snowfall was an event Zaethan had heard more about than actually seen, for in the lowlands and deep South, frost rarely stuck till morning. *Kind of like loyalty*, he sourly commented to himself.

Draped in their thick layers, the Boreali seemed to jitter with unspoken excitement. Over the playful music, it rattled with the bells they all wore—some at their ankles, others about their wrists. Zaethan had even spotted a handful of notably big men who'd strapped them on as a substitute for their belts. The palpable anticipation that shuddered through the courtyard easily clamored up to the seventh story. It was there, among a fleet of impassive drummers, the Clann Darragh stood.

Without his daughter.

Nor was Luscia with the Quadren. The spread reserved no seat for her, had she deigned to dine with them during her own fastidious fete. Strangely, Dmitri's party was the only group eating anything at all.

At distant tables, his prydes cluttered the third story outside Declan's family suite, where every outsider had been segregated from whatever was to happen. The rest of the keep was on the ground. Zaethan shot an uneasy look at Zahra, where yards away, she picked at a leg of meat beside Kumo. His third shook her head at him mistrustingly. He adamantly agreed. They didn't know what to expect, but it was clear that though they weren't to participate, they were intended to watch.

Overloaded with braised elk and rainbow cabbage—an already vile vegetable robbed of its sorry flavor after his experience in the moorland—Zaethan shoved off his plate and buckled his forearms. Drained as he was from navigating the peninsula's surmounting prejudice, he was even more fed up with the political farce as a whole. "Boreal is tarrying with you," he said quietly to Dmitri. "Just another stall tactic disguised as tradition. This celebration is an absolute waste of time."

Setting aside his fork, his king peeked overtop the tufts of his bulky cloak. "No longer concerned for my status as their chosen sacrifice? I'm disappointed, Zaeth." Dmitri's smirk was hidden, but it hooked the corners of his perceptive eyes.

"Ano, not quite. This meal is wrong. The Boreali buried the rest of their food around that dais, yet what little they preserved is being used to stuff you like a pig."

The pinkened tip of Dmitri's nose wrinkled in consideration as his regard waded over the throng and the compacted trench of dirt. "All right, I do admit there is *something* in the air."

"That would be a mixture of gasses naked to the human eye, Sire," said Hachiro. He bent his uncombed head forward to repetitively blink.

"Thank you for clarifying, Lord Pilar," Dmitri wryly said. "I must have forgotten."

"Most Unitarians do, Your Majesty."

Dmitri exhaled, catching Zaethan's eye with a sharpness that warned even he had tired of the shoto'shi's dull candor. Although, his countenance promptly perked up. "Ah, Lord Bastiion, a relief to have you back."

Ira Hastings sailed into his recently abandoned chair, having returned from conspiring with Takoda and Jabari—his newfound gambling financiers—well across the terrace.

"I forbade them from lending you anymore money, Ira," Zaethan informed the yancy.

Ira propped his elbow and leaned in so closely. Seasoned cider flew off his breath. "Oh, my friend, one's imagination is worth far more than one's crupas."

"We're not friends." Zaethan jabbed Ira's slim chest backward with his middle finger.

Pouting, the other haidren resembled a river trout. "So too my business partners say, but not for long. See here?" Ira proudly slapped a couple belled bracelets onto the crammed tabletop. "Traded for these with some seeds I said were magic. The kids here are so dumb."

"Insulting your peers only insults yourself, Lord Bastiion," said Hachiro, emerging like a pretentious little gopher. "That you are adept in the dialect of children is predictable, given how you've repeatedly boasted you are one of so many."

"I sense that you're offending me, but it sounds delightfully like a compliment. So hear, hear!" Ira boosted his growler, sloshing cider into Zaethan's lap.

It felt even soggier at the disturbing reminder that he and the yancy might, in fact, be related. Zaethan's cabbage suddenly smelled of dog vomit. Unlacing his arms, he grabbed his unused knife and grated it angrily against the wood.

Dmitri must have sensed his spell of resentment, for in turning, he placed his hand on Zaethan's shoulder and suggested to his other haidrens, "Lord Pilar, would you favor me by investigating the contents of that sack way over there? Yes, the violet one, by the farthest tables. Lord Bastiion can escort you."

Shrugging, Ira rose and happily brought a pitcher with him. Complying with his regent's request, Hachiro came around their chairbacks. As they walked off together, Ira offered him a pour. "Tickle your whistle, Hachi?"

"I abhor the liberties of tickling." They overheard the shoto'shi's pithy reply. "Unless of course you mean intellectually, then in that case, yes, I should like to be tickled very much…"

With an amused grunt, Dmitri waited until they were alone. "What's wrong?" he asked Zaethan.

"Nothing."

"I'll be an icicle before you formulate your sincerest thoughts." Dmitri tilted his face directly in front of his. "Out with it, Zaeth."

"It's nothing. Or maybe it's everything. Meme ano'qondai," Zaethan replied and slouched further into his chair.

"Tell me, what is everything, brother?"

Letting go, the knife clattered against Zaethan's plate. "I don't why I'm here anymore, Dmitri."

"You're here for me. And to preserve the *real* Darakai."

He rolled his eyes. "A lot of good I'm doing them."

"Perchance your good is still yet to be accomplished."

"Uni? With what to wager?" Zaethan grimaced. "You need leverage to hold your own at any table, Dmitri. The Quadren is no different than a gambling den. Except at your table, my leverage is as hollow as my name."

His friend's forehead creased under his rumpled waves. "I thought you were glad to be rid of his hold on you."

"I was—I am." It incensed Zaethan how his voice broke. And in such a public setting. He glanced up into the trusses instead of at Dmitri's compassionate study. "I spent my life cursing Nyack Kasim. But finally, outside his shadow, I've no idea who I am or what to do with myself."

Dmitri's hand clenched. Then, releasing Zaethan, he too sank back into his seat, watching the animated assembly below. His walking stick lay across the table's edge, much like it always had during regal receptions in Bastiion. Yet this gathering was nothing like those held in Thoarne Hall. This place was packed full of children, each layered in bells and dancing about with their families, their moss-lit courtyard made into a roofless ballroom of wood and stone.

Zaethan had never had a family like that. And he never would.

Something passed over Dmitri's eyes. "Look at our people," he said wistfully. "They need us, Zaeth."

"These people don't need us."

"As Orynthians, they represent those who do. Behold the human galaxy stretched before you. Are they not beautiful?" He made a delicate, introspective noise, the kind Dmitri always emitted whenever pondering a subject valuable to him. "Leaders must find purpose outside themselves, Zaeth, not within. Too late I'm coming to appreciate that humanity is a vivid paradox of dignity and disparity—of our being lost and becoming found. But all of us, no matter that paradox, comprise a constellation of meaning. How rare and wonderful it is when someone else cares enough to chart our own."

Zaethan looked over and discovered that a discomforting sadness had crested his friend's refined features, casting shadows where they did not belong. "Was that supposed to make me feel better?"

"Well, I thought it ought." A wry dimple appeared in Dmitri's cheek. Abruptly, his friend searched inside the heavy cloak and dragged out a small leather-bound book. Pushing the knife aside, he carefully set it in front of Zaethan's restless hand. "You're worth charting, Zaeth. Only you know where to start. So, I bought this for you a few weeks ago in Roüwen."

Zaethan arched his ringed brow. He really hated parchment. "What for?"

Dmitri's chest rose and fell; the long-suffering sigh was drowned by the swelling merriment below. "Because long after you, there will come a day when someone needs to read what you will write."

Zaethan sniffed, uneased by the seriousness in Dmitri's tenor. They were at a party, for Fate's sake. "That's a pretty morbid gift, *Your Majesty*," he stated and poured them both a healthy glass of wine. "Here, drink something for once. It's a holiday."

Dmitri rolled his neck aside. "Let the downcast and the fool seek solace in wine. Sober minds are for kings." He eyed him intently through the fur. "You have a choice to make. Who do you want to become, Zaethan? A fool… or a king?"

"I want to have your drink because you refuse to have fun," he declared, frowning at the morose pit in which their conversation had inadvertently spiraled. Snatching both drinks, Zaethan stood and knocked them back just as the Boreali crowd burst into cheers.

He heard Dmitri billow out a breath.

Zaethan stilled, holding his.

In the courtyard, a glint of moonshine descended the central stairs. She shone apart from everyone else. Brightness refracted off her precise and disciplined pace. It encased her entire bearing as if she were a star falling through the mist, not in a blink but in an epoch all her own.

Without being told, the highlanders cleared a path so Luscia could ascend the wide, dirt-rimmed dais. She stepped up between Bailefore and his elder brother, who presided atop the massive animals of the Orallach. At the striking picture of the three, the courtyard boomed even louder.

Luscia sank onto her knees after a few moments. Her marbled skin shimmered in an array of swirled motifs when she pressed her face against the stone. It was then Zaethan noticed that there were markings carved upon it. Under her touch, the foreign letters glowed.

Melody and merriment dispersed, the Boreali shushing as if one body instead of many. Bemused, Zaethan toed closer toward the railing. Most of the Darakaians did the same, littering the third-story terrace, where they'd crammed between the bizarre powder sacks and their mute keepers.

Arising, Luscia opened her eyes. They shone like suns, more captivating than the iridescent flames dotting her keep. She was not looking at Zaethan, nor at her king.

With the purest of smiles, she was looking toward her father.

Jealousy tinged Zaethan's core when commanding the seventh story, Boreal's Clann Darragh gave her an affirming nod from his drum-clad perch among the heavens.

The people were silent.

Spine straightened, Luscia lifted her heel and broke the calm, slamming it to the dais. Her jangle of bells rattled through the night, echoing from the farthest corners of the mountain. Expectancy seemed to ripple through the crowd. Upon her stomping again, more bells rang from the heights as the Clann Darragh joined her beckoning measure. He beat his heel with her rhythm. One by one, the Boreali accompanied her example. Mothers and fathers, the old and the young, bowed their postures low and raised their feet, then thumped the earth in clinking unison.

Their tolling consumed the keep.

Then the wind changed course.

Inexplicably, the air warmed, thawing the sinking snowflakes like hot breath. It blew in from a place unknown. It strummed the chimes that had been strung around each terrace in concert with the bourgeoning tempo. The hairs on Zaethan's arm stood at attention; he was not imagining the perfection of the wind's timing nor its enveloping cadence. In bursts, it swept in, charged with static.

The heating atmosphere tingled his cheeks.

Having gotten out his chair, Dmitri guardedly reached for his walking stick. He came near Zaethan. "What is happening here?"

"Meme ano'qondai, brother," Zaethan murmured and protectively stretched his arm across his friend.

The keep thundered. Above him, the drummers struck their hides when Luscia's ornamented foot again pounded the stone, awaking the night with an intrepid *boom*. Zaethan grabbed onto the railing. So did Dmitri.

Stringed instruments undergirded their song in slow, melodic progressions, defying the sense of urgency that pounded all around. Yet amid the clamor, it was Luscia's father who roared loudest of all.

His deep, battered voice heralded over his people.

"Darkness abates,

Where Light abides,

We shall pronounce,

He who provides!"

Presiding like a giant oak over his forest, the Clann Darragh stomped his thick leg harder and harder with the hammering drums. An ethereal jingle resonated throughout the courtyard as the same vigor erupted among the Boreali.

"Sown of sorrow,

What might destroy,

Transformed Tiergan,

To reap our joy!

Heal all sickness,

Bind all broken,

We're seeking now,

What was woken!"

On the dais, Luscia's body contorted as her arms snaked out, reaching into the emptiness. Her elbows snapped back and forth as to shake her hurricane of bells, Luscia's mesmerizing dance adding new notes to their otherworldly symphony. The clans mimicked her movements across the overcrowded courtyard. As one spirited sea, the Boreali spun in undulating rings, rippling out from her lead.

The winds increased. Frightened, Zaethan brushed his hand along his forehead, warding off whatever was coming. In his periphery, he saw the sack keepers step forward to his and Dmitri's either side. With their kin below, their lips moved in whispers. Overlapping prayers coaxed Zaethan's timorous ears. The gusts kicked up and so did the leaves, twirling in a rising whirlwind within the keep.

Dmitri's cloak rippled against him. Zaethan gaped at the sack keeper when their prayers turned to chants.

With their Clann Darragh, they screamed the final verse.

"No matter the age,

This people will cry,

Rul'lothadim Aniell,

Rul'lothadim, on high!"

In a unified sweep, the keepers pitched the sacks into the air, shooting teals, reds, azures, and golds into the open. Past Zaethan's nose, time slowed as the powder crashed together, mingled, and sank.

But before he could blink, the colors ruptured with lighting.

Veins of twilight flickered in and out of focus, there one minute and gone the next. Zaethan's mouth fell ajar. Spices seasoned his tongue. The smokey radiance unfurled in tendrils, twisting and cavorting inside the keep's cyclone of color. To the deafening music, hazy lights pranced above the highlander masses. The fractured beams mimicked the direction of the dancing people as if it were one with them, illuminating their faces with an unearthly gleam. The crowd spread out their hands and shouted with brazen delight. Some Boreali fell to their knees. Some even fainted. A shout thundered from the seventh story, the Clann Darragh howling in boisterous exaltation. Zaethan wasn't sure what they'd all been expecting. But he could tell…

It wasn't quite this.

On the next beat, the keepers tossed more pigment over the House of Boreal. Crimson and violet rained from the upper levels in front of Zaethan. He stared into the show of blurred fireworks. Deep into the depth and erratic flare… And then, straight out of the grisly fog, a single beam rushed toward his face.

His feet couldn't move. They dared not. The tendril of light, crisper and so much brighter than the rest, halted right at the end of Zaethan's nose. Every part of him clenched, frozen in fear, for there it lingered. The tip of its sharp, brilliant tail slanted like someone slanting their head in consideration. In challenge. Zaethan could not steal a breath.

But he felt the tendrils eerily fanning his skin in warm puffs. The strand was alive. Mighty and opalescent, just like Boreal's iron.

Just like their haidren's eye.

Zaethan's eyes burned when the strand flickered and disappeared. He sucked in a gulp of air. Dmitri rubbed his back, yelling something into his ear, while in shock, Zaethan leaned over the railing and dry-heaved.

He caught a glimpse of Hachiro around the terrace bend. The shoto'shi's monocular device dropped from his flabbergasted face. Together, his and Zaethan's regard plummeted toward the fourth haidren dancing on the dais.

A mess of ashen abandon, Luscia's hair whipped about her glittering body—her, a revolving hailstorm. He felt as though he were sighting her in her truest form. Because while the orderly cadence had disbanded, many people weeping and embracing each other throughout the courtyard, the beams of light were still moving overhead.

The beams were moving with *her*.

"I thought it was just kakk, how they kept talking about these 'threads,'" Zaethan murmured, piecing it together aloud. "But they're real."

Another surge of vibrant powder blurred the variegated haze. The final particles sprinkled into the courtyard when the sacks had emptied. Vestiges of light dissipated within the coloring as it fell. The fog cleared, returning to what could never again be called normalcy. Despite the rising cheers and reinvigorated song, Zaethan stood stunned beside his king.

"Zaeth." Across the log railing, Dmitri's pinky finger nudged his white-knuckled grip. "Zaeth, the dirt."

Between the bodies of rejoicing Boreali, he spotted the trench about the dais where they had buried their final scraps of produce. The soil wasn't dead.

It was in harvest.

And had spouted with overflowing green.

Zaethan pushed off the wood, stumbling as he backed straight into their deserted tabletop. He caught himself there and froze. A hot shiver chased his dread away, an unfamiliar hope coursing through him in its stead—not because of the miracle below, but the one before his fingertips.

Bleeding its contents through the linsilk table runner, the decanter of wine was overturned on its side. Impossibly, the winds had blown Zaethan's journal open atop the penetrating stain. Amid the mess, the first page stared up at him blankly, preserved and unblemished.

I take it back, he confessed to a supremacy he did not understand. Whatever he had witnessed there that night, it had in no way been a waste of time.

The celebration had spun into a midnight trance.

Three-stringed fiddlers circled the lower terraces with other frolicking musicians. Zaethan traipsed under their festive haunt, his heels padding the leaf-trampled courtyard to the thump and gallop of every highlander hand drum.

He skirted the burrow of dancing bodies. Silks swirled. Wools embroidered in precious stones swayed like ornaments strung throughout a mortal forest. Though the people's bellies were empty, their energies did not falter; they'd doubled. Fasting had done nothing to deter Boreal's jubilation. They fed on something he couldn't identify. Something that, once permitted, had drawn his pryde warriors down into the labyrinth of Northern faces, despite a profound hatred of the sorcery they'd just seen.

Forming a silly, tight-knit trio pranced Zahra, Takoda, and Kumo. Blue and ruby powders mingled in a loud indigo smear across the beta's wide back, where he'd accidentally grazed it against a neighboring reveler. The highlanders were all coated under a thick multicolored film. Boreal's skins stood no contest to the rainbow wash. Their most wintry trait only disappeared beneath it, disguising everyone under the same dramatic brushstroke.

"Alpha Zà!"

Zaethan's hand was eagerly tugged aside, spinning him on his heel. He caught Yhona when she thudded against him in a fit of laughter. Her brother, Sadik, swung around the nearest column, dragging after him a comet tail of warriors from the Mirajii Pryde. It was the happiest Zaethan had seen the sibling pair since Port Khmer, where both prydes had left too many comrades unburied.

Yhona brushed a chunky braid off her forehead, her newly sprung curls divided neatly about her scalp. As she was no longer malnourished, healthy hair covered the patches he'd mourned when rescuing her from the Mirajii. Hiding in Boreal had plumped her reddening cheeks and added muscle to her rickety stature. Giggling, she tried to pull Zaethan along with them into the revelry. But he resisted.

Her brow wrinkled, interpreting her alpha's desire to hang back as disapproval.

So, in a gesture from their homeland, Zaethan dusted his fingers over Yhona, forehead to chin, encasing her near-starved smile into tribal memory forever. "Ho'waladim, you've earned it," he said with feeling and jutted his chin toward the throng. He felt an unmet burden deep in his stomach; she was due so much more than a simple dance. "Go on. Have fun together."

She snatched his palm and kissed it quickly, then eagerly bounced off with the others.

Sadik smacked Zaethan on the bicep. "Zullee, Alpha Zà!" his best archer called, then saluted him fist to chest, cheerfully accepting the charge.

Zaethan leaned against the timber column. He curved his lips as he watched them weasel between the masses toward Kumo and Zahra. The Boreali who noticed their passing hastily jerked away, fearing the contact. But his warriors didn't care. They celebrated anyway.

His attention shifted when not too far off, arms lifted out of the roiling surface. The music shifted to a more melodic minor. With languid twists, the dancer's brightly dusted wrists moved and curled in slow circles—the cords of an ugly, beaded cuff swishing high through the air.

Luscia.

Zaethan's eyes traveled with her across the courtyard, as if she were the fixed point and he the one moving. He didn't remember shoving off the enormous pillar. Nor did Zaethan remember when his feet had started prowling forward to assert himself among those blocking the way toward their haidren.

Though the breeze carried a blister, heat radiated off the swarm of bodies and through his short-waisted gambeson coat. Advancing to the bewitching beat, Zaethan freed the topmost buckles, inviting the cold to lick the sweat that raced for his heart. Pounding flooded his ears when he slid right behind her.

No one decried his nearness.

Because consumed by their own feting, no one was watching hers anymore.

Spices and ground dyes had darkened the gauzy netting of her gem-sewn gown, as if an artist's deluge had painted her roiling form. Zaethan's bootsteps fell into her shadow, adopting the riddle and rhyme of her bare feet. The mesmerizing tune blared. All around him, the Boreali raised their hands and clapped in unison. The entire congregation rotated a quarter step. Anticipating the shift, Zaethan swept his toe backward and altered alongside them. Yet it was not their bodies that his was attuned to, not their figures of which he'd studied every tick and treasure.

It was hers.

Back and forth, Zaethan uncoiled along her spine, nothing separating them but the cushion of her unfettered mane. Rid of her headdress, her tresses swathed her back in a fit of knots and snarls. Zaethan crooked his chin overtop her messy crown. Her head twitched. It was an incremental tilt of her axis, but he knew her too well to be deceived. A thrill channeled his core, and he grinned. She'd become aware of his mirrored presence. The melody recircled, and after trailing his arms above her smaller frame, Zaethan clapped.

Luscia spun, not with the crowd but in a rapid orbit, aiming her three-fingered ring at the base of his throat with villainous alacrity.

A brilliant islet set in a powdered lagoon, her right iris was agleam, casting an opalescent prism across her sharp, teal cheekbones. Sands of gold pigment cascaded Luscia's hairline past her eyelid and down the defiant tilt of her nose. Spellbound, Zaethan fastened onto where a splatter of red flecked her mouth like a spray of blood on a battlefield.

She was a specter untamed.

She was beautiful and beguiling.

And until dawn surmounted the sky, she was in disguise.

They stood at a standstill, the swarm rotating around them. Zaethan spoke as if they were alone. "We can share a dance, Maji'maia."

Her glare only narrowed, and Luscia swallowed. "How can I trust your intent?"

"You can trust it's far from innocent."

With his tongue, Zaethan wet his lower lip and relished how ferally her pupils tracked its regrettable retreat. The witchiron blade hovered over his skin while his hips rediscovered the rhythm of her anthem, rocking invitingly. Though the bluff was buried in their past—though they'd long shed the horsehair rope—the tether between them remained. It was cinched about Zaethan's waist, and that corded flame was still cinched about hers. Luscia's grip on her weapon wavered as he temptingly encroached into the mere inches that cradled their intensified breaths.

Luscia disengaged her ringed blade and steadily dropped her arm. Her shoulders dipped and swung in answer. She said nothing, moving as a mirror to his every stride. Nevertheless, Luscia maintained the defensive inch of separation with her every backstep.

His periphery blurred as pulse by pulse, Zaethan steered them toward the edge of the courtyard and into the dark.

CHAPTER TWENTY FIVE
LUSCIA

She'd been taken in—made hostage to sweet temptation well before the stone column met Luscia's sweat-slickened spine. That was what sin really was… how it was born upon the seat of her own judgment. She was flirting with temptation, knowing full well she was already compelled to give in.

Heat plumed from Luscia's navel as that very compulsion warred with her conviction, one force ultimately giving in to the other when coming to a halt, her naked heels butted the rock.

There was nowhere else to flee.

The music of Ana'Innöx had ebbed and faded into a forgotten dream. Her sensitive ears were instead attuned to every tantalizing creak of lambskin. Each indecent rustle of linsilk and unholy jingle of the bells still strapped down the sinuous muscle of her taut legs. The ravenous pound of two hearts orbiting in the dark, concealed far from the main courtyard.

Luscia's vision adjusted to the dimness inside the abandoned grotto with ease.

Looming over her, Zaethan consumed the shadows. He embodied a confidence buckled with nerve and flecked in hubris. His masculinity surmounted in seclusion; his formerly modest movements shed their bridle of decency and decorum, twin bindings he boldly undressed from his gait with every step taken.

It ought to have felt predatory, were she his prey. But Luscia was the real apex predator. Zaethan knew it more than anyone. And still, he did not shy. He did not slow.

He did not approach her as anything greater or anything less than a woman pressed up against a column in the darkness.

Which made the swing of his strides all the more intoxicating.

Ensconcing his determined gaze, lune-worms dangled from the cave mouth, alighting the way down into the underground riverbed and away from the importance of the keep. The lazy glow frolicked over Zaethan's velvety skin. It emphasized the strong ascent of his cheeks and the uncompromising slant of his wide-set brow, where adorning the left, a pair of golden street-rings flashed. Only Zaethan could wear an article of poor judgment like a prize. Yet that was exactly what made him such a handsome creature.

A creature so very different from Luscia.

Her toes curled, scuffing the frost underfoot, when he planted a palm just inches from her waist. Luscia sidled a fraction, to avoid allowing his thumb to stroke the boning of her corset.

Zaethan's knowing expression changed—not quite a grimace, not quite a smirk. His plunging stare painted a grassy stain down her front as he anchored his other forearm directly above her head.

He sank and suspended himself a finger's breadth off her body.

Though they stood on winter's horizon, a wild summer raged within that meager chasm—spasming, prickling, and taunting Luscia's skin beneath her tiers of linsilk. A blistering surge raised every hair on her arms. Wedged between the pulsing highland stone and the warm promise of his torso, her lungs were sputtering. A very real panic settled in.

Luscia was helpless.

His smile grew. Zaethan's tongue teased his incisor impishly, consideringly, like a cat imagining the ways it was about to play with its mouse. On his next exhale, steam escaped his ample, inviting lips, heating the narrowing chasm between their faces. And gradually—savoringly even—he angled his mouth over hers.

Static electrified the tight space between their flesh. Soon the consecrated color that powdered her skin would be disturbed, and the evidence of his marking it discoverable to everyone in the courtyard.

Everyone—including the woman she'd confront in the mirror after it was too late. Luscia could not permit another stain on her reflection. She already bore too many to absolve.

With a subtle bend, Zaethan nearly closed the gap.

Her conscience broke over her in waves, cleansing Luscia of her weakness and cooling it into a steel resolve. *I am an heir of Tiergan. This cannot happen. Niit, this shall not happen,* she commanded herself.

Luscia darted her chin aside, grazing his. "Zaethan, you can't," she rasped. Her eyes dove for the kurtfierï leashed about her wrist, praying for its help—for it to put a stop to what should never have started and to prohibit her from beginning it ever again. "You can't. Not with me."

"Oh, Maji'maia." A beastly chuckle teased from the base of his throat as lingering even lower, he dragged his breath down her neck in a silky whisper. "I don't need to touch your skin… I live beneath it."

She pressed her lashes shut when Zaethan inhaled deeply. Her heartbeat pummeled her ear as he continued.

"You feel me there. Uni, whenever you sleep. Whenever you're alone. But most especially when you're next to *him*. You feel me where he doesn't belong. And why is this, hm? I will tell you." He returned his mouth to hover it right above hers. "You keep me just close enough to crave but too far to consume. That way, no Boreali can shame their haidren for wanting a nameless, cross-caste bastard like *me*."

Her lashes flung apart. Luscia implored the cynical gleam in his regard. "That is not true."

Zaethan scanned her face, wrinkling his nose displeasingly before he pushed off the column. He stepped back and said, "Even you didn't buy that, Maji'maia."

"Zaeth, I swear."

Putting more distance between them, he neared the entrance to the grotto, shaking his forefinger where he stalled at the edge. "Careful now. That mask of yours is cracking. Do you even know who you are without it? Because after all the confusing shtàka we've shared, it'd be nice to finally find out."

Luscia's mouth opened, then shut. Unable to supply him a fitting response, she suddenly felt naked and natural and anemic. Gone was her euphoria, the transcendent bliss of the lumin ceremony. Though the dust shielding her skin remained unharmed, her heart had spoiled. Her heart that bore his thumbprints. Her divided heart that deemed her unworthy to have graced the dais and usher in the *Other*.

Zaethan lingered there. But fed up with her silent struggle, he ultimately turned and left.

Her chin quivered in anger as much as regret. Having been made emptier by the entire ordeal, she feasted on his departing image. Her hollow stomach grumbled aloud, and she begrudged its vicious pang. It was the first time Luscia felt hunger's gnaw since she'd awoken yesterday morn.

The Boreali fasted during Ana'Innöx for good cause—Luscia, their defective haidren, a living testimony as to why. For time and time again, humans had proven to be forgetful beings who needed to relearn the most basic wisdom of their own sages.

She'd yet to conquer her earliest lesson.

Each soul bows to a master: its body or its spirit.

Both masters lay a table.

One serves everlasting sustenance. The other, enough sustenance to swallow.

Luscia trudged through the frigid muck that fringed the lively courtyard. Her bare feet were numb, no longer shoed by their heavenly warmth—another discomfort of her own making.

Children danced in her periphery, likely delighted to still be out of bed. Even the strictest parents loosened their grip during Ana'Innöx. Luscia crooked a glance at their fun. There was a young girl, a sapling among oaks, spinning with so much abandon, she had caused herself to stumble and slip. Getting back up, she gleefully lifted her hands to the music all the same, as if no one had seen her fall.

Luscia hung her head in shame, stoking a spark of envy.

The girl didn't yet know what it meant to be self-conscious.

Diverting from the main celebration, Luscia kept to the secluded ridgeway that was hollowed in and out of the mountainous walls of the keep. Most of the utility burrows had been excavated by Aksel himself during the mid-Spire Age, employing them for war rather than the transport of livestock and festival supply. Phalen had chased her there when they had been little. Every year, they'd howl and hide from the menacing harvest moon, pretending to be lost lycrans in search of their saving Dönumn.

With petulant bluster, Luscia kicked up the slush as she walked on. Ana'Innöx was so much simpler as a child.

She rounded a more sheltered bend. Ahead, she saw that a small flock of Boreali were huddled in a semicircle, having hemmed in something at the middle—likely an escaped goat or calf. But there came a crack. Then a gurgle. To her absolute horror, supportive yells accompanied the awful sounds.

Luscia broke into a sprint.

They'd cornered no animal.

At inhuman speed, she sailed into an off-duty najjan. Sheer velocity rammed him onto the ground. She gave no credence to the audible dismay of his fellows, instead turning her attentions onto his victim—a bruised, disoriented Darakaian, who, having succumbed to his beating, sagged down the sacred rock face.

Her palm shook where it floated over his fractured jaw. The muscle was inflamed and bloating with fluid from punches too strong for his bone structure to take. Backlighting him, the highland boulder pulsed, casting a twinkling irony across the damage. This land was ordained to heal. To save. To redeem...

By its laws of nature, the Dönumn Lux decreed it.

Luscia swiveled and seethed at the crude mob. Positioning herself in front of the Southerner, she arched her back territorially, guarding him from the assaulting najjan as he regained his footing in one fluid motion. He was a taemplar, by the triple bough on his cloak pin. He made to step forward.

"Heh'ta, brödre!" Luscia threw up her hand, commanding he halt in his tracks.

Disbelief contorted her kinsman's expression. Surrounding them, the gang bore parallel rumples through their brows, their mismatched unity confounding at a glance. She scanned them cautiously but found no pattern among the men's dress and, consequently, neither their association. Some wore totems of agriculture, others of craft and trade… even some, the faded scars of a war Luscia was too young to lament. The taemplar crisply crossed his arms, many Boreali doing the same. Together they murmured.

Their whispers were grating, sowing mistrust for misunderstanding.

Luscia, the esteemed haidren to Boreal, had just come to the defense of Darakai.

Shirking the scandal, she thrust her chin at those bearing brooches of the chosen aelect. For lest they forgot, Luscia was najjan too. "What have you committed here? Violence has not desecrated this holy site in four hundred years. That warrior is a guest of our House. Wem, even nobler, the guest of our king!"

"Ana'Sere," the taemplar started, wiping off the sleeve of his soiled coat. "The pagan was spewing vitriol against Boreal. Then he spoke against you and the blessed Eiide Corün—"

"His words pose no contest to your strikes! They are immaterial!" Luscia cried. She broke from his stare and implored the other Boreali. "You each wield an *infinite* material. Meh'dajjeni Lux, weh'dajjeni Dönumn, meh brödre. What cause have you to forsake your own gift, when the source is but a barrier away from your veins?"

Remorse peppered their postures before a voice shot out from the back. "That pagan blasphemed the threads, cursing that which is higher than you or Tiergan himself!"

The men sucked in a collective breath.

Hearing the voice and recognizing the uncanny way belligerence had curdled its tone during recent months, Luscia twisted around with measured control.

Her own guard stood among the mob's number.

Creyvan pushed through his cohorts and shouldered his way toward the front. With his hair slicked back over his crown, pasted there from sweat or snow, he no longer resembled the sun itself. He hardly resembled his Tearlach twin. Stitched in a radiant florid motif, his fur-trimmed jacket was indistinguishable from that worn by the other men of her personal guard. That was… apart from the maroon splatter seeping through his pocket. Creyvan's copious cups of mulled wine hit her nose well before she'd spotted the aberrant stain. Her face must have betrayed her displeasure, for the blond najjan crossed his bulging, well-toned arms defiantly.

Luscia twisted her gaze at her guard. *When had his form gotten that large?*

Tottering, he eyed the warrior in her shadow and ran his tongue under his smooth upper lip. Creyvan rarely went unshaven, even on the road, always espousing something about the purity of neatness.

Luscia heard that a lot differently now.

"The threads did not condone this, Creyvan," she said. "Thus, under Aurynth's Watchman, such action could be considered sacrilegious. Our resources, as our strength, belong to Aniell and are *His* to dispense."

"If it's dedicated to Aniell, obstruction to such action is a sacrilege too," Creyvan replied with a distinct inflection, like he was a puppet and his orator unseen. Surely that statement was being repeated.

"According to whom?"

"Elder Hinrük." His answer jostled renewed confidence among the small mob.

The atmosphere tickled her fingertips. Luscia formed her fists, incensed by the mention of the Orallach zealot. She knew Creyvan had entertained Hinrük's radical ramblings on occasion, but not that her own guard had fallen in with his fringe sect. The Darakaian behind her stirred, shuffling himself upright with a moan. Luscia wanted to blame the elder for what had happened that night—to blame his incitements and his ongoing discrimination, the same used against Boreal's haidren herself. Yet despite his clear corruption, Hinrük had not committed the travesty.

Creyvan and these men had.

Woefully, Luscia bent to help the unarmed warrior, but his puffy eyelids widened in fear, and with unexpected vigor, he shoved Luscia backward, spitting a mouthful of Andwele slurs. "Y'siti! Doru, y'siti—"

In attack, the mob tore forth at his use of the debased term—*filthy ice witch*—coming to her defense, or maybe even their own.

She meant what she'd said. There would be no contest.

Fire raced through her arm as Luscia held it outright and screamed, "Niit! Stop this!"

The *Other* flared into existence as a disk of incandescent light. Breaking from her palm, the threads knocked back the men like pins.

She'd assaulted her own people; Luscia nearly doubled over in upset. Over their confused and disoriented heads, the lumin coalesced, snaking from the pebbles, the leaves, and even the stone into a cloud of static mist. It crackled in the fresh breeze. A beam brighter than the rest whipped from the brilliant, fabricated core, lashing the space between Luscia and the assembled zealots. Her throat constricted.

The harbinger thread was angry.

But angry with which party?

In their distraction, the bruised warrior ran through the burrow in escape, unable to see the brewing lumin storm. Luscia didn't know what the threads would do, what they were capable of so close to the Dönumn… but she knew everyone needed to get out.

"Return to your families!" She barked at the stunned mob. Luscia then whirled toward Creyvan. "With me this instant. Crestï, or by Aniell, I swear…"

His lips moved instead of his boots. "That was a flagrant abuse of power, a power you shouldn't even hold."

A power Creyvan could disclose to Alora.

Or worse, Elder Hinrük.

Luscia wrenched him by the collar. "I said now! Crestï, Creyvan!"

She towed him out of the burrows and along the courtyard perimeter. Luscia's grip intensified as she hauled the najjan up the flights of a less-populated, curling alfresco stair. Boreali of all ages skittered out of their path, probably afraid of the fever exuding from their haidren.

Rounding the fourth-story terrace, Creyvan said under his breath, "People are looking, Ana'Sere."

"It is my place to correct, not yours. We mustn't forget our stations, brödre."

"Only one of us has."

She spun and slapped him.

Red bloomed across his cheek. His eyes stretched as widely as hers. Luscia abruptly released Creyvan and gulped.

Not twelve paces away stood her aunt, among a trio of clanswomen. Within seconds, her Tiergan iris glowed in a kaleidoscope of suspicion and blatant disapproval. Alora's faraway analysis was succinct. She pursed her mouth into a flat, rigid stroke.

Luscia planted her hands on her najjan's spine and propelled them both out of sight. The blundering bell tones undignified her every stomp up the steps behind him.

Finally on the seventh story of the keep, she flung open the ornate rotary door—an ancient circular slab of interlocking wood panels—and barged Creyvan straight through the entry into her haidren suite.

Boots scrambled upon the spiral-grain floor. Someone blew their nose.

Luscia poked around Creyvan and found that the rest of her guard was gathered around the lustrous, lumilore-plated fireplace that dominated the great room. The mantle was set in an enchanting warren of tinsel ivy. Its ropey tendrils had not turned brittle indoors, protected there from the amassing cold. What a lowlander might assume were spindly candles suspended from the ceiling, the twinkling tinsel ivy had twisted and twined among the joints and rafters. Like the haidrens it sheltered, the greenery grew fuller, brighter, and more complex across the years, eventually having become a part of the dwelling as much as the timber to which it clutched.

Ivy-reflected light mottled the long angles of Noxolo's downturned face. Perched off the edge of the hearth, Marek was patting his thigh in comfort, but the captaen promptly caught Luscia's concerned look. His mouth adopted a bittersweet curve. Declan's arm was slung around Noxolo's willowy shoulder from the other side; Böwen huddled cross-legged beside his upturned boots. Filled with cider, a team of cups sat untouched, appearing to have long lost their steam.

With a kerchief crumpled in hand, Noxolo blotted his beak-shaped nose. When he looked up, he offered Luscia a feeble smile that smashed her heart into pieces.

She'd forgotten.

Out of all people, Noxolo's haidren had forgotten his mother's absence. The haidren had spent the latter hours of the fete enthralled by her own experience rather than applying it in service to those she held most dear.

"Forgive me, Nox…" Luscia hurried toward him—one child of

tragedy to another. She knelt and touched her forehead to his wiry knees in apology. "Meh fyreon, Ana'Brödre. I was being selfish and shortsighted and—"

"She missed it, Ana'Sere." His snot-choked baritone pulled her head upward. Fresh tears spilled from his bright, irritated eyes as he said, "That was a miracle tonight… and meh mamu… Unless we find her, she… She'll never get to see it."

What miracle?

Bewildered, Luscia surveyed her men. Declan's ginger whiskers split, showing his teeth in a grin that stretched to the curve of his eyes. Her favorite guard shook his head at her, and despite the sadness of his stooped frame, Declan let out a rich chuckle, doubling her confusion.

Luscia's search latched onto Marek.

She was taken aback by the favor in his unflinching eyes, as if Luscia were some fabled treasure unburied in the sand. Tenderly, Marek reached over and caressed the length of her tresses until he could scoop up her hand and guide it—along with his kurtfierï—closer. He flipped it over and boldly kissed Luscia's palm in front of the others.

Having disturbed the dusting, his lips pulled away flecked in red and gold.

Guilt sprouted like a weed in Luscia's gut—even though logic guaranteed that according to courtship custom, she'd technically done nothing wrong. Yet were that entirely true, her body would not have wished to hide itself from her suitor. Outside the physical, the mind was not captive to technicality, and neither were the thoughts and feelings repeatedly reenacted across its stage.

Böwen scooted forward. "The captaen told us what he glimpsed that day in the agora. That he somehow witnessed the threads *through* you… But se'lah Aurynth," he said on an exhale. "We didn't believe him, not really. Not until tonight. Ana'Mere never thinned the veil like you did for us, Ana'Sere."

"I also confirmed they saw only a ghost of the truth." Marek snugly cradled her fingers. "That the lumin is so much more substantial than we ever imagined."

"Wem. A miracle sent from Aniell," Noxolo said with a sniffle.

"That miracle was sent for the Boreali. No pagan should have ever seen it."

Together, they all shifted toward Creyvan.

His arms were shackled about himself. The najjan's darkened bearing was altogether unrecognizable, apart from the antlered brooch of the Ranger Aelect pinned at his puffed-out chest. Creyvan had not come to Noxolo's aid… had not submitted to the need of his kinsman.

He'd chosen to wade in his anger near the threshold, alone.

"Come now, Brödre," Böwen said, waving his twin over. "Ana'Sere's power is a precious gift. If Aniell chooses to reveal it to a small handful of lowlanders, then—"

"One handful of pagans carries the malignance of a multitude."

Luscia instantly stood, pointing her finger. "Silence, Creyvan! I've heard enough of your offenses already, for they are too many to tolerate."

"What *offenses*?" Marek's posture snapped into form as he rose beside her, adopting the straight lines expected of an officer of the Order.

"Ock! Smell him! He's sloshed." Declan growled and wrinkled his already-crooked nose. "What've you done now, Creyvan? Gotten into a brawl with the brewer and his cooper?"

"More like an innocent warrior we fought with in Khmer." Luscia signaled a warning before Creyvan could spare a response. "Not another word. I don't care what the Darakaian said to you."

Marek's deep voice doubled in volume. "You attacked a Darakaian?

Shtàka, Creyvan! We set the highest example as those in the haidren's personal guard. What will our clansmen think after this?"

"That they shall sleep easier tonight," Creyvan replied, defying her once more.

Luscia addressed his mortified twin. "Take your brother out of this room, Böwen, before I take out his tongue."

Böwen nodded vigorously, cutting across the room, and hooked Creyvan around his bicep. His twin tried to rip his arm away while Böwen dragged him down the adjoining hallway. It resounded with their scathing whispers. The Tearlach brothers disappeared from view, eventually locking the argument away behind the door to their private quarters.

Noxolo got up from the hearth. "I will attend them, Ana'Sere" was his soft reassurance as he passed.

Exhausted and demoralized, Luscia buried her face in her hands.

They were supposed to be reassuring *him*.

Marek's warm hands cupped her shoulders, though he did not pull her into an outright embrace. He wouldn't, not while Declan was in eyesight—not while they weren't fixed by a formal betrothal.

"It's this influence of Elder Hinrük's." Luscia groaned and knocked her head back against Marek. "You've still family scattered throughout the Orallach. You better than anyone know how Hinrük and his elders regulate Clan Ciann. Creyvan has come to idealize all that tradition and austerity as some kind of backward ideal. Next, he'll be weaving long, woolen hems onto everything he owns."

Declan stepped closer. The burly najjan positioned his back to the hallway and said lowly to Marek, "If Creyvan is corrupted, then he can't be permitted to serve her, Captaen."

"Wem, I know," answered Marek coldly. Blocks of ice seemed to ring his pupils.

"Niit," Luscia replied.

"Luscia, Declan is right—"

"Niit, you can't expel him, Marek." She rubbed his hold atop her shoulder. "If we release him to Hinrük, he will be indoctrinated entirely. The Creyvan we know would be lost to us, to Böwen, to himself… forever."

Declan grimaced. "Then he could convert more zealots of his own…"

"Poor followers make even worse leaders," Marek replied. "Fine. He stays, for now. But he is never alone. Declan?"

"Aye, wem, I'll go see to the weasel." The najjan trudged off in the direction of the twins' muffled bickering.

Heaving a sigh, Marek pulled her against him, and Luscia didn't object. Beaded appliqués poked her cheek where she pressed it against his chest. In winding circles, he dragged his fingers across her back as they stood there, two tired leaders leaning against one another, to better carry the joint burden of their responsibility. It struck her, not for the first time, that a life with Marek would be exactly that.

Luscia's stomach gave an embarrassing gurgle.

So did Marek's. "Arlette left us some fruitcake in the kitchen. Let us eat," he said and lightly kissed her temple. "Your duty has been fulfilled."

The crop had sprouted hours ago. He'd been free to partake when the others had.

Marek had waited to break his fast with her.

Luscia felt unsteady as he guided her toward the kitchen. She was not so different from Creyvan. Her fidelities were just as torn, split not only between her body and spirit but Orynthia and her House, the Quadren and her calling, and her king and her sovereign divine.

The sages had said it best: the soul bowed to something.

Luscia's abdomen chewed on itself. No matter whose table at which she sat, she did not want anyone to starve. Yet by her hand, someone always would.

Chapter Twenty Six

The riches of the royal library slumbered more soundly than the dead. With his heel, the figure tapped the balcony door closed as he stepped onto the cedar planks of the third story, shutting out the sound of Amaranth's beating wings. Were he to permit her inside, the Pilarese hawk would never leave. It was her mistress's domain, and she'd been trained to seek her. Such was a specialty of her lavender breeding. Deserting his sole companion, the figure's ragged boots made no sound against the wooden medallions as he crossed the floor, the pattern akin to that of a massive checklerule board.

A grimace puckered his flaking scabs. Life was a brutal sport, bound and framed by nature's laws.

He should have considered the rules before he'd lost the match.

Emptiness nipped his blistered face. As expected, there were no patrons inside to have lit a fire. No yancy or courtesan hungered for knowledge the way they did a midnight tryst. Winter was sinking her claws into Bastiion, leaving the library barren and cold.

It always was… without Alora there to warm it.

Imbuing the shadow, the figure's threadbare cloak licked the marble columns as he skirted the interior mezzanine. He vaulted his gaze over the scrolling, serpentine banister—cleverly shaped in an hourglass as a nod to all who'd lost time there—then down toward the main level. Squinting in the dark, he scoured the rows of moonlit shelving.

The figure's curse was an acrid gust over his tongue. Not a candle was lit.

Having trailed Tetsu over the past week, the figure presumed this night should have been no different. He'd tracked the chancellor through the Drifting Bazaar, where he had purchased bootleg herbs off a Pilarese ferryman. Through the palace residency to visit the apartment of a Urielean duke, before paying off the sentries who'd permitted him inside. Then back again to his own sil'haidren suite. Yet it was there a letter had arrived, and its response hastily recorded. Knocking out the unsuspecting page, the figure had intercepted the returning correspondence.

It'd been written to Nyack Kasim.

In Tetsu's short, terse message, the chancellor relayed that he could not meet that evening, as the warlord had so urgently demanded. Tetsu was otherwise engaged, for he was to instead "consort with the custodians of old."

The peculiar turn of phrase disturbed the ashes of the figure's memory. It'd awoken his ghost, as he quickly recalled how Tetsu had employed it whenever he'd needed to search the almanacs—such as those neatly housed on the main floor of the royal library.

But no candle had been lit.

No pages crinkled in turn.

No bindings cracked or were being explored.

The sanctuary of study was abandoned to no one except the monster who'd once cherished its every nook and cranny.

He'd avoided going back there. Beneath his unwashed rags, the figure's festering boils began to itch, and he backpedaled into the stacks of books as if they could bury him. It would be better that way. A relief. But his disfigured shoulder—a rotting cavity still missing a hunk of its tissue—ached when it bumped into a long, quartz mantle.

Twisting, he found a two-sided fireplace, holding nothing but dust. The figure's hood fell off his patchy scalp when he angled it back, taking in the entirety of the overmantel's sculpted grandeur. The imposing memorial, tucked in the corner of the third floor, was not easily forgotten. Were his glands not already shriveled, the figure would have broken into a tormented sweat.

In a gilded frame, an oil painting of Thoarne—his founding spear thrust into Bastiion's hill—stared down from the opposing wall. The triumph was out of place and out of time.

Hesitantly, shooting an ache through his every cursed ligament, the figure inched around the corner of the hearth and glimpsed the sitting area on its reverse side. Before King Dmitri's coronation tour had departed the city, it was the last place he'd beheld Alora.

And the only place he'd ever beheld her entirely.

The muscles of his throat convulsed, and he started to choke. The figure's lashless eyes seared as they stared at the design of the rug. Hexagonal lotuses on repeat.

With his sandals tucked neatly under the wing-backed chair, he curled his toes on the plush carpeting, unable or unwilling to believe her words. He didn't understand what had changed… what had triggered her paranoia. Hanging onto her every syllable, trying to compute their gravity, he sat there emotionless as Alora went on.

"Won't you look at me?" she begged and slid their cherished, raggedy codex across the pedestal table. In his periphery, her elegant fingers were reaching for him.

He did not oblige them.

"We knew this day would come, dearest. For us both." Alora carefully set the patinaed locket—an heirloom taken off her father, no doubt—directly beside the tome of their most intimate musings. "I've already rejected five kurtfierï. A sixth is unexplainable to my parents, the Enclave, the Clann Aedan… These swirling rumors will eventually name you. Don't you see? There is no coming back from that for me."

"Who is it?" was all he murmured.

Alora dodged the question, a political forte of hers. "I hold no affection for him," she replied with promise, as if that were a consolation to her marrying another man. "It's an old Orallach family. Traditional. Everyone will assume their haidren had been waiting for such an offer. Frankly, I half expected Emiere to propose courtship by now, were he not so hopelessly in love with Magda—"

"Tell me who it is." His enunciation pricked each consonant, distinguishing their immutable difference, his accent being the least significant.

Delicately, she glided the locket back into her lap. "Girvyn Hinrük."

He'd learned enough Boreali to snort at that. "His name literally means 'rough.' Is that the life you want?" A slip of black hair obscured his vision when he snapped his face toward his beloved. Chin trembling, she was nibbling her bottom lip. "Really, Alora, is it?"

"Niit." She tilted her countenance sadly. Her mismatched irises grew

smokey when her eyes watered. "But I must continue the purity of the line, lest the Higher Gift will depart us. I can't take that away from my people."

"You said your sister, Eoine, wears a kurtfierï right now and won't accept another. She'll surely bear children, so you won't have to."

Alora picked at her cuticles, a nervous habit implying she was summiting the pinnacle of her crushing anxiety. "My reputation. My purpose. This is the only way to preserve both. Even if…" Her voice faltered. "Even if that means losing what and who I want most."

He washed his face with his hands. As he looked over, blood brimmed her nailbeds where she'd viciously plucked at her skin, reviving the scabs that'd only just begun to heal. "No, don't," he said, immediately gliding off the cushion and onto the floor. Sweeping his ankles beneath his robes, he gathered her fingers like costly jewels and kissed their reopened wounds. "Don't hurt yourself for me, my love."

"Meh fyreon," Alora whispered through her weeping. "This is my fault. I should have never entertained you that night in Arune. But from your first inquiry, I adored you so. I will adore you until the day I die. Yet I fear… Niit, I know… Being apart from you will be the slowest death of all."

Alora sobbed inconsolably, cutting a schism deep in his core.

"Shh." Angled against her legs, he hugged her slender knees, wrapped in her dazzling linsilk skirt. The bristles of his shaded jaw raked against the elaborate beading as he gazed into the dancing flames. Her cries shuddered her whole body, vibrating through to his chest to an object beneath the crisp, starched fabric—a pocket journal she knew nothing about. Its secrets suddenly felt heavy and crucial and timely.

"What if," he said daringly. "What if there was a way we could be together?"

Alora sniffled. "What?"

"A way I could become like you."

The library grew hollow, stressing the daring swish as he gradually leaned back on his heels and unbuttoned the top of his robes. He slid the journal out from underneath. It was a brick in his palm. Nervously, he swallowed and parted the pages, revealing a symbol—rather, a theory—made for his beloved.

"What is that?" she asked shakily, though her body felt like stone.

Setting the papyrus across her lap, his finger traced the inky figure eight, then the line down its crux. "A rift in the mammalian course, introducing a reconstitution of lumin into the system." His touch rescanned the curves of interlaced infinity. "Then a regeneration, binding the whole anew. I've not yet given it a name, but it's an experimental eugenic therapy to fashion one animal more like another. You must breed with a Boreali man, yes? Then let that man be me. We've only to harvest enough blood to—"

She ripped the journal out from under his finger and flung the pages into the fire. The embers scattered onto the polished hearth, dying and disintegrating just like his work when it caught flame upon the logs.

Swinging toward her, he saw her hands had clamped over her mouth in horror. And her eyes—her eyes were wild and bright.

"The science is there, Alora. We only needed to follow its strides," he pleaded and gestured toward the crumbling drawing.

She gripped the arms of her chair as if to keep from falling off it. "We do not remake what was already made for us. That evil is not the way forward." Alora searched him frightfully. "We don't become gods to better subjugate our humanity."

"And if that humanity, the immutable granted to us at birth, never fulfills?"

"Then we suffer it!" Alora's statement was laced with uncharacteristic steel. "We suffer it," she said again. After a few strained moments, her voice came much smaller than before. "This is not our only reality. There is greater life beyond the veil."

"According to your sages, I'll only know you on this side of it," he replied, a disharmony of grief and anger lilting his accusation. She'd told him herself; many sages believed that an afterlife in Aurynth was for the Boreali alone.

Renewed tears cascaded her severe cheeks. "We cannot remake what the High One has predetermined. This has to end, lest we damn us both."

From the floor, he read her barren expression as if it were the holiest scroll, condemned by the ardency in her delicate, wrinkled brow. Her faithful resolve straightened her sharp shoulders, bared above the filigree trim of her cream-and-blush gown. Nevertheless, she was everything. Arithmetic incarnate. The magnificent sum of a million microscopic peculiarities. How was he supposed to retreat into isolation and forget each one?

Shifting, he knelt before Alora upon the wing-backed chair, as if he were a worshipper and she one of the chiseled Fates in Bastiion's temple. "Then grant me tonight." He knew it was a commoner's plea, but he made it plainly. "One night with my beloved and I will never ask you again."

A gust escaped her. Alora's incremental nod was a mere crack in her rigid veneer, yet it was enough to spring him off his heels and into her embrace. He encased her with his arms and kissed her as if he could taste her soul… as if the variances between their bloodlines no longer mattered.

As if the very act could not undo them completely.

She clutched at his back, knocking the locket—along with their codex— to the ground. Hastily, Alora undid the remaining buttons down his front. His body ignited when she swept her hands under the muted silk and jerked the heap of it up over his trim abdomen. He'd never been a robust man, but he felt as one then, as all his strength surged toward her promise to come.

With clumsy, urgent fingers, he unhooked her bodice. Dragging her hips forward on the cushion, he made fast work to free her from her stays. Then he untied her overskirt. Unrolled her stockings. And finally, she was sitting in nothing except her linsilk shift.

Rising, Alora unhurriedly permitted it to fall.

Her naked contours were a coastline of crushed pearl. She was divine, a piece of starlight given to earth. Overtaken, he rose onto his soles in one languid exploration. His nose skated up her narrow middle, over her navel, and between her breasts. Kissing her, he drew them together down onto the rug. Alora's hair hung long and loose, falling around him like the first snow. Between the platinum tresses, her eyes were sister galaxies.

The right bluer than sapphire. The left a prism of light.

Although he'd imagined it so many times, having never treaded the path, his body united with hers with as much longing as one rushing home. He held her so close that their legs became a cord entwined. Breath beat their slickened necks, and he was blissfully unsure to whom the rhythm belonged. He left no inch of her unturned. Untrodden. Unknown. Her intonations came like a breeze over water, as in waves of ecstasy, she chimed his name again and again and again.

The bookstands shook alongside their glossy limbs. Gasping, they collapsed against each other. He could die, he realized, and never begrudge it. For a piece of himself just had—the part that had existed before this.

Alora snaked her arms under his ribs and laid her head across his laboring lungs. The fire flickered across her sweat, casting a diamonded sheen he could examine forever. To him, the entire world was cradled within those library walls.

He'd lied to her unwittingly. One night would never be enough. Time suspended beneath his chin as he panted after her, cataloging every sweet intake into memory. It would not simply be their only. It would be their last.

But… It didn't have to be.

Were they the same, she'd be free to choose.

Tempted, he turned his cheek aside and let it rest against the carpeting. Trailing his fingers along Alora's spine, he lowered his sight upon an unburnt remnant of his crimson journal. It seemed to echo a dangerous thesis from the dying embers: remake them the same and he'd free them both.

The library door groaned from the first story, causing the figure to lurch backward, almost tipping over a wing-backed chair. He pressed his wiry form against the plaster. Catching the chair, the figure choked back a gulp of stale air. Darkness consumed him once more, blotting out the most beautiful night he'd ever suffered. She'd returned the codex to Arune after that. Rather than destroying them, Alora had undone her steps as if they hadn't existed.

The empty space was a blunt reminder, where the lotus rug sprawled blank and void. Shame for what had occurred there—and what had come thereafter—was a deeper poison in his veins. He was no longer a man but a wretched thing hauling an eternal stake in his heart. A stake that oughtn't ever be removed.

Animalistically, his blistered ears twerked.

Somewhere, papers were being shuffled.

Aches racked his rawboned legs as he slunk into a crouch and slithered around the corner, closer toward the moonlight flooding in through the dome overtop the mezzanine. Creeping on, he heard the grumble of voices going about their business. The figure stopped and waved his nose at that, ignoring the pang where his decaying flesh—the little left—strained over his cartilage. He couldn't place the faint odor of lilies and sulfur. It was familiar yet polluted. On the second whiff, he caught a sickening hint of marrow. Pus leaked from the figure's lip when he split a venomous smirk.

Tetsu.

You wear your cleverness like a cloak, Chancellor, he thought spitefully, *still neglecting how naked you are beneath it.*

The figure wormed by the railing toward the rancid smell, molding himself within the darkest pools among the bordering bookshelves. Unable to see Tetsu from either angle, he paused and perched directly above where they'd entered. Through the balusters, faint, inky shadows spanned the lobby below. Whoever the chancellor had brought with him into the library didn't carry a candle either.

After a few soft thumps—of someone gathering almanacs, no doubt—the covert conversation resumed.

"Your devices are falling into place," Tetsu was saying, his tone subdued. "Peerage allegiances are shifting in our favor. However, Wendylle is proving problematic. The province worships independence nearly as much as its gold."

There was an eerie silence before a voice—its prevailing rasp like flapping wings—eventually responded. "There is no virtue humanity won't trade for its vice. Discover it, and soon Bastiion will give up her rights for a more glorious end."

Gripping the iron railing, the figure shuddered as the promise seemed to ricochet through the air, not in sound but in the trembling of every particle. The dust both recoiled and responded to the speaker's resonance.

Aghast, his withered organs waded forward against his navel as if summoned, and he nearly heaved. Dark power steadily pulsed through the ether. And though the figure knew it not, it certainly recognized *him*.

"This too shall be accomplished in your name, my lord," the chancellor professed.

The Obscurer is here in the library. The figure panicked, as Tetsu's stark-white robes rapidly swept out from the bookstacks. Pilar's leader strode toward the double doors and greasily slipped out between them, escaping into the palace.

Independently.

The figure leaped over the handrail and dropped two stories, then landed on the compass inlaid in the lobby's marble floor. His bones rattled with the impact, but he swallowed the pain. The figure darted into the rows of almanac shelving, then dashed between them before the Obscurer could flee. But running in circles, he saw no one was there, only the malevolent aroma.

He keeled over and vomited the little he carried in his stomach. A beetle skittered between the torn leather of his boots. The figure wiped his bile with his gloved hand and tracked the insect's course until, coming upright, he was facing a mirror seated in the corner of the library. A string of beetles scurried along its tall, wooden frame, and he practically vomited again.

His hood had fallen backward.

The figure beheld his image in the looking glass. An open wound walking, he resembled death itself, had death refused to die. The bones beneath his scabbed cheeks pierced through his necrotic flesh in unhealed gashes. The hairs of his brow were fully shed above his right eye, the lid infected over his other, and what he'd thought was still a nose was rapidly deteriorating into an open cavity.

It didn't have to be this way, but he'd monstrously remade it so.

He'd surrendered all virtue for one beloved vice. That crimson journal hadn't really burned in a fire, nor was its sin a singular edition. It'd only been the first volume of many.

CHAPTER TWENTY SEVEN
Luscia

"Stop pacing," snipped Alora. "You're a haidren, not a common courier."

Luscia glowered at her aunt as she traipsed this way, then that. The lycran padded dutifully in her shadow before the looming door. Her swinging arms grazed the circular wood. Tall ears and a prolonged snout matching Aksel's were carved into the rotary panels. Every entrance upon the keep's senior floor featured the same interlocking mechanism as that protecting the haidren's quarters, befitting the Clann Darragh to an elder from the lesser clans.

She could hear nothing through the door, though she strained. The thing was bolted shut—padded and reinforced with more resolution than Luscia could muster that morning.

"I can't help it."

Like an extra fixture of luxiron, Alora stood poised and erect beside the locked entry. "Our actions speak more tellingly than our speech," she chided. "After the fete, yours already spoke volumes."

Distrust flexed Luscia's fingers before she could ball them into fists. Not everyone had viewed last night as a miracle. Luscia wasn't sure why, but it upset her aunt. Perhaps it was her jealousy over Luscia's unmistakable manifestation of lumin…

Or something uglier altogether.

Perhaps the reason couldn't be corked in one of Alora's vials.

Keeping from the terrace railing, Luscia avoided the avid glances from those littering the stories below. The keep was shaped like a hive and packed full of busy Boreali bees, and rumors quickly scaled the comb not to the queen but the king. Nibbling her lower lip, Luscia risked a glance over the edge, eased that neither Dmitri nor Zaethan were patrolling the terraces in search of their missing haidren to Boreal. If the chattering pilgrims had already heard of Creyvan's scuffle concerning the Darakaian warrior, then surely had the Quadren.

Luscia smoothed the front of her bodice, reminding herself she was, in fact, slated to be on that particular stoop at that particular hour, and she wasn't at all trying to appear otherwise engaged.

Because as it was the dawn after Ana'Innöx, she was a haidren just that: otherwise engaged.

Abruptly, the overlapping panels clicked, disengaged, and spun in spirals around the sprocket-eyes of the engraved lycran head. Relief doused her nerves when the round door popped forward on its stiff, long-standing hinges, and it was her father who exited the gloom into the still-rising sun.

A masculine mirth crinkled the weathered skin about his brave blue eyes, which held the vestiges of love and loss behind every blink. Boreal's Clann Darragh paused there. He took in his daughter's fresh face and the respectable, high-buttoned surcoat that split at her waist and trailed down the backs of her calves.

Having been cut off from the Enclave's exclusive debates all week, Luscia didn't know if the elders had been lobbying for or against Dmitri. Thus, she'd endeavored to look immaculate for her own meeting. Everything hinged upon it.

This was her one chance to sway the master of the Order of the Najjan.

"He is ready for you, lu'Lycran," her father said. Bending down, he planted a kiss on her head where it was tightly plaited. "May the High One guide my girl."

She shooshed him off. Peeking over her shoulder, she said, "Fappa, bolaeva. They must respect me."

"The haidren is correct, Clann Darragh," Alora said, though only in word as she abruptly straightened Luscia's posture. Letting go, she led the way for her brother-in-law.

He tossed his large palms up in surrender, but by his chortle, he didn't regret his paternal regression in the least. Her father gave Aksel a pat and loitered a moment longer, much like a boy made to go inside when he so badly wished to keep playing outdoors. "Se'lah Aurynth, Ana'Sere," he said, his voice sobering as he bowed his great frame toward his daughter.

She inclined her chin and said in return, "Rul'Aniell, Ana'Frödre."

With a supportive wink, he forced himself to turn and descend the winding stairs. With the sweeping hem of his fur-mantled cloak, he nearly occupied its entire breadth. There stood no authority that would deny it; he genuinely was a *great father*, not merely to Luscia and Phalen but to the grateful multitude who was currently uprooting their miraculously sprouted crops in the courtyard.

Luscia pivoted toward the shaded threshold. From there, she and the lycran were on their own. Though the door had been fashioned on the peninsula, its weathered maroon frame had not. Upon the curved frame read the najjani credo.

Weh yeyisha'shadü tredae lim Lux.
We live in the shadow to walk by the Light.

Reading each character, Luscia stole a sobering breath, then snapped for Aksel and strode inside the darkened corridor.

The entry sealed at her back with a *boom*. With every trace of sunshine expunged, her vision promptly adjusted to the sequence of low-lit lanterns that led a narrow path toward a crescent-shaped chamber.

Luxiron ringed the old stone walls. Brooches of assorted hierarchy and pin design hung off the tips of each set of wraiths, the blade edges heinously battered yet preserved. Still alive with a remnant glow, the metal shone in glimmering testament to those infamous few who'd carried the ancient weaponry into Boreal's most gruesome battles and heroically sacrificed their lives in the process. Though their bodies had long returned to the soil, it was said that in this way, their hearts could remain within the Order and, by the weapons' precise entombment, forever near the source that fueled both metal and mortality.

A table was situated at the chamber's center. The empty chair on either side boasted a high back and the same sleigh-shaped curvature as the prow of a vödalera. Unsure of protocol, Luscia lingered in place.

"Your aunt always chose to sit on the right." Master Rohan's soothing accent came from where he stepped out of a pitch-black passageway, carting a silver tea tray.

He came round the small table. His cloak flowed like water off his shoulders. Up his spine, a two-tone tree decorated it in sterling and indigo-colored beading. The contrasting shades represented either

branch of the najjan, its Order of Hosts and its Set Apart Stewards—
the latter of which included the Ranger Aelect, like Marek and her
guard. Notably, the tree summed seven boughs, a nod to the seven
undertakings it took to purify luxiron ore in the Dönumn.

Master Rohan did not take a seat but waited patiently for Luscia to
make the first move.

She pulled the chair on the left and, swiping her surcoat under,
eased onto its edge.

His freckled lips quirked. "She said you would do that."

Luscia refused to bristle at Alora's predictive interference, though
the desire came faster than Master Rohan could take residence on the
opposite side of the table. "Both chairs are on the right, dependent on
the sitter's perspective," she responded tactfully.

"Wem. But which perspective is most correct?" asked Master
Rohan. His tails of frizzled reddish hair were roped in twine, fencing
his impassive face. To either end of the chamber, his frost-laden eyes
skated toward the door and the pilgrims outside. "Where we are?" Then
across, toward the wall of the slain. "Or where we have been?"

However simple, Luscia sensed his query was a test little to do with
Boreali seating etiquette. Although they were not meeting on the Isle
of Viridis, he would never cease being her favorite teacher. Yet Luscia
could no longer allow him to view her as a student.

He was master of the najjan, and she the haidren to Boreal.

She considered her answer judiciously. "Both and neither. The most
correct perspective comes from above," Luscia said, pointing toward
the largest lantern swung overhead. Its lumilore cutouts painted stars
across her skin. "A higher vantage has a greater scope—not just of who
we are or where we've been but also how the two relate for who we are
meant to become."

"I agree, Ana'Sere." He bent his head. After tossing his long, corded beard over a shoulder, he poured them tea.

"I doubt the elders would," Luscia commented as she took the intricate silver cup he offered. Her nostrils swelled delightedly at her beloved blend of nixberry and essence of Viridi.

"Most in the Enclave would not agree, niit. However, many of their perspectives are not so much wrong as they are incomplete."

"You don't think there is a clear line between right and wrong?" Luscia sarcastically tipped her head at the master.

"Is that line not yours to discern for us now, Ana'Sere?"

Luscia flattened her lips for having walked so foolishly into that. She draped her arm down to stroke Aksel. "Wem, it is, Master. But now without fail. Discerning what is right is proving much more complicated than I'd ever anticipated."

"Then you shall speak, and I shall listen." Master Rohan lifted a small plate of wafers off the tray and scooted it toward her invitingly. Though the exertion was minor, his every movement demonstrated an epitome of complete control. Like a dangerous bird landing without the warning of sound, the master gracefully settled against his chair back.

Luscia stared at the precious wafers and the noteworthy gesture that communicated his hospitality as much as his support. Baked with seven types of seeds collected from the seven prominent peaks across the highlands, the wafers were incredibly rare. She carefully broke one in two, and upon placing a piece in her mouth, tasted all the richness of her homeland.

After a swallow, Luscia stated plainly, "Bastiion will fall if Boreal does not intervene on King Dmitri's behalf. Soon, the entire Orynthian realm with it. Maybe not tomorrow or even the month afterward, but it is, as we speak, progressively falling into the hands of masked men who seek to undo everything Tiergan and Thoarne built. They are not simply chief warlord of Darakai or chancellor of the Shoto Collective… They are a legion bowing to this Obscurer. His cabal spreads like locusts among fields of power." She leaned forward to implore him. "I can only imagine how the elders are campaigning against us taking action, fearful of revealing our small number to the Ethnicam or perhaps exposing to them a weakened border. Either way, I assure you, Master, the stakes here are more complex and more wicked than our elders are willing to accept."

The master set down his teacup. Steam coiled as he considered his reply. "The Elder Enclave is afraid of reintegrating with pagan influences. Historically, the najjan only emerged as wartime reinforcement at a Thoarne's behest. The elders fear that if we hold a noticeable military presence throughout the crown city, then the populace will follow them there. That if we do not adhere to the light of the highland, the House would become… adulterated… by association."

"You mean, they aren't concerned in risking the Dönumn—the very reason for our closed border—just our imperiled purity?" Luscia immediately rose when the master confirmed it with a respectful nod. She couldn't believe their argument. Well, she could from the elders of Clan Ciann, but not the rest. "Niit, they don't care about purity," she said, rubbing her tingling fingers. "They care about control. Meanwhile, our alliance with Razôuel degrades by the day, the loyalists from Darakai are hiding like vermin in Rian, and members of our own House have begun targeting the very people to whom we offered refuge! Whereas I, their *blessed haidren*, am trying to uphold Boreali virtue within the larger realm. They are the ones imperiling it! The elders say they want to 'stay in the light,' but here they are right beside its fount, defying its unchanging virtue. Not us by marching on Bastiion."

"Tell me what happens if we don't."

Luscia nearly sputtered. "Other than the innumerable lives we'd forfeit by inaction? Were the dozens of children who'd been ripped apart by the Obscurer's monsters not enough to convince you?"

"I must ask." Wriggling wafer crumbs from his fingers, Master Rohan calmly laced them in his lap. "This is *your* part in the conversation, to provide me political answers to the outcomes I cannot alone predict. Your senses reach outside my walls, wem? Tell me, Ana'Sere, what will happen if the najjan do not march on Bastiion?"

"Everything falls," Luscia said sternly. "The Accords are tethered to him—to King Dmitri and his heirs. Not Bastiion. If Orynthia is seized, the Ethnicam will ultimately splinter, all treaties therefore annulled. Then… Then the same Houses we barely consider allies might come for us anyways.

"That is where our Enclave has lost touch, Master Rohan. A noose of machinations dangles over the throne, eager to choke out all that is good, including Boreal. Coalitions forged between Pilar, Darakai, and members of the court salivate over our resources. They lay in wait. And by his order, the cult of the Obscurer is drowning our road back to unity with the blood of innocents. A very real shadow has descended the world, Master. Does it not fall to you and me to push it back?"

Master Rohan snaked his beard off his shoulder and took another sip of tea. Thoughtfully, he palmed the leather cordage wrapped about the long, wiry hairs. "It does, Ana'Sere. We aren't called to stay in the light. We're called to bring it into the dark. It may not be the Enclave's charge, but se'lah Aurynth, it is the charge of the najjan. Weh yeyisha'shadü tredae lim Lux."

At a prickle, Luscia scratched at her palm and murmured to herself, "Light can be dangerous too."

"Yet most dangerous when it is withheld," he said, matching her whispered tone. "I must warn you, Ana'Sere, my verdict will not make us too popular in the Grand Tabernacle."

Luscia suddenly looked up. "Niit, but we will be sitting on the right, inside it."

"Then why don't you look more confident?"

"Because I can sit on the right and still surrender the respect of everyone around me." She paced, Aksel scrambling off the stones to lope after her clipped heels. "I've lost the trust of my aunt, of the elders, and now the king—even as I fight for his throne! He doesn't know why we don't serve him foremostly, why we keep his administration at bay… Why the Quadren must be blindfolded from what we hold most dear. He doesn't understand *anything* and is starting to blame me for *everything*. No matter what, I am failing everyone, all the time. And…" Luscia gripped her stomach, turning toward Master Rohan in honest admission. "And it is killing me inside."

A rumble of tears spilled embarrassingly over her cheeks. With alacrity, the master had risen from his chair and was at her side. He gripped her shoulders at a proper distance. "Failure cannot be defined by its voyeurs."

"It is the High One's eye I am considering, Master. Is not this struggle"—she swirled her fist around her navel—"failing Aniell most of all?"

"We are not special because we were chosen; we were chosen because we are anything but. What we were given, Aniell knows he gave it into imperfect hands. Nevertheless, our hands are not the same, and neither are our paths." Master Rohan let out a deep breath as he lowered his body into a stooped pose that would have shaken the legs of normal men. He captured her wavering gaze in his. "I am but a duskling, a child of shadow and light, like she who came before the two. But you, the seed of wrath and bright, are so much more, Ana'Sere."

At the mention of Tiergan's children, Luscia hooked onto his stalwart expression.

"Thus, I will tell you what I told your aunt many, many years ago… You are stitched with contention. Inside your being wars your nature against your significance. Deny it, you become a sickness to yourself and to Boreal. Wield it, instead become a weapon. Release it… Release that contention and you'll become a peril to us all."

Luscia stood transfixed by the icy seriousness that ringed his pupils. Few Boreali referred to themselves as dusklings anymore. They seldom mentioned Tiergan's eldest daughter in their retellings, she who was borne before his reclamation, for in her impermanence, she was nothing to Boreal. Nothing except the mother of those outside his anointed inheritance.

When remembering her, they had to remember their own impermanence too.

People rarely spoke of Tiergan's children at all, yet between Master Rohan and Alora, Luscia had heard them spoken of twice in a matter of months. "Now you're speaking in legends." Luscia scoffed, motioning for the master to rise.

He remained still. "You can't host believing thoughts while living an unbelieving life, can you? Even the wildest legend is woven by a thread of truth, Ana'Sere."

"Be that it may, legends don't tell me how to heal things. What do I do with a king who suspects I am deceiving him?"

"You are the seed of wrath and bright," he devoutly said again. At her confusion, he gave her an incredulous look. "Must you revisit your scrolls? The Wrathling and the Brightling sprouted from the same, reclaimed branch."

The wind left Luscia's lips as she touched her forearm. The lumin in her blood warmed the surface. "I harbor both?"

"Wem!" Master Rohan said, as if it were obvious. "But you are not alone in yourself anymore! Consult them, Ana'Sere. Consult the spirit only you can see."

She saw he meant immediately, right in front of him. Luscia considered escaping his scrutiny, but if he was an ally of the lumin, then he must be an ally to her. Nervously, she closed her eyes and sought the cosmos beyond the black horizon. The veil split apart in her mind eagerly, and a refreshing respite poured from the base of her neck toward her heels in a shivering rush.

Opening to her Sight, Luscia gasped.

The chamber was divided by a river of lumin. The threads were gushing, beaming… burning the fabric of the *Other* and seemingly through the inner wall of the keep. Whispers assaulted her. They were clamoring in chorale tangles when unexpectedly, the harbinger thread rose out of the bright riverbed and curled toward her.

"Reach, Luscia…"

"Reach for what will not rust, Luscia."

She felt a compression around her elbow. Glancing down, she saw the master's strong hand of support. "Ykah lö, what does the lumin show you?"

Luscia searched his features. The concern there was justified.

The threads showed the way to their oldest mystery of all.

The Dönumn Lux.

CHAPTER TWENTY EIGHT
LUSCIA

She'd waited till dusk to mobilize the Quadren. Any sooner would have been civic suicide.

The ancient gate—entrance to the fabled and forewarned—pointed skyward, steering Luscia's thoughts toward Aurynth's lilac underbelly. It stretched high above the hood of her surcoat. She had pulled the garlanded linsilk low to conceal her notoriously two-toned mane, even though most pilgrims were tucked indoors, feasting. Luscia didn't risk being seen by those who could be avoided. The average Boreali would relay almost anything to their respective elder in hopes the loose-lipped favor might someday be returned.

Hence, her window was slim. If she was going to do it, it had to be quick, succinct, and evasively savvy. Soon her kinsmen would finish dining and exit their cottages to start hauling supplies down to the courtyard, in preparation for tomorrow's homeward departure.

Luscia skirted her king's weighty, shadow-rimmed stare as she gave a hard knock against the door's luxiron lattice. Shakily, she dragged her hand away. Luscia bent for her upturned boots.

"Are we seriously going to stand here and not raise what happened last night?" Zaethan demanded. Having rooted himself beyond the closest guard, he'd been glaringly standoffish since he'd arrived.

And not just because the najjan's eyes were disturbingly welded over.

Luscia wished Zaethan's rigidity applied to the mouth he refused to shut. Heat plucked her cheeks, hoping he was implying the harmed warrior instead of the indecent dance they'd shared under the same harvest moon. Fleetingly, she examined Zaethan up through her tawny lashes, seeing she shouldn't be too sure.

He was prodding the inside of his cheek with his tongue, the way he always did whenever his mind raced more actively than his body itched to. His resentment was palpable; angry about the assault and likely hurt by what'd come before it.

Maybe he'd finally understand.

"Remove your shoes," Luscia ordered, slipping off her own. "Everyone. Stockings too."

Gloved in lambskin, Dmitri squeezed his grip atop his bejeweled cane. "Lady Boreal." He sighed, evidently impatient with her too. "This is hardly the season for a bucolic, barefooted stroll."

Hachiro set his slippers directly beside her boots and licked his finger, then raised it in the crispening air. "By standard estimation, the frostbite will engulf our toes in approximately two-quarters of an hour, leading to a guaranteed sequence of amputations."

"But I need my toes! I owe a dance to nearly three of your hand-maidens," Ira told Luscia, even while he dumped his fine, mud-caked footwear onto the pile. "You can't tamper with this kind of talent, gosling."

"*Nearly* three? Were they not all there?" The shoto'shi blinked over his journal at the yancy.

Ira tapped his lip. "Well, lovely as she was, I now think the third might have been a very shapely shrub."

Though the guard's covered eyes could not communicate it, judgment seeped from his stonelike countenance. Luscia hunched, shouldering it in a way Ira never would. She motioned toward Dmitri's feet. After a pause, he wordlessly lifted his heels for her to remove his shoes just as bolts slid and gears clicked into place.

The gigantic, impenetrable gate creaked ajar.

She straightened to whisper to the najjan on the other side. He too paused, much longer than her king and for better reason. Repeating herself, Luscia held her ground. Another breath and the gate widened for the barefoot guests to pass inside.

Winding back around Dmitri's slender frame, Luscia said sternly to Hachiro, "Leave it, Lord Pilar. What I'm to reveal, you may never record."

Hachiro's distraught eyes bulged like he'd just been told he could not have after-dinner sweets. Pouting, the shoto acolyte placed the tools of his trade on the frosty ground and morosely slid his quill into one of his slippers.

She beckoned them into the snug antechamber, no bigger than five men wide and five men deep. Although frost clawed the massive stones at their backs, moss kissed the ones before the Quadren, where a set of identical doors barricaded the opposite end.

Masculine whispers whooshed through the antechamber, and the gate closed to the courtyard, locking them in with the single najjan. Luscia's ears could attest; he had not uttered a sound.

Ira scooted against Luscia's ribs. "Oh, I do not like this. Well, not *this*…"

She slapped his squirmy fingers off her hips.

The yancy was wrenched aside by his coat.

"I don't like it either," Zaethan said, letting Ira go. He traded him for a more instinctive hold on Dmitri's upper arm, thoroughly bundled under his plush cloak.

"Listen, gosling," Ira leaned in to say. "I'm a pony. You got to let me roam." It gave no surprise that the noise he released resembled that of a filly instead of a stallion.

Zaethan smacked him upside the head.

"Ow! What the Depths are you packing, the queen's signet ring?"

Zaethan gave him a sniff. "Depths, are you sober right now?"

"Repressively so."

Zaethan made to smack him again.

"Niit!" Luscia separated the two. "There can be no violence here."

"The floor is warm." Hachiro blinked at his wriggling toes. "Lady Boreal, why is the floor warm?"

"Listen to me," Luscia urged everyone. "There is not much time. What you are about to witness no lowlander has seen since Thoarne himself crossed our border and retreated to build in Bastiion. You stand on holy ground. Here forward, you will not speak." Her glare speared Ira with more ferocity than a she-wolf, then pinned Hachiro. "You will not study. You will not dare to mock." Her voice dissipated when it fell upon Zaethan. Luscia finally slid her focus toward her king. "You will witness, and you will score to memory what it is that Boreal endangers when we elect to lift our sword in your name."

Beneath the brim of his dusky waves, Dmitri's focus sharpened. The mistrust receded from his mossy, wood-splintered eyes. Her king's face ignited with hope and moored onto Luscia when soundlessly, she slid her bare soles before the opposing interior doors.

Taking in a sputtering mouthful, she exhaled into the intricate wheel of intersecting panels. "Weh'dajjeni Dönumn, weh'dajjeni Lux." A ghostly brilliance surged through the maze of lumilore-lined cogs and plates, waking its dormant, scrawling script to life. Luscia pivoted one last time toward her wide-eyed king and his Quadren to sternly remind them. "You will not speak."

With a moan as burdened as the ages, the archaic doors unfolded. Luscia closed her eyes, bracing, and welcomed the balmy gust when it blew her hair off her shoulders.

She smiled at their astonished gasps.

Waedfrel, she thought. *They should be gasping.*

So should all mankind in the presence of what it did not create.

Lifting her lashes, she stilled. Though she had beheld it—the source of everything—many times before, her senses absorbed the overwhelming wonderment once more.

The sweet spice of fir and tree sap basted Luscia's lungs, purging frailty from their ramparts with lifegiving renewal. Like the hands of heaven, branches were wrapped around the Dönumn as if Aniell's own whisper had commanded the holdreheiim into an inexplicable, unified lean. Soaring even higher than the stones that bordered the phenomenon, laid there by its champion, Aksel Bailefore, evergreens dotted the cylindrical walls of entangled nature, shielding every cavity from the purveying highlands outside—as well as those who trod them. Coalescing toward the stars, the boughs circled tighter and tighter yet never growing close enough to fill the round portal left bared to the darkening sky.

Even in day, they did not miss the sun…

For below, another light was born within.

Each bud and bend looked as if dusted by moondust—clad in a lacey landscape of linsilk spiderwebs and bioluminescent fungi. Scaling the evergreen dome, tiny caplets reached for their Maker in Aurynth, just like every twinkling leaf and fir needle, upturned from the ground. Everything fluttered in a self-contained breeze. The warmth did not breach the walls, nor did it come from the keep.

It was billowing off the pooled waters at the center of the glade.

Luscia kept her steps airy, so as not to disturb the hallowed, harmonized chants being sung by the few olive-robed sages. They nearly blended into the shimmering shoreline, where they meditated and prayed. Wisdom was an inherited art, and at the Dönumn's edge, it was preserved.

Under the sages' bare feet stretched a beach of lumilores exuding in concert. The waves tenderly lapped the rocky bank on all sides. From the center came the tide. And off it, steam unrolled like a scroll across the holy ground.

Luscia hugged the gem-laden boardwalk, mindful of the few master luxsmiths whose presence was abided year-round. In many respects, their labor was nobler than hers that day. It was there where Boreal's famed iron was refined. And in its purification, there where its corrosive blade received its flavor. Around the waters, five foundries inset the holdreheiim, and within them, the master luxsmiths' timed their striking hammers to the sages' endless song—never confusing but ever strengthening—the fundamental anthem.

A clatter came from behind. Luscia ceased her humming and turned toward her trailing company.

Ira was bending for Dmitri's cane but stopped midway when his fingertips brushed the warmed earth. Above him, Zaethan gradually helped their slender king to stay upright. Like Hachiro, who fisted his hand in his already-messy hair, Dmitri had halted in the middle of the boardwalk. The king squatted, slack-jawed. His delicate arms were fortified in Zaethan's clenched hands.

All four men, hailing from three diverse corners of the realm, were staring at one singular element.

They did not resemble ambassadors but animals caught in the night. Light haloed their pupils. Their astonishment reflected not the living glade, rather the fount of its brilliance, where from the base of a bubbling pool, eerie, iridescent beams broke the surface in rotating spindles.

Luscia backpedaled toward her smuggled guests; they'd not time to tarry. "With me, Sire." She offered Dmitri her hand.

He clutched it in an instant.

Luscia delicately guided them up the steps toward a gigantic, round slab that protruded over the temperate waves. From there, the verity could be seen. Her advance met a gentle resistance. Though keeping herself to the mortal side of the veil, Luscia felt the fabric of lumin thickening within the *Other*. It was knit more tightly than Arlette's thickest shawl. Straining to climb higher, the others felt it too.

Finally at the ledge, Hachiro sank onto his knees. Ira clutched his shoulder behind him.

"In this world remain things older and truer than our own existence," stated Luscia.

She looked down through the crystalline waters, at where an unnamed energy expanded and collapsed like a lung inside the earth. Deep down, an opalescence swirled amid the deepest parts with more beauty than the skies of the northmost villages.

The same beauty that swirled within her Tiergan eye.

Luscia's bare calves were stippled with gooseflesh; within her veins, the lumin hummed, barely shimmering beneath her skin, as if trying to escape to its origin below.

Beside her, Dmitri twisted and his mouth parted.

Luscia held her fingers up to his lips, silencing them with a weighted nod. "Wem. I am a daughter of the Dönumn Lux." She said with pride before translating. "Our *Gift of Light*. Aniell's tear, shed from Aurynth. This fount is what restored our land after the Forgotten Wars. What sprung it anew and fed light to the darkness. Some say it even predates those wars, that amid their destruction and folly, the High One preserved it from the injury of men.

"Our clans discovered the spring during the Shade Age, initially protecting it from the pollution of the war-tainted multitudes. Though as Boreal healed, so did her infirmities. Throughout the Spear Age, we grew strong and resilient, perceiving that the waters undergirding the highlands were not simply clean but blessed. Then, at the birth of the Sword Age, as tribes and territories arose, there came a leader from the lowlands… a man who charted the unspoiled green up through the flourishing valley and into the cold, where it should not derive. That leader was rumored to have become a king. A king named Thoarne."

Ira pulled his head from the incandescent view. He still carried their king's cane, and pressing it to the stone, he started to bend toward the fount.

"Niit, it will kill you!" Luscia darted forward to wrench the yancy onto the safety of his heels. "The Dönumn heals, but it also destroys. No one can touch it outright, not here, where it is so pure." She reached for the cane and handed it off to Dmitri's slackened grip. "Despite the danger, Thoarne fell in love with these strange highlands," she told her king, her grin reforming. "He found serenity upon them, but most notably, the highlands forged for him a friend in Tiergan the First, a humble, lowly warrior from the Drystan Sea. History tells that he and Thoarne spent two summer solstices together, teaching each other the ways of their vastly different peoples. Yet during their final feast week, this land was assaulted by a herd of war-tainted, who'd overrun the Saoirse coast. Some were lost to the disease, others hunting a cure before it consumed them completely.

"They fought as brothers against the horde, Tiergan and Thoarne. Countless were slain where we stand. But right before their enemy was defeated, an arrow soaked in the blood of so many pierced the sky. And out of love for his friend, Tiergan shielded Thoarne from its sting. As the arrow impaled Tiergan's ribs, he was thrown into the Dönumn's scorching wake."

Dmitri was enraptured, clinging to Luscia's forearm as she continued. It wasn't just her history she was telling.

It was his.

"If touched directly, the Dönumn kills both flora and fauna. Tiergan should have died. In some respects, a human part of him did. But Thoarne, the unbelieving lowland king, prayed to Aniell for mercy. Mercy for his hero and friend." Moisture collected along Luscia's lashes as she spoke in a reverent whisper. "By Aniell'silaem, Tiergan arose, anew yet another, in the demarcating moment we Boreali call 'Ana'Alïstria.' The *Great Reclamation* of he who was not worthy and then became so. His wounds were healed, and once he came out of the water, he embraced Thoarne." Holding Dmitri's unfaltering gaze, she said emphatically, "When Thoarne pulled away, whatever scrapes and bruises Tiergan's blood touched had disappeared. Tiergan made him a vow that day. For interceding on his behalf, for petitioning the miracle, he would serve Thoarne for generations to come."

In awe, Dmitri's slender thumb lifted and stroked his heart, where Luscia could hear his pulse quickening.

"Your children may forget," she told him. "But mine never will. This is why Boreali haidrens hail from a singular descendance. After his Ana'Alïstria, Tiergan the First realized that what was contained in the Dönumn existed all around, behind a veil of dimension. That Aniell's tears threaded our earth back into being. It falls to Tiergan's pureblooded children, sons and daughters like my future own, to *see* and protect the Gift, and to brandish it so that no matter the age, the Forgotten Wars are never repeated."

Painfully, Luscia forced herself to look at Zaethan, who was holding his abdomen in astonishment.

His gaze was piercing and tense. The russet skin shuddered about his bright jade eyes. She prayed it was sympathy that rimmed them, rather than hatred. If the Dönumn couldn't make him see the divine rope by which her hands were tied, then nothing ever could.

Shifting, she swallowed and took Dmitri's sharp cheeks into her palms. "The najjan are going to fight for you, My King, but you must trust them. In bowing to something greater than yourself, they honor your greatness here on earth." His chin trembled when Luscia softly assured him. "And in their devotion, the najjan will honor the greatness of your children after you and I are gone."

She saw him blink back a storm of emotions. From the boardwalk, the najjani guard who'd accompanied them gave a gruff cough, signaling to Luscia the time that'd elapsed. Directing her king, she beckoned for Ira and Hachiro to rise, and retreated them down the other side of the fount through a mossy warren of meditating seers.

Many bordered the path. Out of respect, Luscia did not disturb any in passing, though she knew most from when she was a girl. Cross-legged in their simplistic robing, engraved psalms pulsed over the lumilores they'd placed around their focused bodies.

As she approached the doors to the antechamber, her ankle was suddenly caught in someone's rickety grasp.

Luscia discovered it belonged to a familiar face—an elderly man, veiny and bald except for his long, scraggly white beard. He muttered the incoherent ramblings of someone riding out their own twilight. His eyes were blind but alight, shining through the milky glaze he'd earned during the years he had wielded them on Boreal's behalf.

The accompanying najjan did not intervene.

The elderly seer stared directly behind Luscia. Though he could not see anyone there, he spoke in an unnervingly hollow voice. "King of few, remembered by all. Protect the king who rejects his crown; the answer is found in the eye of the beholder."

Releasing her, the seer picked up a lumilore and chisel and resumed his babbling. A chill raised the hairs on the back of her neck at his unsettling prophecy, despite the Dönumn's warmth. Luscia contorted and glanced back at where Zaethan escorted Dmitri. Their king's skin had drained of its already-tepid color. His pupils darted toward his life-long friend, the one he most wished not to learn of his incurable illness.

Making haste, Luscia stooped and planted a gentle kiss upon the old man's crown. "Tredae'Aurynth, Fapapï." Then, coming alongside Dmitri, she urged his wobbly legs. "Come away, My King. The light is bright as it is alarming…"

The luxiron door to the antechamber swirled and clicked behind them, locking them inside. The seer's words whirled her thoughts. Dmitri was king of few, according to those who no longer recognized his reign. Perhaps the prophecy simply ensured his legacy would survive—

"Why did you kiss that scary man!" Ira blurted, as if he'd been holding his breath the entire time.

"Because he is my grandfather."

The najjan slid the biggest bolt in place to their rear and moved toward the courtyard gateway.

Dmitri hunched in the corner, his tenor distant. "Did any of your grandfather's prophecies ever prove false?"

She bit her lip, already regretting her response. "Niit. Never." Nervousness like she hadn't felt since girlhood sprung up from her belly.

Planted there by both mother and madness.

Eoine was her father's daughter, a beautiful prophetess born to a haidren seer. And though she had sacrificed her sanity to their shared gifting in the end, Eoine's prophesies had never been wrong either.

Phalen slung his fist in the air. He mutely cheered as his lumilore skidded across the rippling pool. The Dönumn was brilliant at the hour, splintered by the clearness of their final morn in the keep.

Expertly avoiding the splash of the caustic, consecrated waters, her brother sauntered back to where Luscia stood along the bank and picked up another stone. He split a grin that bragged more stubble than she preferred a boy could grow at sixteen. "One more try, or you're riding between Fappa and Ana'Mere the whole way back to Roüwen. I won't bear it for you twice."

"Not if you can help it," she replied with a smirk.

"Do you think we'll ever be back here again?" Phalen strangely asked. At her hiked brow, he folded his long arms and rubbed the lumilore between his fingertips. "All of us together like this, I mean. Doesn't today feel off-kilter, like something, somehow, has been altered?"

She tore from her brother's puzzled expression and peered over her shoulder at where their father and aunt were crouching at her grandfather's either side, bidding him their farewells. He was advancing in age, thus his awakening in Aurynth was near, hence why most sil'haidrens opted to spend their last years near the Dönumn.

"Fapapï can't stay with us forever, brödre."

"Niit, that's natural. His passing is not what I meant."

Can Phalen sense I'd brought the Quadren here? He too was advancing in age, and while she'd inherited the family haidrenship, maybe Phalen had inherited something else…

Luscia shied from his study and plucked the stone out of his hold. She chucked it across the shore, then stomped off to find a better one and rummaged through the rocks until her father had joined Phalen.

Returning, she leaned against the trunk of her father's torso, inviting the way his sturdy arms engulfed his children like they were still little.

"Weh'dajjeni Dönumn… My gift is my family, and by the High One, *you* are my strength." Her father hugged them closer. "Believe me, my darlings, your mamu felt the same."

Phalen sniffed gruffly. "Mamu skipped stones a lot better than Luscia."

Their father's belly rumbled. Steering Luscia's shoulders toward the water's glistening edge, he leaned down and said into her ear, "The loudest doubter is the one inside your head, lu'Lycran."

She stole another glance over her shoulder at Alora. Her aunt watched her successor vigilantly from afar, a disapproving bend to her downturned lips. Luscia brought the lumilore close and exhaled. Like always, it shone brighter than any Phalen had found along the bank. Fixing her eyes on the Dönumn Lux, she put her back toward her aunt—the woman whom she used to consider the finest exemplar of righteousness.

The Dönumn bore no shadows… nor lies, nor elusions.

Alora Tiergan sheltered many.

Her father supported her fist and kissed it, then held it out straight before her. "Look toward the light and never hold it back."

His grounding presence vanished from her back. Aiming her stone for the ethereal fount, Luscia let it go.

CHAPTER TWENTY NINE
ZAETHAN

Zaethan reentered Roüwen behind a curtain of crescent wraiths, his prydes closely monitored in line behind him. He'd spent most of the expedition brooding between the Quadren and his warriors—uncertain of the mysteries he had been shown.

Questioning if he was leading them into more.

Plated in evergreen, the holdreheiim seemed smaller inside the city fortress after having come from the seed of their gargantuan supply. Honoring Luscia's wishes, he'd not told anyone about that last day at the keep, not even Kumo or his third. The only kwihila Zaethan had left was the value of his word. And after bearing witness to a kakka-shtàka magicked pool in the middle of the highlands, even that was lacking. He couldn't describe such a sight if he'd tried.

Luscia rode paces ahead as a guide to Dmitri and his haidrens. Their hoods had been removed a few days before. Zaethan tried to fight the lure of her mesmerizing sway atop the dappled mare. Or how every few minutes, she'd reach up and obsessively adjust the linsilk hiding her scar, where in rebellion it slouched beneath her ear. Her collar that day was shorter than those she more often sported.

The measurement discomforted her as much as it did him.

Darakaians bore their scars and the stories they told openly. Zaethan didn't understand why the damaged tissue still paralyzed her, not when she carried so much strength beneath it. The contradiction made her both maddening and magnificent. Were Luscia to ever encounter Tevaár's despicable Prince Darcain again, she'd be meeting her villain.

He'd be meeting his end.

And what a cosmic firework show that would be.

Luscia Darragh Tiergan could explode cabbages and lift boulders and stop a man in his tracks. Could turn massive tree trunks into woodchips. And, evidently, was the descendant of some mythical man, resurrected from some lethal spring and put there by some deity Zaethan had been pretty sure didn't exist, until about a week ago.

What then was a sniveling Tavish ghoul—or his leftover mark—to the mover and shaker of light?

"You're more likable when you're mute." Barging into his periphery, as she'd done almost every hour, Zahra sidled her horse next to his.

"Alpha Zà just hard thinking how to beat the red ogre in tonight's game of darts and dice…" Jabari's Yowekaon prattle sounded from the back of their weary cluster, the mountaineer foolishly untroubled by the vengeful scowl that Declan skewered him with from the front.

"Alpha Zà's aim not too good anymore, ano. Always getting distracted whenever Maji'maia crosses the alehouse."

Zaethan heard someone smack Jabari. He ground his teeth. They ought to smack Kumo for the catchy nickname his beta had given her. Now everyone was using it.

Routed off the town square, they skirted the fountained statue of Tiergan the First and its basin of ever-burning *sky flame*—as Jabari dubbed it. Keeping his distance, Zaethan tailed the Quadren into a multi-story stable burrowed within the trunk of a monolithic holdre-heiim. Inside, the smell was an invigorating cross of cherry and pine. A squadron of shadowmen steered his pryde along the system of rounding ramps and stacked stalls.

Zaethan dismounted Hellion with a grateful stretch of his spine and glanced at Kumo, the real horseman of the two. Born and raised in Halona like their mothers, Kumo would appreciate the spiraling mecca most.

Grinning, his beta sighed through his flapping lips as if to imitate his borrowed mount. Kumo squinted up and down at the gelding, then at Hellion's impressive flanks. "Mine's bigger."

"Keep telling yourself that, cousin," Zaethan said, patting his beta's big bicep before he unbuckled the weather-worn saddle off his Andwele stallion. The cold had done it no favors, not that the leather had been equipped to winter in the highlands.

Abruptly, he was pushed against Hellion's middle. Zaethan spun and saw a pair of shadowmen dashing through the stables toward Luscia and Captaen Bailefore.

"Heard we were back in town, eh?" Kumo elbowed Zaethan. "Our boots hit the hay and they're off running to lock up their yayas."

"I told you not to touch their women, Kumo." A bad feeling furled Zaethan's ringed brow.

"Owàa's chains, Ahoté. It was just a joke."

He shoved Hellion's saddle to Kumo's torso and marched down the row of Darakaian warriors, spurning the way their worried faces wheeled after him.

One of the shadowman had bent down to speak to Luscia in rushes. Yards away, Zaethan couldn't catch their discourse; however, upon hearing the message, Dmitri pulled his fingers to his forehead. It was the only signal Zaethan needed. Whatever they'd relayed to the Northern haidren, he knew it was not good.

Their king's hazel eyes darted across the stable and winced at Zaethan's brisk approach.

All right then, he thought. *Really not good.*

"Zaeth—brother, promise to listen before you jump to conclusions," Dmitri said, going so far as to step between him and the pale messengers.

Past his friend's shoulder, Zaethan spoke louder than the shadowman's nervous speech. "What have you to tell me, Lady Boreal?"

All but imperceptibly, her posture deflated when she turned toward him. "Your scout crossed our border during Ana'Innöx. Meh fyreon, Lord Darakai, but… Dhalili was detained. She's in najjani custody."

Zaethan rebounded his locs three times over before he was permitted to enter the fern-covered holding cell. Like the stables, the lair of living wood was engraved with riddles and rhymes.

Unlike the stables, it featured witchiron bars.

A muscle twitched through his clenched jaw. Sounds of struggle came through the windowed slits above the holdreheiim door, followed by an erratic clatter and a muffled high-pitched shriek. Under Zaethan's glower, one of the shadowmen dislodged the blockading log and promptly spun the metallic lock in a specialized sequence.

With a sobering sigh, Luscia nodded for them to open it. She stepped aside and welcomed Zaethan to go ahead.

He couldn't control the ruthless growl that escaped him, seeing Dhalili there, his tiny scout bound to a splintering chair in the middle of the cell. By its cracking, she'd been thrashing its legs against the floor for a while. By the shards littering the cold floor, it hadn't been the first with which she'd succeeded. A dirty wool blanket had been haphazardly pinned around her shoulders, where beneath, her traditional Darakaian buckskins and breezy gunja pants left her toes starkly bare.

She must have been freezing.

Down her childishly round cheeks slipped a gag, drenched by her feral tears. Dhalili's eyes bulged when she sighted him. She squealed for her alpha through the fabric.

Zaethan rushed in and dropped at her side. Unsheathing his kopar, he sawed through the knotted straps at her bruised wrists. Though unshackled, the reinforced linsilk had harmed her Southern skin as well as any chain.

The rest of the pryde pressed into the space behind him.

"Bolaeva, we had to, Ana'Sere," the other shadowman said. "The trespasser wouldn't listen—"

With his help, Dhalili's gag finally fell. "I told that nasty witchy, Alpha Zà! I told him what you said!" she shouted, jabbing her flat chest furiously. "That I work for the king and his mhàdda queenie, but ano… Ano, witchies don't use *their* ears. So, kàchà kocho, I'm going to chew them off and feed them to each other!"

Dhalili was all teeth when she lurched for her warden. The fair-haired shadowman shrank back against the wall. Zaethan gripped the chair and slammed it back down, where his scout's ankles were still tied. He ran his fingers down the side of her face to soothe her as he crouched and addressed the last bindings.

"Is this true, Armaeger?" Dmitri pushed through and asked the older shadowman, whose freckly nose was as orange as his short mane. Zaethan hadn't noticed the double-branched brooch on the man's tunic. Nor did he think it mattered. "This Darakaian scout is no criminal. Did she not inform you of her status under my special assignment?"

Tensely, the armaeger's eyes snapped toward his haidren. "Wem, yes, she did, Your Majesty. However…"

"However, Boreali protocol is to enforce a closed border, no matter the depositions of those who cross it," Luscia stated. "Waedfrel, Armaeger. You did your duty, despite this unprecedented occasion."

"Waedfrel?" Zaethan sputtered, letting go of his scout's cold, little feet. "Prisoners in Bastiion are better kept. She smells like she hasn't washed in weeks!"

Freed, Dhalili charged at the shadowmen with full verve, her hands hooked like claws.

Zaethan looped his forearm around her belly just before she could swipe.

"We tried, Lord Haidren. She bites!" The younger shadowman stripped his sleeves back to reveal a garden of swelling. Knowing Boreali flesh and how fast it could heal, the bites must have been fresh.

He held his scout like a barrel under one arm. Zaethan snatched her face with his other hand. "Depths, Dhalili. You can't nibble your way out of everything—" Pausing, he rotated her slight jaw into the dappled sunlight.

It looked like a plum.

Zaethan smacked his lips and deliberately glanced up at the shadowmen. Against his palm, so did Dhalili, though with assuredly more glee. "How did that happen?" he questioned. Amid their pregnant silence, he asked again. "How did that happen to her!"

Luscia entwined her arms. "Armaeger? I demand you answer the Lord Haidren."

Dhalili stopped squirming and overtop his fingers, she chattered her teeth excitedly.

"We just… It was like caging a rabid animal," he said, revulsion tossing new gravel into his tenor. "We had to make her stop."

"She's just a Darakaian, Ana'Sere," the other one said in appeal.

Dmitri struck his walking stick on the ground. "Just a Darakaian? Lady Boreal, I thought we were beyond this!"

"We are, Your Majesty."

"Tell that to my scout's fractured jaw," barked Zaethan.

Luscia's dense brows flattened. "It's probably not fractured."

He wanted to shake her, bringing attention to the slickening of his palms. Zaethan lowered to kiss Dhalili's temple and said as controllably as possible into her ear, "Go to big Kumo." Half turning, he made sure she scampered off in the right direction.

After a fleeting reunion, Takoda offered her a leg up. She climbed onto Kumo's colossal back with the friskiness of a squirrel scurrying up a tree.

"This is utterly uncalled for, Lady Boreal," Dmitri warned, clacking his cane until he stood in solidarity beside Zaethan, "and concerns what is possibly my most covert operation in play. Dhalili Pàdoma is a critical asset of the crown. As king, I cannot and *will not* look the other way on this."

Zaethan cracked his knuckles and shrugged. "It's simple really. The Lady Boreal appreciates markings so much, yeah? Let's make them even."

Upon Kumo's shoulders, Dhalili menacingly clicked her tongue at the shadowmen and dragged her thumb across the beta's bared throat. "Witchies getting stitchies…"

"You really do belong in the wild," muttered Zahra, cocking her hip.

In a speed he'd forgotten she could employ, Luscia appeared in the gap between him and the patrolling shadowmen. She held out her hands in their defense. "A wrong has been committed, but further violence won't mend it."

"This makes two—two!—of my warriors injured by your highland regime. The exact number cowering against that wall behind you. I am owed retribution." Zaethan nearly foamed at the mouth.

"Retribution, of course. But brutality? Niit, not here, you're not. They will be punished, according to the Clann Darragh's judgment." Luscia elevated her chin. "Harm them, and you harm the throne. The najjani master has yet to announce his support to the Elder Enclave. Tensions are high enough just by your being here. Then, the prydes did not observe their original confinement to Roüwen, and related or not, a woman went missing. The Enclave is begging for any excuse, Lord Darakai. Proceed violently, and your warriors will be dumped across the border by sunrise."

Dmitri stammered. "You said we wouldn't need the elders' backing if the master offered his."

"Wem, but it will be a hellscape without it," she retorted. "One you don't have political capital to navigate. Sire, right now the House of Boreal is your only ally in the Ethnicam."

Dmitri tucked his walking stick under an arm and washed his face in his hands.

"Ano zà. That Boreal is not." Zaethan huffed and jerked toward his scout. "Dhalili, report."

Luscia held up a pair of fingers. "Wait—Armaeger, take your

patrol outside. And for the love of Aniell, fetch our unfortunate guest a coat."

At the reminder, Kumo rubbed Dhalili's scrawny arms. Her teeth clacked, though hardly from the chill, as the shadowmen sheepishly exited the holding cell.

"Before you say anything, I have to know," Dmitri told the scout. "Did you get my mother to safety?"

Zaethan gave her a sharp nod.

Dhalili cleared her throat. "I stashed mhàdda queenie where the king tells me, with the fancy boar lord in Arune."

At Dmitri's confusion, Zaethan translated. "She thinks Gregor Hastings looks like a hairy pig."

"Ah, an honest mistake," he said absently. "And were you successful with Sayuri Naborū-Zou? Did she accompany the Queen Mother to the duke's estate?"

His scout shook her head of squat, rusty-hued knots. "Ano zà. Western haidren barricaded her door, Your Majesty."

"I see…" said Dmitri in sincere disappointment. He folded one arm over the other. "And what of my appointed commander supreme, Yousif Shà, and his progress? Is there anything worthwhile to relay?"

At that, she cracked a savage grin. "Commander Yousif is being *really* sneaky. He convinced swanky boss man in Rian to let all minor chiefs loyal to King Dmitri encamp in his breakaway haven. Àla'maia winks every night as resistance warriors from the minor tribes tiptoe through Darakai to gather there with Commander Yousif, right under the chief warlord's nose."

Kumo whistled proudly. "Thank the Fates for our Shà kwihila!"

"Yousif brokered an alliance with the magistrate of Rian?" Zaethan clarified, genuinely impressed by his uncle's efforts, despite their personal estrangement.

"From the sounds of it, but for what in return?" Dmitri answered instead. "Rian is a merchant state. It won't give anything for free, especially for a king it hates."

Dhalili giggled. "Swanky boss hates the old commander more."

"Maybe the magistrate permits Yousif's temporary occupation to ensure Rian's long-standing deal with the throne remains intact," Luscia said. "They would not enjoy the same special liberties under the governance of Nyack Kasim. He would snuff out any form of revolt, even that contained within the walls of Rian."

Zaethan tapped his heel. "What of my prydes?"

"Eh, you know how fussy militia can be." The scout dropped her eyes and started coiling sections of Kumo's short hair far too meticulously.

"Dhalili…"

His heart sank when she winced.

"The Eindrulla and the Yachel Prydes are still yours, Alpha Zà. With the Proper and Mirajii Prydes"—she waved toward the town square outside—"that's almost half, yeah? And the Ikaika pryde will do anything for coin, so…"

Dmitri let out a dismal snort. "Great. I'm buying mercenaries now."

Zaethan's hardened expression poked holes in Dhalili's sorry excuse for a smile. Surely Wekesa's divisive hold over the other prydes should have lessened with his death. Zaethan doubted he'd ever be able to trust those from the Valley again, but as for the rest, without him they'd no clear leader to rally behind.

"Wekesa is dead. I watched him sink to the bottom of the Yachel." Zaethan snarled. "Who does the Provincial Pryde—the Andwele, the Khan, or the Foothill—think they are following?"

"The, uh, the Valley Pryde has a new alpha." Dhalili squeaked. "And he is spreading word that he killed you. That himself is the new alpha zà now."

Kumo bent his head upward. "Who?"

"Nigan Hanovi."

Zahra punched the wall, earning herself a pained howl. "That slimy ferret! I should have fed my cousin to a cave python when we were cubs," she exclaimed as she nursed her bloody knuckles.

Zaethan put his back toward them and gripped the cell bars angrily. That was what it felt like. Boreal was a cage, while outside, the realm was crumbling under a heap of deceptions. "They won't join Yousif if they think I'm dead—that I was defeated by a whimpering weakling like Nigan Hanovi." At that, Zaethan beseeched Dmitri. "They need to see my face. You have to let me leave at once—"

"That is a categorical 'no.'"

"You are going to trap me here while your own military mobilizes against you?"

"I will not risk it!" Dmitri's cheeks burned brightly. "Zaeth, you are," he said with a hard swallow, "the haidren to Darakai. And my haidrens will remain safely at my side until my court is restored."

"That's a shtàka plan!" Zaethan yelled at his friend. He heard Luscia's intake, probably offended by his candor, as he pushed off the cell wall and rebound his locs for the fourth time.

But Dmitri leaned over the handle of his walking stick. He held his ground, unruffled and unmoved. "We strategize for the good of our tomorrow, not our today. Think, Zaeth. If I retake Bastiion, yet lack a strong Darakaian haidren, I won't be able to hold the crown city for long. Besides," he said with a sigh. "What forces we forfeit in the militia, we can regain from Razôuel."

Zaethan sputtered. "Like the Zôueli should be trusted to fight our battles!"

"Zôueli would have to get through the Andweles first," piped a small voice.

Together, they spun toward Dhalili.

"The chief warlord, he…" The stare of her big brown eyes bounced between Zaethan and their king. "He's led the Mworran beasties up the Yowekaon tribal territories. They encamped along the border to Razôuel. And even if the Zôueli corps attack the cannibals, they wouldn't make it past the plains. Chief warlord's been building outposts from Halona to Bastiion."

The already-deep hollows under Dmitri's eyes seemed to blacken. "Nyack Kasim knows he can't start his war without its king. So he is invading royal land to choke me out." Sharply, he looked at Dhalili. "Can you get past it—that Mworran encampment?"

"Can I, he asks?" The scout waved him off. To her credit, Dhalili Pàdoma was shiftier than a chameleon in spring.

"I take that as a yes." Dmitri pointed his walking stick at Luscia. "Lady Boreal, you and I will write to Bahira'Rasha immediately. The princess must know this is an insurrection. Bahira'zol'Jaell is a cunning woman, and she'll move mountains to secure her daughter's Orynthian crown; I'm sure of it."

Luscia balked. "Me? I—I'm not sure what to even say to her, Your Majesty."

"Anything. Everything. Language is just spoken music. Sing her an ink-filled melody, Lady Boreal. Rasha favors you." Their king strode toward the cell door with renewed vigor. "That favor could rescue a kingdom."

"Kumo, accompany Dhalili. As beta, I need you to reinforce my leadership to the prydes. You'll certainly encounter them along the way—"

Dmitri halted with a burdened sigh, partly out the door. "Strategize for *tomorrow's* good, Zaeth."

The future.

A future without Zaethan left Kumo in his shoes. His cousin was the Shà heir to the Darakaian haidrenship—the real, pureblooded heir. The House would follow him more easily because of it. Were anything to happen to Zaethan upon retaking Bastiion and Kumo was not there, Darakai's seat on the Quadren would succumb to the avarice and back-biting of those fighting to seize it.

Zaethan passed over his beta. Instead, his scrutiny fell on his third. He marched toward her without hesitation, assuredness weighting his every footfall. "Zahra," he said and cupped the back of her shaved skull, bringing her forehead against his. "Go with Dhalili. Be my voice. Draw the prydes to Yousif in my place."

She locked her honeyed eyes on his. Zahra's breathing changed, and exposing an unusual ounce of hesitation, she risked questioning her alpha. "Is this because I'm more expendable to you?"

His fingers dug into her flesh as if to bury the truth in her head where it could never fall out. "Listen to me now, yeah? You earned your position. Not an inch of your squishy body is expendable to me. Yeye qondai?" Zaethan choked back the lump in his throat. "Because if you get eaten by a cannibal, you'll never live it down."

Zahra punched his shoulder and pulled him into an ironclad hug. "Uni zà, Alpha Zà."

"Don't wait for the sunrise," he ordered, forcing himself to step away from one of his best friends in the whole, rotting world. "Shàla'maiamo to you both."

Zaethan let his feet dangle over the edge of the skyward platform under a darkening sky, too disheartened to lift his chin off a joist of the intricate railing. Swinging them, he noticed the scuffs across his borrowed Boreali boots. Lacquered in beading, they were hideous.

He wished they were lacquered in mud. At least then there'd be evidence of the shtàka sandwich they were stuck in, rather than the glittering facade called Boreal.

The highlands unrolled beneath him, stories below. Shops were closing for supper with their families. The citizens of Roüwen pranced off the streets and up into the canopied heights. Only the Darakaians were left in the square, and they swarmed to the alehouse.

They had no family to run toward here. And none who'd deign to play the part.

Bitterly, Zaethan brought the half-empty growler to his mouth and took a long swig of mead. He almost spit it out, cursing its sweet aftertaste, and tilted the thing toward him. Beneath the glow of the awakening foliage, the liquid sparkled at him mockingly. Zaethan rolled his eyes. They beautified even their alcohol.

Shadowmen bastards.

Someone scuffled along the wooden boards behind him as they summited the climb, doing a poor job hiding their panting as they did.

He needn't turn. He knew who it was, given Zaethan's mood and the intruder's courage. "Can't a man pout in peace anymore?"

Dmitri's chortle was as warm as it was short lived. "Peace is better found in peaceable company," he replied and made a clumsy effort in sitting beside Zaethan. In his periphery, he saw Dmitri was wrapped in an even thicker fur cloak. Its superfluous folds swallowed his thighs, making them look like sticks. His friend swung his thin legs over the ledge, mirroring Zaethan's.

"I can lick my own wounds, Dmitri. I've been doing it for years," Zaethan grumbled and went for another drink of mead.

"Not very well." Dmitri snatched the growler and set it on his other side. "Sober minds, Zaeth."

He hitched his other forearm overtop the joist and tucked it under his chin resolutely. "It's time for a new motto. You've overplayed that one, I'm afraid."

"Hm, well we can't have that," said Dmitri. "Let me ask you this. Is faith a painting or a song?"

"What in the Depths?" Zaethan tugged his neck aside at his friend.

Dmitri twiddled his long fingers airily. "Just something I've been chewing on lately. So what do you think, painting or song?"

Steam puffed off his friend's sallow lips as he repeated the question. Confused, Zaethan tugged his own jacket closer amid the sharpening cold. They should get inside and in front of a fire soon. "Faith." Zaethan snorted. "I don't know what to believe—about anything—anymore."

"I know how you feel," Dmitri murmured but then thoughtfully angled his head the other way. "Then again, maybe I don't know how you are feeling at all."

"That makes two of us."

"Have you written in your journal yet?"

"With what? I'm supposed to be this fate writer—this jwona rapiki—to my people, except I have no idea what it is I'm rewriting. I'm just…" Zaethan plucked a twig off the railing and chucked it into the open. "I'm just stuck between the pages of someone else's story."

Silence fell the way it normally did whenever Dmitri was pondering an issue more than Zaethan cared to himself.

A cough escaped the slender king as he said, "At the keep, you expressed that you were finally out of Nyack's domineering shadow. But you know, I have to disagree. I don't think you were ever really beneath it. I think you've always been casting your own shadow, and the cloud cover is finally in the process of its rightful rearrangement." Dmitri slipped his gloved hand out of the cloak, and he gripped Zaethan's knee securely. The worn, scarlet thread about his wrist peeked overtop the leather trim. "One day, the sun is going to come out for you, brother, when that last cloud has faded away. How magnificent it will be for everyone who lives to see it."

Zaethan's brow creased. Sadness glossed his friend's countenance, and it rattled him to the bone. He hadn't meant for his wallowing to cause any real worry, as if the king of Orynthia didn't have enough worries to contend with already.

Sliding his arm off the beaming, Zaethan took his friend's leather-cased hand. "Dmitri, I'm going to be fine—"

Dmitri's weak grin wobbled, and he quickly shifted his face away, emitting another cough.

Zaethan leaned forward to better catch his gaze but steered it toward the alehouse below when a whooping raucous splintered the tranquility of the night. "The Darakaians are going stir-crazy. We can't trap them here for much longer."

Knocking his rumpled head backward, Dmitri searched the sky, obscuring his expression from Zaethan. "We must teach them how to be content, Zaeth. The gratitude of a king lifts the spirits of everyone around him."

His tenor was frail yet heavy in the same breath. It scraped Zaethan's ears. Dmitri's whole frame shuddered as he issued a slew of hoarse coughs, this time unable to cease until a few minutes later.

Zaethan patted his friend's back and turned him inward. "Are you okay? You look awful."

"Thank you," said Dmitri dryly. Though with an anxious surge, he patted a hand about his cloak. There came a jingle of glass, and in an instant, he eased back against Zaethan's side. "It's just a sniffle. Really, Zaeth."

"Seriously, you don't look well."

"It will pass. All colds do."

Zaethan didn't enjoy the hoarseness of his answer. "Come on, let's get indoors. Along with whatever they call 'dinner' inside you."

"No." Dmitri clutched Zaethan's fingers, as he'd wrapped an arm around his friend's thinned frame. He formed a firm fist and ordered him softly, "Don't strip this moment from me. You said it yourself; we won't be here for much longer."

His heart sank for having neglected their friendship in recent weeks. "Fine. Then it's dealer's choice, and the crown is buying."

Satisfied with the win, Dmitri leaned more heavily against Zaethan. "You're lucky I didn't pack the checklerule."

"I hate that game like hot Uriel pie."

"According to the daughter of its duke, hot pie doesn't hate you." Dmitri chuckled weakly as he chose for them a topic. "Hm. Speaking of delicacies, do you remember that spring, when our blanket fort commandeered the royal pantry?"

"Even the prettier chef agreed. You made a terrible general," Zaethan fondly replied. Securely, he used his hand to warm Dmitri over the cloak.

"Well, the proof is always in the pie, Zaeth…"

They stayed there a while, after his fervent request, reliving the inanest memories for no reason he could conjure. The banalities of their strange life together were all his king wished to discuss until his lids eventually succumbed and shuttered the starlight. It was late evening before Zaethan hauled Dmitri onto his sleepy feet. Holding him close, he half carried his dearest friend all the way to Luscia's manor.

Cold and confused, Zaethan did not go inside.

CHAPTER THIRTY
LUSCIA

Warmth surged along her forearm as she whirled on her heel. Opalescent light ruptured off her skin, blazing for the burgeoning horizon, and arced across Luscia's knuckles, sheathing her grip on the hilt. She spun inside a web of lumin. The threads twinkled against the dawn. Rapidly, they parted like an unraveling seam for an inbound object, flying straight toward her forehead.

She sliced a crescent wraith through the clay disk. Whipping away from the debris and the confident cheers of the brawny najjan who'd launched it, Luscia discovered another disk hailing inches from her nose. She lurched backward. Tugged by her arm, her fist zipped forward and punched it out of existence. The clay burst off the shield of lumin, its ricochet a dusty smear within the *Other*. Flustered, Luscia shook out her hand.

She hadn't intended to strike.

The lumin did.

Beneath her alabaster skin, her veins were sparkling in branches of cobalt and pearl, same as they did near the Dönumn. With most other colors muted inside the Sight, Luscia looked up and quickly spotted Zaethan's brilliant, vengeful grin through the sandy cloud.

He never waited for her to regain her footing as the rest did. Already, she fostered a short-lived bruise over her left kidney. Luscia didn't appreciate his seeming desire to make it a matching set.

The particles cleared as he came fully into view. Zaethan raked his tongue across his teeth. She tried not to chase its movement, noting instead how his thighs tensed, readied for his subsequent attack. The hard muscle puckered the supple stretch of his pants. Luscia found herself counting the pleats…

Suddenly, he pelted his next disk as if it were a spear.

With wide eyes, Luscia bent backward, irate, leveling her spine with the earth. She watched the disk sail inches above her face. Spiking her crescent wraiths into the heather, she kicked up her boots, released one of the hilts, and grabbed the other like a pole, then twisted her body through the air until her foot crashed through a third disk.

Luscia landed. She tore the wraiths from the dirt. Stalling for her to catch her breath, Marek then launched a set of disks from the other end of the circle. She charged the incoming wave with a snarl. Leaping, she spiraled her form, slicing the luxiron in a lethal wingspan through the clay. Luscia hit the earth with a delicate *thump*.

Earthen bits were raining upon the moor, threads of lumin contently drifting in the breeze above them.

More than a little lightheaded, Luscia shuttered her Sight when Böwen excitedly jogged over. A dull pang in her back protested his celebration. She really needed to improve her stretching during morning prayers.

"That was unbelievable! Like something pulled out of a storybook, Ana'Sere!" Böwen exclaimed and batted the chilly air with his best right hook, replicating her triumph.

Marek's steps crushed the clay remnants as he neared. "Aniell'silaem, like a legend of the Brightling."

"Oh yeah, how does the old song go? *By blade of light, the Brightling slayed, yet by his might, the Wrathling paid…*" chanted Böwen.

Declan whistled to the Boreali tune, then playfully backhanded the younger najjan's cheek. "Good to see you've not lost all your dignity over that raven-haired lass."

Böwen turned a shade pinker than the sky. "Bolaeva, not around Creyvan," he begged in a low voice and, scratching his short beard, glanced at his twin where he'd parked himself in the distance, arms crossed and forlorn beside a boulder.

"Tadöm, Noxolo," Luscia said when the najjan silently deposited the crescent wraiths back into her care.

His long arms hung dejectedly at his sides. Her secretive, experimental trainings were not offering a good enough distraction, it seemed. Though Noxolo's father was still leading small parties into the wildwood, the Enclave had ceased mass search efforts for Lady Egon. Some elders even rumbled that it was a lost cause. Noxolo had barely spoken since they had announced their formal decision to give up the investigation—and therefore the hope that his mother ever be found.

"Every day brings a new miracle, brödre." Marek offered him a stiff, yet compassionate smile. "Our Ana'Sere is proof of that much."

There came a vulgar grunt behind them.

Her captaen rotated toward the Darakaian haidren as he trudged across the sparring circle. "You deny what we *allowed* you to witness today?"

"Leave it, Marek. He's not worth it," Luscia said with a dismissive eye roll.

Zaethan nodded when he passed their tight grouping. "Neither are you, it would seem."

"Come again?" She knocked Marek's stomach to step aside.

Halting, the other haidren finished drying his hands on a towel and whipped it over his shoulder, then planted his hands on his trim hips. "One out of five," Zaethan barked. "Out of five pitches, only once did you do what you set out to do—and that was because you didn't see it coming. *That* was instinct. *That* was real. But four times you did what was comfortable. You defaulted to your precious blades. Shocking, yeah? I won't always be there to provoke you into getting your hands dirty, Maji'maia. Eventually you have to do it for yourself."

She sneered. "Believe me, I do it for myself," Luscia replied through clenched teeth, feeling her face heat at her own choice of words.

His pupils dilated in a flash. "Now that I'd like to see."

"You just did." Recovering, Luscia gestured toward where her wraiths had pierced the moor. "Are you calling me a liar?"

"Only in word and deed."

She knew then that her training was the last thing on his mind. A more tangible anger rumpled his brow, the way it only did whenever he felt betrayed. He was talking about Dhalili and the awful conditions those najjan had kept her under.

Luscia implored him. "I consulted with my father this morning. They will face punishment by week's end, Zaeth."

He nearly flinched, as if he'd been slapped by his own name. "Since when do the Boreali martyr themselves for Darakaians?"

Since the moment your foot met our soil.

"I think it's time for you to leave," Marek said, widening his stance.

"Don't have to think very much when he does it for you, yeah?" Zaethan fastened his stare on Luscia. "But the captaen might be onto something. I was never supposed to be here… Maybe it's time I stopped coming back."

"Maybe so."

Her chest caved inward when he gave no rebuttal. After a few tense moments, Zaethan strode onward down the winding path leading down into Roüwen.

When he crossed Creyvan's boulder, the najjan crooked his chin up off his forearms. "Keep walking, mutt."

"Creyvan!" Luscia barked, mortified.

Zaethan only laughed. It was a bitter, resentful melody. Without stopping, he replied, "Mutt or not, it won't stop your haidren from watching me leave."

Luscia hitched her weaponry under an arm, and her hand flew to tauten the material about her throat, where a shameful blush had scurried up from her breast. Evading Marek's loaded stare, she deliberately bent to sift the broken pieces of clay from among the undergrowth.

She hated that he was right—about her reliance on her blades, but most of all, her reliance on *him*. Because in the margin of her periphery and humiliation, nothing, not even the chiding of her own conscience, had stopped Luscia from watching him leave.

Marek slipped his hand into hers as they walked.

His touch, though not unwelcome, disrupted the disobedience of her thoughts. Frost-armored boughs formed a charming winter's canopy where the noonday sprinkled in above them. It'd taken Luscia far too long to gather that they were not traversing the usual path—or that the rest of her personal guard weren't artlessly muttering about the pair in their shadow, as was custom. Along the rural highway, signals could be heard between the outlying laborers as they worked on the west side of the moorland.

She and the captaen were strolling alone. Heavy-hearted, Luscia didn't really mind it.

"Where have you brought me?" she asked.

Marek gave a wry smirk. "Do you not recognize this place? It's the backdrop to so many of your impassioned threats. See it there, between the break in those trees?"

When he stepped behind her, his grasp melted around her hips to twist them northward. The rivets of hardware in his braided tunic pressed against Luscia's back when, leaning in, Marek pointed at a clearing beyond two holdreheiim.

Luscia pursed her lips, denying her smile, when she saw it was no clearing but a sheet of immature ice. Stretching from the trees, the crystal-clear lake was stocked with schools of bobbing red dots.

She laced her arms. "I didn't want you to actually go take a swim in a berry-loche." It'd been a favored suggestion during her stay on the Isle, particularly during Marek's ill-fated stint as her tutor.

"Oh, I think you did." His body separated from hers. She watched the farmers push their wheelbarrows to the lake's edge to dump in their pickings, preserving them until the spring thaw. There came a rattle when he said, "Specifically with iron weights on my ankles, if I recall."

Pivoting, Luscia found Marek pulling a set of chains from a sack she'd earlier paid no mind. "What in Aurynth?"

Methodically, he unbuttoned his jacket.

"That was years ago, Marek. I was a child. You cannot be serious."

"I'm nothing if not a serious man," he said, throwing his coat onto the frosty leaves. He peeled off his undershirt. A well-defined riverbed was soon revealed underneath. Alert as ever, Marek caught her notice. The captaen hiked his brow brazenly.

Luscia flitted to cover her swallow. "Really, I don't know what you're trying to prove, but you don't have to do this—"

"Wem," stated Marek as he kicked off his upturned boots and coiled the chains about his naked ankles. "I really think I do."

In nothing but his breeches, the captaen stood to his full height, stretching out his wide shoulders. With an approving nod, he plodded toward the water's edge.

Bewildered, Luscia plodded right after him.

At winter's onset, the calm waves would barely be above freezing temperatures. Boreali blood or not, it was cold enough to cause real harm to anyone who stayed under for too long. But Marek waded straight out into the depths. He shivered only once when it met his navel, then he collected and controlled himself until he was neck deep in berry brine. There he gradually turned and held her puzzled stare, the determination on his face heavier than his chains.

The farmers paused in their toil to witness whatever ritual the heir of Bailefore was performing for the heir of Tiergan.

"What the Depths are you doing?" she shouted against the whipping breeze, spitting out pieces of her hair.

Discomfort started to warp his countenance. "Hear me when I say this, Luscia Darragh Tiergan," Marek called back. "I can and will endure whatever you ask of me…"

"Wem, I get that!" Luscia hurriedly waved for his return.

"And whatever it is you won't," he said. The water reflected the clear sky—and how desperation replaced the determination across his face, which was rapidly descending into pain. "Because I'm not blind to it, Luscia. I'm not blind to what you won't tell me aloud."

Shaking, Luscia cupped her elbows, and she ripped her gaze aside, blinking back her emotion. He'd not brought her there for a show of strength, but endurance.

Endurance to a pain she hadn't known was brewing. A pain she'd caused.

Marek wasn't dumb, as it'd been stupid, insulting even, to think he'd not see the magnetism between Luscia and her new tutor. Though nothing could ever come of it, Zaethan posed a biting reality for her and Marek both.

They'd never been masterful at wielding their words to each other, and so he wasn't using them. As substitute, Marek leveraged his entire body to tell her one hard certainty: he was hurting. Badly. But he'd suffer it as long as she required.

Frantically, Luscia clutched his kurtfierï over her heart. "I never want—" Her voice failed her with pathetic weakness. "I never wanted this to happen. Bolaeva. Bolaeva, please come out."

He heard her plea, though it was no louder than the waves. Marek waded forward, water spilling down his strained, reddening physique as he came upon the icy bank. The iron chains clinked with his every surge.

Luscia rushed toward him but stopped short of an embrace—conscious of the many voyeurs overseeing the lake. She took his trembling fingers and blew hot breath onto them. Her exhalation matched his brusque pants. "Tadöm, Marek" was all she could articulate.

His soaked, scarlet hair dripped from where it was half-knotted. He reached around and guided her head against his wet chest. "I believe in you, Luscia. I don't understand it, but you're... By the High One, you're like the Brightling reborn. So I must trust in us too—in whatever it is we're together being called to build."

One suitor, one courtship, and therefore one date she couldn't bring herself to set filled the gulf between them. Luscia whispered against his drenched braids, "That doesn't make our choices any easier."

"Everyone wants to be chosen," he replied. Propping her chin up with this shivering forefinger, Marek searched her eyes. "But I can wait." Marek drew his lips over hers in a dizzying quest. "If my belief is real, it should have much less to do with what I abandon than what I chase."

She wished she could say the same.

In the privacy of her inmost being, Luscia wept when he lowered and kissed her with a devotion she did not deserve.

"One at a time, brödre," Boreal's Clann Darragh begged of his brethren. "By Aniell, I'll not remind this Enclave again."

Around the chancel, their fiery remarks faded into backbiting disputes, while Elder Yarlven continued to convey the misgivings of those from Clan Ödetha. He was the kind of man who sucked in a breath at the start of each sentence, none of which were proving helpful in the least. Luscia panned her attention back to her father, where he prayed up into the sacred script that luminously ringed the interior of the Grand Tabernacle.

Orien Darragh's patience was waning. She'd seen the signs all her life. Emitting a helpless sigh, he barreled his fur-mantled shoulders forward with the regrettable curve of a parent readying to reprimand his children, rather than a leader attempting to mobilize his troops.

It ought to have been a standard commissioning hearing. Who knew a dead reingafier could cause so much discord.

"Simply cannot pull the najjan from Boreal when such nefarious acts keep taking place every time we blink," Earl Yarlven said, emphatically pointing his finger at the butchered carcass strewn at the foot of the Prajja'Veriidim as he finished.

A vulgar offering, the reingafier lay before the altar. Its hind legs were missing, and its entrails were spilt between the slashes down its enormous ribs; the dried, crusty gore was crassly dressed in the twinkle of their raw highland stone. Supposedly, the animal had been found desecrated deep within the wildwood. Then, in showy display, had been unceremoniously dumped in the Grand Tabernacle by Earl Hinrük's lackeys.

Miraculously, just as Master Rohan had dispensed his decision to support their king.

Luscia tautened her grip on the luxiron chair. By the najjani master's unruffled stance, his suspicions stood in line with hers: the whole exhibit had been staged.

"Meh fyreon, but I confess my verdict remains unchanged by this… illustration," said Master Rohan. "The Order will aid King Dmitri in his plight. Najjan are to usher him back to the crown city as a statement of Boreal's fidelity and a warning to those who plot to defy it. I've already sent word to the Isle, Ana'Brödre. The appointed squadrons are set to arrive and extract His Majesty within a fortnight. From our coast, we'll cross the Gate and sail for Bastiion."

Dmitri's sigh was louder than the Enclave's silence. At the other end of the altar, he knocked his head back in relief. The waiting had worn trenches beneath his eyes, each a deeper shade of purple than normal. Hearing the news from Luscia was one thing—hearing it publicly confirmed by the master, quite another.

Their king inclined toward him. "A debt to your House I shall endeavor to repay again and again, Master Rohan."

"Ock!" Earl Morratagh's knees popped when he sprouted up from Clan Ciann, nearly toppling over in the process. "We cannot allow these savage perils to ensue on our blessed lands. The pagans should be banished before the najjan leave us and march with the king!" Sympathetic hollers arose from the clusters of clansmen. The man's prejudice was older than anyone else in the room.

"Statistically speaking, it's less probable that a Darakaian would have committed an offense of this nature," interjected Hachiro from where he and the rest of the Quadren were lined behind Dmitri. At the lilt of his voice, Ira anxiously glided his enchained snuff canister below his nostrils. "You Boreali are more characteristically associated with draining your livestock prior to consumption, ritual or otherwise. We've reports of the blood practice dating as far back as the Sword Age—"

Zaethan clamped a hand over Hachiro's mouth before the elders could descend upon him and sew it shut. "Enough fun facts, Lord Pilar."

The shoto'shi mumbled the rest of the sentence against Zaethan's unmoving grip.

She could empathize. In her experience, facts were seldom as useful as they ought to be. Scooting to the edge of her chair, Luscia spoke over the renewed yelling. "That is true, Lord Pilar, but not applicable in this case. Our faith prohibits it, you see. We are permitted to eat an animal, not to consume its lifeforce."

"Wem!" Supportive shouts fired from the Enclave. "It was the heathens from Darakai!"

Picking up his byrnnzite cane, Dmitri drilled it against his forehead.

Zaethan glowered at Luscia unforgivingly over his shoulder.

No one seemed to listen when she beseeched the elders. "Niit, that is *not* what I implied—"

A cool hand clammed atop her shoulder with more force than a woman of middle age should yield. Elegantly, Alora bowed into

Luscia's ear. "You speak for your House, niece, not any of theirs." Luscia dubiously looked up at her aunt, the pillar of modesty and decorum amid the clamor. Alora's pastel brow was scored with a stern line, and beneath, her Tiergan eye glittered at her successor. She flicked a glance at the haidrens on the tabernacle floor—one, specifically, Luscia knew. Luscia's stomach twisted when Alora craned her long neck. The movement shaded her glowing, right iris with unsympathetic warning. "Control yourself," her aunt said under breath, "before you destroy everyone along with you."

A frosty draft chased her return behind Luscia's iconic chair.

"My people didn't do this!" barked Zaethan.

The Clann Darragh was on his feet. "Lower your tone in this chamber, Lord Haidren—"

Suddenly the doors creaked apart, letting in jarring beams of afternoon sun from the outside. The small assembly swung toward the intrusion. It'd been another closed session.

Her eyes adjusted quickly to the backlit najjan occupying the slim gap. Emiere Tallaesen dipped his chin at her father. "Meh fyreon, Clann Darragh," he apologized, then swung toward the haidren pedestal. Distress stretched the slit scar down his mouth into an ugly omen. The well-worn warrior considered Luscia, as if debating rank, and passed her over for his charge.

Luscia cheeks heated at the slight.

"Ana'Mere," he said. "We have an issue outdoors."

It was then the Enclave heard a commotion in the distance, having been so caught up with their own inside.

Emiere granted her aunt a deferential bow and exited before he could be asked more.

Luscia immediately pushed off her seat, as did many of the elders, following Alora's clipped walk to investigate. Her father's strides quickly caught up with Zaethan's, and together they swung open the doors onto the tabernacle's gem-plated veranda. The Quadren and the Enclave piled in behind their abrupt halt, shocked by the riotous portrait below.

People had flocked to the square. Crammed between the holdreheiim, they were pressed in from all sides with their fists clenched, shouting at a pair of fair-skinned captives, who in their ragged dusters were butted up against the floodlit fountain. A set of blond, fur-clad traders loomed over them—a father and son by their ages, inland pelt suppliers by their garb.

One held up a rucksack and shook it over the crowd. Herbs fluttered to the ground. The crowd grumbled and pushed forward, but it was not for them that Luscia feared.

Caught in the human net was a group of innocent Darakaians. Huddling together, the warriors were being inched closer and closer toward the middle of the conflict.

"Why are those men on their knees?" Dmitri strained his voice above the noise.

"Tavish pickers, poaching our southern outcroppings," her father answered. His thick finger was set with steel when he pointed it toward the dark-haired men from Tevaár. Like her friend Mila, their features were striking, even from afar. Though complexion was the only thing they'd in common with the Boreali. "Our enemies cannot grow what we do, and so they steal it before the winter ice cuts them off from the cures they once enjoyed. Now, pickers enjoy the price they fetch instead." The Clann Darragh stepped back from the banister to lead the assemblage down the spiraled stair. Resentment weighted his steps. "Tevaár will take nothing from Boreal—or my family—ever again."

Luscia molded her collar over her scar, wishing she could stitch it in place, and trailed after her father. Angling her body in front of her king, Luscia warily told Dmitri, "Stay behind me and Lord Darakai no matter what happens."

Zaethan hastened down the steps beside her, his intuition likely the same. He scowled at where her fingers were still pinned at her neck.

She dropped her hand. When her upturned boot met the hard earth, Luscia instantly searched for her guard, finding Marek first among the angry throng. With either hand, she indicated the haidrens to Bastiion and Pilar. Marek mimicked the motion in the air, and out of the masses, Böwen and Declan emerged. Her najjan surrounded the Quadren within seconds.

"Why can't we ever settle things over a smoke and a pint?" objected Ira, nestling in between Dmitri and Declan. "But no… It has to be a murderous parade, a headless dinner party, a human hunt through the Mirajii… not to mention a suicidal sailboat ride across a haunted lake."

"While Captain Nabhu exhibited demonstrable deviance from nautical protocol, need I remind the Ghostly Gate phenomenon is created not by spectral stimulus, but by a disparity in saline—"

"Shut up, Hachi!" said Luscia, Zaethan, and Ira in unison.

They cut through the crowd in the ravine that had formed for the Clann Darragh as he neared the Tavish pickers.

Up close, the men were raggedly thin. Sovllim, the capital trading post in Tevaár, must have lost most of their autumn crop—a slim yield to begin with in a terrain more dead than alive.

A stump had been passed overhead toward the fountain and placed before one of the pickers. The older Boreali trader had the man's dirt-stained palm spread atop the wood. After grabbing a hatchet off his belt, he isolated the man's first few fingers—a loss for each sack they'd stuffed and stolen—and waited for permission from the Clann Darragh.

Her father didn't hesitate to give his nod.

"Wait!" the other picker unexpectedly wailed. Undernourishment had chipped his teeth where they hadn't turned brown. "That woman you want. We saw the woman you want!"

Salacious speculations rounded the square in waves. Luscia wasn't surprised the tale had reached the ears of sailors and bordering merchants. The search for Lady Egon had stretched from Clan Ödetha to Ciann. Surely a rumor's trek over the border wasn't too far-fetched. Cries, hopeful and disbelieving, sprung up among the onlookers.

But the Tavish man being held under the blade only smiled and spat at the trader's feet.

Boreal's Clann Darragh raised his hand, in attempt to quiet the mob. Folding his arms, he stooped before the picker who'd spoken. "Describe the woman or I will take your entire hand, just as I did your prince."

"King," sneered the other man. "Darcain is *king* of Tevaár now."

Luscia felt the dirt spinning underfoot, as if the trees were uprooting themselves, fleeing the soil the way she couldn't as a girl. Because it couldn't be. It was too unjust.

Her monster was wearing a crown.

While she hid at home.

"*Luscia…*"

She absently flicked the air. Nothing had changed. While Darcain had gained power, she'd only lose more of it.

"Describe the woman," her father repeated with force.

"Mature enough to have born adult children. Hair long and bright as the moon," the talkative picker prattled off Lady Egon's description in fear.

My monster wears a crown, Luscia thought again. Her chin quivered, and she held back indignant tears.

"Where?" her father yelled.

"Port Tadeas" was the response. "In chains, being boarded onto an unmarked vessel."

My monster wears a crown.

Her fists boiled when she squeezed them tighter.

"*Relent, Luscia…*" the lumin hummed.

Her Sight flickered in and out through her brimming tears. A web of frosted threads was nested high above the square, rotating, twisting… cavorting. The lumin sparkled, beauty mocking the ugliness of the world. Her nose burned when she turned it away from their light, angry that Aniell's goodness had not prevailed. That it lingered there in the heavens. That it hadn't interceded… hadn't stopped the nightmare from becoming real.

That it had let the monster win.

"You took my wife!" Eitri Egon burst through the bevy of citizens, a distraught Deidre and an even taller Noxolo on his heels. The supposed widower shrieked at the Darakaians, "You took my wife and sold her to slavers!"

Luscia blinked at him through her errant tresses whipping her cheeks. Eitri Egon had grown gaunt, and the look in his bloodshot eyes was made wilder when the wind picked up. It riled the crowd, as it did the multicolored flames in the fountain's basin.

"I assure you, my warriors from Darakai did no such thing, good sir." Dmitri boldly came forward and splayed his hands. At his invitation, Kumo and Takoda cautiously broke from the cluster and edged toward their sovereign. "They are honorable and don't deserve—"

In anguish, Noxolo restrained his father when Lord Egon exploded. "Give her back to me, you pagan pig!"

"Your own kind sold that woman, yeah?" Zaethan roared in turn. "Because mine wouldn't touch her even if she asked for it!"

Dmitri pulled on his arm. "Zaeth—"

"Uni zà!" echoed Kumo with the others.

In droves, clansmen in traditional tunics came to the forefronts, their hems patterned in identical red, green, blue, and white threading—a counter-militia from the Orallach Mountains. Talï stones glittered among the party of zealots, their knuckles free of mitts but armored with Boreali bone, who positioned themselves across the Darakaians.

The only barrier between north and south was the king of Orynthia and his unarmed Quadren.

"Dissention is not the answer," Dmitri called to his subjects, a wheeze rattling his panicked voice. "I tell you today that we are not each other's enemy."

Someone bellowed from the rear, "The Darakaians have brought their evil upon us!"

"And evil is the enemy of Aniell!" shouted the zealots.

Rage rippled through the people, and a riot sprung to life. Clashing currents merged in a violent storm. Punches cracked like thunder as men grappled each other into the gravel.

"*Luscia…*"

Luscia pivoted, seeking a weapon off her najjan, only to realize she was about to use it on her own House. Her Sight cut into the *Other*, and she scanned the lumin-lit square. Her notice landed on the assemblage of elders, protected at the base of the tabernacle stair.

At the center, Elder Hinrük tucked his arms and watched the havoc ensue. A smug expression creased the murky veins beneath his translucent skin. Sighting Luscia, he raised a wheaten brow at his haidren, as if they were competing in darts and dice, and he'd just struck the center.

A body was flung into hers, and she hastened aside in time for Marek to throw the person into another as they charged Takoda. Her back met Declan's, and with her following his movements, they did a quarter spin. Feet away, a pair of zealots were hanging from Kumo's trunk of a neck. Although smaller in stature, their Boreali grip was stronger than his, and he thrashed like a bull. When a third rushed the beta, Kai appeared, knocking him out with one blow.

Out of Luscia's periphery, Zaethan barreled into a Boreali tradesman and slung the alpha away, taking the punch for him.

"Relent and reach, Luscia…"

The lumin raced through the treetops, spiraled the holdreheiim, and crackled above the fighting. Declan pivoted, and Luscia went with him. Atop the fountain rim, her father was ordering the riot to end while he caged his arms around her aunt, shielding her from the barrels and bins starting to be thrown. Luscia saw it then, tearing her community apart.

Not all monstrosity was external.

Some came from within.

"Luscia…"

Fed up with the voices, she screamed into the wind. "What do you want with me!" Her arms became rails, shooting outward from her torso as she spun away from her protector.

"Luscia." Dmitri wheezed her name and teetered over his byrnnzite cane. Out from under him, the last vestige of Unitarian decadence plummeted into the muddied snow.

His subjects warred around him, and his hazel eyes pleaded with her, beginning to roll backward.

"Dmitri!"

Blinded by hate, no one else saw the king of Orynthia fall into Luscia's embrace, uncrowned and unconscious.

Chapter Thirty One

Councilmen grumbled to each other as they piled into the rising pews of the grand legislative chamber. Their velvet-swathed chests puffed and heaved under the large gilded pendent worn by each man, signifying the nobility of his represented province. Beneath the radiant byrnnzite dome, they gathered despite the hour, tugging their stately robes as tightly as they did their coffers.

It was not *their* coin that had paid for recent renovations.

With hooded scrutiny, the figure sidled his eyeline over the balcony, where he was crouched.

The Peerage of Nobility was anything but noble. Over his decades—

those spent under the sun and those shying from it—the figure had witnessed the reality: councilmen were a breed of bloated rats in a grandiose cage, polished and paid for by the sweat of those they merely let in to clean it.

In snapping fortune's handcuffs around beneficiaries, taxes worked both ways. Debts even more. And in this case, debts had forced the councilmen out of their warm, overstuffed beds for a clandestine meeting called not by their minister and sil'haidren, Gregor Hastings, but rather the most powerful man in Pilar.

The Peerage was not used to amassing in the dead of night, though their duplicitous deeds often merited it. They squirmed as Tetsu Naborū stalked through the bone-pale beams that poured through the vaulted black windows. He stationed himself before the glass and waited for the Unitarian elite to settle into their seats. The tall oil lamps did little to disguise the chancellor's worsening jaundice or the darkening leer that cut a slant to his features, as if the rich scholar were a pillar of wax between the prickling flames. Clasped behind the swell of his voluminous, pearly robes, Tetsu tapped his forefinger against the back of his other hand—a modest, erratic gesture the figure remembered well.

Whatever his purpose, Tetsu was excited to begin.

Trepidation stirred inside the figure as he raked a scale of decay off his blackened tongue, and he lowered beside the grime of the thick balusters. He'd trailed Tetsu across the House of Bastiion for too many nights to count. Followed him to Agoston, Hildur, and Galina—even into the gutters of Marketown, where many a duke could be found toiling among a pair of legs instead of his fields. The chancellor was amassing votes, but for what legislation, the figure did not know. Except that through the most inopportune encounters, it was whispered to the councilmen in the Obscurer's name.

With stone-shaking gusto, the grand chamber's doors were thrown open for a parade of battle-scarred chieftains.

Tetsu had no intention of leveraging all those encounters alone.

Shouting broke out across the benches.

"Order, order!" At his fellow Unitarians' uproar, Gregor banged his gavel against the podium, having to hastily adjust his steep, cupola-topped hat when it slid off his head. No longer their original sable, the curly gray triangles bearding his either cheek emphasized his blustering jowls. "First you demand a covert conference with the Peerage, and now you've dragged the Darakaians into it too? What kind of circus do you think we run, Tetsu?"

"An armed one, in violent need of a ringleader," the chancellor drawled. "Your court of jesters simply won't do, Minister."

Nyack Kasim led the way into the round chamber as if it belonged to his outfit instead of Gregor's—a pissing match that should have died with the warlord's wife.

Cyra would have spit on them both.

Korbin should have silenced the opposition of his sil'haidrens when he'd had the chance; their rot had only festered outside his grave. A bittersweet brine wafted off Nyack and his warriors up toward the balcony, their leather seasoned by stonewashed slaughters, sweat, and endorphins. The figure fought its thrall, focusing intently on the mortal games at hand.

Fanning out, the tribal leaders flanked Nyack where he halted and anchored his wrists, one over the other. Unlike the councilmen, he bore vestiges of battle. A sheathed kopar. Mixed medals, forged of bone, bronze, and iron. His long, dusky yak-hair cape absorbed as much light as did his scarred grimace.

Discomfited, the figure leaned closer, hating how it plucked his blisters apart. Beneath the imposing fall of Nyack's cape, the Darakaian leader donned a tailored Unitarian vest and matching baroque trousers.

But Nyack despised yancies and everything they touched…

The gavel landed once more. "It is late," said Gregor with an angry yawn, "and I sense no emergency except your breaching three hundred years of protocol. Explain to me, Chancellor Naborū, why was I lured out of my bed—on false pretense—to meet with Darakai's chief warlord?"

"Did the minister forget the king was murdered, or did it shrink from his mind when his balls shrank from his manhood?" questioned Nyack.

Behind the podium, Gregor sputtered. Cackles jittered through the Darakaian frontline with the mirth of a pack of hyenas.

A councilman from the Wendyllean bench tossed out an arm and yelled, "The king is in Pilar on his coronation tour along with your own haidren! No wonder there are rumors that King Dmitri wishes to replace you as commander of his armies. You've already lost track of him!" He earned more than a few ignorant laughs of his own.

Nyack's nostrils flared at the jab, but he only bolstered his shoulders. Many in the Peerage did not know of the events in Darakai. Nor that a rebel outfit had splintered from the prydes under the command of his brother-in-law, Yousif Shà, and was assembling as an underground force at the behest of their young king.

"A commander cannot be replaced if his king is missing," crooned Tetsu as he crept from the windows and came toward the grand eight-pointed star pattern in the center of the mosaic floor. Each Orynthian spine was testament to the sharpness of the four Houses and their governing bodies, which together formed the Ethnicam. "Dmitri Korbin Thoarne is not in Pilar, as he was scheduled. To the contrary, gentlemen, he sailed himself to Boreal."

The figure expected the nobles' upset.

"The insult," one scoffed.

"Political games," said another.

"Through the Ghostly Gate? A dangerous deviation, that." The duke of Uriel rose from his bench and cricked his back. "Do we know what drove the king into the witchlands?"

"Weakness!" Nyack barked and, snatching his cape, swept it after him until he was opposite Tetsu across the mosaic star. The moonlight shone caustically upon his pockmarked cheeks. "In Darakai, I humbly presented him the head of his father's *authentic* assassin, an Andwele smuggler and traitor to the crown. But your kingling could neither stomach the implications to his engagement with the Zôueli princess or demonstrate the basic fortitude to defend his own throne—his own kwihila! For the assassin revealed to us that the plot to poison King Korbin was authored by the queen of Razôuel, Bahira'zol'Jaell!"

The figure tongued his incisor at the playact. Nyack had spread his arms theatrically for the Peerage, feeding their shock and dismay as if they were audience to one of the classic tragedies. The impact was evident; the best lies parodied the truth.

At least one in the Peerage's number knew what had really happened in Darakai, because the proof was being harbored in his wine cellar.

Gregor smacked his fleshy lips. "We already executed the murderess, Salma Nabhu. These speculations come from illiterate mountain-dwellers…"

"Regicide is no speculation, Minister. Must one read their journals to know when they've been played by an ally?" With his silver nailpiece, Tetsu thoughtfully hooked his taloned forefinger through his short, tapered beard.

"The treaty is broken!" shouted a sprightly councilman from Galina. A Hildurean yelled, "Peril is upon us!" There was a vacancy beside him on the bench, belonging to his missing earl. Tetsu must have bribed others besides Darius of Hildur, to ensure the nobles had gathered.

Dead skin flapped off the figure's nostrils with his impatient sigh. Humans inherited their instinct to fear first and to consider later, never learning from the generation before. Then again, the most senior Galinean had nodded off beside the younger noble and was offering him nothing except his wheezingly bad breath.

Broadening his stance, Nyack bellowed over their panicked debates. "Uni, peril is upon us. Razôuel has infiltrated this city, bloodied the throne, and is now preparing to invade. But where is the kingling, eh? He hides in Boreal." The warlord spat the House's name. "Behind their witchiron and spells. He's abandoned Orynthia to her enemy!

"The Western queen plots to steal the land and coin we reclaimed in the Shield Wars. She aims to steal it from the Peerage. Will she stop at your fields? Your manors? Razôuel slavers for everything the nobility has attained." Nyack jerked his dark finger toward the windows, which extended away from the building like spokes on a bejeweled wheel, and the streets of Marketown's upper class. "Razôuel will trample over every poor Orynthian soul just to seize what is yours! The kingling is too weak to lead. So he ran to the y'siti."

Plenty of councilmen mock-spit over their shoulders.

"Darakai has forged a new alliance. Powerful and strong, Mworra will stand with Orynthia while the kingling cowers behind the Ghostly Gate—"

"Mworra?" Gregor called over his podium, gripping either edge with fervor. "Nyack, are you insane? Orynthia has warred with the cannibals since Thoarne fought them himself!"

"Outpost camps have already been peacefully established along the Andwele ridgeline, within the borders of my House. Mworra is here and with us, gentlemen," Nyack replied, shrugging off any concern. "The monsters you dread are ready to fight at your side."

"For what in turn, a bite of my firstborn?" a middle-aged noble asked flippantly, earning the nods of his fellow nobles from Uriel. "Or a levy on my laborers for their meat supply? I'm already down two slaves as it is. Those rabid animals keep ravaging my livestock."

"Imagine the money you'd lose to an invasion, councilman," Tetsu stated.

The Urielean's face slackened. He then leaned over and whispered to a provincial peer, who seemed to agree with whatever comment he'd made. Clenching his fists, the figure growled as Uriel debated selling out the realm just to better keep their stock.

Tetsu knew it best: strip truth of its nuance, and every evil becomes a partisan issue.

"The time is upon us," Nyack declared. "The Orynthian armies must march."

"War is not yours to declare… Commander," Gregor warned and straightened under his velvet mantle.

"Yet we are in want of a king." Tetsu's mouth curved, stretching his slick, jaundiced skin disconcertingly.

Gregor's complexion reddened, hosting the same splotches as when he'd drunk too much. "We have a king, Chancellor. He is in Boreal."

"He *conspires* with Boreal," Nyack spat. "Runaways don't send for their mothers."

Multiple eyes widened, connecting Lourissa's absence with her son's.

The figure hunched, changing his vantage of the duke who was concealing her beneath his estate, perhaps to the ignorance of his duchess—though Lourissa Thoarne was hardly the first woman he'd ever stowed down there.

"They have turned the king against us!"

"The y'siti intend to recover control of the realm!"

"And will hex anyone who resists their compulsion!"

It didn't take long; animosity spread faster than any pox or plague. It needed but a sneeze to consume everything it touched. The figure had witnessed it spread throughout his entire life with her. Embodying such unmerited grace, Alora had shouldered the Quadren's hostility her whole tenure. Ironically, hatred for her was the one thing upon which Nyack and Gregor had ever agreed.

Nyack drilled his fist against his palm. "It took centuries to purge the y'siti plague from Bastiion… to push it back into the moors where it belongs. Dmitri Thoarne betrayed us all when he ran into the Boreali's diabolical arms. And if he still lives, he is a king no more!"

"Treason to the realm at worst. An outright abdication at best," stated Tetsu. "And here we are, left to the slaughter because of our own Accords. What to do, what to do… Ah." He licked his finger and held it upright. "Perhaps a proxy regent."

"You cannot submit that," Gregor said through his teeth. "The Ethnicam is not here."

"Aren't we?" Tetsu gestured plainly toward the men in the room. "Boreal violated the Accords when they took in a rebel monarch. As heads of House and state, do we not then represent a quorum of Bastiion, Darakai, and Pilar?"

The figure rocked forward onto the soles of his worn-out boots, pressing his blistered face between the balusters. *Why are you doing this? One Unitarian is as good as another…*

Gregor started pilfering through the pages of the fat bedecked book of legislation atop the podium.

Tetsu smirked when he went white. A vote was in the bylaws.

"*Though the regent Unitarian, a proxy may be nominated from any House*," Gregor said, reading in a fearful murmur.

"Chief Warlord, do you second the motion to install a proxy regent in the absence of Dmitri Korbin Thoarne?"

With his chest puffed, showcasing the costly sheen of his Unitarian garb, Nyack appeared all too enthused to oblige—a man who'd tasted too much power for one lifetime, whetting his appetite for more.

The figure felt the walls closing in as he absorbed the loaded glances between both sil'haidrens on the floor. They'd planned this. They were really going to war, and in their greed, they were taking Orynthia too.

"Uni zà. I, chief warlord and commander supreme, second this motion."

With invisible clockwork, Tetsu sprang into motion, gliding around the rim of the eight-pointed star in perfectly measured steps. He fixed his attention on the tiered benches. "To choose from Bastiion's most noble would surely ensue in civil war, a tariff we cannot withstand. Darakai has proven steadfast and capable to carry the realm to victory over Razôuel."

At the praise, Nyack grinned and even bowed his head in feigned humility.

"Orynthia needs a leader politically tactile and shrewd in spirit, one able to mediate between our formidable territories."

Shadows seemed to creep forward when Tetsu lowered his stare onto individual noblemen.

The figure watched as one by one, those scattered through the assemblage scratched at their wrists. As the heavy, ceremonial fabrics were pulled aside, a symbol repeated across the bronzed flesh, branded there by the Obscurer.

His cult had pervaded the Peerage of Nobility.

Suddenly, the duke of Agoston jumped up from the higher benches. He seemed no different than when he'd scrabbled upon the floorboards of the inn at Littleling Eaves. Sweat again doused his brow, as if he was fighting a virus of conscience. With a gulp, he said, "I nominate... Tetsu Naborū as proxy regent."

The figure's bones heaved forward as the world tilted on its axis.

"What!" Nyack screamed. He ripped the precious rings from his fingers. They prattled across the marble as he stormed toward Tetsu.

But when the chancellor clicked his tongue in reprimand, Nyack's knees unnaturally buckled under him. He clutched his wrist, biting back pain as he mutely seethed at Tetsu.

"I second the nomination," asserted the earl of Galina abruptly, scratching at his sleeve.

"No. This is a sham." Gregor's hands sliced the air, and he stepped backward. "And you're a morrow addict, looking for your next fix. As minister, I announce this conference closed."

Tetsu's snakelike brow coiled higher, and he sinuously twisted his head on its side. "The vote is already underway, Gregor. You wouldn't want the Peerage to question your fidelity. I thought you were as faithful to the crown as you were your intriguing wife."

At the comment, Gregor Hastings slowly pulled off his lofty, ministerial hat and wrung it between his hands. The figure snarled from deep within his barren belly when Korbin's old friend looked downward in defeat.

Blackmail was the coin of the realm. And in Bastiion, it weighed more than gold.

Their imbalance formed a trilateral puzzle box: a cadre of Darakaians on one side, Bastiion's congress of nobles on another, and then there was Tetsu Naborū... alone yet hardly outnumbered. He'd trapped everyone's treasure inside.

Tetsu always liked solving puzzle boxes. He liked constructing them even more.

What did the Obscurer ask you to build him? the figured pleaded within.

Gregor rubbed his creased forehead. "All those who favor Tetsu Naborū as proxy regent, say 'aye.'"

Across the benches, many a man trembled, afraid his own secrets would be threatened next. Together, their voices struck like a surreal cymbal.

"Aye."

Pleased, Tetsu showed his teeth—yellow and stained—to his new subjects. He bowed to them, mocking every ruler who'd ever been coronated within those halls. Arising, his words resounded like a prophecy. "The Thoarne Dynasty is reaching its close. One kingdom arises when another falls away. Good evening, gentleman." He turned from their stunned, helpless expressions and strode toward the doors.

Nyack gasped like a muzzle had been loosed. Grasping his wrist, he bolted after him. "Declare it, Tetsu! Declare my war!"

The figure's stomach turned when Tetsu quoted the children's rhyme. "*Listen as the teacher speaks. Patience before havoc wreaks.*"

Reaching out, he stroked his metal talon along the symbol burned into his pawn's mutilated skin. The figure suspected that same clinical instrument—crafted by the shoto guild from silver for its purity and sharpened for its function—had been used to drain unascended crosscastes upon the altar of the Obscurer.

"Do you hear your teacher, Nyack?" Tetsu crooked his ear. "He is called 'Your Majesty' now."

The figure's breath was sucked from his lungs when he laced his fingers and hooked the nailpiece overtop. Departing the devastated chamber, Tetsu tapped his skin excitedly, signaling one sickening certainty: those children were merely fodder to his darker machine.

CHAPTER THIRTY TWO
Luscia

The sun had risen, fallen, and risen again through the window overlooking his bed before the king of Orynthia had finally woken.

Absentmindedly, Luscia toyed with the delicate, lacey caps of the minmalïss morels in the basket as she rested her head against the doorjamb and listened to Dmitri's soft conversation inside. It was Ira's turn to sit with him; he must have relieved Zaethan while Luscia had been retrieving another bushel of mushrooms from her aunt's cottage. The Eastern haidren murmured something profoundly inappropriate, eliciting a tired chuckle with enough vigor to travel between the cracks and into the hall.

The basket in her arms lowered as Luscia relaxed her shoulders.

Dmitri was laughing. That was good. They had so little left to laugh about.

She wanted to grant them privacy, as much as her Tiergan ears would allow, so positioned her back toward the slightly agape entry, recalling how she'd used to stand eagerly outside, in that very same spot, when it'd been Phalen who'd slept on its other side. Luscia had snuck into that room to rouse him for so many midnight adventures, she'd often found her young brother already waiting, bow staff in hand and suited in bear mitts, ready to disappear into the wilds where Alora could never find them.

All of which had ended when he'd relinquished the bedroom to Luscia. For hers had been locked away.

Along with her innocence.

She ground her teeth at the bedroom across the circular landing. Though it came silently, her ears were attuned to its ever-present dirge, mournfully telling of the girl within who'd been taken and torn. Brick by brick, Luscia had built her reputation back from the rubble, having buried everything else. Yet a single door was undoing all her labors. It hadn't been that way on the Isle of Viridis, nor in the crown city.

And so Luscia hated its image. Hated how she had to walk past her worst monument every morning and every night. Hated the motif of lycrans running along the wooden trim. Hated their whittled eyes that watched whenever she passed going up or down the stairs. Luscia stared at them bitterly. Those carvings used to represent freedom. But coming back from Bastiion, she hated most that she hated being *there*—in the home that'd created her.

My monster wears a crown, she reminded herself as her gaze bored into the luxiron padlock. Out of the two of them, she was the only person locked inside.

Luscia rolled against her shoulder and glared out the round, floor-to-ceiling window, into the canopy instead. Through the glass, flurries were descending upon Roüwen between the boughs, dusting the verandas of the neighboring holdreheiim manors in a hopeful varnish, masking each pristinely for their flawed inhabitants. She felt small standing there, probably because she *was* small—at least in char-acter—for she'd done nothing to prevent the turmoil that was tearing her community apart. Clansman against clansman... some Boreali defending the Darakaians, most not. As the fighting had broken out, Luscia had frozen in the square.

Just like she had in her tent in Rian.

Same as she had inside that cursed bedroom.

Worst of all, Alora had seen her failure too. Disappointment agitated her aunt's entire countenance whenever she came by the main manor to check in on Dmitri's recovery. Until yesterday, the contention was mutual. However, in this case, Alora's curt replies and dismissive gestures were justified.

While her father and aunt had worked to subdue the rioters, Luscia had huddled over their fallen king, desperately trying to wake him. But he hadn't. Dmitri had gone cold, and for a moment, she'd feared forever. She'd left herself then, in some respect, not even realizing when the factions had parted ways and retreated bruised and sullen into their residences. They'd told Luscia that a dozen zealots, now in holding, had been arrested by the najjan... but she couldn't remember anything after Dmitri had collapsed.

Luscia wasn't ready for what that meant, not for herself or the world he'd almost left behind.

A thump reclaimed her interest. Ira must have returned his chair legs to the rug.

"Sometimes this is all too much," the haidren whispered, having shed his blasé facade. Luscia's ears quirked toward the tremor in his statement. "I just want to go home."

"I know," Dmitri gently replied, "but I also know that you can bear it too. Without vice, Ira. You can bear this burden with me."

Ira made a noncommittal noise. "Vices would do you a great service, Your Majesty. You ought to try mine."

At the jingle of chain, Luscia barged into Dmitri's quarters and found him holding Ira's snuff canister between his thumb and forefinger, as if observing one of his succulents.

"Return that trash to him right now," she ordered her king. "I leave you alone for an hour, and he's got you resorting to drugs."

"We've been caught out. I must gladly return this into your care, Lord Bastiion," Dmitri told him conspiratorially. After handing the canister back to its rakish owner, he sank back against his barrage of pillows. His complexion hadn't improved much. Even the fire wasn't helping, considering how Aksel was hogging its crackling warmth.

Ira looped the enchainment over his head as he stood. "The point of life is to enjoy it, gosling."

"That's absurd," she retorted and stepped over her dozing lycran, curled in front of the hearth, to set the basket of minmalïss morels atop the dressing table.

Luscia plucked a rhali sprig and dusted some pollen into a mesh. She ground the filigree mushroom cap, then plopped the reflective goop in after, hoping the minmalïss would soon stimulate his appetite. Dmitri was more stubborn than a child when it came to eating what was good for him.

After splashing hot water through the mesh into a sterling teacup, she rested the kettle aside. Luscia covertly slid a vial of Dmitri's elixir out from her apothecary and into her pocket, wary of Ira lingering in the doorway. Carefully, she walked the cup toward their king's bedside.

"If this is Boreali hospitality, then sign me up for the plague." The other haidren ogled Luscia as she bent over to tuck the blankets around Dmitri's legs.

"You've been excused," she sniped and claimed his chair. "Now, bolaeva, please go away."

Coughing, Dmitri said to Ira's back when he stepped into the hall, "Do not forget, Lord Bastiion. Meme ràtomdai na yeye."

Ira turned in the threshold, clutching his snuff canister. His expression went serious behind his ribbon of mahogany hair. The yancy stretched his fingers beneath the chain, over his heart.

Exactly where Dmitri had placed *his* during the Holiday of Hands in Darakai.

The two noblemen inclined toward each other in some private agreement before Ira left. Listening after his fading footsteps, Luscia twisted toward her king suspiciously. "I don't suppose you're going to tell me what that was about?"

"No, I don't suppose I will," Dmitri dryly replied. "Another so soon? I just took the last dose two days ago."

"Right before you fainted, you mean. Crestï. Now, drink." She watched his nose crinkle at the original elixir's musty flavor, wishing her stronger batches had worked. She'd reverted it after his fall. Her idea had only made his illness worsen. "And wash it down with this."

"I miss the old blend." He smacked his lips and set the teacup to the side.

"Even expediting the wedding, you need every herb in the highlands to get you down that aisle to Rasha."

Dmitri grunted. "Right."

"Once the Order arrives, we send another envoy to have Rasha meet us in Bastiion, so she can conceive an heir before it's too late—"

"Did you hear about the Mirajii Pryde?" he asked sharply. "Zaeth just informed me."

Her head hung. "Wem."

"They think it is more dangerous to stay here than to flee to the mercy of my enemies. As I lie on your mattress, the warriors who bled for me are packing for your border." His words ended with an impassioned wheeze.

"I can provide my kinsmen's excuse, but it will not suffice," Luscia confessed, washing her hands in her lap. "If that pryde can merely wait a little longer…"

"People reveal their true selves when they're waiting. That's why so many try to rush through it."

"Maybe I can speak to Lord Darakai or to his alpha, Kai, directly," Luscia hurriedly said.

"I wasn't talking about *them*."

Reluctantly, she lifted her chin. Her king was in shambles. Unlaced, his undershirt stuck to his torso from his recently broken fever. Veins were visible beneath his emotive gaze, depleted of its usual generosity. Scathingly, it pinned her to the chairback like an insect on display.

"I'd like—" She took a sobering breath. "I'd like to think my truest self is worth trusting, Your Majesty."

"Of which self are we talking? The longer I know you, the more versions I meet."

She recoiled as if he'd punched her in the heart. Luscia's mouth moved, but the only words to escape were "a person can only really serve one sovereign."

"Then tell me, who were you serving in Bastiion?" Dmitri pointed his nose toward hers as he said, "Because whoever it was, for them you'd never withheld your spine." He swerved his face back toward his crackling fire. "Sometimes I barely recognize the woman sitting beside me in Boreal."

A tear rolled down her cheek, and she angrily swiped it away. "All these generational politics are so messy. I don't know how to set things right, when they never were in the first place." Luscia aimed her focus away from Dmitri and at the knots of the macramé shades across his window. "Even the Watchman sees me plainly. Sees my every flaw. Meh fyreon. I don't know how to repair it, Your Majesty."

Dmitri released a shallow sigh. "I don't blame you entirely, Luscia. The Boreali are a… potent… people. They're different from the rest of us—you most especially—and so is whatever this force is, living among you all." He surprised her when he charitably reached for her fingers, as his skin was no warmer than the room. Dmitri reclined his tangled waves against the sleighed headboard and stared at her. "But this turmoil? This division ripping everything apart? It may not have been your fault, but it's certainly your problem to fix."

Luscia's grip went cold against his as Dmitri let his eyelids close, leaving her to the lonely snap and pop of the flames. Restraining herself, she did not permit her eyes to flick toward the hall and to the padlock looming behind the stairwell. Every hair on her arm had risen, rallying to run away.

He adjusted his feet underneath the heavy, sheepskin fur while Luscia debated how best to excuse herself…

"Is faith a painting or a song?"

She sputtered, securing the front of her collar. Luscia didn't remember touching it. "Are you still fixated on that?"

"Unitarians believe in the Fates, as do most Darakaians. We burn articles for their pleasure, the luxuries we won't miss, attempting to appease either their desire or wrath—I can never recall which. Though, that's neither a painting nor a song, rather a barbecue." Dmitri turned onto his side, planting himself in the pillows. "According to Hachiro, in Pilar the shotos profess that 'any faith in the unmeasurable is a long con for man's unscrupulous sentimentalism, for itself comprehends no bounds.'"

"Hachi also believes his sciences will never fail him. Watch how sentimental he gets about his calculations the next time one of his morbid statistics is proven wrong," Luscia replied. Forgetting her heaviness, she leaned forward intently. "Why is this so important to you?"

"Death clouds my horizon. It's well in view," said Dmitri distantly, "coalescing inside my bones like your highland mist. At the end of a man's life, he is less concerned about what to believe than how he ought to have believed it. Otherwise, he may draw his final breath, unsure if he ever really believed in anything at all. I remember what you showed us at Ana'Innöx. I've committed it to memory. I may never understand your Aniell, but I do understand that genuine faith must be more than simply bearing witness to His apparent mystery."

"Mysteries don't subside the more you believe in them," she murmured in turn, flexing her free palm.

The lumin pulsed under her skin. Defiant. Unruly. In charge.

"Hm." His eyelids fell once more, his thick, dark lashes twitching as he fought much-needed sleep. "Enough philosophy. A king should not be consumed by his own lips. Sing me something sweet. Something to chase my grave away."

Knocking her head back, she blinked at the rings in the ceiling, covering her mouth so he wouldn't hear her choking back a sob. Luscia swallowed hard. Recounting the only song to ever soothe her slumber, she hummed her mother's lullaby… flinching from the bittersweet tune of a prophetess gone mad.

When I was young, my mother told,

Tales of Aniell on nights so cold,
For He sings, for He sings, for He sings to you,
O Child of mine, I'm near to you.

With an exasperated growl, Luscia tossed atop the bedroll, wrenching the quilt out from under Aksel's unmoving poundage. The manor was soundless, the tall windows circling the aerial loft locking out the sounds of the wilderness. Under the soft glow of her mother's tented, crystalline canopy, the spherical room was vacant and still. It would seem Luscia was alone with her lycran.

Except she wasn't.

"Luscia…"

Burying her face in her pillow, she grumbled, for her thoughts were already in tangles. Finding rest was a tall enough feat without the lumin squawking in her ears. "Just let me sleep!"

The whispers abated. An owl hooted on the other side of the glass.

She let out an exhausted moan. Pulling the quilt higher, she drew it snugly over her head.

"Luscia…"

"Niit."

"Luscia…"

"Shut up!"

"Luscia…"

She ripped off the covers. Luscia stormed toward the stairwell, snatching her robe along the way, while the *Other* flashed in and out of view. Giving Aksel a harsh snap to follow, she hastened down the steps.

On the lower landing, Luscia paused.

The door was dark… restless and frighting. Its demon never slept.

My monster wears a crown.

Her hand skated the knobby banister, and she whipped round the stair, continuing by the guest floor down to the main. Her lycran dashed ahead through the front door before her desperate toes could cross the threshold.

The night blasted her cheeks. Clean, fridged air scrubbed her lungs as her soles beat a freedom song along the veranda, across the suspension bridge, and down the spiraling stone flight. Whispers joined in chorus with the breeze, sweeping through the shimmering leaves and twisting boughs. Luscia's heels met the gravel. She took off into the highland forest, racing toward the only safe place she could think of.

Holdreheiim blurred in her periphery. With audible thunder, the veil collapsed, and her full Sight erupted through the trees like lighting. The earth rumbled beneath her escape. But no matter how swiftly she lifted her feet, Luscia could not flee the threads. Their network thickened as she embarked deeper into the wildwood. The lumin chased her as in a full sprint, she smacked the closest threads away.

With a splintering *crack*, a tree fell in her wake.

As did two more.

Nearing her and Phalen's childhood hideaway, she slowed to a frustrated trot, her mouth falling ajar. Flurries melted into her tears. Over the logs, the harbinger thread hovered in the air, brilliant and unrelenting. Aksel howled at the ethereal occupation as if it were the moon incarnate.

A cry escaped Luscia. Nothing was her own anymore. Nothing was as it should have been. And nothing would ever return that way again.

"Why are you tormenting me?" Luscia dug her heel into the dirt and wailed at the harbinger thread. "I've done everything you want! Why is it never enough?"

Like an arrow snapped from its bow, the thick thread zoomed

toward her throat. Its nearness prickled her flesh in a euphoric irritation, and her scar began to burn.

"*Relent, Luscia...*"

"Niit! I will never relent to her madness!" she screamed back and lunged for the harbinger thread without thinking.

In indiscernible harmonies, the whispers roared when her fingers curled around the energy. Luscia shrieked at the sensation—at the valiant fury she felt coursing from the thread and into her body, as the dimensions distorted and snapped back into place.

But even as her skin boiled, she didn't let go, and wrenching her arm, she hurled the harbinger thread into the others. The nest of light bowed between the trees, snapping off their limbs, and flung the most brilliant right back at Luscia.

The supernatural force pummeled her onto her backside. Luscia skidded through the slush and into the base of a holdreheiim, dividing the monolith in half. She rasped, wide-eyed, as the harbinger thread coiled around her torso, constricting against her thrashes.

"*Relent, Luscia...*"

Something pelted Luscia's side. Suddenly, the threads loosened and delicately floated off as if their constraint hadn't been severe. Pain throbbed across her bicep. Luscia looked down at the small rock and scoured the forest. She growled when she discovered who'd thrown it.

For he was quickly priming another.

"Get up," Zaethan barked. Hiking a leg over a cluster of broken branches, he stalked toward her. "Get off that entitled ass and explain why you've let this happen."

Aksel loped toward his approach. Yipping, the lycran circled the other haidren.

She formed fists in the snowy dirt. "I didn't make Kai's pryde pack their gear."

"Ano zà, you packed it for them. Packed their bruises!" Zaethan chucked a stone. "And their bandages." He let loose another. "Your people painted mine black and blue for an outgoing parade!"

Luscia dodged again, letting the stone strike the bark. "Yours don't need mine to conjure bruises. They do that just fine on their own!" she shouted, scrambling to stand. Indignantly, Luscia smoothed the grime off her dressing gown. "Turn around, Lord Darakai, and go back to them. You shouldn't be in this place."

The stadium of lumin and bioluminescent wildlife shimmered over his darkened, angular features. "You don't own these woods."

"Wem. I kind of do," answered Luscia. Hand on her hips, she flicked her forefinger.

So, turn around and leave."

Zaethan clicked his tongue, exciting something in her middle. "You are so *arrogant*."

"Truth cannot be arrogant. It's naturally superior."

His laugh was curt and biting. Unbound, his sable locs decorated his chest, shifting with his every riled pant. An emerald Boreali jacket hung open off his musculature, showing the topmost lacing of his lambskin breeches was loosely tied, as if he too had climbed from his bed. Zaethan's ringed brow had hiked.

She wasn't the only one performing an inventory. Barefooted, Luscia felt for the fur trim of her robe and drew it over herself.

He palmed his jaw, his brightened eyes tracking her movements. "Depths, when will you ever stop hiding?" he asked, and with a shake of his head, Zaethan started toward her.

A new sweat beaded down between her breasts beneath the linsilk shift. Instinctively, Luscia backpaddled, as if that old lead rope were strung between their navels.

Like a raven, he swept his arm low without slowing and collected more stones.

Luscia's foot rolled over the rootage of a fractured trunk, and she ducked clumsily. A rock whizzed overhead. The lycran darted after it, disappearing into the shadows with the same exuberance had the haidren thrown him a stick. Sneering, she patted her hips awkwardly, remembering she carried no weapon, not even her radials.

Zaethan sailed another stone, this time with more vigor, and Luscia whipped around the closest tree. She hastily snatched a busted branch. Awaiting his nearing footfalls, she spun out and pelted him across the middle.

Surely bruised, he cradled his ribs as she made to leave, but then his rock bashed her ankle, and she tripped.

And he threw another.

From the ground, Luscia snarled and struck out her arm. The lumin raced forward, and the rock disintegrated.

"Uni! Again!"

"You are not in command here!"

"Neither are you," Zaethan bellowed and flung a larger stone.

Furiously, she swept her leg, evading it. "This is madness!"

"You were stronger a world away from here." He quickly soured the undergrowth for something heavier and barked, "*Why is that?*"

"Why do you even care?" she exclaimed.

"Because you have all this power," Zaethan roared, stampeding toward her. "And you're throwing it away while stripping us of ours!"

Anger surged from her insides. Luscia shoved her hands toward his relentless approach. A translucent bowl of light broke over her fingertips and blasted him backward. But as he was knocked back, Zaethan seized her calf and tore her down with him.

Rolling through the slush, Luscia tried to snake her knee around his neck. He was all too familiar with her instincts. Zaethan grabbed her by her thighs, his strong fingers imprinting their shape along hers. He pushed up between her knees, turned himself over her, and penned her between his legs, then threw them both to sit against the base of a tree.

Luscia's body sailed the currents of his heartbeat, which was clamoring through her tensed back. She melted against his rigid abdomen. Her nostrils were overcome by his scent, bolder than anything in their midst. Spicier than pine. Richer than cedar. Earthier than the soil itself. His forearm flexed over her heaving breast, restraining her not unlike the harbinger thread. Lightheaded, Luscia gripped his jacket sleeve, her other hand digging into his thigh. She was as determined as she was confused.

His breath was hot on her temple when, more tenderly than the rest of his touch, Zaethan brushed her dirtied hair back between them. And invoking a gasp, he stripped back her robing.

Off her wrist, the leather ties of Marek's kurtfierï dangled against her barely clothed chest. "Don't," Luscia begged him, not from fear but resolve.

His mouth did not meet her skin. Instead, his right hand took hers off his forearm, and he lowered their entwined fingers into the cold, snowy muck, flattening them out. "What hope does he have to claim you, Maji'maia, if you still can't claim yourself?" After lifting her out of the mud, he guided her hand—the same that bore the mark of her testimony before the Enclave—to her throat. Zaethan pasted her handprint against the elder, much uglier scar that marred her lobe to clavicle.

Cupping with pressure in place, he did not let go.

The ice sank deeper than her scarring. It thawed into her body and pierced a grotto in her soul. Luscia uttered a noise even the animals could not define. With her Tiergan eye, she searched the wood and the lichen-lit emptiness beyond, until she found the harbinger thread lurking in the distance… watching. And in a languid motion, it seemed to nod in agreement.

With little force, Zaethan nudged her head aside with his jaw so that his mouth hovered over their conjoined hands. His warm cheek covered her ear, but somehow his voice was a gong, clanging in her deepest places.

"Your mask is cracking. So let it fall." Wavering against her temple, he disentangled his limbs from around her and stood. Zaethan bent. He removed the last undamaged stone from his pocket and gently put it between her filthy feet. "The choice is yours. We *need* your mask to fall, Luscia. And so do you."

Invisibly, she felt their lead rope stretch and snap when he turned and walked away from her, into the night.

Clambering up the stairs, Luscia kept her heels from sounding her return home. She was too numb to scrape herself clean, and the prints on the floor would reveal her escapade in the morning.

She stopped and listened for her father's notorious snores at the top of the third story, as was her and her brother's custom. At her back, Luscia felt the whittled lycrans watching her from next door. Felt their proverbial fangs gnawing down her vertebrae. She stood there, frozen in the dark, for too many moments.

"*Relent, Luscia…*"

Static scratched at her temples. Luscia tapped Aksel's matted hindquarters, directing him up into the loft.

"*Relent and reach…*"

Wavering on the balls of her feet, she did not follow the lycran. Luscia closed her eyes. In her mind, she dropped the veil like a sheet. It was so flimsy and lightweight, as if the segregation between dimensions were a ruse. Crooking her chin over her shoulder, Luscia creaked open her eyes.

Her lips parted.

Tributaries of lumin were flowing under the door and into the locked room.

Before she could change her mind, Luscia let go off the banister and retreated down to the main floor. Her heart hammered as she silently padded across the great room to the floor-to-ceiling fireplace laminated in lumilores. They gleamed at her advance, brightening as her nervous breaths greeted their surfaces. She splayed her fingers atop the mantle where the miniature replica Prajja'Veriidim sat.

Two end bowls of gold, the center of stone. Steeling herself, Luscia hastily flipped it upward. Underneath lay a luxiron key.

The truth of man, precisely where she'd last left it.

Luscia swiped it before her bravery dissolved, then marched back up to the third floor, the key cutting into her palm. *Just another scar in my collection*, she thought and halted among the current of threads flowing along the floorboards.

She hesitated before the padlock. It was large and obscene. Her lashes grew wet, sticking together. After shoving the key into the hole, Luscia rapidly turned it until there was a *click*, and the bolt withdrew.

The door crept back on its hinges on its own. Her legs moved her forward in pantomime. Tears streamed from her eyes, though Luscia could not believe their Sight.

The bedroom—unchanged and inhumed in dust—was awash with light.

Spindles of lumin waded through the musty air. In glittering tangles, the energy gathered about in specific spaces. It sat at the desk where she used to meditate. It cavorted as a tower in the corner, atop the child's klödjen she'd used to teeter. It formed a half-moon up the side of her round windowsill, as if reading the scriptures in her stead.

Luscia turned in a circle, facing down the bed.

It was neat and tidy, and sprawled across the quilting, the lumin had threaded into the shape of her sleeping form—both arms tossed above her pillow carelessly. Luscia clutched her belly, nearly falling forward. For at the base of her bed, the lumin had taken another form—one beautiful and prostrate in prayer.

The lumin was imitating her mother.

A sob was liberated from her lungs, and Luscia plunged to her knees. Yet there on the floor, through her weeping she saw the majority of threads pooling under her bedframe.

"Relent and reach for what will not rust, Luscia," the whispers instructed.

Wiping her nose, she pushed upright off the rug. In a frenzy, Luscia shoved an old trunk out the way and hastily wrenched the bed from the wall. And she stared. She stared as if she were beholding the Dönumn itself.

The lumin congregated in a radiant mass, snaking along Boreali script that had been etched by someone's hand into the living floor.

Lux aemida hen. Hen mii'orr vida.

The Light is within her. She will not fall.

Luscia's hands trembled over the lettering, every curve and flick belonging to the woman she so often missed and cursed—the prophetess who'd written it there long before a monster had ever entered her prayerful domain.

Cupping her mouth, Luscia cried and cried, pressing so tightly, not even the najjan could hear. When her eyes went raw, she eventually got up. Luscia caught the door handle and dragged it closed. But at the last second, she stopped. Instead, she left the key in the padlock and pushed the door open.

There was nothing to be ashamed of inside.

Chapter Thirty Three
Zaethan

He slung the axe and piked it through the maple wood as if it were his enemy. Swabbing the sweat from his forehead, Zaethan chucked both logs into his heaping pile on the outskirts of the agora. No one had bothered him there. With the mood he was in, it'd be dangerous to try.

Snow covered the fruit of his labors in a pristine sheet, coming in steady flurries since that morning. He tugged his kidskin gloves higher and prepped the next hunk of wood atop the stump, then flexed his shoulders and made to swing.

"Eh, Boreal must have snuck our servitude somewhere into the

Accords," someone said, coming up from behind. "Because Owàa's chains… I never thought I'd see the day my haidren was forced to labor for them."

Zaethan jerked, saw it was Kai, and replanted his footing. He brought the axe down with a bite. "I wanted to hit something," he muttered and elevated the borrowed tool. "Declan obliged."

He swung it down, and the wood chunked apart.

The lesser alpha harrumphed. Raising his sights, Zaethan assessed Kai as he adjusted the sack slung across his chest. Despite the cold, he had traded his woolen pants for loose, Darakaian gunjas. Whereas his fur-lined jacket was buttoned closely to compensate.

Zaethan squinted against the sun. "I searched for you this morning for hours." He didn't ask where Kai had been. Being alpha zà, he shouldn't have had to.

"Making the final arrangements," he bluntly replied and shifted his weight onto his other leg. Even without crutches, he still favored it.

Kai was in no condition to trek the Valley of Fahime, nevertheless hostile territory. They wouldn't survive it. And neither would Zaethan. He'd already lost enough.

"Don't do this."

"The pryde voted, Alpha Zà," said Kai apologetically. In Darakaian fashion, he wriggled his fingers away from his middle. "They're determined to flee these witchlands at sunrise."

Zaethan shoved the axe toward the alpha. "In Mirajii, you swore you'd follow me anywhere."

"And we did! Depths, we followed you all the way to Fates-forsaken Boreal." Kai was all eyes, round and bulging as he gestured at the giant, neighboring holdreheiim. "And look where it got us, yeah? Freezing and frightened."

Tossing his hands, Zaethan argued, "So you'd rather lead your warriors into Fahime? Wekesa's old pryde is devoted to my fa—" He pressed his lips furiously. "To Nyack Kasim."

"Kwihila rapiki mu jwona. Easier to write over the enemy you know, uni?" Kai shrugged miserably. "No one died in this last riot, but the next one? Meme ano'qondai."

"The king would never stand by and let that happen. He will honor your sacrifice in time. Gaibai will be danced about under Àla'maia's shine. But he needs you *now*, Kai. More than ever," Zaethan said, pleading. "The Quadren will negotiate more protections with the Enclave. The king will make it so."

"With what authority, Alpha Zà? He is at Boreali mercy, just like the rest of us."

Zaethan stared at him, mooring onto the kindred desperation exuding from the other man. "He's a good man, Kai. He's good for Orynthia."

The lean alpha deflated, almost at a loss. "Wars aren't won by the goodness of their kings," Kai said. Grabbing the sack's corded strap, he stepped closer and held onto Zaethan's arm. "No one is abandoning you, Alpha Zà. We'll find the new commander, bolster Yousif's numbers, and send word as soon as able. Uni zà?"

Kai tilted the angles of his triangular face, waiting for Zaethan's pained affirmative.

"Uni zà," he said through his clenched jaw.

"We're still with you," Kai said again as he bumped his fist against his heart in Darakaian salute and began to walk away. "Shàla'maiamo, Alpha Zà."

Zaethan gazed after Kai until he disappeared behind the candle-maker's stand and into the local foot traffic. Releasing an enraged howl, he twisted and pelted the axe into a tree. Stuck in the bark, it ripped out of his grasp and he stumbled forward with a curse.

The shaft had fractured from the hit. The natives really weren't jesting about the strength of holdreheiim, even those hollowed out. Zaethan wrenched it back and forth from the trunk and judged the damage. "Shtàka."

He heaved a sigh and spun to locate the closest smithy. If he didn't get it fixed, the Athdaras would. Zaethan shrugged his coat on with a grumble and started moving, lest the lady of the house charge him twice.

Ducking under a fern-covered awning, the loose snow dusted Zaethan in a shiver as he entered the excavated hollow. Heat blasted his grimace from the rival forges situated between the monstrous bends in the exposed root system. It was a marvel the furnaces didn't light the sheltering tree on fire. Daringly, the luxsmiths had implemented a thorny system of pipes, routing their smolder up through the rootage in cloudy spires along the outside. It made the smithies easy to spot from a distance.

Kaleidoscopic light danced across the scooped-out ceiling as men hammered their najjani blades to the beat of a collective chant. It called to mind the constant songs of the priestesses in Bastiion, but merrier and more masculine. With belly-rich voices, their iron clamor conveyed a hardier kind of finesse than the warriors who would wield their handiwork. Bright, fair eyes watched him guardedly as he passed, the lone Darakaian cross-caste in their midst.

A quick glance around and Zaethan spotted Luscia's brother singing too.

Granted, far more distractedly.

After walking up to his cluttered counter, Zaethan set down the busted axe and planted his hands on either side. He stood there a handful of minutes while the young luxsmith snatched a sword from the flames and doused it in a bucket, swiveled to shove a swatch of cloth into a lumpy satchel, pivoted, and popped a sandwich between his teeth before again grabbing his mallet.

Hunched over, Zaethan gave an awkward cough.

"Ah! Lord Haidren, allöh! I didn't see you there!" he exclaimed and wiped his face, leaving behind a streak of coal.

Phalen Tiergan was the near image of his sister, were she rugged, squared, and stretched taller. Much like Zaethan beneath his coat, he wore a cross-body tunic that was tied over his ribs, though his sleeves were rolled up in bunches over his sooty forearms. Unlike Zaethan, his ghostly eyes glinted with the neighboring witchiron when he cracked a crooked but friendly smile.

"Can you fix this?" Zaethan nodded toward the axe, saying, "It's not mine…"

"I'd still fix it if it was, Lord Haidren," said Phalen wryly as he carried it to his anvil.

Pushing off the counter, Zaethan rebound his locs, knotting them high. No wonder Phalen was pasted in sweat. The heat he'd originally found comforting quickly became a swelter.

Phalen kicked the large satchel on the ground, granting himself more legroom as he assessed the damage.

"Going on a trip?" asked Zaethan sourly as he mulled over what might've just been his last conversation with Kai Wakhan.

"My söhlo," Phalen muttered, holding up the bit. "Shores of Aurynth… You were really pelting this thing, weren't you?"

He ignored the insinuation and leaned against the rustic slab with folded arms. "What's a 'söhlo'?"

"Ritual at sixteen years. It's my birthday tomorrow." The luxsmith grinned. Phalen dumped a ladle into a molten pot and drizzled it in delicate threads as he spun the axe's shaft underneath, in the manner of a glassblower. "Two days and two nights in the wilderness before Aniell. For the blessed few," he explained, walking the red-hot weapon to a barrel, "it is the only time we ever hear Him speak."

Voices from the sky? Zaethan eyed him piteously.

Too many hillman fools chased the voices of their so-called Fates, only to turn up bone-thin and hallucinating, or dead, in the Andweles. It was why tribes like Jabari's were so superstitious. The Yowekaons hadn't woken to the real world, which made them gullible and enchained to silly practices in everyday life. Jabari still threw dirt over his shoulder after swallowing a fistful every time he saw a raven. Kakka-shtàka mountaineer.

Then again, come to think of it, Luscia talked to herself regularly. Zaethan had caught her screaming at the wind just the other night…

"What's the point then, of your *söhlo* ritual?"

Phalen splashed the ground as he brought the newly fixed axe out of the waters. "Everyone brings their own into the highlands."

"Yours being?" Zaethan asked. He'd initially been making conversation so the other smithies would see he wasn't a threat to their apprentice. But he'd grown mildly curious.

Phalen started to polish the metal in thought. "It'd be pretty miserable to live out my life wearing other people's definitions. Being son of the Clann Darragh and meh mere… my, uh, mother, that is… There are certainly enough theories to go around," he said as a bead of sweat rolled off his chin. "Ock. I suppose I'd like to learn the real definition once and for all."

The statement settled heavily on Zaethan. He hated to admit it, but he ached for the same thing, were he not scared to learn the truth. He pushed the thought aside. The truth was what he made it. "I'm Darakaian. I write my own definition."

Unexpectedly, Phalen laughed, bright and airily. "Better hope you're a decent author."

Zaethan bucked at that. Standing taller, he took the axe when it was returned to him. "Thanks. Eh, tadöm," he offered flimsily.

"Yeh'maelim. My help is always welcome to you, Lord Haidren," Phalen said, and peering at Zaethan, his eyes narrowed. He scratched his scalp between its short, blond plaits as Zaethan turned away. "Heh'ta! Just stay there." Slapping his pockets, Luscia's brother scurried to his satchel and rummaged through its folds. Having located something, he sat back dumbfounded. "I tell you, the High One really has a sense of humor." He got up and carried whatever it was to the counter. Unrolling his palm, he said, "I think these are for you."

Seated in Phalen's smeared, calloused hand sparkled a pair of tiny, witchiron posts. At the look of confusion he got in return, the luxsmith tapped his eyebrow, indicating the pair of gold rings adorning Zaethan's.

He stared at the posts cautiously. "No one asked you to make those."

"Well, I wouldn't say that. I caught myself sleepwalking last night. Waking up… They were nearly completed. Don't think too much of it—kind of thing runs in the family. Until now, I wasn't sure whom they were meant for," Phalen said with an encouraging smirk and dumped them into Zaethan's grasp. "It won't hurt you. The iron's edges were safely sealed before I even came to."

The prismatic metal was warm. Intimately so. Zaethan might've imagined it, but he could almost feel a pulse thrumming from the posts, in time with the resonant song being sang throughout the forge. Hair rose along his nape, and he quickly scooped the witchiron away and into his pocket. "Your fellows wouldn't take too keenly to these being worn by someone of my birth."

Phalen sidled his hands above his wide belt, seeming much older than his sixteen years. "My fellows taught me that greatness isn't born, Lord Haidren. It's forged."

Her news was dire. The Quadren sat in shock, scattered around Dmitri's bedroom, opposite where Boreal's sil'haidren stood gravely in the doorway. She hadn't yet told the elders, nor the clann. She'd come straight to the king.

Tetsu Naborū had been named proxy regent.

In Dmitri's absence, the Peerage of Nobility had voted it so.

Orynthia was now scepter and shield to the House of Pilar.

In the muteness, Ira was an irritating gnat, nervously dropping his snuff canister on the floorboards for the second time in five minutes. No one else turned toward his disruption except Zaethan. After picking up his gilded chain, the yancy settled back into his chair, threw his slim leg over an arm, and went back to nibbling on the canister's rim. In the adjacent corner, Hachiro had put his quill to paper as if about the write. But he hadn't begun. An ink blot spread under his troubled facial features where the tendons fired in their erratic spasms. Seated beside the bed across from Ira, Luscia sat unnaturally still—a hidden cosmos shuttered from them, surely swirling behind her closed eyes.

Upon the furs, their king sat against the headboard, his ankles crossed and his elbows perched atop his knees. Dmitri tapped his steepled forefingers. Anguish had warped his elegant countenance. Were he on a battlefield instead of a bed, one might have believed Zaethan's friend had been run straight through with a spear.

By all intents, Dmitri had been—in being betrayed by his native House.

Pilar could do nothing in Bastiion without the votes.

Wordlessly, Zaethan rotated against the dressing table and grabbed the pitcher of mulled wine. He didn't even like mulled wine, but he knocked it back as if it could drown reality nonetheless.

Alora Tiergan hadn't revealed her informant, not even when Dmitri had outright asked how she'd come to learn of Naborū seizing his throne. Or how the chancellor had even managed it. Luscia's aunt had skirted the question as she so dexterously did others, Zaethan had observed. The hour slowed the longer she remained as an ominous statue, hemmed rigid and taut in her sterling, high-neck gown. The sil'haidren made no attempt to console Dmitri. Had she any feeling at all, Alora Tiergan had exorcised it before entering the room.

It riled Zaethan when she stiffly dipped her height in deference for their king.

"I will excuse myself, Your Majesty," she solemnly stated, "so as not to impede your Quadren's deliberation. Should you request my counsel, I will be gathering the Enclave promptly in the Grand Tabernacle." Picking up her narrow skirts, Alora Tiergan withdrew into the hallway.

Luscia's eyelids flew open, and she skidded her chair backward. "Aunt, wait," she called, crossing him to trail after her sil'haidren.

The door swung shut on its fat hinges. Zaethan's gaze traced her outline through the wood, still feeling the impression of her body against his arms after their volatile encounter in the wildwood. He grunted and rolled back toward the dresser to pour himself a second glass.

An understanding of Luscia Darragh Tiergan was like a fistful of water; the moment he thought he had one, it slipped right through his fingers.

"Sober minds, Zaeth" came Dmitri's admonishment over his caged forearms.

"If I can do it, surely you can, my friend," Ira drawled. "What I wouldn't give for last year's Wendyllean blend and a slice of Uriel pie in a time like this."

Hachiro rewet his quill, alertly inching forward. "Perhaps we can solve for the monetary value. Does a specific price come to mind?"

"Well," Ira replied, angling the canister at him. "Flourette does make quite the diversion in Father's will..."

"And Arune's estate must be worth at least a quarter of Vien," Hachiro murmured as he etched a system of hatch marks.

Zaethan glowered at Ira. "Your only friend is whatever that is you've been snorting this entire time."

"You think you know everything, but you don't, do you, big alpha!" the yancy snapped right as the door reopened. "If you're so smart, then why are your men deserting us, huh?"

Zaethan's face went tight, his frustration at Ira simmering as Luscia returned to her seat far more slowly than the way she'd flown from it. Fluidly, she situated herself and clasped her hands stoically in her lap once more. Whatever she'd hoped to get from her aunt, he doubted it'd been received.

Good, he thought. He knew that feeling well.

Dmitri pinched his nose, then slid the ancient puzzle box out from under his pillow. In listless, methodical steps, he unraveled the panels until it was a flat pentagon pointing away from his toes overtop the bedding. Bleakly, their king leaned over the Quadrecipher to twist the petite turntables so that they reflected the crest of each haidrens' respective House.

Zaethan stepped up to the footboard before Darakai's panther.

"This Quadren is now in session," Dmitri said, settling against the headboard. He looked up at them all. His eyes were darkened pits. "Tetsu Naborū has stolen control of Bastiion. What do we do now?"

No one spoke a word.

Propping on an elbow, Luscia eventually uttered through her fingers, "Tactically speaking, nothing has changed. The Order of the Najjan should be here next week. With Lord Darakai's remaining troops, we will retake Bastiion as planned."

"That's a significant decrease in troops, by my tally," Hachiro stated. "Simply by the law of averages, that'd assuredly impact any attempt of a siege."

"Those aren't najjani averages. And it won't be a siege but an infiltration," Luscia said without apology.

Zaethan had seen firsthand the najjan in combat. It was a frighteningly honest boast; one najjan really was worth twenty enemies. But even still, the librarian had a point.

Hachiro lifted his quill and blinked four times. "Even factoring in your deluded statistic, Lady Boreal, given the pryde's defection, we're at a significant disadvantage."

"They aren't defectors." Zaethan began to pace at the end of the bed. "Kai's going to lead them to my uncle, Yousif."

Ira clinked his canister on the chair. "We can't exactly call them 'stayers,' Lord Darakai. Deserters, maybe."

"You scrawny little brat!" he shouted. "Those warriors bled for you in Port Khmer and now they're being persecuted for it!"

"Boreal was persecuted for centuries," Luscia stiffly replied. "Yours can endure it for a few months."

Zaethan gaped at her, and she finally held his gaze. In a speechless exchange, Luscia gestured at Dmitri, pointedly suggesting his people weren't as loyal as hers. Sucking through his teeth, Zaethan violently shook his head.

"Should we wait then? Yet what of the people?" Dmitri's desperate tenor cut through their glaring, causing Zaethan to swerve. "Are we to hold for Yousif—Commander Shà, rather—to fully organize before we launch our attack?"

"Yes," Ira and Hachiro said in unison.

"Niit."

"Ano zà," Zaethan stated, angrily agreeing with her. "Weakness breeds violence because only strength can rein it in. You want to protect everyone left in the proper, Dmitri? Then we cannot wait. You're getting on the boat, and we're taking back Bastiion."

His friend wrapped his arms around himself. Dmitri leveled his regard at Zaethan, and his woodsy eyes filled with mist. "You can say that today. But who will leave me tomorrow?"

Zaethan had never feared a look so much in his life. It was pure hopelessness. Gripping the footboard, he tried to calm down. Dmitri could not lose, not yet. Not before he'd even begun his reign. Not before they tried to save it. Toeing his edge, Zaethan felt himself about to explode.

"Perchance we ought to dangle a diplomatic carrot, so to speak," Hachiro said. "Offer the deserters a title, a plot of land, or a chest of aurus from the royal treasury. People seem to take to that sort of thing."

Zaethan fired up at him. "Diplomacy will not fix this!"

"Do not raise your voice at him," Luscia warned, driving herself up off the chair arms. "That was a fair proposition, Lord Pilar, and I second it."

Ira cheers'd her with his canister. "And I, third. Where there's a money problem, there's never *really* a problem."

"Coin is not everything. And neither is diplomacy." Zaethan shoved off and loomed over Luscia, his finger pointed. "They don't trust you! Show them why they should trust you, Lady Boreal, or accept that you did nothing—absolutely nothing—to keep them from marching to their own executions, instead of with us to dethrone his usurper!"

"Zaeth, please…"

He ripped his vehemence from her and threw it toward his friend.

A tear was rolling down Dmitri's cheek.

Zaethan smacked the dressing table. A glass clattered to the floor in shards. "I need some air."

After storming into the hall, he raced down the corkscrewed staircase. Zaethan braced against the biting cold and slammed the door to her manor. On the veranda, he butted his back against the bark while his breath came in short bursts.

Seconds later, the entry opened and shut. Luscia had joined him outside.

The wind lashed through her unbound hair where she stood before an ethereal backdrop of lichen and lamplight. Without warning, she soundlessly moved toward him and pressed her hand over his heart. And bending her forehead, she leaned against him overtop it.

His heart pounded. Fighting. Raging against her touch.

After a time, she raised her chin and searched him, as if she could scrape the barrel in one caustic glance. "Give me till the morning," Luscia said, retracting her hand.

Whether absently or intentionally, she wiped it off on her skirt and went back inside.

Chapter Thirty Four
Luscia

Flurries clustered upon her lashes. Batting them against the bitter wind, she steeled her concentration toward the southwestern trees. It was taking them too long. Something was amiss.

Luscia wriggled her fingers. They stung in the cold. Fighting the urge to worry, she slid them back into her fox-trimmed parka and assumed her unyielding stance at the top of the moor, a blunt contrast to the man pacing shallow trenches behind her through the snow.

"It's nearly dawn," he said, griping. "If I miss their sendoff because of this, I'll never forgive you for it. They could die the second they cross the border."

"A moot point, considering you don't believe in forgiveness, Lord Darakai—though it has been generously bequeathed to you in the past," Luscia replied without humor. At that, she heard the irritable crunching pause.

Luscia smelled the whiff of smoke and camphor before he dangerously crooked his chin over her shoulder.

"He's barely recovered. He shouldn't be out here," Zaethan sniped.

"It won't work if he isn't."

Through her periphery, she risked a look at their king, who off at the edge of the stone circle was bundled inside a parka much like hers. Yet where hers cut at the knees, Dmitri's swelled about his ankles. He drew the hood tightly with his sealskin mitts. The eastward gusts battered the long wisps of white fur against his reddening nose, his lone feature poking out. It was the brightest blot of color she'd seen on him in weeks, and not for good cause.

Luscia took a cleansing breath. Even a Tavish witchdoctor could tell that Dmitri should not be outside in his condition; risking his exposure was more perilous than Zaethan even realized, as he believed the recent bout to be a mere cold. But if the king of Orynthia was not sighted alive and well that morning, the jeopardies Luscia was risking might be for naught.

Not that a haidren from Darakai would ever grasp that.

"*What* exactly isn't going to work? We hiked out here before Owàa could spread his wings without a hint as to why, yeah? You didn't even drag most of your own men from their beds."

The accusation only appeared true, for only the twins had joined the Quadren at the moorland. Sidling Dmitri, both najjan were mirrored in stature, though hardly in deportment. Böwen—ever faithful—stood with his hands clasped at his back, attentive yet seemingly at ease, as if the winds were warming with the pinkening sky. Creyvan clearly did not share his brother's confidence. His arms were interlocked before him. It did not miss Luscia's attention how a new, distinct pattern decorated the hem of his coat sleeves. Threads of white, blue, red, and green had been handstitched there—the colors of Orallach traditionalists. Thus, she had been forced to bring him along. In that, Böwen had quickly become his brother's keeper. Creyvan's ears were still being seduced by Hinrük's sympathizers, making it too dangerous to leave him behind.

Creyvan had pinned his sneer at their foreign elites for most of the morning. Alongside him, the other haidrens were huddled together under a massive bear pelt. Ira's teeth chattered as, shuffling through his monocular lenses, Hachiro examined the flurries catching on the end of his quill. The contraption made the shoto'shi look like a squished chipmunk, magnifying his vexation every time Ira would blow the snow back into the chilly gusts.

She would have preferred locking the rest of the Quadren in a room with Creyvan for a few hours. But given the najjan's zealotry and Hachiro's obsession with recording the minutia of everything that ever happened to him, that political blunder would have been transcribed for generations to come.

"Trust that my guard rests far less than you do, Lord Darakai. Seek their beds and you will not find them," Luscia said as her ears quivered.

"Maji'maia, it was trusting you that's going to get my pryde killed—"

"Submit emotion to reason," Luscia replied, quoting her aunt, then rapidly shifted her face a few degrees west. Branches snapped in the distance. Böwen and Creyvan heard and angled toward it too. "They're here."

Behind her, Ira hissed to Hachiro, "Fates, I hate when they do that. Be sure to write that part down…"

The quill eagerly scraped the shoto'shi's pad when at the base of the moor, movement pierced the timberline. In a single-file row, their

Darakaian guests slowly appeared between the base of the holdreheiim, like foxgloves cropping up in springtime. Skittish and confusedly, they trailed each other, hand to shoulder. Each wore a sleeping cap over their eyes—a suggestion that'd come from Declan, who gently guided one group forward. It'd be best if witnesses couldn't later prove they had been ushered to the site of Luscia's breach. She didn't want to count how many Boreali laws she was about to break, nor those her men were breaking with her.

Yards off, Noxolo emerged, towing his row of warriors more slowly as he helped a female at the front navigate her way over an icy log. When he offered her his hand, she vehemently slapped it away and nearly fell over, had he not caught her first.

Lastly, Marek marched his line in from the rear. A spray of scarlet against the backdrop of fir and frost, he came much more gradually, for the leader of his group was bound in his possession. As was the sharp spindle Marek held at the alpha's throat.

Luscia frowned.

"What the Depths is *this*?" Zaethan whirled on her. She couldn't blame him. Things were off to an unpalatable start.

"The invitation had to come from our side."

"Invitation? This is an abduction!"

The warriors gracelessly hiked up the moorland. She kicked her upturned boot out of the gathering snowfall and pointed at the flimsy weapon Marek eased away from Kai's neck. "Where you see a scandal, I see a stick," Luscia replied as she walked on.

On her approach, the captaen slid the nightcap off an exceptionally unhappy alpha.

Kai wrestled against the linsilk tied at his wrists, and when the fabric cleared his overlarge eyes, he stumbled back from Luscia in surprise. His rucksack bumbled against his thigh. Suited up beyond him, those from the Valley Pryde were outfitted to leave. A scowl crumpled his upper lip. "You've got some nerve, uni. Curse these highlands!" The alpha spat on the ground, then spewed toward Marek. "And curse him too!"

Her captaen spread his hands placatingly to reveal the jagged stick Kai had assumed was a blade. It probably had been at one point, considering the dagger strapped to Marek's corded thigh. One look from the captaen confirmed Kai wouldn't have succumbed otherwise. And where an alpha goes, so does his pryde.

Luscia beckoned someone to unknot the alpha's binding and thanked her najjan in a relieved whisper. "Tadöm, meh brödre."

But Zaethan promptly stepped in. "I didn't know about this. I swear," he told his comrade, pricking his heart with his pinky and dragging it up his forearm in some rushed Darakaian gesture. He furiously ripped the linsilk off Kai. Zaethan corkscrewed his upper body, searching the moorland. "Where's Kumo? Kumo!"

From the back, a megalith broke from the gathered mass and bumped his path through the other warriors. The huge beta shook out of his cap—a lacey rendition that had likely originated from Arlette's drawer. "Eh, Ahoté… Hate to complain, but we're getting pretty sick of wearing lady rags." He soon received whoops of support from Takoda and Jabari, who once unmasked, trotted up beside him.

Zaethan snatched the wadded cap and fisted it in front of Luscia's face. "You're a real piece of work, you know that?"

It took a brisk pass to spot the few warriors who were curious about her unorthodox summoning. The rest were incensed, and their haidren's bombastic temper wasn't helping. Those on the outskirts were bearing down like spooked oxen, ready to charge anyone who tried to pen them in. Packs and bedrolls folded off their dark frames, packed with the only belongings left to them. Kai's pryde wanted to leave, as probably did most of the Proper Pryde too.

This was her final opportunity to convince them to stay.

Meaning it *had* to work.

The warriors hissed when Declan and Noxolo encouraged the Darakaians to pile in closer to the boundary line before Luscia.

Standing behind the stones, she swallowed her anxiety. "Tadöm—I thank you for coming. All of you."

Grumbling rippled through the dozens of disgruntled Darakaians. Some cheered when Kai contested. "Didn't give us much of a choice, ano? Just like we didn't have much choice when you hauled us up into this Fates-forsaken highland!"

Luscia didn't bother arguing the point. It was valid. "You'll get that choice after this morning. I guarantee it. As does your king," she said, backstepping aside to gesture toward Dmitri at the far end of the sparring circle. Searching the suspicious eyes of each warrior, Luscia opened her arms and curtsied herself before Kai. "Will you, Darakai the brave, bid us this final boon before you go?"

He laced his arms and sniffed.

"Just… shamàli, Kai. If you see fit," Zaethan said quietly.

"Fine. Uni zà." The lesser alpha smacked his lips. "Then we're gone for good."

Hope inflated Luscia's lungs. Undoing the toggles of her parka, she backtracked deeper into the circle, Zaethan furiously marching after on the right—just as she'd planned—and Marek flanking her on the left. At the center, the captaen extended his hands. Luscia slid out of the overcoat and rested it across his forearms. Then, making a show of it for the onlookers, she stripped off her weaponry. She laid her mother's dagger in Marek's gentle care and skated off Phalen's three-fingered radials, until it felt as if she stood naked in front of those she'd once called her enemy.

"Are you sure?" he asked, beseeching her one last time.

"Wem. Se'lah Aurynth."

"Rul'Aniell." Marek bowed his head reverently, then took her things with him to the apex, the northmost position along the stones.

Creyvan and Böwen joined him there, claiming the spurs along the east and west. An icicle animated to life, Noxolo towered over the prydes and stole the fourth, southwestern spur. From the southeast, Declan stepped up and assumed the fifth and final spur. He held her tense gaze, pawing his snarly, ginger beard, and with a wink, the najjan tapped his fist against his chest in Darakaian salute.

Steeling her breath, Luscia turned toward Zaethan. The oddest expression distorted his full lips. It was almost as hostile as it was befuddled.

In a ravenous sweep, he raked in her lower half, where Luscia's legs were swathed by a pair of gunja pants. Shaking his head of freefalling locs, he breathlessly asked, "What kind of charade is this?"

"This is me offering them more than diplomacy," Luscia replied and tightened the thick belt around her quilted tunic. "Now, unsheathe that kuerre, and don't you dare hold back when I tell you to use it."

Zaethan confusedly lowered his hand to the luxiron hilt when she pointed for him to claim nadir, by his people to the south. Together the men formed an Aurynth star with Luscia surrounded in the cradle, though not for the sake of her protection. In the sweetest whine, iron kissed iron when her najjan unleashed their crescent wraiths from their backs.

"Bastiion has been overthrown," Luscia pronounced to the prydes. The news recaptured their attention from the specialized weaponry, inciting alarmed chatter. "Tetsu Naborū, the leader of Pilar, crowns himself your regent, whilst the heir of Thoarne is here, braving the highlands with you. He and I know you are patriots. And many of you have been mistreated."

It would be counterproductive to apologize for it. To throw herself at their mercy. Darakaians didn't even apologize to each other, seeing it only as retraction. As a weakness.

Luscia had to deal in their own language.

She had to offer them kwihila.

"Wem, yes, you can risk the Valley to join arms with Commander Shà," she continued. "Or… You storm Bastiion with the Order of the Najjan. Because when we confront the chief warlord's claim on the city, I tell you today, we are going to win."

Some warriors tossed up their hands. Plenty of others scoffed at the premise.

Luscia stole a glance toward Hachiro. "Some say this confidence is a delusion. Yet I ask you, House of Darakai, where is the line between faith and delusion? Is it not marked by what it has the power to overcome? The odds are not against us! For we are outnumbered in number alone."

Closing her eyes, she reached for the veil in her mind. It swept back with a gust, pushing her lids apart as it thrust Luscia into her Sight. The *Other* repainted the highland horizon in a glistening, muted tapestry. Under the rust of the resplendent sunrise, threads of lumin were spiraled in tight, quivering bands around the circle and its voyeurs. Beyond it, the mist rose in spires over the mountains like phantoms rousing from their tombs. The luxiron solrahs through her septum awoke with their spirits—whether in excitement or in warning, she could not discern.

Luscia reached into her gunjas and produced a strip of linsilk. "There are forces in this world you cannot see," she declared, wrapping the blindfold over her eyes. "And though we may be blind to them, they are never blind to us."

Earth crunched when she knelt into the wet snow. Luscia bowed forward, balancing on two fingers, as she prayed in a whisper. "Bolaeva, Aniell. I am relenting to you."

Static pricked her skin in response. There would be no bomaerod or homing echo. It would be Luscia trusting the Light in the darkness.

Weh yeyisha'shadü tredae lim Lux.

Crooking her forefingers at her either side, she beckoned her men to charge.

An unnatural breeze brushed her cheek. She heard the warriors gasp when within her self-imposed shadow, Luscia rolled aside in its direction and onto her soles just before a body slid through the snow where she'd been kneeling. Energy rushed through her thighs, driving her into a backward somersault. Her boot landed on metal, and she sprung through the air onto the lip of his other wraith. Luscia ran up the blade as its axis tilted. Her arm was jolted aside, releasing a rush of warmth. Iron shattered, and the prydes shrieked in surprise.

She landed, crouching on one ankle, and swung her other leg out, cutting someone at their knees. With a masculine *oof*, her najjan hit the ground. But just as she rose, an otherworldly force, as if hands from the sky, pushed her down. A hot, euphoric sensation broiled Luscia's knuckles as her fingers were squeezed into a fist. The lumin shoved her elbow forward, and she struck a new attacker in the abdomen beneath the swipe of a wraith.

The light-fueled impact threw her skidding across the moor. Something impaled the earth right beside her face, sending vibrations under her skull. Disoriented, Luscia hooked her heels overhead, catching a blade's edge between her boots, and stole the wraith from its najjan. With it, she blocked his next strike. The air shifted as he dodged her haphazard hits. Luscia pitched the weapon afar and kicked him instead.

A high-pitched whizzing neared as she stood. Luscia spun and grabbed a dagger midair by its hilt and discarded it like trash. They were going too easy on her. They always did.

But *he* wouldn't.

Neither would Creyvan.

Scenting him, Luscia revolved toward the bracing, honeyed smell of drösarra leaf. Every good zealot stuffed his linings with the holiest herb. She rushed the wayward twin, freeing her disappointment and anger in him through every rapid swish of her legs. Somehow, Luscia sensed Creyvan doing the same.

It was his chance to take it out on her. To that, she grinned.

Luxiron nicked her bicep, and Luscia whistled in pain. As her flesh burned, she leaped and screwed her legs around his strong arm, within the cage of his crescent wraiths, to knee the najjan across the jaw. Blood or spit splattered her forehead. Creyvan grunted as she dropped from him, who was surely coming back for more. Faking, he whirled in the opposite direction, but a gust from the *Other* guided her footing to his dance. Evading his blades, Luscia pivoted, and in a gush of molten vindication, the lumin exploded from her conjoined palms.

The Darakaians swore. With a distant thump, Creyvan hit a bordering boulder past the stone perimeter. Suddenly they started to cheer.

Their haidren was stirring from nadir.

Luscia bent low, quirking toward the sound of his panther-like steps. She'd recognize the tempo anywhere—slick, confident, and loaded with the assurance he was about to win. Her hips slunk with his predacious pace as they rotated about each other. A whistle went through the air as he rotated his kuerre cockily, rallying more excitement among his prydes. And she was glad for it; the emotion would aid their cause. Yet Luscia did not wait for him to make the first move.

That was hers.

Inside the darkness, she ran for Zaethan. Anticipating his first swipe, Luscia flipped twice over, hooking her heel around his ankle and walled her back against his. She bowed her spine across his firm backside and rested her head in the muscle between his shoulder blades. A torrid shiver scurried up the sinuous line of their spines, fusing them together. In tidal waves, his ribs expanded, and the two haidrens took on the same breath, which rushed in and out as his footing grew erratic but no less predictable. No matter how he moved, she matched it as his shadow. He'd smugly forgotten: she knew his body too.

Then, relishing his rumble of irritation as he reversed the angle of his hilt, Luscia broke away when he swung the Boreali sword backward. She chuckled darkly. Her nostrils flamed; the luxiron had sizzled the fibers of his jacket instead.

Dipping under another pass of his kuerre, her arm was lurched aside by the *Other*, and energy speared through her palm toward something on her left. Metal debris fell in clattering clinks. Distracted, Luscia was abruptly jerked back by her double braids, like a wild mare being reined in by its master. She slammed against Zaethan's hard torso.

His heart throbbed behind her ears. It drowned out the whooping and applause as he pinned her temple with his chin.

The haidren had the audacity to click his tongue.

Growling, she leaped off the earth and revolved over his head. He lost grip of her hair as her legs crooked around his navel. Zaeth tried to buck her off, but she seized him by his own locs, clicking her tongue at him in kind, and used them like a rope to bounce off his hip. Luscia flung herself over his arm, dislodging his kuerre with her heels.

Vibrations thrummed through her entire body. She caught the hilt of the backsword before she landed and brashly threw it back at him when she did. Luscia felt the thread of light leave her after the blade.

Her fingers again curled inward, the euphoria building within her fists. In warm, prickling bands, the lumin wrapped around her and bent her body like a slingshot.

Then it let go.

Coming down hard, Luscia pummeled the ground.

A mighty avalanche coursed through her and blasted forth, flinging her backward in a booming shockwave across the moorland.

The blackness was consuming. Cold and soundless, she lay there with ringing in her ears, unable to move. Yet unexpectedly, Luscia felt herself being lifted out of it. Shaken more like, by a harsh grip on her uninjured bicep. A muddied raucous slowly penetrated her hearing.

Gasps. Cheers. Swearing.

Roughly, her blindfold was stripped away, and the world's brightness whited out her vision. Refocusing, all she could see was an intense pair of wide-set eyes.

In sparkling ribbons, the lumin wafted behind the intimacy of Zaethan's stare. She saw her image dwelling within the heartland of his bright-green irises. There her Tiergan eyes were tenacious and aglow. Spreading his free hand over her face, Zaethan gently skimmed his middle finger down her nose, and pulling away, he mimed removing a mask with it.

"There you are," he rasped.

Locked in his clutches, Luscia couldn't shirk the weight of his penetrating gaze, not even when Kai jogged up behind him. "Uni! Uni zà, the Valley Pryde will fight with you, Lady Haidren!" sang the alpha as he held his head in shock. In the *Other*, the reflection of lumin traced brightly across his deep skin. "Fates, this kakka-shtàka witchery is wild."

"She's not a witch," Zaethan said, his voice charged with gravel from the blast. More delicate than his hold, he dusted her blondest strays off her cheeks and into her hairline.

"Eh, course not, meme qondai." Kai chuckled. "Just another day in Boreal, yeah?"

Luscia blinked a few times, shuttering her Sight. Over Zaethan's shoulders, the highland range returned to its wintry picture, the sky blossoming in a mature sunrise overhead. People were gathering alongside Kai, and she suddenly realized how long she'd been in their haidren's arms.

She pushed away just as Marek extended his hand between them. "I'll take her from here," he said with so much composure, it had to be contrived. Luscia grabbed onto him when Marek scooped her up from the mess of ice and dirt. He set her down a few paces away, then carefully adjusted the kurtfierï on her wrist and let go.

Luscia cupped his cheek. A tendon snapped through his jaw as quickly as it disappeared. "Tadöm for being my partner today," she stated.

Abruptly, Marek slid behind her, for both king and Quadren were sloughing through the snow toward Luscia as fast as they could manage.

"Lady Boreal!" Hachiro was shouting, clicking on his monocular device while he ran—or tried to, under his ocher robes. "Is it a solution you first drink before dolling the carnage? I must document the grammage." He took a gulp, apparently having forgotten to breathe, and switched to the violet lens. Bending down, he panted. "And might I render a diagram of your p-palms over dinner?"

"Have I taught you nothing about wooing a lady, Hachi?" Ira rubbed his arms against the chill as he joined them. "'The stronger the kick, the sweeter the lick,' as the former duke of Wendylle always contended. From our first meeting, I sensed you had a rarefied, nuggety center, gosling. Care to be nibbled later?"

"Niit," she and Marek said in tandem.

"See, Hachi, that's how you properly proposition a lady—wait a minute…"

Hachiro clicked on the yellow lens. "I have always repudiated palm readers as toothless, bunkum hawkers, but perhaps there's something substantial in your conduit lines that we could study—"

"Let her breathe, Lord Pilar," Dmitri chided, raking his cane through the snow in slower haste as Declan guided him through the rocks strewn out of place. "Though she is magnificent. I didn't—I had no idea such things existed in this life, Lady Boreal." Collecting her fingers, he bowed his forehead toward them. "Thank you for disclosing it. Thank you for winning back the pryde."

Humbled, Luscia could only bend her knee before him. "You needed to see this too. Believe it, My King. Together we are going to take back your throne."

Luscia belted her mother's dagger securely over her thigh and removed her boot from the boulder, then lazily fastened the toggles up her parka while her stomach grumbled. She was utterly depleted. Ravenous too. Shoveling the rest of her gear under her arm, Luscia patiently waited as her guard finished aligning the stones back into their original circle.

After plunking a rock into the snow, Creyvan dusted his hands. He was the first to march off in her direction, but by his pace, he did not care to pause.

As he passed, she awkwardly said, "I appreciate your help, Creyvan—"

"You waste miracles on heathens," he snapped and continued down the moor.

Luscia nearly dropped the gear, for her heart sank with it. No matter what she'd told her king, she couldn't win. Never fully. Not with those closest to her, or who ought to have been.

"He'll cool down, Ana'Sere." Böwen's steady reassurance jolted her when he stepped up beside her. "He participated at least."

Her expression soured as she nudged him with her sliced bicep. "Wem, I'll wear his gracious memento the rest of my life. The High One's mercy on me, Böwen, I truly don't know what to do with him anymore."

"Ock. It's really me meh brödre is mad at, Ana'Sere. Not you."

Perplexed, Luscia regarded him. Though trimmer than Creyvan, Böwen seemed to have gained in age rather than poundage during their season apart. Böwen's short beard had filled in, now abundant like harvested flax. Lines rutted his sparsely freckled brow—from nights spent worrying over his twin, she supposed. But his expectant, crystal-blue observance was unchanged, anticipating her response as if it ought to have been obvious.

It wasn't. Luscia's face said as much.

"Mila accepted my kurtfierï," Böwen replied and shrugged the straps of his sheathed wraiths into better position. "That copper necklet, it's Unitarian. I obtained it from her mother. Mila's been wearing it since before Ana'Innöx."

"Oh, she ascended in the summer…" Luscia trailed off.

How had she not noticed? Had Mila said something she'd chosen not to hear? Luscia was aware of the affection that'd blossomed between them. Frankly, it was hard *not* to notice, all that staring longingly at each other and the like. Had Luscia become so self-involved, mulling day and night about her own problems, that she'd overlooked the life-altering events of those she considered friends?

Am I a selfish person? she asked herself. *Surely not.*

"Ana'Sere?"

I'm a haidren to Boreal. All we think about is other people.

"Ana'Sere, are you listening?"

"Hm?" Luscia blinked. "What is it?"

"I said, 'The Order will be here next week, so we don't want to wait,'" Böwen replied, an out-of-place giddiness making him bounce on his heels. "With your daeünna, naturally."

"My blessing…"

"To—to marry her."

As she quirked her head at him, Böwen instantly bent in subservience so that his height did not supersede hers. Though he was trained to control it, his breathing hurried with his nervousness.

"So soon?" she asked.

"Who is to say how long we will be in Bastiion? And anything could happen there. This will secure her status in Roüwen in my absence. My name will guard her when I cannot. And, well," he said, splitting the happiest of grins—the kind lit from within, "I can hardly wait another day. When you've spent every waking moment with someone, a few months is the most moving eternity."

Her eyes welled at his happiness even while her chest ached. Luscia fought it as her face turned toward the tree line and those who were no longer there.

A moving eternity it had been.

"I know the feeling," said Luscia. "Wem. Of course. I wish you both a lifetime of joy."

Böwen engulfed her in a tight hug. Unceremoniously, he jumped her up and down in celebration while the other najjan rushed over, clapping for him.

Böwen and Mila did not need another's blessing; they'd sown enough in each other.

Set down in the snow, Luscia found Marek. She slid her hand determinedly into his, willing that they could sow it too.

Chapter Thirty Five

Death perfumed the figure as he crept deeper through the long-forgotten tunnel. His dim torchlight painted shadows on the wall of tombs, their inscriptions as faded as the memory of their dwellers. The bone-sated niches were buried beneath Bastiion's spirited surface. The figure felt in company with their number.

These corpselike halls were barren, feeding only ghosts and rats. He lurked easily by both. The dead did not judge the living.

And the figure was neither.

Down the slickened stones, faraway screams echoed from the dungeons. No prison guard would venture this far into the catacombs, but the figure shrouded the torchlight nevertheless, the labyrinth so dark that his eyes required its aid.

Bile seeped from the palace. Under the ominous flicker, a record of refuse and revelry stained the burial sites in mineralized streaks. Waste festered in puddles where the court had pissed on its regents of old.

Columns of stacked skulls lined the tunnel in macabre arches, their servants attending them even after death. Patterns stretched the passage length, fashioned from the lower-class skeletons shepherding their royal stewards into the supposed afterlife, were the Fates gracious enough to permit their renewed appointment.

Few remembered the catacombs and those who had been laid there to rest centuries before the early Shield Age, when Queen Roma Julius Thoarne had refused to be buried alongside her ancestors. Forfeiting the once-revered footpaths, she'd moved Bastiion's prisoners many feet under, lifetimes below the surface where the nobility would never see their shackles, hear their shrieks, scent their smut, nor taste their responsibility in the making of all three.

Ages upended because a dead queen was said to be afraid of the shadow and did not wish to sleep under its eternal oppression.

Holding her infamous misdeeds to account, it was *her* shadow that she'd truly feared.

The figure feared his own that much more.

It was why he'd delayed coming there… waiting and hoping for weeks that Tetsu had gotten himself caught in a web not of his own making. But he *had* made it—remade it, in fact—and with a research not his own. The chancellor was not working off theory or an old scribble on a scrap of parchment. If Tetsu could transform the Obscurer's creatures, and do it with an altered procedure, just how much had been discovered about the figure's?

Questions abounded, forcing the figure to embark on this most wicked retreat. If the answers he needed could not be observed aboveground, they might be inferred below, amid what should have stayed entombed with the corpses twenty terrible years ago.

The figure ran his tongue along the blistering of his inner lip and rounded the final turnoff to his despicable destination. His feet could not miss the way, no matter how many attempts he made to confuse them. He slowed, nearly dragging himself to the entry of the old mausoleum.

Holding up the torch, he saw the threshold was laminated in cobwebs—a slight reassurance of the years it'd gone uncrossed. The mausoleum belonged to a duke from the Scourge Age, and the family's name had been engraved beneath an eagle-hewn insignia, where one wing had crumbled to erasure. Glutted by inherited opulence and prosperity, their descendants weren't mourning them, nor did they mourn what he'd done inside—how he had desecrated their unvisited resting place.

How he'd desecrated his soul along with it.

The figure recalled when he'd found the mausoleum. The catacombs were brimmed with such familial crypts, but it was this one that was so poorly maintained, he knew it would be safe. The figure had searched for the proper location for months, somewhere he could research. Where he could test. Somewhere neither would be denounced or discovered.

He never told Alora where it'd happened.

Never told her to burn it.

Never thought Tetsu would seek it out, come behind, and rob the evil from its crib.

Unclenching his hand, the figure swept the cobwebs aside. He pressed his gloved hand to the splintered door and paused. A tide of shame broke upon his disfigured shoulders and curved beneath his heavy, tattered cloak. The figure refused the dank air to splash his shriveled lungs, as if breathing might revive the man he had once been or had the audacity to call himself. For all intents and purposes, his name had died well before his body had rebirthed. It had died the minute he'd first opened that door.

He pushed the rotted wood inward, throwing his weight against the stronghold of a thousand secrets.

The resultant dust cloud almost snuffed out the torchlight. He wished it had. Shudderingly, the figure stepped into the arched cavity. In a cruel unveiling, the stale particles settled over what had served as his hidden laboratory.

Along either side, crypts fenced the abandoned workspace, their deceased the silent and solitary witnesses to his crimes. Papers were still plastered across the tallest wall at the end of the lab. Others cluttered the dirty floor. The brittle parchment curled away like a birch tree shedding its bark in telltale strips. Some had been robbed by the chancellor's hand. And until the figure had stolen them back, those papers had been well preserved under lock and key in Tetsu's office.

Anguished, the figure stared at the notes that clung there. Those that had failed to fall away. His thumbprint had transformed the noble family's memorial… had vandalized it with shocking charts and diagrams, hypotheses, and conjecture. None of it had amounted to science, only savagery and heartache. These were the writings of a madman wrecked by love and his desperation to keep it. A man ruined by a chronic symbol he'd sketched over and over again on practically every surface displayed.

Beneath the figure's boots, it lay—the conundrum, the accursed theory, scored into the stonework upon which he stood. Twin bends spanned from one corner of the lab to the other, shaping a symbol of infinity, existence and hereafter divided at its crux.

Of genes splintered.

Of life paused.

Of creation ended and creation renewed.

A theoretical fissuring to become like his cherished Alora so that they would no longer have had to be apart. But he wasn't supposed to have replicated her attributes. Was never supposed to have cherished her at all.

Intended for gifts and floral deposits, a bench stretched below the vile exhibit. The figure hesitantly moved toward it while averting his gaze in the process. Clothed in cobwebs, book stacks were strewn about. Undone scrolls were splayed under a dusty film, the resources amassed from every library he'd ravaged during the beautiful, thought-pro-voking, tortuous years after his and Alora's introduction in Arune. With his finger, the figure drew a line through the grime toward one of his research journals. He flipped it open. The page was damning at a glance.

Counting the neighboring journals, the figure exhaled for the first time since entering the makeshift laboratory. Fear escaped him in a rush.

A journal was absent.

The journal—the only one that really mattered.

His past tapped him on the shoulder, imploring the figure to turn around… to face what he had started. Dread skated his spin when he did. In want of tears, his eyes chafed as he took in the table at the center of the lab.

And the skeleton that he'd left upon it.

Blood dribbled over the table edge, spewing from the most recent incision. It was too close to the artery. Scrambling, he shoved the scalpel aside and thrust a rag against the wound. Crimson soaked the fabric through to his shaking hands. He wasn't a surgeon and needed sleep. He should have waited. If he lost the candidate, then tonight was the only chance to make the attempt. Outside the body, the samples would not keep to tomorrow.

There may never be another candidate; such arrests were rare. Alora's people weren't like the rest of the Ethnicam. They avoided Bastiion, except in trade.

Atop the table, the man moaned in his sweat-sodden delirium. No one would overlook a missing Boreali prisoner, especially of the murderous variety. The midnight guard had voraciously taken the bribe of two aurus. One so lowborn wouldn't reject gold from someone of prominence. As such, secrecy was sold with the backstory: the full-blooded trader had gotten into a tavern brawl and been convicted for the death of his aggressor. The man had been set to hang in a month, and there wouldn't be another like him, a Boreali so easily obtained. Not for years.

Years were not an option. Her courtship was well underway.

The tincture of pipe marrow and cyanide salt was metabolizing faster than anticipated. Faster than the gore draining from the man's ashen, muscled thigh. Soon the prisoner would be fighting the restraints where they were buckled to the tabletop.

He removed the rag and let the blood pour. Racing around the lab, he snatched a bowl to catch the precious runoff. It had to be fresh. There were too many variables otherwise. He wiped away the perspiration collecting on his brow, along with his trepidation, envisioning her face—her perfect, moon-kissed face and the tears that had showered it the last time they'd spoken. His body still thrummed from its memory of hers holding onto him tightly, desperately, ardently… having finally come together. Her token embrace clung to his very soul. Alora had called it a mistake, even as her drowning eyes argued her own assertion.

Thrown in the fire, his theory had turned to ash with her daydreamed hopes, whispered in their youth. She was seated on the Quadren now; it had gone too far. They were to return to their lonesome… to an existence deprived of one another while sharing its occupancy. But Alora would see how mistaken she was. He could become anew; he'd found the way.

He could become whatever she wanted.

Doubt had lost its voice amid his prepared beakers and vials. His hands were already bloodstained. He sloshed a clean cloth into the warm, soapy water as the prisoner rustled into consciousness, and he scrubbed the crook of his arm, quickly ensuring his own flesh was not contaminated. He took his hypothesized concoction of ground stimulants and underdosed poisons and set it before him on the bench. Then, he sterilized another scalpel over the candlelight. With a cut to his wrist, he drained some blood into the beaker. The prisoner started groaning behind him as the concoction turned scarlet and indistinct. Bubbles formed on the surface, the chemical reaction beginning before his eyes.

He documented the result in an open journal and hurried back to the table. His steps splashed where the bowl had overflowed. Covered in incisions, the Boreali's body was a carnage.

"Ykah…" The prisoner's voice rasped. "Ykah lö?"

"Shh. I promise it's almost over. I promise it is. I promise," he said to himself and poured the lumin-enriched blood into three vials—their ingestion interval to be painstakingly timed.

The bubbling concoction followed, fizzing when it splashed into the Boreali samples. He lowered his gaze to the glass, scrutinizing every pop and flash that sparked through the liquid. His breath hitched; the lumin was dormant, but it was there.

The bloods were mingling.

It was going to work.

Consumed with glee, he swished the vials to encourage the merge of their opposite lineages, even as the prisoner stirred and thrashed. If the ratio was correct, the Boreali should be dominant. Should be—

The man screamed. There was no one to hear.

He briefly glanced over his shoulder, barely a blink away from his possibly fatal experiment. Perhaps they were both going to perish and then it wouldn't matter anyway.

Perhaps he would live—live like he never had lived before.

Fevered by the rising stakes, he scribbled more notes and picked up the first vial. Cradled it like a jewel. The Ethnicam had no clue what pumped in Northern veins. And soon, he was going to share in it. Soon, he would be Boreali too.

He brought it to his lips, those which had known every inch of her, and drank.

Hot iron doused his tongue, though he felt nothing when he swallowed. He blocked out the prisoner's cries for help and counted the seconds until the next interval. Nineteen, twenty, twenty-one. With determination, he threw back the second vial.

His throat itched. Excitement swung him around toward the table and panted over it. The Boreali's shouts had tapered to whimpers, having either lost hope or the energy to scream. Sweat and tears drenched the matted, flaxen hair that swabbed the wood.

His blue eyes, lacking the splendor of hers, twisted toward him. "Bolaeva… Bolaeva…"

Nineteen.

Twenty.

Twenty-one.

With an ecstatic grin, he pivoted back toward the bench and drank the third formula, then slammed down the vial in triumph. There was a rumble through his torso. Then a spasm along his limbs. Prickles of ecstasy overtook his core, the transfused lumin doing its work as it dispersed up his spine and down to his toes, transforming him. He would be new.

He would be hers.

Fire speared his abdomen, the pain flinging him to the ground before another surge impaled his insides. He contorted across the stone. His teeth throbbed, his incisors pushing in and out of his gums. Unforgiving embers consumed his skin, and before his eyes, patches of it boiled off the backs of his hands under the smeared blood of his captive.

The calculations, the method… Something had gone horribly wrong.

He looked up at the Boreali prisoner, whose renewed weakening cries stuck his ears like cymbals. He heard everything. It came in tides: the torture in the dungeon, the nibbling of rats… But louder than them all was the tear-choked prayers of the man he'd carved like meat upon a butcher's block.

With his windpipe closing, or maybe it was his lungs, he crawled to the leg of the table and used his remaining strength to pull himself higher until he came face-to-face with the prisoner.

"Bolaeva… Aniell…"

His vision blurred, then refocused, sharpened, and blurred again. He fumbled for the scalpel. "Forgive me for what I've done. Meh fyreon," he whispered in the man's tongue.

And slid the blade into his temple.

Blood oozed down his forearm as he slid back to the ground, and the scalpel clattered out of his slacked grasp. His heartbeat slowed. It ceased to beat. The room descended into cold darkness. Not yet dead nor alive, he was absolutely alone. And while the sound of the rats faded to dust, he still heard the man crying.

The figure heard it now.

Pressure panged his sinuses, though no moisture came. He doubled over the tabletop in a silent wail, one only understood by those who'd preceded him into the Depths, where he so surely belonged. There was no agony like a sin unforgiven. It was a parasite, eating away at his necrotic heart. When would it be finished with him? When would his tissue decay to the point of forget? He longed to be forgotten… erased to nothingness like the insignia of the family tomb.

He dragged himself to the head of the table, where the Boreali trader's skull was crowned in cobwebs. "Meh fyreon, brödre." The figure leaned his forehead down and brushed it against the bone. Hardly a murmur, his voice quaked as he said, "I did not know my own depravity then."

Crouching, he found the blade, and twenty years too late, he took it and sliced the restraints, cutting the skeleton free. The figure dropped the scalpel and backed up the short steps.

Fleeing from the mausoleum, he digested the reality. He'd committed unthinkable acts on an altar of passion. Deeds driven by an obsession masquerading as love.

Love would have walked away. Obsession had opened a door.

A door that he'd cracked for another without realizing it.

Tetsu Naborū had been here; his drawer was riddled with the artifacts to prove it. He'd seen the corpse. He'd read the lettering. He had taken the results with him.

They had been taught that ideas should never be suppressed.

Their teaching was wrong. Some ideas were damned upon their conception.

The journal missing was unparallel to the rest, for in it he'd recorded how the experiment had been performed. Every heinous step. Every descent into a treachery that could not be undone.

All of it, delivered into the hands of the Obscurer and his incarnate kingdom.

His footfalls splashed through the polluted puddles down the catacomb corridor. The figure felt the bones of his departed jurors pressing in from their macabre prominence in the walls. His depraved spirit begged for their judgments to burst forth and bury him alive.

Inside, he was already dead.

CHAPTER THIRTY SIX
LUSCIA

A hasty knock heralded from the base of the staircase to her loft. Luscia set the book of psalms aside. "What is it?" she called down while peering over the windowpane and at the moon's position in the inky sky. It was much later than she'd realized.

Arlette's plume of silver curls grew like a dust bunny as she tottered up the steps—ironic, considering that the finnicky old housekeeper had always reminded Luscia of a plump rabbit. Her father loved Arlette, for she'd tended his parents' home before theirs, and therefore did *not* love whenever Luscia and Phalen had reenacted the inexplicable hop in her ever-purposeful stride, age be damned.

"I'm to give you this," Arlette announced, pushing herself up the banister with a fold of parchment in hand. "Ock, not *you*, you mangy overgrown mutt." Offering Aksel her grumpiest harrumph, she hobbled overtop the yipping lycran where he blocked the path to Luscia's pillowed fortress.

Arlette despised Aksel. Almost as much as the dead things he so often brought home to her.

Luscia chuckled affectionately, taking the crinkled note from Arlette. Yawning, she unfolded it, turning it toward her. A stone formed in her belly. The script belonged to her aunt.

Find me forthwith.

Do not dawdle, Niece.

Propping her fists on her hips, Arlette smacked her wrinkled lips. More nanny than housekeeper, the woman had tucked Luscia in more nights than her aunt ever had. "She's in the cottage…"

"The High One save us," Luscia grumbled and tilted her empty cup toward her with a sizable pout. It'd been a perfectly pleasant night.

She was going to need more tea.

Pots were piled everywhere across the narrow, circinate veranda. Careful not to disturb the glowing heads of wintry cabbage or snag her dressing gown on a thorny nixberry shrub, Luscia scraped a fall of frosted ivy aside and clicked the handle inward.

Alora's cottage was a portal into an elder world, tended by gardeners and gatherers. Stalks laden in seed pods hung from the rafters, casting an ominous, spindly shadow across the overlapping rugs. Dried eüpharsis. The scent did little to calm Luscia as she crossed behind her aunt.

"Sit down."

The order was blunt. Alora's tone carried no invitation.

Luscia's hackles seditiously rose even as she migrated toward the sheepskin armchairs before the quaint, glimmering hearth. Reluctantly, she sat upon the cushion's edge.

Alora was unturned from her workbench and the series of herb-filled mortars she was rigorously grinding. She paused after a few tense minutes, not to greet her niece—her haidren, rather—but to offer Amaranth a nibble off the end of her forefinger. Hopping from its luxiron perch onto the counter, the lilac-feathered hawk snatched it with a beak designed to shred her mistress's flesh in place of her leafy offering. Amaranth raised her wings and rubbed against Alora's caress.

"Yeh'maelim, dearest," her aunt said quietly—and with more tenderness than she'd ever shown another living soul.

Luscia scrubbed her hands together before stuffing them between her knees. She despised that spoiled bird nearly as much as Arlette despised Aksel.

The fire's crackle was stale. Uneased, she cleared her throat when Alora roughly capped a vial and clomped shut the pages of her thick, legendary tome. Not all of the inscribed remedies were her own. Rather, they belonged to those entrusted to guard them since being originally penned there by the father of the apothic arts—Tiergan's son, his bright and morning star.

And like some bright things, not all remedies intended to heal.

Luscia eyed the vial of purplish liquid trapped in her aunt's grasp when Alora turned and sputtered, "You're in your nightgown."

"Well, I *was* planning to sleep."

"We host the king of Orynthia, Luscia," chastised Alora. "A reputation requires vigilance if it is to remain intact. Yet another lesson you have refused to learn from me."

Crossing her ankles, Luscia stifled her irritation. "I'm confident the king could stand the sight, were we to cross paths." *It's nothing he hasn't seen before*, she inaudibly added.

"Confident," her aunt said derisively as she stopped short of the modest tea table, becoming a tower of gray and indigo linsilk that loomed overtop it. "I am less concerned with your self-esteem than I am your self-control."

She laughed; the sound was curt. "What more could you possibly ask me to control? My whole life, I have observed your every decree."

"Wem?" Alora asked, issuing a sinking feeling from Luscia's gut when she pivoted toward the mantle. Retrieving the miniature Prajja'Veriidim, her aunt planted it on the tabletop and spun it before Luscia as if it were a cordial tea set. Alora bent her willowy form. Deliberately, she set the fresh vial directly beside the small altar. "Then drink it."

The small room shrank, trivializing every happy memory it'd held.

She knows.

Luscia's inhalations came quickly as she stared at the tonic, just as she'd done at the onset of puberty. She'd thought it her deliverance then. Now it drowned her in the truth. Her debilitating headaches had washed away with every vial she'd poured out her window. There had been no episodes, no bouts of pain, and no fear of the Sight and the strengthening Light therein. Luscia was no longer crippled by her girlhood affliction, an affliction her aunt was determined to prolong.

Sweat threatened her neck. She carefully considered her aunt's miniature altar resting behind the bitter fluid. The three tiny bowls symbolized the preservation of the utmost and the unerring. What happened when the keepers of truth kept lies alongside it? Truth could always be trusted.

Its keepers could not.

And neither could Alora.

Luscia could placate her—could keep up the ruse and drink this fleeting swallow of poison. Debating within herself, her lumin-rich bones screamed through her skin in dissent.

"Drink the tonic, Luscia."

Uncertainly, she reached toward the vial, and her vision began to fracture. Threads of lumin flashed around as her Sight phased in and out. Luscia's finger wavered. Hovering it above the stopper, whispers, indiscernible yet known, blew in currents over her ears.

From the *Other*, the voices loudened, raging and roiling, the longer she stalled. Steadily, Luscia withdrew her finger.

With a *pop*, the storm swiftly dissipated.

Fueled by a newfound fire, Luscia disobediently twisted her face up toward her aunt and, with all the courage she could muster, said, "Niit."

A spasm fled through Alora's pursed lips. Yet whatever had cracked her detached veneer, it clearly wasn't shock as she elegantly circled behind the woolly seat. She measuredly spread her palms over the chairback. Still-healing scabs decorated her cuticles in gruesome crescent moons, a rare sign of disrepair in her carefully cultivated midst. Alora's Tiergan eye flashed, and through the *Other*, she let her suspicion scour the air about her niece.

"You've been keeping secrets from me, lu'Lycran."

Brow arching, Luscia tipped her chin and countered, "As have you, Ana'Mere."

Alora's head half turned as if she'd misheard her successor.

"Having me followed through Darakai all the way to Port Khmer. Transmitting with your agents about the king's maneuverings and scheming ahead of us as if we are your pawns," Luscia said and bent to explicitly slide the vial across the table toward its maker, "to name a few."

Her aunt's mouth parted, and she snaked a glimpse over her shoulder toward Amaranth's preening. Lumin crackled in tight, coiled tendrils between her and the hawk. Alora's scowl snapped forth. "My networks don't retire when I do. They exist for Boreal's benefit. I'm neither inclined to explain such things nor am I obligated to, niece."

"That is where we fundamentally disagree… aunt." Luscia tapped her pinky finger on the cushion. Squeezing the material, she winked out of her Sight, opting to stay on the natural side of the veil and in the room of rustic color.

A statue, except for her hands, Alora stiffly drummed her scabbed fingers along the chairback.

Luscia repressed a shiver. Though unseen, she could feel pinpricks plucking the draft as the threads responded to Tiergan's heir within the *Other*.

"You gave quite the demonstration today."

Said as an indictment, it posed no inquiry.

There was no use in lying; the threads would betray her if she did. Luscia straightened her spine. She'd only relented to the powers at play as the lumin had ordained. "I gave the king what he needed."

"Oh, you gave away far more than that."

"By whose account?"

"One most loyal to the seat of his haidren," snipped Alora.

Marek. Luscia seethed. It'd only been her guard that morning, and no Darakaian would approach the woman many deemed a "white demon." Her jaw clenched, wanting to rip the beaded cuff from her wrist with her teeth. The knowing glow in Alora's scrutiny made Luscia want to shrink.

Resolutely, she stood.

"Was it not charged to us by Tiergan himself to speak for those whose tongues have been cut by the evils of the world," Luscia replied, gesturing northward toward the men and women who'd been on that moor, "and to fight for those whose limbs have failed them in the process? It is I who am haidren to Boreal, not you. And it is I who have the right to demonstrate whatever I see fit!" Her Sight splintered into the *Other* once more, illuminating the round room with her aunt's widening eyes.

Like beating wings, the lumin fluttered back from Alora as she stomped in front of the chair. "You can't talk about your rights without accepting your responsibilities!" Her tone reached a new height as she pointed at the undrunk tonic. "Sick and ungrateful is what you are! What right did you have to abandon your treatments? To betray your House's mysteries, hm? To nurture errant, *unstable* manifestations that ought not be in your custody and to then parade them before a panel of impious outsiders. Do you recognize the gravity of what you've disclosed to those warriors? Many of whom still harbor ties to our enemies. Or to the Quadren, political leaders who do not share our fidelity to that which is higher? Did it ever occur to you what they could do with that information? Why they might play our king—might pretend to aid him, just to sacrifice his throne in a two-faced attempt to take our lands, and our keep, for an unpredictable power you made them think one human can hold?"

Luscia's fists unclenched at her sides, marginally, as she searched the aged rings of the wood underfoot. She knew she'd broken Boreali law. But she'd never considered someone else might go against Dmitri, and consequently Orynthia, because of it.

Had she just given the prydes—the other haidrens—reason to betray their king?

Who would want a throne when they could have the Dönumn?

"Niit, of course you didn't think. By the Watchman, you never do!" Alora slapped her hips, insulting Luscia's slackening expression. In twinkling tendrils, the light energy snapped irritably about her animated hands. "Because of your capriciousness, you thought of yourself, Luscia—and of your hazardous, all-encompassing, futile infatuation with Cyra's son."

Steel brandished Luscia's knuckles, turning her skin white hot under Marek's kurtfierï. The room darkened in contrast to the brightening threads that were looping around them at mounting speed. Her fingernails dug against her palms. The whispers returned, lapping her ears, and whipped up the flames like a hissing firestorm.

Hotly, she stated through gritted teeth, "I have done nothing wrong."

The lumin skipped with a glittering jolt when Alora made a choking noise. "Chemistry without character is just spun sugar. It melts at the first sign of hardship," she stated, "right along with your virtue."

"Only a woman *so* noble as you could make the claim," Luscia spat, tasting the biting aftertaste on her tongue though, feet away, the deceptive tonic sat uncorked. "Because you've never lied to our people, have you? Never misled anyone you love? Never put your aims, your desires, above theirs?"

Alora was slow to answer. "I have not."

A thick, brilliant strand slithered up behind her aunt's back, although she did not seem to detect it. The harbinger thread hooked high above her face in an eerie interrogation. Struck by the lumin's reflection, the fissures in Alora's stonewalled features sharpened to shadowy canyons.

"*Lies.*"

Luscia liberated a shrill laugh in disbelief. Sheer vindication overtook her as she shoved her finger at the other woman and boldly proclaimed, "It calls you a liar!"

A deep blush painted her aunt's cheeks like a cheap night-caller. She stumbled backward. The harbinger thread unwound to the side as Alora's eyes darted toward the lumin spiraling around them in the *Other.*

Heat seared Luscia's limbs, coursing through them with righteous anger.

Slowly, Alora hunched beneath the roiling threads. Her chin quivered. "I'd asked if you heard voices…"

"I hear His light, and it says you've been deceiving me for a very long time, aunt."

"Only Tiergan communed with the Logoth—the voice. The Brightling danced with its lumin—that which is redeeming, that which is *seen*. As their heirs, we are to merely witness the presence throughout the *Other*… to testify to our people that the spirit of Aniell moves among us still," she whispered as the dried stalks overhead lashed back and forth against the rafters in an unnatural wind. Alora gaped at Luscia, clutching the chairback in one hand and reaching out guardedly with the other. "But you are neither Tiergan nor his Brightling, Luscia. We don't hear. We don't dance. We *see*. It is not for us to bear those Gifts…"

"The Logoth?" Luscia shouted the ancient term, having never heard it before, her arms rattling at her sides. Her hair battered her eyes in the static gusts. "You hide everything from me as if I can't handle the truth! Yet here I am controlling it!"

Alora's gaze fearfully shot to either side and locked onto Luscia. "Are you?"

Luscia looked down. Lumin unfurled from her body in dazzling webs toward the walls. Pots and planters and books and tools were all coiled by the light energy, suspended high off the ground. In alarm, Luscia enclosed her arms about herself.

The lumin retracted with her, and in pieces, everything crashed to the floor.

Parchment scraps, clumps of soil, and terracotta chips flew across the rug, seating her toes in a garden of her own folly. Desperate to escape the Sight, Luscia blinked angrily as tears rushed in. Debris clung to her wet cheeks.

Before her predecessor, she stood mute for what felt like a century.

"You poisoned me," Luscia said on an exhale.

Alora shakily rose from behind the chair. "I rescued you," she stated. "That power neither belongs to you nor is yours to command." Her aunt picked up a busted pot and sourly set what was left of it on her workbench. "You don't know what I've given up all these years. How hard I'd strived just to see you to your Ascension."

"See my Ascension?"

"Wem!" Her aunt wiped specks of dirt from her forehead and flicked them into the rubble. "I made you, Luscia. With those tonics. For Eoine, for Boreal—I made you into a vessel that could endure your nature so you wouldn't be destroyed by it."

"I don't understand…"

With a weighted sigh, Alora curtly gestured toward the sheepskin chairs, covered in debris.

Following her movements, Luscia numbly swept it clean and retook her seat as a broken and bruised girl once more.

"There is a ledger hidden in that bookcase," her aunt said over steepled fingers. "Nearly two hundred years ago, the haidren to Boreal recorded an encounter he had with an orphaned child during the Mworran Wars.

"'Eye of blue, eye of bright,' he'd written. The child was very young, undocumented with a parentage unknown and unclaimed. It heard things too, presumably the Logoth, and exhibited an effortless ability to *play* with the lumin. To even draw forth pictures with it. Miraculously, as the lumin was too potent in the blood, its gifts surpassed the Higher Gifts. They were so unpredictable and intense that our brödre haidren referred to this child as a 'beacon.'"

At the pinched folds cradling Alora's cold eyes, an eerie sensation skittered down Luscia's spine. "I don't follow."

Her aunt forcibly swallowed. "Luscia, you exhibited much the same. Not at first, not so young. But when you did, the lumin used to awaken you in the middle of the night, and we'd find you playing with it in the wildwood. It was…" She paused to shake her head. "It was extraordinary."

"Then why would you stopper it?" Luscia asked with more resentment than surprise. Tiergan's heirs could only initiate their Sight *after* their Ascension. Yet she couldn't remember anything except the enchanted fables her mother would spin once she'd been carried back home.

Luscia rocked in the chair. Perhaps wanton headaches had not been the only side effect of Alora's tonics.

"Because the extraordinary threw you into vicious fits. Unascended and unable to heal fast enough, we knew something was hazardously wrong. So, your mamu and I poured over the haidren's writings, scouring them for answers. And then we found that single entry from two centuries ago. Eoine… She refused the idea of an apothic therapy. She started to prophesy—fervently—that you'd outgrow it, and later, it'd grow *into* you. But when she…"

Luscia's heart ached when Alora's pained expression dipped toward her lap.

"Well, afterward I decided if you were truly a beacon, Boreal just couldn't risk it."

Scoffing toward the ceiling, Luscia tartly replied, "Right, wem. Far too dangerous to let me someday do something you cannot."

"Luscia," said Alora tiredly. Her lids closed over her pregnant stare, and she reopened them with renewed focus. "The child didn't survive. There exists no record of it ever reaching adulthood."

Her lips parted, inhaling a harsh taste of mortality and spilt earth.

"Everything I did was to keep you alive. In due course, I theorized the High One allowed this so you could eventually save Orynthia's ailing king," Alora said as one by one, the strongholds in Luscia's mind collapsed. "*Save the king who rejects his crown.* It's all your fapapï says anymore… But still Dmitri deteriorates before us. Thus, in that, I too was wrong."

Running her palms atop her thighs, Luscia quietly said, "Maybe to fight this evil, Aniell wanted me to use it to win the Quadren to our side."

"It is man's greatest malpractice to suppose the thoughts of Aniell."

"But after hearing the Logoth… In my heart, I know this must have been given to me for a greater good."

Luscia jumped when Amaranth lurched from her perch and flapped to Alora's chair, then hooked her talons into the snowy pelt. Her aunt curved toward the hawk. "The heart commits as many charities as it can atrocities. It cannot be trusted. Believe me in this," she murmured. Mist welled along Alora's bottom lashes, though unexplainably in her gut, Luscia detected those rare tears were neither for her nor her mother, Eoine. "We are born of flesh, Luscia. And it is by our flesh we always fail."

Skulking amid the bark of the holdreheiim's contorted roots, Luscia sheepishly padded into the abandoned luxsmith district of the tasseled agora. It was odd to see it in the quiet hours while its masters were still sleeping. There rang no hammers within the spacious smithies. No sturdy songs. No roaring forges illuminated the underside of the ancient, excavated trunk, except the embers of a lone workspace near the back.

Luscia noiselessly carved her way toward her distracted brother. Above, garlanded by barren vines, faded traces of lumin dotted the living wood like the stars still clinging to the skies.

Perhaps he'd been unable to sleep too.

Phalen tinkered with a project. Pitching it aside, he went back to trolling through a rucksack strewn across the adjacent bench.

Behind his back, she boosted herself onto his anvil and sank onto it like a feather. "Rüsha'silaem," she said morosely, wishing him ears of grace before anyone else could, as he was set to leave for his söhlo that morning. "Happy Hearing Day."

"Ock!" Her brother bumped his skull on a tool hanging from the rack above and swung round. "How you've always been able to sneak up on me, I'll never know. Woah—you look like you lost all your acorns in a race with a scürie."

She shrugged under his gaze as it scanned her mess of hair and bloodshot eyes, then landed on her mismatched fur-trimmed boots. Phalen's eyebrow curved at the apple she was rolling between her palms.

"Is that my birthday present?"

Her motions stalled. "I'd forgotten I was holding it."

Phalen sighed through his nose and set down his bag. He pinched a stool from the neighboring forge, dragged it beside the anvil, and plunked down. Though seated a foot lower, they were nearly the same height.

"Go on," said Phalen.

"Don't you have somewhere to be?"

"Sixteen can wait."

Luscia slanted her grimace at him. There were so few traces of boyhood left in his physique. Although, he'd always been better at sharing his toys. Selflessness loosened his new muscle as her brother knit his hands behind his head and inclined for her to continue.

She hardly knew where to begin.

Or if she even should.

In her lap, the fruit shined under the wood's twinkle, and crossing her ankles, Luscia idly handed it over to him. "Do you recall the parable of the golden apple? Of the farmer who climbed the tallest tree for it only to let everyone else starve?"

The face he made buckled his button nose. "Shores of Aurynth, I hate that dumb folk story."

Luscia swung her interlaced feet and replied with a yawn, "It's a favorite of our aunt's."

"Wem, well, it doesn't tell the whole truth."

Her feet stopped midswing. "How do you mean?"

"The farmer was the only person in the village brave enough to try," said Phalen, tossing his soot-stained hands at the obvious. "They were starving. Anyone could have climbed for it. No one talks about *that* part. Everyone focuses on how he chose the fruit and not the grain. Never that he was the single person who underwent the struggle to reach better food."

Perplexed, she wadded her fingers inside her belled sleeves and shoved them into the warmth of her underarms. Having whirred all night long, her mind ached from its conflicted ruminations. Luscia had desires, and she'd suffocated them for the superior good. She had duties, which she'd fervidly fulfilled. She had a king who desperately needed her help, and the light within had sprung forth to the occasion.

She wanted so many things and pushed them aside. Therefore, this singular wish—to truly know herself and the voice that had designed her that way—shouldn't be too much.

Nevertheless… if Luscia was really a beacon… then not a soul knew her limits. She was playing with fires from another realm, not of flesh but of spirit and shadow.

Alora had betrayed the family, likely the entire House, by her repeated deceptions. But in the way that counted, she had not lied. Luscia had *never* been in control. It'd been arrogant, foolhardy, and dangerous to think she ever could be. She was a faulty conduit; the power wasn't hers to begin with.

And soon, someone, if not herself, was going to get her because of it.

Her legs resumed their rocking. "Were the farmer's wishes worth his family's life? Is that your answer then?"

"Niit, I don't know what the answer is. Just that we aren't asking the whole question." After a handful of minutes, Phalen got up. He withdrew something from a case beside his furnace. Bringing it to Luscia with a gangly slouch, he presented what looked like an ordinary, polished belt buckle. "It's no golden apple, but here—in case you all lose the fight for Bastiion and find yourself locked in a dungeon again."

Bemused, she flipped it around. He'd fashioned the buckle to resemble the head of a lycran, the opposite end snapping its snarling snout between a set of elongated fangs. It was beautiful, though knowing her brother, there was more to it. She stuck her fore and middle fingers through the small, decorative loops welded to the nose and lower jaw. Giving them a tug, a hidden blade slid from the mouth like a lethal inverted tongue.

Attached to the backside, a lockpick collapsed.

"Funny." Luscia could barely maintain her sneer before it cracked. Rising, she gave him a tight hug. As they parted and he reached for his rucksack, she caught his wrist awkwardly, seeing the excitement igniting his eyes as he made to embark on his much-awaited söhlo. "Not everyone hears something," she worriedly cautioned.

"You did," said Phalen, taking a big bite out of the apple. "Not that you ever told me what He said."

"It was enough."

"What was?"

"That's all I heard. *It was enough*." Luscia let go, a rough sensation on her tongue. Phalen seemed as if he wanted to push the matter but didn't. Instead, he grabbed a canteen, along with two bloated wineskins off the floor with a cheeky wink, causing Luscia to grimace at his youthful naivete. "Phalen, not everyone hears something," she said again.

He rolled his contradictory, Tiergan eyes. "Most people listen for what they want, not for what is. I'm ready, really," he assured. "Whatever it is, I know it's going be better and more profound than whatever I want it to be."

Behind his mischievous smirk, Luscia saw that he was earnest. Her stance deflated. "You should have been haidren."

"*Man's greatest malpractice is to assume to the mind of Aniell.*" Phalen's grin widened as he quoted Alora in a nasally whine. "He could have easily made me haidren, Ana'Sere," he said, suddenly serious, and deposited the apple back into her hands. "But he didn't."

Clutching it, Luscia gaped at the bitemark in the apple's red flesh. She reflexively reached up to her collar, only to remember her neck was naked and bare. Luscia's tangled waves fell away as she let her fingers thoughtfully trail the awful scar.

She'd been allowed to suffer.

She would surely suffer more to come. Yet what kind of person would willingly undertake pain for a purpose unknown?

The only person brave enough to try.

Swift, confident footfalls sifted through the straw toward the wilderness as she heard Phalen excitedly hike the rucksack higher onto his shoulder. When she looked up, her brother was already gone.

Chapter Thirty Seven

Zaethan

He'd never felt so displaced—or idiotic—sloughing through the tundra with nothing but a knife, a borrowed bow, and an overstuffed bedroll.

The cold was overwhelming. Temperatures dropped with the sun when it sank through the colossal canopy. The highland days were shortening, passing as unforgivingly as Zaethan's patience. But if a sixteen-year-old could endure it, then so could any alpha.

That was the excuse he'd given his pryde, at least, for taking a temporary leave. What he didn't mention was the need to get away from their prying eyes, all watching… waiting for him to fall apart. Taking heavy steps, Zaethan felt the Mantle of the Fallen lugging him down, as on the day the arrowhead cape had been dumped on his shoulders. He'd been told during Dmitri's coronation that all of Darakai was looking on, waiting for him to crumble beneath it. And they were, more than ever before. Though it was worse. Everyone wanted to help, except no one could. Zaethan was suffocating and desperate to breathe.

No matter how bitter the air.

He took a deep, sobering breath where no one could see. Then crisply let it out.

This was a stupid idea, Zaethan scolded himself, bundling the woolen cloak more securely around his neck. He didn't know where he was going nor how to get back. It served him right, following the advice of a sheltered, adolescent luxsmith, espousing his fanciful Boreali tales.

What had he really expected to find, coming out into the freezing wilderness on his own? As if the answers to all his problems would be hidden within the forests outside Roüwen… What did he hope for, a do-over of last year tucked in some fallen log? His kwihila sprouting between the ferns? A new family waiting up for him, as they happily shared supper in a hut?

Zaethan acknowledged that a power resided within the North. It'd gloriously manifested for Luscia on the moor. There was no unseeing the fount from where it came and why it was so heavily guarded at the keep.

That power was no myth.

The myth was that the divine who'd put it there would take any interest in *Zaethan*. Bearing neither the mark nor piety of a Boreali man, his sixteenth year was well buried in the past with the beast who'd raised him. So, trudging between the trees, Zaethan heard only the crass crunch of his own boots as the tenuous trail took him farther into a lonely, barren reception.

As consolation, there was peace in the wilds, amid his self-chastising thoughts. And no screaming cubs crawled under his legs as they had during breakfast, to Lady Athdara's devout chagrin. One would have assumed that losing Zahra as an emissary to Razôuel—and then to Yousif—would have lessened how much she loathed her Darakaian houseguests. Somehow, it'd only spurned her more.

Zaethan paused and rolled out his ankle to prompt circulation. Lady Athdara had resorted to laying out children's socks after swiping his adult pair for so-called washing. A brilliant play, to her credit, for his treading the winter without them would only lead to frostbite.

While the wind bit, it did not carry Kumo's relentless probing. That was the drawback to such an intuitive beta; he caught onto Zaethan's mood and sank his teeth in like a starved jackal, never let it go.

"*What's wrong, Ahoté?*" Zaethan mimicked aloud. "*Talk to me, Ahoté.*"

Dmitri was much the same. He'd tried to hide it, but his friend saw through the plastered smiles and forced laughs. No longer bedridden, their recovering king had spent less time consulting the elders than he had bothering Zaethan to open up. Bordering obsession, Dmitri had hitched his wellbeing to his, as if the two were entwined.

Zaethan loved his friend… maybe more than himself, or what he'd diminished into being. Yet there was nothing to say that hadn't already passed between them. The consequence of which just gnawed the soul of one man more than the other.

As did the hollow grumble of Zaethan's stomach.

He hadn't fully thought his walkabout through.

Near the base of a trunk grew a thicket of shrubs. Zaethan popped a couple berries off the stems and angled his fist over his open mouth. The image of Luscia smacking them out of his hand materialized with vengeance. He instantly dropped the edibles.

He could no longer discern safety without her.

An ache more akin to the ripping of sinew tore through his torso as the vision left him. Knocking his head back, he placed his mitten over his heart, imagining they were still standing together on the veranda. Luscia had made him a promise that night to convince Kai to stay in Boreal. But she hadn't just changed the tide. She'd shattered the seawall.

His lashes twitched, catching the flurries. There was no language to describe all that Luscia Tiergan was, and all she was becoming. Thwarting every attack, her counters were whirlwinds of power, beating an unparalleled thrill all the way to his core.

He'd seen her wholly then, unabashed and unashamed—her flaws on equal display as her strength. She was light incarnate, blistered by shadow. And there she *really* had been, reciting their repeated refrain.

Zaethan yearned to hear her repeat those words once more in kind. Yet how could she? How could anyone see him when amid the smears of heartache and betrayal, Zaethan scarcely saw himself?

Frost was settling on his Southern skin, accosting him to rejoin the nothing. Owàa had dipped behind the closest mountain, dragging hope with his enchained legs deeper into the moonless Depths.

It was too late to turn back. Resolving to hike into the village fortress at first light, Zaethan scoured the darkening gloom for a place to camp against the gusts rolling down the range. Like the wings of a raven, an ominous evening fast enveloped him, the emptiness made blacker as the glorious glow known only to Boral overtook nature. Squinting, his options for shelter—and a meal—were bleak.

Zaethan would not find what he sought here. Only a fool would have sought it in the first place—proof that he still mattered, written somewhere in the snow.

Stoking a weak fire, he picked the succulent meat out of his teeth, savoring every bite. Zaethan reclined against his bedroll and bunched his brows at the bow staked in the ground where feathers were piled about. *Dumb bird*, he thought. The grouse had just wandered into its predator's lair.

As he tossed the bare thigh into the flames, he moved onto the main carcass. Zaethan held the sustenance in one hand, grateful he didn't have to share. He drew his attention to the endless folds in the ghostly wood. The animals were mute. Even the leaves had abated their rustling. There seemed no life for miles. It struck Zaethan then, that at no point during the last decade had he ever been so solitary. He'd been alone of course, constantly in contact with a member of the court, his House, or his prydes, but never in total isolation.

Had he any hackles, they would have risen to the silence. Its vacancy was severe.

He didn't favor it.

The irony was cruel and pierced him like ice. Zaethan had spent most of his youth desperate to get away, to gain real independence, and now that he finally had it, there was only one person he had left.

Himself.

What a kakka-shtàka deal *that* was. Zaethan couldn't restore anything—political or personal—let alone save himself from his own misery. Dmitri's gifted leather-bound journal poking out from Zaethan's bedroll stared at him blankly as if waiting for the supposed jwona rapiki to finally crack it open.

He'd been stupid to bring that too.

Crossly, Zaethan chucked the grouse bones at the fire, scattering the embers so much that only a measly flicker remained. He'd have to rekindle it all over again or he'd be ice within the hour. "I give up." He moaned and hung his head, crushing his temples between knees.

Branches snapped to his left.

Zaethan tensed, alert and ready, and reached for the bow as stealthily as he could. Alarm flooded his ears, pulsing loud. He'd been sure he was alone… but he'd not accounted for any zealots who might have followed him into the wilds, hungry for Southern sport. Feigning ignorance, he kept his face low, twisting it slowly in that direction while his fingertips eased the weapon out of the earth. Long range was not his forte, but even the worst Darakaian archer was better than most.

His breath came in steamy puffs. Through it, two trees away, was a massive dusky bear. Its size was frightening, with paws the width of wagon wheels. And its eyes, unblinking and aglow, were watching Zaethan intently.

It didn't move when with his other arm, he inched forward for his quiver and scooted it gradually onto his back. Heart racing, Zaethan reached behind himself to pull forth an arrow. He nocked it and, with strained slowness, rotated his upper body toward the animal.

Zaethan drew the string back, and at his exhalation, the bear turned and ambled away. Puzzled, he lowered his weapon. Not five paces and the bear halted, slinging its colossal skull backward.

It stared on fixedly.

Resting the bow atop his lap, Zaethan stared back. The animal started to budge again. And after another five steps, it stopped and did the same.

Does it want me to follow?

Zaethan scoffed at the absurdity. "There was something funky in that grouse."

At that, the bear grunted, curling its black nose with exposed jaws.

Heeding the warning, Zaethan scrambled to his feet. He clutched the knife on his belt, ensuring it was there as he warily stepped toward the waiting beast. At his trepid advance, the bear resumed its late-night stroll, weaving among the holdreheiim.

Over the hour that he stalked it, glimmering striations radiated more and more intensely through the neighboring tree bark. Farther into the thickets, the vegetation grew obtrusive. He climbed over slick logs and through webs of frosted ivy to keep up, slicing himself on the thorns.

The cuts stung. "Shtàka!" he swore, bringing his bloody palm to his lips.

Zaethan glanced up and spun in a semicircle, unable to find the bear. He took a shallow, measured inhale. Listening, he heard only the wind. Letting out the breath, Zaethan pivoted toward camp and yelped.

A ferocious snarl met him, black lips rippled back to reveal his certain death. The bear's head was so huge, it blotted out the trees. Zaethan stumbled back in retreat.

Teeth tore after him.

His heel caught on the rootage, and stumbling, he dropped his knife among the artic brush. The beast swiped its forepaw. Claws resembling lethal hooks nearly tore open Zaethan's throat as he dived to the ground, trundling. He fumbled to find the knife. His mittened fingers nudged the hilt, but he rolled when the bear slammed down overtop it.

Trapped between its shaggy legs, Zaethan panicked. He grabbed onto them like rods and scooted himself under its belly. He threw out his arm and cupped the largest rock he saw. With all his might, Zaethan struck the beast in the gut.

Loosing a mean growl, it thrashed back and forth. He scuttled out from underneath and onto his feet. The bear stood on its hind legs, twice his height and ready to charge, but there was nowhere for

Zaethan to run. Frantically, he bent and sifted the snow for more rocks or his blade. For Fates' sake—

Agony blasted through his ribs when he was batted like a sack of grain into a holdreheiim, slamming his skull. His vision dotted in stars. Zaethan flipped over, planting his spine against the trunk and punched the thing in the snout, all but cracking his knuckles on its iron-hard skull. Huffing, he kicked off the bark and drilled his shoulders into the fur of the animal's abdomen—each step against its poundage draining his vigor.

The bear snorted, as if at his futile efforts, and slugged him across the side. Bone cracked like thunder. Zaethan's hip exploded in pain. He could barely move his leg. Thumping over into the snow, he watched in terror as with snarling jowls, the bear descended. His eyes enlarged frightfully at the threads of ethereal light that writhed through its irises.

This is the end, he cried inside. Zaethan smashed his eyes shut, awaiting his suffering.

Yet none rained upon him. He lay there, his heart ravaging his chest. Zaethan tempted a glance, rocking his gaze side to side.

The bear had vanished.

He stayed there gasping, the base of his head buried in the snow, and gaped up at the heavens that keenly watched him through the netting of evergreen leaves. With retribution, the quietness returned. Though it was not empty-handed. It came with a whisper of trickling water.

Along the branches throughout the canopy, the shimmering foliage began to swirl like pinwheels in the opposite direction. And a chill from the belly of the earth cradled him still.

"Arise, Zaethan."

His loins shrank at the sound of his name, spoken in a voice unlike any man's. Its command reverberated from every direction. Its tone was a deep, disturbing harmony of power and knowing and otherness.

Zaethan knew not what to do, except obey.

Pitching onto an elbow, he groaned and, with shaking biceps, raised himself up, coming face-to-face with a shallow pool set in the recess of an outcropping. Luminous, variegated stone rose high around the collected waters. The rocks were robed in rich, unseasonable moss. At the center, water fell in a thin glittering cascade from the heights. Straining his neck, Zaethan could not see from where it came.

With a rough swallow, he struggled to stand, collapsing onto his knee.

The strong, soft voice persisted. *"Zaethan, rise and remove your shoes."*

He nodded bewilderedly, pushing himself through the pain, and kicked off the upturned boots. Ice scalded his soles.

"Reach past the water's edge."

With a cry, Zaethan dragged his injured body toward the pool. Thinking himself crazy, he splashed his naked feet into the few inches of water. At his immersion, the sleeping algae that coated the surface sprang to life. The bioluminescence lapped his toes, coming in ripples from the descending stream. Zaethan sucked in a breath. Warmness chased the agony upward and out his limbs.

"Who are you?" he asked in fear.

At his question, the trickling water discharged more light, refracting in glorious prisms across its unhewn, stone hedge. The beams swelled as if embodying the brightness of the sun, causing him to squint until it hurt. *"I am the one who poured your foundation and wrought you for my purpose,"* the voice declared. *"It was I who was there before the beginning and will be after its end."*

Zaethan's legs tried to buckle under the resonance, even while something else was supporting him upright. The light shifted, subduing itself so he could bear it. The algae took on an opalescent cast, identical to that which Luscia had shown them behind the fortified walls of the keep. That which plated their luxiron. The element Zaethan now bore through his brow. The same brilliance that flashed behind her eyes each and every time she'd proven there was more to this desolate life.

This was the High One.

This was Aniell.

"My son… My son…" The power repeated the phrase with authority and unrelenting claim. Zaethan released a wounded noise, unable to prevent his eyes from finally shedding their hard-held tears. In a rush, his weakness, his exhaustion, and his sorrow flowed down his cheeks. *"Lay down your kwihila,"* the voice whispered, *"and see what I do not return void. Yours is a name written long ago, but mine endures forever. My son, for which will you live?"*

Zaethan shuddered. As if outside himself, he felt his head nodding in timorous understanding. His victory—his boasted kwihila—had failed him, and even if it hadn't, it would only turn to ash upon his finishing pyre.

In eternity's eyes, his name was rubble.

There stood no contest. Yet he was free to choose one all the same.

Trembling, Zaethan uttered, "I choose yours."

In a seismic wave, light blasted from the falling stream. The forest whimpered and moaned. Rocking him on his heels, it blew through his battered body like a refining hailstorm. And after a matter of suspended, ferocious moments, it dispersed in a *whoosh*, and the trickling was no more.

Zaethan rocked there, his hands clumsily held in the air. The stone hedge returned to an ordinary outcropping. Instantly, he peered down at his cold toes, where ice was already creeping along the water's surface in fervent spindles. Shuddering, he fled from the bank and shirked into the discarded boots.

A pang shot through his hip. Zaethan prodded the injury with a wince, staggered at the bone's assessment.

Bruised but no longer broken.

He turned and paused. A fresh sheet of snow had blanketed his tussle with the bear, along with his surviving tracks to the pool, as if the man who'd walked there had never been. Taking one step and then another, Zaethan curiously angled his chin over his shoulder, looking back. The only evidence there was that of the new man walking away. He took a cleansing breath. Facing forward, Zaethan thumbed the warming luxiron posts staked through his brow—fashioned just for him.

The living metal had awoken too.

Zaethan rubbed his arms against the cold and, favoring his hip, aimed toward his excuse for a bed. Moonlight sparkled across the forest floor, illuminated as though it were a looking glass. And where it was frigid and bleak and dark, it was the brightest night he'd ever known.

⁂

The next day, he reentered Roüwen shaking icicles out of his locs. With his quiver strapped over his chest and the filthy bedroll unfurling off his shoulder, he aimed for the lively alehouse with a hankering for a hot drink.

Traipsing past the fountain, Zaethan felt a strange kindship with the ever-burning, pastel flames in the elevated basin. His muscles throbbed. His step faltered, yet he walked an inch taller. Zaethan held no knowledge of how the unearthly fire was made, only that it'd burned up something within him.

There was only one person he wanted to tell.

Amid the flurries, the square was teeming with newfound business. Merchants had step-up stalls outside the agora with excess goods. A meat trader rolled his rickety trolly to make room for the swaths of iron-winged warriors pooling in from the winding side streets—najjani reinforcements, just arrived from Viridis, no doubt. The Order must have come inland to restock itself, he presumed. Zaethan civilly moved himself out of their way, biting back any response to the dirty looks he received. The shadowmen were an imposing force, one that'd come to Dmitri's aid against some of their own leaders' wishes.

Not surprisingly, many of the men were funneling into the alehouse. Zaethan scowled as the passersby cleared. Outside the excavated holdre-heiim, he saw Captaen Bailefore leaning against one of the gigantic, gnarled roots. His penannular brooch, bearing its specialized antler, gleamed off his pinned cloak. Growler in hand and one leg hitched behind him, Bailefore bowed his head in deference as the Northern warriors filtered by, exchanging words with a handful of his fair-haired kinsmen. Each were high ranking, as demonstrated by their brooches of two and three branches, stopping to show their respect in turn.

Zaethan gingerly rubbed his hip, then hardening his grip on the bow, started that way.

Celebratory luting and rhythmic bells were played over the jovial laughter that flowed from the crowded interior. Though Zaethan sensed the captaen's vigilant watch, the shadowman did not inter-rupt his conversation to extend a greeting when Zaethan neared the natural archway.

"Bailefore," Zaethan yelled over, earning a guarded reaction from his brothers-in-arms. The subtle twitch of the captaen's ear was the only sign he'd heard him while he casually took another drink of ale. "Your haidren, is she inside?"

A tendon leaped through Bailefore's set jaw. "What are her whereabouts to you?"

"It's a matter of…" Zaethan drawled, playing along, "divine importance."

He enjoyed how quickly the lips of the other shadowmen shuffled, even though he couldn't distinguish their riled comments in witchtongue.

With a few fingers, Bailefore calmly gestured for the warriors to move aside. His cerulean eyes were sharper than the luxiron crisscrossing his back. "Our blessed haidren takes no interest in the divinations of a pagan lowlander."

Amusement broadened Zaethan's features, and he clicked his tongue. "Eh, is it her husband or her warden you're so desperate to become? Meme ano'qondai," he said, scratching his temple with the tip of the bow. "I can never tell."

Ire flashed across the captaen's sculpted face. He lifted his agile frame off the bark.

With a satisfied nod, Zaethan hobbled onward.

"Bastard."

Zaethan swung round. It wasn't spoken in witchtongue. Bailefore had wanted him to hear it.

Murmurs of his being cross-caste—or an *unwanted mutt*—promptly echoed among those in vicinity to the alehouse. Animosity fueled Zaethan's sore legs. Inelegantly, he marched up to the captaen and seized him by a handful of his linsilk jacket, butting him against the enormous tree.

Zaethan's shabby title was the only thing keeping the observing najjan from joining in on the fun.

The tension between their jutting chins was raw and material.

Bailefore's free hand snapped around Zaethan's wrist and contracted with shocking force as he flicked his eyes downward.

"You have a limp, Lord Haidren," he sneered, satisfied by the observation.

Zaethan twisted the fabric and smirked. "Wrestle the divine, walk away with a limp."

Bailefore searched him, his glare landing on the Boreali posts pierced through Zaethan's lowland skin. The captaen's scarcely freckled nose rumpled when he boasted in a low baritone, "She's made her decision."

"There's only been one on the table."

Bailefore's steely confidence fractured in microtremors. Zaethan made to say something else, but he winced when there came a tender pang through his bruised hip. Irritated, he squinted up toward the clear, cloudless heavens, taking it as a reproach. Aggressively, he let go of the captaen and shoved off into the alehouse.

He pressed between the shadowmen, edging along the long, clustered tables. Scanning the rowdy cheers, he spotted Declan and the kinder twin. Across from their benches was their haidren, sitting up on the bar above the meadow of gilded heads. Like a bard, Luscia threw up her growler, leading the warriors and their supporters in song. Devotion captured many, some planting a hand over their heart as a masculine accord joined her melodic tune.

That was most frightening aspect of a woman's power—her ability to make a man feel as if he were invincible.

Especially when the evidence was to the contrary.

Zaethan dropped his bedroll onto the wood chips and plunked onto the bench beside Declan without taking his eyes off her.

In his periphery, the shadowman wiped his braided beard and drew his tunic over his nose. "Ock, you're ripe as a turd."

He sucked in through his teeth. "That kurtfierï custom," Zaethan said. "Tell me what to do."

Chapter Thirty Eight

Rain spat upon the slums that choked the outer bank of the Drifting Bazaar. The inky waters sloshed the crumbling seawall, swallowing the runoff of disease and human waste—a visceral taxation, ferried out into the Vasil where the poor might finally be overlooked.

Closed were the colorful, floating stalls of which Bastiion was proud, not that their merchants often steered such beauty or provision that far down into the hopeful view of the lower class. The dispiriting aroma matched those upon whom it festered.

Neither were good for business.

Buildings were rotting, and so was the food—could one afford it. This was not a place for courtiers to spend their frivolous coin. It belonged to the impoverished, vagrant, and lame.

Aside from any financier adept at exploiting them.

The figure catapulted his gaunt form under the cover of a dilapidated roof, keeping close watch of one such man. Below, Tetsu's robes were a stark-white seal against the stained floor of the abandoned depot. With his arms tucked patiently within his belled sleeves, he stood awaiting an unarrived party.

That he was unaccompanied only put the figure more on edge. Patience was Tetsu's most hazardous virtue.

From a higher landing, the boathouse was in shambles, the assortment of broken ships looking more like a boneyard than a former station of commerce. The stench was revolting, brined by blood and dead fish. It overpowered his heightened senses, turning over the figure's husk of a stomach. His leather gloves creaked as he stiffened them around the railing of the damaged landing.

Tetsu's neck twisted at the subtle sound.

The figure slunk deeper out of the moonlight, careful to avoid the notice of both the chancellor and his Pilarese hawk circling overhead. He'd already sent word to Alora in Boreal and couldn't rely on Amaranth to thwart the other bird. Like her savage sister, she too had been trained to alert her master.

Anxious, the figure reminded his barren lungs he need not use them, that air gave nothing but the empty promise of calm. Pressing against the splintering slats, he stealthily drew his hood to conceal his sores from the night, welcoming the chafe against his ever-gaping wounds. The trappings of his humanity were vengefully creeping back in, the more he walked these disturbing intersections of past and present. He could not pretend to be a man, not for a second. He was the firstborn of the unborn. The eldest of the unmade.

Only a monster of that magnitude could face the blight he'd helped to create and crush the cult that was spreading it further. Because she shouldn't have to. Alora had bathed in his sins long enough, so long she called them her own. The figure cricked his head at an unnatural angle as he glared down at the chancellor who'd robbed him from the grave.

His itchy eyes dilated with predatory ire when Tetsu's short, pointed beard suddenly snapped toward the opposite direction.

The figure's ears heard it after his had.

Clacking against the soiled flooring, a sapphire walking stick protruded out from between the skeletons of two dismembered ships. A ringed hand encased the jeweled handle. A matching cobalt satin coat sleeve emerged next, and an overly dressed yancy stepped out. He strutted toward Tetsu and where he loomed under a spill of silver moonlight.

The figure could scent the costly oil that slicked the noble's receding, dark, gray-streaked hair against his scalp. He hissed through his decaying teeth when the man tilted his ugly, notoriously hooked nose up at the chancellor with a snobbish grin.

Yannis, the slaver.

Animalistically, the figure sank lower and pinned his attention on the wealthy noble's gold tooth. He should have killed him that night in Bastiion. Tonight would be different; Amaranth was not there to stop him from making the same mistake twice.

"A delivery involves a package, Yannis," said Tetsu. Feigned tolerance slickened his voice into that of a practiced politician.

The slaver set his wide face askew, showing off a set of poorly healed scratches in his reddened flesh, marking him ear to mouth. "Package didn't come easily," Yannis said, bloating the vowels of his otherwise-Hildurean lilt in a fashion suggesting he'd wasted more of his life conversing with miscreants than the aristocracy. "Price has risen to thirty aurus."

"Steep, considering you're not in a position to bargain. You are unforgivably late," replied Tetsu.

"Had to hunker in Tadeas. People looking for this one."

"As they did the last," Tetsu caustically replied. "Your skill was well worth my coin back then, when you were nothing but an ambitious crook, and I your gracious benefactor, Yannis. The price has fallen to fifteen."

He'd always relished the haggle, the figure recalled, especially whenever he held twice the money. Though something didn't add up. The Orynthian skin trade had two sides to its hideous coin. On its face was indentured servitude, a lawful avenue for the poor to pay their debts in a field instead of a cell. But morally gray avenues always led to darker destinations. In its shadow had surged a black-market playground for the domesticated debauchery of dukes and lords… not a distinguished shoto prime. Were word to get out that the leader of the Collective was indulging an industry so vile, it would cause a realm-wide scandal, perhaps enough to knock him off his stolen throne.

However, this could have been precisely what'd placed him there. Tetsu Naborū had gained his fortune by playing every side. For once assimilated, he adeptly extorted each one.

Yet what pitiable person could be worth so much to him? Fifteen aurus—nevertheless twenty or thirty—was the value of a small estate. Even the most exotic cross-castes were illicitly purchased for no more than five pieces of gold.

Yannis prodded his fat tongue inside his cheek. "She still bleeds. Good hips. Lots of yancies can put her to proper use, making more. That's supply and demand, Chancellor."

The figure growled, tasting iron as his fangs throbbed in his gums.

"Is that so?" In a flicker, the chancellor ripped his hand from the cover of his sleeve and held up his contorted fingers like a claw, their tips stained black. His silver nailpiece glinted in a deadly arc. "Is she for your profit," demanded Tetsu, gradually screwing his hand as Yannis squealed in pain, "or is she for the Obscurer?"

The slaver shrieked and tore at the brocade material to reveal a brand on the underside of his wrist, which burned as if put there anew. His bronze, Unitarian skin bubbled around the white-hot lemniscate, a vertical line severing its eternal twin loops.

Looking on in horror, the figure gawked at his symbol and then the raw power Tetsu was wielding in order to control him through it. His sketch, his manifested theory, was no longer mere instruction on paper…

It was a mode for anatomical control.

"For the Obscurer!" Yannis cried out as he repeatedly snapped for someone else, hiding in the back of the depot. "Forgive me, Low Lord. Forgive me."

Low Lord? What have you become, Tetsu…

Muzzled noises foretold the sweaty miscreant who lumbered into the light, hauling with him a woman in a torn, filth-sodden dress. A hood covered her face. As if she were chattel, rope was slung from her neck and leashed to her pale, black-and-blue arms.

The man pulled at his belt and shoved her to her knees. "Get down 'ere, y'siti mongrel."

She collapsed as if she were made of twigs.

"The product is of no use to me if it is destroyed." Tetsu enunciated his words threateningly.

"She'll polish like new, won't you, lovie?" Yannis gripped his wrist as with that same hand, he ripped off her hood. A heap of knotty, platinum hair slumped forward with the slack angle of her neck. The woman was barely alive.

"Look at 'er." The miscreant splayed his hands the way he would a hog at a fair. "Bath'll make 'er nice and shiny."

Lacing his arms neatly, Tetsu tapped the nailpiece as he drifted toward the woman. His loop of slick black hair slid across his upper back when he crouched before her. Tetsu propped the iron talon under her chin and crooked her features toward a spindle of moonlight.

The figure nearly leaped from his perch. Despite the swelling and the massive bruise disfiguring her mouth, she resembled Alora so much, it hurt. Roughly the same age. Nearly the same height. Though she was identical in stature, he pinpointed the differences too. They were subtle, but they were there.

"Pry open her eyes," Tetsu commanded them.

The figure's intestines knotted. There was but one reason to examine the eyes of a Boreali.

Yannis swatted her matted hair, and cupping her head backward, he pried her lids open with his thumbs.

After a pause, Tetsu clicked his tongue and rose. "The deal is voided," he said, once more lifting his black-tipped fingers in menacing angles as he coolly strode away.

Yannis instantly dropped the woman and writhed in agony. She slumped to the mildewy floor, giving hardly a whimper. Tetsu revolved his wrist, and the miscreant flopped on his belly with a *boom*. The man's stumpy legs shuddered as if he were swimming. Over his hip, the sapphire walking stick clattered as the slaver mewled for their torture to end.

"You failed me, Yannis," said Tetsu, winning more cries. "You failed *him*. The Obscurer will give you one last chance to fulfill your oath. Return to Boreal, find her, and bring her to my doorstep. Do you understand me?"

Red-faced, Yannis trembled in acknowledgment while his partner suffocated on his own dribble.

"Good." The chancellor released them, revolving his open palms toward the shadows. Like inkblots in water, the darkness quivered and curled at the crooking of his fingertips. The figure pivoted with the changing scent, fetid air souring by wrongness and necrotic tissue. "A much larger accompaniment will assure that you succeed, Yannis. Though, it would please them more if you were to fail…"

Suddenly the shadow birthed form. Humanoid creatures on all fours clawed their way toward their master. Blackened limbs jutted out of their sockets and in unnatural shapes as they moved. Talons clicked against the rotting floor. Needlelike incisors dripped. Crimson shone from their eyes, no longer burdened by their whites. From their decaying muscle, the relics of civilization hung in tatters where there'd once hung shirts and trousers. And scarring the hide of their throats was the same symbol, oozing blood so putrid and dark, there was nothing fresh enough to run red.

The figure spun and pushed his blisters against a hole in the slats, bewildered as to from where and when they'd come. Adrenaline coursed through his legs. Hurriedly, he slithered along the scaffolding, his mouth brimming with saliva while he counted them in their misshapen ring, closing in around the chancellor.

Six in total.

Six more had been made—all because the figure had unmade himself first.

Six that would faithfully obey Tetsu Naborū as lord and master.

"Seek me in Lempeii," Tetsu stated. Then after he spoke in a guttural tongue, he waved his abominations toward Yannis. In Unitarian, he addressed the slaver once more. "I've provided your crew, and the hull is hungry. Now, set sail. Arabax will clean up your mess."

A creature with scaly gray skin hungrily crept toward the woman.

"You're… Low Lord, you're quitting Bastiion…" Yannis gulped as he backpedaled beside his miscreant. "After you were just named proxy regent?"

Tetsu strode in the opposite direction without a glance at his followers. From beneath his robes, a cluster of beetles chittered after his heels. "I have a navy to prepare."

The figure lashed his tongue in anger. He swung himself side to side, his vision sharpening as it latched onto the chancellor, who was sinuously exiting under a fallen beam, then back onto the slaver slinking out the back with his cadre of monsters.

Were he to stop Tetsu, Yannis would sail to Tadeas and infiltrate Boreal.

Were he to stop Yannis, Tetsu could abscond into deeper hiding with the Obscurer.

Running, the figure kicked off his heels and leaped over the railing, plunging toward the floor. He rolled his damaged shoulder and onto his bootheels. The figure shifted in either direction.

Then he heard the woman sob.

The cry's weakness wrenched his focus from the door closing after Yannis. The creature—called Arabax—had dragged the Boreali woman toward a nest of crates. Its claw was buried in the tissue above her knee. Strings of its hair were sprayed with scarlet where it crouched, devouring her thigh. Anguish animated her expression, and from across the gap, she fixed it on the figure.

Though her thin, colorless lips did not move, he heard Alora's voice escape the listless fold; his name quaked through the caverns of his mind.

"There is still hope for redemption."

With a raging howl, he screwed his heel and stormed the creature, then struck it back from its prey. Arabax warped around and shredded the figure's back with a screech. Up close, he saw the patterned scarification down its arms. The creature was Mworran.

It fought ravenously, a cannibal converted into its craving.

Snarling, the figure yanked its wrist and sank his teeth into the blackened veins. He ripped tendon from bone before snapping it at a hideous slant. The creature reared and flogged them into the crates, attacking the figure, and he was thrust down. A section of wood speared his calf. Arabax snapped its inhuman fangs, flashing a row of sharp, filed teeth.

Gelatinous slaver, laced with bile and undigested blood, splattered the figure's eyes.

Releasing every reserve of strength, he caught the creature by its jaws and wrenched the mandible from its skull, bashing the Mworran's rancid brains into a nail that projected from the wall. By the fourth hit, the creature crumbled to dust. The figure watched its fibers dissolve through his gloved fingers. In less than a minute, all that remained was a mound of powder and strips of decomposing cloth. Hunched over, he hooked a glance at the Boreali woman.

Her chest was no longer lifting.

He pushed off his knee and scrambled to her side, pulling her limply into his hold. Down her body, a river of blood streamed from her thigh, soaking through his pants. Her neck fell slackly over his forearm. His eyes arid and burning, the figure rocked her securely.

The figure petted her off-white tresses as if to soothe her transition to the heaven he could never enter. The world seemed to be ending. Her world had ended because of him. He hid his face in her dirtied crown. Torment ripped through him, and he released a dry, ragged sob. He pulled away in gasps, her hair sticking to his snot, as mortality laid before him like an unrighteous mirror.

Death was his legacy.

The woman was another casualty of his transgression, killed by the crossfire. The Obscurer had not put a bounty on her head. He'd put the bounty on Alora.

Chapter Thirty Nine
Zaethan

A fair, young clanswoman handed them each a pine cone from her basket. Ira elbowed Zaethan in the ribs and made a comment as to its size, which she didn't comprehend. He wriggled his fingers after the poor yaya as she crossed the spruce-and-pine-laden aisle.

Zaethan snatched his playful gesture and wrenched him back toward the platform that'd been constructed before the fountain.

Their cones rolled underfoot. "Don't. Just be quiet and keep your sticky fingers to yourself," he said, grimacing. Zaethan wiped his palm on his linsilk pants. The crisp, Northern material wasn't as broken in as his weathered lambskins.

From the corner of his eye, he tracked the many shadowmen armed in attendance. Though the wedding had not yet begun, the last thing the Quadren needed was for them to overhear Ira Hastings offering to spread his inbred seed among their Boreali orchard.

Ira straightened the beaded cuffs of his skintight, fox-lined coat. Having traded his everyday alternative, which was two sizes too large, he'd opted for something more embellished and two sizes too small, giving him the air of a street performer who'd just had a growth spurt.

Zaethan heaved a long-suffering sigh. The yancy looked ridiculous, and so did he by association. He peered up, petitioning the clouds that fleeced the crowded square to open their floodgates and douse the other haidren.

Caging his arms against his abdomen, Zaethan cursed the cold, wishing they would speed things along. Roüwen had certainly gone to enough trouble. Around the congregation, knotted linsilk ties fell from the holdreheiim in panels, swaying in the wind to the melody of delicate chimes. At his back, the Boreali were humming along with the notes, somehow recognizing the song though nothing was being played. Fir draped the skies in woodsy teardrops, festooned there by gemstones and billowing ribbons. Zaethan suppressed a grumble. He flicked some shed pines off his shoulder and onto Hachiro to his left. The shoto'shi merely plucked the greenery from his open journal, then without comment, drew it.

At least one of them was having a good time.

The flurries sparkled, descending like diamonds over the gathering guests while more people eagerly squeezed into the rows of benches behind their king. Others had climbed higher to watch from overlooking verandas. He'd been told that the controversy had drawn many witnesses that day, each outfitted for the occasion. From their necks to the backs of their hands, the Boreali had decorated themselves in swirling patterns and shimmering script, as if they were all shards cut from the same jewel—awkwardly accentuating every unpainted foreigner who shivered among them.

Still, it was beautiful, Zaethan had to admit. But the beauty stood out of place in contest to their terrible tomorrow, when ushered by the Order of the Najjan, the Quadren would depart the peninsula and set forth to lay siege on Dmitri's palace. It was no time for a wedding.

The yancy was ogling another maiden. Aggravated, Zaethan tugged Ira by what little of his coat he could grab and pinned him in place. She scoffed in response and, nose upturned, paraded along toward her seat.

"I'm so fond of that standoffish, highland patois," Ira wistfully said after her. "The constant rejection, it's tantalizing."

"No locals, Ira," Zaethan reminded him.

Nervousness pinched his gut as he formally nodded at the Clann Darragh across the aisle, who was taking his place beside their najjani master, sil'haidren, and elders. The few with stones in their cheeks also wore patches of plain skin, a possible sign of disunity. Declan had mentioned civil disputes about the coupling. Or rather, the idea of the cross-caste bride residing in Boreal after they left. Evidently, her husband-to-be would have legally been expelled... were it not for their haidren's intervention.

Ira tossed an arm around Zaethan chummily. Though, as he was unable to lift it in that preposterous coat, his grip settled around his stiffened elbow instead. "Don't dismiss the resident appeal, my friend. Weddings are proof there's someone for everyone... especially that blonde iced crumpet over there." He waved at her with an airy flick of his wrist. "Oh, yes, 'allöh' to your friend too!"

"A mathematical falsehood, I'm afraid," Hachiro stated, his nose planted in his parchment. "There were far more women than men counted in the last census. Consequently, there is certainly *not* someone for everyone. I would say best of luck to Lady Boreal, but luck too is a myth."

Cocking her hip, Luscia slanted around Dmitri and cleared her throat.

Hachiro paused his quill's scratching. "What? By all estimation, my prospects of a union far exceed yours."

Their king stifled a chuckle. His elaborate, bespoke suit was hidden, as was the effort of those who'd worked through the night to construct it. Encased in a cocoon of regal fur, Dmitri leaned over his byrnnzite walking stick to greet the family as they settled in. Coming to sit directly in front, he offered them his mittened hand. The smears of lilac hadn't fled his under eyes yet, but Zaethan was glad for the genuine smile he bestowed on the bride's mother—a clear effort to set the Unitarian woman at ease. She and her daughter shuffled down the bench to grant room for a brood of flaxen-headed cubs. Joining them were a pair of happy parents, their likeness falling flat on the bitter son, who trailed glumly behind.

Zaethan felt Luscia's eyes pass him over and descend frostily on the twin. He covertly glanced over and found her holding the sister's hand in casual conversation, her mannerisms tense.

It was hard to drop his stare as Luscia moved. In iridescent gossamer tiers, her long-sleeved gown glimmered like opal, the effect blurring the edges where it met her alabaster complexion. She was a lampstand among men, shining in elegant glyphs. She'd left her pale mane the way he'd always favored it, unbound and rebellious. It tumbled down to her waist, tickling the tight corsetry there. Zaethan's eyes slowly climbed the rungs of her stays, over the cropped rabbit stole clasped around her biceps, and up the slope of her bare, illustrated shoulders, ending back at her pinched expression. Luscia had carried it with her into the square that afternoon. And between her tight smiles, it'd only worsened when Captaen Bailefore had arrived.

Zaethan flattened his smirk and steered himself forward.

"A wedding is exactly what we need right now," Dmitri cheerfully remarked as a veiled sage in an olive robe ascended the platform and took residence between two large gilded basins. Outstretching his arms, the man resembled a haunting cypress from Hagarh.

"We *need* to brief the prydes and start loading ship," Zaethan stated.

The distant rhythm of bells shuddered through the trees. "Is it starting?" he asked Luscia with hushed excitement. Beyond Hachiro's disheveled head, his friend's hazel eyes rounded when the sound neared, and the whole assembly hummed more stridently.

Twisting in place, Zaethan saw a dueling parade of children coming from the side streets in pairs, toward opposite ends of the long platform. In unison, they each thumped a short stick covered in bells, timed in song with the advance of their tiny feet. Tailing them came both bride and bridegroom, each seated in splendor atop a mighty reingafier.

The beasts entered the square. On one rode Böwen, strong and tall. From the cushion of his wheatlike beard, his smile beamed as he beheld his betrothed. Zaethan understood the quarrel between the brothers now. With blue eyes wide as an ocean and raven hair crowned in a coronet of braided herbs, the girl was stunning. Cross-caste and all.

Böwen eagerly slid off his reingafier and onto the platform, grabbing the heavy cloak of gray fur after him.

"Wolf. From the valley," someone behind them murmured.

Zaethan didn't know what that meant, only that there was respect for the shadowman in their tone.

He rushed across to help his bride off her antlered steed. When he lifted her out of the saddle, the lacey willows of her pale-green cape snagged on the horn. Something passed between them as they laughed, lost in a realm of their own, despite the thousand people looking on.

The cubs with their belled sticks lined the base of the platform like a henge, watching and giggling. A mother shushed her son from the closest benches as the sage invited everyone to sit. Lowering his flattened hands, he spoke from behind the swath of translucent material.

An expectant stillness fell upon the Boreali.

Words were exchanged between the couple and then with the sage in a language Zaethan barely understood. He'd never been one for ceremony. Darakaians mated in private, by one oath and one witness. He couldn't imagine his own parents, nevertheless Nyack Kasim, ever having undergone this kind of pomp for anyone. Zaethan could hardly imagine Dmitri suffering it with a Zôueli princess. Seeing how it had turned out for Cyra Shà, Zaethan wasn't sure such oaths really mattered. Those were the most commonly broken.

Guided by the sage, the couple broke apart. Each waded toward a gold basin. The mystical tree-man came around Böwen first, motioning wide. Reaching under his wolf cloak, the shadowman retrieved a blade sheathed against each thigh. He handed them to the sage, who elevated them high for everyone to see: a perfect set of consort daggers, the hilts fashioned in the heads of wolves.

Böwen hovered his downturned palm over the bowl; its orientation was important, Zaethan had learned, indicating he gave without requiring in return. The sage restored one of the daggers into his grasp.

Pacing toward the bride, the sage repeated the gesture. "What is happening, Lady Boreal?" Dmitri softly asked.

"They are to cut a covenant," she affectionately replied.

Ira squirmed beside Zaethan. "Why are you outer Houses so obsessed with carving people up?"

A subtle ripple went through the guests. Glancing around, Zaethan noticed each of the Boreali was holding a scrap of brown, a scale snapped off the pine cones. With his boot, he prodded the earth beneath their bench for the one he'd lost.

Trading that maddening journal for his pocket lexicon, Hachiro flapped through the pages to keep up with their statements as Böwen and his bride set their luxiron blades underneath their palms, where it was sure to leave a mark—even on Boreali skin… which Zaethan then suspected might be the point.

Across the aisle, the townspeople had their palms raised over their laps.

Böwen beamed at the girl. "Enjjen anar," the couple said at the same time, slicing the phrase through their flesh. In a telling rustle, their Boreali brethren did the same, slashing the pine cone spines against themselves throughout the square.

Zaethan peeked down their row. A bright-red line marred Luscia. She and her captaen were no different.

"*To none other*…" Hachiro muttered the translation. Like Zaethan, he thoughtfully observed how upon the platform, the joyous pair squeezed their fists, flowing blood into their separate basins.

Stopping the drip, the bride bent down toward the cubs. One upheld a piece of cloth for her to wrap around her wound. Böwen left his station and went to assist in gently tying it for her. His own wound had already clotted. Taking her by the hand, he presented her before the sage. More words. The tree-man retreated, and again the children beat their bells.

With his eyes locked onto his bride, Böwen escorted them around her basin, then crossed the center of the platform, around his own.

"What are they doing now?" Dmitri inquired quietly. Intersecting the other way, the couple repeated the path about each bowl of blood.

Zaethan caught Luscia's subtle motions as she leaned closer to their king and explained. "They will walk about each other. Tread their lived experience. Revere who they were before today," she said. An unusual yearning seeped into her smokey voice. "They will walk each other eight times. On the seventh, they will be wed."

Quickly switching books to notate it in his journal, Hachiro questioned, "Then what purpose serves the eighth?"

"To ensure the first steps of their union honor from where the other came."

With each turn, the couple drew nearer to each other. On the fourth, Böwen adjusted her leafy coronet. On the sixth, his fingertips brushed her cheek. Upon the seventh, he kissed her forehead, and the people cheered. On the eighth, the bride nestled her face against his arm, laughing through her tears.

Zaethan fidgeted, cold and numb on the bench. Though they'd hardly touched, the ordeal seemed too intimate an exchange for him to have witnessed.

The sage shuffled aside. A few shadowmen broke from the flanks. Together, they dragged a larger stone basin and fixed it at the center, between the two of gold. Zaethan comprehended the pattern, thinking back to the altar in the Grand Tabernacle, as the couple stood opposite each other. They clasped hands across the rim.

In pairs, the assisting shadowmen elevated the independent bowls and, at the sage's direction, poured both bloods over their conjoined hands. Blending in a scarlet glaze, it spilled over them into the third basin.

"They are a new person now," Luscia said on an exhale, just loud enough for those closest to hear.

Through Zaethan's periphery, his watch inched toward her, faltering when she absently toyed the beads of the cuff on her wrist. He couldn't see her face, but he didn't need to. It had waned her voice. She wanted this kind of match, the kind that bled two into one.

A rock formed behind his navel. Zaethan again glanced at her father, a boulder among the other leaders, and her aunt beside him. The sil'haidren's countenance was so rigid, it could have been cast in steel. Yet just when Zaethan thought she must have disapproved, he caught her erasing a tear of her own, wiping it so briskly, it was as if she were afraid someone might see.

The sage raised a sterling pitcher above them and spoke. With the crowd, Luscia chanted as he poured clear water over the couple's hands, washing them clean.

"Pricta'siim, fojjünaet'Aurynth, benadicta'anar."

The wind added to their measure. Chimes resounded throughout the canopy, almost drowning Hachiro's translation. "*Tested by iron, quenched by Aurynth, separated by none.*"

Another cub waved a clean cloth, and this time Böwen stooped to grab it. He dried his wife's dainty hands while the sage came to the front of the stone basin. Bending, the tree-man placed a sparkling vessel underneath a slit in the rock and slid back a metal panel. The pastel mixture flowed into the glass, filling it to the brim. The sage corked it.

Kneeling before the couple with his back toward the crowd, he gave the vessel up to Böwen.

Taking it, the flaxen shadowman kissed his wife's hand and threw his arm triumphantly into the air. "Se'lah Aurynth!"

To which the bride led their people to merrily bellow, "Rul'Aniell!"

And the celebrations began.

Takoda stole his second helping from the butcher board when the huffy matron wasn't looking. He attempted to blow the sticky nettles off the seared boar. "The best part of storming Bastiion will be our homecoming feast, free of these kakka-shtàka stems."

With his half-eaten meal discarded, Zaethan bounced on his heels, antsy as he craned his neck around Kumo. The beta was a rampart in the middle of the festivity. He lowered back onto his heels, annoyed that the flock of elders had not dispersed. "Uni, it's the *food* we're after, Takoda," he sarcastically replied.

"Food and a hungry yaya," Kumo said with a full-bellied chortle as he rolled his bulky shoulders to the frisky tempo of the panpipe. In maddening circles behind a parade of lutists, the pipe player had looped once more through the warren of roasting fires and barrels of mead.

Zaethan cracked his knuckles. He wasn't much for praying. But he prayed to Boreal's High One that after tonight, he'd never have to hear the panpipe ever again.

Kumo gave his bicep a sharp pat. "Eh, you look like your stomach is about to brawl your bowels, Ahoté."

"Meme qondai, it's too many nettles," Takoda said and gripped his belt, a sympathetic screw to his long face.

Zaethan bristled. "It's not the nettles." Collecting his nerve, he smacked his own cheek and finally stepped around his giant cousin.

"Doru, Zaeth. Eh, stop, why are you walking like that?" the beta called after him.

But Zaethan ignored him. *Now or never, it must be tonight*, he coached himself, beelining for the elders. Shoulder-to-shoulder, they were herded around their high clann, Orien Darragh. Zaethan's determined step was frustrated by the procession of musicians, whose glazed eyes spoke to their many passes around the mead. Zaethan broke past them and awkwardly halted outside the revered ring of Boreali men.

He was saved from announcing himself. Having noticed the lingering Darakaian, they promptly parted.

Orien Darragh rotated, and the considerable cloak, threaded with gemstones, skated after his broad frame. Though his daughter was more than a foot shorter, it was evident from whom she'd inherited her imposing countenance.

Clearing his throat, Zaethan squared his stance. "Allöh'jomn'yeh, Clann Darragh. May we speak?" Even as he recited Declan's instructed greeting, his focus pitched between the beady, onlooking glares and her father. "In confidence?"

Despite the mumbles of suspicion, their leader regarded Zaethan down his bulbous nose. He then worded something soundless through the side of his mouth. An order in witchtongue, by the disgruntled way they promptly scattered.

Politically, the Accords guaranteed a foreign haidren an audience with the leader, should he or she make the invitation known. It was in his subject matter where the legalities thinned. The audience could end as soon as it began.

The Clann Darragh stoically awaited Zaethan's request.

"I wish to…" Zaethan clamped his jaw, hating the feel of the phrase as it left his tongue. "I'm here to surrender myself to your discrimination."

The folds in Orien Darragh's mottled skin smoothed, then swiftly intensified. He cupped the wiry hairs of his beard. In harsh assessment, his shock scanned Zaethan as if he were a misplaced bolt on a wagon wheel. Hitching his gaze onto the luxiron posts his son had made, Orien Darragh lowered his wide, calloused hand.

"With me," he abruptly said. Revolving, he wiggled his fingers searchingly, then plucked a bowl of seasoned oil and a fresh-baked loaf off a nearby table. "Let us find common ground, Lord Haidren, and eat upon it."

Confused, Zaethan mutely followed Orien Darragh along the perimeter of the square and down a tight, winding path away from the music. He said nothing as they walked into the thickening trees. Eventually they stopped at a crooked, stone stair that disappeared into a dense thicket. Halfway up the steps, the Clann Darragh nodded to himself, tucked the loaf under his chin, spread his cloak, and sat.

He arranged the bread and oil next to his knee in the manner Dmitri would a picnic. Raising a bushy brow, the leader of Boreal beckoned Zaethan to join him.

Zaethan stiffly complied.

Orien Darragh ripped the loaf in half. He took one, then split it again and dipped the quarters into the oil. He offered one to his guest. "When two men eat, they see each other first as human. Companion second. Ally or adversary third."

Mimicking the man, Zaethan bit into the sweet, herb-laced bread.

The Clann Darragh swallowed. "This is difficult for you. That much is plain."

Zaethan adjusted his posture uncomfortably. "I'm not in the habit of submitting… especially to someone I do not know." He tore a smaller bit and brought it toward the oil.

"We all submit to something, summoning joy or madness by the master we choose. Niit, like this." He placed his fingers atop Zaethan's and pushed his bread deeper into the bowl, swirling it around. "It's good for the bones. Waedfrel." Again, he gestured for Zaethan to eat. The Clann Darragh spoke while he chewed. "Now… convince me why I should entertain this conversation. You are not Boreali. Your title was all but stripped. Ana'Mere does not even permit you to lodge in my home. And to be frank, Lord Haidren, whenever I look at you, all I see is a lost boy roaming in my woods."

Zaethan's mouth hardened around the soggy food. Hunched forward, he laced his fingers and answered, "There was a season when that was painfully true. I came here a man in shambles." Rubbing a remnant throb in his hip, he sought the lamplit wilderness, recalling the presence he'd encountered there. "But I'm not lost anymore. Out there, I stepped away from myself and into something… *other*. And by the other, I was found."

When the Clann Darragh didn't respond, Zaethan curved his face around, knowing he sounded foolish. Yet he was pierced by the man's watchfulness. It was unyielding and bluer than the spotted morels glowing upon the tree trunk behind him. He measuredly leaned backward against the bark. Hitching a knee, Orien Darragh propped his elbow and thoughtfully rolled the bread between his thumb and middle finger.

"Did you know that my wife is dead?"

Zaethan's lips stalled. "Pardon?"

"She's dead, in some ways."

"Some ways…"

"Wem, well, her body has been accepted by the earth," he casually explained, "but she is down there across the square, in the corner of my daughter's mouth whenever she is laughing. In my son's creativity and every crack of his hammer. In the richness of the soil. In the threads we cannot see dancing in the night. My wife lives on, happy, joyful… free with her Maker in Aurynth. What is that silly phrase your people love to say again? Oh, wem, 'every gain has a loss.'" The singsong tone had a mocking edge, though it was softened by the crack in his firm facade. "I have lost Eoine but briefly, while she has gained eternity. It seems petty, after some time to think on it, to hold a grudge against the High

One for what He's allowed to pass. Sometimes, I wonder if He must have missed her even more than I do and brought her home to Him."

Conversations with the Boreali seemed a never-ending puzzle. The man's reception was even more confounding. Firm yet gentle, guarded yet unthreatened… He seemed so different than the menace who'd raised Zaethan. "While I used to think a love like that was merely in myths, Clann Darragh, I fail to see your point."

"The point is this, Lord Haidren. The heart cannot quote a poem it has never read, unless it was written there from the very start," said Orien Darragh, his keen observation arrowing onto Zaethan. "Perhaps by Aniell's mysterious design, He etched that same poem onto your heart too. Understand?"

"I understand the Boreali love riddles."

His lips quirked as if he found that amusing. "We do. As did Eoine's fappa. So, out of sheer respect for the High One and my bride, this is what we'll do… I am going ask you the same four questions that he once asked me. I will repeat them only once."

Zaethan nodded at his look of caution. Situating himself upright, he anxiously rubbed his palms together.

"She is precious to me," he said as a final warning, then gave a blustery sigh. "Meditate on my daughter, fulfill these four, and receive my verdict.

If she were a tool, what would she bring?

Were she a song, what would she sing?

If she were a picture, what would she show?

And were she to bloom, how would she grow?"

Keeping his word, Orien Darragh tore four bits of bread and, one by one, set them in a dividing line between their feet as he ran the stanza once again.

An owl hooted. The trees shuffled and groaned. Zaethan studied the scraps like they were uncut gems, careful not to reach out until he was certain.

A tool. What would she bring? He'd learned the haidren to Boreal was intended to restore and reconcile her people in some way. That, Luscia had. She'd healed plenty of Zaethan's own pryde out of Hagarh. But that was a byproduct of her presence, not its function. Ano, if she were a tool, then in his life she'd become a dagger. Cutting through the darkness. Separating truth from lies and exposing the intentions of those around her. A dagger could kill, but it could also save.

In many ways, she'd splintered his nature. Now, he was becoming new. That was her rescue.

"Division," he said decidedly, grabbing the first piece and placing it one step higher.

Orien Darragh's eyes broadened with intrigue, trailing Zaethan's hand back toward the bread.

A song. What would she sing? "Justice." *A picture. What would she show?* "The truth." He plucked the third piece as her father crossed his arms and inclined closer.

Were she to bloom, how would she grow? Luscia was the only person he knew who put upon herself a chain so flimsy that with her every step she feared it might break. What would the world look like if she were brave enough to stride and let it snap off?

Zaethan tenderly placed the final piece on the ledge. "She would grow in courage." When he peered up, Orien Darragh had his hand over his mouth again, his gaze boring into Zaethan. "I mean, what good is strength if she's so afraid to leverage it?"

Her father scratched his nose. After a moment, he let out another loaded sigh and stared at his right hand. Zaethan's heart leaped when, miraculously, he slipped a plain silver ring from his thick forefinger.

Holding it between them, he presented it to Zaethan. "Meh'daeünna'yeh, Lord Haidren, but heed this portent. My daughter *will* deny you, as she should," he said humorlessly. "I raised her. She will not turn from her duty, not even for you."

"That is all but certain, Clann Darragh."

"Then why seek my blessing?"

"Because I'm shackled to the question. And because her refusal might finally set me free." Zaethan's throat caught as he carefully took the ring from him. As it shined under the surrounding glow, he noticed a faded Boreali script engraved within the inner rim. "What does it say?"

Whatever the message, it meant a great deal to Orien Darragh, by the tremor that went through his clamped countenance. Rising, Boreal's leader grabbed the quaint bowl and rotated it so that the oil slid around the surface in strange patterns that reflected the highland light. "It says what only her mother can relay."

CHAPTER FORTY
LUSCIA

"A wish of endless happiness to you both," Luscia said sincerely, letting go of Böwen's hand before relinquishing Mila's. "Meh fyreon, dear friend. I regret how I must take him away from you so soon."

"Tadöm, Lady Luscia," the young bride replied. She laced her arm securely around her husband's waist.

Böwen brought the rare beauty closer and planted yet another kiss atop her forehead. "We are just grateful to have found each other at all, Ana'Sere."

Lingering behind her, Marek slid his hand across Luscia's lower back before he grabbed the shadowman into a firm, congratulatory hug. Backstepping, he said, "We ought to leave you to your bevy of guests… Seems even your worst critics stayed for supper."

The jest was wasted on Luscia. She'd maintained a stubborn detachment from him throughout the ceremony, at least as much as courtesy would allow in public. His deep chuckles nettled Luscia. She crossed her arms over herself as she spared the merry couple a drawn-out good-bye and permitted the next family in line to take their place.

Weaving through the throng of dancers, Luscia aimed for her king, who had enthroned himself upon a squat stump between the agora and the mill. A flock of bright-eyed children surrounded him, enraptured by whatever tale he told and the theatrical way his cane twirled above their heads.

"Ana'Sere, Ana'Sere," people respectfully uttered as she marched by.

Her pasted smile faltered when the procession of lutists surged around the bend and steered her away from Dmitri's storytelling and toward the dancing masses. She ought to have been spinning among the celebration. She ought to be brimming with cheer. Instead, she was compressing her anger in polite greetings and forced nods.

Luscia fought the urge to smack the tambourine player when his fleeting footwork allowed Marek to fall in step beside her.

With trained poise, the captaen rotated on his heel, circling to confront her. "Are you going to tell me what I've done to upset you, or am I to keep guessing?"

"Wouldn't you rather discuss it with Ana'Mere?" Luscia dodged him.

"Heh'ta." He tugged her by the arm, turning her round. The jerky move caught the attention of the dancers. Marek dropped his voice, along with his hold, but his eyes were frozen lochs beneath his ginger brows. "What was *that* supposed to mean?"

Luscia scratched the skin of her wrist beneath his kurtfierï, aware he cataloged her every motion—as did the citizens of Roüwen, prancing with their partners on either side. Her grin returned, albeit more strained than before. She waited for the lutists to finish parading by to respond. At least the raucous melody afforded some semblance of privacy among Boreali ears.

"Next time you're ashamed of my conduct," said Luscia, tipping her nose beneath Marek's sharp chin, "take it up with me, your haidren. Don't tuck your tail and tattle to my aunt."

He released his lower lip from his teeth, relaxing a fraction. "Tattle to her? About what? Your ever-increasing gifts? How you revealed those spectacular gifts to the prydes to persuade them to stay with our king? Or that you secretly escorted him and his Quadren to the Dönumn while we were at the keep?" Marek tucked a lock of his crimson hair behind an ear, and folding his arms, he leaned downward. Each lash a flame, fire licked his scowl. "Wem, I know about that too. And though you didn't have enough trust to 'take it up with *me*,' my brother's najjan absolutely did."

That he'd not reproved her for her unlawful act itself spoke more about him than it did Luscia. Mortified, she hugged herself tighter. "If the betrayal was not yours, then whose?"

Marek rustled his head, be he baffled or exasperated outright. His face hardened when it angled westward. "Is it really so hard to piece together?"

Luscia tracked his gaze. At the base of the Grand Tabernacle lingered Creyvan, conversing with Elders Hinrük, Dagmar, and Kalf. Unlike the iridescent gossamer layer stitched over Marek's jacket, Creyvan's was detailed in wools from the Orallach.

Her guard's garments officially matched Hinrük's more than hers.

Luscia kneaded her temples. "This is a trying time for me, Marek. Forgive my assumptions."

"Perhaps I should be pleased that I came first in your mind," he replied with a cagey shrug and brushed the beads of her cuff. "You are continually surrounded by men…"

She regretted the ice her voice carried. "It's a man's world. Am I supposed to avoid it simply because there are so many of them?"

"It's not the many I worry about," Marek muttered, his focus drifting from Luscia and back toward their troublesome zealot. "I'll deal with him. You must ready for tomorrow. You're right. Things are trying enough."

"Tadöm," Luscia replied when he promptly stormed in Creyvan's direction and disappeared into the crowd. An energetic song overtook the square, and her steps quickened to escape the spirited throng. He'd truthfully spoken; the dawn was fast approaching, and with it was coming a multitude of hardships, hardships from which Roüwen would be gratefully spared. She needed to prepare—to sharpen her blades, to brew a crate of Dmitri's elixir, and if she was lucky, to sleep.

Contorting with the music, she bobbed and whirled with the revolving ring, lithely escaping the dancers toward the rim. Homeward bound, Luscia set her sight on the nearest spiral stair that led into the roost of skyward villas.

A warm pressure suddenly slipped down her forearm like a second skin and took grasp of her hand as someone sinuously interlocked their strong fingers with hers. Their hold was sure and inviting, and she was pulled to follow. Confused currents raced along Luscia's flesh as she took in his secure, cinnamon-hued grip. Wide-eyed, she scanned its muscled arrow up into the crisp shadow of his jawline.

Zaethan didn't bother looking down at her alarm. He determinedly strode them past the outlying fires, between the abandoned carts, and away from the festivity.

The rush of tambourines died, and the plucking strings dulled. All she heard was her drumming heart as she ambled after his jarring strides. She should have wrenched away, returned to the Quadren…

anything but fixate on the hypnotic gallop of his taut body beneath the sheen of his coat. The lantern-lit boundary fell behind them.

In the margins, her vision blurred into smears of bark and pulsing evergreen as they crossed into uncharted territory.

Luscia felt herself sinking into the earth as they passed under the colossal roots of a holdreheiim and into a vast, dark hollow. Straw crunched underfoot. Moss and wood sparkled above. Zaethan didn't speak. Instead, he abruptly turned on her and bent low to scoop his strong arms beneath her.

She gasped, her intake grassy and sweet. Zaethan lifted her as if she were nothing, as if her burden were weightless. He adjusted her so that one of his arms could slide up her spine, curling her against him. Luscia's arms reflexively turned to water, cascading over his shoulders. At her touch, he split a grin so bright, it contested the lumin sparking the nature all around them.

With his forehead pressed against hers, his breaths challenged Luscia's in combative bursts. Out of nowhere, Zaethan laughed—the relaxed, rippling texture tantalizing and new. She was intoxicated by the sound, and her thighs constricted. How she'd missed his closeness, where against all rationale, she fit like a tailored piece in his renegade puzzle. Her legs instinctively locked around his hard abdomen. And with a satisfied groan, he began to spin them senselessly in circles.

Her thoughts struggled to keep up as her world faded away. Senselessly, Luscia closed her eyes and leaned back into his sturdy hold. As they twirled, her arms slipped and hung loose, and for a few moments, it felt like flying.

Zaethan slowed. His course changed, as did the masculine tension that braced his frame. The edge of his thick belt scored her backside through her dress as he carried her toward a stack of hay.

Luscia was unblinking when, biting his lip, he boosted her over a bushel and thumped her indelicately upon the hay. He stepped away. She swallowed a blazing flush as he rocked back on his heel and allowed his parched regard to drink her in. Clutching fistfuls of straw, her nails dug in while as a man caught in a drought, he took his time, quenching a thirst she'd no idea she could inspire.

Studying the disheveled fold of her skirts where they hiked over one knee, Zaethan raked his thumb across his ample mouth in consideration. Then he cricked his neck. And reaching up, he wound his sable locs out of the way.

Luscia's pulse fled her chest.

Any appeal leaving with it.

With aching slowness, Zaethan dragged his knuckles down her stocking as he bent at her feet. He became a beast tamed. A storm contained, he pressed the most delicate kisses up her leg as strikes of lightning. At her knee, he broke away, stealing from her a ragged gasp. His tongue toyed with his teeth. Her toes curled at the image, seeing him so thoroughly pleased with himself.

It'd been so long since she'd seen that face.

Luscia arched forward involuntarily when he planted a hand beside each of her thighs. Biceps bunching, Zaethan leaned in and ran the very tip of his nose along her stays, between the valley of her breasts, toward the base of her throat. She felt him slide something from his pocket and palm it before curving her chin back with his forefinger. Luscia panted as he brought his face just above the lacey trim of her bodice.

Hot breath was only his prelude.

There, Zaethan penned attestations with his tongue across her supple flesh, and she savored each torrid message. Overwriting the luminescent scrollwork, he scraped his teeth atop her bare shoulder. Up her throat. Below her ear. Tingles shot through her extremities, and for a second, he was all there was.

Her heel scraped against the bundle of hay. Luscia reopened her eyes. As her pupils dilated, the area behind him brightened. A large wheel leaned against the hollow. The outline of tools and shards of straw sharpened, and her heart sank.

He'd carried her to a threshing floor. The place where chaff, the unusable seed, the deceiving harvest, was separated from the good and true.

Alora's warning thundered through her ears as if from the sky.

It is by our flesh we always fail.

All vigor leaked from her body, and shame adeptly took its place. This was not her calling. He was not her charge, her purpose to fulfill. This thing of theirs was a ritual distortion. She wanted him, so badly it felt like peeling her own skin to reinstate an inch between them. Yet she wanted what was better—what was righteous—even more.

Luscia lifelessly rocked with the impact of his fervent kisses. She flattened her cheek against him. "I cannot, Zaeth…" she whispered, spurning every syllable. "I cannot have you."

She heard the issue of her phrasing, the reason why his hands continued to skate around her middle. "Which is why I have something to show you, Domàa'maia," Zaethan said breathily.

"Niit," Luscia croaked, torn by the name and how it longingly stroked her ears. With both hands, she gently pushed him back. "This confusion of ours is all my fault. I should have mended it from the onset."

Although she barely flinched, it was as if she'd slapped the simper right off him. Backing off, Zaethan widened the ravine. Seconds later, he extended his hand like it were a lifeline. "We are not a problem to be solved, Luscia."

"But a problem rages within me because of us," she openly confessed.

Hurt turned him to leave, as was their pattern, but Zaethan swung right back around. "Is that why you're with him? Bailefore gives you no problems?"

"Marek grounds me," stated Luscia flatly.

"You don't need to be grounded."

She steeled her spine upon the straw. "Then what do I need?"

"To be free!"

Amazed, and insulted, Luscia untucked her skirts and resentfully hopped down onto the circular, stone slab. "Freedom is not the same as anarchy," she said and waved between them. "Freedom is the liberty to exert self-control, not that you ever trouble yourself with anything like that!"

Smacking his lips, Zaethan shoved whatever it was back into his pocket and pecked at his puffed chest. "If you're to reject me, just do it outright."

Her upset ceded to remorse and pity for his pain. "My line must continue, Zaethan," Luscia explained with deflated gestures. "I thought… I was certain after showing you the Dönumn, you would understand that now, but apparently—"

"I understand you have a brother!" Zaethan spurted. "You act like you're an only child."

"I act like I am haidren!" She was unable to miss how he flinched, but she spurred on nevertheless. "Under Aurynth, the responsibility is mine. If we all shirk duty onto our fellow man, then it would never be accomplished or preserved!" exclaimed Luscia. "What good is love without duty?"

His green eyes brightened at her slip of the word, and he beckoned wildly. "What is duty without love!"

"I love my people," she staunchly replied. "I love Aniell."

Zaethan's fist proudly struck himself. "Eh, at least I am my own."

"Well, I want to be more." Luscia searched him intently after he winced and started kneading his hipbone. Caging her arms, she spoke tiredly toward the floor. "Don't begrudge me my duty, Zaeth, just because you've been stripped of yours. I'm not the one who is lost here."

She brought up her chin when he didn't reply, only to find him nodding as he took the edge of his palm and sliced it across his navel. Zaethan then flipped his hand outward and imitated painting his entrails over his heart. Clenched, the muscles of his face quaked with feeling, yet in an unusual effort, he shuttered them from her, adopting a mask of stone. "Your tongue cuts sharper than any blade, Maji'maia, and you've no remedy to dull its sting. The day you entered my life you tore it asunder," he professed. "Most days I hate you for it."

Her eyes shot toward the underside of the holdreheiim. Luscia choked back animosity. Hurt. Loss. The statement was so unfair. Her tongue might be sharp, but as the master himself, he'd trained her how to wield it. And within her, he'd set his hooks so deeply that just one wrench of his whim drew blood.

Emotion pounded through her at revolting speeds. Uncontrolled, her Sight distorted the veil, and a whirlwind of lumin flickered at the fringes of her vision.

"*Luscia…*" the Logoth—the voice from the *Other*—disconcertingly called.

She ignored it.

Hooks had two ends; he should feel them too.

Luscia lowered her glare onto his. "There are days I hate you too."

"*Luscia…*" Sparks from the *Other* coalesced above her hardened brow.

With a jerk of his head, Zaethan acidly replied, "Then I think we're done here."

"I think we are."

But he'd already started toward the hollow's exit. Energy pricked her fingertips, and a cold gust swept through the threshing floor, whipping up the discarded chaff around his departing heels. Luscia observed the cadence of his steps in anger, only then detecting their mismatched hitch.

"You're limping," she blurted, shuffling after him in concern. "Zaeth… You're limping…"

Lumbering off, he tossed his hands. "That I am! Uni! Maybe if you'd looked up from your *duty*, you might have noticed—"

A shade blacker than the most sinister shadow tore across her vision with inhuman velocity, crumpling Zaethan like he were a stalk of grain as it drilled him into the other side of the hollow. Luscia shrieked. The lumin crackled and lashed her arms in tendrils of hot static. Zaethan struck the stack of hay, the impact sending chaff flying with a foul plume. Her nose repelled from the familiar scent of contaminated carrion.

It couldn't be.

Not there, not in Boreal.

Rearing itself up, the sinuous shape showcased a protruding spine, sharp enough to punch through its putrid, blackened hide like teeth down its rounded back. A petrifying screech tore from its rotting jowls. The air grew fetid and dry, lifting the ends of her tawny hair in response. To her dread, the creature's elongated talons swiped down upon Zaethan.

"Zaeth!" Luscia cried, reaching for him.

Light flashed. Cords of lumin snapped in line with her outstretched arms and bolted for the creature. Bright energy sizzled when it lassoed it by the neck and drew the thing off the ground. Like the carcass it was, the blazing threads spread the creature wide. Erratically, the lumin sputtered around its form, creating a vacuum in the air—a black abyss in the *Other*, devoid of light. Fresh crimson foamed and dribbled from its incisors, alighting the red of its swollen, hellish eyes.

She and Zaethan were not its first prey.

Before Luscia could charge, a thick stick exploded sludge from the devoid's chest cavity. The inky slurry turned to dust, raining upon the slab. Behind the settling particles, Zaethan stood, huffing in shock, a slimy threshing flail slipping from his grasp.

He held onto the top of his head as if surprised it was still there. "Is that… Is that what Ambrose almost became?"

That evil had been lurking right outside, where no one expected. Luscia gathered up her skirts in horror and dashed toward the opening of the hollow, Zaethan sprinting right after her.

Screams, the kind hailing only from nightmares, filled the open.

She shoved icy ferns out of the way along the choked, nature-lit path. Nearing the edge of the square, Luscia's feet faltered at what she beheld.

Zaethan stopped short of knocking her over, and she desperately whirled toward him. Splitting a shrill breath, they both expressed the same terrible certainty, the one that tethered them for a lifetime.

"Dmitri!"

Death perfumed the city, a reek that choked both the living and the slain. Creatures came from everywhere. Too many to count. It was as if the Depths had opened wide. Seemingly multiplying, its infernal spawn scurried up the holdreheiim in hordes. Jumped from the verandas. Plagued the avenues. And feasted on Roüwen's bounty.

With her sweat-wracked back pressed against Declan's, Luscia fastened her focus forward, high above the grisly red streaking the snow and the ravaged bodies from which it flowed. Their haidren couldn't stop to mourn them. She had to press onward.

Somewhere was the king of Orynthia, trapped among the massacre.

Luscia's feet slid trustingly with her najjan's as Declan rotated them without notice. His wraith squelched into something wet. At the bloodcurdling cry, a creature's head went rolling, disintegrating into a demonic rain over the icy gravel. A freckled, lifeless arm lay there, as if the dead man were reaching to catch it. Garbed in Boreal's finest linsilks, his petrified eyes were as empty as his torn-open abdomen.

"Hold!" she shouted to Declan, and gripping his curled bicep, she laterally sprang off the ground to kick back another abomination galloping toward them on all fours.

It wasn't alone.

Swinging over Declan's spine, Luscia hooked her ankle around his thick calf like a pole, then slammed *Ferocity* down upon the partly decayed skull of the next devoid. Fetid, sticky tar sprayed when she withdrew her consort dagger. She blinked, passing back into the Sight. Lumin shuddered in hectic, incensed patterns throughout the air and in tangles around the pods of warring najjan; citizens of Roüwen herded within them as the doomed chaotically fled for their lives between the abandoned cooking fires.

Thermal shivers cascaded her fingertips. Careening her neck, she saw the first devoid creature doubling back. Its bones had dislocated from her impact, but its inhuman speed only increased, and a long, blackened tongue flailed from a hellish visage more bone than meat.

Luscia reached through the *Other* for the threads, petitioning Aniell for their cooperation. Grasping onto spindles of lumin, she sprang off Declan and looped the energy around the wicked thing as if by the reins. She planted her boot against it and drove it into the earth. A howl went up. Seconds later, Aksel barreled through the fray and, with his elongated canines, speared the creature by the temples, shredding it asunder.

She jumped back when beneath her, the carcass crumpled to ash. "Creyvan!" Declan barked in relief.

After wiping her mother's dagger against her skirts, Luscia retied the hem higher up her leg and backed herself against them, forming a defensive trinity. To her left, Creyvan was covered in gore, most of it dark and vile.

Winded, the najjan swiped his brow with his ruined sleeve, the stitched Orallach tradition fraying and stained. "Where is she?" Creyvan frantically asked. "Bolaeva, tell me you've seen her…"

He thrust a crescent wraith up through a set of snarling jaws.

Luscia's hair whipped as she wildly shook her head. She'd already lost Zaethan. Declan was the only person she'd found before the worst of the onslaught. "What of the king?" she yelled back.

"Niit." Creyvan's head shifted fitfully in every direction.

She elbowed him, wedging closer against Declan once more. "Go. Crestï, Creyvan. Find Mila and Böwen." Her animus subsided at the sound he made before tearing off and madly slicing a path through the chaos. Had she known where to turn, Luscia would be doing the same.

Luxiron arced around her middle, nearly tearing her ribs, as Declan shielded her behind his brawny stature and drove either wraith into a charging demon. The devoid creature shrieked, a guttural tone that reverberated from one world to the next.

Perspiration ran down her face. Ribbons and wedding wreaths collapsed around them, catching fire. Luscia howled in frustration.

Her Sight scoured the field of fleeing victims, the light energy flaring in hectic bursts each time the fallen were slaughtered. "Show me where he is!" Luscia furiously screamed to the sea of lumin.

At her voice, the opaline tendrils parted like drapery, creating a tunnel through the *Other* toward the statue of Tiergan rising from the center of the square. Within the shadow rift wavered a blazing beam of light.

There, the harbinger thread beckoned.

It quaked and darted around the fountain bend right before the lumin crashed back into itself. Luscia barely heard Declan's protest when her boots pummeled the earth, praying her sovereign was alive. She shouldn't have left him. Whatever happened… The blame would be hers alone.

Luscia hopped over a cadaver, running toward a najjan who by himself battled three slavering devoid. Heat poured from her palm as the lumin raced ahead and impaled one gruesomely in the heart. After rolling over the najjan's shoulders with her momentum, Luscia locked her legs around another creature. She grunted in pain when its talons cut into her thighs. As she drilled her consort dagger through a putrid cavity that had once been an ear, her soles touched the snow, and she sprinted for where the harbinger thread had vanished around the fountain.

Aksel flanked her. Snapping and snarling, the lycran thwarted a devoid coming at her right side and dragged it off so Luscia could leap upon the stonework. Atop the fountain's rim, she found the harbinger thread winding among the tides of thrashing figures. Luscia's heart lurched. The radiant beam of light arrowed toward one man, remarkably huddled between a heavily muscled Darakaian and a tall, luxiron-clad Boreali.

Dmitri.

And not far off advanced a fresh swarm.

"Nox, watch out!" She signaled the najjan, leaping.

Breaking from their king, Noxolo cut through a decomposing torso in ferocious revolutions, circling his crescent wraiths back into place opposite Kumo. But severed in half, the creature kept clawing after them.

Luscia piked it through its nest of wiry jet-black hair. "Sever the head or take the heart," she bellowed over its deafening screech and whirled under Noxolo's towering cover.

Inky bile slipped from his kaleidoscopic blades into the snow. The rest he wiped off his slender cheek. "Tadöm Aniell," Noxolo praised. "We'd thought the worst, Ana'Sere."

"Shtàka, the Fates sent their worst upon us! But glad to see you, Maji'maia," Kumo threw over his shoulder.

She anxiously rotated toward Dmitri, who was barely standing. "Sire, are you injured?"

"Not yet." He wheezed. He was hunched over the cane he shrinkingly clutched. Even were he healthy, no king was ever meant to be foisted upon the frontline. Perspiration dotted his sallow complexion, pasting his unruly umber waves against his forehead. Skeletal shadows loomed under his eyes. "Zaeth," he blurted in panic. "Is he dead? I cannot—we cannot lose him."

"I don't think so," she said. Guilt arose at the ardency in his weak voice.

His eyelids sank, allayed by her meager assurance. "These… These are the beasts you warned us of?"

"Wem." Luscia bolstered his cane, which was slipping under his weight.

"I am afraid, Lady Boreal. I'm afraid to die." Dmitri shot his gaze beyond her.

Spinning, her stomach plummeted.

A wave of creatures was stampeding straight toward them.

"So am I, My King," Luscia replied, shoving the dagger into the sheath strapped at her thigh. "Take my hand."

Pitting him behind her, Noxolo and Kumo shifted to flank her. She gripped her lycran by the scruff and held him fast.

Creatures charged through the *Other*. Threads of lumin lashed at their hides as they drew near. Snow and gravel were shrapnel under their menacing tread. Luscia's lips moved as she sent a desperate prayer to Aurynth, begging the High One to save them.

From the gloom of her periphery, the mighty tendril of light wound forth.

The harbinger thread traced hotly around her free arm and fingers, coiling in brilliant bands. Static popped through her ears, and a feverish power, a euphoric agony, tore down her limb into her middle. Luscia centered her regard on the devoid at the forefront; its eyes shone redder than the bleeding sun.

And clutching the hand of her king, she smashed her outspread fingers to the earth.

Thunder quaked the surface. Otherworldly ripples exploded across the square, blasting the creatures backward when the harbinger thread unraveled and spread into a great, crystalline dome over Luscia's and the men's heads, protecting the four from the subsequent assault.

Terrified, she jumped when talons suddenly ripped at the lumin shield. A muffled screech could be heard on the other side. Claws of the devoid corroded when it touched the harbinger's defensive field.

How can this be?

Luscia gradually looked down at her and Dmitri's conjoined hands. Then up at him.

But the king of Orynthia was transfixed, his eyes alight at the mesmerizing iridescence of the opal dome and the multitude of tiny, interlocking threads holding it together. Dmitri's lips parted as if he'd seen his first dawn.

He was seeing the *Other*.

She stared at their hands again. Just like Marek, that day in the agora.

"I'm not so afraid anymore," he whispered.

Flabbergasted, Luscia stared through the translucent dome and into the ugliness of battle. Across the fountain, Alora stood—her eyes gaped and fixed in horror, not at the slaughter but at her niece safe inside the dome of lumin.

Luxiron slashed away her image as with alacrity, Emiere spun in front of her, sweeping his crescent wraiths in a deadly arc. In her stead, smoke and cinders descended from the heights. Luscia choked back her next scream.

Roüwen was aflame.

CHAPTER FORTY ONE
ZAETHAN

"Dmitri!" he shouted, his throat hoarse and torn open by the gathering smoke. Braced against the base of the alehouse, Zaethan shoved Ira's curious head back down into hiding behind a barrel. The yancy was going to get himself killed. "Stay put, you limp-wristed ingrate!"

He whooped to Jabari.

Heading the signal, the lanky Yowekaon speared his kopar through a bull-rushing creature, and having moored it in place, Takoda lobbed off its monstrous head.

Thus far, it was the only method that worked.

"Hillman three," Jabari said, out of breath as he counted his fingers for Takoda. "Faraji boy two."

"That devil huwàa would've chewed your leg off!"

"One-legged hillman better than three-armed warrior and his pretty yancy," Jabari called back as they positioned their footing for the next wave.

Said yancy couldn't resist his own mention.

Zaethan palmed Ira's head and drove him lower behind the barrel, holding him still with one arm. "Dmitri!" he roared again.

"I am a noble lord," Ira announced, weaseling out from under Zaethan's protective grip, "not a chambermaid in your closet. You can't tell me what to—ack!"

Blackened guts went flying, dousing the haidren to Bastiion in a sheet of filth where he'd risen from his crouch. Nasty, mold-crusted intestines slid down his overly tight coat.

Ira wicked his hands petulantly. "Anything but the suit… Someone fetch the servants to clean this up."

"You don't have any servants, Ira," said Zaethan, wrenching him aside when a creature dodged Takoda's swipe and barreled up the tree trunk, its claws scattering the bark below.

"I surely do!"

Zaethan growled, and with his fist buried in the putrid fabric, he wrangled the yancy to the other side. He threw his arm out against the rough bark. His kuerre, commandeered from the dead, severed the creature between its searing eyes. The lower half crumbled to dust below the highland blade.

He tipped his skull against the holdreheiim, panting toward Ira. "Not here you don't."

The other haidren was clutching his snuff canister as if one hit would fly him into blissful oblivion. With a gulp, Ira plucked his sullied linsilk collar. "Then can I borrow your servants? Time is of the essence."

It took everything in Zaethan not to strike him. "Dmitri!"

"Alpha Zà!" exclaimed Takoda, pointing the tip of his kopar toward the mayhem at the center of the square. "Is that…"

"The librarian," he said in a bluster. "Kai and Bailefore with him."

Past the barricade of whirling luxiron and snarling beasts, he spotted the flash of ocher robes atop the wedding platform. Hachiro cringed behind Captaen Bailefore. He nearly blended into the spreading wildfire, as the shadowman slashed his iridescent wraiths in mesmerizing, downward arcs, hacking away at the abominable swarm clawing up over itself from the gravel, as though the creatures were one beast instead of a dozen. From the other end, Kai was retreating toward them when a creature scraped its way onto the platform. It dropped on all fours, its advance uneven and predatory.

Wherever the librarian was, their king would be close by. Dmitri needed every warrior he had. Hastily, Zaethan scanned the battle raging in the gap.

Ira would never make it on foot.

"Get on." Zaethan squatted before the yancy. "Rhaolé ono, or I'm leaving you behind."

The hesitation was short lived. Ira leaped onto his back, interlocking his ankles and arms in tight, terrified loops about Zaethan's torso—armed with a dull spoon ladle in hand. Zaethan snorted. Like that'd help. Though on second thought, he hitched his weight higher and scoured the base of the holdreheiim, until he uncovered a large, discarded pot lid.

Gripping it by the knob, Zaethan raised it as a shield just below the level of his eyes. His swallow was hard against the restraint of Ira's forearm. Zaethan hooted to his Darakaian warriors. Flanking him, they pressed forward together and into the havoc.

Evil encircled them. Whatever was fueling the demons, it never stopped. Was never satisfied. Was never extinguished.

She'd called them "devoid." He understood it now; they fed on nothing and everything at once.

The platform stood only a stone's toss away, but by Zaethan's odds, it might as well have been on another continent. Blood seeped down his thigh. A gash across his elbow weakened his grip on the kuerre. Another throb tore through his hip, feeling as if Ira had somehow gained fifty pounds. Adrenaline pumping through his veins, Zaethan threw their conjoined weight to the left, their momentum hurling his blade into another creature's entrails. Sick secretions gushed when he drew the kuerre up through its ribcage, splicing the heart.

Zaethan seized his hipbone with a frustrated moan. Under beads of sweat, he narrowed his eyes toward the reputed heavens, biting his tongue from cursing it.

At Jabari's threatening ululations, Zaethan instinctively swerved on his heel. He flipped the pot lid and drilled it into a cavern of barb-like teeth. Foul, dark saliva slid down the wood in sticky rivulets as the thing ravenously snapped its incisors. Holding it at bay, he yelped in disgust when a flurry of horned beetles scuttled out of its blackened throat and raced toward him over the sticky dribble.

Zaethan hated beetles, especially the kind that bred in the bellies of the dead.

From under his nose, a stick darted out and jabbed the creature in its leathery forehead. As it dissolved into dust, he saw the weapon was Ira's soup ladle.

Using it, he flicked a beetle off Zaethan's bicep. "I am *not* limp-wristed," the yancy haidren shrilly declared in his ear, twirling the tool like an imperial scepter.

Ira's grip constricted, and he jabbed Zaethan in the clavicle.

Breaking from the melee, a devoid creature dragged a shadowman by his leg, then ripped it clean off the way a rabid dog would rip its kill. The highlander's screams breached the bedlam and tragically broke. Spitting out the limb, the creature slunk round. Its eyes gleamed, their permanence paranormal, like a dead man's rubies from an under-world unknown.

It bent its neck at an impossible angle and issued a chilling screech.

Then hurtled straight toward them.

It eluded his first swing, and the devoid's talons slipped in the contaminated slush underfoot. Zaethan threw a leg over its back and spiked the kuerre through its eroded scalp. The Northern iron blistered brain and gristle. With a shove, it spewed sludge into the snow.

"Look out!" Ira cried.

Revolving, Zaethan bashed his pot lid into another disfigured face. Cartilage crunched. Fractures splintered down the crude shield, and the ferocious creature busted through the battered halves. Black claws hooked around each hunk of wood. Its tongue writhed, tasting the air in front of Zaethan's brow.

A chip of metal exploded from its crushed snout. Sooty powder showered before him, and he swiftly caught the arrow—the fletching helical and of longtail pheasant.

"Shtàka…" sputtered Zaethan at the Andwele feathers. He instantly looked up into the throng. "Sadik! Yhona!"

He staggered toward them, the limp worsened by the slash in his leg. Yhona, outfitted in mire and her Darakaian buckskins, sank against Zaethan's widespread arms. Fiercely, he kissed her crown of slinky braids. Sadik too. Wrapping around the siblings, he brought the three of their heads in together.

"This is charming." Ira stroked his cheek with the ladle. "I so relish seeing this side of you, Zaeth."

Whacking it away, Zaethan hitched the yancy with an *oomph*. "To the platform," he told the warrior pair. "The king must be near."

Training snapped them into motion. Joining with Jabari and Takoda, they pegged their backs against one another, and as a unit, kopar beside kuerre, they drilled farther into the hysteria.

The rhythm of home overtook his fatigued limbs. Alongside his Darakaian comrades, the drumming of war lifted the soles of his feet, strengthening their reflex. Zaethan gritted his teeth and swerved, putting weight on his bum leg when he cut a devoid at the knees, Jabari shattering its skull before the decomposing torso hit the ground. Another instantly replaced it. Terrible talons sliced him over the ribs, flaying Ira's upper thigh in the same attack. The yancy haidren wailed at his first taste of profound pain.

All at once, blades of opal swept in and upward, quartering the creature. Onyx gore splattered the fair-haired fighter as he caught a second devoid on the tip of his crescent wraith and drove it through a third. The shadowman nodded at Zaethan—whom he'd just saved— and whirled away.

Fighting beside the ruthless, alien najjan, armed with their other-worldly speed and steel, it was abundantly clear: he was nothing but a man caught between realms. And Zaethan was afraid.

Yet he feared for his friend—his sovereign, his better half— even more.

His bootheel touched the bottom step. Battering his way up the boards, Zaethan stole an unpromising glimpse over the multitude, seeing that his prydes were scattered and lost among the carnage. Feathers flew, flecks of turquoise flashed, and kopars clanked.

They needed their alpha. And he couldn't spare him. From the edge of the platform, Zaethan let out an enraged war cry over the square.

From the across the battle, their whoops met his. Aggrieved yet invigored, Zaethan turned his back on his people.

Bodies… More bodies than he'd expected littered the wedding stage. Some were strewn over the gilded bowls, their Boreali blood streaming in offering to the Depths.

"Alpha Zà!" shouted Kai, kicking a creature's severed member off the wood. "Thank the Fates—"

"Hachi is unharmed?" Zaethan demanded and deposited Ira unceremoniously. He cricked his spine like a turtle freed of its shell.

The shoto'shi poked around Kai's athletic frame, swinging his head back and forth. Animated by his uncontrollable blinking, Hachiro indicated the fat journal he'd used to barricade his vulnerable middle. "While improbable, I'm delighted to report that neither are the annals…"

"Well done, Hachi." While sarcastically said by Zaethan, the shoto'shi stood taller. Zaethan then addressed the captaen. "Bailefore. The Quadren is in your debt."

Bathed by the slaughter, Bailefore resembled every bit the vengeful spirit from Darakaian ghost stories as he tore himself away from the brink of the platform to regroup. "Niit. The debt is null, Lord Haidren," he replied. His grim, blue eyes pierced Zaethan. "We serve the king and those in his care."

"And those in his care," Zaethan echoed in rare accord.

An arrow whizzed past Bailefore's clenched jaw and landed in a creature scraping its way up the risers with only one arm and half a leg. It rented a bloodcurdling screech. The arrow had just missed its heart.

Bailefore twisted, winding his wraiths, and shaved its neck off its emaciated shoulders. Bent over, he quickly unsaddled a quiver from a shadowman who no longer needed it.

"Try these next time." He tossed Sadik the bundle of luxiron arrowheads. "The corrosive point will eat at the tissue until it reaches your mark."

"Zullee." Sadik accepted it with honor and nocked one. The highland weapon refracted the pastel flames in the overarching basin as well as the oranges rapidly spreading throughout the square.

Suddenly, a burst of dawn exploded beyond the fountain. Zaethan covered his eyes before it blinded him. He grabbed Hachiro when the boards popped nails and a tremor ripped the earth beneath the platform.

Where there was light, so was she.

Squinting back involuntary tears, he combed the masses and found her crouching over their king.

"Dmitri! Dmitri, I'm coming!" Zaethan screamed until he was hoarse. But once he was about to spring, someone seized his bicep.

He spun, irate.

It was Ira. The thin yancy held on with one hand and rattled his bronze snuff canister in the other. "You can't, Zaeth. I swore we'd stay together!"

Zaethan's brow puckered, and he shoved him off.

"Listen, I don't like it either, but the king is safest at *her* side." Bailefore stepped defensively toward Zaethan to tighten their makeshift squadron. "If anyone survives the night, it'll not be us but them."

A deafening boom interrupted his argument. They swerved northward toward the Grand Tabernacle and found a newfound horror trapped upon its great, winding stair.

Stories up, dozens of little children, and mothers carting their infants, were bottlenecked along the passage to the sacred place. Gigantic boughs had fallen and shattered, blocking them from ascending any higher behind a massive blaze. Their precarious position was girded by elders as well as the Clann Darragh. It was a safety protocol gone awry.

The cubs could not descend in retreat to the square, for the beasts were crawling up the stairs, hungrily pursuing the group closer to the flames. There was no escape. The altitude offered them too great a jump, even for the men.

At the lowest point, Luscia's father boosted his blade and brought the backsword down savagely. From Zaethan's place on the platform, it appeared the other leaders were unarmed. With a single sword to defend them, Boreal's Clann Darragh was all that stood between the innocent and the devoid.

There was a great cracking, and fragments of more holdreheiim crashed onto the stair, already aflame. Cinders went flying, and the intensified screams stole the attention of more creatures nearby. As if summoned, they scrambled like locusts and started up the surrounding trunks toward the heralding cries of much younger prey.

Zaethan's grip steeled around the hilt of the kuerre. He pivoted back toward his king, his indecision fleeting. His hip throbbed in raw opposition.

Bailefore had spoken true; Dmitri was safest in her care.

But what of everyone else?

On the ground, a warning rang out. High-pitched whinnies foretold the stampede mere moments before the horses barreled out from the holdreheiim stable. Burning bark showered the animals' terrified escape. Broken straps and bits hung off their snouts when they plunged into the mass of raging bodies.

The devoid dived for the first unlucky steeds, but a chestnut stallion leaped over a fallen horse, galloping toward Zaethan.

"Kai, Takoda, Jabari, defend the haidrens. The rest save the cubs. Sadik, with me!" he declared and ran alongside the platform edge. With the archer on his heel, Zaethan launched onto the stallion.

Sadik landed seconds after. The archer swung his legs around to ride reverse, his Northern quiver bolstered between them. Zaethan buried his fingers in the horse's mane. Bareback, he kicked it urgently. Over his shoulder, Bailefore rode a white mare fiercely behind them, Yhona spotting him with her bow.

Dipping his upper body, Zaethan slashed the kuerre through a barrier of devoid, the acidic blade searing their decay in one fell swoop. Bailefore gained and advanced past him as the Grand Tabernacle sharpened through the smoke. Its gem-encrusted pillars sparkled like jewels on a tombstone.

Nearing the lowest point of the stone stair, Sadik's protection was wrenched off the horse. Yhona wailed, a sound so awful, it panicked Zaethan to the core. He jerked the chestnut around.

He slid off the instant he did.

Gurgling on his own blood, Sadik lay torn open where a creature was gorging on his entrails. Hatred colored Zaethan's vision as it locked on the thing's bright-red eyes. He sprinted toward his warrior and slid through the gravel. Zaethan swerved on his shins and thrust the backsword up into the devoid's heart.

Dust fell upon Sadik as the deep, lively color of the Andweles melted from his slackened face.

Zaethan roared in fury. His archer was already gone and spent for whom? No Boreali would ever grasp the value of the man who, on their own soil, took his last for those who smeared him a *pagan*. Darakaians were braver because they were more breakable. To the highlander, he was profane. To Zaethan, and to history, he was valor—a warrior who had sacrificed without hesitation. He ripped a button from his jacket and grabbed Sadik's forearm. Quickly, he cut a deep slit and let it flow, capturing the stain across the rare metal.

"For Zwaàlu Ghopar. Your memory will mark our Kindred Bridge," he hoarsely vowed and pocketed the button. Swiping the quiver of sparkling arrowheads and the Darakaian bow, Zaethan surged to his feet and into motion.

Atop the stallion, he reached the tabernacle stairs. A quaking mass of dark figures plagued the bottommost steps.

"This way. Make haste." Bailefore beckoned from where he and Yhona had climbed farther up the broad, curving banister.

Behind the captaen's nimble ascent, the landscape unraveled as they got higher. Roüwen was burning. The ornamented well wishes of its citizens were collapsing from the canopy like falling stars. Swing bridges sizzled in tatters, sliding down the image of Tiergan.

Smoke suffocated the skies. "Àla'maia has turned her face." Yhona sobbed for her brother ahead of Zaethan. "The Fates have forsaken us…"

He pulled her back by the shoulder. "We never needed them," Zaethan declared. Snatching her chin, he twisted it toward the flashes of ethereal light among the ghastly haze, where wielding a higher power, Luscia still covered their king. With his thumb, he wiped Yhona's undereye. "Grief later. Kwihila now."

"Uni zà, Alpha Zà." She steeled her trembling lips and took off faster after Bailefore, a partly empty quiver bobbing against her sweat-soaked spine.

Steam rose from the bark in his periphery. It cloaked the holdre-heiim with the reek of bile and demise. Though the great tree seemed unwilling to burn, fire littered the rising steps in blazoned ribbons as the limbs of other holdreheiim continued to snap.

Finally, they reached the harrowing chokepoint.

The Clann Darragh was a gatekeeper, warring within a passage so narrow between two smoldering piles of wood, his sleeves were catching flame. He yelled, in agony and wrath, as he wildly hacked at the creatures. "Clear the path for the children!" Boreal's leader ordered them between strikes when Bailefore slowed to help him.

Eyes wide, Zaethan jumped over the busted boughs and chased after the captaen, cutting down the devoid attempting to follow through the licking flames. Mothers shrieked backward, pulling their crying bundles closer. An elder, the female from the inlands, dived out and pushed the last creature away from the cubs and over the edge. Round, tear-stricken faces watched Zaethan pass along the banister, their little destinies left to the courage of three renegades against a deadly legion.

Huddled along the opposite end was a group of the elders, many branded by the same colorful yarns. At first glance, Zaethan thought them heroic—unarmed, the first defense behind the bookending fire. But he soon realized the truth: those elders had been the first to flee.

The children were their buffer.

A huge, flaming log lay across the breadth of the steps. After Yhona, Zaethan hopped down from the banister on the other side. His assessment was immediate. By the time they sawed through, it'd be too late.

"Watch out. Huwàas in the heights!" shouted Yhona, pointing upward, where scurrying along the outspread boughs, the devoid were beginning to descend.

"We have to douse it somehow." Bailefore stripped off his coat. He beat the blaze with it but to no avail.

Zaethan whacked him with the bow. "The dust! You drive them over, and we'll make it rain!"

At the idea, Bailefore's sapphire eyes ignited, and he dashed up the stairs and around the bend toward the foremost veranda.

"Get back!" Zaethan hollered to the people.

Getting into position, he and Yhona nocked their arrows. They stared into the curling smoke where it thickened. A whistle rang out. Immediately, a creature was rammed over the edge and came writhing from above.

Expertly, Yhona's arrow sank into its decayed skull. Zaethan lowered his bow, grabbing the feet to yank the thing over the tail end of the log. Dust showered the blackened bark.

His shot struck the next. Alternating with Yhona, they compounded the dead, slowly but surely suffocating a portion of the blaze.

"Alpha Zà, the rear," warned Yhona. In the other direction, she snapped her bow in repeated strikes. A ruckus could be heard from the veranda too.

Together, the elders had started to heave the smothered part of the log off the banister. Children were already trying to wiggle to freedom through a narrow fissure between the stone and the slanted log. An earsplitting shriek sounded right behind Zaethan. He tossed his bow and unsheathed the kuerre. Protectively, he threw out his arm to barricade the cubs.

The creature's fangs anchored into the meat of his forearm. The cubs squealed. Zaethan cried in agony as the worst torment he'd ever experienced charred through his veins. His tendons seized, and his grip surrendered, relenting the kuerre over the edge. Weaponless, Zaethan twisted and repeatedly punched the devoid as hard and relentlessly as he could. But its jaws only tightened, threatening to snap the bone.

Furiously, he called out to the High One while claws filleted his skin. "Help me!"

"Lord Haidren!" Bailefore answered, unseen.

Zaethan bashed the creature against the barrier and looked up into the darkening vapors. Suddenly a beam of refracting light fell from the heavens. Biting back the pain, he reached for the hilt.

And caught the wraith by the middle.

Without hesitation, he thrust the najjani blade into the abomination's heart, impaling a cavity of mutation and rot. The creature burst into dust. He pulled away, alive and astonished. Zaethan raised the crescent wraith—a weapon so revered, it was despised—while the log was dislodged and the Boreali broke through in droves.

Yhona backed into him, gulping for air. Blood spilled from slices running from her temple to her chin. The doors to the Grand Tabernacle were heard thundering apart, and more cubs rushed by the two Darakaians toward the refuge. He leaned over the banister and searched the square as snow came down over Roüwen in fat, wet clumps.

The battlefield was scarce, but for the slain.

Using his teeth, Zaethan made a tourniquet for his arm with his belt. He slung it around Yhona's limber shoulders, which upon his embrace heaved and shuddered. As he held her under his chin, the tears for her brother finally broke.

Out of nowhere, Bailefore madly came barreling down the stair, skipping steps at a time.

Moments later, Zaethan heard a penetrating cry from below. He slid from around Yhona and disembarked after the captaen. Stories lower, Zaethan stopped in his tracks.

His breath deserted him.

Shadowmen had assembled securely around their haidren, who on a bed of blood and snow was rocking on her knees before the fallen Clann Darragh.

His body lay burned, linsilk singed to his seared skin. Hefts of his muscle hung loose, devastated by the demon scourge. But that was not what had summoned her torrent of tears.

There was a luxiron knife standing out from his chest.

"Ana'Mere!" Luscia wailed for help, her hands trembling over his wounds as if she didn't know where to begin. Her words cracked and gushed, pouring with moisture over her dead father, as she called for her aunt again and again and again.

But no one came.

A shadowman with long silvery hair broke through the others. He dumped his wraiths to the ground. In stark alarm, he scratched at his heart and disbelievingly stated, "I cannot find Ana'Mere."

CHAPTER FORTY TWO
LUSCIA

While they were young, Orien Darragh would often steal away his children on the days his wife did not protest it, to journey them far beyond the conventions of men. It was there in the highland wilds where he taught them how to tune their ears to a single leaf flapping in the wind. Yet in all those years, not once had he ever taught them how to listen—or what to hear—if the wind was ever extinguished.

Though the nature bordering the stark meadow swished, Luscia could not harken to its sound. To her, all surrounding air had been stripped but for the rasp of leather and linsilk each time her brother tried to beat away his tears.

Luscia had none left to shed. Raw as sandpaper, her eyelids stuck together whenever she blinked.

Sorrow flanked the siblings where they stood before their father's unlit pyre. It drew her limbs heavy as if weighted to the cold ground. She'd no strength. The thought of a meal repulsed her. That murderous knife might as well have landed in Luscia's gut.

Roüwen had gathered to honor him outside the city limit—those who could walk the distance through the rubble. They had wrapped her father in clean linen to conceal his mangled form upon a bed of fir. He'd been lowered partly into the ground, just deep enough for his memory to take root. In countered circles, a pair of moss-cloaked sages scattered the body of their Clann Darragh with seed.

A task that should have been performed by her aunt.

With both Boreali giants taken in one night, she and Phalen had been made orphans on three accounts. An empty niche had been dug on either side of Orien Darragh. One to represent his wife. The other, the sister who'd preserved her legacy. Alora wasn't their mother—but nearly, and in the ways that counted.

Luscia sniffed harshly, reflecting on each parent. She'd lived the curse of the first, the joy of the second, and the disappointment of the third.

Death had only sealed it so.

Aksel sat against her thigh. With his damp muzzle, he prodded her limp hand and emitted a slow whine. The massive lycran was a fearsome fixture between Luscia and her king. The Quadren formed a somber line behind them. Beside her, Dmitri watched on as the sages finished their sowing and gestured for the najjani master to depart his station next to Phalen.

Master Rohan shared beautiful verses, though she scarcely perceived them. That too should have been her aunt's obligation.

Emerging from the vast ring of citizens, the widows of Roüwen stepped out and onto the untread meadow, its joyful colors dormant beneath winter's blanket. The seniormost of their association removed a fur-lined hood over her white plait and sang. Her frail voice led the dirge of the fallen, sang as much for Orien Darragh as those who'd perished before him. Together, the women lifted Boreal's lamentations to Aurynth.

Their haunting melody carried across the highlands. In the distance, clouds rose off the alps as if they were on fire, but instead of flame, there was fixedness and the eternal frost clinging to their caps. Luscia's heart could have been cut from the peaks. For when the Elder Enclave replaced the widows, it became hard and cold.

Bearing their ceremonial torches, the elders came forth and lit them in a blazing urn that held the ashes of the najjan, collected from the square. Luscia kept her gaze locked on her father's bundled feet, where alongside his betrayer, they formed a circle about his body.

Not one could ever fill his footsteps. While great, Orien Darragh had never wanted to lead. Yet he'd led as if it was for that unwanted purpose he'd been born.

The torches lowered, and Luscia's exhalation roughened.

Dmitri gently wrapped her arm around his. "Fight it, Lady Boreal," he said with a cough into the secret space between them, his lips blocked by the ample scruff of his fur cloak. "Bitterness is the root of defilement. Give it no ground, lest it corrupt you whole."

Steadily, Luscia twisted toward his reddened nose, pointed down at her.

Loss wreathed his hazel eyes. Dmitri suppressed his next cough, his olive complexion waning on its borrowed time. The lines had deepened around his mouth, not from laughter but atrophy and grief. A part of him had never recovered from losing his own father.

Luscia wondered what part was about to burn away with hers.

It was barely a nod, yet she gave it in deference, and with her other hand, she caught Phalen's calloused fingers. Without hesitation, her brother seized her lifeline. Although heads taller, he was still a boy, left just as alone—if not more so—than she.

The elders touched their torches to the body. Instantly, iridescent flame sprang from the layer of seeds, sprouting a fog of sparkling spores. It rose in tendrils. The spicey aroma stemmed over their people. Her father's formidable frame crumpled under the fragrance of heaven, a tangible totem of their foretold reunion. The son of herdsman, he'd held her entire world upon his broad shoulders; he was the only man to never regret her. The last vestige of moisture cascaded Luscia's cheek.

She'd have to suffer a lifetime before she could tell him just how much she loved him.

The elders rotated toward their haidren, as did all those present from their House. In silence they waited.

Luscia closed her eyes and harnessed her strength. Aksel's voluminous tail tapped her upturned boots in tempo with her beating heart. Boosting her chin, she declared as loudly as she could, "Onymn'fierï, weh iishra dahir."

In nature's echo chamber, the Boreali recited the burial verse across the meadow.

Planted by fire, we bloom evermore.

Retreating, the elders gave way to a team of najjan, who shoveled the hard, mineral-rich dirt into the shallow niches. Minutes passed before the flames disappeared with her father's silhouette.

Dmitri repositioned his cane and curled closer. His question came hesitantly. "Meh-meh fyreon, Lady Boreal, for my ignorance... but why do we quench his pyre?"

"Because the fire has played its purpose," Luscia whispered. "The seed only opens once it is burned. We are standing in the most vivid, bountiful field on the entire peninsula."

Before her reply could trail off, the buddings of green had already begun to push through the soil, despite the frost. They stood there and beheld the mystery a while, as Roüwen's mourners took their leave in solemn clusters. She knew it was the end on this side of the veil, but it took everything within her to walk away.

Finally, Luscia nudged her feet forward.

Her king's stride faltered. Wheezing, Dmitri's weight slanted into her hold, and he regarded her with a bereaved smile. "Know that just once, Luscia, I wish it could be me who was supporting you."

Luscia somberly traced the grooves of the venerated chair, feeling the old markings along the arm made by their forebears, the ancients who'd believed every good thing traced its root to the Dönumn—to the source—and that if their descendants simply abided in that covenant, all would be well.

Yet next to nothing was well.

Good had only triumphed by principle and marginal number.

Her lashes lifted lethargically as Luscia drifted her eyes back toward the elder chancel. The Grand Tabernacle had survived the raid, though another attack from within was rapidly unfolding. The Enclave's debate had migrated from the issue of Bastiion and back to the subject of her father's office.

Not the butcher who'd removed him from it. That would be too vulgar, directly following his funeral.

Nor her father's title as clann. That would be too obvious. Niit, *that* the vipers would save for tomorrow or the week thereafter, for each man expertly hid his spittle, salivating over it.

The issue rather arose of an impromptu eldership appointment to replace Orien Darragh in Roüwen's congress of five. Aniell forbid they entertain matters of war and state without a warm body to fill his empty seat, each of the bureaucrats masquerading as priests.

Despicable. Every last one. She fumed inside. Luscia couldn't trust a soul up there, quarreling beneath the consecrated lanternlight.

Long-suffering, the king of Orynthia loitered behind the Prajja'Veriidim beside Master Rohan as the Enclave's arguing ensued—his most decent ally among them underground. His byrnnzite cane tapped the floor, and he covertly coughed into his shoulder, robbing her brittle gaze.

His stare was almost as sad as hers.

"Ana'Brödre," entreated Master Rohan, raising his voice with his hands in peace, despite the gravel in his battle-struck tone. "Do not be deceived. These creatures—these *devoid* beasts—have not been vanquished." In deference, he dipped his long red beard toward Luscia's podium before continuing. "The crown city could be overrun as we speak. Thoarne's throne must be retaken and upheld before all Orynthia suffers this wicked plague."

From Roüwen's star-shaped recess, Elder Tabish shook his veiny fist at Master Rohan. "So the Order of the Najjan abandons Boreal to defend another House!"

"You hear that? Thaddeus Rohan would see us invaded!" shouted Elder Yarlven across the elevated chancel. "That is if Ödetha isn't occupied by Tevaár first!"

The master washed the air of him and barked, "Tavish iron is seagrass to our own."

"But not that of a lowly farmer," said Elder Hinrük, bowing his yarn-and-wool-patterned torso as if he was one himself, instigating bellows from the inland agrarians among the lesser clans. Cut into the base of the Orallach, Clann Ciann was not renowned for something so innocent as farming.

His lackeys, elders Dagmar and Kalf, did a poor job of hiding their sneers when it was Elder Sheridwen, from Roüwen's faction, who took it a step further.

"Perhaps we leave the Unitarians to their own corruption," the middle-aged elder advised. "We should withhold the safeguard they never wanted and grant it to our own!"

Affirmations sprouted around the chancel with invigored fervor from the inlands.

In rare demonstration, Dmitri released a noise of anger, thwacking his cane in retreat to where the rest of his Quadren was huddled toward the back of the closed session. Statements were exchanged between him and the others. The king chucked the cane across the ringed floor and scrubbed his face.

Statecraft was never straightforward. And the only power a regent really had was that granted by those who observed it. Elsewise, the crown was merely a wreath of impotent metal, leveraging less impact than the pauper's plow or till.

Picking up Dmitri's cane and handing it back to him, Zaethan motioned for Luscia to do something. Yet what was there to say? How was she to convince them otherwise? The Enclave held the final say, and both Boreali law and the Orynthian Accords acknowledged it.

Alora would have known what to do, Luscia thought despondently. Her aunt always knew the right course, at least that written on paper…

Master Rohan approached her chair while the Enclave deliberated Elder Sheridwen's mildly seditious recommendation. "Drive them under the proper yoke, Ana'Sere," the master whispered in rare reproof, "before we lose them to the wrong one."

"I am not an elder" was all Luscia could say.

"They are dusklings!" Master Rohan seethed. Still-healing scabs stretched harsh and taut across the folds in his freckled skin. "*You* are the seed of wrath and bright. Consult the threads and do their bidding, Ana'Sere. Do it now."

He indignantly pushed off her podium to storm back toward his place before the Enclave. The najjani master slipped his arms into either sleeve and waited for her to act, as names for Roüwen's replacement were once again tossed into discussion. None of them were favorable to Bastiion's plight.

A flush crept up Luscia's cheeks at his criticism. Counting the seven branches of the sacred tree stitched into his linsilk robe, she blinked miserably into the Sight, harboring little hope of what she'd find there.

The veil fluttered aside, not with a jolt but softly, the way fabric was dragged off furniture years after it'd last been used. In the *Other*, lumin was weeping from the vaulted ceiling in crystalline twists. Luscia angled her face toward the ethereal glow; the threads were in mourning. Just like her.

At her attention, the licks of lumin dropped lower, coalescing into a multi-strand cord. She watched it curiously as it coiled midair and snaked into the shadow. There it hovered around a soundless najjan standing guard. Luscia's lips parted. In the dimness, his clear-blue eyes tensed at her questioningly.

She was not an elder.

Nor did she need to be.

Suddenly, Luscia stood. "I appoint Marek Bailefore the next elder of Roüwen."

Her husky voice reverberated throughout the tabernacle, blotting out any other noise. The lumin laced about Marek's temples as if reacting to his thoughts. Though bewildered, he dutifully exited the shadow and humbly padded toward the center.

The lanternlight kissed the captaen's crimson head. And in an instant, the men's shouting resumed, more thunderous than before.

"The haidren shall not govern the Enclave," croaked Elder Ejnarök for Roüwen, a whistle at the end of his words. "In my day, your grandfather surely knew that!"

"Don't you see? The daughter of Tiergan doesn't wish to relinquish her family's hold over this body, Brödre." Elder Hinrük prowled from Ciann's grouping and onto the brightest, more-prominent portion of the chancel. "The only reason Orien Darragh was voted clann was because at the time, his wife was not sitting in his daughter's place."

Luscia's spine went stiff, and she held her ground atop the podium. "I welcome you to revisit our Boreali bylaws, Elder Hinrük. Your haidren retains the right to appoint one elder from each clan during his or her lifetime. I employ one of mine today."

The zealot's blocky face puckered, rumpling the slit stones embedded in his splotchy cheeks. "Convenient that the chosen is your suitor. Is that what the High One ordained? For one family to monopolize so much power?"

Those from Ciann clapped, emphasizing their agreement. Their praise clung to him like maggots on a corpse while he inched down the top of the widening steps. In a flickering web, the lumin descended alongside him. More threads spooled under the rim of the chancel beneath the notorious spot where he'd stopped.

Hinrük had planted his feet in the space normally occupied by the high clann. He elevated his square chin as if he'd already garnered the votes.

Her father's death had given him the perfect opportunity to use them.

Luscia's breathing sped, and the lumin shuddered with her rough intakes. "We must break through this one-sided reasoning, meh brödre," she said levelly, despite the clamping of her fists.

"Break through a wall, you might just get bitten by a snake," Hinrük replied.

She felt her eyes flash with long-denied rage. The threat wasn't hidden. It was openly touted with the casual lace of his stout arms. Although he ate well, given the hardship of his people and the swell overtop his belt, his bony shoulders poked through the wool. The Enclave silenced themselves, utterly fixed onto the exchange. "For too long we've overlooked these compromises. Boreal's garden must stay pure."

Snapping into erratic shapes, the dazzling threads quivered about her ankles when Luscia dragged herself down the steps of her podium with predatory grace. "Beware the snake in the garden who calls himself a saint. Your clan was the most pagan before Tiergan. Did you think we would forget its dark practices? Ciann is the reason they"—she pointed at where Dmitri had assembled with his foreign Quadren—"have been afraid of us for five hundred years! Your piety strips nothing away, for your conviction is self-seeking and dead. Be zealous, wem, Ana'Brödre. Be zealous in this: we must ransom ourselves for our king and those supporting him, march with them into Bastiion, and flesh out his traitors!"

Luscia came between Marek and Master Rohan, where on the testament side of the altar, they together stood in the gap between her forefathers and her failed sovereign.

Behind the panel of inscribed wood, Hinrük showed his teeth. "All this from an eighteen-year-old girl."

"Woman, Elder Hinrük."

"One who thinks her reflection will sway wisdom twice her age." He scoffed, gesturing up and down. Arrogance greased his expression. "It may enthrall a prince, but this Enclave is not so fleshly as your devotees or your heathen… traveling partners."

It was not Unitarian royalty to which he'd referred and brandished like a sword. His fellows murmured about her Tavish brand behind him. Hinrük would have never treated Alora so irreverently. However, his allegiance to her seemed to have vanished with the sil'haidren, for he was with the Enclave and not Emiere, nor one of the dozens of other search parties.

Fire burned up the reach of her scar, and Luscia froze. Yet shame wicked off her spirit when the lumin abruptly unspun from under the chancel. It rose higher in threatening shoots. Breaking through the root, a thick, glittering cord more radiant than the rest snaked over the half wall. Luscia tracked the harbinger thread to where it targeted a lumpy pocket in Hinrük's elaborate tunic.

She'd been looking for something.

Righteous wrath displaced all shame.

Luscia drifted up to the Prajja'Veriidim and the three bowls sitting atop it. Her hands fell upon the uncut stone, an altar fashioned not by men but their Maker.

There, she suggestively ran her fingertips along the thin luxiron blade.

"Do you know why Aniell made me beautiful?" Luscia boldly asked the hypocrite. "It's so that when I speak of Him, Elder Hinrük, you will pay attention. For the High One has spoken to me, many times over. Now, *relent and reach*... into your pocket... and expose the contents before your brethren."

In unison, the Enclave twisted toward him. Hinrük paled, but his arm did not move.

"Relent. And reach," she commanded again through her teeth.

His veins bulged more prominently. The hypocrite shakily dipped into the multicolored cloth and produced his closed fist. Wildly, the harbinger thread encircled it, gaining speed.

Luscia could feel its momentum spinning her blood.

"When I found my father, his killer had stolen off his hand his two most prized possessions," she feverishly said. "The first, a ring fashioned by my mother. The other, by our forebears—the symbol of his position as clann.

"Open your hand, Hinrük."

"Wem, he must show us!" someone bellowed among the Enclave.

Whispers whooshed her ears in haunting harmonies. Within the *Other*, the lumin emitted a searing light around his stippled skin, and like a clam under the sun, his fist winched apart. Gasps permeated the tabernacle.

There, in his palm, shone a heavy luxiron ring, set with the same gems as the pillars outside.

"I only found him!" Hinrük declared, his heels creeping back toward the elders. "I merely wanted to preserve the token for the next clann!"

"*Liar.*"

The Logoth's voice shook the walls, though it was only Luscia who heard its spoken verdict. Her pale hair floated in her periphery. "Liar," she said, reciting its word.

As she did, the harbinger thread wound around Hinrük's neck and, to the terror of the Enclave, seized him up off the chancel like a puppet doll. Hoisting his short legs over the altar of unhewn stone, a golden bowl bordered his either foot. Thin spindles of water pattered into their bases from above. The truth of creation rained into one, the truth of Aurynth into the other.

The bone-dry bowl of rock waited to be quenched.

Hinrük's eyes doubled in fear at the lengthy, corrosive blade she held in her grasp. He clawed at the unyielding harbinger thread, unseen by the elder and his peers, as it choked his appeal. "Bolaeva—Ana—Sere—Innocent—Just—"

The Logoth spoke before Luscia could brandish the blade.

"Murderer."

She screamed when a beam of blazing light tore open his chest, pouring forth the fruit of his heart—the truth of mankind. Hinrük's jaw quailed as scarlet bathed his lying tongue, dripping past the harbinger thread's brilliance and into the central bowl.

Aghast, Luscia stumbled backward. Both Marek and Master Rohan leaped out of her way. The men were staring at the living wood underfoot. Their fearful gazes climbed the walls.

Patterns of light illuminated the stanzas that curved with the tabernacle in rising tiers. But the source wasn't coming from the veridaedill or the mound of testimony. The light refracted off from the harbinger thread, on either side of the veil.

In fright, the Enclave absorbed that Hinrük was guilty. Those from Clann Ciann showed the backs of their hands and tapped their glowing talï in ritual prayer.

The High One had painted the proof for all to *see.*

The harbinger thread retracted itself, and the corpse flopped onto the floor. Filling her vision, the commanding lumin wavered before her eyes. The harbinger thread took its tip and tapped the solrahs in Luscia's septum. Warm static pricked along her entire body when the luxiron fell back against her skin.

Stunned, she slowly turned, the harbinger with her.

The newly appointed Elder Bailefore hurriedly fell into step behind.

Luscia ignored his pace. It was anxious, as was the look on her king's face. Drawn and wane, Dmitri clasped his cane as if it were a fencepost. His other haidrens cowered behind Zaethan's protective stance. He mouthed something at her, but she disregarded it. There was nothing left to hide anymore.

She was the seed of wrath and bright.

Anchoring her sights on the double doors, she took her strides toward the freedom of day. The harbinger thread descended upon Luscia's shoulders and clothed her in a majestic stole, not one of fox or hare but of pure, unadulterated light.

Cross-legged on the charred floorboards, she blinked in and out of the Sight, meditating on the stark contrast between worlds. The old bed was scooted off from the burnt wall. Her mother's script was on full display where it had been carved into the exposed wood. On the natural side of the veil, Eoine's writings were black and tarnished. Unpromising. Dead.

Again, Luscia blinked, and the same message shined, the coarse grooves embossed with lively lumin.

There came a knock on the doorframe.

Phalen entered without invitation and sat in the same manner, touching their knees. His plaits loose, his blond hair fringed the bottom of his ear as her brother lowered his face in consideration.

She didn't tell him who'd inscribed the message. Phalen would recognize the author.

He looked at his sister.

Atop her thighs, Luscia lay her palms bare. Hinrük's blood still stained the creases. Phalen must have heard, by then, of the reluctant testimony and their haidren's part in it. At his sound of understanding, she curled her fingers inward.

Phalen readjusted and looped his forearms around his legs. Sadness and grief cloaked his curved postured. "Did I ever tell you what Fappa said the day he took that man's hand?" He needn't indicate the bed, for the memory was scorched into them both—when their father had charged into their manor, his shoulders slumped and the front of his tunic soaked by the justice he'd taken on his daughter's behalf.

Luscia shook her head.

"He told me, 'Son, goodness is truly good. But that does not make it safe.'"

Giving no reply, she blinked back into the *Other*. Threads of lumin streamed toward the underboards. The light sealed every flaw and divot in the wood, repairing whatever it passed toward the carved text. It was beautiful as it was deadly.

Each strand radiated wrath.

Each strand radiated mercy.

"What's it like?" Phalen murmured toward what he could not yet see.

Another two years of boyhood, and his adult eyes would see it all too well. Luscia made a noise of irony. Her father had had no idea.

"The lumin is good. But it is not safe." Her lips trembled when she asked him faintly, "What is to become of me, Phalen?"

Her brother offered her a saddened yet sympathetic shrug, inclining his muscled frame at their mother's message. "I think that was prophesied a long time ago, Ana'Sere. Lux aemida hen. Hen mii'orr vida," he read aloud and bumped his shoulder against hers. "Whatever she is—whoever she's to become—the Light is within her. *She will not fall.*"

CHAPTER FORTY THREE
ZAETHAN

The cuts were deep, like ugly crags in the clay. Minty moss had been packed down Jabari's back, where the devoid had narrowly missed his spinal cord. Having popped out of the quilt, the warrior's gangly toes twitched against the bitter draft that swept through the open infirmary. He would still walk.

Eventually.

Zaethan shuffled aside for the healer to sponge the rest of Jabari's upper body free of debris. Her elderly hands shivered with age as she worked under the attentive watch of a Darakaian alpha and his superstitious beta. On wiry knees, the gray-eyed healer stacked her bowls of green paste, then dipped her veiny finger into the saucer of oil. Tapping some onto the unconscious warrior's either temple, she soothingly whispered to him in witchtongue.

"No spells!" Kumo lurched forward, scaring the woman off.

But Zaethan showed his hands obligingly. "Thank you—erm," he said, bowing awkwardly as he tried to recall the phrase. "Tadöm. Tadöm…" He smacked Kumo's middle to do the same.

"Eh, you want to be in a Boreali's debt, Ahoté?

"We already are, cousin."

Obliging, Kumo grumbled out the highland syllables, though his flexed stance didn't hide how he felt about it. The woman's bones popped as she rose from under his shadow and frightfully took her supplies to the next patient a few gurneys over.

There, she passed one who could not be revived.

Passed out, Yhona was prostrate beside her brother's bound feet. A linsilk blanket had been draped around Sadik's remains and tied as if he were a gift to the underworld. The infirmary housed not only the lame but the lost awaiting burial—for those of whom enough had been recovered to lay to rest. It served a small comfort to Zaethan, amid his bouts of rage, that Sadik had received the same consideration as Boreal's fallen najjan. For sheathed in beaded silks, their bodies too were scattered about the gurneys, more joining their number every hour. There were some wounds even the great Order of the Najjan could not withstand. A year ago, that thought would have elated Zaethan.

Now, it chilled him to the bone.

Wrapped in their own bandages, healers migrated through the infirmary, tucked under the shelter of a charred holdreheiim off the blackened square. Outside, the Boreali were sorting whatever could be salvaged from the putrid ash. The rest was to be burned. A cub would occasionally trot under the overhanging burnt roots to show a family member something he'd found. Thus, Zaethan had sent Takoda, along with Kai and the Mirajii Pryde, out to help the cleanup. For once, the Boreali had not refused them.

There was little worry about Darakaian stain after the very Depths had crossed onto their homeland. Some locals were calling it the Twilight Massacre. Others, those of an Orallach slant, had dubbed it the Wicked Wedding. But all Zaethan saw was death. And loss. And despair.

He'd brought the prydes to this place.

And they'd loyally followed him to the slaughter.

Zaethan sank across from Jabari's bed and scrubbed his face. "Shtàka. They give everything for me and get the grave in return. Meanwhile, here I sit—with a busted hip—still unscathed for their sake."

Kumo's hulking weight depressed the cot, sinking it toward the cold earth. He bumped his bandaged wrist against the dressing on Zaethan's torn bicep. The beta gestured toward the skinny Yowekaon. "He gives his life for ours. I give mine for both of yours. But you are not just alpha zà, Ahoté. You are *haidren*. Ano, your life? You lay that down for no one less than a king."

Zaethan reached across his knees to carefully pluck one of Jabari's spiraled curls out of his wound. He drifted his cross-caste fingertips lower to tuck the quilt around his warrior's puckered flesh. "Is one man's life really worth more than another's?"

"Uni zà, if the Fates have any say about it," replied Kumo.

"They don't." Hip aching, Zaethan shook out his grimace and heaved his eyes toward where his archer slept across her sibling, a sibling who was never going to wake. Sadik had protected Zaethan's back that night. But who'd been protecting his?

With his head hung low, Zaethan fiddled with one of his mother's five gilded beads clasped throughout his sable locs. Cyra's rune, crusted in dried blood, stared back.

Heart.

A haidren was never meant to play two roles. Cyra Shà never had. It was why the brave dared to whisper her name in Faraji. She'd served her king, for the good of her people, from one powerful seat. She'd committed herself completely to one cause, even to her end. The haidrenship required privilege to succeed. An alpha was to forgo his own. Serving two aims—albeit three, as ruthlessly modeled by Nyack Kasim—was hazardous. There in the infirmary plainly lay why: split priorities always favored the common denominator.

Zaethan had just never realized that it was him.

Metal scraped wood at a grating and tactless tempo. Zaethan swiped his arm across the ruined surface of the lengthy table and smacked the butter knife flat out of Hachiro's probing grasp.

"Doru," he ordered as quietly he could. "Stop that."

The shoto'shi clicked the blue lens over to the green on his monocular device. Before his bloated, magnified eye, Hachiro rubbed the sooty flakes between his forefinger and thumb. "These scorched particles don't act as they ought—"

"Neither do you," said Zaethan, ripping the contraption off him. He placed it to his left, out of Hachiro's reach.

He refrained from saying more when Arlette, the Darraghs' housekeeper, bustled through the discolored doorframe, carting another tray of whatever she could recover from the kitchen. Scooting past Kumo, Declan, Böwen, and his wife and down the line of other najjan hugging the walls, the housekeeper came between Luscia and their king. Amid the silence, she lowered the tray into the gap. A raisin loaf—toasted unintentionally—was cut into pieces and placed at the center of the table next to Dmitri's unlocked Quadrecipher.

Arlette poured a pitcher of steaming mulled wine into a fresh goblet. She set it directly before her new mistress, just as she had with the one untouched beside it. The housekeeper worriedly waited for her to take a drink.

Everyone tested a glance at their hostess, sitting mutely on the other side. An eerie glow was cast upon her hollow, unnerving features. Scattered among the discarded plates, lumilores lit the wrecked room more tellingly than the candles. The vision shown was arresting, her face an unreadable tundra. Her unbrushed hair snarled like desert cobras at her chairback. Bared in a collarless tunic, the narrative of her scar was an unadulterated exhibition, slicing a ruthless path down her neck. Her sunken eyes were as luminous as the stones—the right, an unquenchable sea, and the left, an iron storm. Luscia had her arm listlessly slung over her gigantic wolx, his piqued ears twitching under her preoccupied strokes. After the lethal spectacle within the Grand Tabernacle, they'd all granted her more breadth than normal. Even her own brother, Phalen, had scooted his chair some sensible inches in Ira's direction.

Only Captaen Bailefore risked a position right behind her.

Zaethan toyed with the ring hidden in his pocket, remembering his final interaction with the man missing from the head of her table. They'd shared a meal unlike any other. One that'd budded joy and bloomed in pain.

He didn't know how to tend that outcome. Or what he was supposed to feel after his last conversation with her. Whatever it was, it was far from the freedom he'd hoped for.

She appeared unreachable to him now, were she ever in the first place.

To Arlette's dismay, Luscia was not tempted by the cup. Her fingers instead fluttered absently in the air, as if she were picking the strings of an imagined instrument or twirling invisible ribbons in maddening circles, wherever she was trapped, deep in thought. From the hardened expression carved into her face, it was not to a dimension they should wish to follow.

Pitching her fists atop her plump hips, the housekeeper scowled, then flicked the wolx's muzzle off the table when he hungrily inched forward to steal Luscia's uneaten bread. Arlette glanced at the captaen questioningly. "Emiere?"

Bailefore scratched his brow in a rare sign of unease. "Niit, not yet," he replied.

The rest didn't need saying; the elder captaen's search party hadn't returned, meaning they'd made no discovery worthy of report. Wailing and echoes of grief were carried in through the manor's shattered window. Roüwen was faint. The Clann Darragh had departed; their celebrated sil'haidren, disappeared.

Across the Quadrecipher, Luscia continued revolving the dust floating in with the draft.

Zaethan heaved up from his slouch and slid a plate toward Dmitri, urging his friend to eat as well. Sighing, he caught the pitcher and granted himself a healthy pour of wine.

"Sober minds, Zaeth," Dmitri muttered past the fur blanket bundled under his chin.

The goblet slid out beneath him. "Then I take it I'm off the hook," said Ira, who gulped it down with a shiver. "I would like a rather unsober mind right now, thank you very much. Memory's serving a bit too sharply." The yancy paled behind his flop of mahogany hair. "Much like all those teeth…"

"We should have waited to wed." Bowing in regret, Böwen squeezed the posts of an empty chairback. His beautiful young bride consolingly stroked his blond head. "My King, you should've been on a boat far away from here. This is our fault. Se'lah Aurynth, Ana'Sere, meh fyreon. It was too much, too selfish for me to ask."

Cross-armed against the wall in the corner, his twin snorted. "Selfish."

Declan thwacked him with his plate.

"Had we left," their king replied, sloping his reddened aristocratic nose toward the warrior, "there would have been too few najjan left to protect Roüwen. Your union saved people's lives, Böwen."

From under the blanket, Dmitri reached out toward the couple. The bride clutched his thin fingers in gratitude as Böwen covered his eyes with a sob.

"Those weren't *our* people," grumbled Kumo as he pushed off the round window frame. "But eh, yet again, us Darakaians had to die."

Zaethan signaled beneath the tabletop for his beta to cool down.

Luscia's sharp, husky voice garnered their attention. "They were *your king's* people. It will please you to know that plenty of them perished too." Her pitch sank, as did the wolx's flattened ears. "Or would you prefer we count the bodies and compare?"

"Why is he even in here?" asked Noxolo.

"Because he's supposed to be," Zaethan answered curtly. He twisted the frayed, red threading that was still miraculously holding onto his wrist and caught the anxious wrinkle that darted through Dmitri's forehead. Before his friend could question it, he shot back at the snowy shadowman. "Why are so many of you?"

"Well, it's not for the refreshments. They're dreadfully short lived." Ira tipped his goblet upside down.

"I live here," said Phalen from the opposite end, where Zaethan had forgotten her brother, his chair tilted back, had his hands laced over his belting.

Across the fanned reeds, Zaethan swiveled the panther crest back and forth on the Quadrecipher. Letting go, he'd aimed the illustration more toward his beta than himself. "Fine. Then everyone tuck your kwihila back in your pants, and let's settle the issue at hand."

Hachiro was poised to write. "What's going in my pants?"

"I'll show Hachi later," Ira told Zaethan with a wink.

Captaen Bailefore leaned over Luscia. "Is it always like this?"

"Wem."

"Uni," Zaethan said at the same time. She held his gaze, emptying his stomach, before he offered it to Dmitri. "The king must regain control of Orynthia from Bastiion as soon as possible. Can the Order march tomorrow?"

It was Bailefore who confirmed. "Theoretically. But the issue is we've lost our supply."

"Captaen, we could push to Tadeas," Declan suggested, palming the braids in his carroty beard. "Take the port and its reserves. Establish a new base from which to launch?"

"Sire?" Zaethan asked, though his friend's eyes were pinned on the Quadrecipher and the angle of the panther crest. "Dmitri, your thoughts?"

He tore from the board, and looking up at Zaethan, he suppressed a cough. The winter had not let him fully recover. "The world is changing. We cannot afford to delay any further. Whatever it takes," Dmitri said to the captaen. "The people need us now."

"The war is changing too," Luscia said, her sentiment more chilling than the night air. "Are we prepared for what we might meet in the crown city? Boreal was just attacked by a horde of devoid. Undoubtedly, the Obscurer's reach stretches far beyond our naive assumptions. What if Bastiion is already consumed?"

The slashes down Jabari's back raced through Zaethan's mind. "It always haunted me… Before I killed him, Wekesa had said, 'You have your sorcerer, now we have ours.' Meme ano'qondai. I never understood it until now. If Darakai allied with the Obscurer, then how many of these creatures plague the realm?"

Jarringly, the room fell quiet and afraid.

And the wolx rumbled.

Swiftly, Luscia and her shadowmen jerked their ears at an unnatural angle, their necks twisting toward something unseen. She breathed deeply. Her nose contorted as if it'd struck something vile.

Zaethan mirrored her as he too carefully pushed away from the table. He heard the gentle whine of luxiron leaving their sheaths. Kopar in one hand and kuerre in the other, he blocked Ira. To his hip's protest, Zaethan sank his thighs into a strained crouch, and together the blended warriors steered their stances toward the shattered window.

The wind whistled, and nothing happened.

Hinges creaked, and they pivoted toward the entry. The door inched apart, then swung wide as the housekeeper scuttled backward in through the gap, her arms full of more food. She yelped when she turned. Zaethan relaxed his shoulders. Whatever was in the pot, it certainly stank. He put his gifted kuerre back in its scabbard and chuckled with the others.

A blackness soared in through the window, and a menacing figure hit the floor.

The housekeeper shrieked, dumping the pot onto the rug, as a spear of light erupted from Luscia's extended palms. Lurching to action, Zaethan targeted his kopar at the cloaked creature, alongside her guards, primed to strike.

"Don't," the thing rasped.

Shaken by the utterance—a grating, vibrating growl from its decomposing vocal chords—they watched as the pile of tattered cloth horrifyingly arose on two legs and took the shape of an average-sized man. Concealed by a hood, the dark figure daringly leveled the bottom of his shaded face up toward the crackling tip of the opalescent light-spear.

"You speak," Luscia stated.

"Wem."

The najjan gasped when it responded in their tongue.

Holding the brilliant beam steady, Luscia cautiously reached down and grabbed a lumilore off the table. More light flooded the space at her shaky exhale.

Begrimed blisters ravaged the exposed portion of his chin. Through a hole of missing skin, a visible tendon snapped with his jaw when he told her, "The haidren to Boreal cannot sail to Bastiion."

Dmitri coughed again, though likely at the rancid reek shedding from the figure before them.

Zaethan covered his mouth, and raising his kopar, he demanded, "Why the Depths not?"

The thing's snarl came threateningly. "The Obscurer has taken my mistress to Lempeii." Its hood dipped in his direction. "Stave your weapon, son of Cyra."

He knows me. Backstepping, Zaethan gulped, baffled by the mention.

"Is the Obscurer not your master?" Luscia asked with contempt. "You've the look of a leper yet the scent of the damned."

"That is because I am the firstborn of the unborn," the figure rattled in answer. "That is why I have come."

Her question was timorous. "What does your making have to do with Boreal?"

"Search it in your veins. If the Obscurer takes Alora's blood, the world will be as damned as I am." At her intake of breath, the figure tempted a step toward her. The ring of crescent wraiths clinched in response, despite his allegiance to their missing sil'haidren. The light-spear singed his deteriorated flesh, and an acrid fume bubbled off the fresh wound. "The sullied waters of the past are flowing into the streams of the present. I can no longer cross them without you."

"Truth, spoken aloud, has the power to reverse the tides—as it can the tip of this spear. You are an abomination." Behind the table, the wolx snapped his serrated fangs when Luscia pressed the light deeper into the figure's marred throat. Taint burned off him like a noxious gas. "Why should the Quadren trust you?"

If it hurt, he did not let it show. Instead, the figure reached for his ragged hood and steadily swept it back onto his hunched shoulders. Luscia's lumilore ascended as she lifted it high.

He flinched when they all recoiled from the sight.

Zaethan's eyes bulged while he inventoried the man's disfiguration. Patches of skull were presented among tufts of his hair. The ominous glow revealed he had no nose, just a cavernous void of rotting gristle. Above it, half an eyebrow was seated on a canvas of boils and battered tissue.

Settling his bloodshot eyes not on the king of Orynthia but on the shoto'shi beside him, the figure stated, "Because once, in another life, they called me the haidren to Pilar."

CHAPTER FORTY FOUR

AKITO

Akito Naborū cataloged the too-familiar face of his sister's son. He didn't contest the torment that pressed deeper into his throat. Nor could he conjure tears to fight the burning sensation as he gazed over the glaring beam. It hurt to behold the young man. Yet inexplicably, having left his shelter of shadows, he would be pained even more to stop.

He seldom permitted himself memories of Masumi. But there she sat in the rounded apples of her son's cheeks and the delicate crook of his forefinger while his thoughts whirled quickly past it. Masumi's darkly gold irises were set in the shape of her husband's stare—lilted, with a sharp humor their child didn't appear to possess. Ryoto Zou had been a rescue for her in that sense. The farther he'd taken Masumi from her lineage, and the world that'd corrupted its core, the better.

Far better off than their children would ever be.

Under Akito's acrid watch, the interim haidren's blinking worsened, becoming acute. His tics were less subtle at that age, having never suppressed them. Few could camouflage their nature with the frightening expertise of an artist painting a fishing village as if it were not a slum, editing the perceived overtop a canvas of the actual. Yet that wasn't what made such a painting valuable enough to hang in a chancellor's suite in the royal palace. The strokes had been deceivingly coarse and unrefined, fashioned not by horsehair but unwanted scrap. Such was Tetsu's brush of choice.

Akito hoped his nephew was not another tool in his collection.

"Uncle?" Hachiro sputtered, emptying of his sun-kissed color.

Stationary and indifferent, Akito was an undead man in a sanctuary of the living—empty, save the urgency that animated his aching bones. There came no impulse to shirk their weapons or capture the young haidren in familial embrace. Those instincts had perished before Masumi had ever conceived.

The overgrown wolx shoved past his nephew's chair, barking incessantly, though its extensive canines panicked the housekeeper more than their intruder. He had teeth too. And with them, he had committed greater atrocities than any Orallach hybrid.

"You—you're Akito Naborū?" asserted the sickly king, having studied his Orynthian history, certainly more than his predecessor could ever boast. Korbin's heir regally clutched his cane. Like the editors of the archives, he seemed just as adept at concealing secrets of his own. "They say you died early in my father's reign..."

Careful not to behead himself on the scorching spear of light, Akito deliberately bent with the beam and bowed in the manner of shotos for the flabbergasted King Dmitri. He cared nothing for the crown, except for how it might be brandished. His wretched body shuddered against his will. A mind made monstrous, even his most flexible sinew knew it belonged to a butcher rather than the scholar he had once been. Dipping side to side, it'd been two dark decades since he'd cracked his spine in the double undulated motion he'd last afforded to Alora.

To his beloved.

Akito would sever himself in two and be cleaved between worlds in order to bring her back to her own. He'd do the same to anyone who tried to stop him.

That was if her successor didn't do it first. Carving the light up the blistered flesh of his neck, Luscia tipped Akito's chin toward her. "The title of the devoid means nothing," she stated. Being in Alora's confidence, he knew her niece was special, that a naturally occurring mutation had multiplied the lumin within her bloodstream… although nothing so spectacular as the way she'd just folded the *Other*'s unseen threads into an immortal spear. "Ask the late Lord Ambrose how he forfeited that credibility when, like you, he traded his humanity to the Obscurer."

Fury wound wildly within her. Beneath her radiant, unmatched eyes, her grief practically foamed off her lips. She thirsted for a fight more savagely than her wolx for its next kill.

That was as good, Akito assessed. She would need that.

"Calculate the variables against the constant, Lady Haidren," he told her flatly, detaching emotion from fact. Fear—his own real, unmitigated fear—would not stoke trust, only more chaos. "Your aunt has been taken for terrible purpose. During the creatures' attack, no doubt, by the slavers Tetsu hired. My legs could not run fast enough to stop this. To warn her before it began."

"Ana'Mere is in the custody of slavers?" The stockiest najjan swore and swung his thick, wiry beard toward his neighboring najjan. "Shores of Aurynth…"

Although her weapon did not falter, Luscia's marble edges softened a fraction. "My aunt faces the skin trade?"

"Niit, it cannot be," said the firm-faced captaen. His protective stance slackened beside her.

"First a coup in lockstep with the Darakaian insurgence." Hachiro drew Akito's attention to where his quill was teetered over an open chronicle. Ink dripped with the acolyte's trembling. "Then the usurpation of the throne. Now my Uncle Tetsu is responsible for this calamity? Here, where so many innocent people were slain?"

Life's most petrifying perplexity wrinkled the bridge of his nephew's slender nose: evil was intrinsic not to numerals or equations but rather the hearts of mankind, and multiplied by that infinite human potential, evil therefore existed in an incalculable state.

Akito stood a sum of that tragedy.

"I learned too late. I tried," he said, clamping his aching gums as if he were still in that cursed boathouse. He'd made the wrong choice then, trying to save the woman in Alora's honor. Now her soul hung in the balance. "It must not have been Tetsu's first attempt. They had a woman who resembled your aunt in captivity."

There came a cry from the tallest najjan, and his crescent wraiths clattered to the floor. His periwinkle eyes widened with foolish hope. "Meh mere—my mother! She is alive! Rul'Aniell!"

Akito garnered enough pity to spare him the details. "Be comforted that she is not."

The najjan made a gagging noise and stumbled backward.

"Tetsu Naborū has my throne! Your brother already took Bastiion," the fledgling king said above the wolx's relentless barking. When he coughed, the fur blanket glided off him to showcase a frame more with-ered than his skeletal fingers had initially let on. King Dmitri shoved his hand through his dark, turbulent waves. "Why Alora Tiergan? What more could he want?"

"It's unclear, just that he is operating as a devoted agent for the Obscurer's ends. I've not uncovered who he is," Akito replied as King Dmitri's pallid lips shaped the question. "Yet every second we waste is another second he can harvest Tiergan blood for his infernal devices." Luscia's light-spear boiled the tissue of his gullet. His own charring flesh cleansed his nostrils. Akito's vocal cords vibrated against the pressure, his voice an inhuman wheeze as he cautiously directed his gloved hand through the open window toward the massacre outside. "See what the Obscurer can accomplish without the power locked in her veins."

Gruesome realization bathed their collective faces; King Dmitri laid his byrnnzite cane across the table and grievously leaned his sunken shoulders overtop it. Gregor's yancy son shrank farther back to cower behind Cyra's. The bastard reared his Southern kopar higher, as if Akito's statement had been a threat instead of a warning.

But Luscia's Tiergan eye glowed brighter, searching the space around Akito. Her head slanted as if she'd been made curious by what she saw. "The threads… They don't flee from you like the devoid. You said you are in my aunt's service?" Luscia's brows hiked, and she suddenly retracted the light-spear into nothingness. "It was you who saved me in Rian."

Akito staggered forward, clawing at his wounded windpipe. The cartilage shuddered as he tested it with a needless inhalation. Whatever had been pierced would not grow back.

"And us in the Mirajii," Cyra's son pieced aloud. With reluctant respect, he tipped his dimpled chin up at Akito in the same stiff, guarded manner his mother always had. Their likeness was off-putting.

Up close, Cyra wasn't the only one detected there.

Following Luscia's lead, the ring of weapons lowered, if only so that their bearers could retreat and shield themselves from his stench. Akito curved his mauled shoulder, unused to the sucking sensation that plucked his middle. Humiliation, he classified it. Of course, the necrosis of his walking corpse had nauseated the enclosed space. Akito knew he was rancid. Even he could scent his own reek.

But Alora never showed that she could.

Flame touched his tear ducts, though nothing came. Akito strengthened his command. "To save her, we must leave as soon as able."

"The king is to march on Bastiion—and I, with the entire Order of the Najjan, at his side." Luscia slid closer in solidarity with her sovereign. Her head shook away an apparent inner battle. "We can't afford to divert forces to Pilar, nor can we delay for them to return. Emiere will have to lead the rescue effort at our behest. He is trained and he is vigilant, and he will not rest until she is found."

Akito's fangs descended. "Obstinate child, you cannot go with the Quadren!" His baser instincts surged from his glands, and he nearly pounced over the table. A menacing rumble played from the back of his throat. It took his last iota of willpower to contain himself as he harshly entreated Alora's niece. "The only reason you still breathe is because I've safeguarded you on the darkest of nights. For no other reason than that extraordinary woman. You, Luscia Darragh Tiergan, are the one person who can feasibly penetrate the nefarious forces shrouding the Obscurer's stronghold. And as I was the first to unmake myself, I am the only one bearing knowledge of how he might be multiplying his army of creatures. You and I are leaving the House of Boreal. Because you and I are her only hope."

Luscia hung onto his gaze. Pitted priorities warred within the same tensed expression so often etched on her aunt.

The picture cut Akito; he may never see it again.

"Shtàka. How—why would you have done this to *yourself?*" whispered Cyra's son.

Saliva ran the length of his incisors as Akito twisted toward him animalistically, then toward the object of his clear desire where she stood across the room. In desperation, he couldn't keep the misery from his grated, honest answer. "I wanted to become like one who was never meant to be mine."

He watched as the nature of his devotion sank in. Alora would crumble, hearing his admission. Yet Akito would do or say whatever it took to wrench that young woman from this tree. His love was prepared to strip bare each and every lie, even though Alora would later hate him for it.

Better to damn her reputation with his than her spirit.

Luscia's jaw flinched tautly, and the tails of her hair began to drift, her deportment evolving into something dangerous and unpredictable. Abruptly, she waved her palms at him dismissively. An unhinged, disbelieving laugh cracked her stern mouth. Luscia wiped moisture from below her noise where it'd started to angrily stream. "So she knew! About the cross-caste children, about the devoid. Alora knew this *whole* time… all while she… at me… as if I…" The haidren bellowed in disjointed bursts.

"She saved me as a boy," the king murmured in disbelief.

Static clipped the tops of Akito's scabbed ears. A daunting feeling battered his gut. He'd uncaged something within Alora's niece. And soon it would poison whatever narrow ground he'd won.

There was no path to Pilar that included her refusal.

"We need to go." Akito's guttural voice broke. "Now, Lady Haidren."

The sconces on the wall rattled as her kohl-rimmed eyes widened violently. "She is a *liar!*"

Around Akito, everyone backed away, including her own guard. He glimpsed up at where the burnt, antlered chandelier was swaying on its chain.

"Sentence your aunt to the Depths, sentence all Orynthia with her," Akito worriedly reasoned.

"Lady Boreal." King Dmitri brushed one of her shaking arms. Bracing his weight against the table, he beckoned her to sit. His relief was palpable when the chandelier stilled. Using his cane, the king shakily took residency beside her and said, "Luscia, please, my people. The Obscurer's curse cannot out-strengthen us."

Dusk fell upon her features where she simmered. When the remainder of her Quadren had retaken their places, Luscia folded her hands over her lap as if nothing had occurred. Her voice came thickly. "We must have faith the High One will deliver Alora from this fate. I go with my king."

Akito's vision flushed red, and his knees readied to launch him across the room.

But King Dmitri said to her softly, "Is faith a painting or a song?"

Dragging her face toward him, every particle between the two seemed weightily strung upon the regent's strange question.

Coughing, he put his fist to his mouth and continued. "In this case, as in most, I suspect faith is the one demanding our participation."

Her intent stare traveled with his hand to where he hid it underneath the table.

Akito's tongue swelled pleasingly; his senses alighted, recognizing the presence of blood.

Luscia shook her head at her king, so adamantly it could have been perceived as defiance. "Niit, I'm not leaving you."

King Dmitri inclined past the arm of his chair and tucked a strand of her chaotic hair behind an ear. He murmured in a tone too low for anyone but Akito and their Boreali spectators. "Sometimes we don't get to see the harvest, Luscia. But there'll never be one if my soil is dead."

Angling her unreadable expression at her weakened sovereign, she curtly addressed her brother. "Phalen, did Ana'Mere train you in the apothic arts?"

The boy gave an awkward snort. "Menially."

She didn't turn her face from her king. "We need to talk before I quit this peninsula."

"I will go with you." The najjani captaen rounded the room faster than any common man and loyally placed his vow of support atop her shoulder.

The trenches striking his forehead smoothed when she reached up and held him there. "You must stay in Roüwen."

Wind poured from his stern lips, their short argument no louder than the nervous scraping of the yancy haidren's boots.

"Because, Marek, you have to become the clann," Luscia finished aloud. Her fingers slipped off his. "Clann Bailefore. Our *Mighty Shield*. That is what Boreal needs now."

Stepping back, the captaen covered his mouth.

"We will go, Ana'Sere." Together, two other najjan, the stout ginger and the silvery one who'd lost his mother, edged toward the table.

Akito pivoted toward his nephew when his journal snapped shut. "No…" said Hachiro, blinking. "The only Boreali who enter Pilar do so as slaves. Too many of you and they will detect why you are there."

"The rest of the guard remains with the king," agreed Luscia.

"You expect us to let our haidren to walk into a rogue House," exclaimed the captaen, "with nobody but Emiere and an abomination?"

"And a shoto'shi." Hachiro unexpectedly stood, smoothing the buttoned panel of his stained, amber robes. "Ashore Lempeii, they will need a guide."

"And a sword," uttered Cyra's son.

"No!" their young king declared, with so much feeling he started hacking into his clean fist. "No, Zaeth, I prohibit it."

"The realm succumbs if the Obscurer gets a Tiergan, right?" the cross-caste passionately replied. "You really want to risk giving him two?"

King Dmitri's eyes pleaded with him. "Anyone else. You are my haidren. Send one of your warriors. Anyone but you."

His genuine affection struck Akito. No one would have predicted it to grow so strongly between them. Then again, ignorance covered a multitude of sins.

"You once accused me of having abused your love for me," said Cyra's son, his long locs swinging as a pendulum as he scooted out of his seat and rose once more. Showcasing his wrist, he tugged a red string tied there. "Brother, you have my heart." He held the chair and turned toward the taller Darakaian behind him. "But my birthright was always his."

"I don't care!" The king blared. The veining beneath his eyes protruded in violet sprays. "That doesn't mean you forfeit your mother's seat!"

"I was never the real haidren, Dmitri. Kumo Shà is," he replied, ushering the other man to take his place. Upon the Quadrecipher splayed across the table, Cyra's son leaned past the shocked warrior to straighten the panther crest. Forming a fist, he bumped it against his chest and offered his subordinate a slight bow.

Akito didn't understand, except that the full-blooded man was just as surprised as everyone else. "Ahoté... Ano zà, you can't mean..."

"Darakai won't follow a cross-caste. But the militia might. Alpha Zà is the only thing I've ever truly earned. And I want to be the man who earned it." Cyra's son grabbed a rolled journal from his coat and threw it on the tabletop. "Every gain has a loss, Dmitri. All this time, while I was safe with you, my prydes were risking their lives for me. This time I do it for them."

It stunned Akito, him giving up his seat even though he was no longer eligible to hold it. Cyra died having done everything to secure it in his name, by granting him the name of her tyrant husband.

That was not a move his mother would have made.

That was someone else entirely.

Akito chewed a canker inside his cheek. The cross-caste coming to Pilar created a grave complication.

"But you're supposed to stay together!" the yancy spewed from the other end of the table, holding some sort of pendant. "We can't—"

"Ira, that is enough!" hollered King Dmitri, causing the haidren to Bastiion to slide lower into his chair. The regent rotated a matching red thread about his wrist. He crisply said, "The sil'haidren has set his mind on Pilar. Please welcome my new Lord Darakai to the Quadren."

Remarkable, Akito thought, his patience for politics expiring. Alora wasn't the only one tending secrets on Boreali soil.

To Luscia, Akito said, "Gather what you can, Lady Haidren, and get on your knees. Pray to your divine, for I cannot." He dragged his heels away from their tangled web toward the open window. "A darkness you cannot fathom is fast unfolding."

The cloak waved behind him as he disappeared over the sill and rejoined the night. Vaulting onto a scalded bough, Akito swung his body up into the sparse canopy and bolted across the wreckage of the destroyed verandas. He didn't stop until the voices of the Quadren vanished like ghosts.

Being there, reentering Alora's waking world and speaking to them, was too much. However, it was nothing, Akito saw, gasping from the heights, compared to the annihilation he'd caused below.

The destruction stretched for miles. Leaves burnt upon their branches, holdreheiim stripped of their limbs, homes destroyed… swing bridges incinerated and hanging in strips. Bioluminescent lichens and fungi had been seared from the striated bark, condemning Roüwen to a cryptic gloom.

His beloved would not survive his shadows.

Shrouded in shame, he descended the altitudes. Akito's feet hit the blood-soaked snow. He rolled his gnarled spine against an ancient trunk, searching deep into the graveyard of colossal trees. Death's dominion choked the air, human dust plaguing it with a gray smog between nature's tombstones.

Akito doubled over, producing nothing but curdled bile. He could not fail to save her from himself. Not again. Akito had broken his covenant of concealment to set her story to rights, restoring her not to more lies but to the truth. And for it, they would never be the same again.

Upon her liberation, Alora would condemn him as the miserable monster he was. Then, without her, he'd finally be damned to the infinite dark.

Weakly, Akito allowed himself one fleeting look into her skies, sparkling far above the barren branches. *Perhaps*, he hoped deep within that empty, quiet place, *perhaps the High One will release me to the Depths if I keep her from joining me there.*

A shockwave pounded from his chest, suddenly pitching him against the bark.

Akito scraped his gloved fingers atop his sternum where his shriveled heart was caged. Scared and confused, Akito ripped the coat off and searched his decaying body as it hoped beneath his frayed garments.

Dead flesh stretched across his protruding sternum. The ghost of life, one that shuddered so rarely beneath it, seemed to have passed with the next sweeping wind. He parted his lips after life's haunt, only to choke against the cold.

It could not have been. Akito was dust in motion, no more than any other monster.

A second, arduous, powerful beat wracked the bone.

He cried in pain. His heel rolled over something, and there was a foreign jingle. Looking down, Akito found a broken bracelet of bells mashed underfoot. The sound rattled the night, echoing an improbable refrain. Sprouting around the burnt bells in glittering shoots, fresh ivy was climbing up his ankles. Dormant, highland light pulsed through the dirt beneath his boots as a third beat battered his undeserving heart. After all he'd committed, Akito ought to have been standing in his grave.

But this was the land of Tiergan.

This was resurrection ground.

Epilogue

Akito

Roüwen had cried itself to sleep, unaware that in the stillness of night, the arbiter of anguish lingered outside their sil'haid-ren's door.

Amaranth's talons bit into his shoulder where she'd perched. The Pilarese hawk was reluctant to enter; she smelled it too. Alora's solitary cottage soared before him, the entry pitched black and the herbs in her pots dissolved to soot. A branch protruded through one of the vaulted windows where it'd crashed during the fire and busted in across the framing.

Akito's cloak caught on the rubble as he hesitantly approached the doorknob. It wasn't usually how he'd enter. His heart laboriously thumped, the reaction new and unsettling. The corrupted flesh had healed where the ivy had touched his leg… yet no other tissue, apart from Akito's beating heart, had been revived.

The last time he'd knocked on a door that had been hers was in Korbin's palace, on a night so much like this. He wished he could lock it away and swallow the key.

Torture wrapped in tentacles around his appendages, the beet-red corruption spreading up the veins of his arm toward his heart. Painted in the prisoner's blood, Akito slammed his forehead against the door and hammered it harder than the pounding through his skull. He could feel the transformation happening, the wrongness drowning his system. Frantic, he cried her name like a prayer through the silent corridor.

"Help me! I'm so sorry, Alora. Help me, please, I beg you!"

The wood shuddered out of its threshold, and Akito caught himself, his crimson prints staining the mosaic border to her apartments—the singular place he was forbidden to appear.

Alora shrieked in the entry.

The captaen of her guard ran into the common room behind her, kuerre drawn at the ready.

Akito nearly collapsed. Fresh faced and her hair loose—falling in a pale sheet past the waist-tie of her white shift—Alora was his priestess, there to cleanse him of his terrible error. "Beloved…" He moaned, reaching for her aid.

But her hands shuttered her mouth while she absorbed his tainted robes and the gruesome tale they foretold. Horror cradled her question. "Akito, what have you done?"

He flinched from the handle, then girding himself, cracked the door open and advanced into the quaint cottage.

The interior resembled a coal mine. Tenebrous streaks marred it wall to ceiling, her cuttings having vanished from their racks. Akito trudged over a heap of burnt furniture where he cut a path through the valley of cremated plants and broken pottery. Launching from him, Amaranth flew to her luxiron perch lying on its side. Sorrowfully, Akito crossed to where she'd kept her books.

When he selected one, the binding fizzled in his grasp. The ruined vellum hung in bitter scraps, a material unable to carry a flame nor the written word any longer. Parchment littered his feet in disintegrated clumps. Her writings, her research, were destroyed. Alora was gone, and yet Akito still smelled her pine and bramble beneath the ashes.

Falling into the spoiled bookshelf, Akito's knees gave way as his heart struck another backbreaking beat. He wept without tears.

Alora's home was in ruins, and so was he.

"She told us you were dead."

Rotating in the wreckage, Akito peered past his hood at where Emiere Tallaesen's robust stature filled the doorframe.

The middle-aged captaen came out of the shadow and into the moonlight, taking his strides as soundlessly as he had decades prior. He was unchanged by age, save the lines that furrowed his angular face and the swath of gray hair cupping his chin. Long, silver hair outlined the hostile buckle in his expression. "Told us she couldn't revive you that night. That she'd disposed of the body on her own to protect the guard from prosecution. Made us believe it was political precaution," said Emiere, his tone darker than the room. "That was a fiction, one she's maintained for twenty years."

Akito moved his ragged frame with the captaen's as he fluidly rounded the sitting room.

"You did this to her," Emiere stated. "Stole the life she should have led. I never understood why she chose isolation… why she never married, never bore her own legacy. The reason was you, you despicable fiend. I confronted her once, but she assuaged my concern. Swore it was an allyship, between Boreal and Pilar." He halted short of her cast-iron teapot, buried in the dust. "Niit, it was a theft. You stole everything Alora Tiergan was meant to become."

Head bent, Akito reached for a stray teacup and gently poured the ash from it. "Wem, I know I did—"

"Don't dare to speak our tongue to me. You have no right, not with that sin swimming in your veins!" The slit scar became a jagged arrow through Emiere's lips. "And now, Ana'Sere tells me that Alora's been stolen again, by your blood. That he is going to destroy her."

Akito croaked the admission. "Yes."

The hawk flapped her lavender wings and launched through the charged silence, then landed on the workbench. Dissatisfied, for her mistress was not there, Amaranth left the bench for a ledge across from the captaen. She crooked her beak predatorily when he wavered over the hilt of his kuerre.

Emiere lowered his hand. "What are you willing to lose to bring her back?"

"Everything I have left in this life, and whatever awaits me thereafter."

"Thereafter…" Sneering, the captaen glanced toward the moon. A promised reckoning ringed his emerald irises. "Not everyone can be redeemed."

"No," he agreed. An ache strummed Akito's ravaged throat with his revived pulse. "But she can."

Emiere locked his oath-sworn eyes onto his foe. "She must."

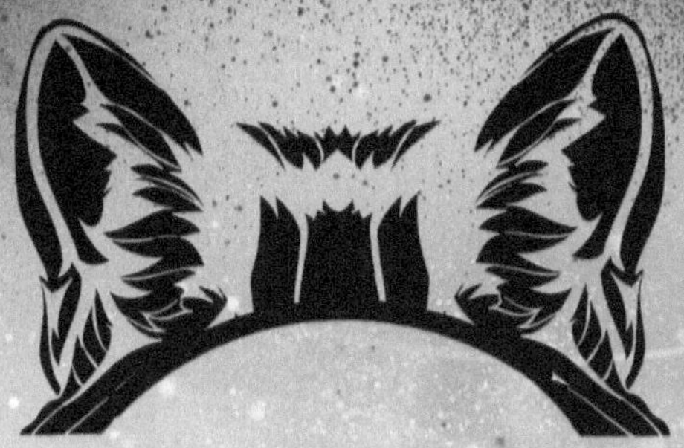

GLOSSARY

—

REGIONAL LEXICON

Visit www.TheHaidrenLegacy.com/Glossary to access digital references on your mobile device.

For a comprehensive list of terms, please consult the Master List succeeding this Regional Lexicon.

ORYNTHIA
⸺UNIVERSAL⸺

al'Haidren: /al-Hay-dren/ The next representative in line to sit on the royal heir's Quadren, typically the closest blood relative from the generation behind the current haidren

Breakaway: Member of the outer Houses who chooses to live in Unitarian lands, typically in Bastiion proper

Cross-caste: One of split lineage; an individual born of two separate Houses

Ethnicam: The assembly or association of all four Orynthian Houses

Forgotten Wars: The unknown events that led to the old world's destruction

Hagarh: /HAY-gar/ Wetlands opposite the Mirajii Forest, inhabited by nomadic peoples

Haidren: /HAY-dren/ A legal, judicial, and social representative on behalf of his or her corresponding House, seated on the current ruler's Quadren

House: The collection of a people and their preserved, self-governed territory within Orynthian borders, though still beholden to the throne

Interim Haidren: The next familial relation to the Haidren, though sometimes elected by the House, put in place when the rightful Haidren is deceased or incapacitated

Orynthia: /OR-in-thee-Uh/ Central kingdom comprised of four Houses; governed by the royal line of Thoarne and the Ethnicam

Outer Houses: Self-governed Houses on the outskirts of the Unitarian lands

Quadren: The committee of advisors encircling each Orynthian ruler, consisting of one haidren from each House

The Wastes: A barren, uninhabitable wasteland on the eastern side of the Yachel River

War-taint: Residual, toxic poisoning as a result of the Forgotten Wars

War-tainted: An individual, animal, or land harboring the symptoms of war-taint

Witchiron: Najjani weaponry (slang)

HOUSE OF BASTIION
⋙LOWLANDS & PLAINS⋘

Aurus: /AUHR-ruhs/ Gold coin of Bastiion origin; adopted by all Houses

Bastiion: /BAHS-tee-on/ Crown city of Orynthia

Byrnnzite: /BERN-zite/ An organic composite of petrified ash, wood, and Old-World metallics

Crupas: /CROO-pahs/ Copper coin of Bastiion origin; adopted by all Houses

Drifting Bazaar: Merchant market of floating stalls along the bank of the Thoarne Bay

Dromas: /DROH-mahs/ Silver coin of Bastiion origin; adopted by all Houses

Inner Proper: Walled and fortified inner city of Bastiion, encompassing the palace, Marketown, and upper- and lower-class districts

Marketown: Mass market within the streets of Bastiion's inner proper

Outer Proper: Royal land encircled by the noble provinces; the outskirts of the city of Bastiion

Pipe Marrow: A highly pungent opiate often smoked in the tents of Marketown

Province: Land bestowed to the heads of the nobility and their heirs

Vàssa Ship: /Vaah-sa/ Leisure vessel

The Veiled Lady: Popular tavern and night den in Marketown owned by Salma Nabhu

Unitarian: Primary language spoken in the House of Bastiion and the Unitarian lands; general mixture of ancient languages, refined over time

Unitarians: Orynthian bloodline comprised from a blended ancestry from centuries past

Yancy: /Yan-see/ Universal slang for any wealthy Unitarians; the nobility

UNITARIAN

Shtàka: /ShTAH-kuh/ Shit (slang)

Y'siti: /Yuh-ZEE-tee/ Filthy ice witch (derogatory slang)

HOUSE OF BOREAL
⋙ HIGHLAND PENINSULA ⋘

Aelect: /Aye-lect/ Chosen graduate warrior on the Iris of Viridis, its penannular brooch marked by the single branch

Aniell: /AHn-ee-eL/ High One; sole deity of Boreal

Armaeger: / AR-may-jer/ Officer within the Order of the Najjan, its penannular brooch marked by the double branch

Bomaerod: /BOH-may-rahD/ Vented staff utilized by the najjan; typically made of bone and/or wood; used to created audible reference points in a space while training

Boreali: /Boar-eell-ee/ Primary language spoken in the House of Boreal; term for the people of Boreal

Clann: Ruling leader of the clans inhabiting the Boreal peninsula

Clann Darragh: /Klan Dahw-rah/ High leader of the Boreali clans; named as Boreal's governing mighty oak

Clan Elder: Elected leader of a Boreali clan

Consort Daggers: A set of short, curved luxiron daggers; ornate in design

Crescent Wraiths: A set of long, arced luxiron blades used in unison; gripped at the center, serrated or scooped at the ends

Feidierdanns: /Fee-DYER-dons/ A braided whip used to increase the agility of footwork in najjani training

Ghostly Gate: Protective phenomena shielding Boreali shores from invaders

Great Harvest: Annual holy festival observed at Aksel's Keep during the autumn equinox

Isle of Viridis: /eyeL of Ver-EE-dees/ A remote island off the coast of Boreal; fortress where najjani train

Klödjen: /klode-Gen/ A wooden globe surrounded by a horizontal ring wide enough to hold a man; used in elementary training by the najjan

Kuerre: /Koo-AIR/ Luxiron backsword; curved blade

Kurtfierï: /Kert-FYE-ree/ Courtship token; an article of the father's clothing or dress, typically worn by the suited

Linsilk: Boreali fabric made of silk harvested from spiders around the banks of the Dönumn

Lumin: /Loo-men/ Sacred light energy native to the Boreali highlands

Lumilore: /Loo-meh-Lore/ Lux-stone; lumin-infused stone gathered near the banks of the Dönumn

Luxiron: Specialized najjani iron, forged in undiluted lumin; warm to the touch, prismatic in color, corrosive in nature, and lightweight; trade restricted

Luxsmith: A najjani smithy, dedicated to the creation of luxiron (i.e., luxcrafting)

Lycran: /LIE-kran/ Orallach fox-wolf (wolx) hybrid; genes enhanced by war-taint

Master of the Najjan: Nonpartisan leader of the Order of the Najjan

Najjan: /Nah-zhahn/ Elusive sect of the warrior faction; elite Boreali warrior(s)

Orallach Mountains: /Orr-uh-laK/ Range of frigid mountains; uninhabited

Order of Hosts: Core martial branch of the Order of the Najjan

Radials: Hidden luxiron blades; worn as three-fingered rings; fans open when triggered

Ranger Aelect: Operatives on covert assignment within najjani Set Apart Stewards, its penannular brooch marked by a reingafier antler

Roüwen: /Roe-OO-wen/ The village fortress; capital of Boreal

Sanctuary of Scribes: Sacred hall of scribes within Aksel's Keep

Set Apart Steward: Branch of specialized operatives within the Order of the Najjan

Shepherd of the Keep: Head najjani protector of Aksel's Keep; descendant of Aksel Bailefore

Söhlo: Ritual two-day period spent in the wilderness upon one's sixteenth birthday; Hearing Day

Solrahs: /SOL-rahs/ Half-moon shaped septum piece made of luxiron; worn by the haidrens to Boreal

Taemplar: Senior officer within the Order of the Najjan, its penannular brooch marked by the triple branch

Talï: /TAHL-ee/ Traditional prayer stones embedded down the wearer's cheeks

Teller's Bane: Flowering ivy planted at the base of the Altar of Truth

Tiergan: /TARE-ghan/ Sacred bloodline of the haidrens to Boreal; direct descendants of Tiergan

Vödalera: /Voh-duh-LARE-uh/ Najjani longship outfitted with a sleigh-shaped prow

Wreath of Wisdom: The ceremonial headdress passed from predecessor to successor during the haidren's Seating ceremony

BOREALI

Allöh: /AH-loe/ *May peace convene with you* (informal greeting)

Allöh'jomn'yeh: /AH-loe zhoM-yay/ *May peace convene with you* (formal greeting)

Ana'Brödre: /Ahna-Broe-DRuh/ *Great Brother(s)*

Ana'Frödre: /Ahna-Fro-derr/ *Great Father*

Ana'Innöx: /Ahna-ee-NOCKS/ *Great Harvest*

Ana'Mere: /Ahna-Mare/ *Great Mother*

Ana'Sere: /Ahna-Sare/ *Great Sister(s)*

Aniell'silaem: /AHn-ee-eL see-lame/ *Aniell's grace*

Aurynth: /Aur-rinth/ *Eternal resting place; heaven*

Bolaeva: /Bo-LAY-vah/ *Please*

Crestï: /CRES-tee/ *Now; this instant*

Dönumn Lux: /Doe-nuM Lux/ *Gift of Light*

Eiide Corün: /Eye-dee-kor-OOn/ *Wreath of Wisdom*

Enjjen anar: /En-zhen ah-nar/ *To none other*

Daeünna: /Day-oo-nuh/ *Blessing*

Fappa: /Fah-puh/ *Daddy*

Fapapï: /Fah-pah-pee/ *Grandaddy*

Heh'ta: /HEH-tuh/ *Stay; halt*

Lothadim'Aniell: / Loth-uh-dim AHn-ee-eL/ *Glory to Aniell*

Lu'Lycran: /Loo LIE-cran/ *Little Lycran* (nickname)

Lux aemida hen. Hen mii'orr vida: /Lux aye-mee-duh hen Hen MEE-or vee-duh/ *The Light is within her. She will not fall*

Mamu: /Mah-Moo/ *Mommy; Mama*

Meh fyreon: /Meh Feer-ee-on/ *I'm sorry; I apologize*

Meh'daeünna'yeh: /Meh Day-oo-nuh yay/ *My blessing to you*

Meh'dajjeni Dönumn, weh'dajjeni Lux: /Meh Dah-zhen-ee Doe-nuM, weh Dah-zhen-ee Lux/ *My strength in the Gift, our strength for the Light*

Niit: /Neet/ *No*

Prajja'Veriidim: /Prah-zhah ver-EE-dim/ *Altar of Truth*

Pricta'siim, fojjünaet'Aurynth, benadicta'anar: /PREEK-tuh-seem foh-zhoon-aTe-aur-inth BEN-uh-diK-tuh-ah-nar/ *Tested by iron, quenched by Aurynth, separated by none*

Rul'Aniell: /Rool-AHn-ee-eL/ *In and to Aniell*

Rul'Lothadim Aniell: /Rool-Loth-uh-dim AHn-ee-eL/ *All Glory in and to Aniell* (formal declaration)

Rüsha'silaem: /ROO-shuh see-lame/ *Ears of grace*

Se'lah Aurynth: /se-Lah Aur-rinth/ *Until the shores of Aurynth*

Tadöm: /tah-Dome/ *Thank you*

Tredae'Aurynth: /Tred-AYE Aur-rinth/ *Walk in Aurynth* (parting)

Veridaedill: /veR-eh-DAYE-dil/ *Teller's bane*

Veriidim: /veR-EE-dim/ *Pure, untainted truth*

Waedfrel: /Wade-frell/ *Good; great; exemplary*

Weh yeyisha'shadü tredae lim Lux: /weh yeh-YEE-shuh Shah-doo tred-AYE lim Lux/ *We live in the shadow to walk by the Light*

Wem: /whem/ *Yes*

Yeh'maelim: /Yeh-may-lim/ *Welcome to you*

Ykah lö: /Eye-kuh Loe/ *What; huh; come again*

HOUSE OF DARAKAI
⋙SOUTHERN MOUNTAINS AND LOWLANDS⋘

Alpha: Leader of a regional pryde of militia

Alpha Zà: Leader of the militia prydes

Andwele: /An-DWEE-lee/ Native language of Darakai

Andwele Mountains: Mountain range forming the western border of Darakai, separating it from Razôuel and Mworra

Arrowball: Darakaian field game consisting of three baskets, two archers, and ladle-like sticks

Beta: Second to the pryde alpha

Beta Warlord: Official second to the chief warlord; second to a Darakaian tribal chieftain

Bwoloa: /Beh-WOE-lo-ah/ Golden liqueur imported from Darakai; made of fermented grain and citrus blossoms

Byumbé: /Beh-YOOM-bay/ Octagonal daub and rock dwellings built into the City Nest

City Nest: Soaring city carved into the towering, rounded cliffsides of the Faraji canyon

Chief Warlord: House leader of all native tribes and minor chiefs, appointed by the Darakaian War Council

Commander of the Orynthian Armies: Supreme military leader over the united Orynthian realm, of Darakaian descent, appointed by the king

Cub: kid (slang)

Darts and Dice: A Darakaian game coupling a set of dice, a hung board, and a blowpipe; adopted by gambling houses in Bastiion

Faraji: /Fah-rah-zhee/ Capital of Darakai; fortified mountain city; location of War Council and tribal leaders

Gunjas: /Goon-Juh/ Loose-fitting pants, wrapped at the waist and ankles; worn for drills and combat

Halona: /Hah-LOE-nuh/ Major tribe in the foothills of the Andwele Mountains

Holiday of Hands: Annual Darakaian holiday wherein tribes claim one another with their handprints

Kindred Bridge: Historic natural stone bridge stained by the blood of ancestors past

Kopar: /Koh-PAR/ Sickle sword carried by the Darakaian military

Mantle of the Fallen: Historic cape constructed of ancient, bloodstained arrowheads; typically worn by the haidren to Darakai or the chief warlord

Pammu: /PAH-moo/ Fermented pam sap; brewed with beetles in the base of the bottle

Pryde: Localized group of Darakaian militia

Yowekao: /Yow-uh-KAY-oh/ Remote mountain tribe within the Andwele Mountains

ANDWELE

Ahoté: /Ah-HO-tay/ *Restless Bobcat* (nickname)

Àla'maia: /Ah-lah MY-ah/ *The Moon* (name)

Ano: /Ah-noe/ *No*

Ano'puwàa dim'hakku, yona alpha ni ràtomdai: /ah-noe-POO-ah dim-hah-koo YOHN-uh Al-fuh nee rah-tohm-dye/ *Unworthy and wanting, an alpha's blood will be claimed*

Ano zà: /Ah-noe Zah/ *No* (final; absolute)

Chombà ano'ruko yon namàa tswé: /Chom-buh ah-noe-roo-koh yohn nah-MAH tet-sway/ *The pot is not named by the tool that shapes it*

Doru: /DOH-roo/ *Stop; wait; pause*

Fàkkadim'Chalim: /Fah-kuh-dim-Chah-lim/ *Holiday of Hands*

Fhàdda: /Fah-duh/ *Dad* (informal)

Gaibai: /Guy-buy/ *Story-dance*

Hérumaa: /Hare-oo-mah/ *Mercy*

Hewe hai Darakai: /Hay-way hi Dare-uh-kye/ *We are Darakai*

Hewe ràtomdai na hewe: /Hay-way rah-tohm-dye nah hay-way/ *We claim us*

Ho'waladim: /Hoe-wall-a-dim/ *As is due to you* (in place of "you're welcome")

Jaha: /Jah-Hah/ *Pretty thing*

Jwona rapiki: /Jeh-wahn-uh rah-pee-kee/ *Fate writer*

Kàchà kocho: /Kah-chah Koe-cho/ *This or that; so-so; either*

Kakk: /Kak/ *Babble; ramblings; nonsense*

Kakka-shtàka: /Kak-uh ShTAH-kuh/ *Dumb; shitty thing; useless* (slang)

Kwihila rapiki mu jwona: /Kwih-hee-luh rah-pee-kee moo Jeh-wahn-uh/ *Victory writes over fate*

Làtoh Ché: /la-TOH Chay/ *The City Nest*

Maji'maia: /Mah-zhee MY-ah/ *Witchy-Moon* (nickname); full moon

Mhàdda: /Mah-duh/ *Mom* (informal)

Motumbha: /Moh-TUM-buh/ *Arrowball*

Na huwàa tàkom lai na huwàa: /Nah hoo-ah tah-KOM lie nah hoo-ah/ *It takes a hound to hunt a hound*

Ni yeye ràtomdai na wewe: /Nee yay-yay rah-tohm-dye nah way-way/ *Do you claim rights to him/her/them/it*

Owàa: /Oh-WAH/ *The Sun* (name)

Owàamo: /Oh-WAH-moe/ *The Sun greets you* (greeting)

Papyon: /Pap-ee-on/ *Love; sex* (slang)

Qondai: /Kon-Die/ *To understand; to know*

Rhàana ne'Etswégo: /RAH-na neh-et-SWAY-go/ *Mantle of the Fallen*

Rhaolé: /Ray-OH-lay/ *Hurry; speed up*

Rhaolé ono: /Ray-OH-lay OH-no/ *Hurry faster*

Shàla'maiamo: /Sha-lah my-AH-moe/ *The Moon watch you* (farewell)

Shamàli: /Sha-mah-lee/ *If you see fit* (in place of "please")

Shumabin: /SHOO-muh-bin/ *Paladin's aloe*

Uni: /Oo-nee/ *Yes*

Uni zà: /Oo-nee Zah/ *Yes* (final; absolute)

Yaya: /Yah-Yah/ *Honey; an attractive woman* (slang)

Zullee: /Zool-lee/ *Accepted with honor* (in place of "thank you")

Zwaàlu Ghopar: /Zwah-loo goh-PAR/ *Kindred Bridge*

HOUSE OF PILAR
⸎EASTERN COAST⸎

Chancellor: Head of the Pilarese Shoto Collective

Gakoshū: /Gah-koh-shoo/ City of Learning

Lempeii: /Lem-PAY/ Port city; station of the Orynthian navy

Shoto: /ShOH-toe/ A philosopher or scholar; statesman dedicated to the pursuit of learning

Shoto'shi: /ShOH-toe-shee/ A shoto acolyte; training in the ways of the Collective

Shoto Collective: Pilarese congress of scholars and politicians

Shoto Prime: Senior leader within the Shoto Collective

PILARESE

Kiataki: /Kee-uh-ta-kee/ *Sword-keeper*

Pyō chakrit: /Pie-oh cha-KREET/ *Wisdom affirmed* (statement of accord)

Pyō jien: /Pie-oh JYEN/ *Knowledge accepted* (statement of accord)

GLOSSARY

MASTER LIST OF TERMS

Aelect *Boreal-Boreali* /Aye-lect/ Chosen graduate warrior on the Iris of Viridis, its penannular brooch marked by the single branch

Ahoté *Darakai-Andwele* /Ah-HO-tay/ Restless Bobcat (nickname)

Àla'maia *Darakai-Andwele* /Ah-lah MY-ah/ The Moon (name)

al'Haidren *Orynthia-Unitarian* /al-Hay-dren/ The next representative in line to sit on the royal heir's Quadren, typically the closest blood relative from the generation behind the current haidren

Allöh *Boreal-Boreali* /AH-loe/ May peace convene with you (informal greeting)

Allöh'jomn'yeh *Boreal-Boreali* /AH-loe zhoM-yay/ May peace convene with you (formal greeting)

Alpha *Darakai-Andwele* Leader of a regional pryde of militia

Alpha Zà *Darakai-Andwele* Leader of the militia prydes

Ana'Brödre *Boreal-Boreali* /Ahna-Broe-DRuh/ Great Brother(s)

Ana'Frödre *Boreal-Boreali* /Ahna-Fro-derr/ Great Father

Ana'Innöx *Boreal-Boreali* /Ahna-ee-NOCKS/ Great Harvest

Ana'Mere *Boreal-Boreali* /Ahna-Mare/ Great Mother

Ana'Sere *Boreal-Boreali* /Ahna-Sare/ Great Sister(s)

Andwele *Darakai* /An-DWEE-lee/ Native language of Darakai

Andwele Mountains *Darakai* Mountain range forming the western border of Darakai, separating it from Razôuel and Mworra

Aniell *Boreal-Boreali* /AHn-ee-eL/ High One; sole deity of Boreal

Aniell'silaem *Boreal* /AHn-ee-eL see-lame/ Aniell's grace

Ano *Darakai-Andwele* /Ah-noe/ No

Ano'puwàa dim'hakku, yona alpha ni ràtomdai *Darakai-Andwele* / ah-noe-POO-ah dim-hah-koo YOHN-uh Al-fuh nee rah-tohm-dye/ Unworthy and wanting, an alpha's blood will be claimed

Ano zà *Darakai-Andwele* /Ah-noe Zah/ No (final; absolute)

Armaeger *Boreal-Boreali* /AR-may-jer/ Officer within the Order of the Najjan, its penannular brooch marked by the double branch

Arrowball *Darakai* Darakaian field game consisting of three baskets, two archers, and ladle-like sticks

Aurus *Bastiion-Unitarian* /AUHR-ruhs/ Gold coin of Bastiion origin; adopted by all Houses

Aurynth *Boreal-Boreali* /Aur-rinth/ Eternal resting place; heaven

Bastiion *Bastiion* /BAHS-tee-on/ Crown city of Orynthia

Beta *Darakai* Second to the pryde alpha

Beta Warlord *Darakai* Official second to the chief warlord; second to a Darakaian tribal chieftain

Bolaeva *Boreal-Boreali* /Bo-LAY-vah/ Please

Bomaerod *Boreal-Boreali* /BOH-may-rahD/ Vented staff utilized by the najjan; typically made of bone and/or wood; used to created audible reference points in a space while training

Boreali *Boreal* /Boar-eell-ee/ Primary language spoken in the House of Boreal; term for the people of Boreal

Breakaway *Orynthia* Member of the outer Houses who chooses to live in Unitarian lands, typically in Bastiion proper

Bwoloa *Darakai-Andwele* /Beh-WOE-lo-ah/ Golden liqueur imported from Darakai; made of fermented grain and citrus blossoms

Byrnnzite *Bastiion-Unitarian* /BERN-zite/ An organic composite of petrified ash, wood, and Old-World metallics

Byumbé *Darakai-Andwele* /Beh-YOOM-bay/ Octagonal daub and rock dwellings built into the City Nest

Clann *Boreal* Ruling leader of the clans inhabiting the Boreal peninsula

Clann Darragh *Boreal-Boreali* /Klan Dahw-rah/ High leader of the Boreali clans; named as Boreal's governing mighty oak

Clan Elder *Boreal* Elected leader of a Boreali clan

Chancellor *Pilar* Head of the Pilarese Shoto Collective

Chief Warlord *Darakai* House leader of all native tribes and minor chiefs, appointed by the Darakaian War Council

City Nest *Darakai* Soaring city carved into the towering, rounded cliffsides of the Faraji canyon

Commander of the Orynthian Armies *Darakai* Supreme military leader over the united Orynthian realm, of Darakaian descent, appointed by the king

Consort Daggers *Boreal* A set of short, curved luxiron daggers; ornate in design

Cross-caste *Orynthia* One of split lineage; an individual born of two separate Houses

Crupas *Bastiion-Unitarian* /CROO-pahs/ Copper coin of Bastiion origin; adopted by all Houses

Crescent Wraiths *Boreal* A set of long, arced luxiron blades used in unison; gripped at the center; serrated or scooped at the ends

Crestï *Boreali* /CRES-tee/ Now; this instant

Cub *Darakai* kid (slang)

Daeünna *Boreal-Boreali* /Day-oo-nuh/ Blessing

Darts and Dice *Darakai* A Darakaian game coupling a set of dice, a hung board, and a blowpipe; adopted by gambling houses in Bastiion

Dönumn Lux *Boreal-Boreali* /Doe-nuM Lux/ Gift of Light

Doru *Darakai-Andwele* /DOH-roo/ Stop; wait; pause

Drifting Bazaar *Bastiion* Merchant market of floating stalls along the bank of the Thoarne Bay

Dromas *Bastiion-Unitarian* /DROH-mahs/ Silver coin of Bastiion origin; adopted by all Houses

Eiide Corün *Boreal-Boreali* /Eye-dee-kor-OOn/ Wreath of Wisdom

Enjjen anar *Boreal-Boreali* /En-zhen ah-nar/ To none other

Ethnicam *Orynthia* The term used when referring to the assembly or association of all four Orynthian Houses

Fàkkadim'Chalim *Darakai-Andwele* /Fah-kuh-dim-Chah-lim/ Holiday of Hands

Fappa *Boreal-Boreali* /Fah-puh/ Daddy

Fapapï *Boreal-Boreali* /Fah-pah-pee/ Grandaddy

Faraji *Darakai* /Fah-rah-zhee/ Capital of Darakai; fortified mountain city; location of War Council and tribal leaders

Feidierdanns *Boreal-Boreali* /Fee-DYER-dons/ A braided whip used to increase the agility of footwork in najjani training

Fhàdda *Darakai-Andwele* /Fah-duh/ Dad (informal)

Forgotten Wars *Orynthia* The unknown events that led to the old world's destruction

Gakoshū *Pilar-Pilarese* /Gah-koh-shoo/ City of Learning

Gaibai *Darakai-Andwele* /Guy-buy/ Story-dance

Ghostly Gate *Boreal* Protective phenomena shielding Boreali shores from invaders

Great Harvest *Boreal* Annual holy festival observed at Aksel's Keep during the autumn equinox

Gunjas *Darakai* /Goon-Juh/ Loose-fitting pants; wrapped at the waist and ankles; worn for drills and combat

Halona *Darakai* /Hah-LOE-nuh/ Major tribe in the foothills of the Andwele Mountains

Hagarh *Orynthia* /HAY-gar/ Wetlands opposite the Mirajii Forest, inhabited by nomadic peoples

Haidren *Orynthia-Unitarian* /HAY-dren/ A legal, judicial, and social representative on behalf of his or her corresponding House, seated on the current ruler's Quadren

Heh'ta *Boreal-Boreali* /HEH-tuh/ Stay; halt

Hérumaa *Darakai-Andwele* /Hare-oo-mah/ Mercy

Hewe hai Darakai *Darakai-Andwele* /Hay-way hi Dare-uh-kye/ We are Darakai

Hewe ràtomdai na hewe *Darakai-Andwele* /Hay-way rah-tohm-dye nah hay-way/ We claim us

Holiday of Hands *Darakai* Annual Darakaian holiday wherein tribes claim one another with their handprints

House *Orynthia* The collection of a people and their preserved, self-governed territory within Orynthian borders, though still beholden to the throne

Ho'waladim *Darakai-Andwele* /Hoe-wall-a-dim/ As is due to you (in place of "you're welcome")

Inner Proper *Bastiion* Walled and fortified inner city of Bastiion encompassing the palace, Marketown, and upper- and lower-class districts

Interim Haidren *Orynthia* The next familial relation to the Haidren, though sometimes elected by the House, put in place when the rightful Haidren is deceased or incapacitated

Isle of Viridis *Boreal* /eyeL of Ver-EE-dees/ A remote island off the coast of Boreal; fortress where najjan train

Jaha *Darakai-Andwele* /Jah-Hah/ Pretty thing

Jwona rapiki *Darakai-Andwele* /Jeh-wahn-uh rah-pee-kee/ Fate writer

Kàchà kocho *Darakai-Andwele* /Kah-chah Koe-cho/ This or that; so-so; either

Kakk *Darakai-Andwele* /Kak/ Babble; ramblings; nonsense

Kakka-shtàka *Darakai-Andwele* /Kak-uh ShTAH-kuh/ Dumb; shitty thing; useless (slang)

Kiataki *Pilar-Pilarese* /Kee-uh-ta-kee/ Sword-keeper

Kindred Bridge *Darakai* Historic natural stone bridge stained by the blood of ancestors past

Klödjen *Boreal-Boreali* /klode-Gen/ A wooden globe surrounded by a horizontal ring wide enough to hold a man; used in elementary training by the najjan

Kopar *Darakai* /Koh-PAR/ Sickle sword carried by the Darakaian military

Kuerre *Boreal-Boreali* /Koo-AIR/ Luxiron backsword; curved blade

Kurtfierï *Boreal-Boreali* /Kert-FYE-ree/ Courtship token; an article of the father's clothing or dress, typically worn by the suited

Kwihila rapiki mu jwona *Darakai-Andwele* /Kwih-hee-luh rah-pee-kee moo Jeh-wahn-uh/ Victory writes over fate

Làtoh Ché *Darakai-Andwele* /la-TOH Chay/ The City Nest

Lempeii *Pilar* /Lem-PAY/ Port city; station of the Orynthian navy

Linsilk *Boreal* Boreali fabric made of silk harvested from spiders around the banks of the Dönumn

Lothadim'Aniell *Boreal-Boreali* / Loth-uh-dim AHn-ee-eL/ Glory to Aniell

Lu'Lycran *Boreal-Boreali* /Loo LIE-cran/ Little Lycran (nickname)

Lumin *Boreal* /Loo-men/ Sacred light energy native to the Boreali highlands

Lumilore *Boreal* /Loo-meh-Lore/ Lux-stone; lumin-infused stone gathered near the banks of the Dönumn

Lux aemida hen. Hen mii'orr vida *Boreal-Boreali* /Lux aye-mee-duh hen Hen MEE-or vee-duh/ The Light is within her. She will not fall

Luxiron *Boreal* Specialized najjani iron, forged in undiluted lumin; warm to the touch, prismatic in color, corrosive in nature, and lightweight; trade restricted

Luxsmith *Boreal* A najjani smithy, dedicated to the creation of Luxiron

Lycran *Boreal-Boreali* /LIE-kran/ Orallach fox-wolf (wolx) hybrid; genes enhanced by war-taint

Maji'maia *Darakai-Andwele* /Mah-zhee MY-ah/ Witchy-Moon (nickname); full moon

Mamu *Boreal-Boreali* /Mah-Moo/ Mommy; Mama

Mantle of the Fallen *Darakai* Historic cape constructed of ancient, bloodstained arrowheads; typically worn by the haidren to Darakai or the chief warlord

Master of the Najjan *Boreal* Nonpartisan leader of the Order of the Najjan

Mhàdda *Darakai-Andwele* /Mah-duh/ Mom (informal)

Marketown *Bastiion* Mass market within the streets of Bastiion's inner proper

Meh fyreon *Boreal-Boreali* /Meh Feer-ee-on/ I'm sorry; I apologize

Meh'daeünna'yeh *Boreal-Boreali* /Meh Day-oo-nuh yay/ My blessing to you

Meh'dajjeni Dönumn, weh'dajjeni Lux *Boreal-Boreali* /Meh Dah-zhen-ee Doe-nuM, weh Dah-zhen-ee Lux/ My strength in the Gift, our strength for the Light

Motumbha *Darakai-Andwele* /Moh-TUM-buh/ Arrowball

Na huwàa tàkom lai na huwàa *Darakai-Andwele* /Nah hoo-ah tah-KOM lie nah hoo-ah/ It takes a hound to hunt a hound

Najjan *Boreal-Boreali* /Nah-zhahn/ Elusive sect of the warrior faction; elite Boreali warrior(s)

Ni yeye ràtomdai na wewe *Darakai-Andwele* /Nee yay-yay rah-tohm-dye nah way-way/ Do you claim rights to him/her/them/it

Niit *Boreal-Boreali* /Neet/ No

Orallach Mountains *Boreal* /Orr-uh-laK/ Range of frigid mountains; uninhabited

Order of Hosts *Boreal* Core martial branch of the Order of the Najjan

Orynthia /OR-in-thee-Uh/ Central kingdom comprised of four Houses; governed by the royal line of Thoarne and the Ethnicam

Outer Houses *Orynthia* Self-governed Houses on the outskirts of the Unitarian lands

Outer Proper *Bastiion* Royal land encircled by the noble provinces; the outskirts of the city of Bastiion

Owàa *Darakai-Andwele* /Oh-WAH/ The Sun (name)

Owàamo *Darakai-Andwele* /Oh-WAH-moe/ The Sun greets you (greeting)

Pammu *Darakai* /PAH-moo/ Fermented pam sap; brewed with beetles in the base of the bottle

Papyon *Darakai-Andwele* /Pap-ee-on/ Love; sex (slang)

Pipe Marrow *Bastiion* A highly pungent opiate often smoked in the tents of Marketown

Prajja'Veriidim *Boreal* /Prah-zhah ver-EE-dim/ Altar of Truth

Pricta'siim, fojjünaet'Aurynth, benadicta'anar *Boreal-Boreali* / PREEK-tuh-seem foh-zhoon-aTe-aur-inth BEN-uh-diK-tuh-ah-nar/ Tested by iron, quenched by Aurynth, separated by none

Province *Bastiion* Land bestowed to the heads of the nobility and their heirs

Pryde *Darakai* Localized group of Darakaian militia

Pyō chakrit *Pilar-Pilarese* /Pie-oh cha-KREET/ Wisdom affirmed (statement of accord)

Pyō jien *Pilar-Pilarese* /Pie-oh JYEN/ Knowledge accepted (statement of accord)

Qondai *Darakai-Andwele* /Kon-Die/ To understand; to know

Quadren *Orynthia* The committee of advisors encircling each Orynthian ruler, consisting of one haidren from each House

Radials *Boreal* Hidden luxiron blades; worn as three-fingered rings; fan open when triggered

Ranger Aelect *Boreal* Operatives on covert assignment within najjani Set Apart Stewards, its penannular brooch marked by a reingafier antler

Rhàana ne'Etswégo *Darakai-Andwele* /RAH-na neh-et-SWAY-go/ Mantle of the Fallen

Rhaolé *Darakai-Andwele* /Ray-OH-lay/ Hurry; speed up

Rhaolé ono *Darakai-Andwele* /Ray-OH-lay OH-no/ Hurry faster

Roüwen *Boreal-Boreali* /Roe-OO-wen/ The village fortress; capital of Boreal

Rul'Aniell *Boreal-Boreali* /Rool-AHn-ee-eL/ In and to Aniell

Rul'Lothadim Aniell *Boreal-Boreali* /Rool-Loth-uh-dim AHn-ee-eL/ All Glory in and to Aniell (formal declaration)

Rüsha'silaem *Boreal-Boreali* /ROO-shuh see-lame/ Ears of grace

Sanctuary of Scribes *Boreal* Sacred hall of scribes within Aksel's Keep

Se'lah Aurynth *Boreal-Boreali* /se-Lah Aur-rinth/ Until the shores of Aurynth

Set Apart Steward *Boreal* Branch of specialized operatives within the Order of the Najjan

Shàla'maiamo *Darakai-Andwele* /Sha-lah my-AH-moe/ The Moon watch you (farewell)

Shamàli *Darakai-Andwele* /Sha-mah-lee/ If you see fit (in place of "please")

Shepherd of the Keep *Boreal* Head najjani protector of Aksel's Keep; descendant of Aksel Bailefore

Shoto *Pilar-Pilarese* /ShOH-toe/ A philosopher or scholar; statesman dedicated to the pursuit of learning

Shoto'shi *Pilar-Pilarese* /ShOH-toe-shee/ A shoto acolyte; training in the ways of the Collective

Shoto Collective *Pilar-Pilarese* Pilarese congress of scholars and politicians

Shoto Prime *Pilar-Pilarese* Senior leader within the Shoto Collective

Shtàka *Bastiion-Unitarian* /ShTAH-kuh/ Shit (slang)

Shumabin *Darakai-Andwele* /SHOO-muh-bin/ Paladin's aloe

Söhlo *Boreal* Ritual two-day period spent in the wilderness upon one's sixteenth birthday; Hearing Day

Solrahs *Boreal* /SOL-rahs/ Half-moon shaped septum piece made of luxiron; worn by the haidrens to Boreal

Tadöm *Boreal-Boreali* /tah-Dome/ Thank you

Taemplar *Boreal* Senior officer within the Order of the Najjan, its penannular brooch marked by the triple branch

Talï *Boreal* /TAHL-ee/ Traditional prayer stones embedded down the wearer's cheeks

Teller's Bane *Boreal* Flowering ivy planted at the base of the Altar of Truth

Tiergan *Boreal* /TARE-ghan/ Sacred bloodline of the haidrens to Boreal; direct descendants of Tiergan

Tredae'Aurynth *Boreal-Boreali* /Tred-AYE Aur-rinth/ Walk in Aurynth (parting)

Uni *Darakai-Andwele* /Oo-nee/ Yes

Uni zà *Darakai-Andwele* /Oo-nee Zah/ Yes (final; absolute)

Unitarian *Bastiion* Primary language spoken in the House of Bastiion and the Unitarian lands; general mixture of ancient languages, refined over time

Unitarians *Bastiion* Orynthian bloodline comprised from a blended ancestry from centuries past

Vàssa Ship *Bastiion-Unitarian* /Vaah-sa/ Leisure vessel

Veridaedill *Boreal-Boreali* /veR-eh-DAYE-dil/ Teller's bane

Veriidim *Boreal-Boreali* /veR-EE-dim/ Pure, untainted truth

Vödalera *Boreal* /Voh-duh-LARE-uh/ Najjani longship outfitted with a sleigh-shaped prow

The Veiled Lady *Bastiion* Popular tavern and night den in Marketown owned by Salma Nabhu

Waedfrel *Boreal-Boreali* /Wade-frell/ Good; great; exemplary

War-taint *Orynthia* Residual, toxic poisoning as a result of the Forgotten Wars

War-tainted *Orynthia* An individual, animal, or land harboring the symptoms of war-taint

The Wastes *Orynthia* A barren, uninhabitable wasteland on the eastern side of the Yachel River

Weh yeyisha'shadü tredae lim Lux *Boreal-Boreali* /weh yeh-YEE-shuh Shah-doo tred-AYE lim Lux/ We live in the shadow to walk by the Light

Wem *Boreal-Boreali* /whem/ Yes

Witchiron *Orynthia* Najjani weaponry (slang)

Wreath of Wisdom *Boreal* The ceremonial headdress passed from predecessor to successor during the haidren's Seating ceremony

Yancy *Bastiion-Unitarian* /Yan-see/ Universal slang for any wealthy Unitarians; the nobility

Yaya *Darakai-Andwele* /Yah-Yah/ Honey; an attractive woman (slang)

Yeh'maelim *Boreal-Boreali* /Yeh-may-lim/ Welcome to you

Ykah lö *Boreal-Boreali* /Eye-kuh Loe/ What; huh; come again

Yowekao *Darakai* /Yow-uh-KAY-oh/ Remote mountain tribe within the Andwele Mountains

Y'siti *Bastiion-Unitarian* /Yuh-ZEE-tee/ Filthy ice witch (derogatory slang)

Zullee *Darakai-Andwele* /Zool-lee/ Accepted with honor (in place of "thank you")

Zwaàlu Ghopar *Darakai-Andwele* /Zwah-loo goh-PAR/ Kindred Bridge

CAN'T WAIT FOR MY NEXT BOOK RELEASE?

Get access to early chapter drops, exclusive character art, behind-the-scenes videos, and new world illustrations! Best of all, come partner with me in developing Orynthia by voting on terms, apothic elements, creepy creatures, and more!

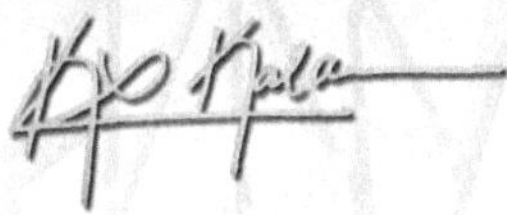

WWW.PATREON.COM/KLKOLARICH

Acknowledgements

This book tried to kill me.

It would have succeeded too, had certain realities not been strong enough to uphold me. Realities both temporal and transcendent, superficial and supernatural, which while at odds in their sacredness, are of nearly equal import to an author sporting a migraine and a healthy dose of imposter syndrome.

Simply put: doing hard things is *hard*.

We want things to be easy, yet none of us ever get the easy way out. We see a mountain. We dream of its summit. Though to get there, we actually have to do the climbing. We must endure the trudge. Our legs must burn. Our backs must ache. Sweat must pour. All the while it's in that refining process, whenever we pause to catch our heaving breath, do we finally realize that we are so much weaker than we ever imagined.

I thought this would be the easiest book in the series to write. That was rational; *House of Boreal* speaks to what I hold most dear. Yet, how often is the mind's rationale proven foolish by the heart? My experience—my walk through the wilderness—in writing this book was no different. My own insufficiencies, and my rationale, were not sufficient to see it through. I needed others. I needed divine inspiration. And you better believe I needed carbs.

These tangible needs became apparent shortly into the manuscript, the drafting of which was akin to pulling nails. Aside from implementing a new vitamin regiment, I spent the subsequent eighteen months clearing my mind of unhelpful influences, books, etc. and instead devoted myself to nourishment. *House of Boreal* was depleting; every page consumed my soul. So, I prayed, and I fasted. Then I dove into the past, into texts enriched with meaning, those revered writings that for millennia have wrestled with the most fundamental questions about humanity. I poured over Aquinas and Augustine. Josephus and segments of the Talmud. Waded into the Apocrypha. Hid in the caves of Qumran. Walked ancient roads with Edersheim. Witnessed the building of Alexandria. Devoured the papers of Newton. Suffered with Frankl and healed with Lewis.

Because as much as my flesh would love to boast it... I was not enough to write this book.

It should be self-evident that I'm a devout individual, personally speaking. It would be sheer hokum, nevertheless a great ruse, to pretend otherwise. Thus *House of Boreal* presented an unavoidable dilemma. Where analogies exist, blasphemy cannot. Nor where imagination reigns, should conviction cede. I agonized over this book, you see. How could I write from my deepest pools without retaining the flavor of their waters? It is impossible to undo the fusing of my composition. Or in other words, though it would be folly to try, how could I be expected to bear a fruit separate from the branch upon which I grow? I carry the seed within the core of my being.

For too long, I feared how this installment would be received. The Quadren was traveling to a theocracy, after all. And although I do not wish for any theocratic imposition on the free masses—nor does Luscia, by the way—painting that experience in this book was a scary endeavor. Not to mention complicated. Here I introduced multi-faceted tensions unlike those in the previous books. Boreal boasts incomparable beauty. However the humanity of its stewards boast a counter dose of malice, hypocrisy, and greed. This produced a tough dichotomy within myself, even though I'd planned to express it all along. I really had to wrestle with these themes. Themes that were personal to me both individually and communally. Then, had to interpret them onto paper. I had to give the themes to you…a gift I wish could have encompassed more fantasy than its inspiration.

Because of the toll, my longsuffering husband took the brunt of mine. There were many nights he ate alone. On more than one occasion, he had to stomp up to my office and remind me that we are, in fact, a married couple. Though somehow, Aaron remained more steadfast than me. An irony, considering he has yet to read this book as of my typing his acknowledgement. If asked, he would tell you that he never needed to. He continues to meet my needs regardless, even when I don't have the energy to adequately voice them. I delayed this book twice. Each time was at my husband's bidding. He thought his urging was for my sake, and perhaps in part it was. I certainly needed to rebalance. But in the end, it really proved to be for the book's. *House of Boreal* needed more time. Its flavoring needed to ferment, its themes to age and integrate into every atom of its design. Had I not listened to Aaron, had I rushed and not delayed, innumerable factors would have never materialized. Those who honor the Sabbath often say that we were intended to "work from rest". Not for the first time and assuredly not the last, Aaron protected my rest. And from that consecrated place did Boreal bloom.

I dedicated this book to two people who deserve it more than anyone else: my parents.

While they did not write this novel, they absolutely inked the most defining pages of its author. It was my parents who introduced me to the principle of truth—the central theme shooting throughout Boreal like barrage of lightning. I was obsessed with the concept as a child, always filtering topics into crude buckets of black and white. A weird way of processing the world, considering I was a very persuasive liar by the age of six. Yet they endured. In our home and at our dinner table, truth always prevailed. Meals are significant in Boreal because it was there that my parents executed the majority of their corrective work. Over plates of chicken tetrazzini, my mother would help us morally navigate social dilemmas. My parents would discuss their day and the choices they had to make during its trying hours. And when a disrespectful remark flew from my brother or me, my father would reorient our training by telling another story of old—the same parables which had oriented him into becoming the man he demonstrates himself to be each day. This is why the pain I gave to Luscia and Zaethan—the joint loss of their mothers—was never a statement about mine. It's the exclamation mark on a statement about fathers. Moreover, on the stark contrast between one like Nyack Kasim, and one like my own. My father, by his sheer existence, saved me during my worst time of need. Just as Luscia's saved her. Good men do exist. One raised me, even when wolves were prowling upon our doorstep. For not everything in life can be easily sorted into my cherished buckets of black and white. More often than not, those carcasses must first be broken down. Dissected. Analyzed. And with grace and fortitude…forgiven. It is the worldview my parents instilled that taught me to make sense of the ugliest, most confusing gray. There is no Luscia without my parents. Like me, they raised her just the same.

Writing a book this long can be a lonely, arduous process. Gratefully, that was not entirely the case with *House of Boreal*, thanks to Sana, Brandy, Laura, Alexandria, and the rest of the Orynthian Elite. Their ever-zealous patience and excitement stood a reminder that readers will forgive the delays as long as I gave it my all. The Patreon crew kept Orynthia alive and visceral when, from the outside, it probably seemed dormant. Because of their support, we are now curating a Louvre of character artwork. Their comments and discussions give me a private space for constant ideation. You can also thank them for the "scürie" who ate Zaethan's hair…that was their fault.

Bless them for it.

As I mentioned, there was a lot of anxiety in finally relinquishing this book, even to my beta readers. However, per usual, they offered the perfect proving ground. I cannot thank my betas enough—this fairly insulated little team of people whom I trust more than myself sometimes. The reason being is that they genuinely know these characters. They breathe this world. They can now sense when I am doing "a thing", when I'm planting a seemingly odd egg to hatch later on, as I love to do. I would be lost without them, honestly. My internal compass tends to go haywire near the end of drafting, when all my self-doubt creeps in. The betas embolden my convictions and keep me honest with myself, and the story. They deserve all the credit I can possibly give them. Orynthia is made brighter with them in the margins.

Speaking of margins, and the comments littered there… My editor,

Angie Wade, has earned all the badges for being such a trooper through the drafting of this behemoth. My husband might have been the person who encouraged me to delay, but it was Angie who made it possible. She was gracious with me and my internal struggle. Twice. Those adjustments had to impede her business, in some form or fashion. I'll never forget that. Though Angie's unwarranted compassion is not the real treasure she brings to the series. Stating it bluntly, she makes me better. Angie preserves my voice in the writing while simultaneously calling to attention anything that detracts from it. She accomplishes both with poise, kindness, and too few quips—a talent of hers I've ordered more of in future projects. My editor is a rarity among her peers. My books, and the industry at large, are better because they bear her thumbprint.

Aiding the cause is my clever assistant, Amber Garcia. It is only by her continual efforts that I do not come across like a complete recluse to the book community at large, nor to my own fans. She keeps me connected, on my toes, and on schedule. Immense thanks go to Amber for dealing with my grumblings and the countless GIFs sent in lieu of actual responses. Not to mention the many projects I randomly chuck at her, yet rarely complete myself. Amber is an angel who really deserves a card. Though knowing her, I should expect an email relaying she's already sent herself one on my behalf.

Wrapping all these ramblings into a pretty, readable package, would be Brent Spears. Or as we call him, the patron saint of interior revisions. Many thanks to Brent for constantly updating published versions of work I've already made him do, not because he didn't do it right in the first place, but because I'm a perfectionist who can never make up her mind. He has truly attained a level of Orynthian martyrdom not even a Boreali zealot could hope to obtain.

I think we'd all agree that the cover of *House of Boreal* is the most stunning of the bunch. Fiona has been with us since the beginning, and like her partnership, her artistry never wavers. It was a divine appointment to have found Fiona at the beginning. Most debut authors choose to re-cover their flagship series years after publishing. We won't have that problem—we have Fiona. Working with her is a recurrent pleasure. In a myriad of ways, her contributions laid the groundwork for Team Haidren to assemble. She's an OG, like Brent. I could not do this without them.

Which leads me to the most critical person of all.

You.

Thank you for taking a chance on this series, and for traversing its saga into the highlands. Readers are the backbone of every book, especially those well-loved, with their bindings tattered and pages marked by those who've held them close. My hope is that this book may one day mean so much to you, it wears the traffic of your many revisitations. You have walked this path with me, traveler. You've supported my lagging steps and carried the banner down the dusty trail into the unknown.

We *can* do hard things.

We can do them when we aren't alone.

K.L. Kolarich is a bestselling and award-winning epic fantasy author, based out of Nashville, TN. An individual plagued by sarcasm, conviction, and a constant distraction of fable and lore, she dreams in the day and writes through the night. Often hearing her characters argue in the background, Kolarich stifles the daily temptation to abandon reality and lose herself in the realm of Orynthia.

When fully present in the real world rather than another, she explores local waterfalls, habitually frequents the same Thai restaurant, adds to her ever-growing spice collection, and maintains a thoroughly messy kitchen for the sake of colorful vegan feasts.

With too many cats and not enough wine, Kolarich resides in the woods away from the noise, happily married.

THE HAIDREN LEGACY

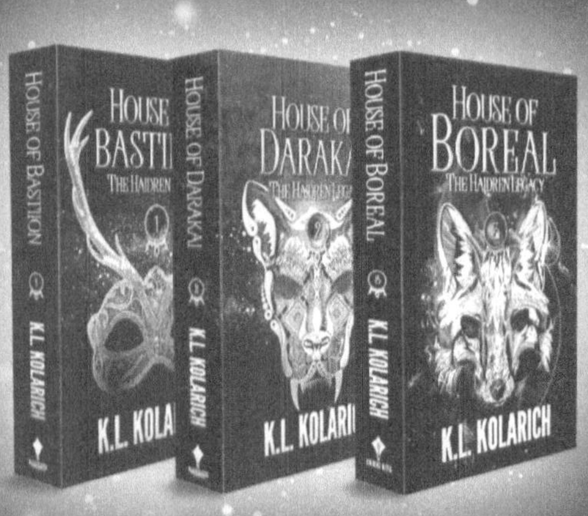

PYŌ JIEN. PYŌ CHAKRIT

THE TREACHEROUS SAGA CONTINUES…

www.thehaidrenlegacy.com/series